ESTRANGED
THE CHANGELING KING

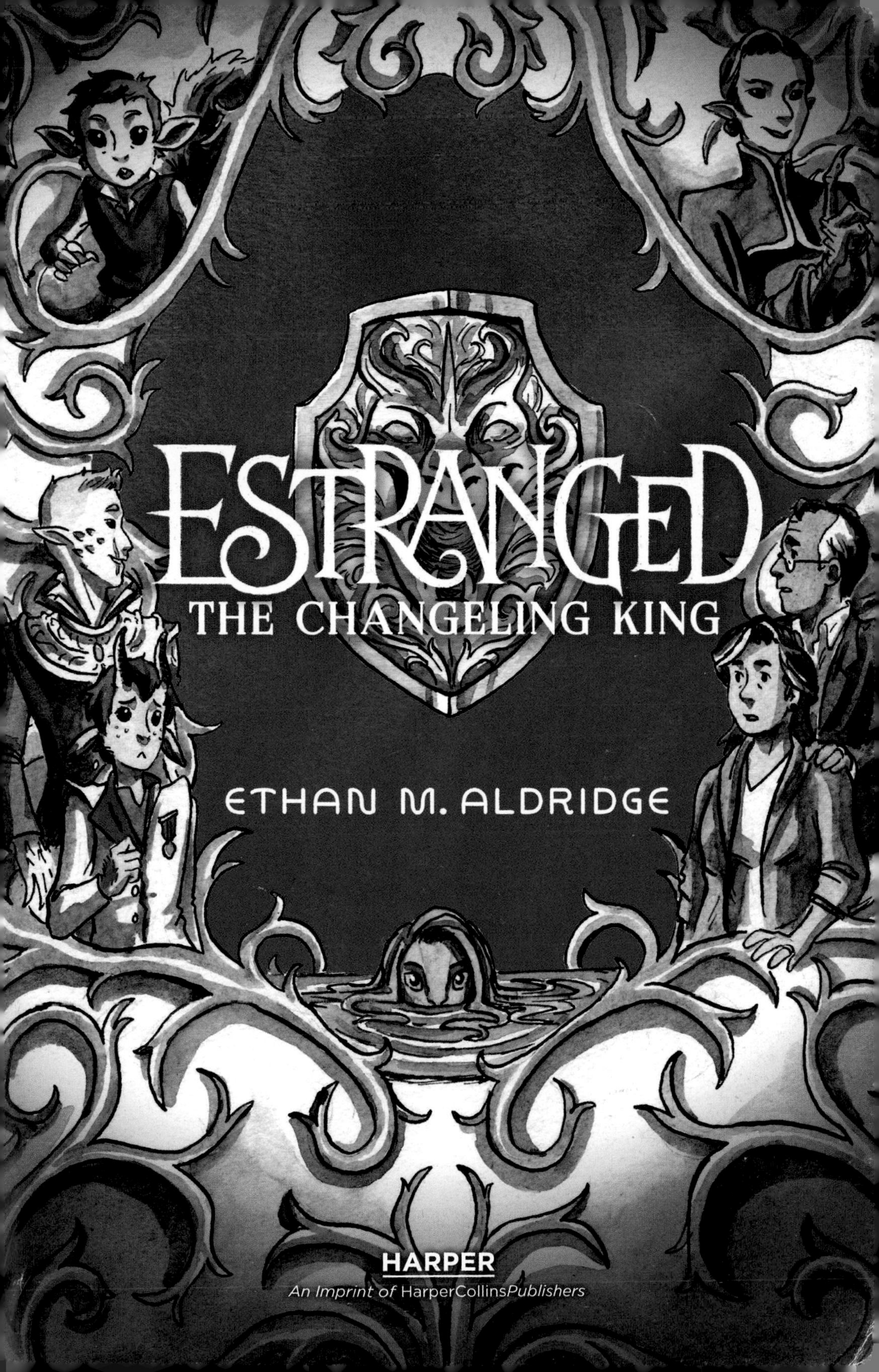

ESTRANGED

THE CHANGELING KING

ETHAN M. ALDRIDGE

HARPER
An Imprint of HarperCollinsPublishers

Estranged: The Changeling King

 For information address HarperCollins Children's Books, a division of HarperCollins Publishers, 195 Broadway, New York, NY 10007.
www.harpercollinschildrens.com

ISBN 978-0-06-265389-5 (paperback) – ISBN 978-0-06-265390-1 (hardcover)

The artist used watercolors, ink, and Photoshop to create the illustrations for this book.
Typography by Catherine San Juan
19 20 21 22 23 SCP 10 9 8 7 6 5 4 3 2 1
❖
First Edition

To Matthew,
the ideal adventuring companion

CHAPTER
ONE

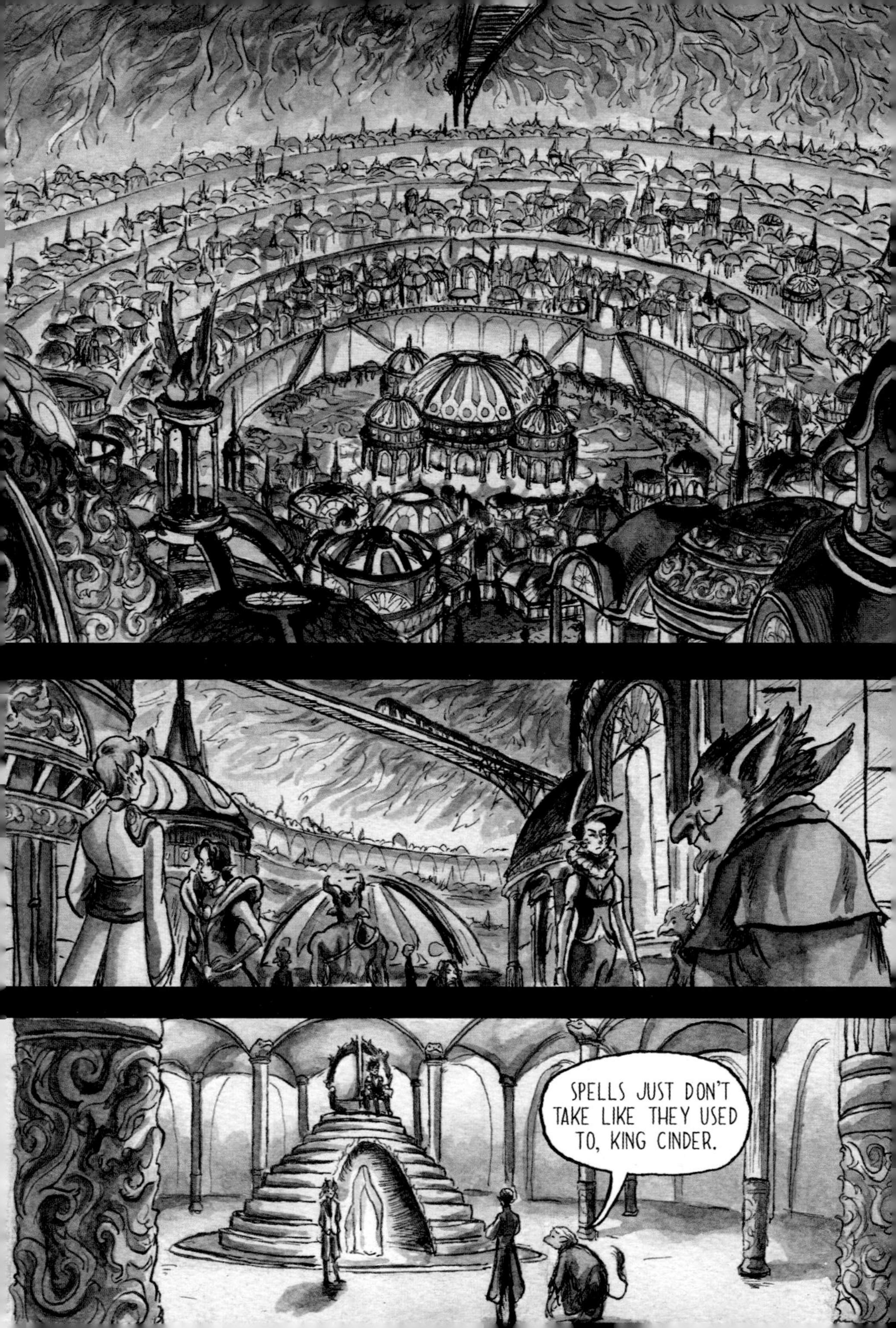
SPELLS JUST DON'T TAKE LIKE THEY USED TO, KING CINDER.

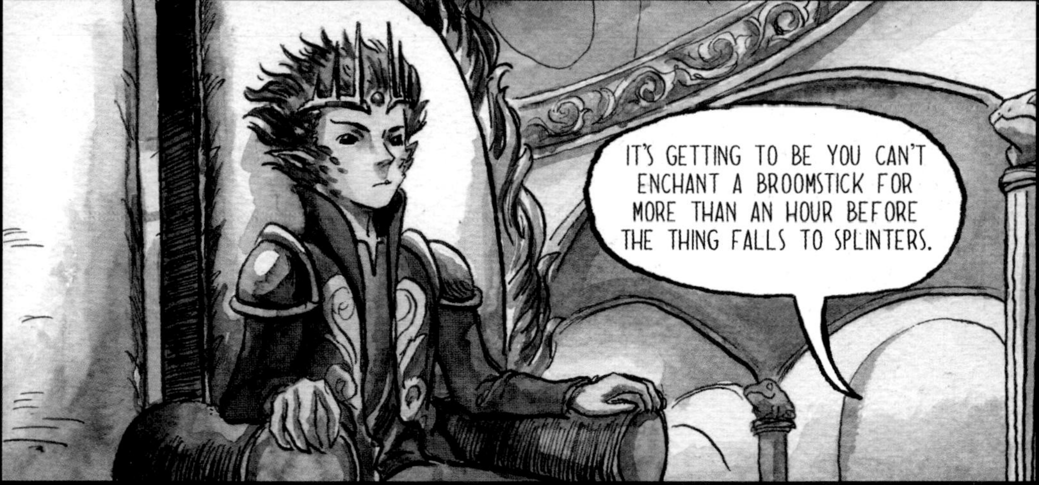
IT'S GETTING TO BE YOU CAN'T ENCHANT A BROOMSTICK FOR MORE THAN AN HOUR BEFORE THE THING FALLS TO SPLINTERS.

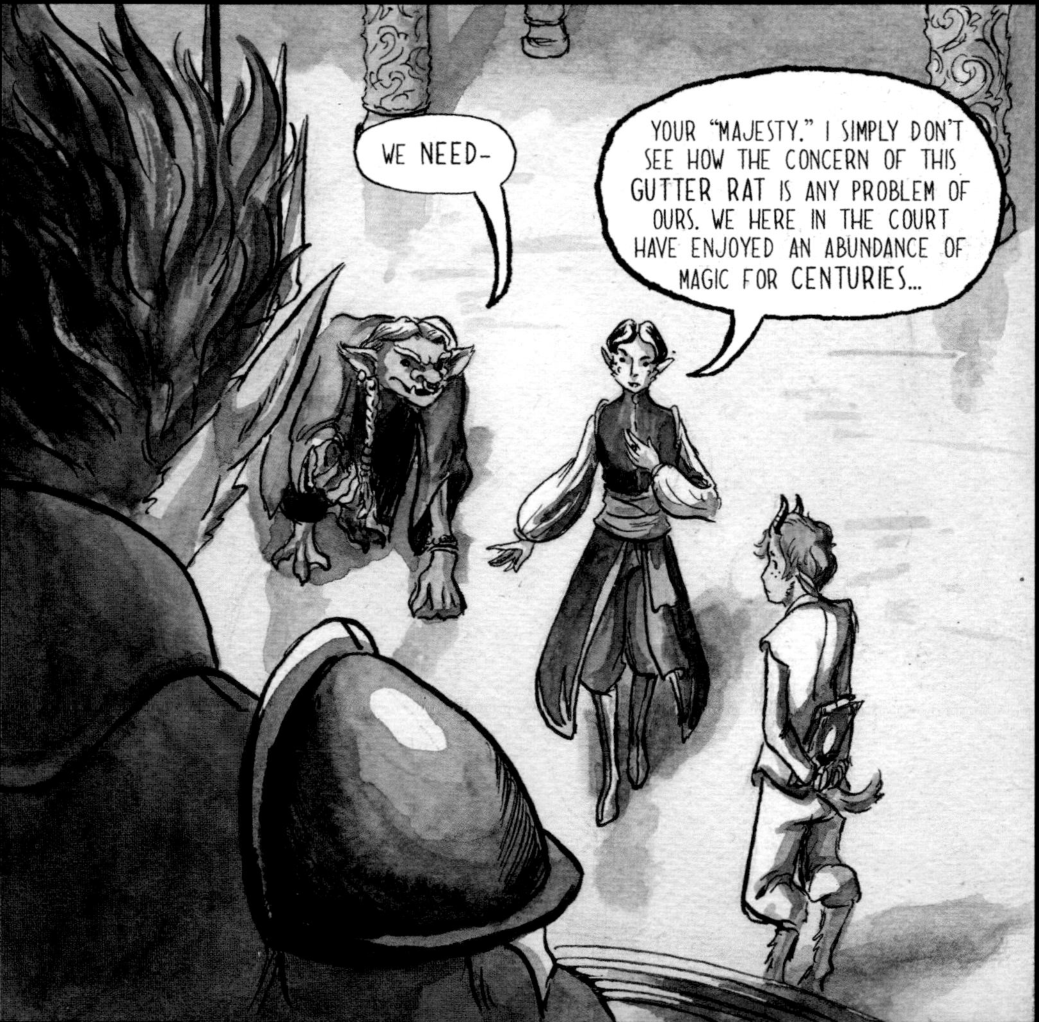
WE NEED-
YOUR "MAJESTY." I SIMPLY DON'T SEE HOW THE CONCERN OF THIS GUTTER RAT IS ANY PROBLEM OF OURS. WE HERE IN THE COURT HAVE ENJOYED AN ABUNDANCE OF MAGIC FOR CENTURIES...

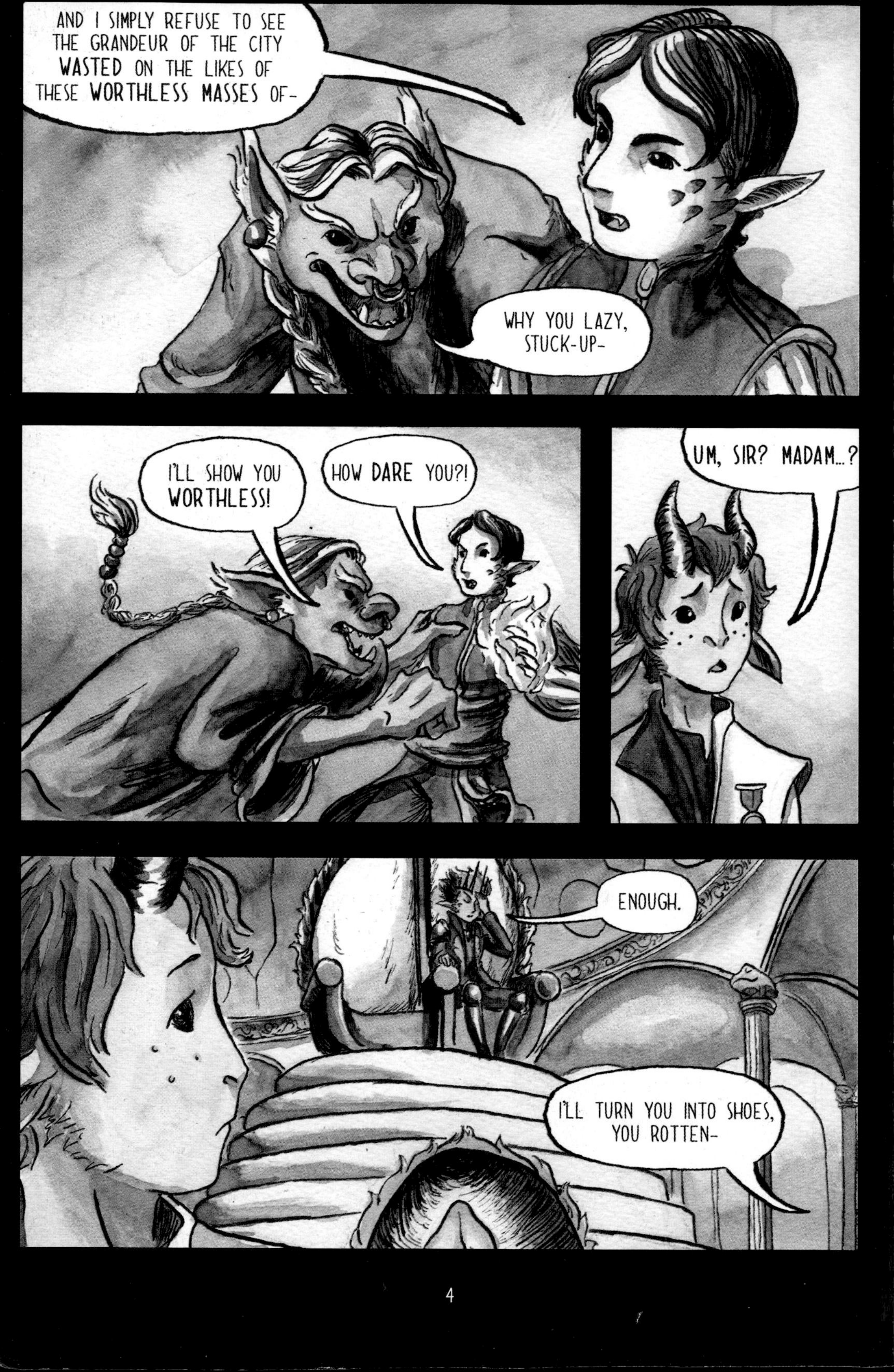
AND I SIMPLY REFUSE TO SEE THE GRANDEUR OF THE CITY WASTED ON THE LIKES OF THESE WORTHLESS MASSES OF-
WHY YOU LAZY, STUCK-UP-
I'LL SHOW YOU WORTHLESS!
HOW DARE YOU?!
UM, SIR? MADAM...?
ENOUGH.
I'LL TURN YOU INTO SHOES, YOU ROTTEN-

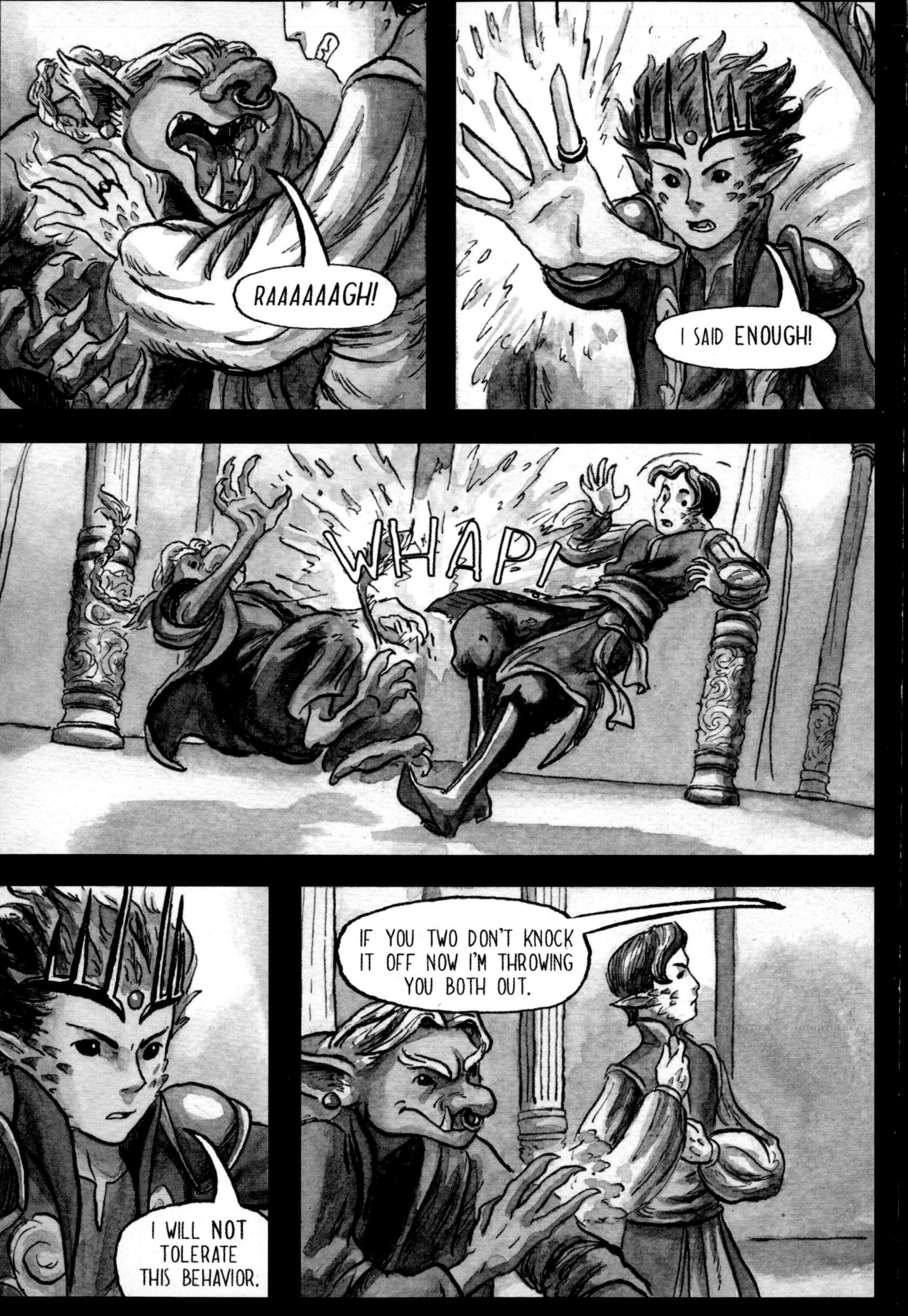
RAAAAAAGH!
I SAID ENOUGH!
WHAP!
I WILL NOT TOLERATE THIS BEHAVIOR.
IF YOU TWO DON'T KNOCK IT OFF NOW I'M THROWING YOU BOTH OUT.

NOW, MS. UM...

MOSSGUTS, YOUR MAJESTY.

...RIGHT. MS. MOSSGUTS—

JUST MOSSGUTS, YOUR MAJESTY. MS. MOSSGUTS WAS THE ANCIENT MOUNTAIN HEART THAT SHATTERED AND MADE MY WHOLE CLAN.

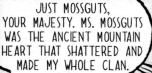

WHAT, REALLY? HOW...DOES THAT WORK EXACTLY? DO YOU ALL—

AHEM...

AH, RIGHT. MOSSGUTS, THEN. I AM AWARE OF THE SITUATION ON THE OUTSKIRTS.

WITH MAGIC IN THE BELOW THE WAY IT IS, WE—

AND Y'ALL HERE IN THE COURT HAVE MAGIC TO SPARE!

6

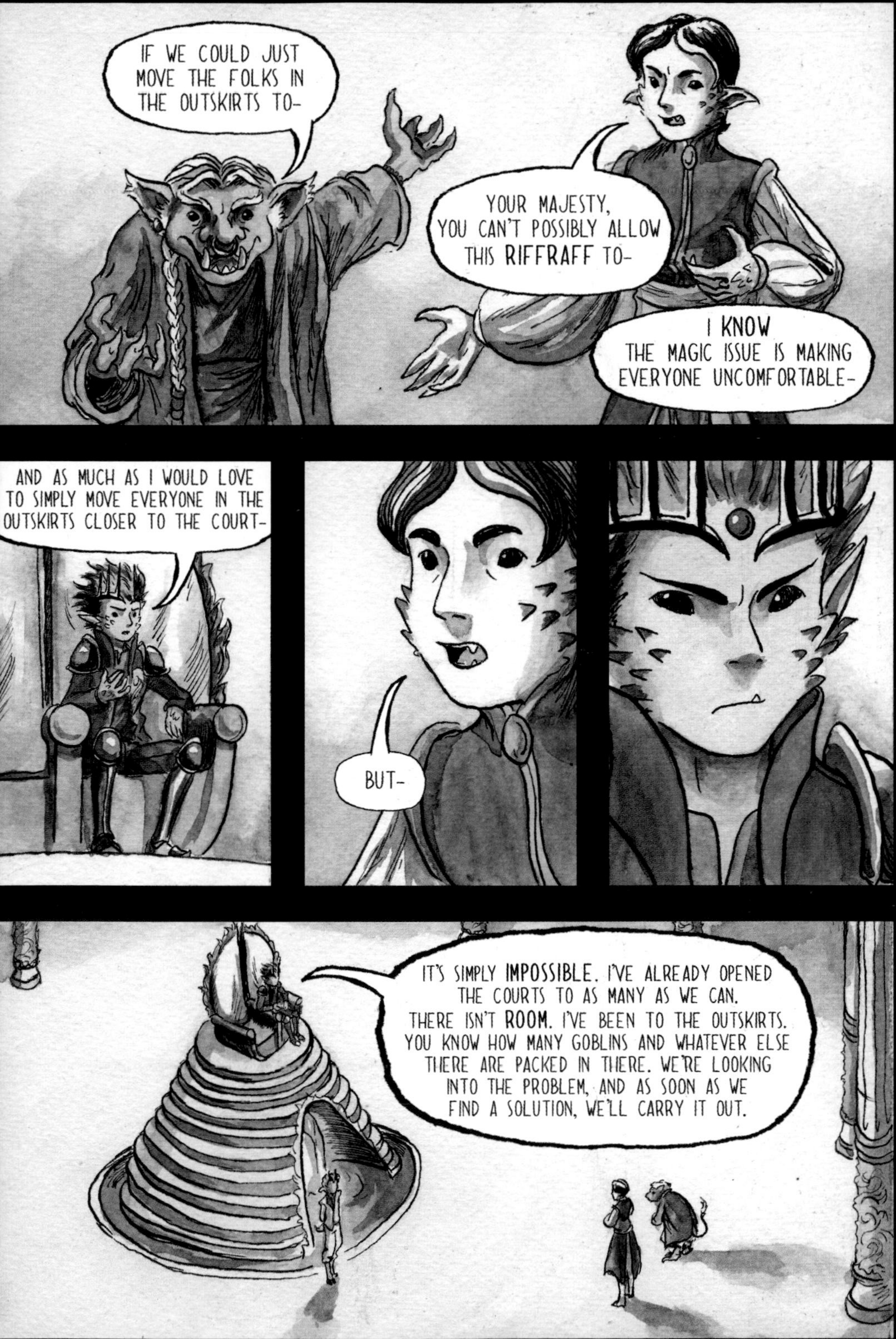
IF WE COULD JUST MOVE THE FOLKS IN THE OUTSKIRTS TO-
YOUR MAJESTY, YOU CAN'T POSSIBLY ALLOW THIS RIFFRAFF TO-
I KNOW THE MAGIC ISSUE IS MAKING EVERYONE UNCOMFORTABLE-
AND AS MUCH AS I WOULD LOVE TO SIMPLY MOVE EVERYONE IN THE OUTSKIRTS CLOSER TO THE COURT-
BUT-
IT'S SIMPLY IMPOSSIBLE. I'VE ALREADY OPENED THE COURTS TO AS MANY AS WE CAN. THERE ISN'T ROOM. I'VE BEEN TO THE OUTSKIRTS. YOU KNOW HOW MANY GOBLINS AND WHATEVER ELSE THERE ARE PACKED IN THERE. WE'RE LOOKING INTO THE PROBLEM, AND AS SOON AS WE FIND A SOLUTION, WE'LL CARRY IT OUT.

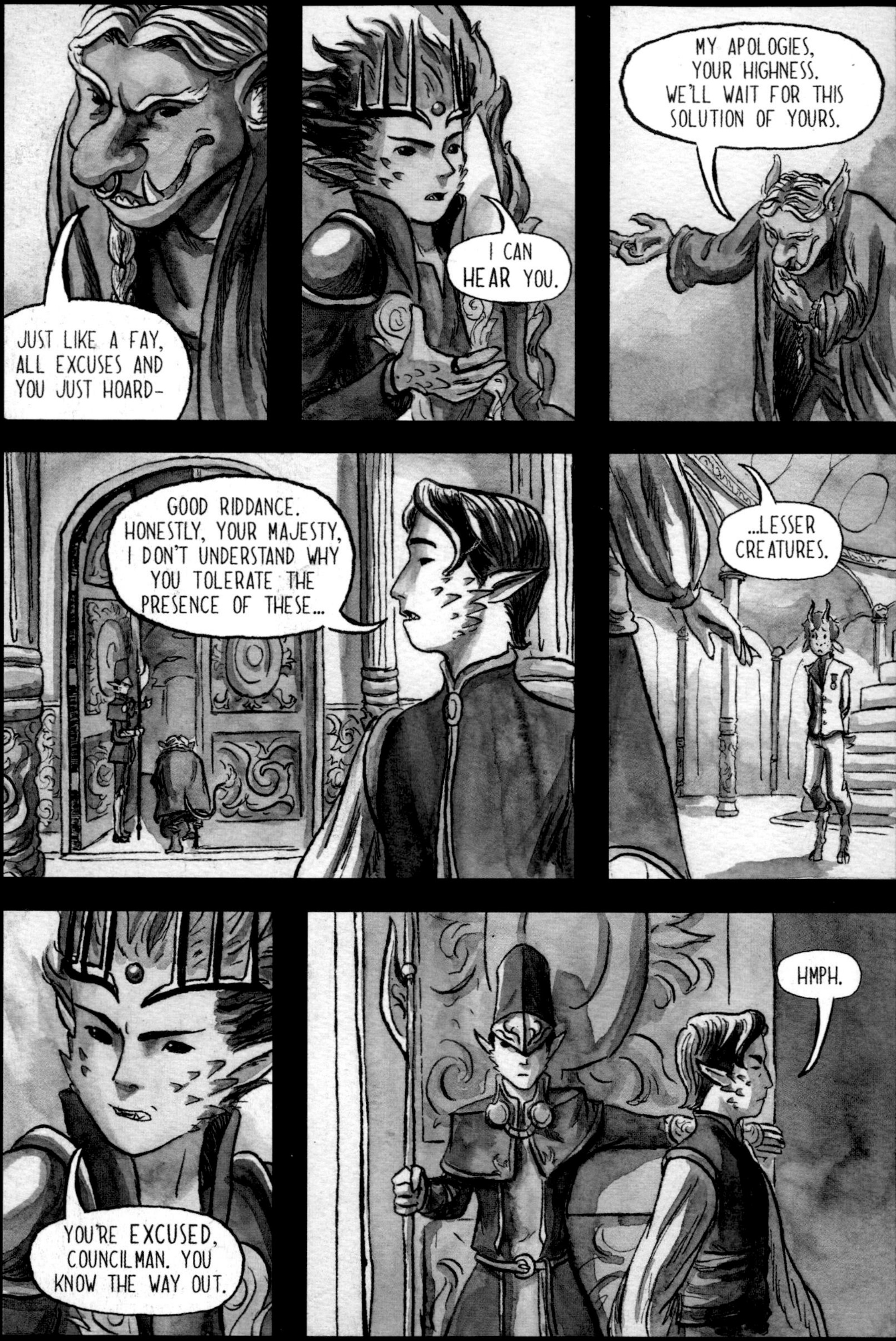
JUST LIKE A FAY, ALL EXCUSES AND YOU JUST HOARD-
I CAN HEAR YOU.
MY APOLOGIES, YOUR HIGHNESS. WE'LL WAIT FOR THIS SOLUTION OF YOURS.
GOOD RIDDANCE. HONESTLY, YOUR MAJESTY, I DON'T UNDERSTAND WHY YOU TOLERATE THE PRESENCE OF THESE...
...LESSER CREATURES.
YOU'RE EXCUSED, COUNCILMAN. YOU KNOW THE WAY OUT.
HMPH.

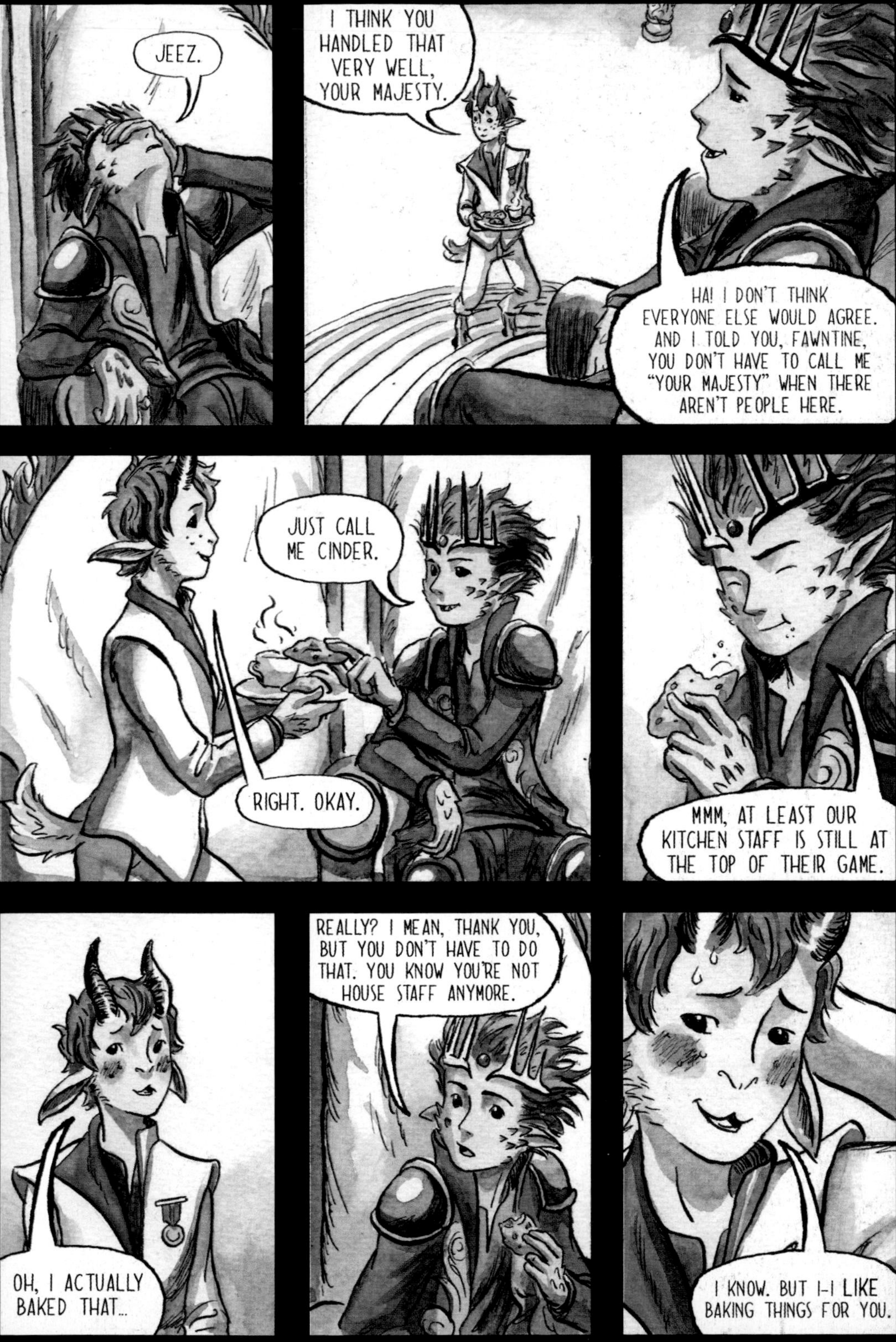
JEEZ.
I THINK YOU HANDLED THAT VERY WELL, YOUR MAJESTY.
HA! I DON'T THINK EVERYONE ELSE WOULD AGREE. AND I TOLD YOU, FAWNTINE, YOU DON'T HAVE TO CALL ME "YOUR MAJESTY" WHEN THERE AREN'T PEOPLE HERE.
JUST CALL ME CINDER.
RIGHT. OKAY.
MMM, AT LEAST OUR KITCHEN STAFF IS STILL AT THE TOP OF THEIR GAME.
OH, I ACTUALLY BAKED THAT...
REALLY? I MEAN, THANK YOU, BUT YOU DON'T HAVE TO DO THAT. YOU KNOW YOU'RE NOT HOUSE STAFF ANYMORE.
I KNOW. BUT I-I LIKE BAKING THINGS FOR YOU.

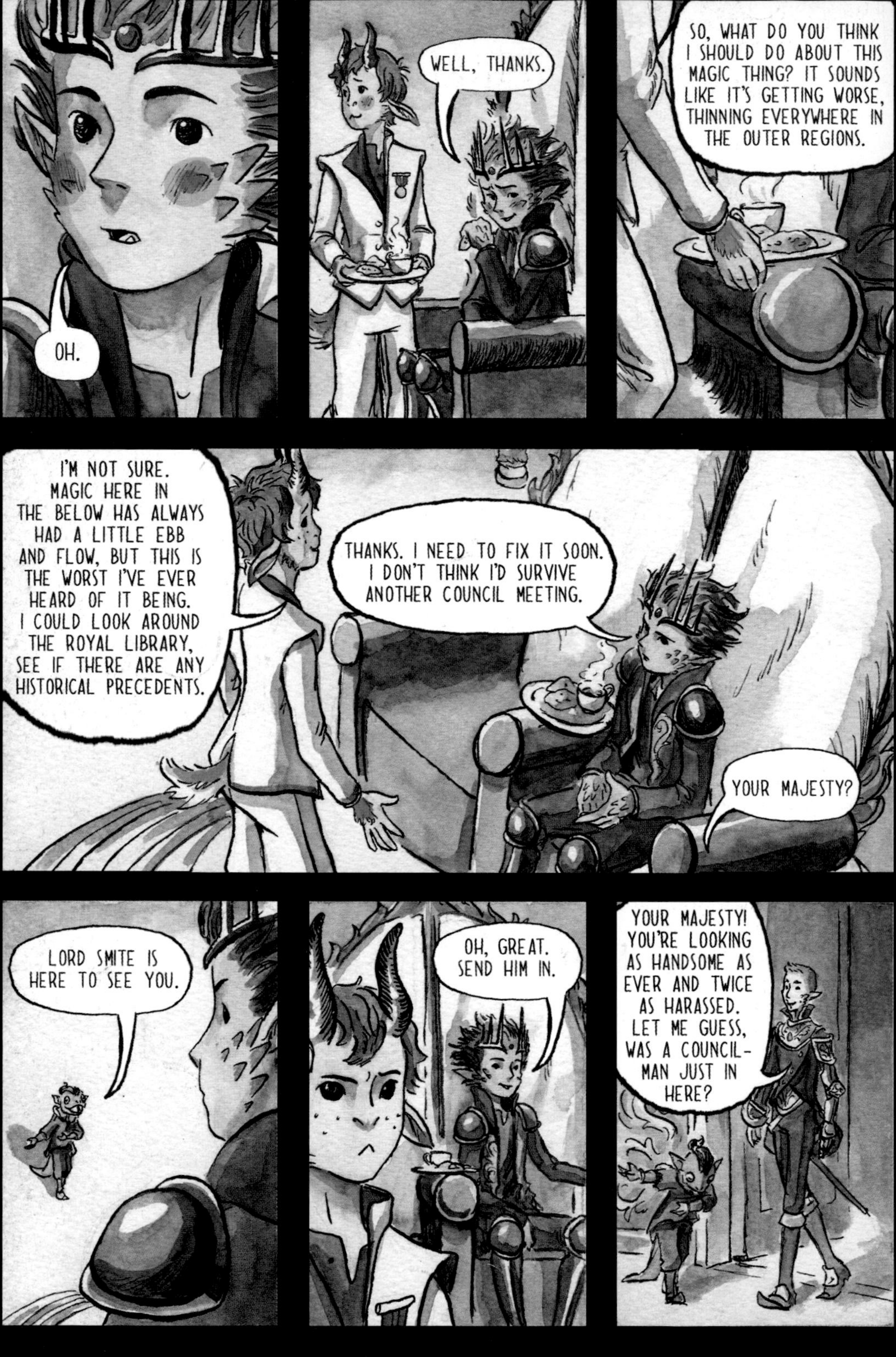
OH.
WELL, THANKS.
SO, WHAT DO YOU THINK I SHOULD DO ABOUT THIS MAGIC THING? IT SOUNDS LIKE IT'S GETTING WORSE, THINNING EVERYWHERE IN THE OUTER REGIONS.
I'M NOT SURE. MAGIC HERE IN THE BELOW HAS ALWAYS HAD A LITTLE EBB AND FLOW, BUT THIS IS THE WORST I'VE EVER HEARD OF IT BEING. I COULD LOOK AROUND THE ROYAL LIBRARY, SEE IF THERE ARE ANY HISTORICAL PRECEDENTS.
THANKS. I NEED TO FIX IT SOON. I DON'T THINK I'D SURVIVE ANOTHER COUNCIL MEETING.
YOUR MAJESTY?
LORD SMITE IS HERE TO SEE YOU.
OH, GREAT. SEND HIM IN.
YOUR MAJESTY! YOU'RE LOOKING AS HANDSOME AS EVER AND TWICE AS HARASSED. LET ME GUESS, WAS A COUNCIL-MAN JUST IN HERE?

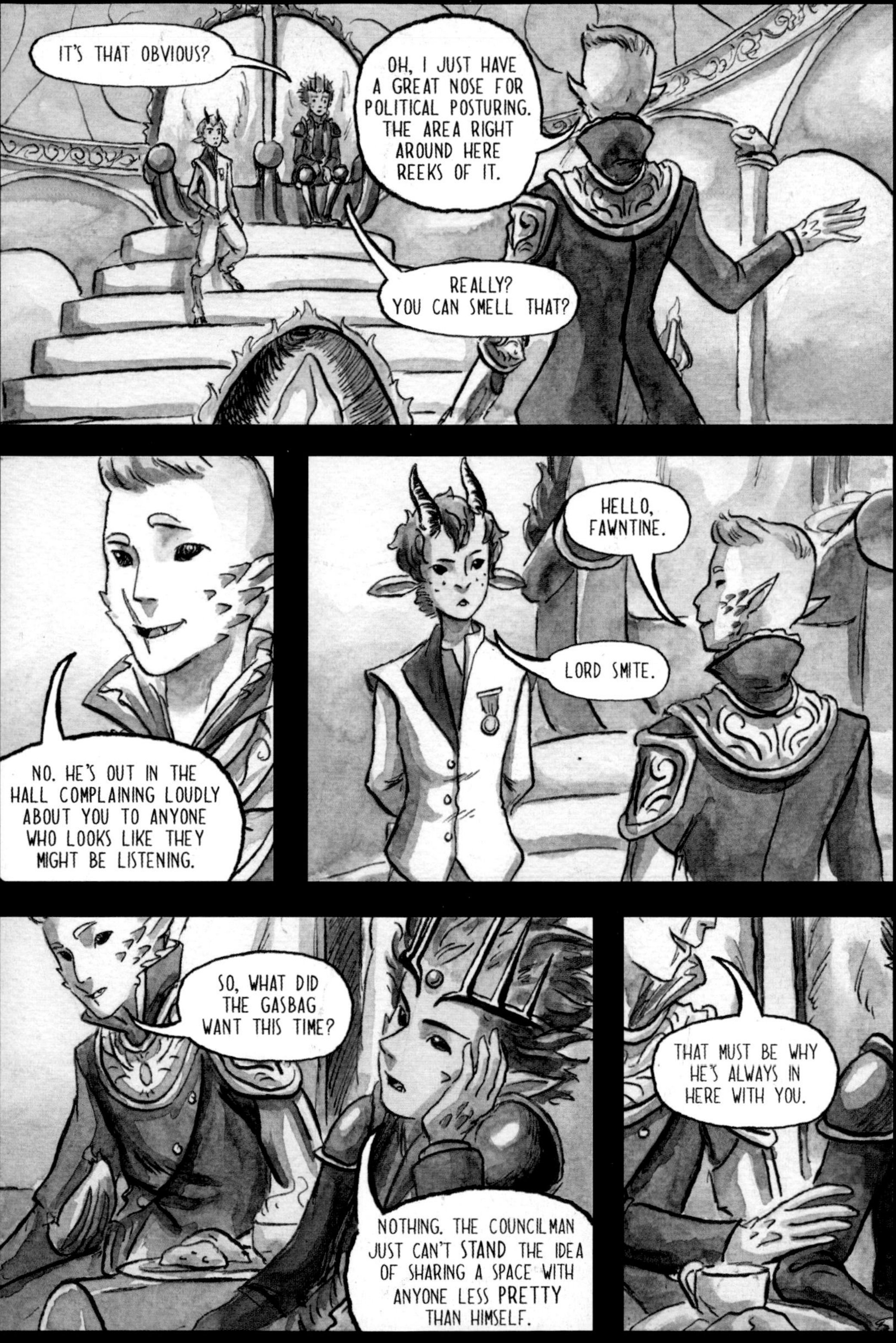
IT'S THAT OBVIOUS?
OH, I JUST HAVE A GREAT NOSE FOR POLITICAL POSTURING. THE AREA RIGHT AROUND HERE REEKS OF IT.
REALLY? YOU CAN SMELL THAT?
NO. HE'S OUT IN THE HALL COMPLAINING LOUDLY ABOUT YOU TO ANYONE WHO LOOKS LIKE THEY MIGHT BE LISTENING.
HELLO, FAWNTINE.
LORD SMITE.
SO, WHAT DID THE GASBAG WANT THIS TIME?
NOTHING. THE COUNCILMAN JUST CAN'T STAND THE IDEA OF SHARING A SPACE WITH ANYONE LESS PRETTY THAN HIMSELF.
THAT MUST BE WHY HE'S ALWAYS IN HERE WITH YOU.

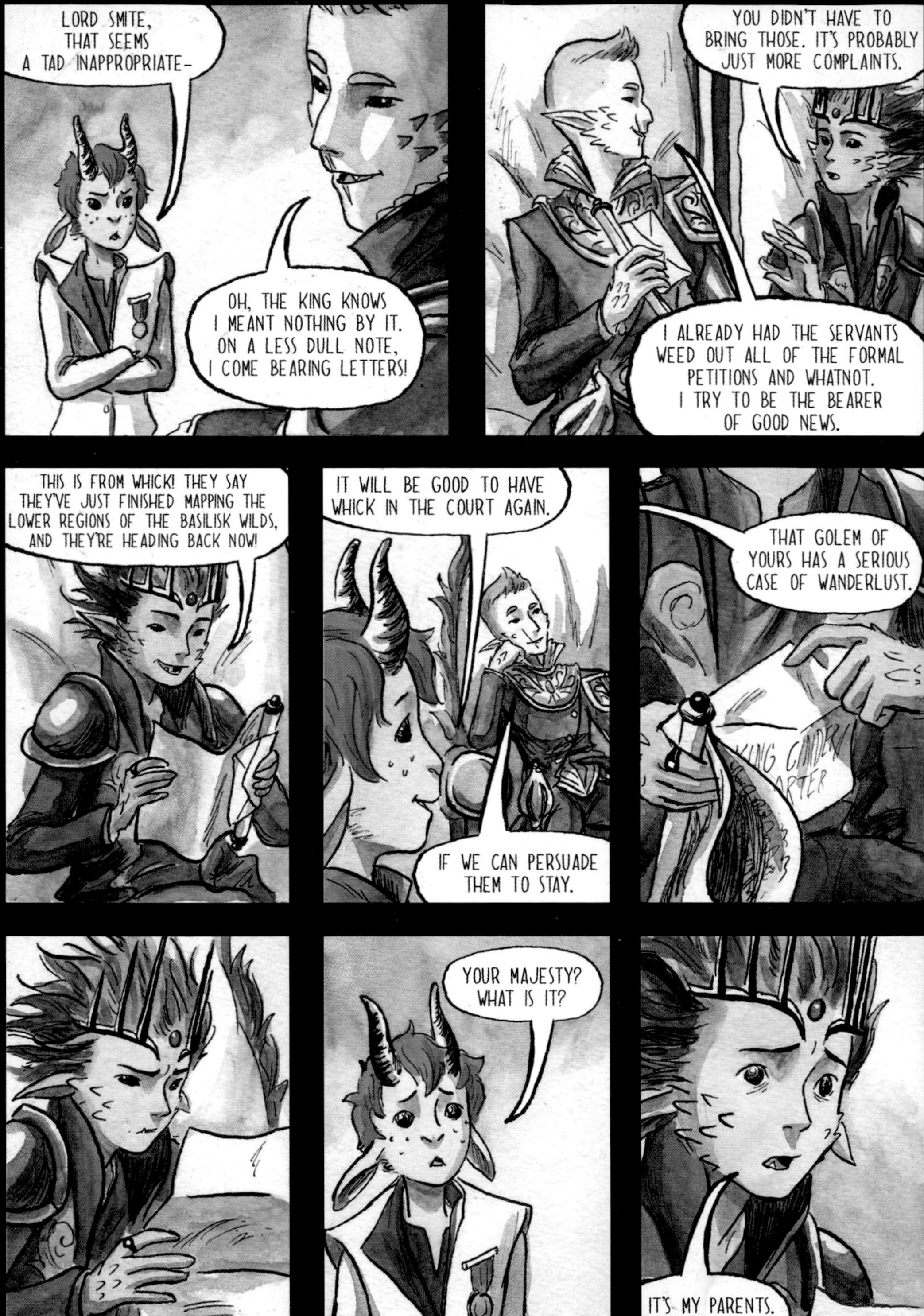
LORD SMITE, THAT SEEMS A TAD INAPPROPRIATE-
OH, THE KING KNOWS I MEANT NOTHING BY IT. ON A LESS DULL NOTE, I COME BEARING LETTERS!
YOU DIDN'T HAVE TO BRING THOSE. IT'S PROBABLY JUST MORE COMPLAINTS.
I ALREADY HAD THE SERVANTS WEED OUT ALL OF THE FORMAL PETITIONS AND WHATNOT. I TRY TO BE THE BEARER OF GOOD NEWS.
THIS IS FROM WHICK! THEY SAY THEY'VE JUST FINISHED MAPPING THE LOWER REGIONS OF THE BASILISK WILDS, AND THEY'RE HEADING BACK NOW!
IT WILL BE GOOD TO HAVE WHICK IN THE COURT AGAIN.
IF WE CAN PERSUADE THEM TO STAY.
THAT GOLEM OF YOURS HAS A SERIOUS CASE OF WANDERLUST.
YOUR MAJESTY? WHAT IS IT?
IT'S MY PARENTS. THEY...WANT TO COME VISIT.

CHAPTER
Two

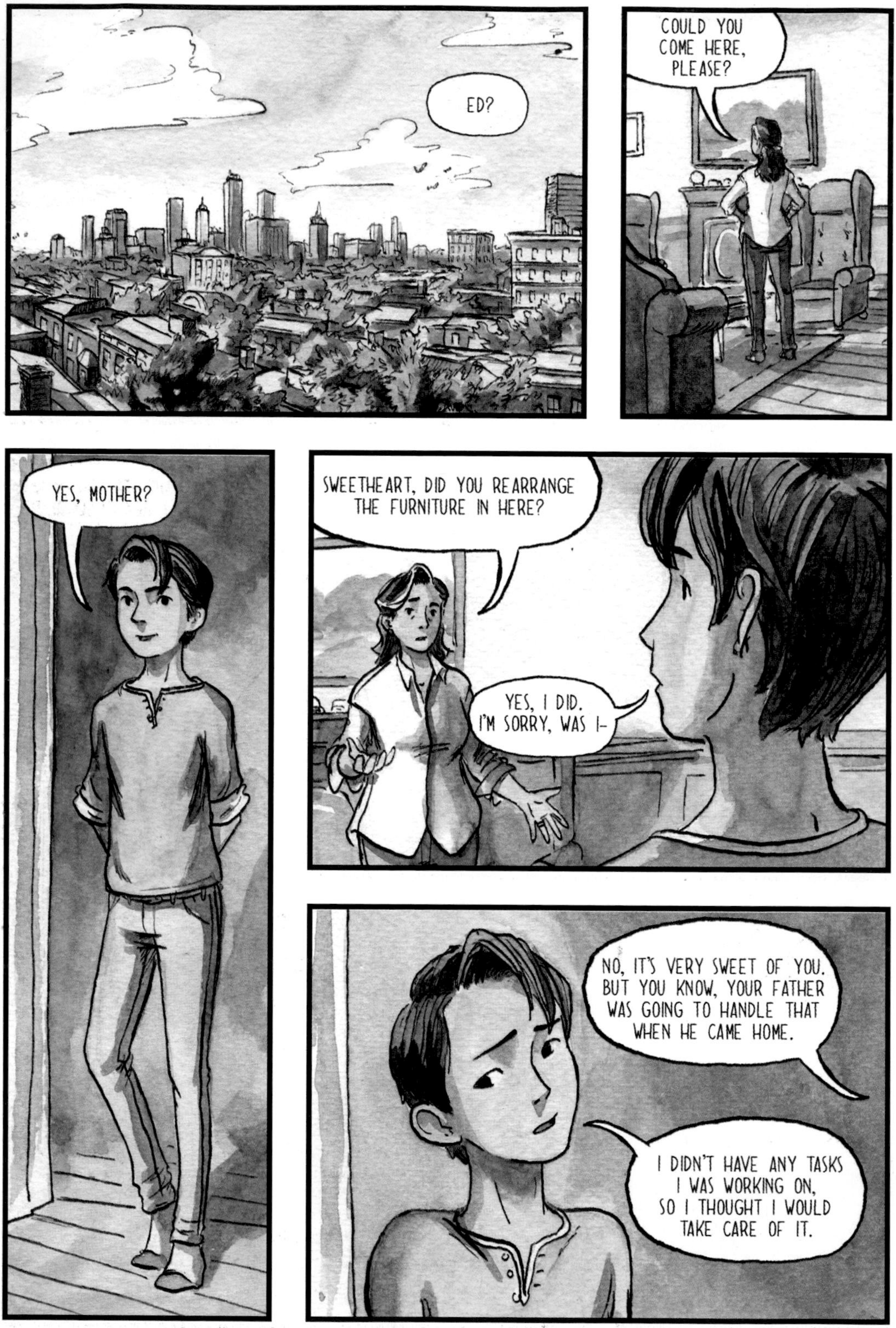
ED?
COULD YOU COME HERE, PLEASE?
YES, MOTHER?
SWEETHEART, DID YOU REARRANGE THE FURNITURE IN HERE?
YES, I DID. I'M SORRY, WAS I-
NO, IT'S VERY SWEET OF YOU. BUT YOU KNOW, YOUR FATHER WAS GOING TO HANDLE THAT WHEN HE CAME HOME.
I DIDN'T HAVE ANY TASKS I WAS WORKING ON, SO I THOUGHT I WOULD TAKE CARE OF IT.

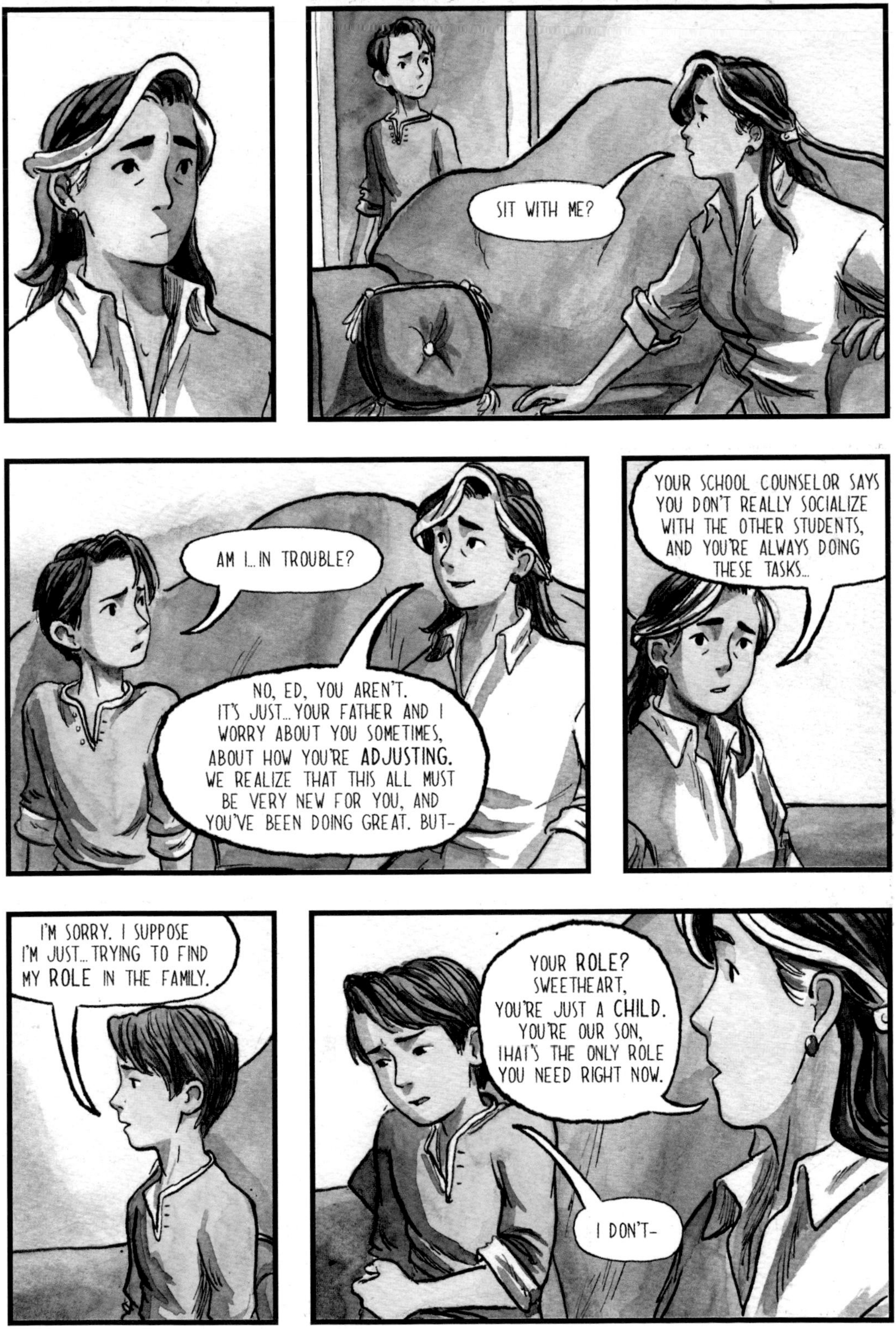
SIT WITH ME?
AM I...IN TROUBLE?
NO, ED, YOU AREN'T. IT'S JUST... YOUR FATHER AND I WORRY ABOUT YOU SOMETIMES, ABOUT HOW YOU'RE ADJUSTING. WE REALIZE THAT THIS ALL MUST BE VERY NEW FOR YOU, AND YOU'VE BEEN DOING GREAT. BUT-
YOUR SCHOOL COUNSELOR SAYS YOU DON'T REALLY SOCIALIZE WITH THE OTHER STUDENTS, AND YOU'RE ALWAYS DOING THESE TASKS...
I'M SORRY. I SUPPOSE I'M JUST... TRYING TO FIND MY ROLE IN THE FAMILY.
YOUR ROLE? SWEETHEART, YOU'RE JUST A CHILD. YOU'RE OUR SON, THAT'S THE ONLY ROLE YOU NEED RIGHT NOW.
I DON'T-

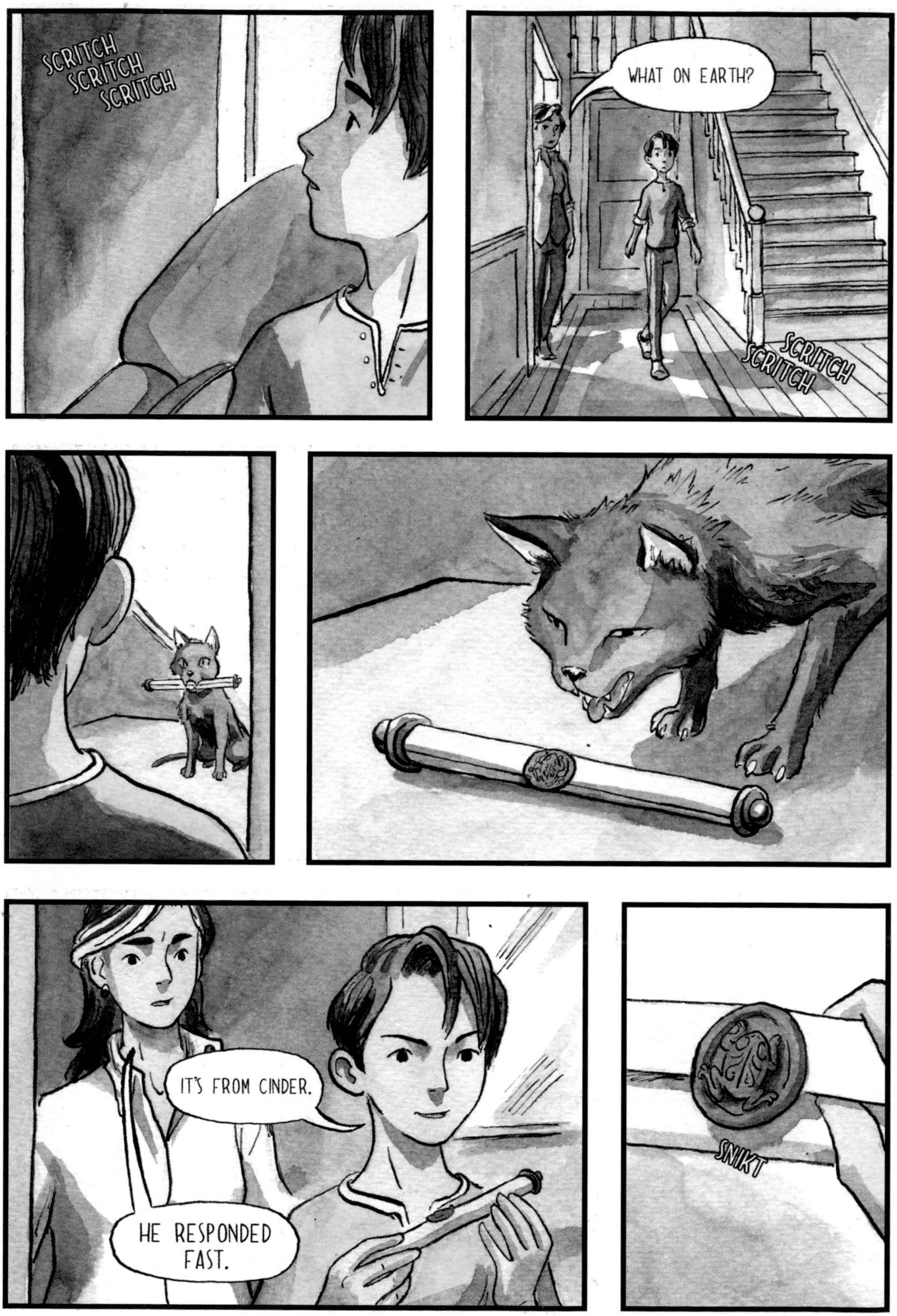
SCRITCH
SCRITCH
SCRITCH
WHAT ON EARTH?
SCRITCH
SCRITCH
IT'S FROM CINDER.
HE RESPONDED FAST.
SNIKT

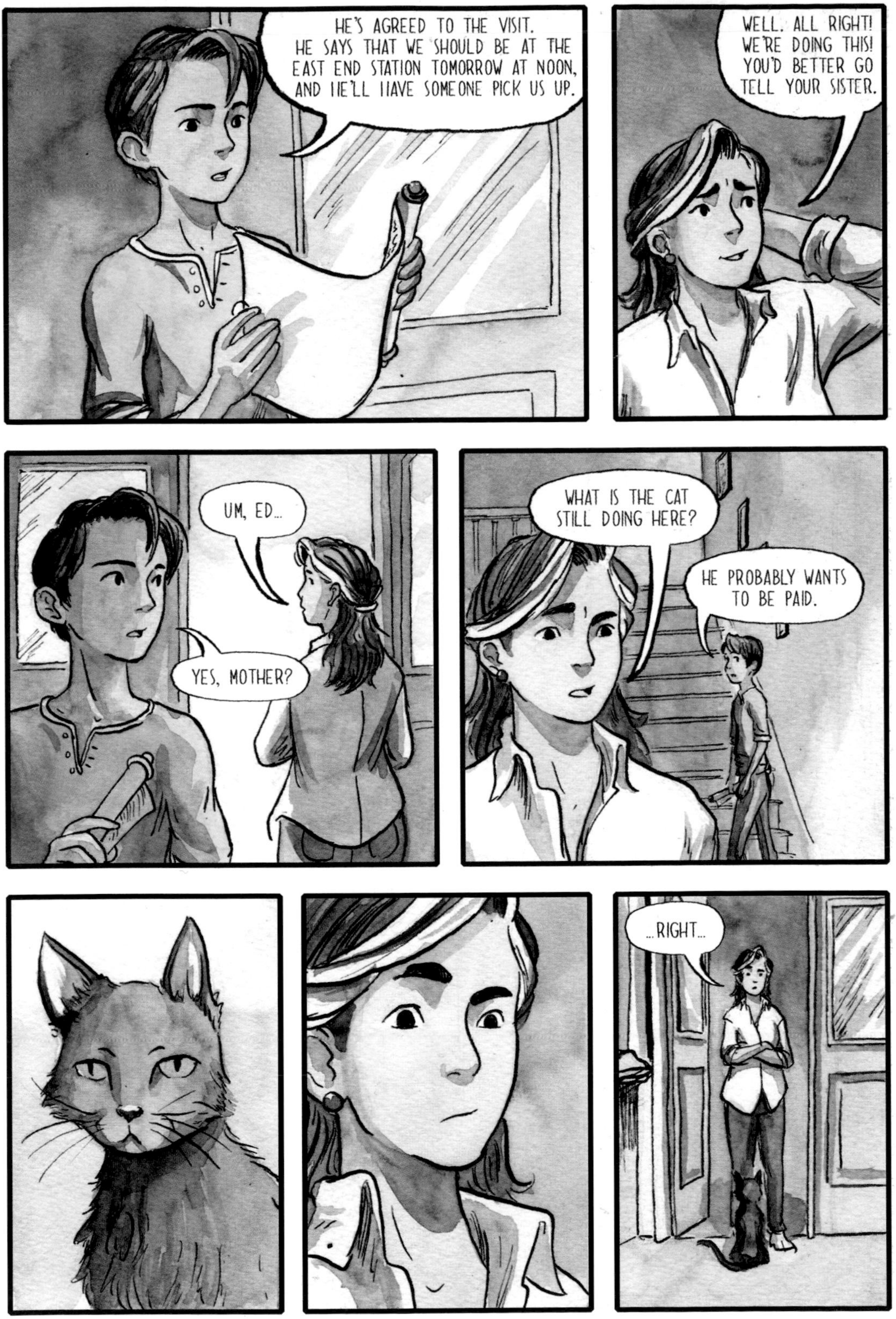
HE'S AGREED TO THE VISIT. HE SAYS THAT WE SHOULD BE AT THE EAST END STATION TOMORROW AT NOON, AND HE'LL HAVE SOMEONE PICK US UP.
WELL. ALL RIGHT! WE'RE DOING THIS! YOU'D BETTER GO TELL YOUR SISTER.
UM, ED...
YES, MOTHER?
WHAT IS THE CAT STILL DOING HERE?
HE PROBABLY WANTS TO BE PAID.
...RIGHT...

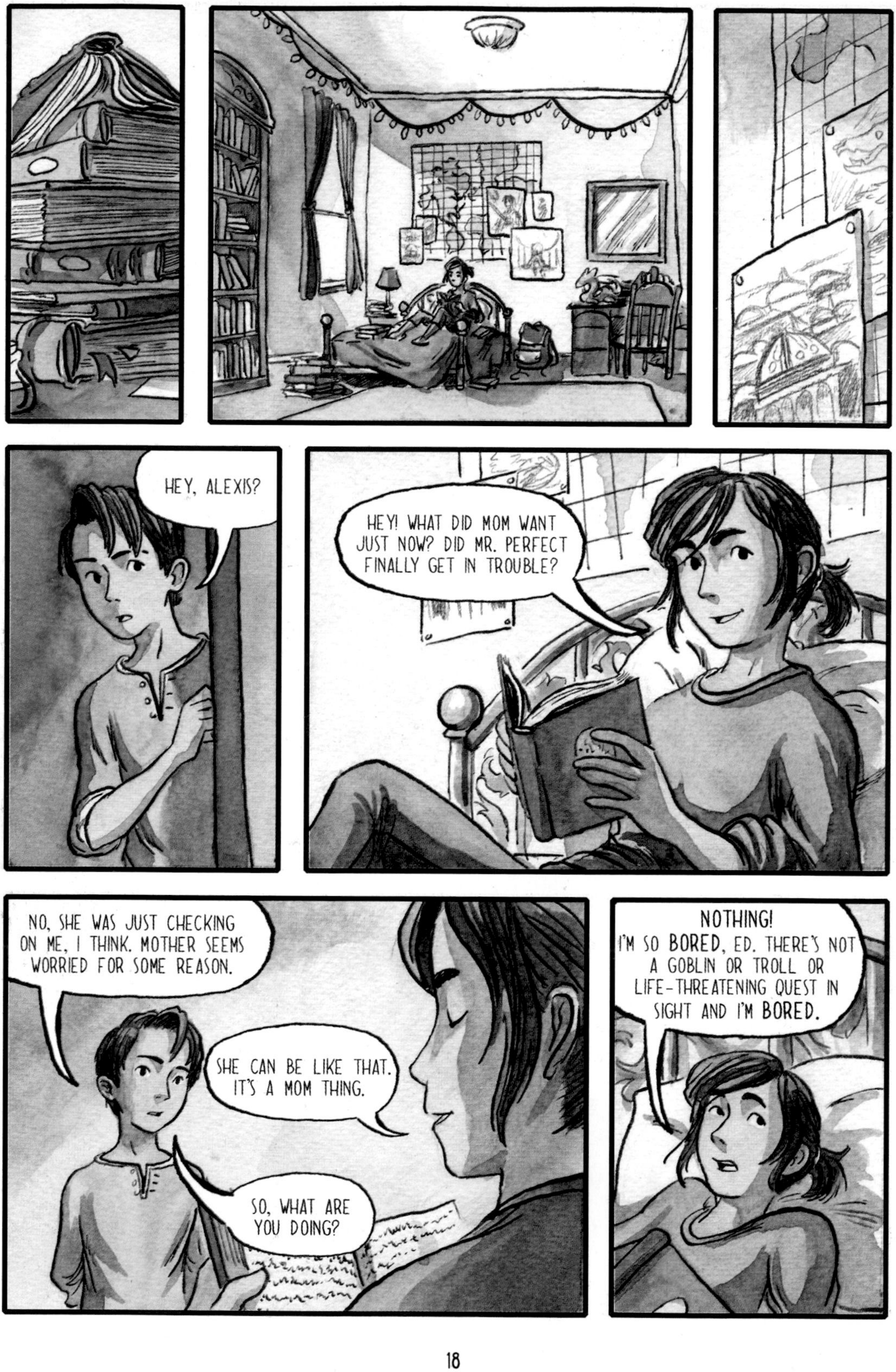
HEY, ALEXIS?
HEY! WHAT DID MOM WANT JUST NOW? DID MR. PERFECT FINALLY GET IN TROUBLE?
NO, SHE WAS JUST CHECKING ON ME, I THINK. MOTHER SEEMS WORRIED FOR SOME REASON.
SHE CAN BE LIKE THAT. IT'S A MOM THING.
SO, WHAT ARE YOU DOING?
NOTHING! I'M SO BORED, ED. THERE'S NOT A GOBLIN OR TROLL OR LIFE-THREATENING QUEST IN SIGHT AND I'M BORED.

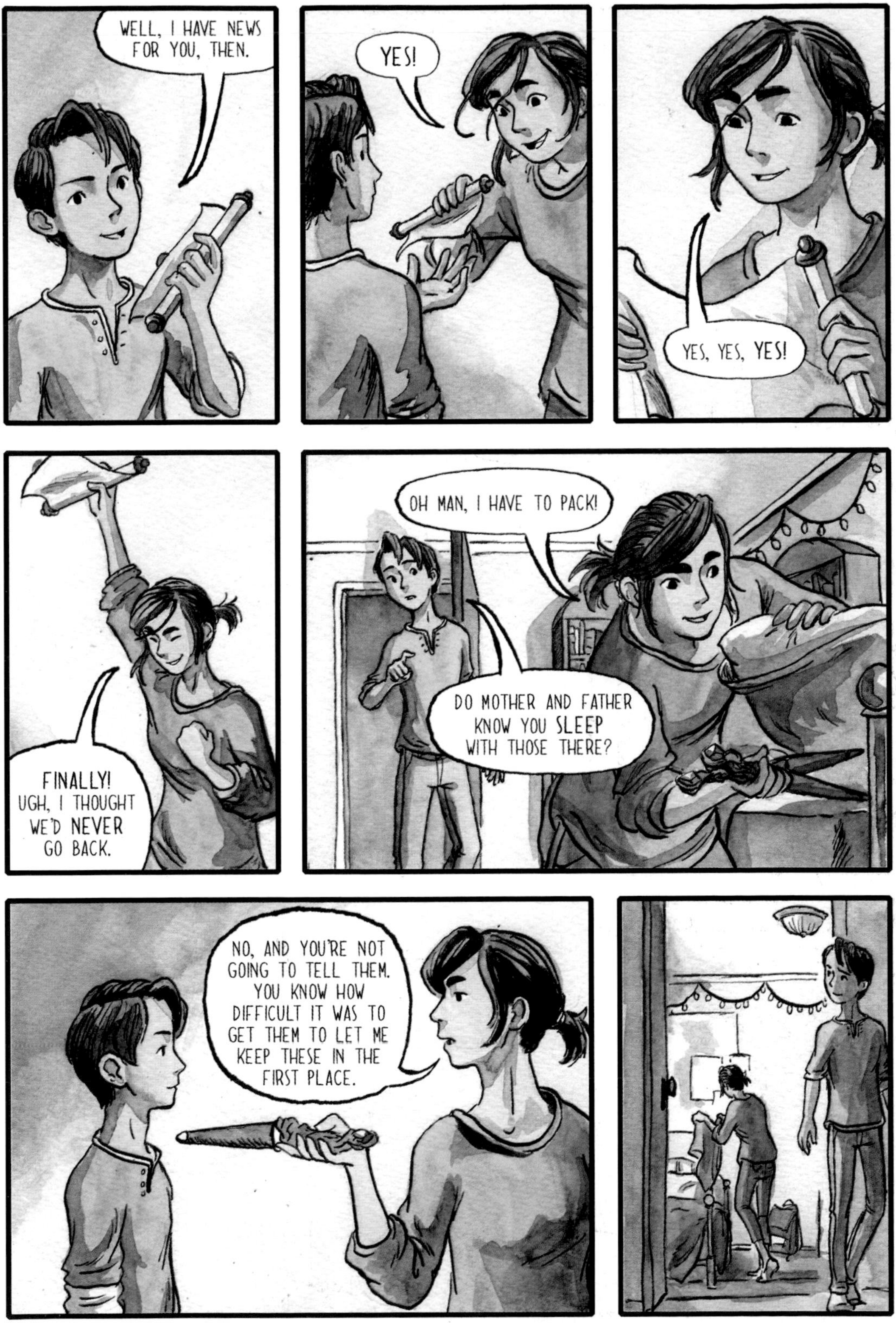
WELL, I HAVE NEWS FOR YOU, THEN.
YES!
YES, YES, YES!
FINALLY! UGH, I THOUGHT WE'D NEVER GO BACK.
OH MAN, I HAVE TO PACK!
DO MOTHER AND FATHER KNOW YOU SLEEP WITH THOSE THERE?
NO, AND YOU'RE NOT GOING TO TELL THEM. YOU KNOW HOW DIFFICULT IT WAS TO GET THEM TO LET ME KEEP THESE IN THE FIRST PLACE.

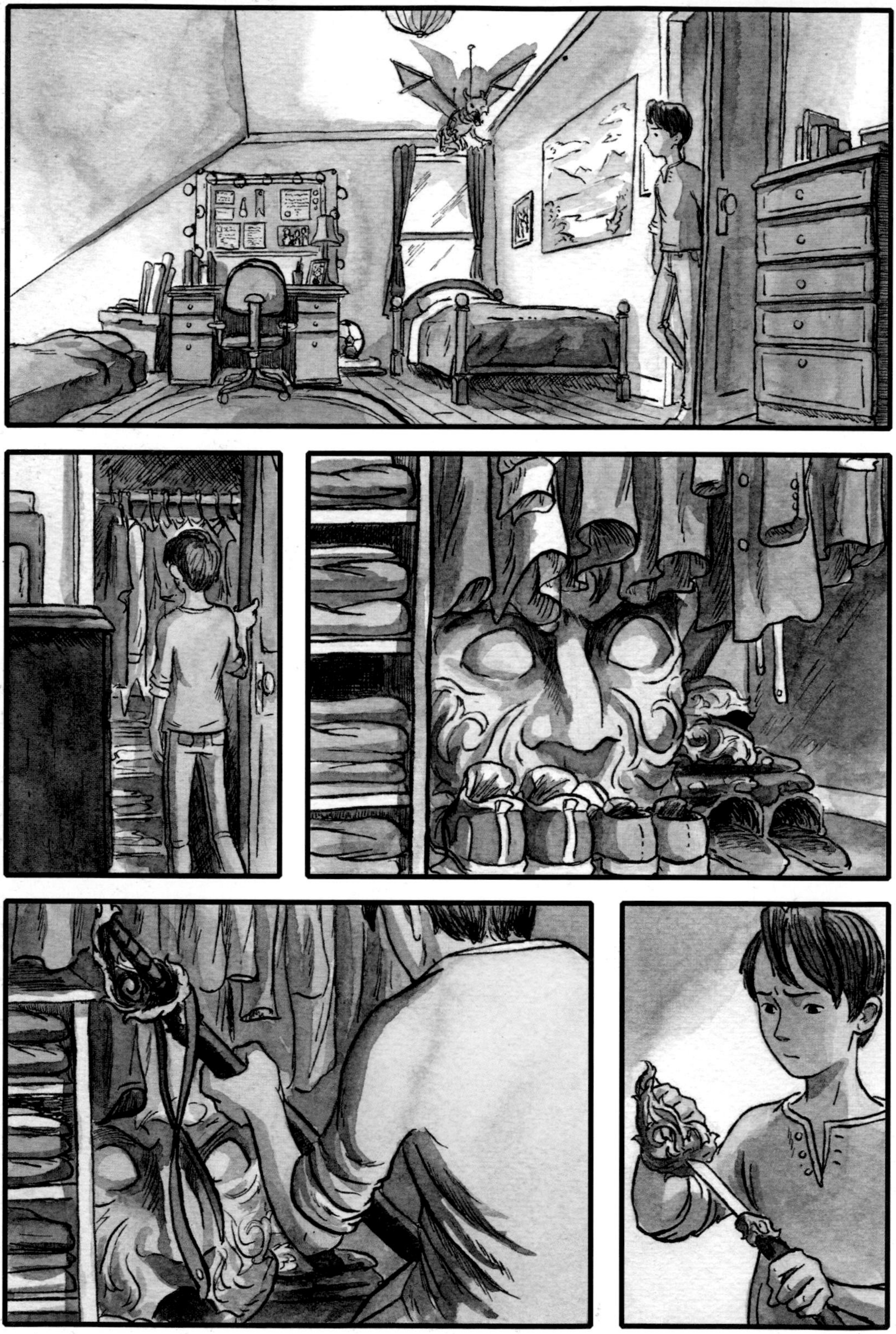

CHAPTER THREE

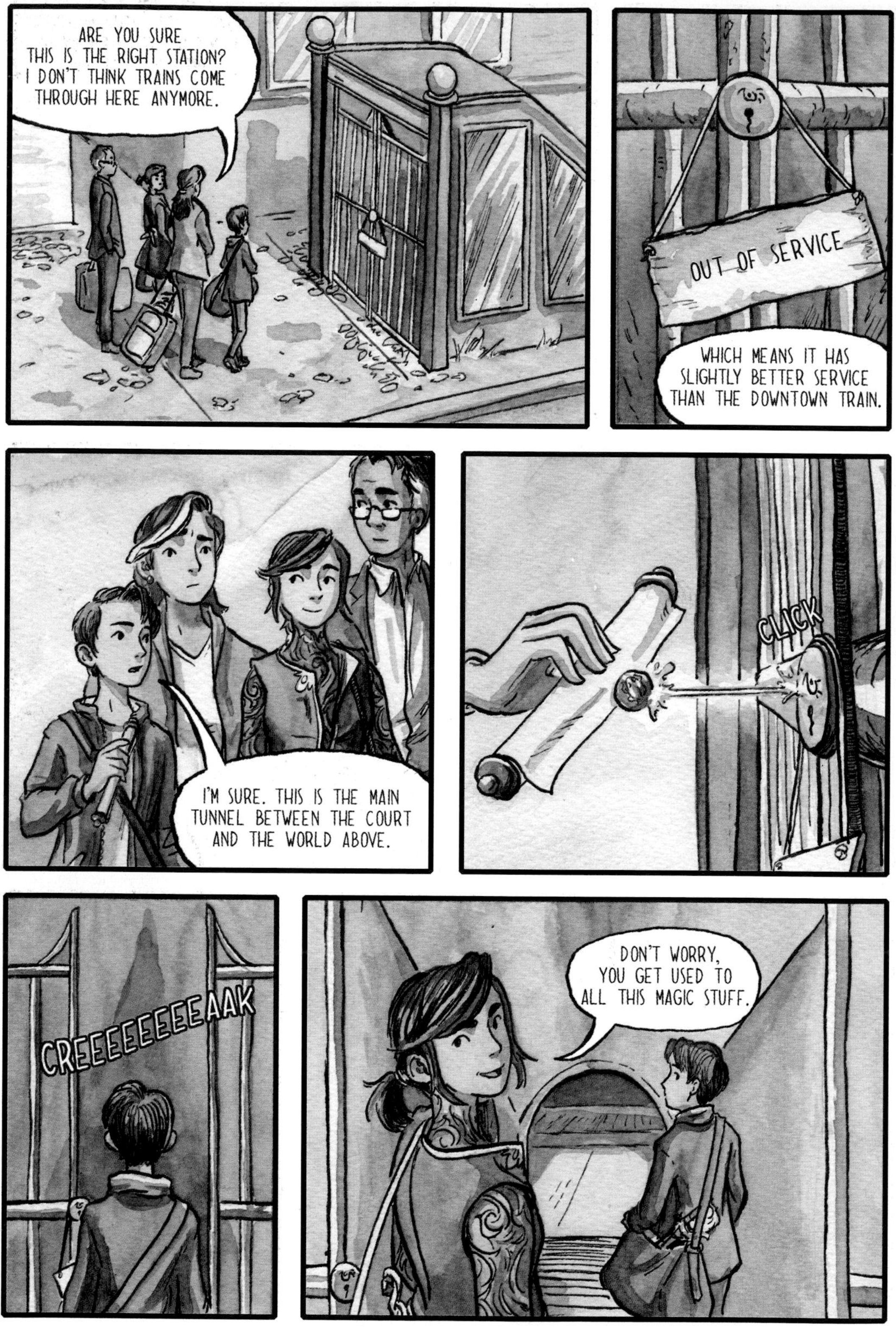
ARE YOU SURE THIS IS THE RIGHT STATION? I DON'T THINK TRAINS COME THROUGH HERE ANYMORE.
OUT OF SERVICE
WHICH MEANS IT HAS SLIGHTLY BETTER SERVICE THAN THE DOWNTOWN TRAIN.
I'M SURE. THIS IS THE MAIN TUNNEL BETWEEN THE COURT AND THE WORLD ABOVE.
CLICK
CREEEEEEEEAAK
DON'T WORRY, YOU GET USED TO ALL THIS MAGIC STUFF.

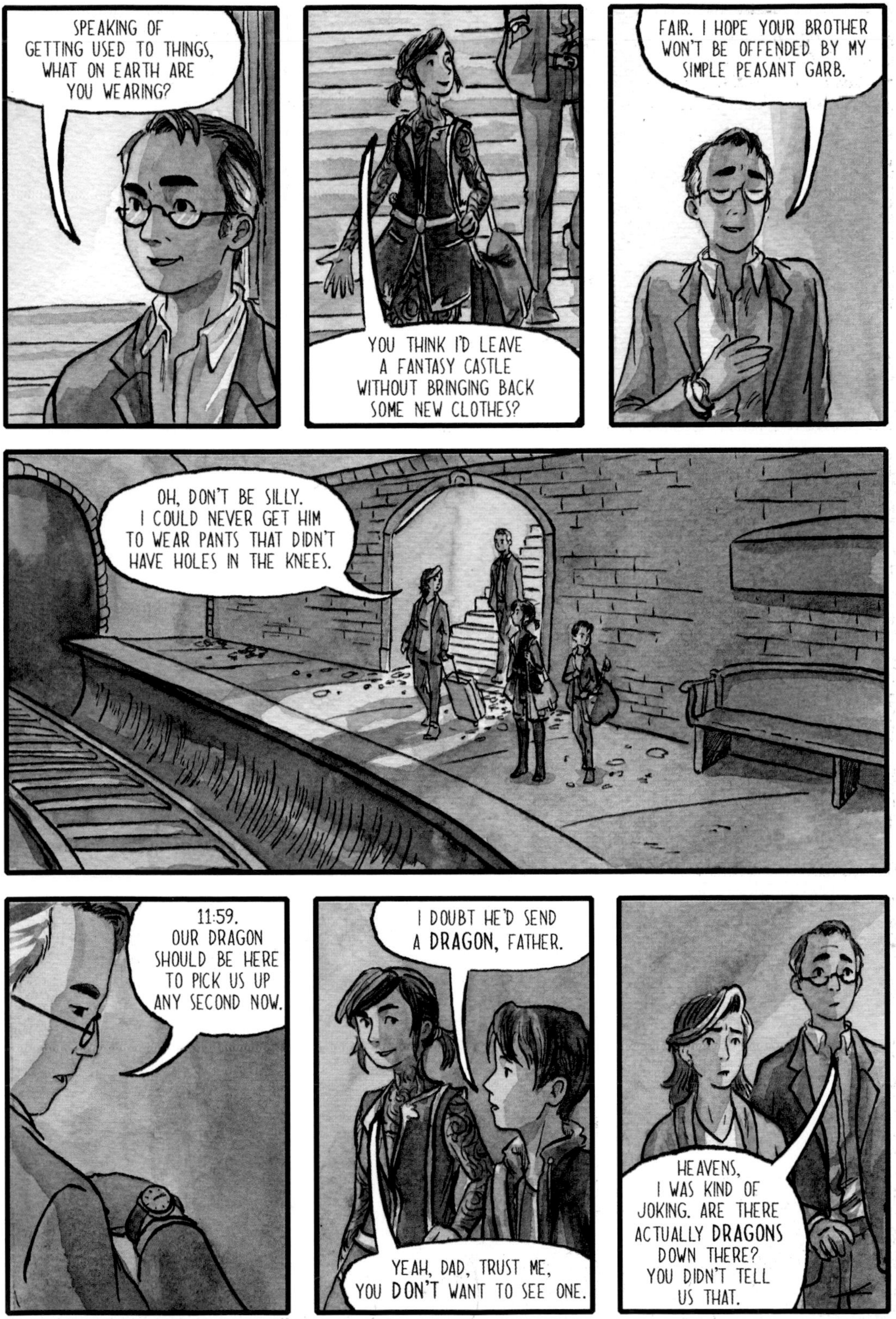
SPEAKING OF GETTING USED TO THINGS, WHAT ON EARTH ARE YOU WEARING?
YOU THINK I'D LEAVE A FANTASY CASTLE WITHOUT BRINGING BACK SOME NEW CLOTHES?
FAIR. I HOPE YOUR BROTHER WON'T BE OFFENDED BY MY SIMPLE PEASANT GARB.
OH, DON'T BE SILLY. I COULD NEVER GET HIM TO WEAR PANTS THAT DIDN'T HAVE HOLES IN THE KNEES.
11:59. OUR DRAGON SHOULD BE HERE TO PICK US UP ANY SECOND NOW.
I DOUBT HE'D SEND A **DRAGON**, FATHER.
YEAH, DAD, TRUST ME, YOU **DON'T** WANT TO SEE ONE.
HEAVENS, I WAS KIND OF JOKING. ARE THERE ACTUALLY **DRAGONS** DOWN THERE? YOU DIDN'T TELL US THAT.

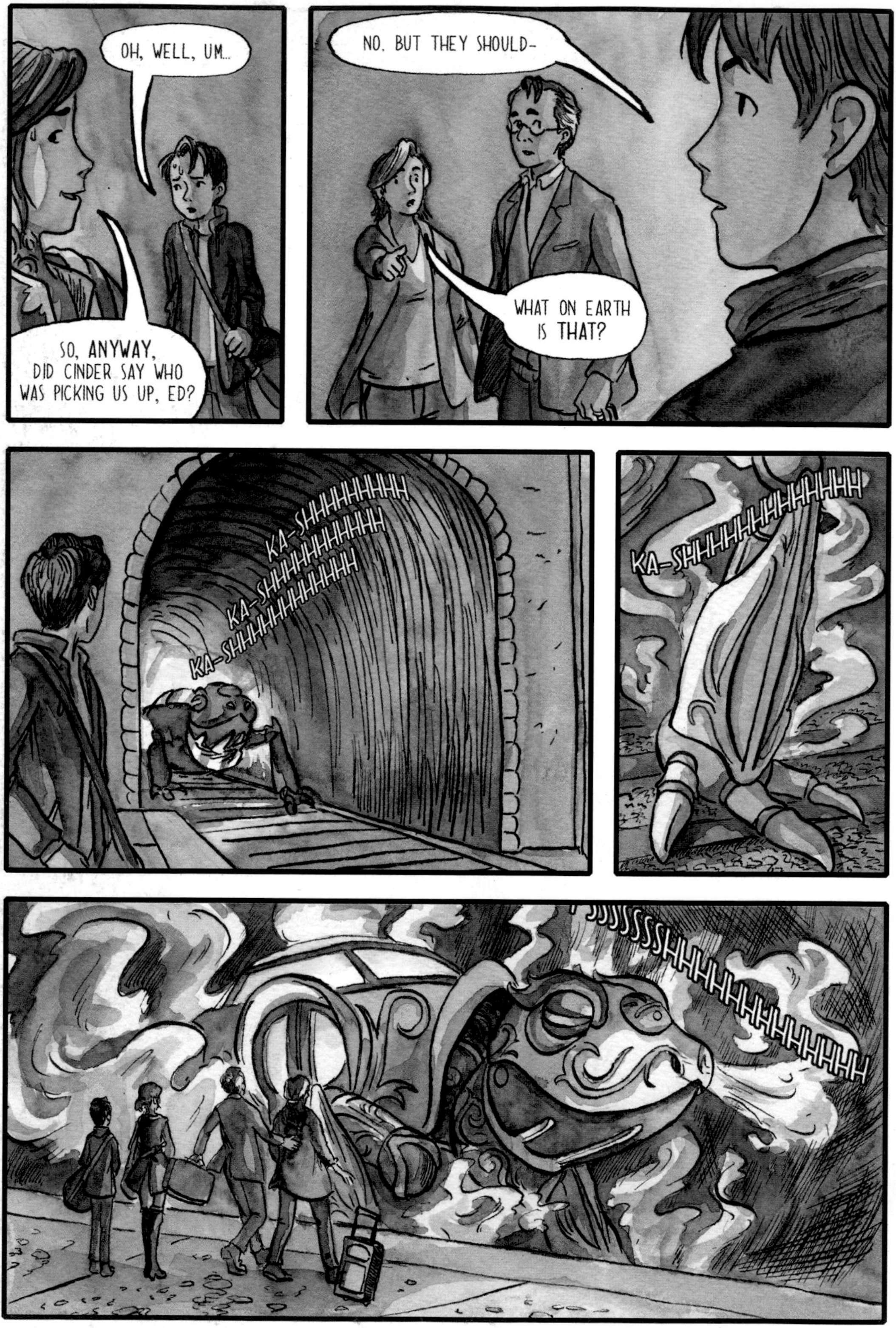
OH, WELL, UM...
SO, ANYWAY, DID CINDER SAY WHO WAS PICKING US UP, ED?
NO. BUT THEY SHOULD-
WHAT ON EARTH IS THAT?
KA-SHHHHHHHHHH
KA-SHHHHHHHHHHH
KA-SHHHHHHHHHHHH
KA-SHHHHHHHHHHHH
KA-SHHHHHHHHHHHHH
SSSSSSSSHHHHHHHHHHHHHHHH

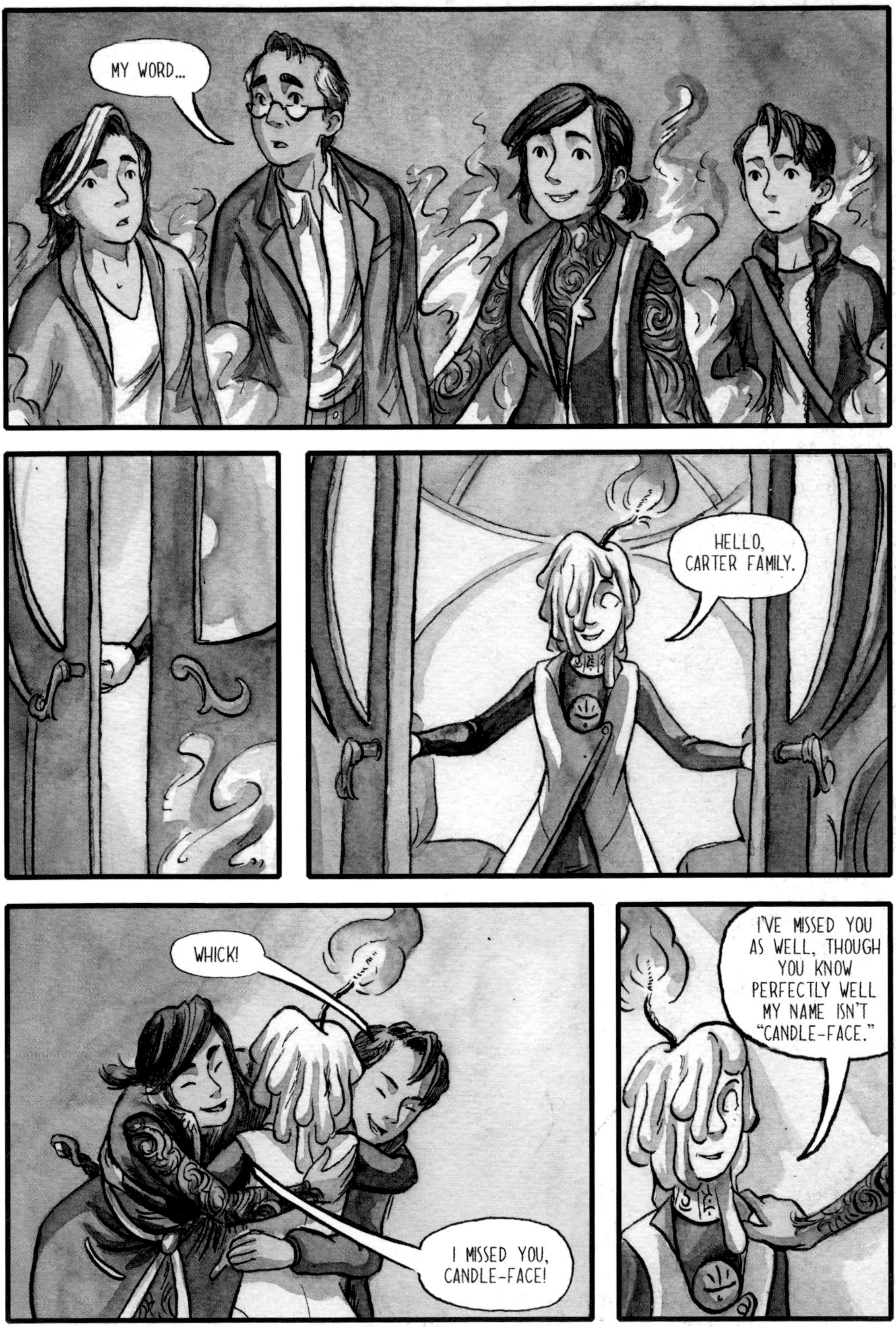
MY WORD...
HELLO, CARTER FAMILY.
WHICK!
I MISSED YOU, CANDLE-FACE!
I'VE MISSED YOU AS WELL, THOUGH YOU KNOW PERFECTLY WELL MY NAME ISN'T "CANDLE-FACE."

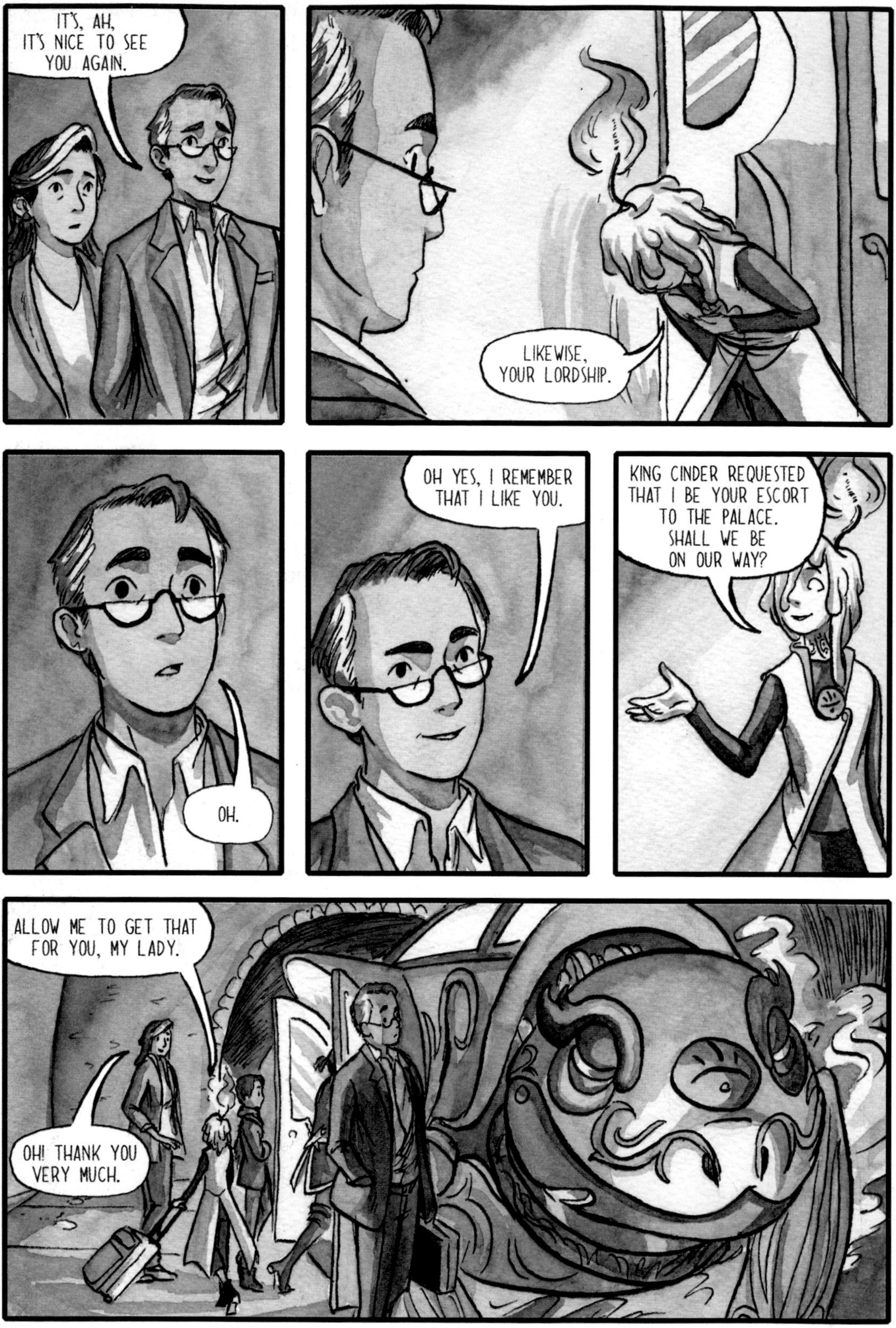
IT'S, AH, IT'S NICE TO SEE YOU AGAIN.
LIKEWISE, YOUR LORDSHIP.
OH.
OH YES, I REMEMBER THAT I LIKE YOU.
KING CINDER REQUESTED THAT I BE YOUR ESCORT TO THE PALACE. SHALL WE BE ON OUR WAY?
ALLOW ME TO GET THAT FOR YOU, MY LADY.
OH! THANK YOU VERY MUCH.

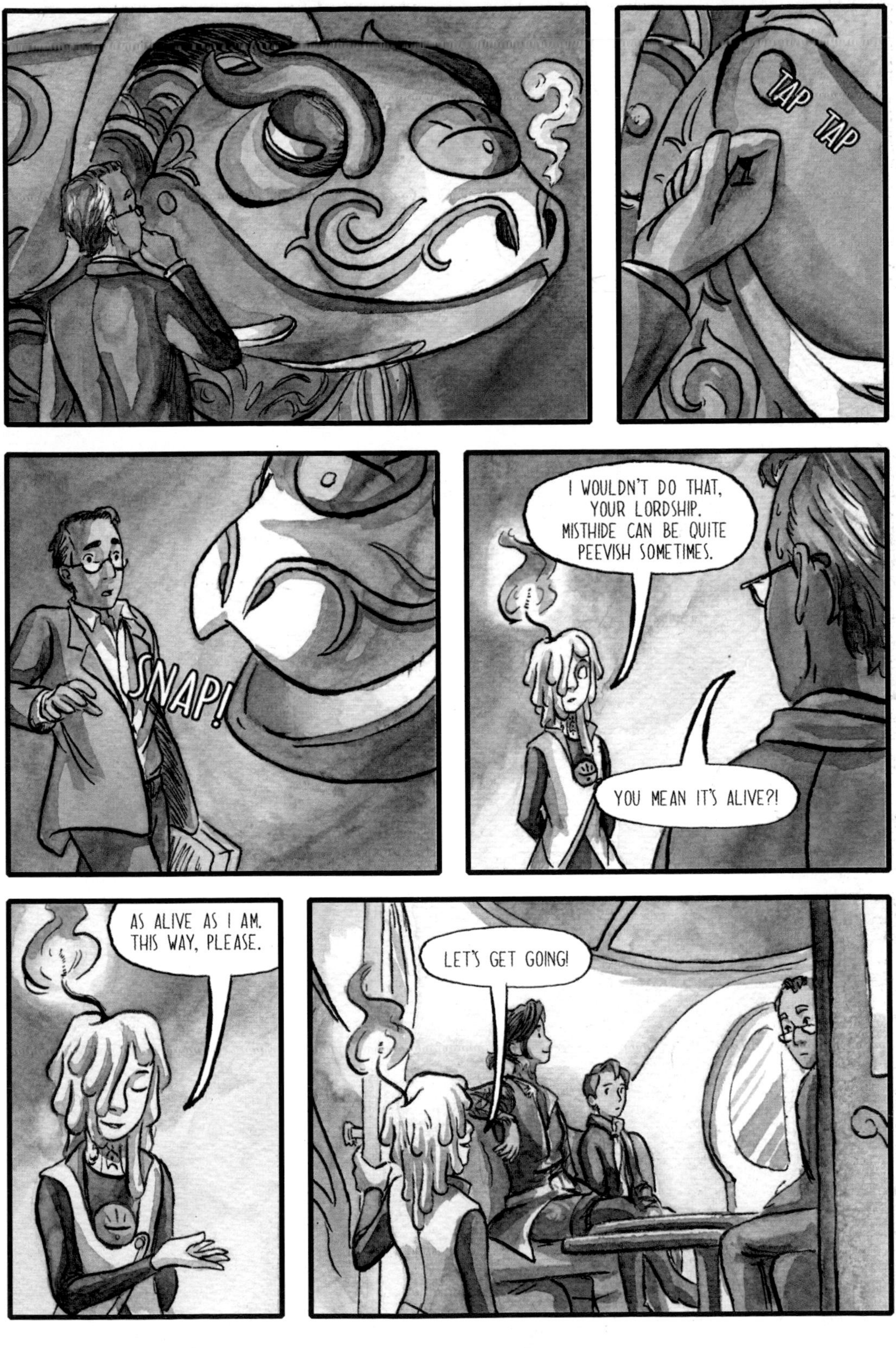
TAP TAP
SNAP!
I WOULDN'T DO THAT, YOUR LORDSHIP. MISTHIDE CAN BE QUITE PEEVISH SOMETIMES.
YOU MEAN IT'S ALIVE?!
AS ALIVE AS I AM. THIS WAY, PLEASE.
LET'S GET GOING!

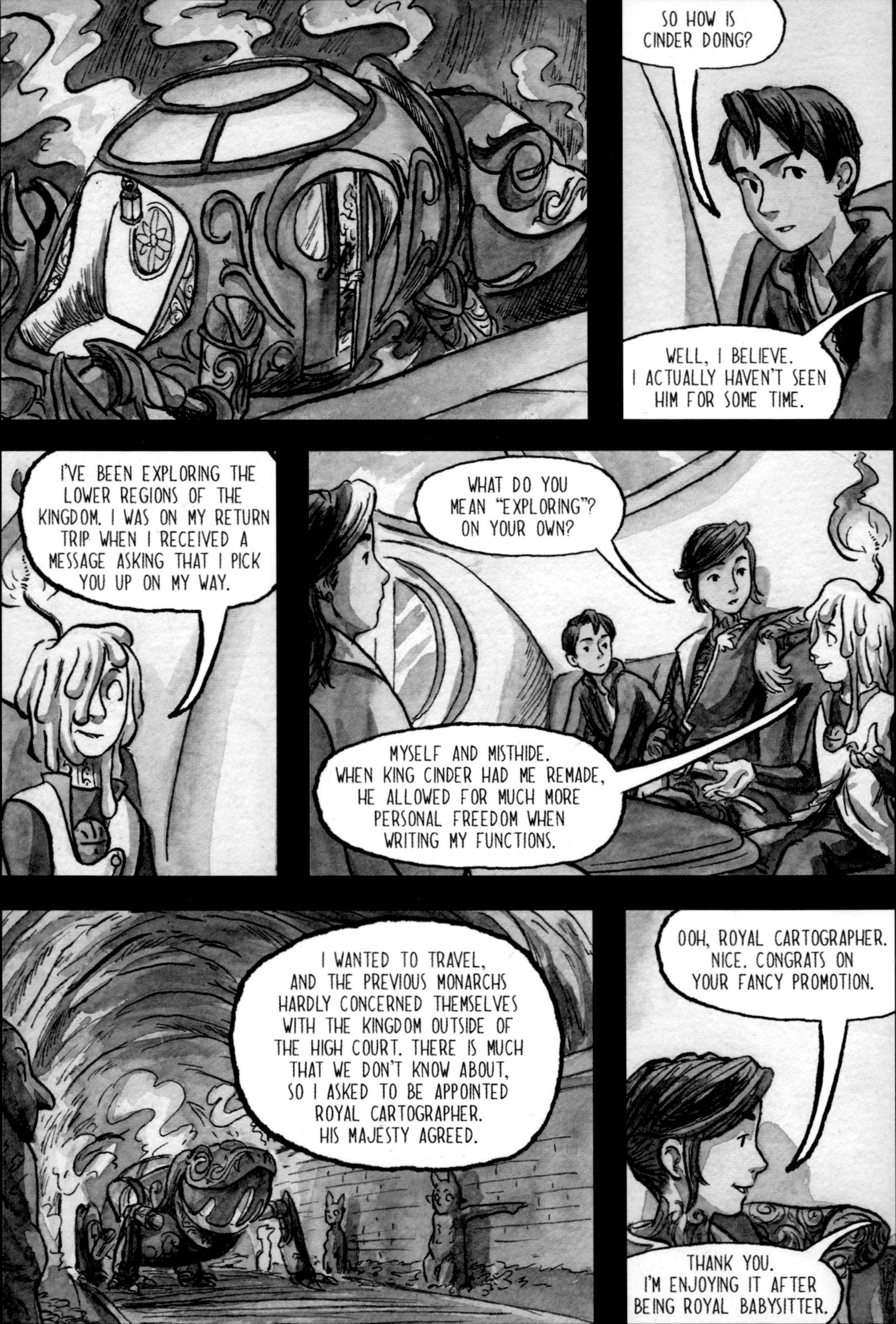
SO HOW IS CINDER DOING?
WELL, I BELIEVE. I ACTUALLY HAVEN'T SEEN HIM FOR SOME TIME.
I'VE BEEN EXPLORING THE LOWER REGIONS OF THE KINGDOM. I WAS ON MY RETURN TRIP WHEN I RECEIVED A MESSAGE ASKING THAT I PICK YOU UP ON MY WAY.
WHAT DO YOU MEAN "EXPLORING"? ON YOUR OWN?
MYSELF AND MISTHIDE. WHEN KING CINDER HAD ME REMADE, HE ALLOWED FOR MUCH MORE PERSONAL FREEDOM WHEN WRITING MY FUNCTIONS.
I WANTED TO TRAVEL, AND THE PREVIOUS MONARCHS HARDLY CONCERNED THEMSELVES WITH THE KINGDOM OUTSIDE OF THE HIGH COURT. THERE IS MUCH THAT WE DON'T KNOW ABOUT, SO I ASKED TO BE APPOINTED ROYAL CARTOGRAPHER. HIS MAJESTY AGREED.
OOH, ROYAL CARTOGRAPHER. NICE. CONGRATS ON YOUR FANCY PROMOTION.
THANK YOU. I'M ENJOYING IT AFTER BEING ROYAL BABYSITTER.

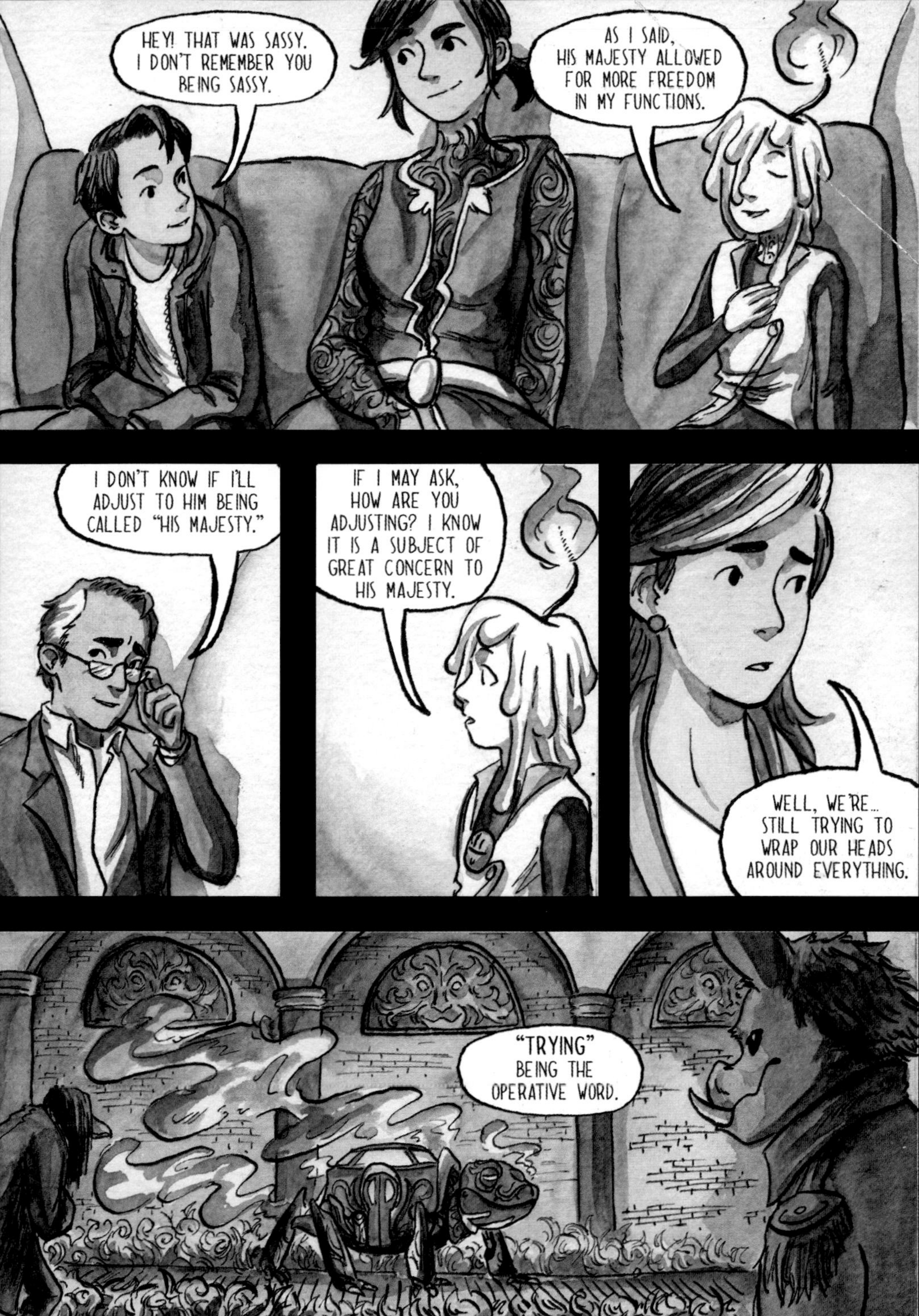
HEY! THAT WAS SASSY. I DON'T REMEMBER YOU BEING SASSY.
AS I SAID, HIS MAJESTY ALLOWED FOR MORE FREEDOM IN MY FUNCTIONS.
I DON'T KNOW IF I'LL ADJUST TO HIM BEING CALLED "HIS MAJESTY."
IF I MAY ASK, HOW ARE YOU ADJUSTING? I KNOW IT IS A SUBJECT OF GREAT CONCERN TO HIS MAJESTY.
WELL, WE'RE... STILL TRYING TO WRAP OUR HEADS AROUND EVERYTHING.
"TRYING" BEING THE OPERATIVE WORD.

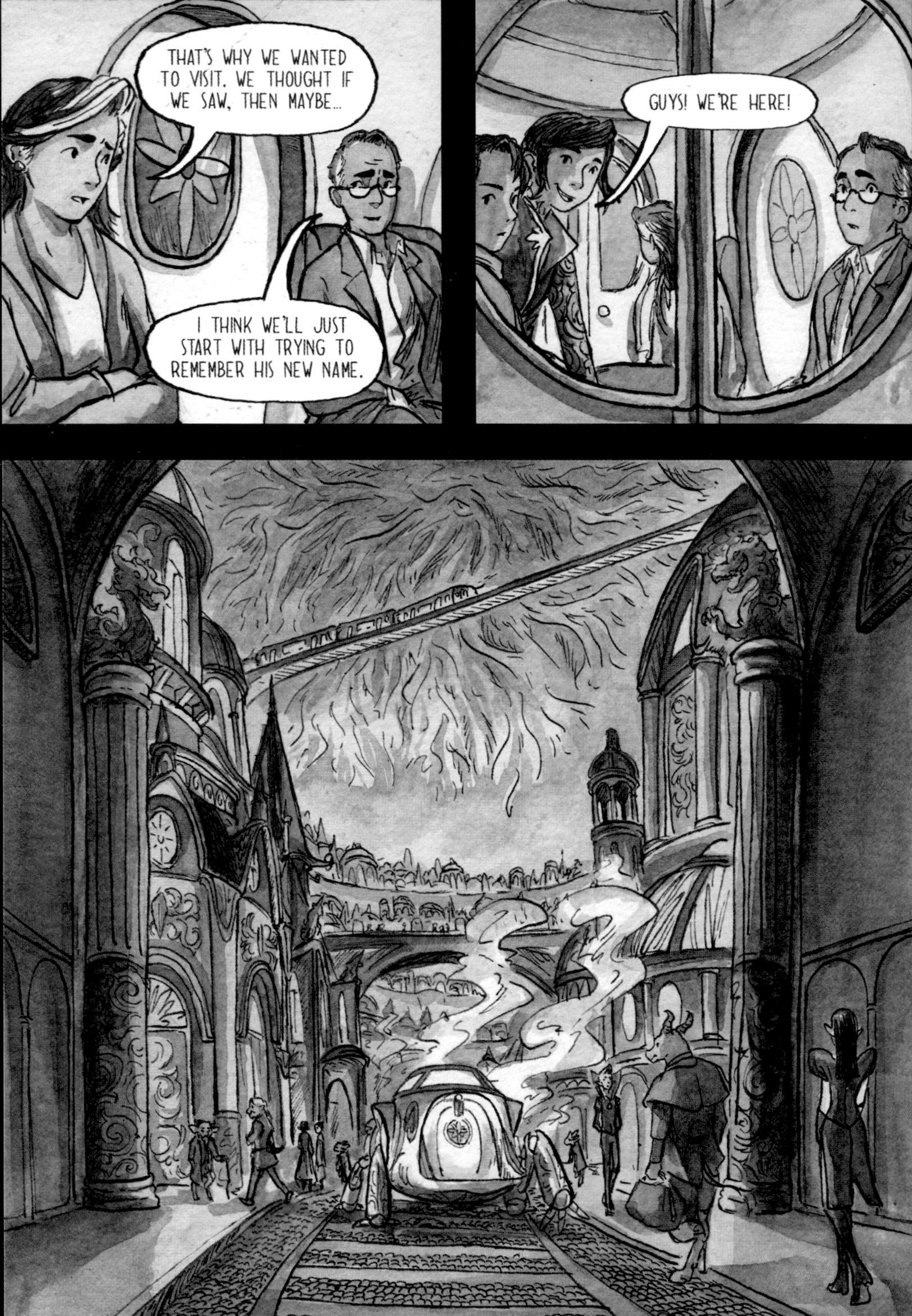
THAT'S WHY WE WANTED TO VISIT. WE THOUGHT IF WE SAW, THEN MAYBE...
I THINK WE'LL JUST START WITH TRYING TO REMEMBER HIS NEW NAME.
GUYS! WE'RE HERE!

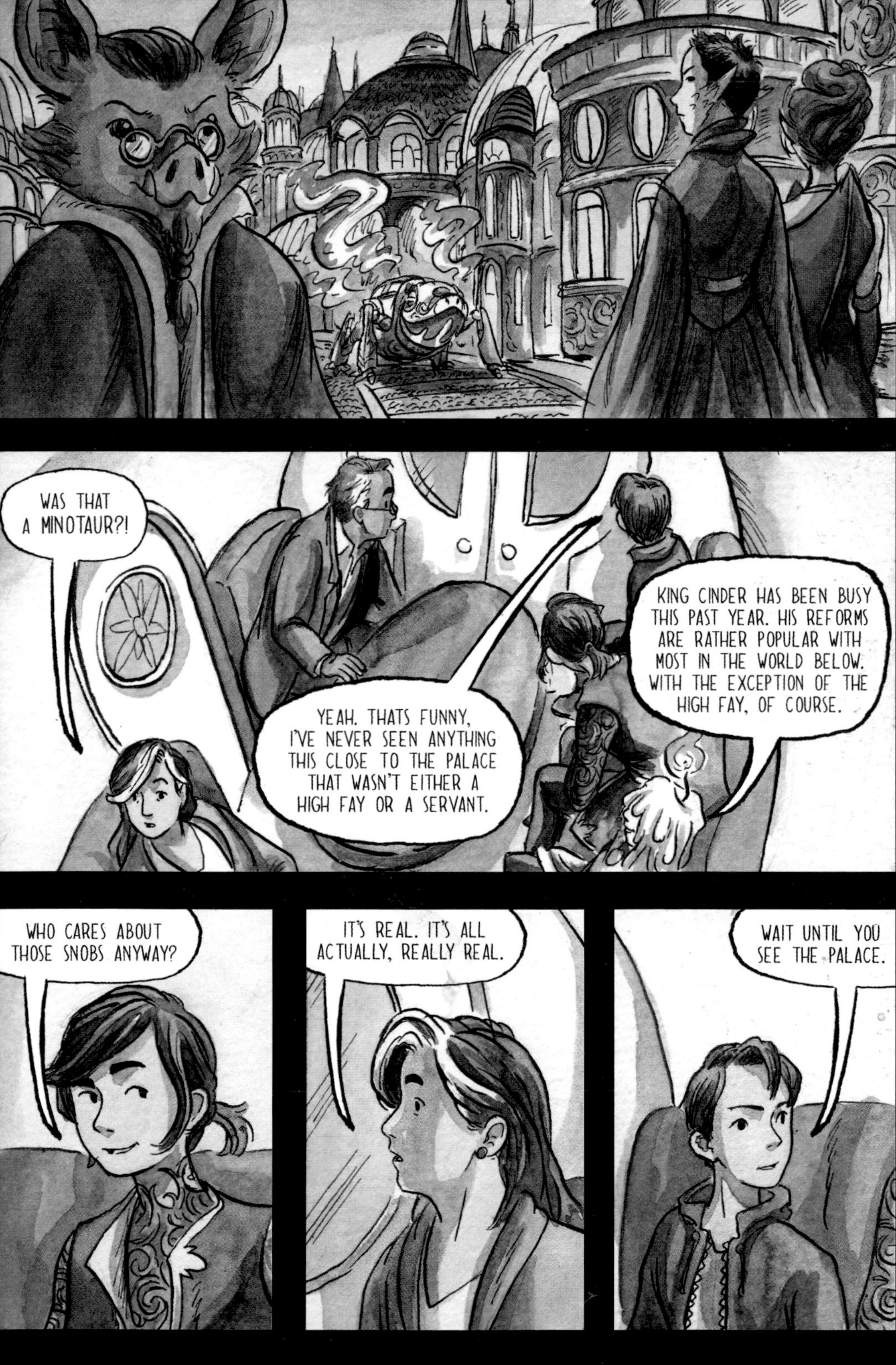
WAS THAT A MINOTAUR?!
YEAH. THATS FUNNY, I'VE NEVER SEEN ANYTHING THIS CLOSE TO THE PALACE THAT WASN'T EITHER A HIGH FAY OR A SERVANT.
KING CINDER HAS BEEN BUSY THIS PAST YEAR. HIS REFORMS ARE RATHER POPULAR WITH MOST IN THE WORLD BELOW. WITH THE EXCEPTION OF THE HIGH FAY, OF COURSE.
WHO CARES ABOUT THOSE SNOBS ANYWAY?
IT'S REAL. IT'S ALL ACTUALLY, REALLY REAL.
WAIT UNTIL YOU SEE THE PALACE.

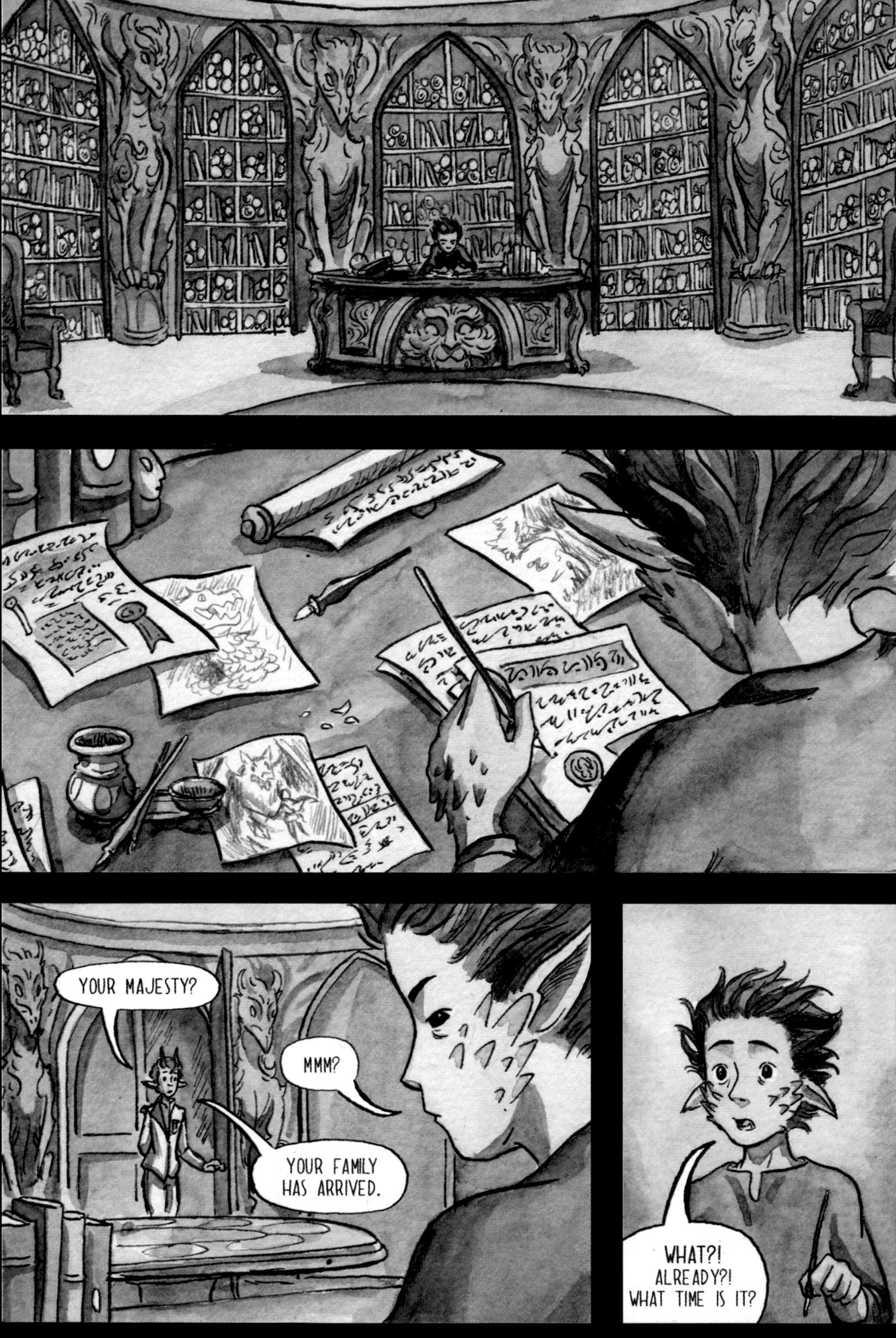
YOUR MAJESTY?
MMM?
YOUR FAMILY HAS ARRIVED.
WHAT?! ALREADY?! WHAT TIME IS IT?

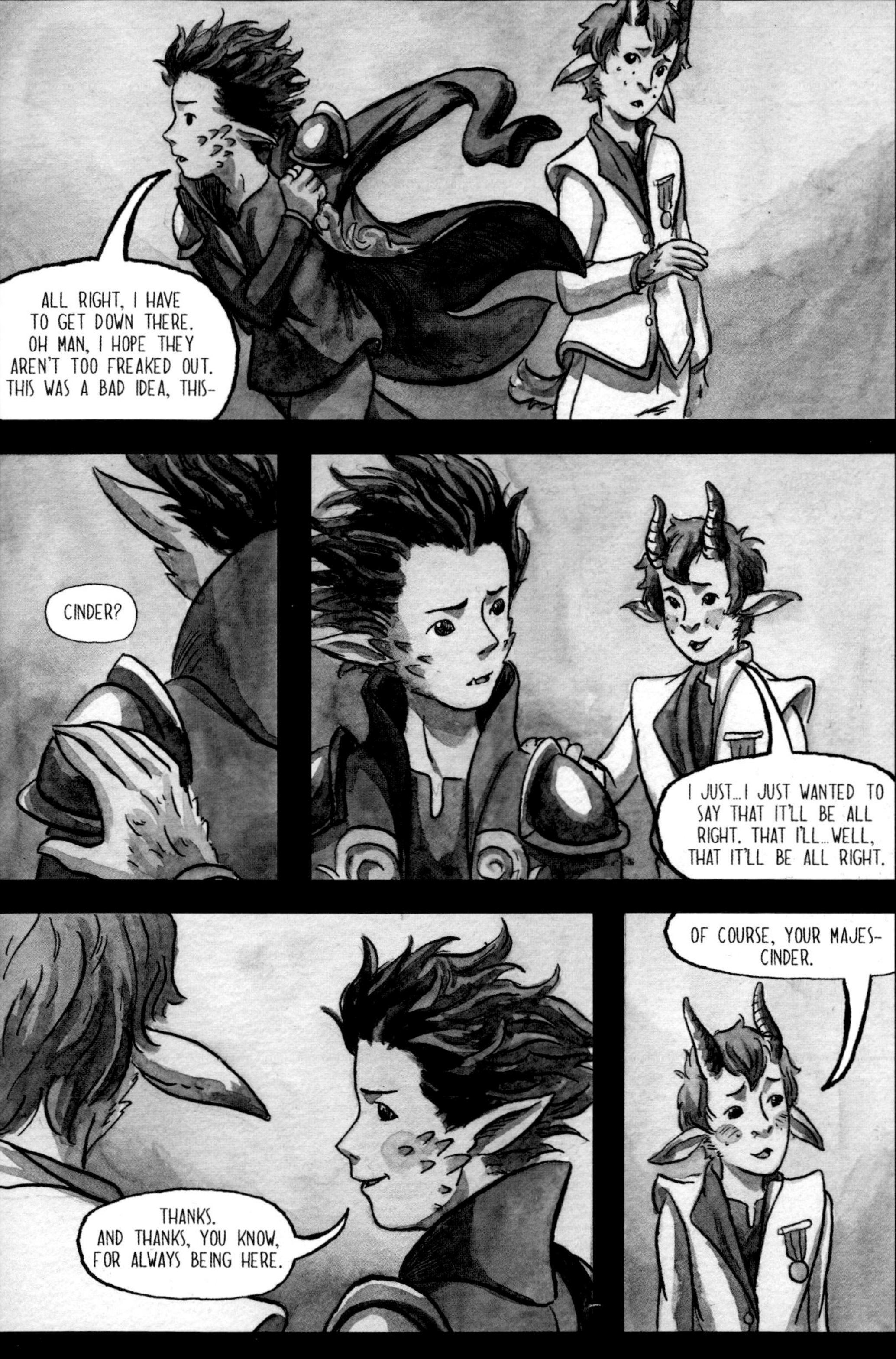
ALL RIGHT, I HAVE TO GET DOWN THERE. OH MAN, I HOPE THEY AREN'T TOO FREAKED OUT. THIS WAS A BAD IDEA, THIS-
CINDER?
I JUST...I JUST WANTED TO SAY THAT IT'LL BE ALL RIGHT. THAT I'LL...WELL, THAT IT'LL BE ALL RIGHT.
THANKS. AND THANKS, YOU KNOW, FOR ALWAYS BEING HERE.
OF COURSE, YOUR MAJES- CINDER.

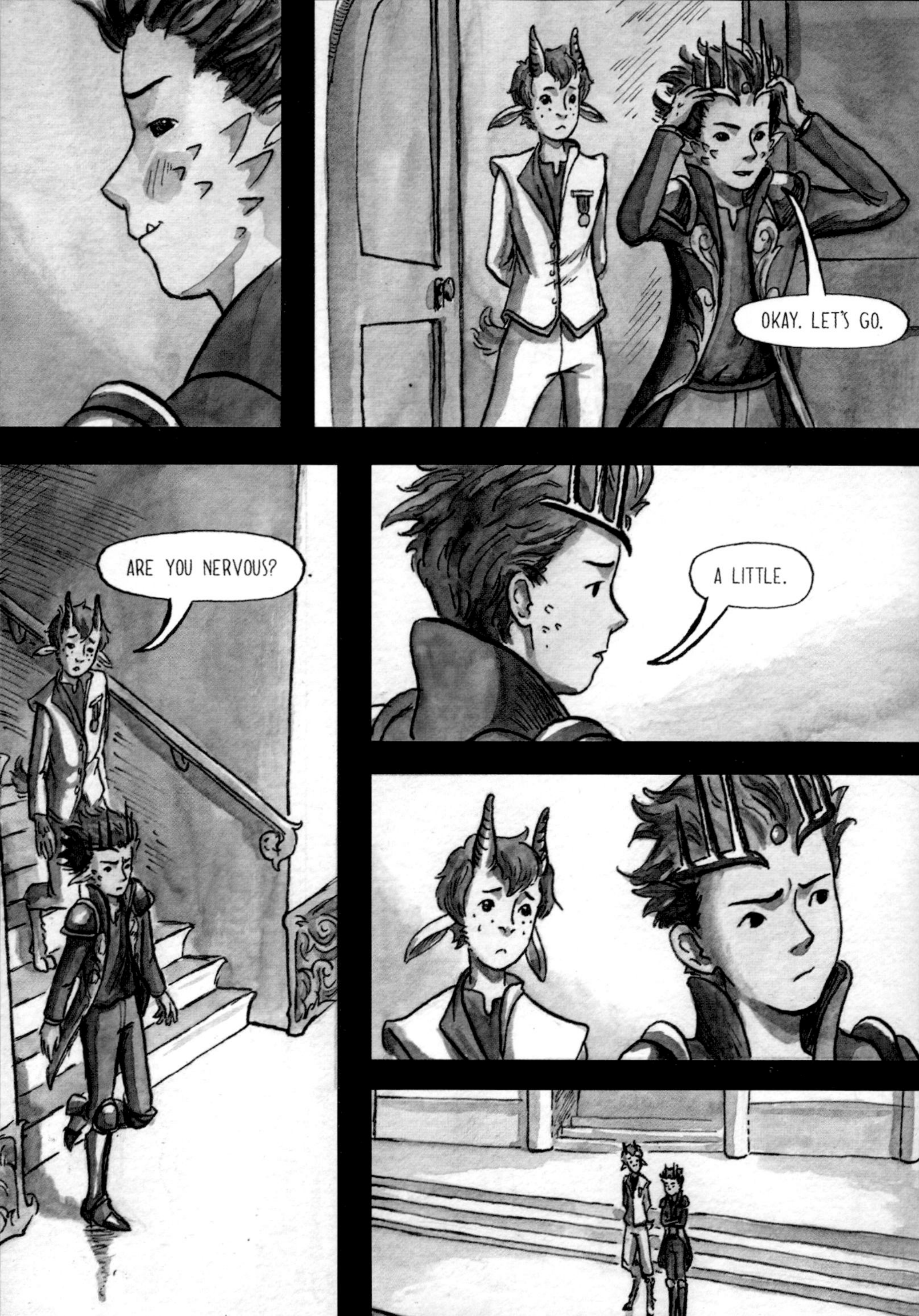
OKAY. LET'S GO.
ARE YOU NERVOUS?
A LITTLE.

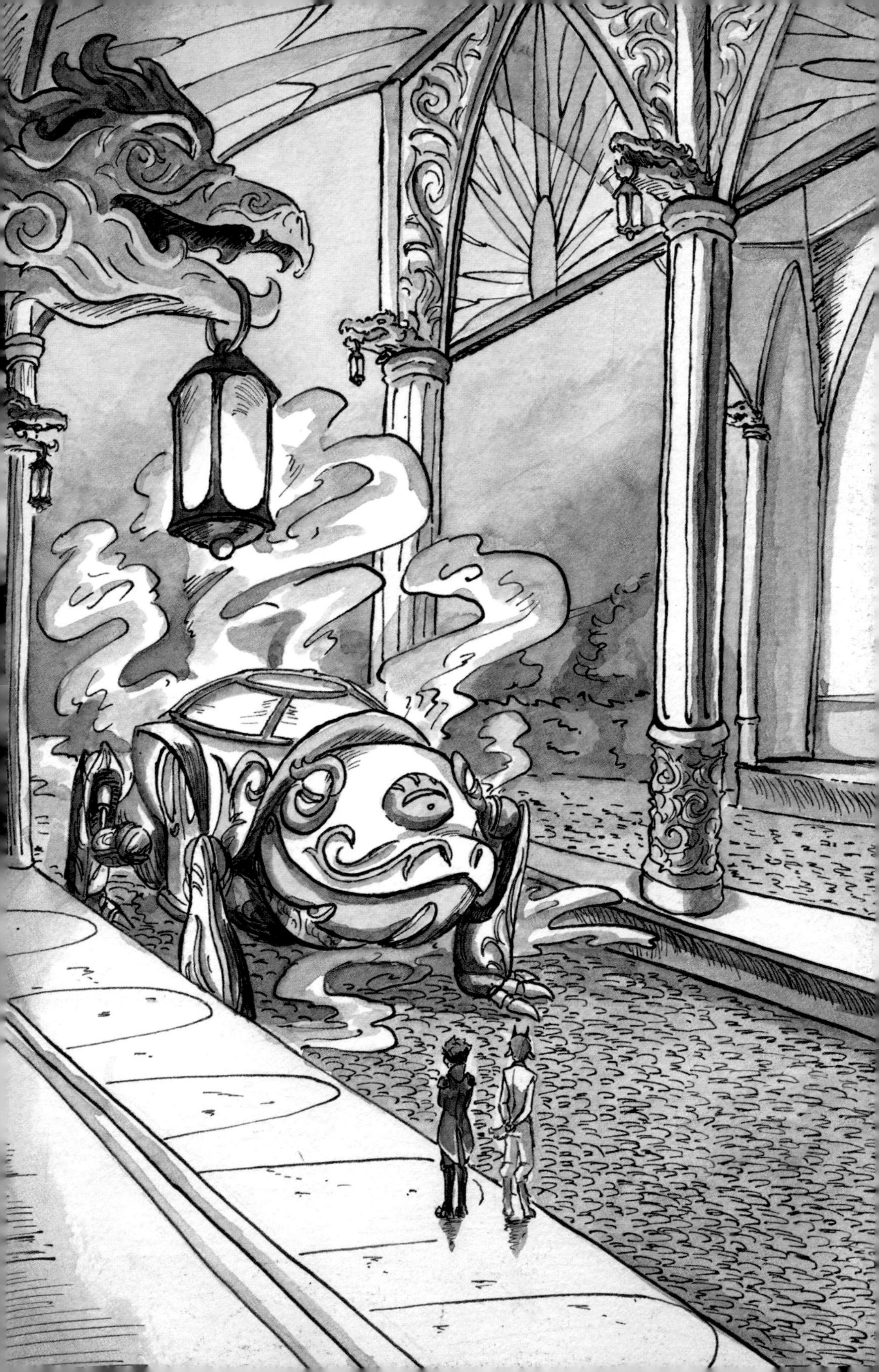

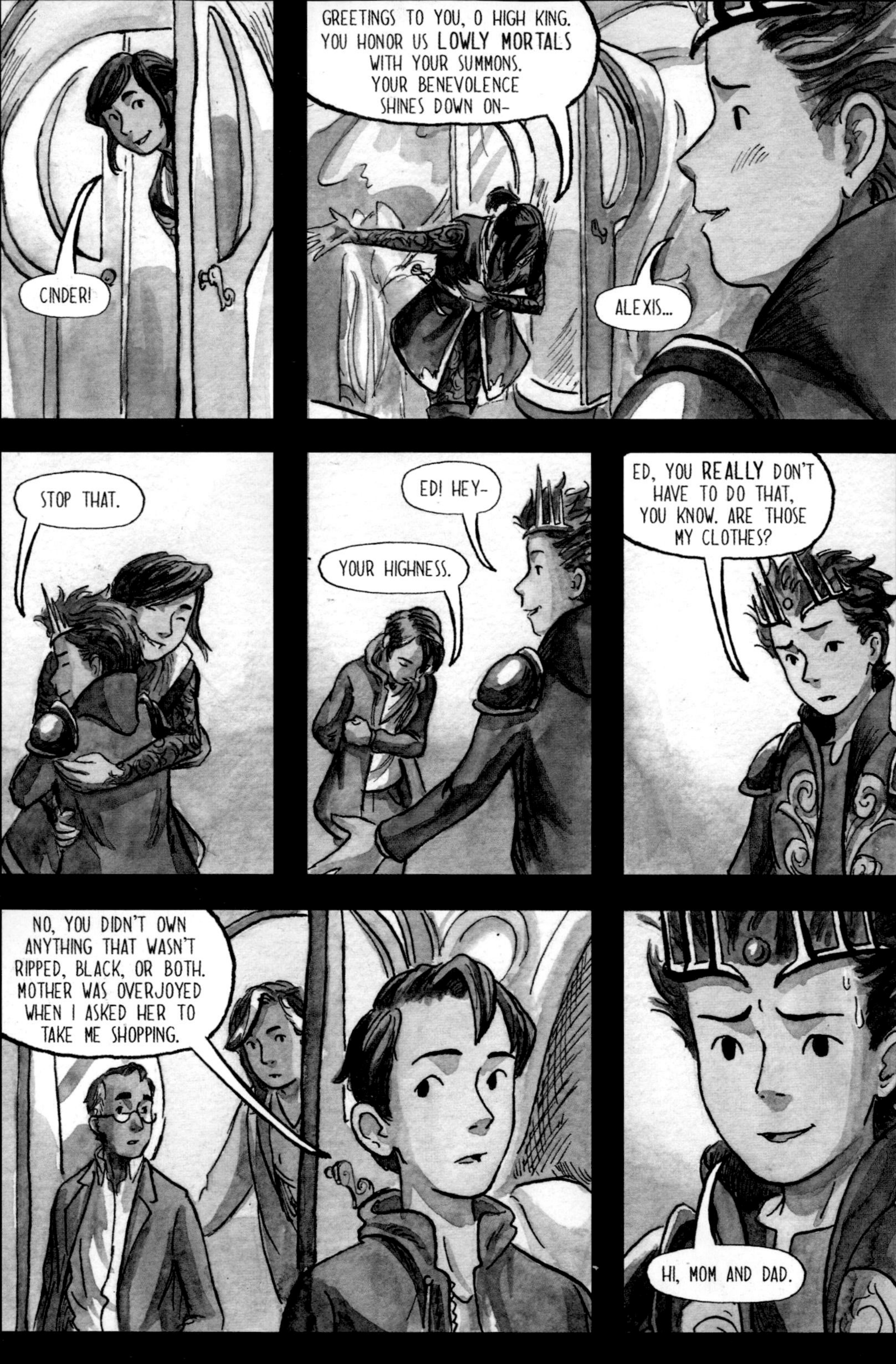
CINDER!
GREETINGS TO YOU, O HIGH KING. YOU HONOR US **LOWLY MORTALS** WITH YOUR SUMMONS. YOUR BENEVOLENCE SHINES DOWN ON-
ALEXIS...
STOP THAT.
ED! HEY-
YOUR HIGHNESS.
ED, YOU **REALLY** DON'T HAVE TO DO THAT, YOU KNOW. ARE THOSE MY CLOTHES?
NO, YOU DIDN'T OWN ANYTHING THAT WASN'T RIPPED, BLACK, OR BOTH. MOTHER WAS OVERJOYED WHEN I ASKED HER TO TAKE ME SHOPPING.
HI, MOM AND DAD.

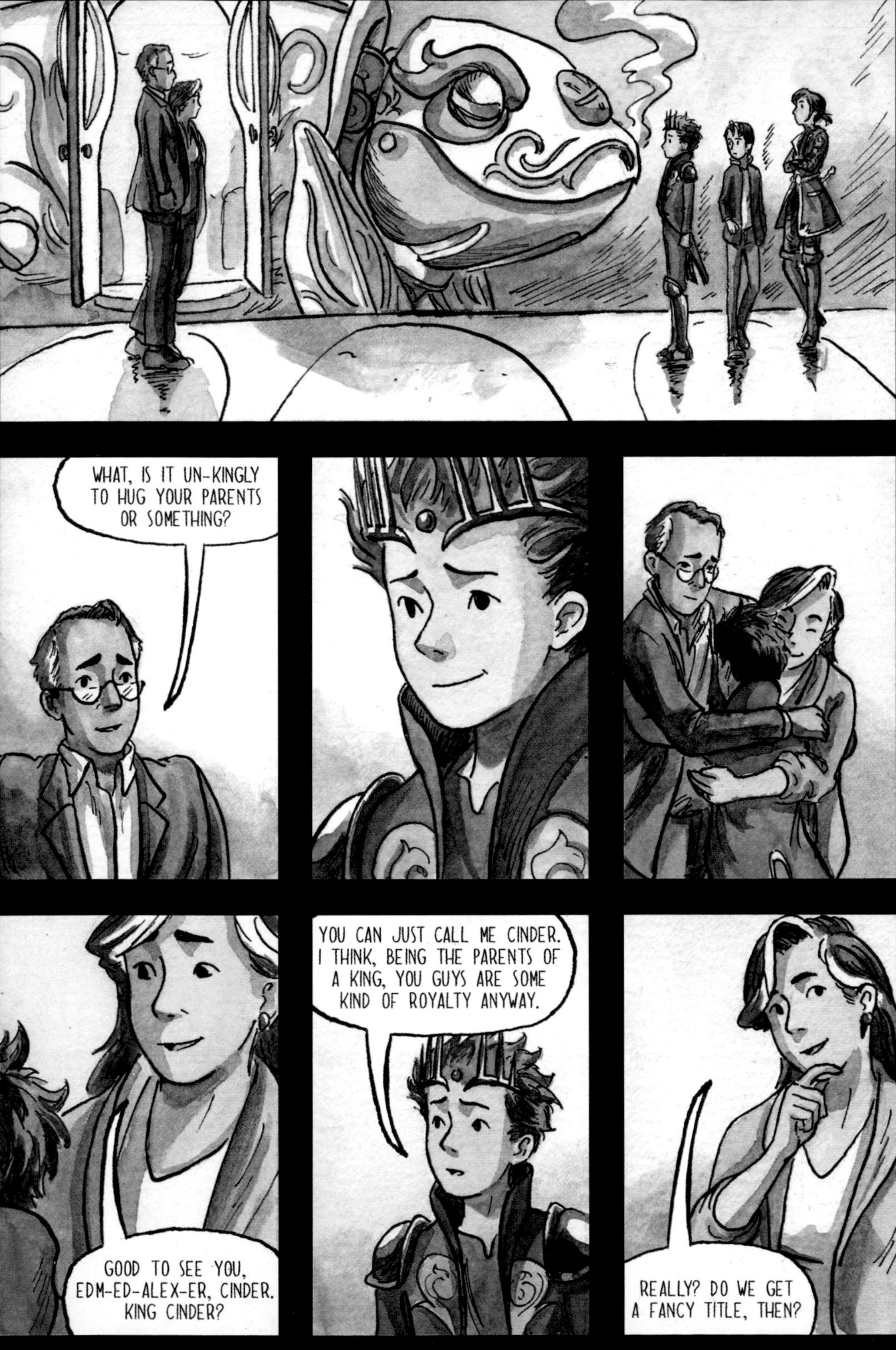
WHAT, IS IT UN-KINGLY TO HUG YOUR PARENTS OR SOMETHING?
GOOD TO SEE YOU, EDM-ED-ALEX-ER, CINDER. KING CINDER?
YOU CAN JUST CALL ME CINDER. I THINK, BEING THE PARENTS OF A KING, YOU GUYS ARE SOME KIND OF ROYALTY ANYWAY.
REALLY? DO WE GET A FANCY TITLE, THEN?

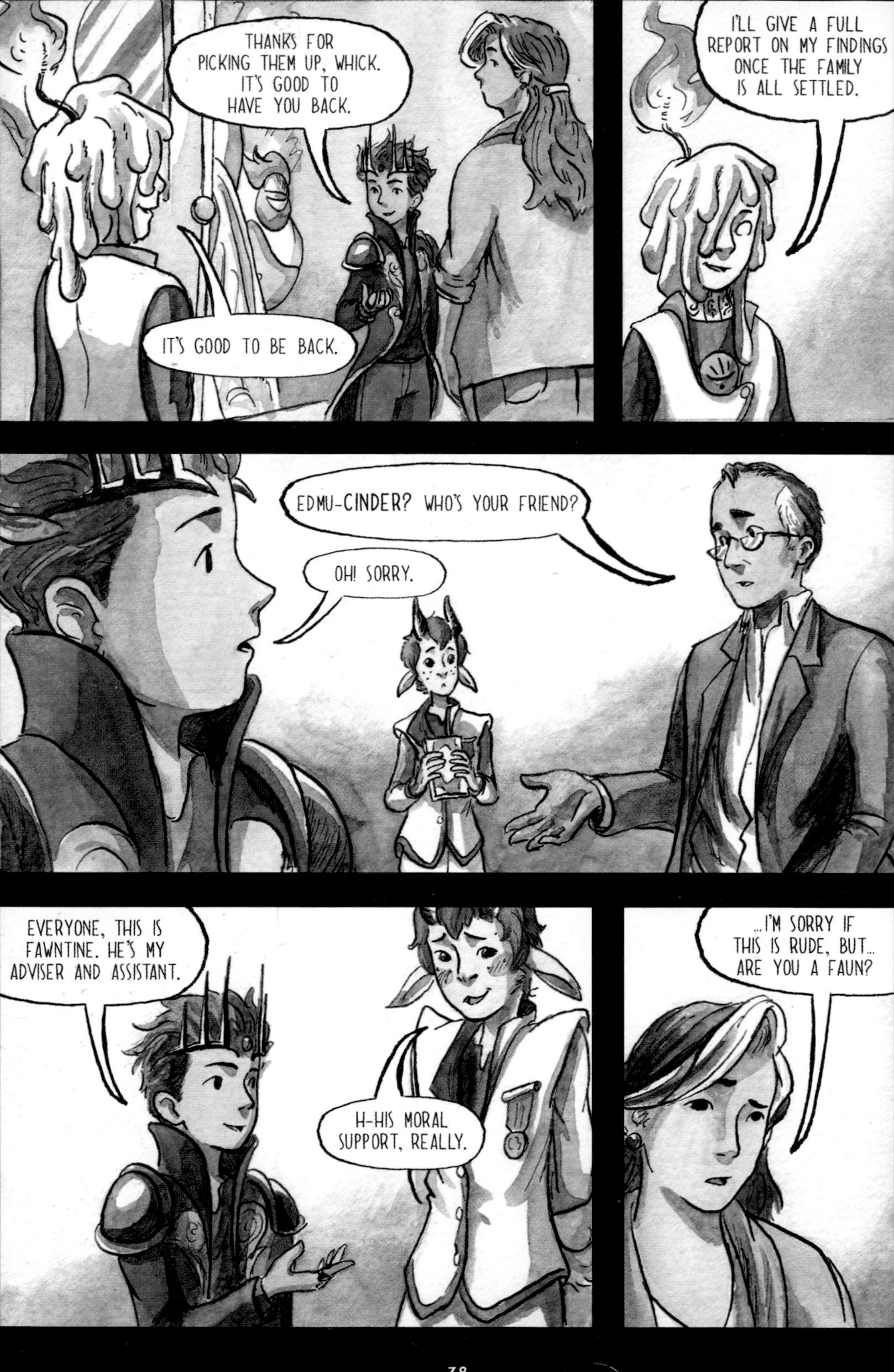
THANKS FOR PICKING THEM UP, WHICK. IT'S GOOD TO HAVE YOU BACK.
IT'S GOOD TO BE BACK.
I'LL GIVE A FULL REPORT ON MY FINDINGS ONCE THE FAMILY IS ALL SETTLED.
EDMU-CINDER? WHO'S YOUR FRIEND?
OH! SORRY.
EVERYONE, THIS IS FAWNTINE. HE'S MY ADVISER AND ASSISTANT.
H-HIS MORAL SUPPORT, REALLY.
...I'M SORRY IF THIS IS RUDE, BUT... ARE YOU A FAUN?

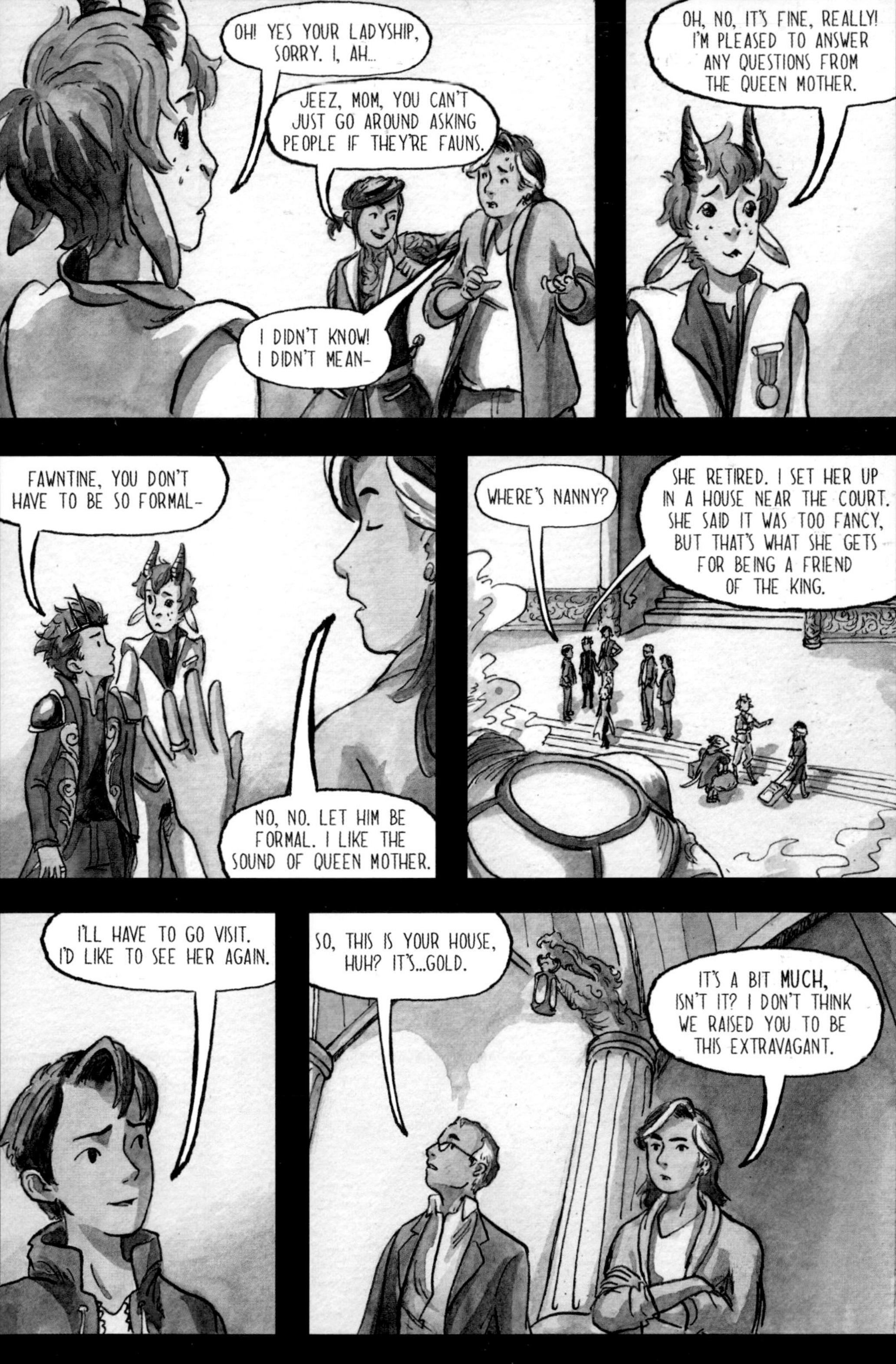
OH! YES YOUR LADYSHIP, SORRY. I, AH...
JEEZ, MOM, YOU CAN'T JUST GO AROUND ASKING PEOPLE IF THEY'RE FAUNS.
I DIDN'T KNOW! I DIDN'T MEAN-
OH, NO, IT'S FINE, REALLY! I'M PLEASED TO ANSWER ANY QUESTIONS FROM THE QUEEN MOTHER.
FAWNTINE, YOU DON'T HAVE TO BE SO FORMAL-
NO, NO. LET HIM BE FORMAL. I LIKE THE SOUND OF QUEEN MOTHER.
WHERE'S NANNY?
SHE RETIRED. I SET HER UP IN A HOUSE NEAR THE COURT. SHE SAID IT WAS TOO FANCY, BUT THAT'S WHAT SHE GETS FOR BEING A FRIEND OF THE KING.
I'LL HAVE TO GO VISIT. I'D LIKE TO SEE HER AGAIN.
SO, THIS IS YOUR HOUSE, HUH? IT'S...GOLD.
IT'S A BIT MUCH, ISN'T IT? I DON'T THINK WE RAISED YOU TO BE THIS EXTRAVAGANT.

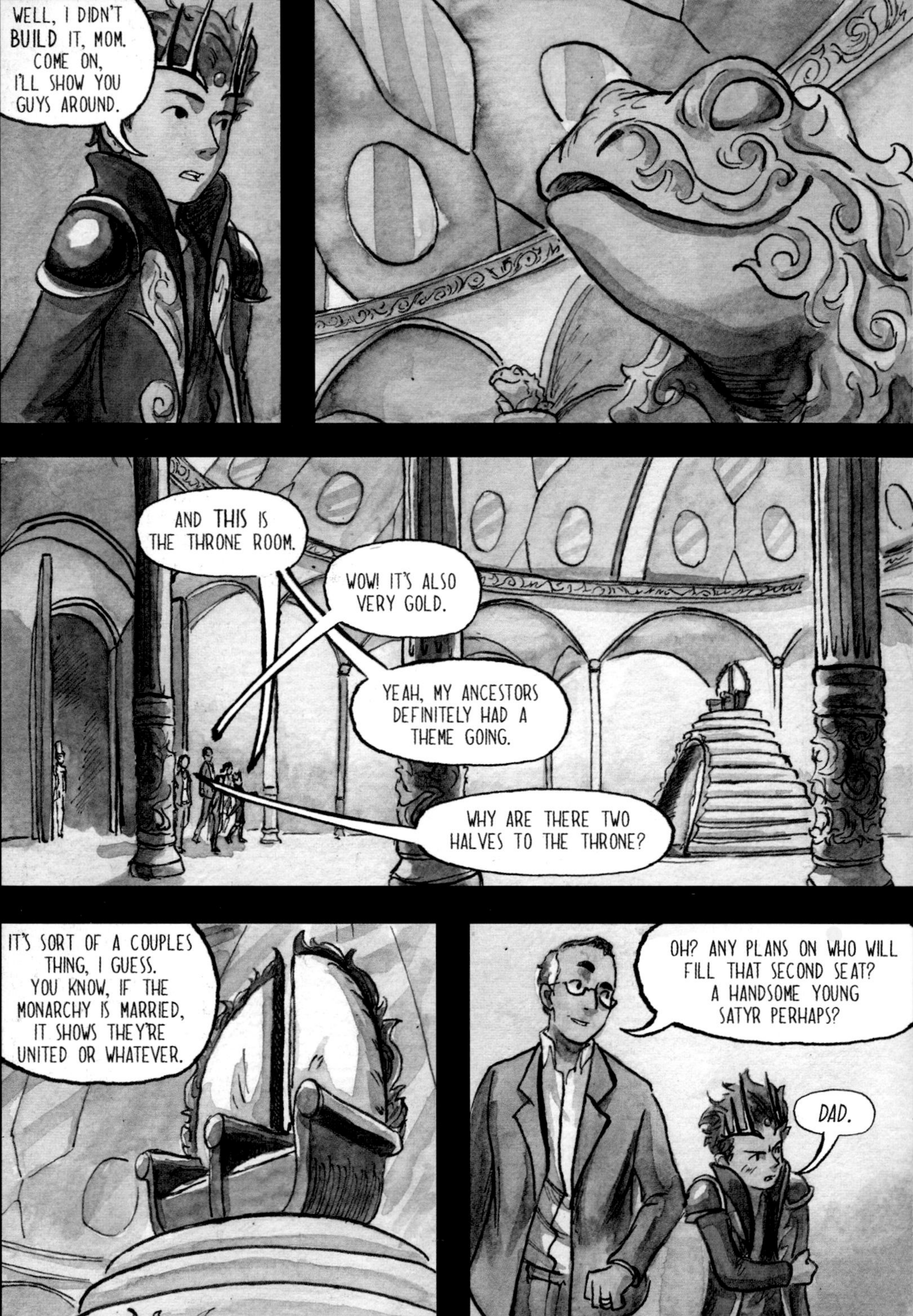
WELL, I DIDN'T BUILD IT, MOM. COME ON, I'LL SHOW YOU GUYS AROUND.
AND THIS IS THE THRONE ROOM.
WOW! IT'S ALSO VERY GOLD.
YEAH, MY ANCESTORS DEFINITELY HAD A THEME GOING.
WHY ARE THERE TWO HALVES TO THE THRONE?
IT'S SORT OF A COUPLES THING, I GUESS. YOU KNOW, IF THE MONARCHY IS MARRIED, IT SHOWS THEY'RE UNITED OR WHATEVER.
OH? ANY PLANS ON WHO WILL FILL THAT SECOND SEAT? A HANDSOME YOUNG SATYR PERHAPS?
DAD.

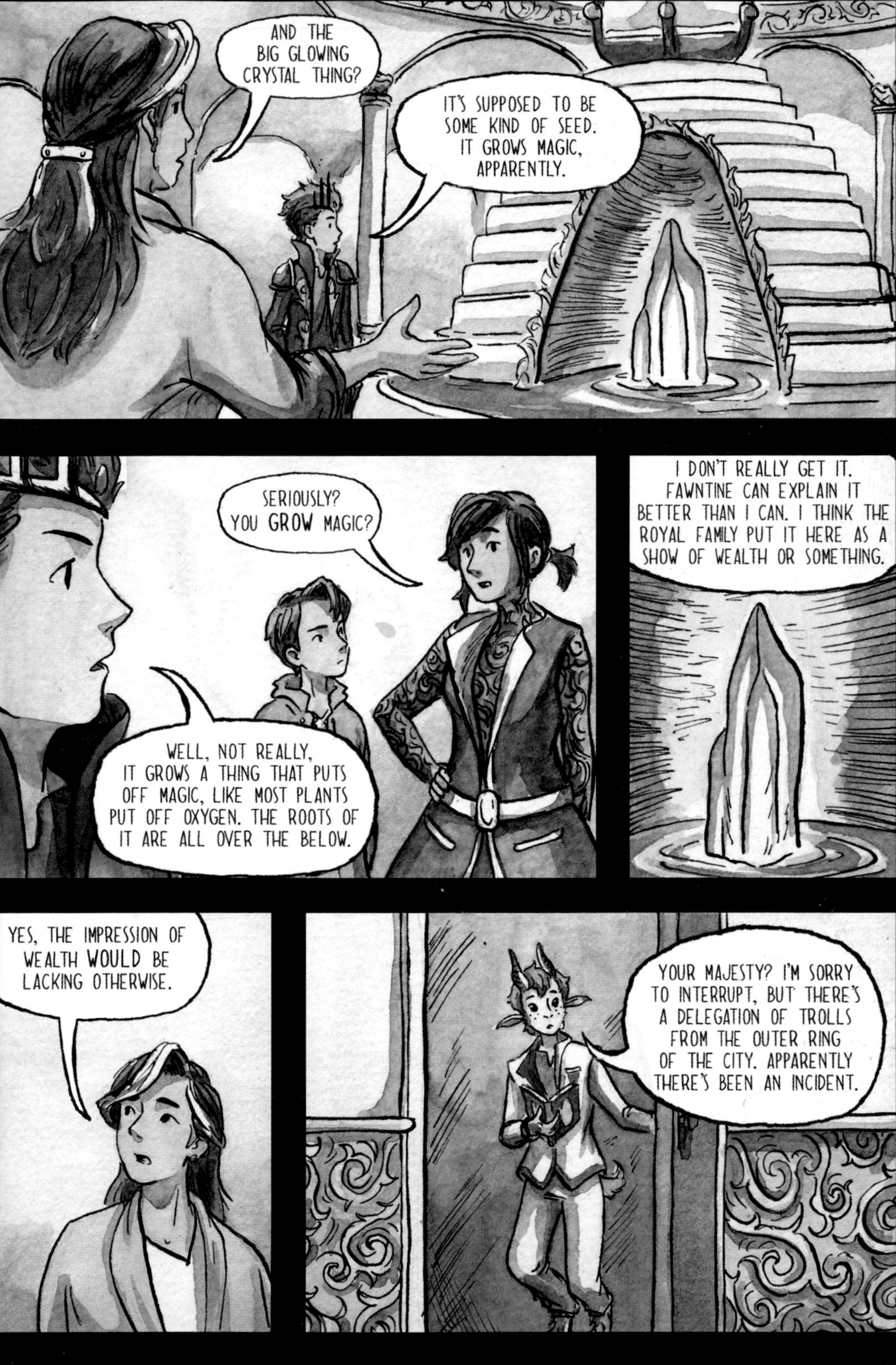
AND THE BIG GLOWING CRYSTAL THING?
IT'S SUPPOSED TO BE SOME KIND OF SEED. IT GROWS MAGIC, APPARENTLY.
SERIOUSLY? YOU GROW MAGIC?
WELL, NOT REALLY, IT GROWS A THING THAT PUTS OFF MAGIC, LIKE MOST PLANTS PUT OFF OXYGEN. THE ROOTS OF IT ARE ALL OVER THE BELOW.
I DON'T REALLY GET IT. FAWNTINE CAN EXPLAIN IT BETTER THAN I CAN. I THINK THE ROYAL FAMILY PUT IT HERE AS A SHOW OF WEALTH OR SOMETHING.
YES, THE IMPRESSION OF WEALTH WOULD BE LACKING OTHERWISE.
YOUR MAJESTY? I'M SORRY TO INTERRUPT, BUT THERE'S A DELEGATION OF TROLLS FROM THE OUTER RING OF THE CITY. APPARENTLY THERE'S BEEN AN INCIDENT.

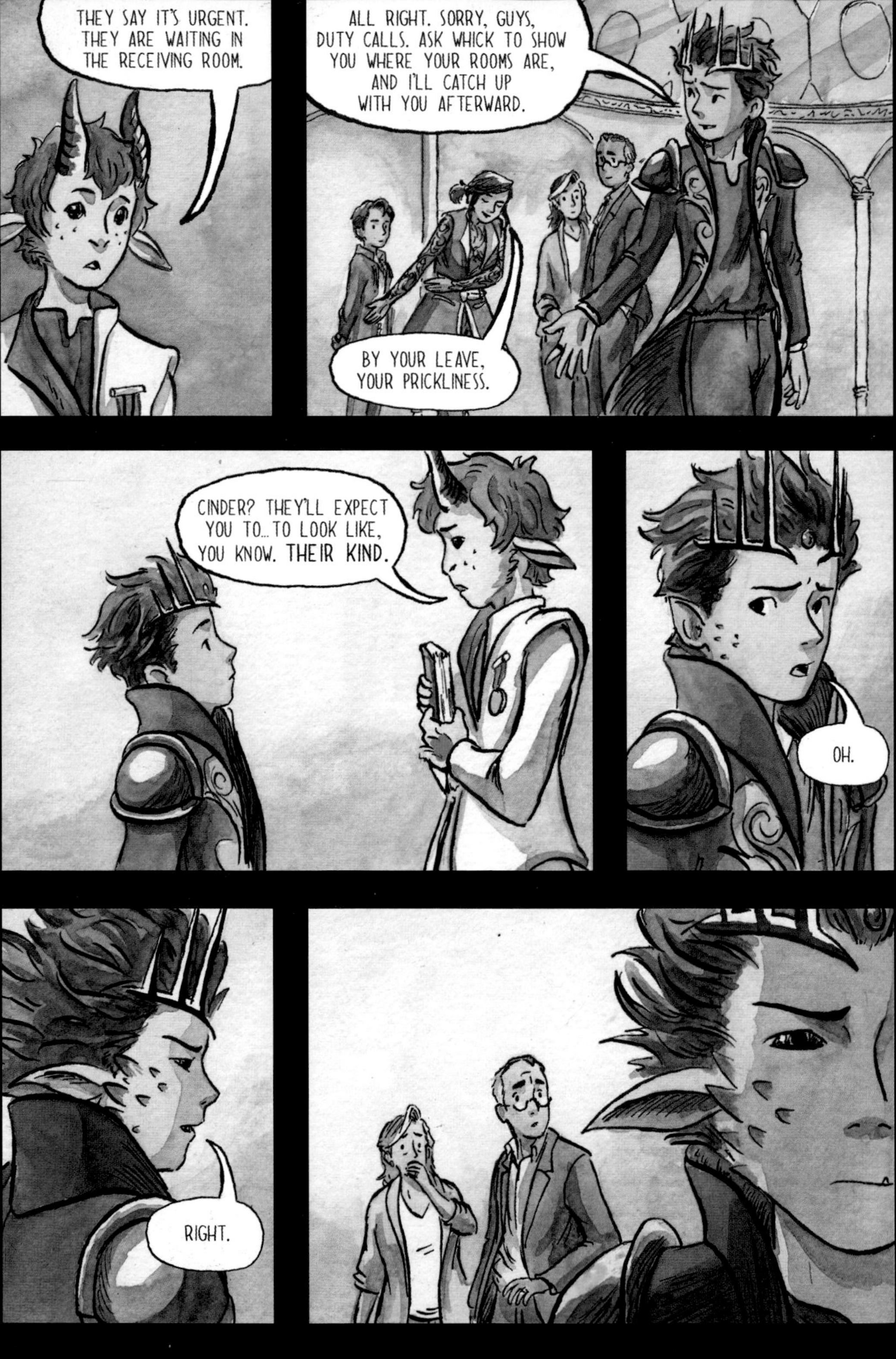
THEY SAY IT'S URGENT. THEY ARE WAITING IN THE RECEIVING ROOM.
ALL RIGHT. SORRY, GUYS, DUTY CALLS. ASK WHICK TO SHOW YOU WHERE YOUR ROOMS ARE, AND I'LL CATCH UP WITH YOU AFTERWARD.
BY YOUR LEAVE, YOUR PRICKLINESS.
CINDER? THEY'LL EXPECT YOU TO... TO LOOK LIKE, YOU KNOW. THEIR KIND.
OH.
RIGHT.

CHAPTER
FOUR

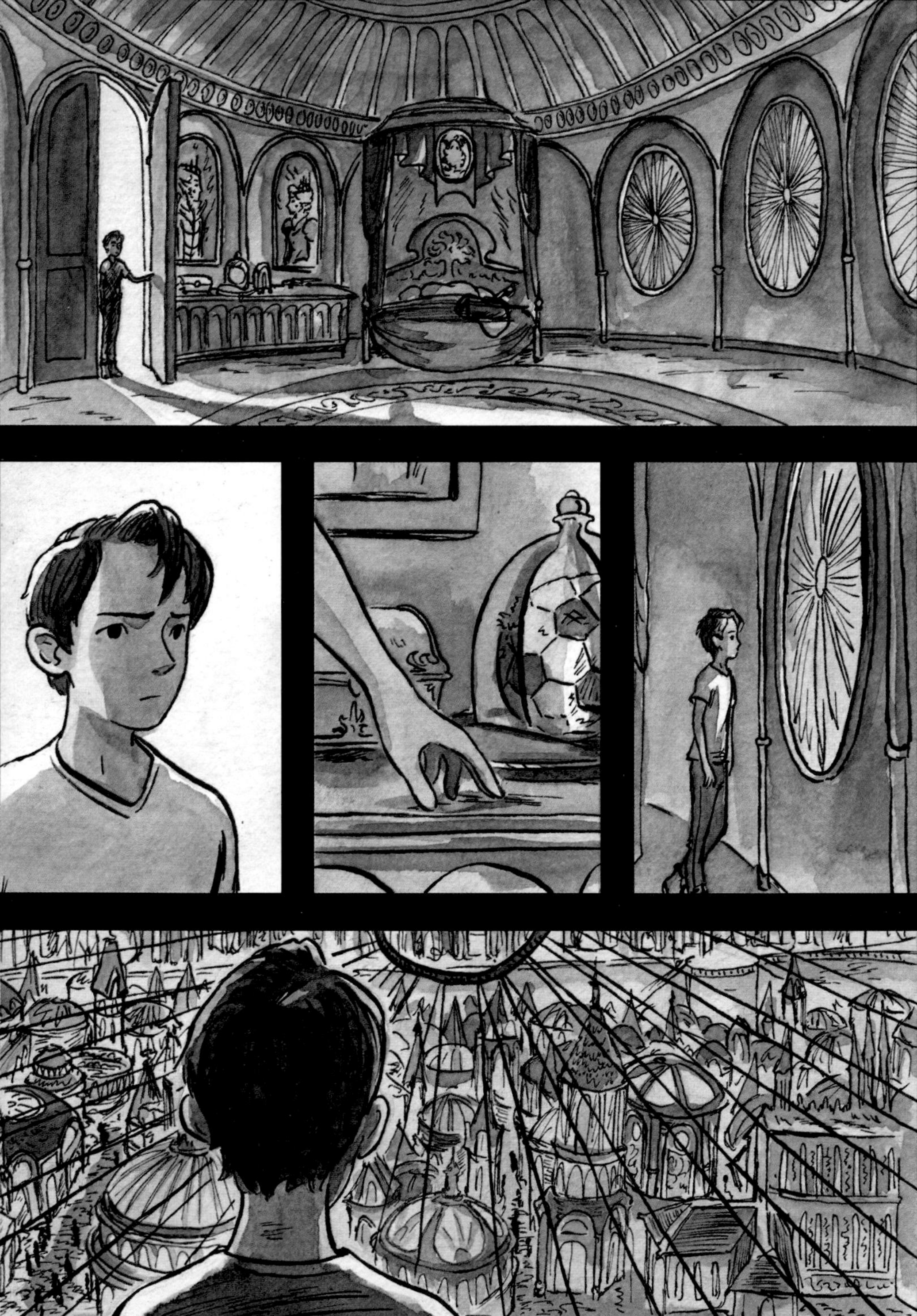

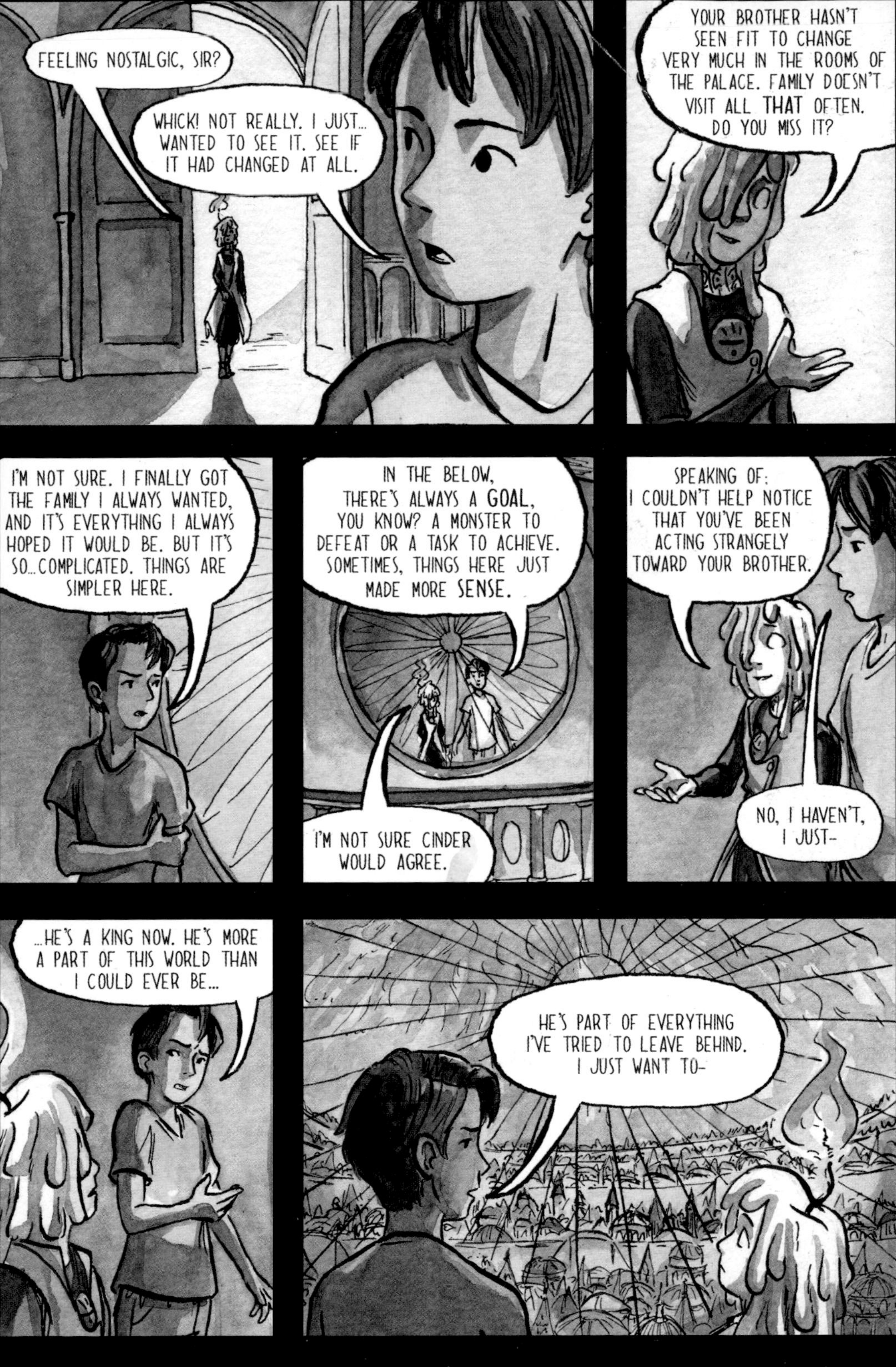
FEELING NOSTALGIC, SIR?
WHICK! NOT REALLY. I JUST... WANTED TO SEE IT. SEE IF IT HAD CHANGED AT ALL.
YOUR BROTHER HASN'T SEEN FIT TO CHANGE VERY MUCH IN THE ROOMS OF THE PALACE. FAMILY DOESN'T VISIT ALL THAT OFTEN. DO YOU MISS IT?
I'M NOT SURE. I FINALLY GOT THE FAMILY I ALWAYS WANTED, AND IT'S EVERYTHING I ALWAYS HOPED IT WOULD BE. BUT IT'S SO...COMPLICATED. THINGS ARE SIMPLER HERE.
IN THE BELOW, THERE'S ALWAYS A GOAL, YOU KNOW? A MONSTER TO DEFEAT OR A TASK TO ACHIEVE. SOMETIMES, THINGS HERE JUST MADE MORE SENSE.
I'M NOT SURE CINDER WOULD AGREE.
SPEAKING OF: I COULDN'T HELP NOTICE THAT YOU'VE BEEN ACTING STRANGELY TOWARD YOUR BROTHER.
NO, I HAVEN'T, I JUST-
...HE'S A KING NOW. HE'S MORE A PART OF THIS WORLD THAN I COULD EVER BE...
HE'S PART OF EVERYTHING I'VE TRIED TO LEAVE BEHIND. I JUST WANT TO-

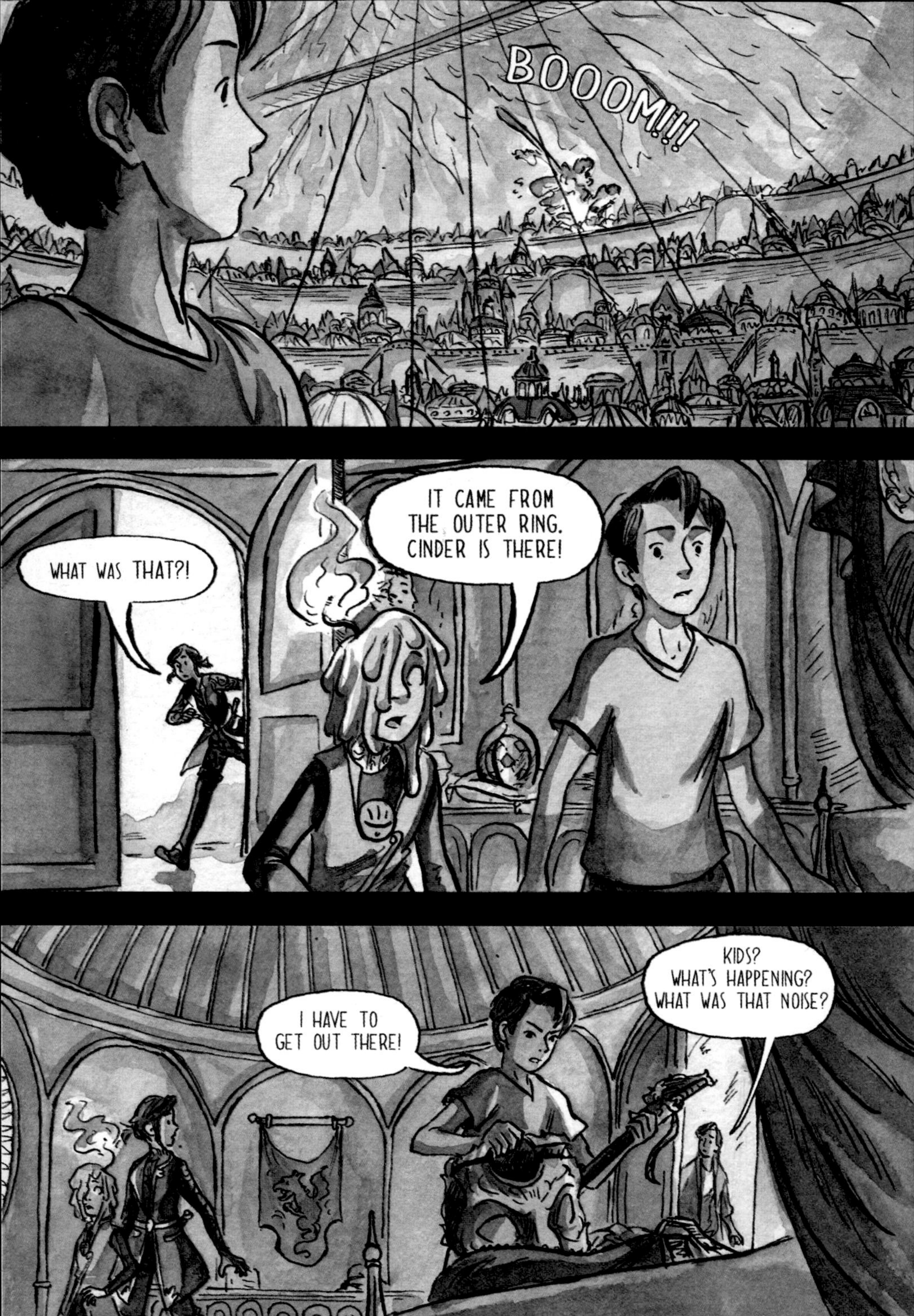
BOOOOM!!!
WHAT WAS THAT?!
IT CAME FROM THE OUTER RING. CINDER IS THERE!
I HAVE TO GET OUT THERE!
KIDS? WHAT'S HAPPENING? WHAT WAS THAT NOISE?

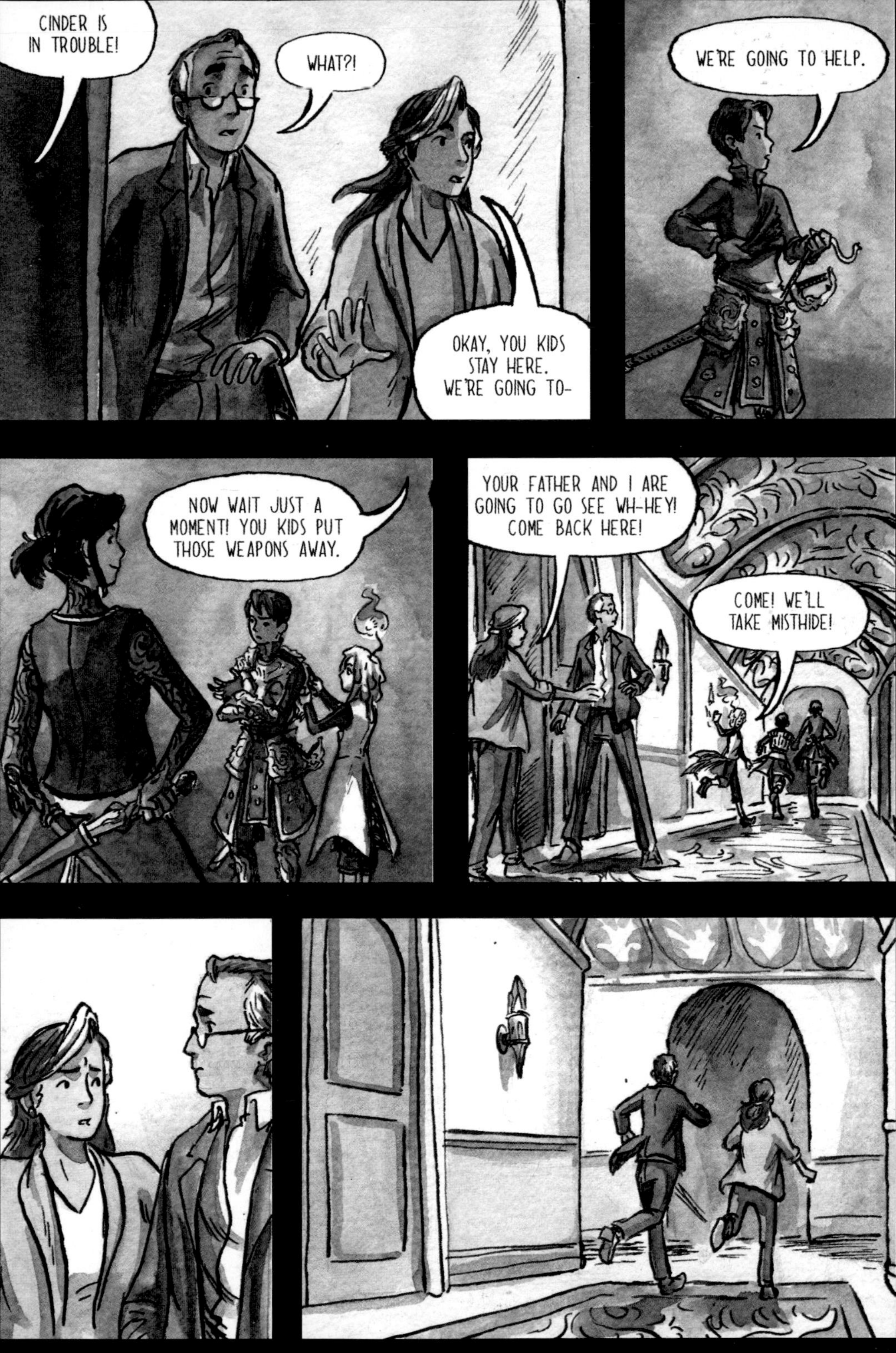
CINDER IS IN TROUBLE!
WHAT?!
OKAY, YOU KIDS STAY HERE. WE'RE GOING TO-
WE'RE GOING TO HELP.
NOW WAIT JUST A MOMENT! YOU KIDS PUT THOSE WEAPONS AWAY.
YOUR FATHER AND I ARE GOING TO GO SEE WH-HEY! COME BACK HERE!
COME! WE'LL TAKE MISTHIDE!

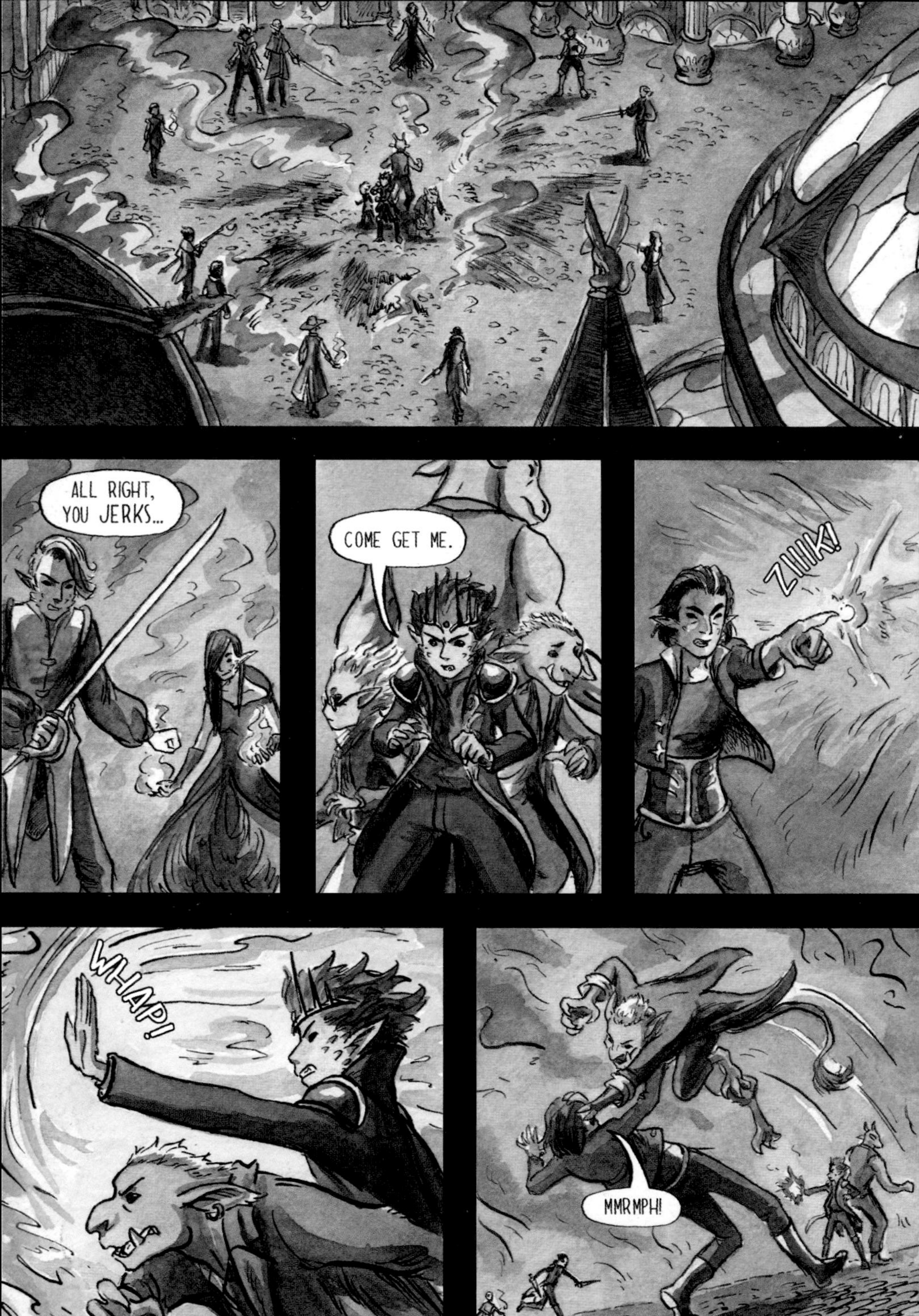
ALL RIGHT, YOU JERKS...
COME GET ME.
ZIIIK!
WHAP!
MMRMPH!

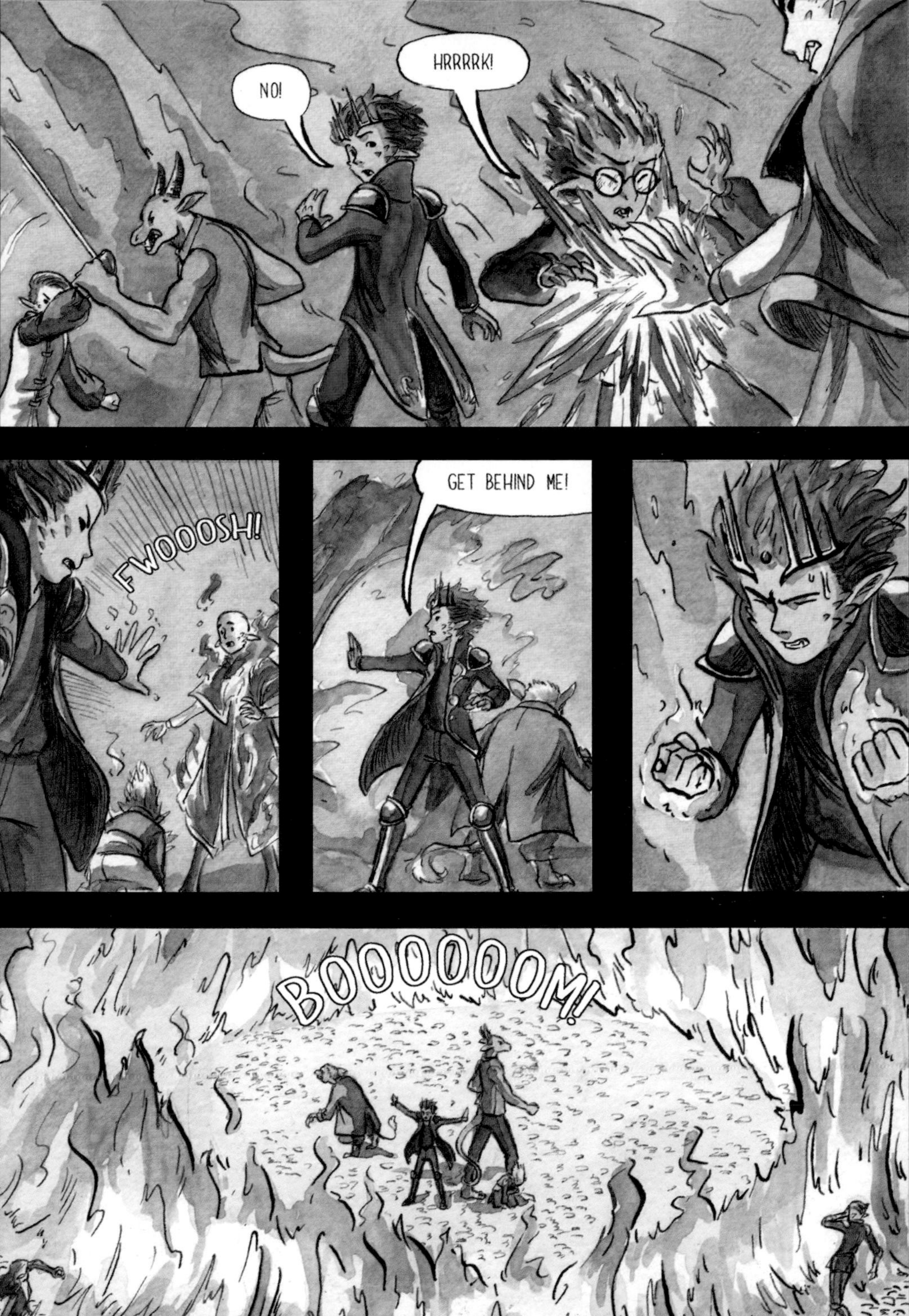
NO!
HRRRRK!
FWOOOSH!
GET BEHIND ME!
BOOOOOOOM!

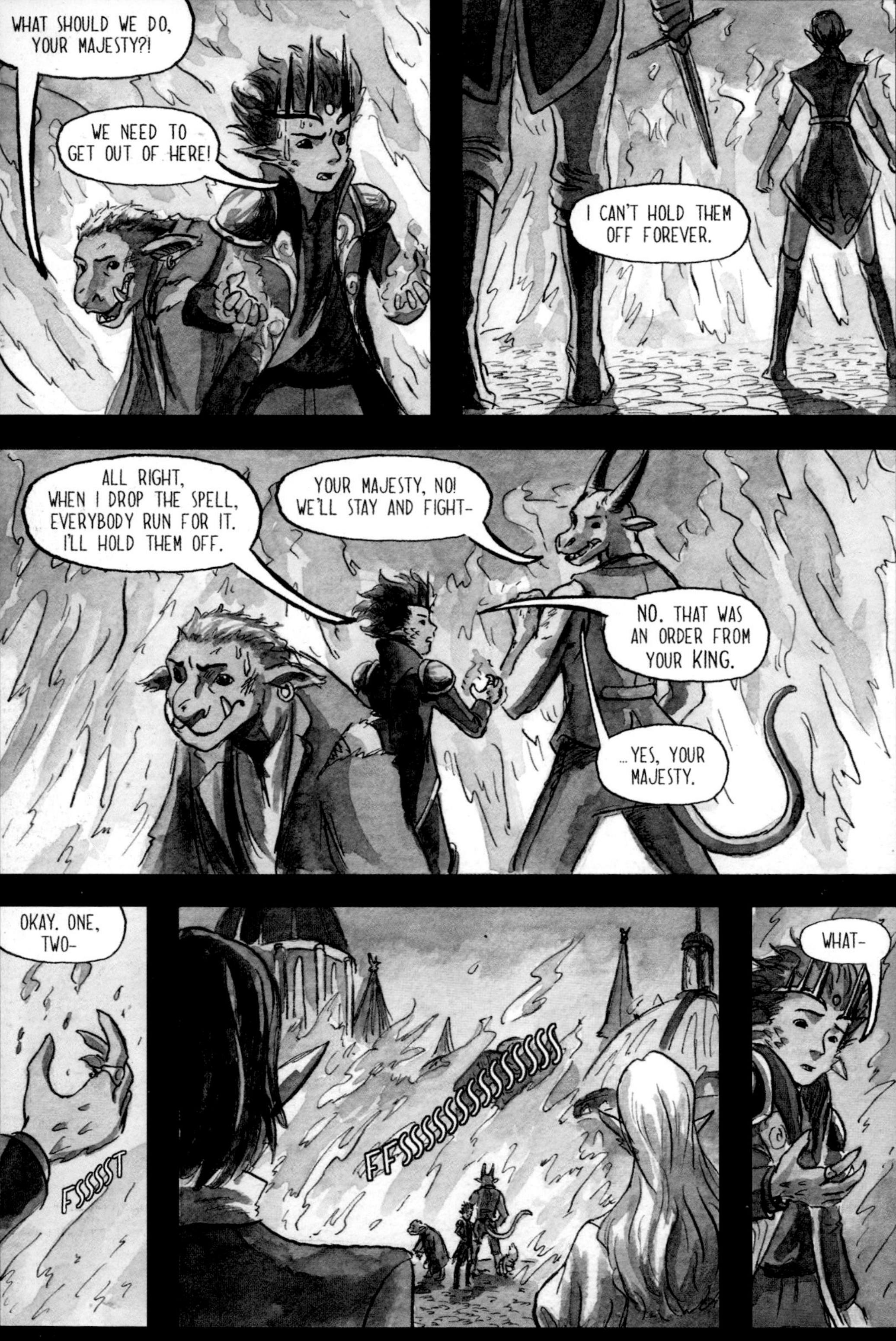
WHAT SHOULD WE DO, YOUR MAJESTY?!
WE NEED TO GET OUT OF HERE!
I CAN'T HOLD THEM OFF FOREVER.
ALL RIGHT, WHEN I DROP THE SPELL, EVERYBODY RUN FOR IT. I'LL HOLD THEM OFF.
YOUR MAJESTY, NO! WE'LL STAY AND FIGHT-
NO. THAT WAS AN ORDER FROM YOUR KING.
...YES, YOUR MAJESTY.
OKAY. ONE, TWO-
FSSSSST
FFSSSSSSSSSSSSSSS
WHAT-

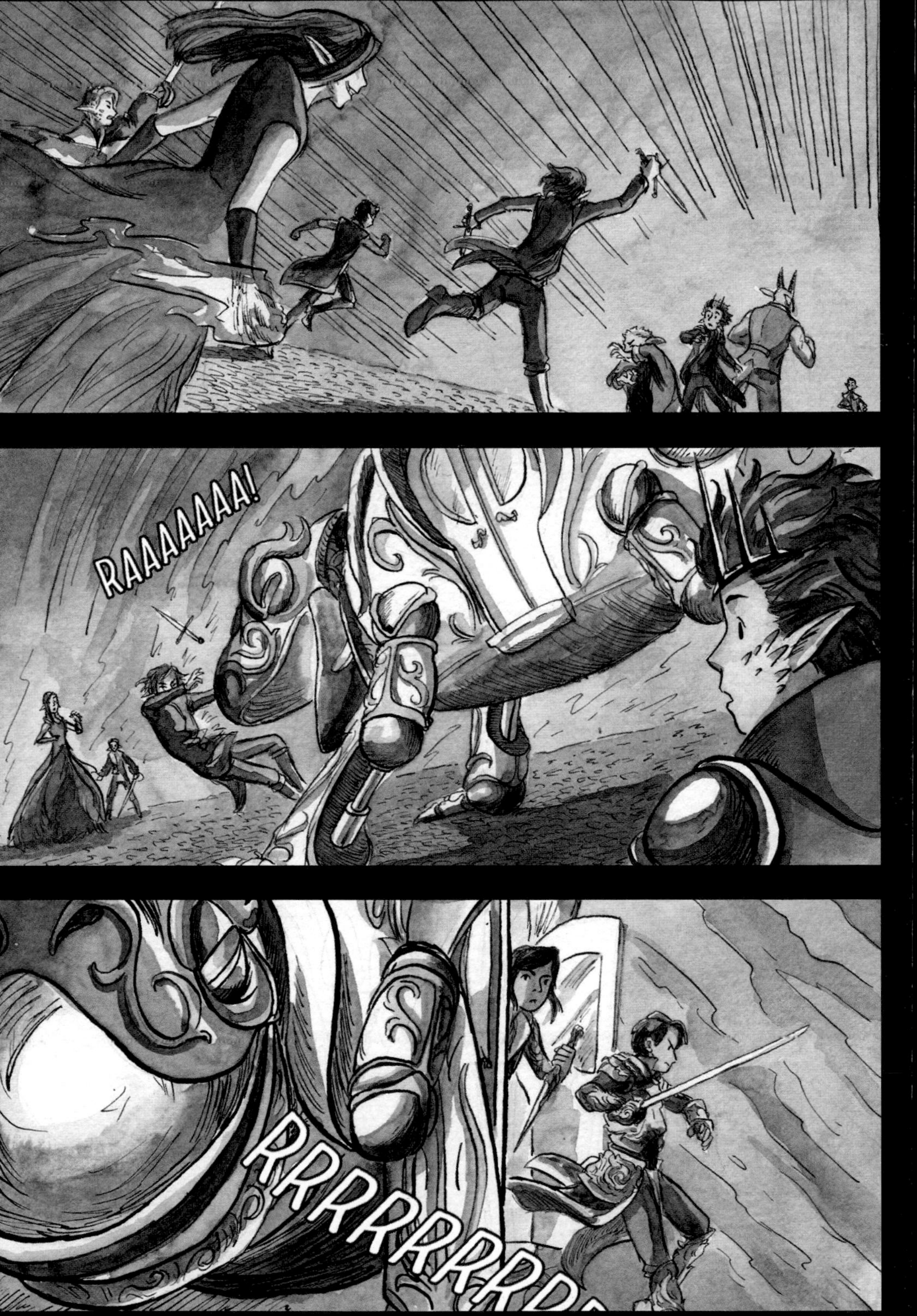
RAAAAAAA!
RRRRRRRRR

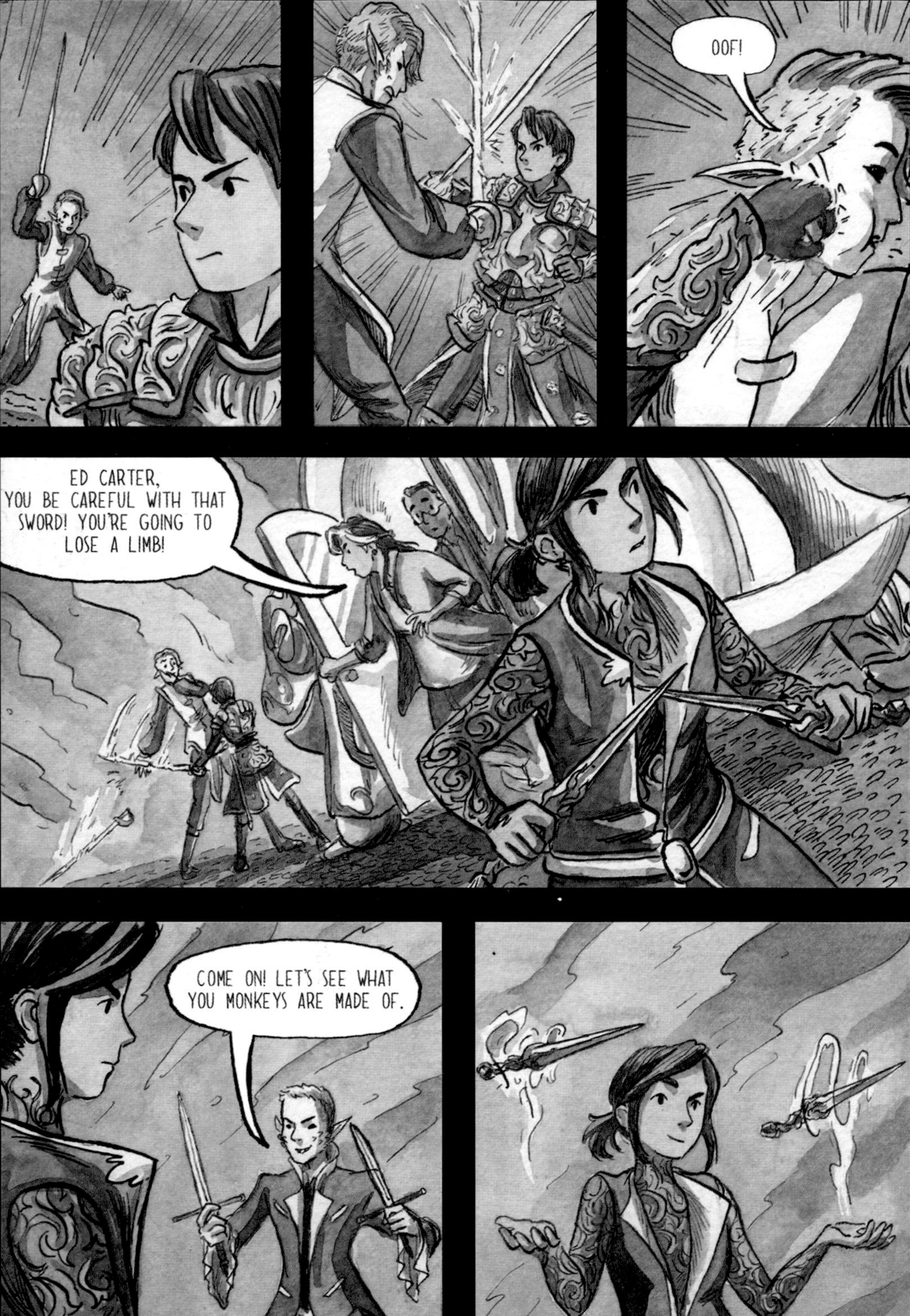
OOF!
ED CARTER, YOU BE CAREFUL WITH THAT SWORD! YOU'RE GOING TO LOSE A LIMB!
COME ON! LET'S SEE WHAT YOU MONKEYS ARE MADE OF.

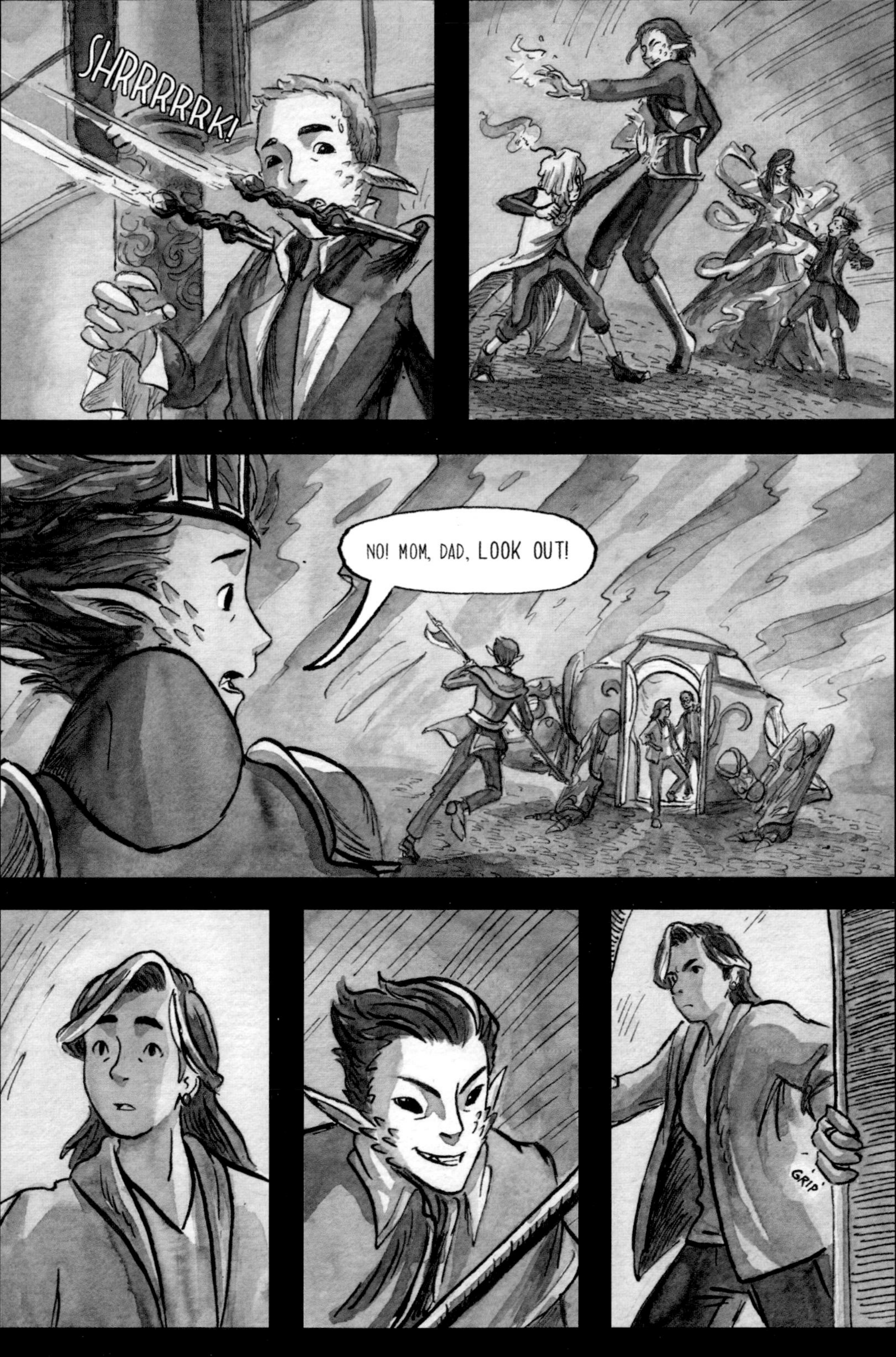
SHRRRRRRK!
NO! MOM, DAD, LOOK OUT!
GRIP

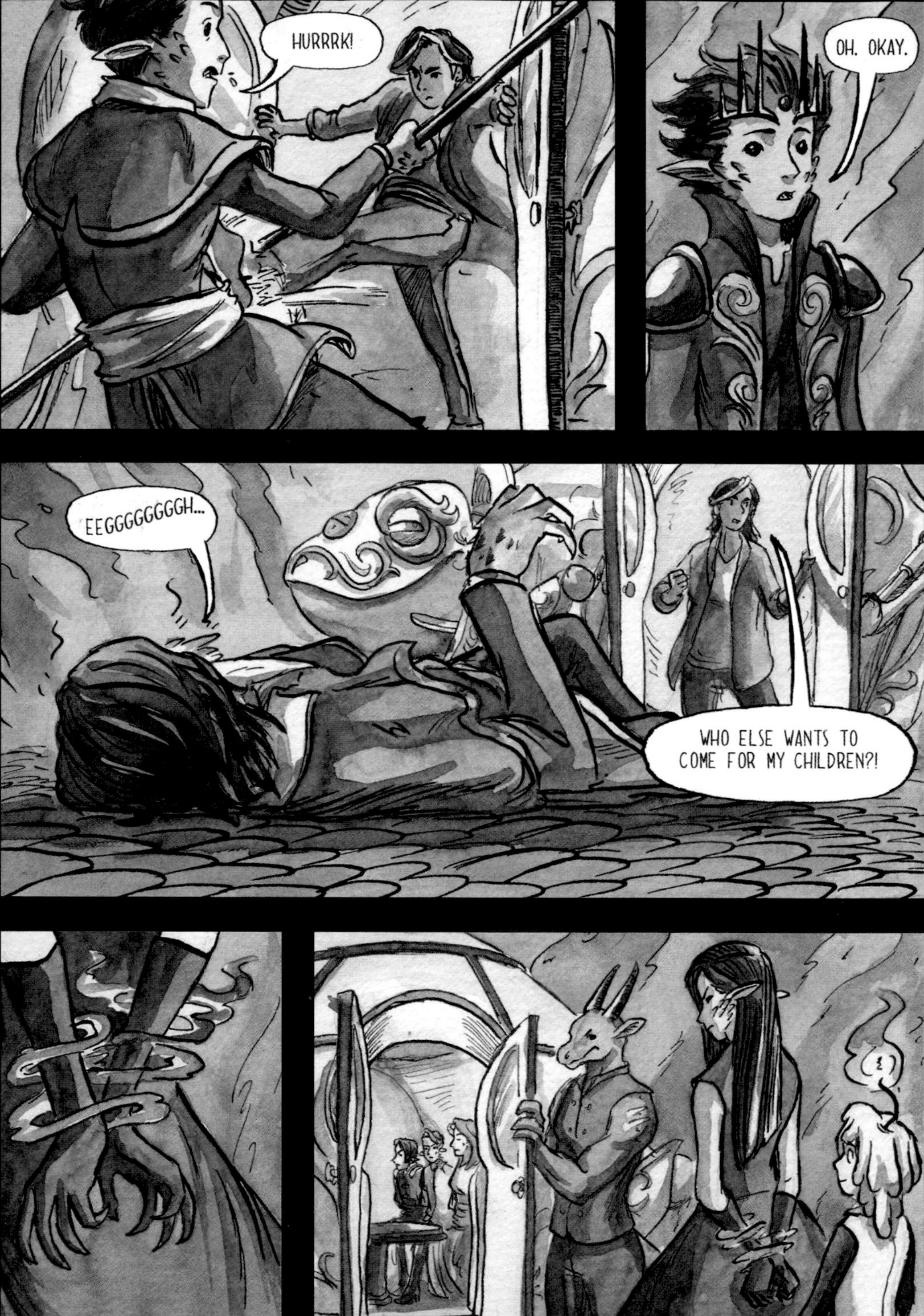
HURRRK!
OH. OKAY.
EEGGGGGGGGH...
WHO ELSE WANTS TO COME FOR MY CHILDREN?!

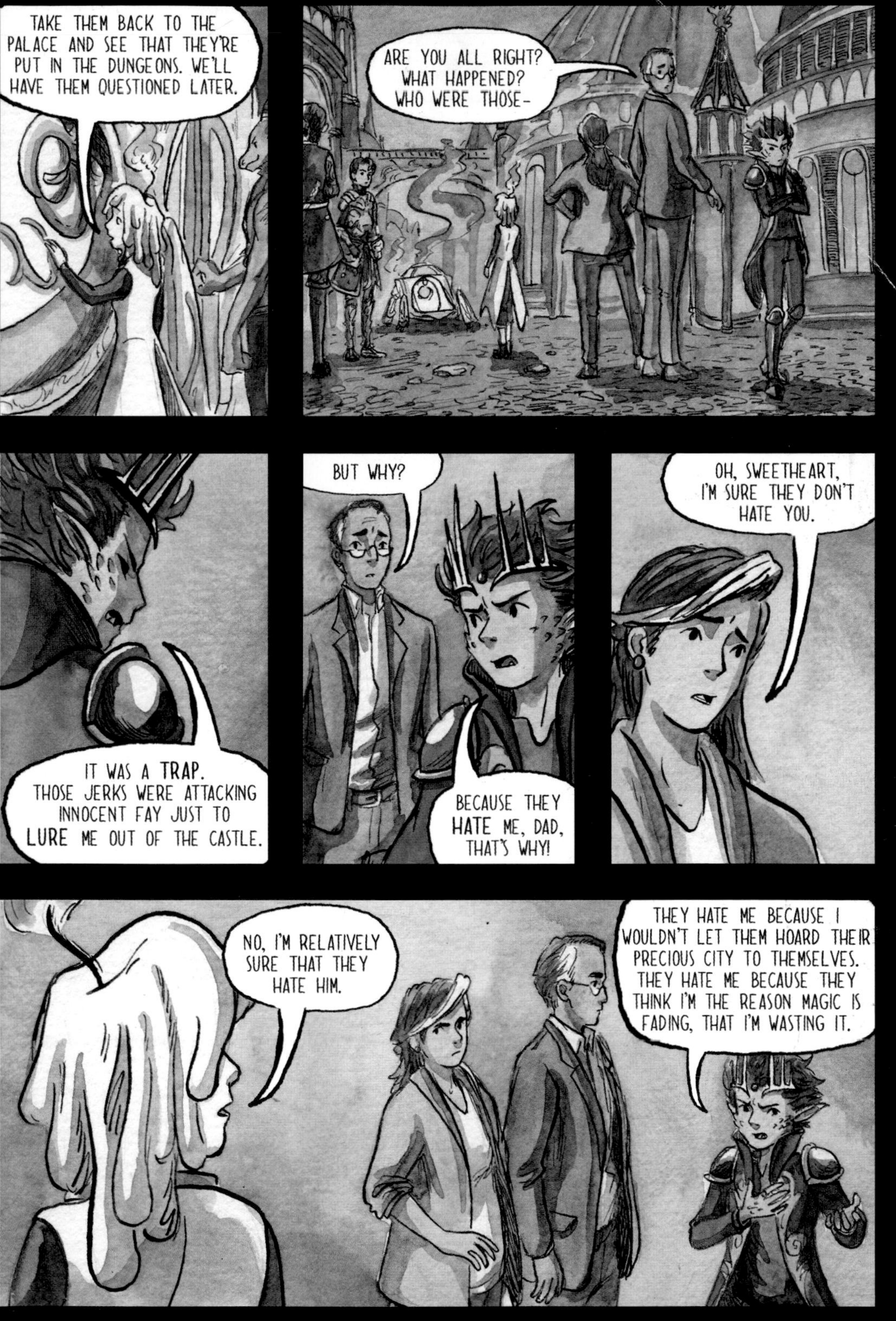
TAKE THEM BACK TO THE PALACE AND SEE THAT THEY'RE PUT IN THE DUNGEONS. WE'LL HAVE THEM QUESTIONED LATER.
ARE YOU ALL RIGHT? WHAT HAPPENED? WHO WERE THOSE-
IT WAS A TRAP. THOSE JERKS WERE ATTACKING INNOCENT FAY JUST TO LURE ME OUT OF THE CASTLE.
BUT WHY?
BECAUSE THEY HATE ME, DAD, THAT'S WHY!
OH, SWEETHEART, I'M SURE THEY DON'T HATE YOU.
NO, I'M RELATIVELY SURE THAT THEY HATE HIM.
THEY HATE ME BECAUSE I WOULDN'T LET THEM HOARD THEIR PRECIOUS CITY TO THEMSELVES. THEY HATE ME BECAUSE THEY THINK I'M THE REASON MAGIC IS FADING, THAT I'M WASTING IT.

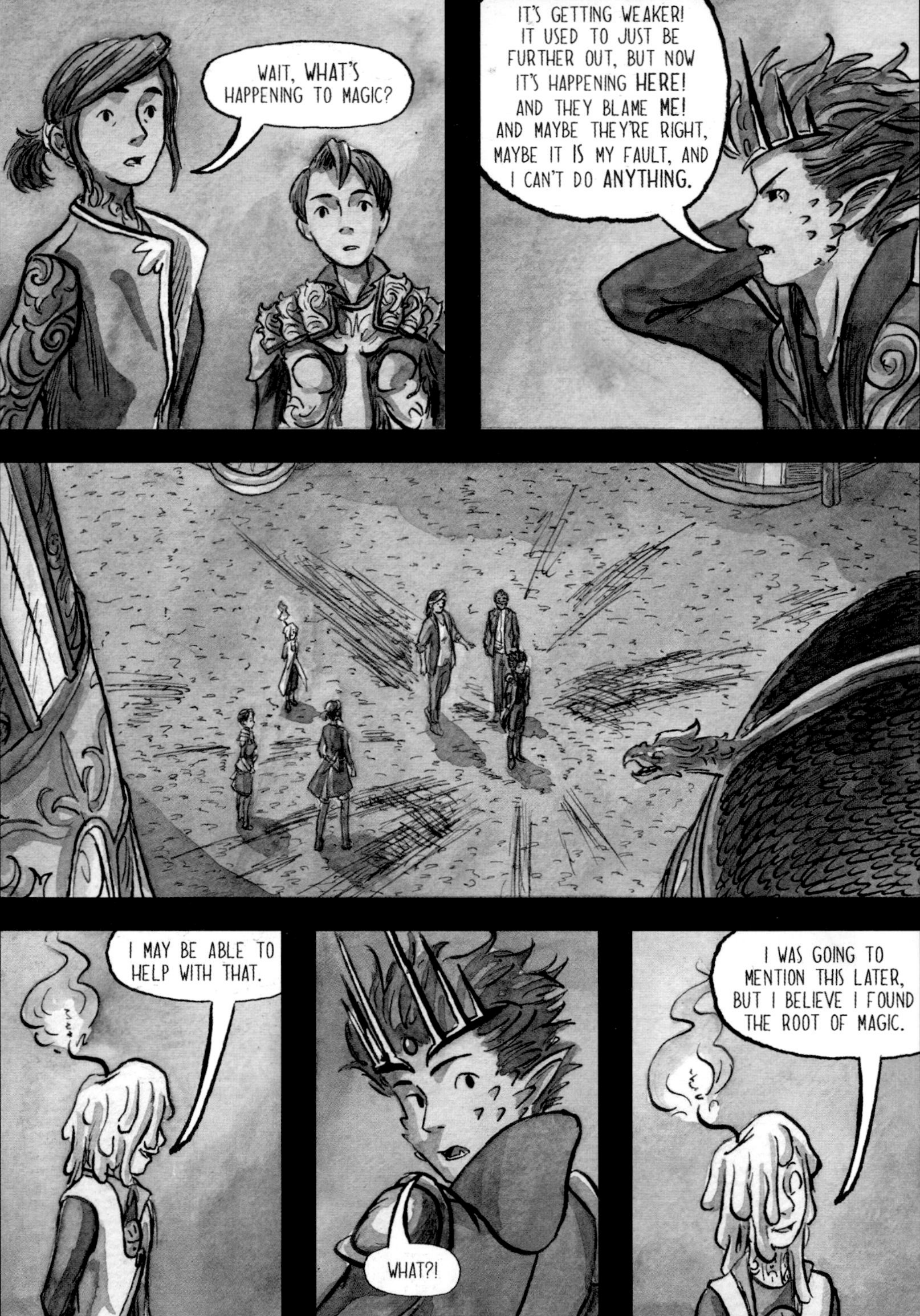
WAIT, WHAT'S HAPPENING TO MAGIC?
IT'S GETTING WEAKER! IT USED TO JUST BE FURTHER OUT, BUT NOW IT'S HAPPENING HERE! AND THEY BLAME ME! AND MAYBE THEY'RE RIGHT, MAYBE IT IS MY FAULT, AND I CAN'T DO ANYTHING.
I MAY BE ABLE TO HELP WITH THAT.
WHAT?!
I WAS GOING TO MENTION THIS LATER, BUT I BELIEVE I FOUND THE ROOT OF MAGIC.

Chapter Five

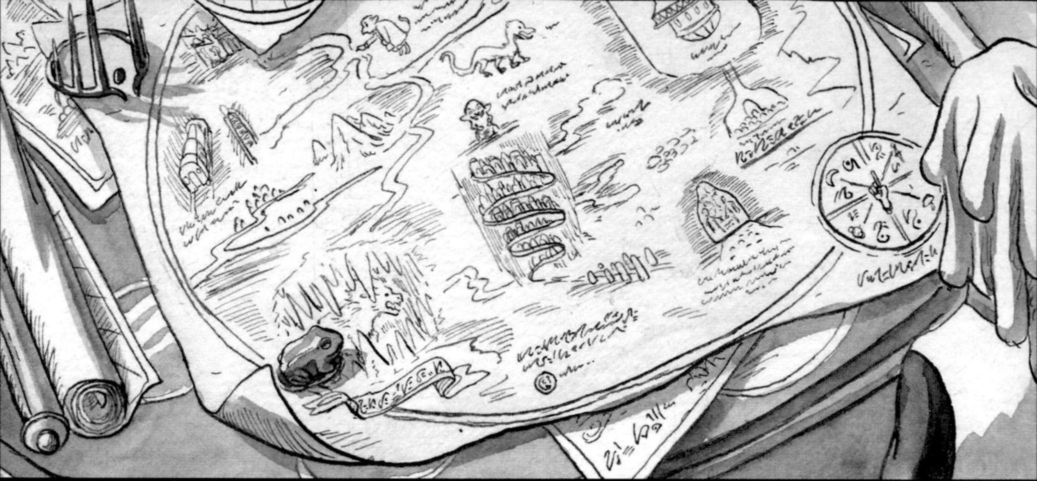

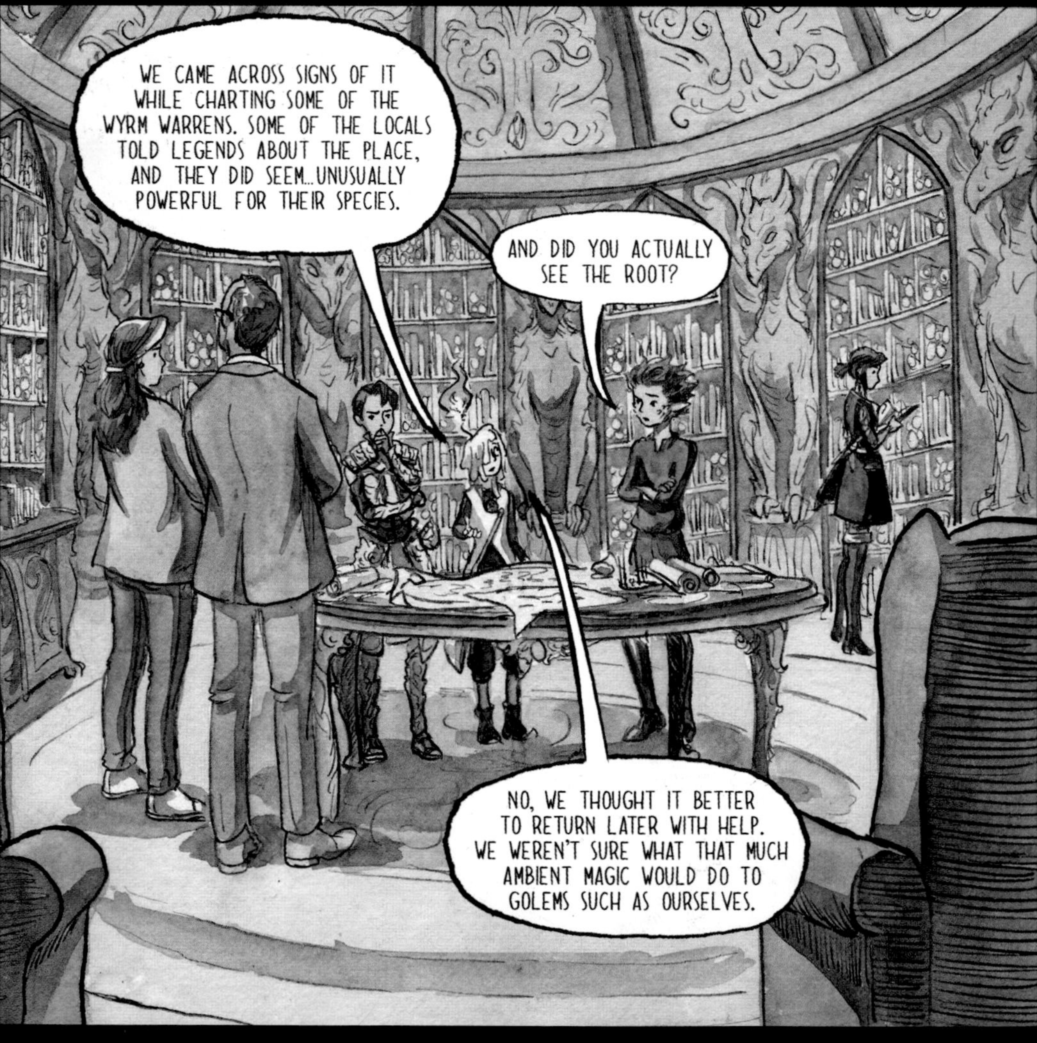
WE CAME ACROSS SIGNS OF IT WHILE CHARTING SOME OF THE WYRM WARRENS. SOME OF THE LOCALS TOLD LEGENDS ABOUT THE PLACE, AND THEY DID SEEM...UNUSUALLY POWERFUL FOR THEIR SPECIES.
AND DID YOU ACTUALLY SEE THE ROOT?
NO, WE THOUGHT IT BETTER TO RETURN LATER WITH HELP. WE WEREN'T SURE WHAT THAT MUCH AMBIENT MAGIC WOULD DO TO GOLEMS SUCH AS OURSELVES.

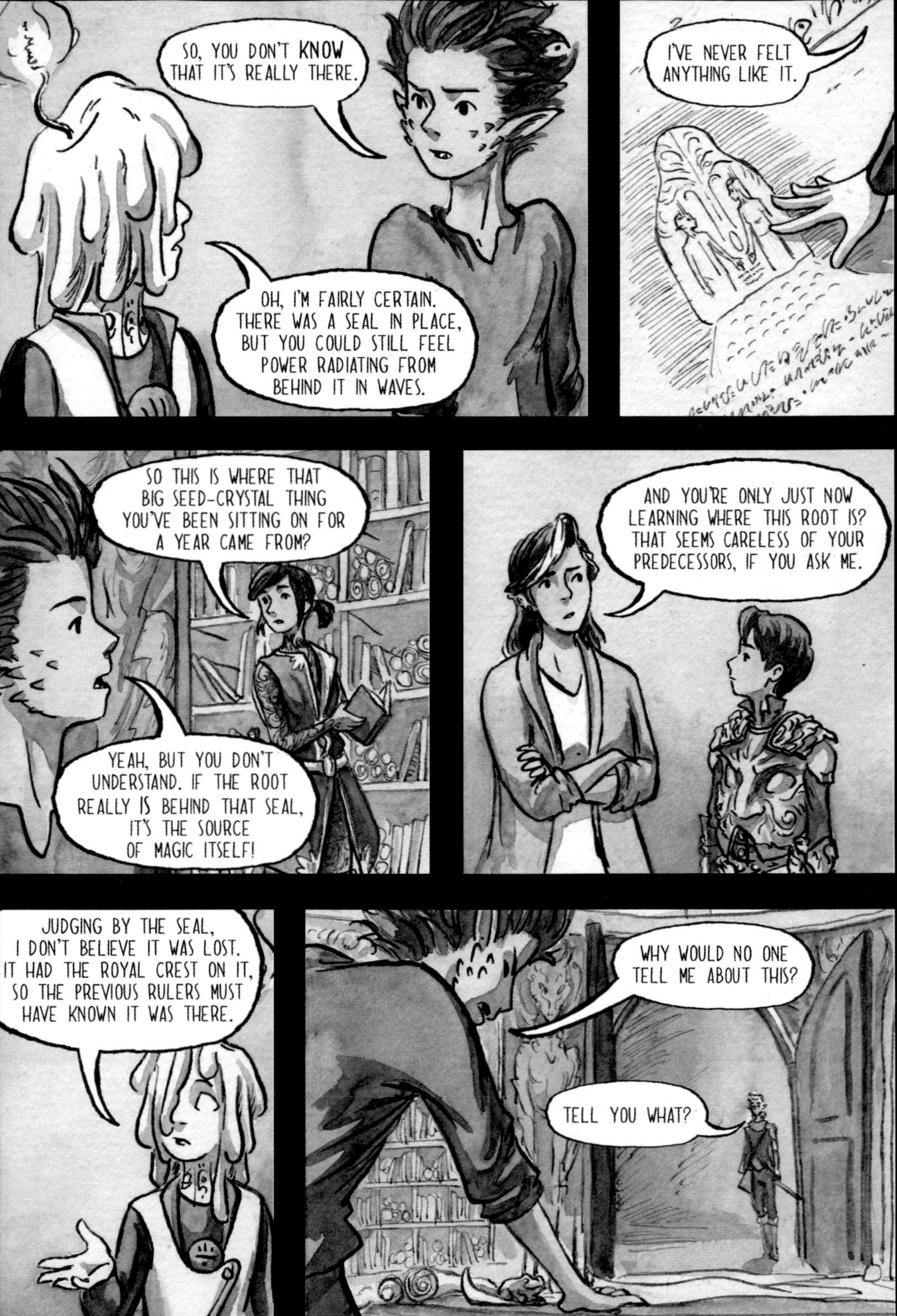
SO, YOU DON'T KNOW THAT IT'S REALLY THERE.
OH, I'M FAIRLY CERTAIN. THERE WAS A SEAL IN PLACE, BUT YOU COULD STILL FEEL POWER RADIATING FROM BEHIND IT IN WAVES.
I'VE NEVER FELT ANYTHING LIKE IT.
SO THIS IS WHERE THAT BIG SEED-CRYSTAL THING YOU'VE BEEN SITTING ON FOR A YEAR CAME FROM?
YEAH, BUT YOU DON'T UNDERSTAND. IF THE ROOT REALLY IS BEHIND THAT SEAL, IT'S THE SOURCE OF MAGIC ITSELF!
AND YOU'RE ONLY JUST NOW LEARNING WHERE THIS ROOT IS? THAT SEEMS CARELESS OF YOUR PREDECESSORS, IF YOU ASK ME.
JUDGING BY THE SEAL, I DON'T BELIEVE IT WAS LOST. IT HAD THE ROYAL CREST ON IT, SO THE PREVIOUS RULERS MUST HAVE KNOWN IT WAS THERE.
WHY WOULD NO ONE TELL ME ABOUT THIS?
TELL YOU WHAT?

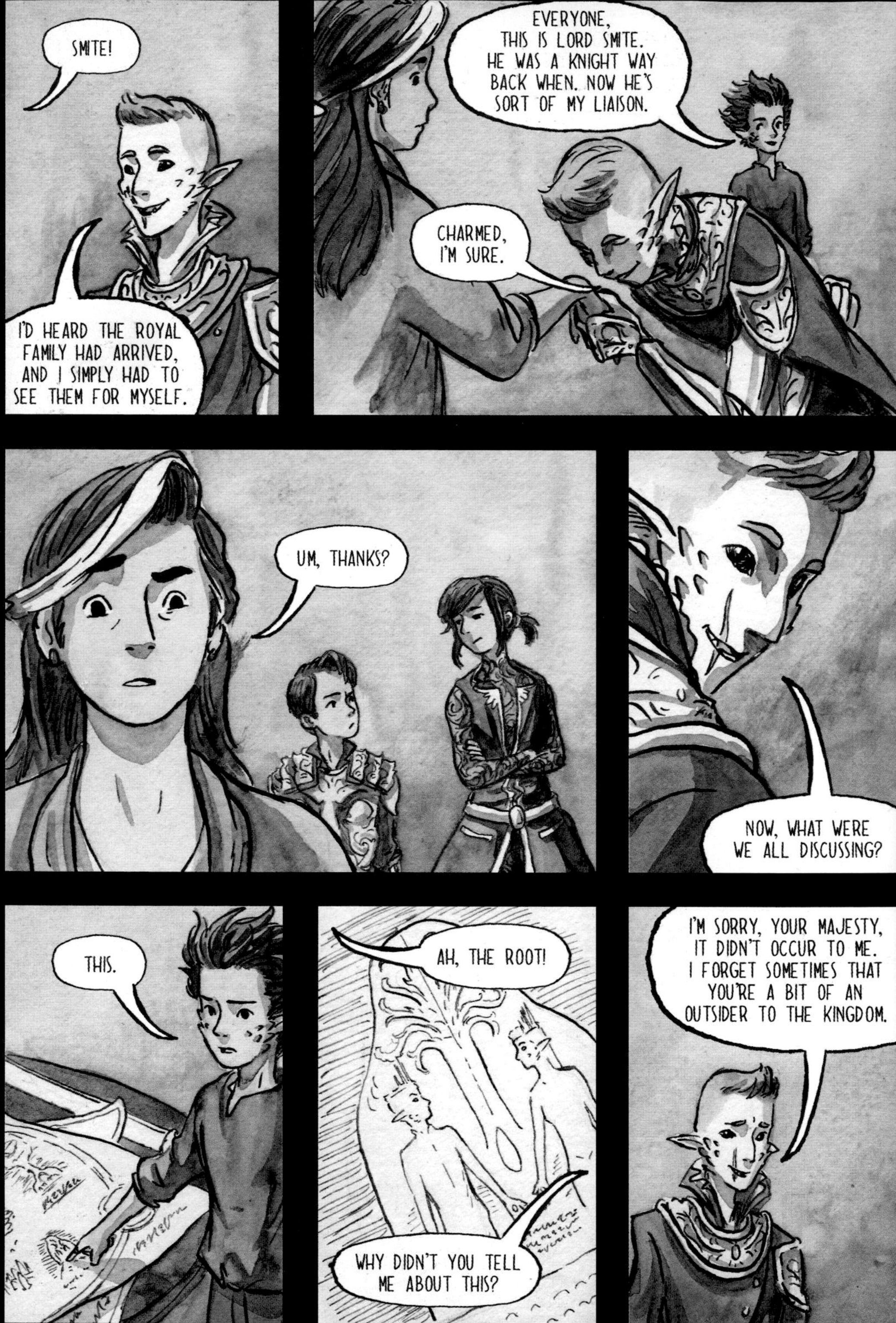
SMITE!
I'D HEARD THE ROYAL FAMILY HAD ARRIVED, AND I SIMPLY HAD TO SEE THEM FOR MYSELF.
EVERYONE, THIS IS LORD SMITE. HE WAS A KNIGHT WAY BACK WHEN. NOW HE'S SORT OF MY LIAISON.
CHARMED, I'M SURE.
UM, THANKS?
NOW, WHAT WERE WE ALL DISCUSSING?
THIS.
AH, THE ROOT!
WHY DIDN'T YOU TELL ME ABOUT THIS?
I'M SORRY, YOUR MAJESTY, IT DIDN'T OCCUR TO ME. I FORGET SOMETIMES THAT YOU'RE A BIT OF AN OUTSIDER TO THE KINGDOM.

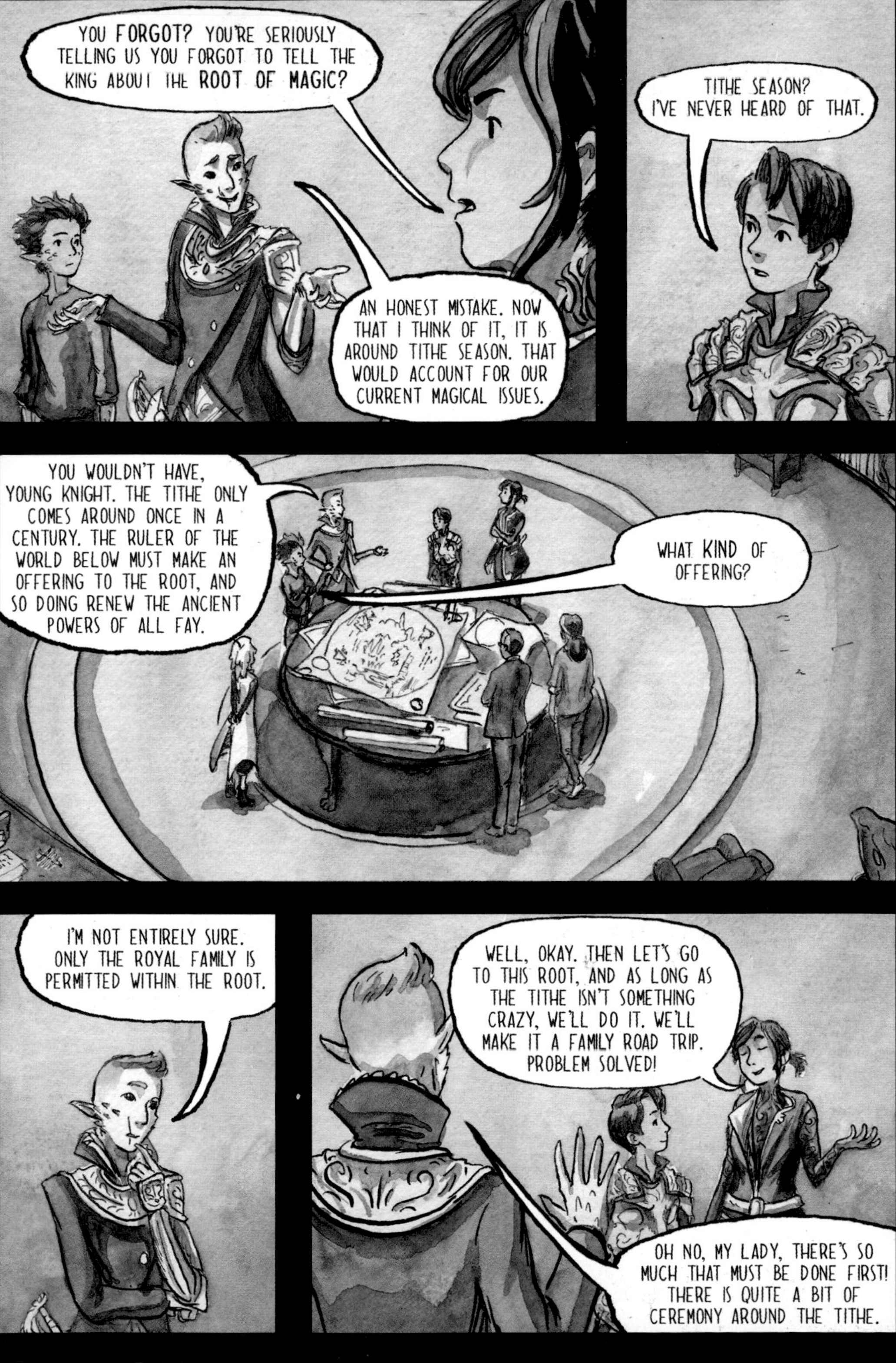
YOU FORGOT? YOU'RE SERIOUSLY TELLING US YOU FORGOT TO TELL THE KING ABOUT THE ROOT OF MAGIC?
AN HONEST MISTAKE. NOW THAT I THINK OF IT, IT IS AROUND TITHE SEASON. THAT WOULD ACCOUNT FOR OUR CURRENT MAGICAL ISSUES.
TITHE SEASON? I'VE NEVER HEARD OF THAT.
YOU WOULDN'T HAVE, YOUNG KNIGHT. THE TITHE ONLY COMES AROUND ONCE IN A CENTURY. THE RULER OF THE WORLD BELOW MUST MAKE AN OFFERING TO THE ROOT, AND SO DOING RENEW THE ANCIENT POWERS OF ALL FAY.
WHAT KIND OF OFFERING?
I'M NOT ENTIRELY SURE. ONLY THE ROYAL FAMILY IS PERMITTED WITHIN THE ROOT.
WELL, OKAY. THEN LET'S GO TO THIS ROOT, AND AS LONG AS THE TITHE ISN'T SOMETHING CRAZY, WE'LL DO IT. WE'LL MAKE IT A FAMILY ROAD TRIP. PROBLEM SOLVED!
OH NO, MY LADY, THERE'S SO MUCH THAT MUST BE DONE FIRST! THERE IS QUITE A BIT OF CEREMONY AROUND THE TITHE.

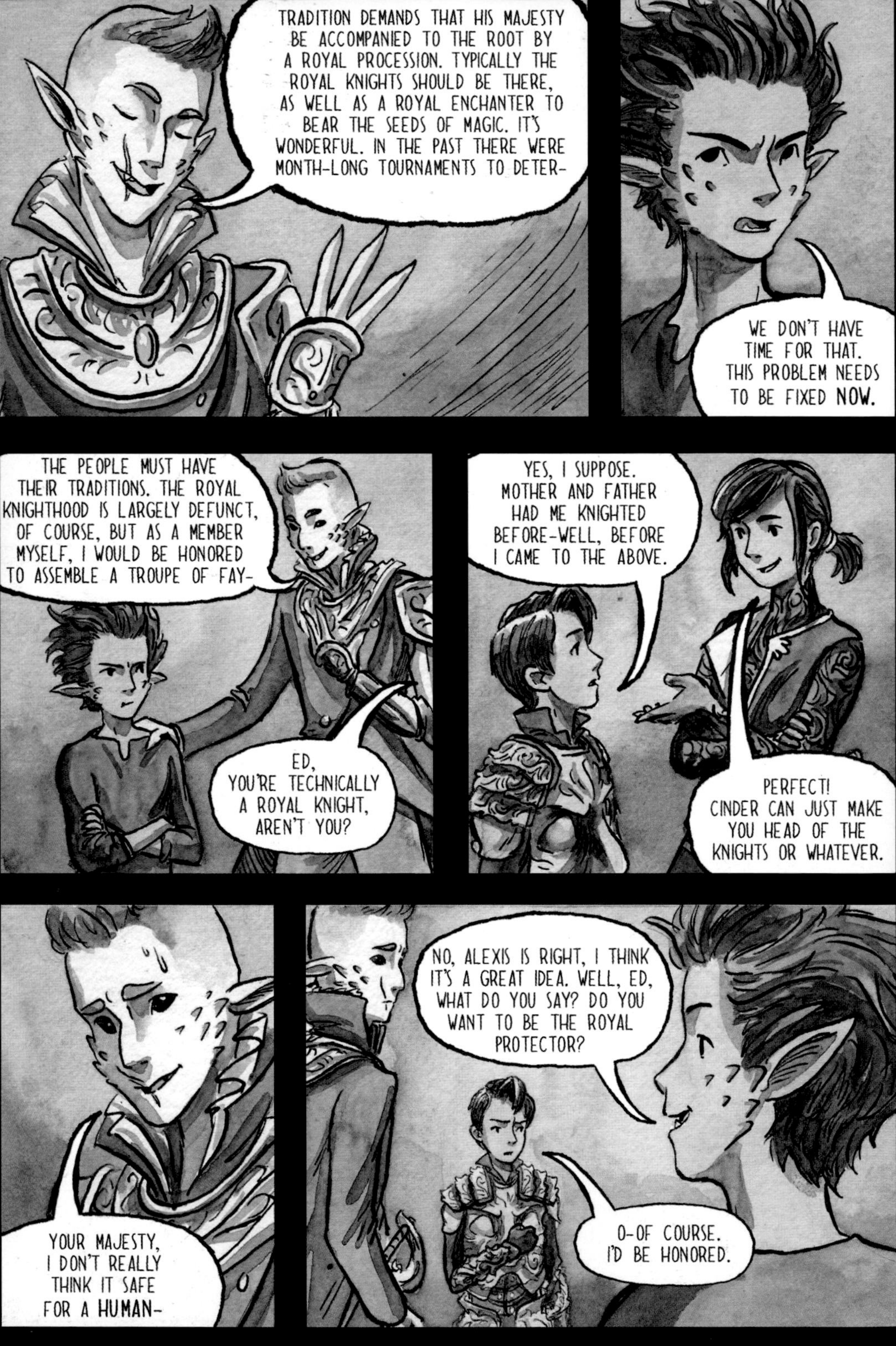
TRADITION DEMANDS THAT HIS MAJESTY BE ACCOMPANIED TO THE ROOT BY A ROYAL PROCESSION. TYPICALLY THE ROYAL KNIGHTS SHOULD BE THERE, AS WELL AS A ROYAL ENCHANTER TO BEAR THE SEEDS OF MAGIC. IT'S WONDERFUL. IN THE PAST THERE WERE MONTH-LONG TOURNAMENTS TO DETER-
WE DON'T HAVE TIME FOR THAT. THIS PROBLEM NEEDS TO BE FIXED NOW.
THE PEOPLE MUST HAVE THEIR TRADITIONS. THE ROYAL KNIGHTHOOD IS LARGELY DEFUNCT, OF COURSE, BUT AS A MEMBER MYSELF, I WOULD BE HONORED TO ASSEMBLE A TROUPE OF FAY-
ED, YOU'RE TECHNICALLY A ROYAL KNIGHT, AREN'T YOU?
YES, I SUPPOSE. MOTHER AND FATHER HAD ME KNIGHTED BEFORE-WELL, BEFORE I CAME TO THE ABOVE.
PERFECT! CINDER CAN JUST MAKE YOU HEAD OF THE KNIGHTS OR WHATEVER.
YOUR MAJESTY, I DON'T REALLY THINK IT SAFE FOR A HUMAN-
NO, ALEXIS IS RIGHT, I THINK IT'S A GREAT IDEA. WELL, ED, WHAT DO YOU SAY? DO YOU WANT TO BE THE ROYAL PROTECTOR?
O-OF COURSE. I'D BE HONORED.

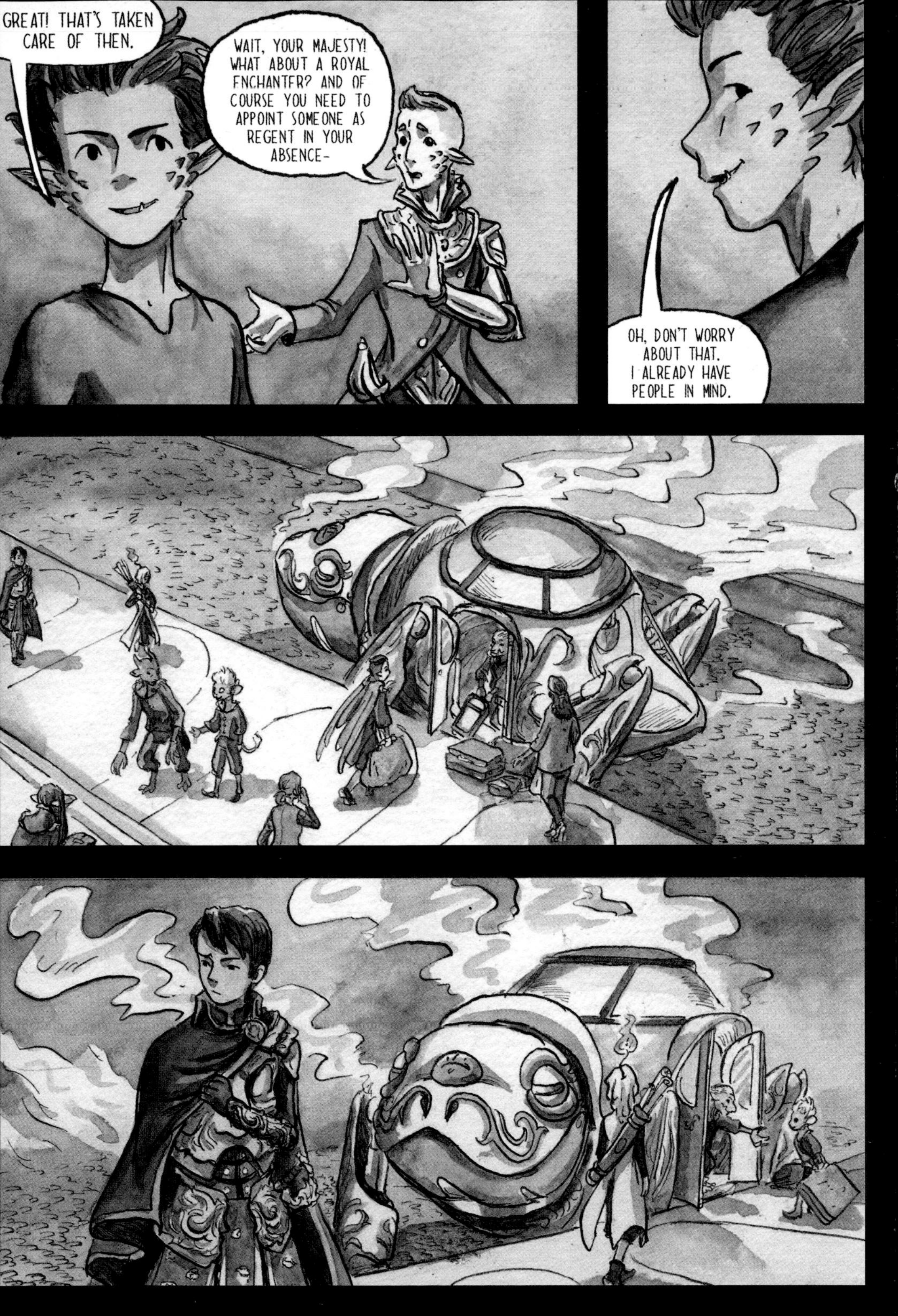
GREAT! THAT'S TAKEN CARE OF THEN.
WAIT, YOUR MAJESTY! WHAT ABOUT A ROYAL ENCHANTER? AND OF COURSE YOU NEED TO APPOINT SOMEONE AS REGENT IN YOUR ABSENCE-
OH, DON'T WORRY ABOUT THAT. I ALREADY HAVE PEOPLE IN MIND.

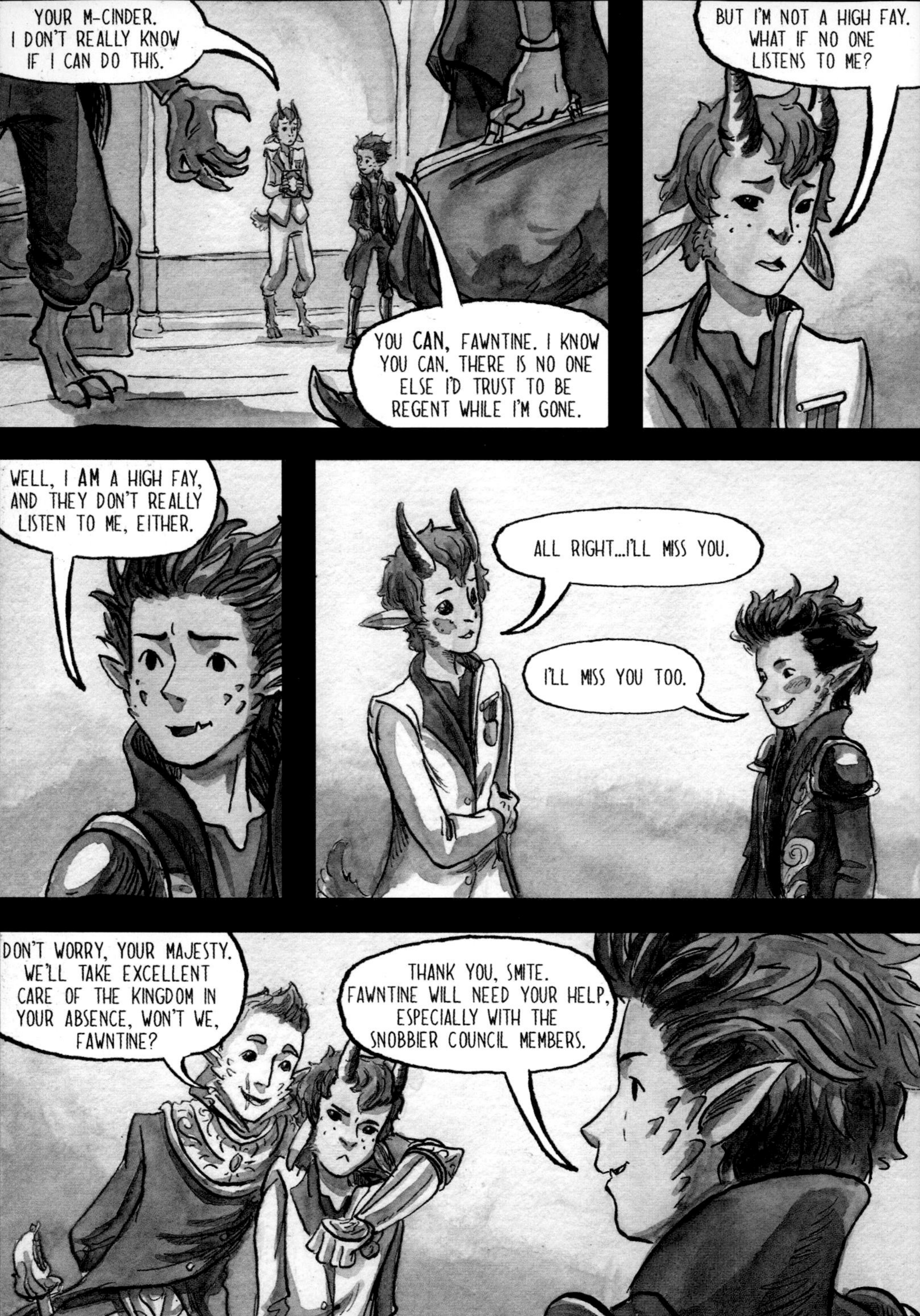
YOUR M-CINDER. I DON'T REALLY KNOW IF I CAN DO THIS.
YOU CAN, FAWNTINE. I KNOW YOU CAN. THERE IS NO ONE ELSE I'D TRUST TO BE REGENT WHILE I'M GONE.
BUT I'M NOT A HIGH FAY. WHAT IF NO ONE LISTENS TO ME?
WELL, I AM A HIGH FAY, AND THEY DON'T REALLY LISTEN TO ME, EITHER.
ALL RIGHT...I'LL MISS YOU.
I'LL MISS YOU TOO.
DON'T WORRY, YOUR MAJESTY. WE'LL TAKE EXCELLENT CARE OF THE KINGDOM IN YOUR ABSENCE, WON'T WE, FAWNTINE?
THANK YOU, SMITE. FAWNTINE WILL NEED YOUR HELP, ESPECIALLY WITH THE SNOBBIER COUNCIL MEMBERS.

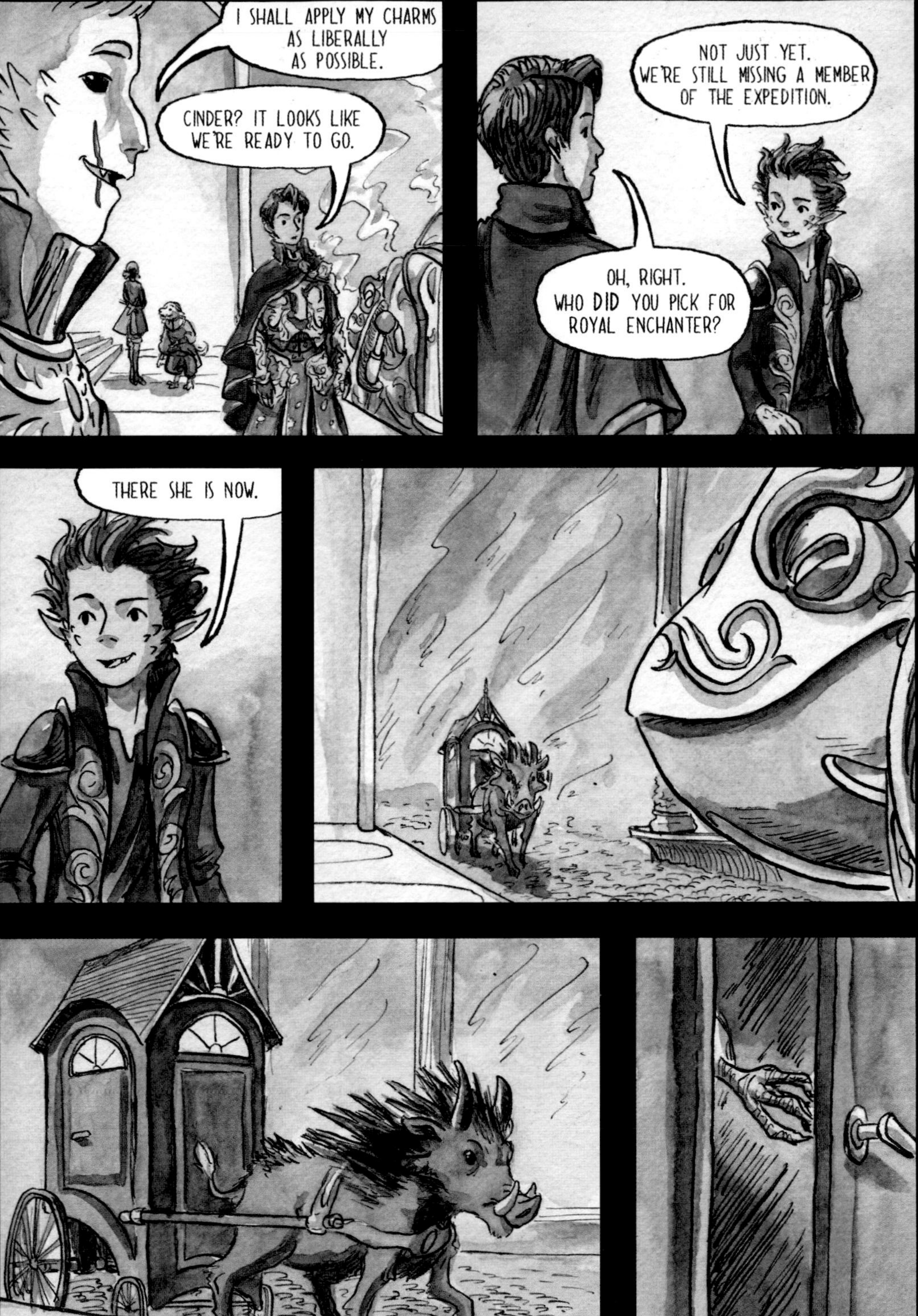
I SHALL APPLY MY CHARMS AS LIBERALLY AS POSSIBLE.
CINDER? IT LOOKS LIKE WE'RE READY TO GO.
NOT JUST YET. WE'RE STILL MISSING A MEMBER OF THE EXPEDITION.
OH, RIGHT. WHO **DID** YOU PICK FOR ROYAL ENCHANTER?
THERE SHE IS NOW.

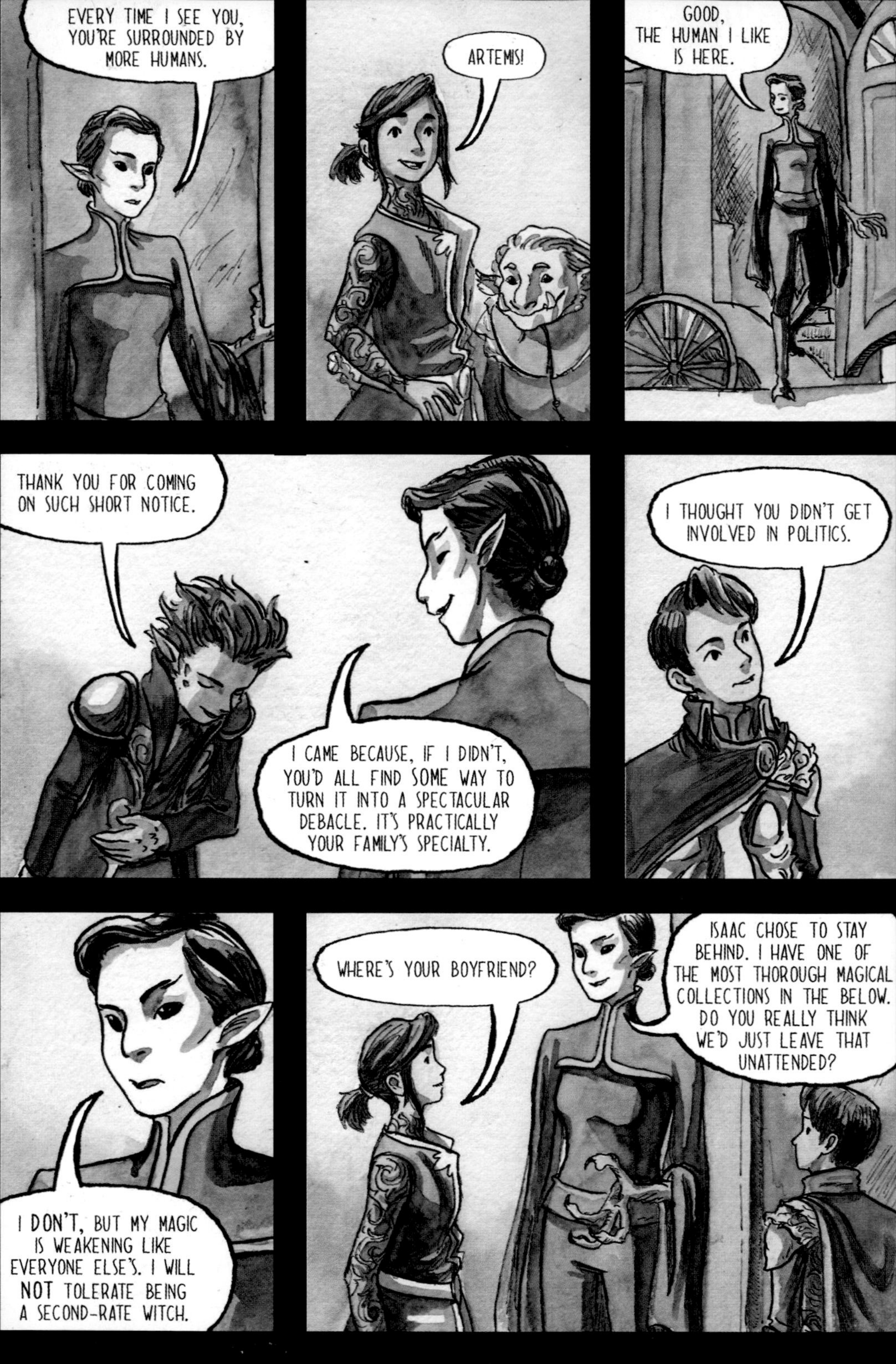
EVERY TIME I SEE YOU, YOU'RE SURROUNDED BY MORE HUMANS.
ARTEMIS!
GOOD, THE HUMAN I LIKE IS HERE.
THANK YOU FOR COMING ON SUCH SHORT NOTICE.
I CAME BECAUSE, IF I DIDN'T, YOU'D ALL FIND SOME WAY TO TURN IT INTO A SPECTACULAR DEBACLE. IT'S PRACTICALLY YOUR FAMILY'S SPECIALTY.
I THOUGHT YOU DIDN'T GET INVOLVED IN POLITICS.
I DON'T, BUT MY MAGIC IS WEAKENING LIKE EVERYONE ELSE'S. I WILL NOT TOLERATE BEING A SECOND-RATE WITCH.
WHERE'S YOUR BOYFRIEND?
ISAAC CHOSE TO STAY BEHIND. I HAVE ONE OF THE MOST THOROUGH MAGICAL COLLECTIONS IN THE BELOW. DO YOU REALLY THINK WE'D JUST LEAVE THAT UNATTENDED?

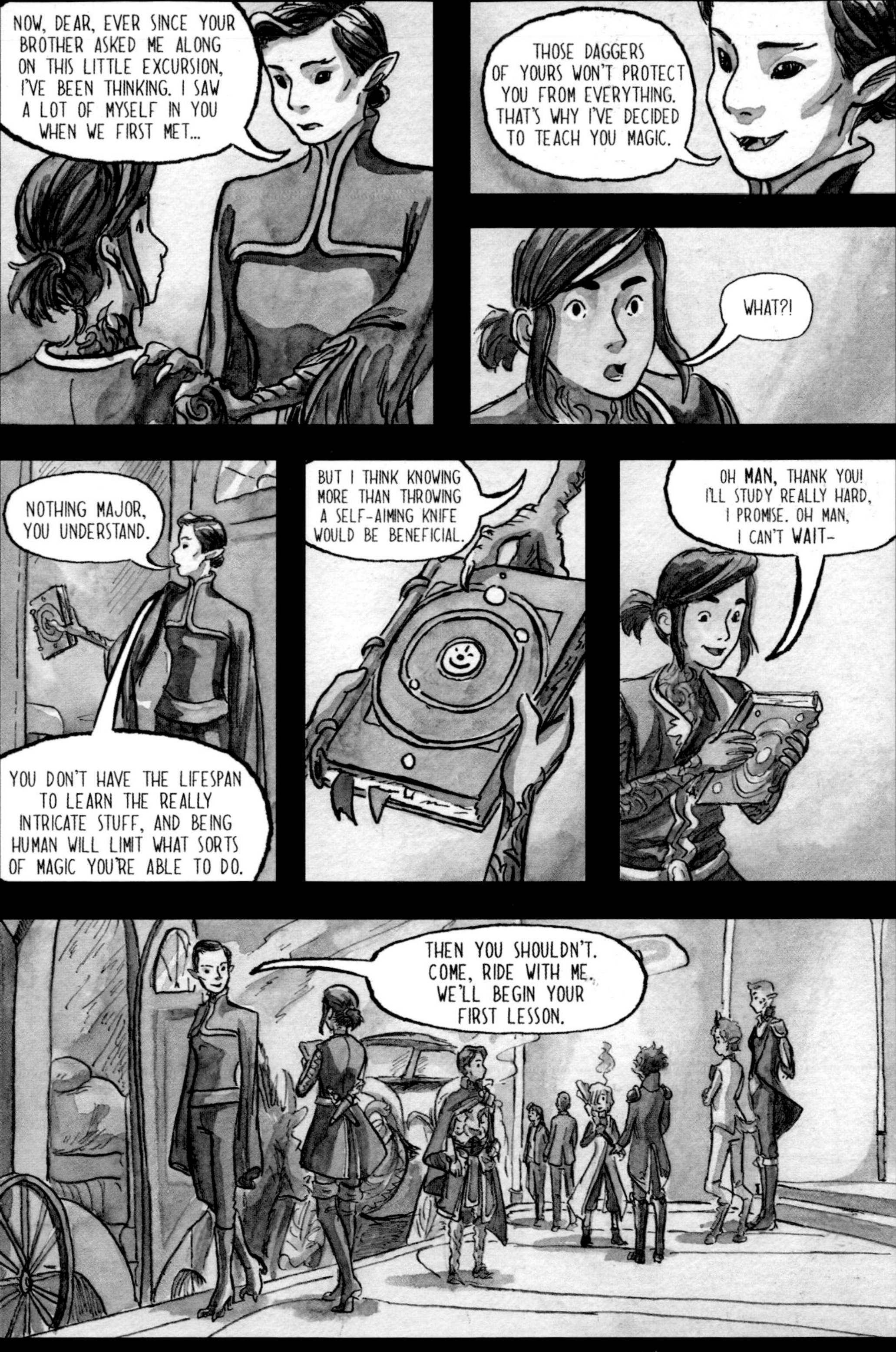
NOW, DEAR, EVER SINCE YOUR BROTHER ASKED ME ALONG ON THIS LITTLE EXCURSION, I'VE BEEN THINKING. I SAW A LOT OF MYSELF IN YOU WHEN WE FIRST MET...
THOSE DAGGERS OF YOURS WON'T PROTECT YOU FROM EVERYTHING. THAT'S WHY I'VE DECIDED TO TEACH YOU MAGIC.
WHAT?!
NOTHING MAJOR, YOU UNDERSTAND.
YOU DON'T HAVE THE LIFESPAN TO LEARN THE REALLY INTRICATE STUFF, AND BEING HUMAN WILL LIMIT WHAT SORTS OF MAGIC YOU'RE ABLE TO DO.
BUT I THINK KNOWING MORE THAN THROWING A SELF-AIMING KNIFE WOULD BE BENEFICIAL.
OH MAN, THANK YOU! I'LL STUDY REALLY HARD, I PROMISE. OH MAN, I CAN'T WAIT-
THEN YOU SHOULDN'T. COME, RIDE WITH ME. WE'LL BEGIN YOUR FIRST LESSON.

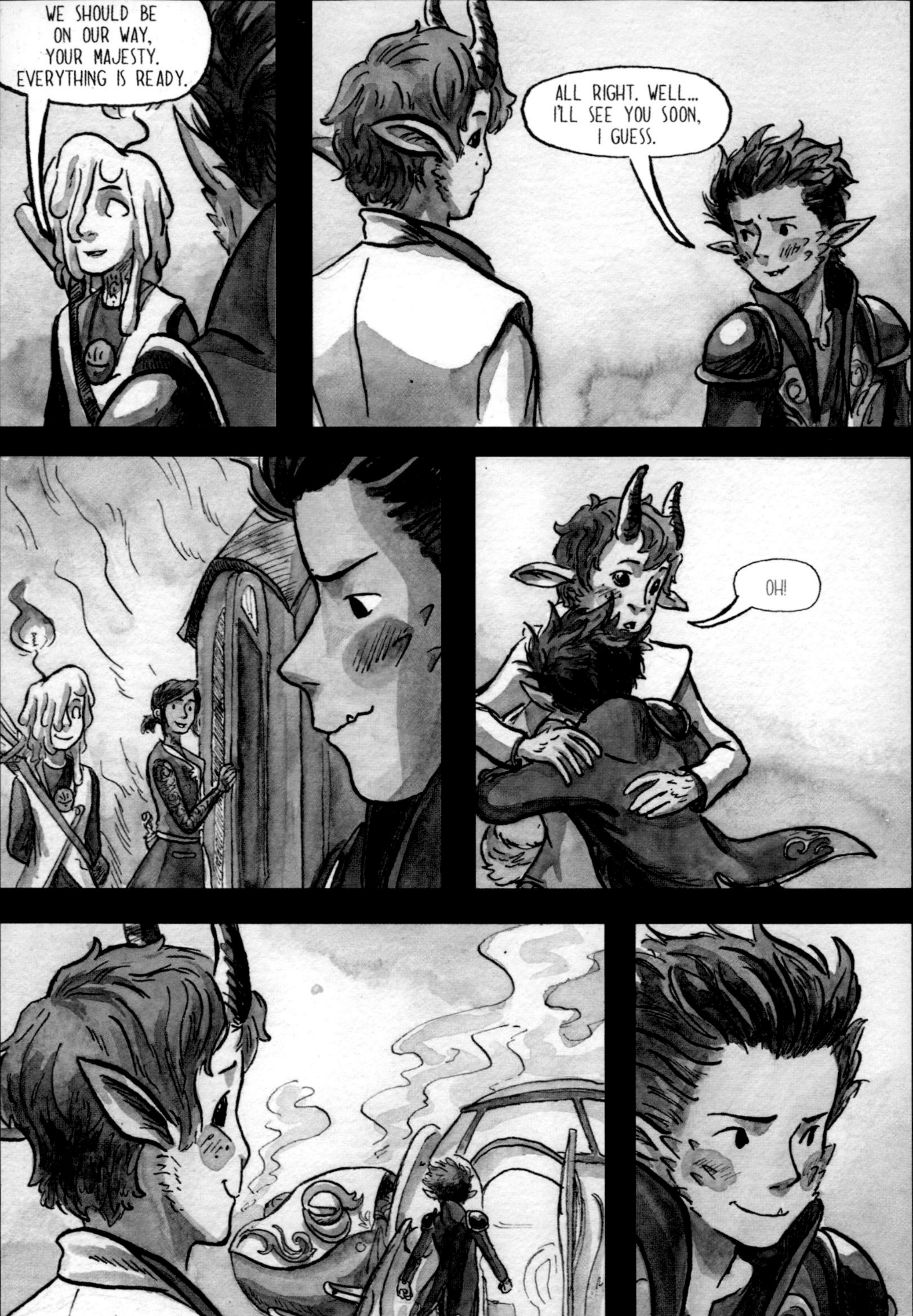
WE SHOULD BE ON OUR WAY, YOUR MAJESTY. EVERYTHING IS READY.
ALL RIGHT. WELL... I'LL SEE YOU SOON, I GUESS.
OH!

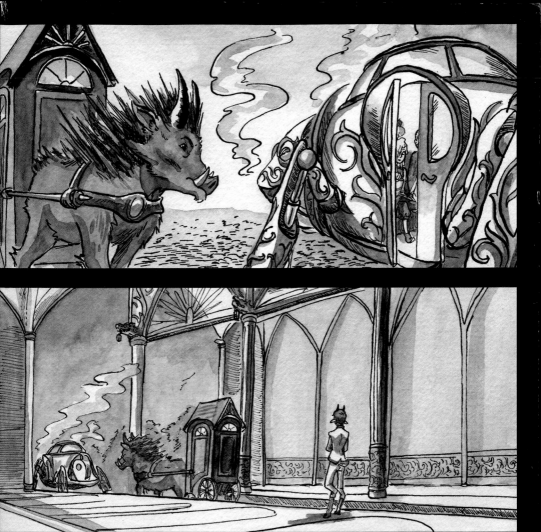

RIGHT. WELL. I GUESS I'M DOING THIS. LORD SMITE, WOULD YOU—

LORD SMITE?

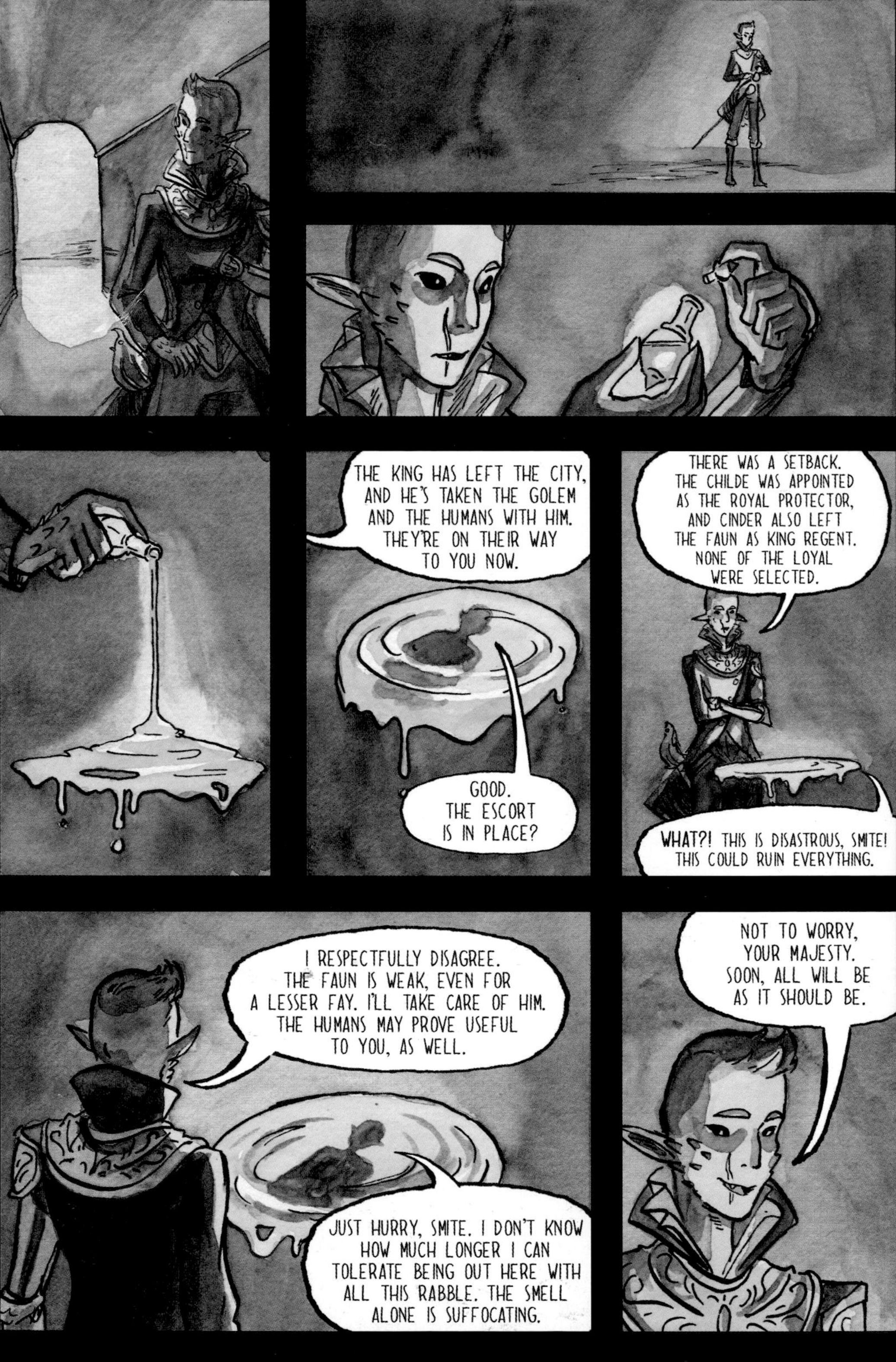
THE KING HAS LEFT THE CITY, AND HE'S TAKEN THE GOLEM AND THE HUMANS WITH HIM. THEY'RE ON THEIR WAY TO YOU NOW.
GOOD. THE ESCORT IS IN PLACE?
THERE WAS A SETBACK. THE CHILDE WAS APPOINTED AS THE ROYAL PROTECTOR, AND CINDER ALSO LEFT THE FAUN AS KING REGENT. NONE OF THE LOYAL WERE SELECTED.
WHAT?! THIS IS DISASTROUS, SMITE! THIS COULD RUIN EVERYTHING.
I RESPECTFULLY DISAGREE. THE FAUN IS WEAK, EVEN FOR A LESSER FAY. I'LL TAKE CARE OF HIM. THE HUMANS MAY PROVE USEFUL TO YOU, AS WELL.
JUST HURRY, SMITE. I DON'T KNOW HOW MUCH LONGER I CAN TOLERATE BEING OUT HERE WITH ALL THIS RABBLE. THE SMELL ALONE IS SUFFOCATING.
NOT TO WORRY, YOUR MAJESTY. SOON, ALL WILL BE AS IT SHOULD BE.

CHAPTER
SIX

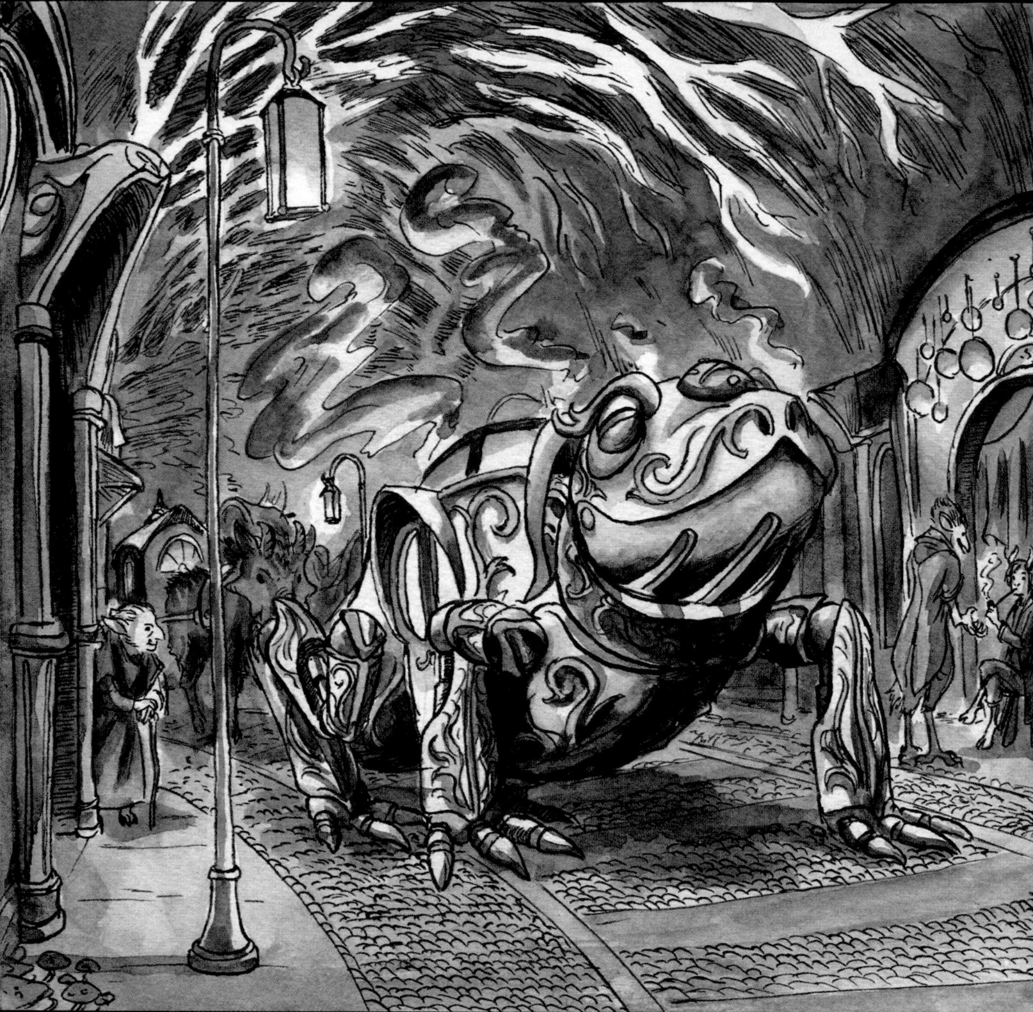

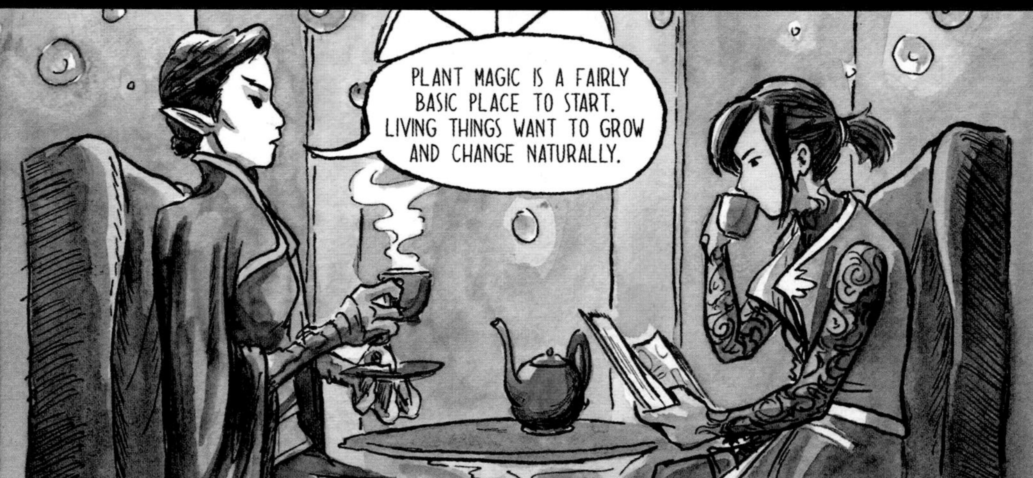
PLANT MAGIC IS A FAIRLY BASIC PLACE TO START. LIVING THINGS WANT TO GROW AND CHANGE NATURALLY.

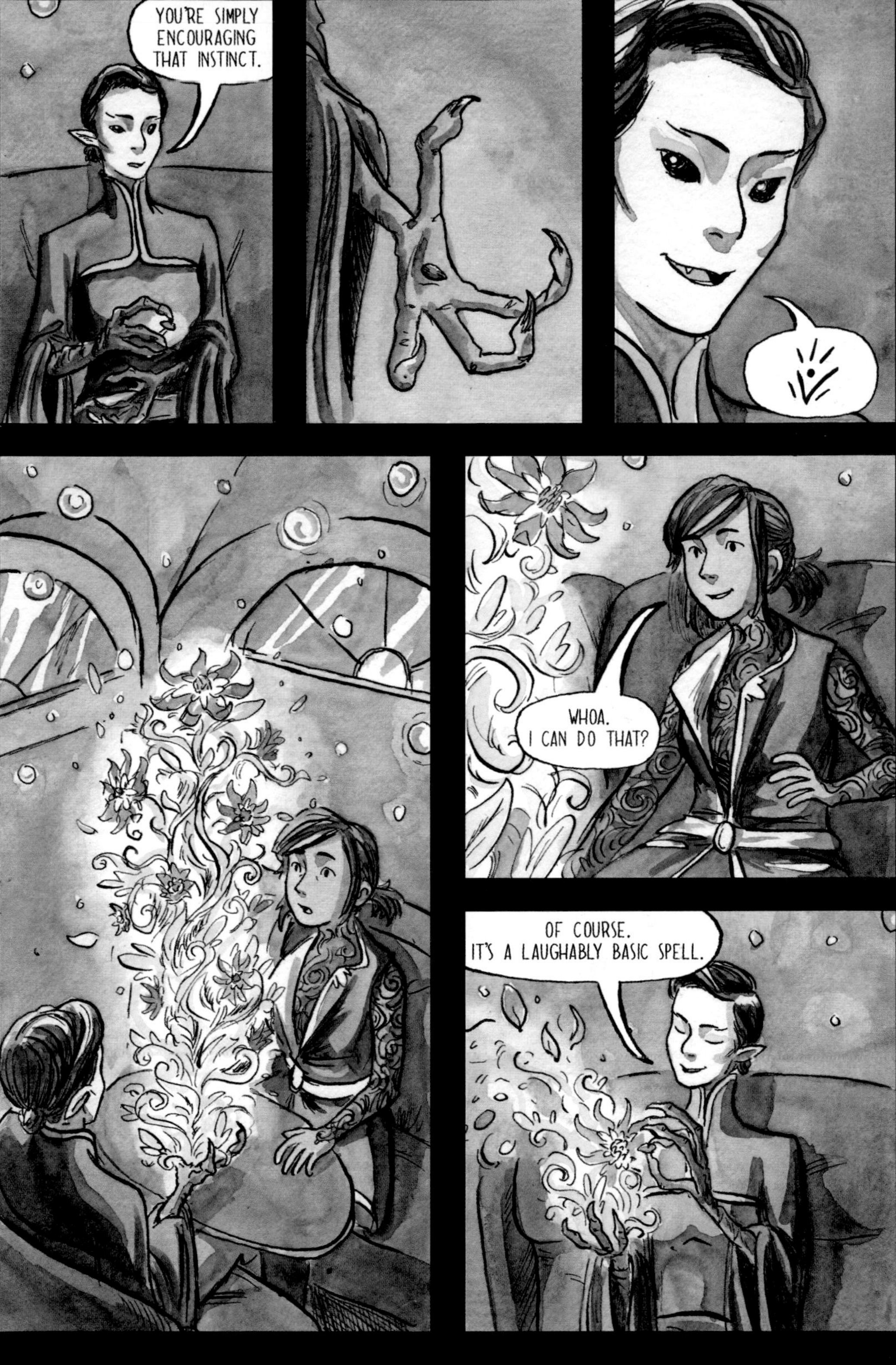
YOU'RE SIMPLY ENCOURAGING THAT INSTINCT.
WHOA. I CAN DO THAT?
OF COURSE. IT'S A LAUGHABLY BASIC SPELL.

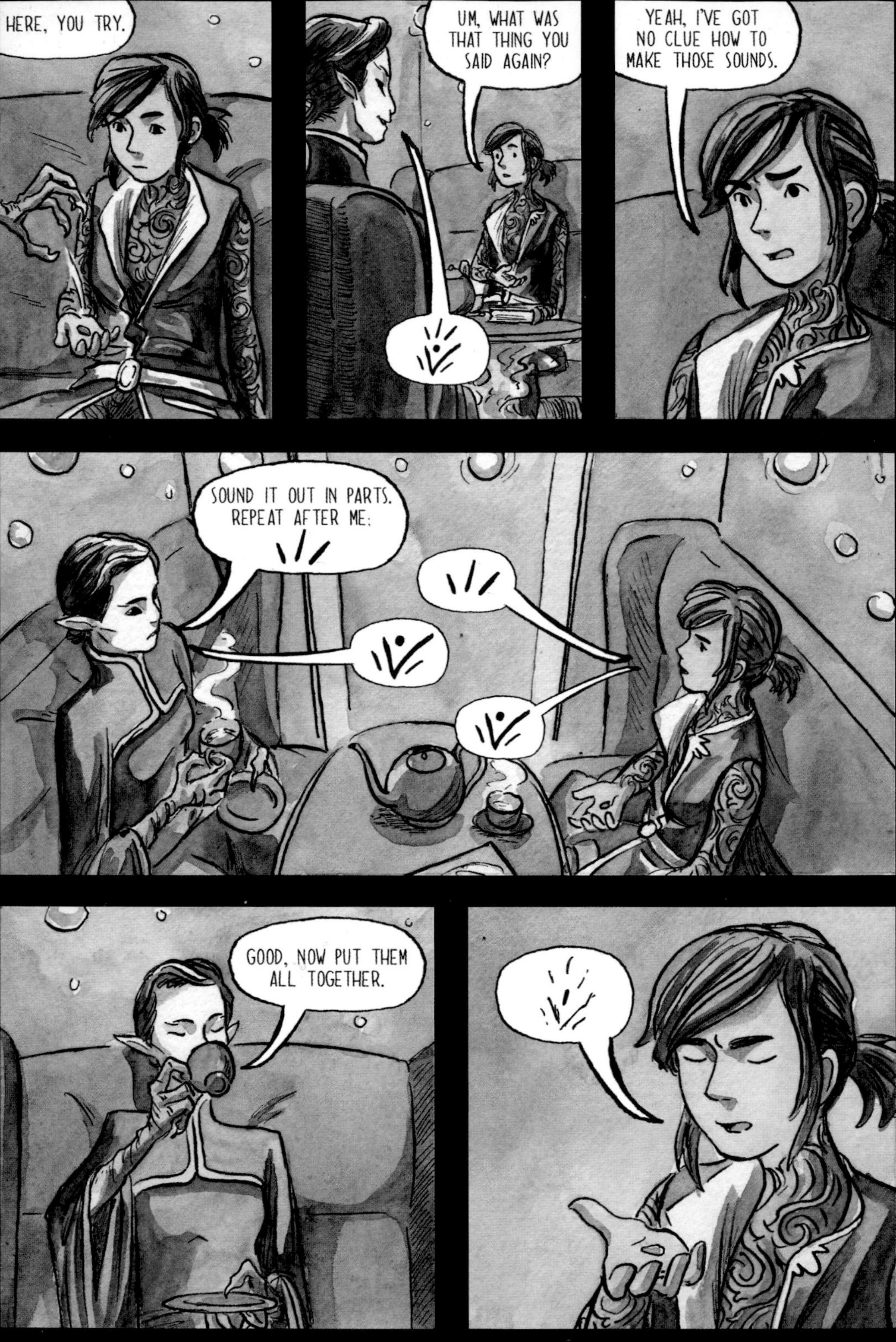
HERE, YOU TRY.
UM, WHAT WAS THAT THING YOU SAID AGAIN?
YEAH, I'VE GOT NO CLUE HOW TO MAKE THOSE SOUNDS.
SOUND IT OUT IN PARTS. REPEAT AFTER ME:
GOOD, NOW PUT THEM ALL TOGETHER.

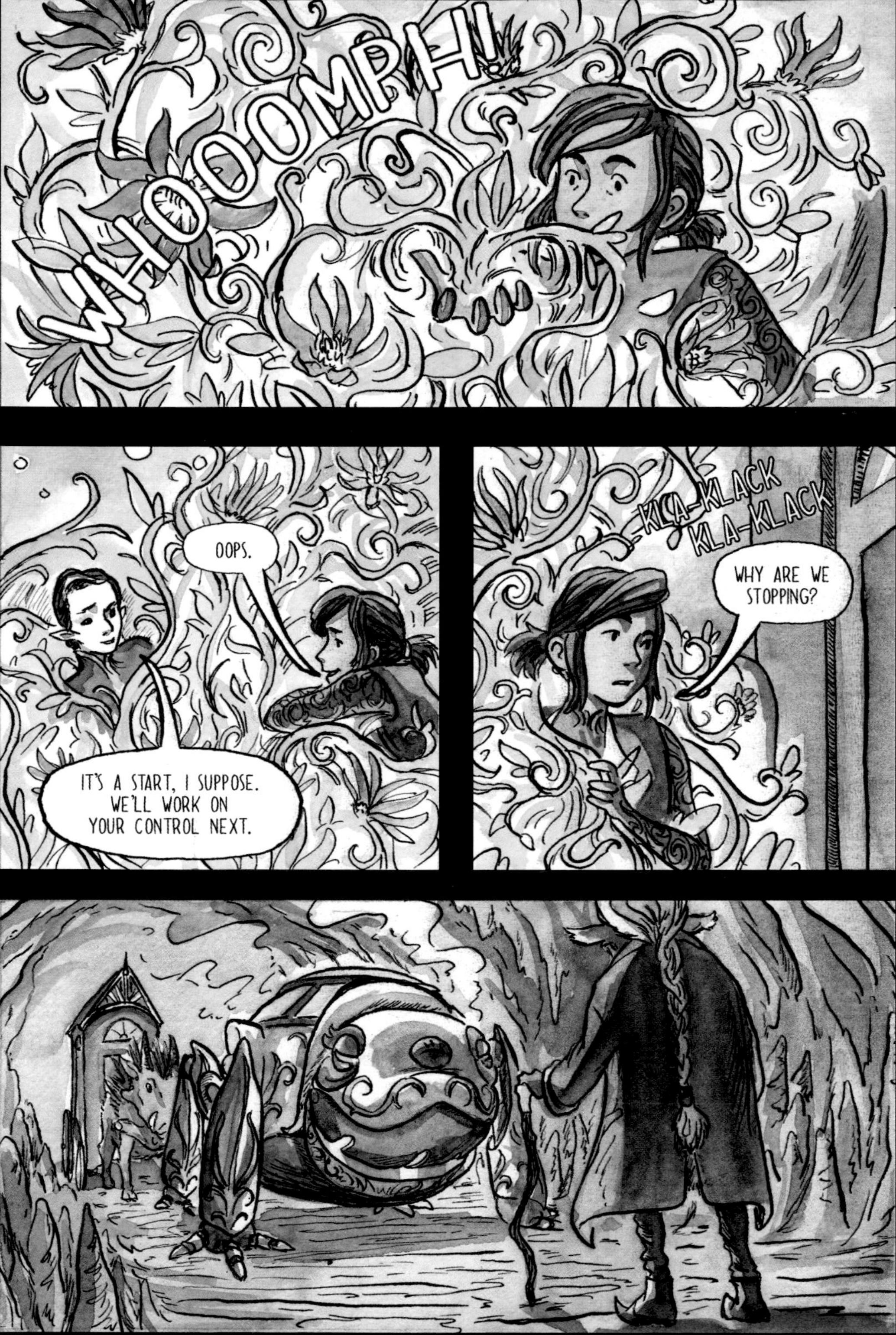
WHOOOOMPH!
OOPS.
IT'S A START, I SUPPOSE. WE'LL WORK ON YOUR CONTROL NEXT.
KLA-KLACK KLA-KLACK
WHY ARE WE STOPPING?

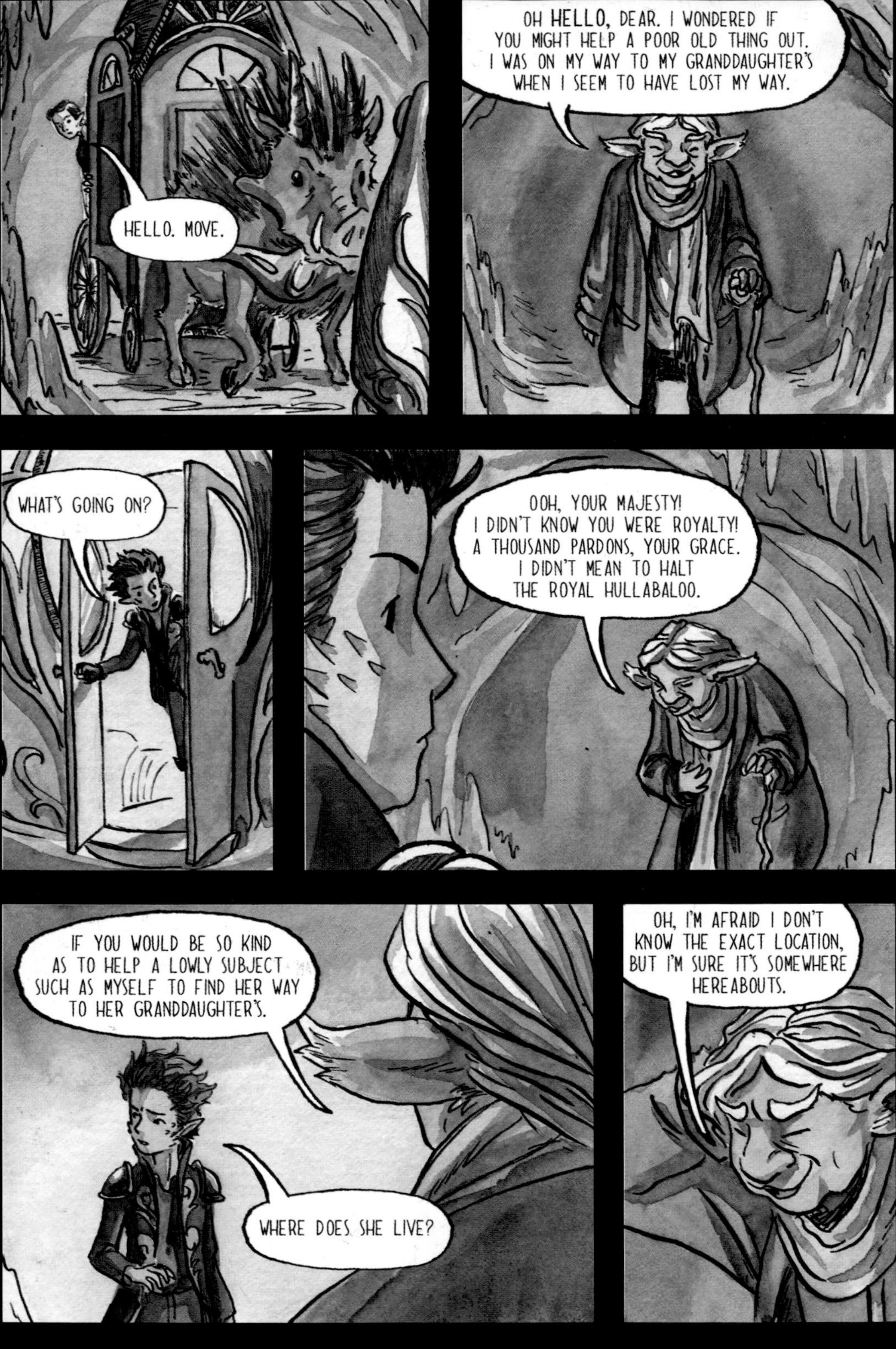
HELLO. MOVE.
OH HELLO, DEAR. I WONDERED IF YOU MIGHT HELP A POOR OLD THING OUT. I WAS ON MY WAY TO MY GRANDDAUGHTER'S WHEN I SEEM TO HAVE LOST MY WAY.
WHAT'S GOING ON?
OOH, YOUR MAJESTY! I DIDN'T KNOW YOU WERE ROYALTY! A THOUSAND PARDONS, YOUR GRACE. I DIDN'T MEAN TO HALT THE ROYAL HULLABALOO.
IF YOU WOULD BE SO KIND AS TO HELP A LOWLY SUBJECT SUCH AS MYSELF TO FIND HER WAY TO HER GRANDDAUGHTER'S.
WHERE DOES SHE LIVE?
OH, I'M AFRAID I DON'T KNOW THE EXACT LOCATION, BUT I'M SURE IT'S SOMEWHERE HEREABOUTS.

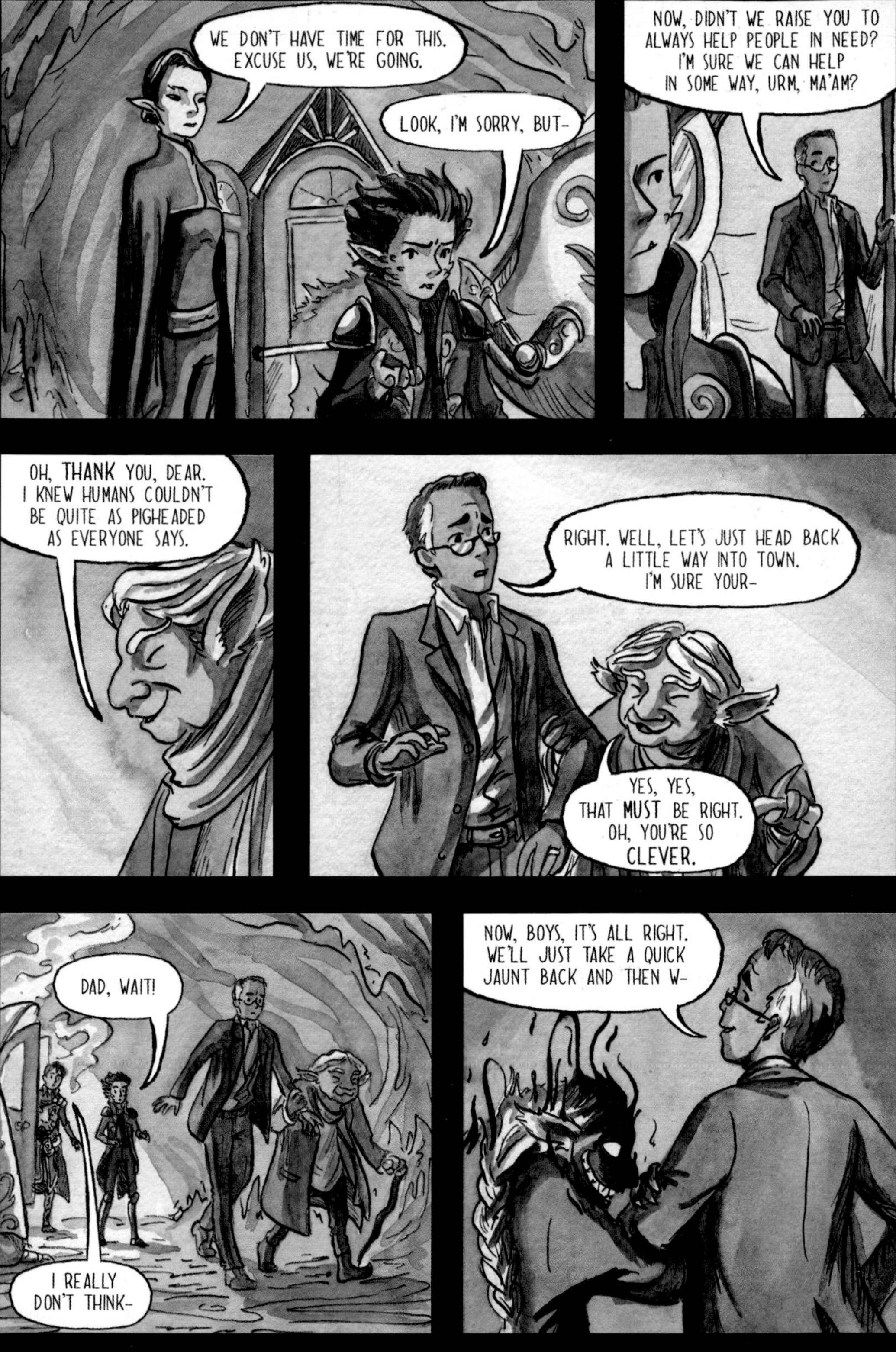
WE DON'T HAVE TIME FOR THIS. EXCUSE US, WE'RE GOING.
LOOK, I'M SORRY, BUT-
NOW, DIDN'T WE RAISE YOU TO ALWAYS HELP PEOPLE IN NEED? I'M SURE WE CAN HELP IN SOME WAY, URM, MA'AM?
OH, THANK YOU, DEAR. I KNEW HUMANS COULDN'T BE QUITE AS PIGHEADED AS EVERYONE SAYS.
RIGHT. WELL, LET'S JUST HEAD BACK A LITTLE WAY INTO TOWN. I'M SURE YOUR-
YES, YES, THAT MUST BE RIGHT. OH, YOU'RE SO CLEVER.
DAD, WAIT!
I REALLY DON'T THINK-
NOW, BOYS, IT'S ALL RIGHT. WE'LL JUST TAKE A QUICK JAUNT BACK AND THEN W-

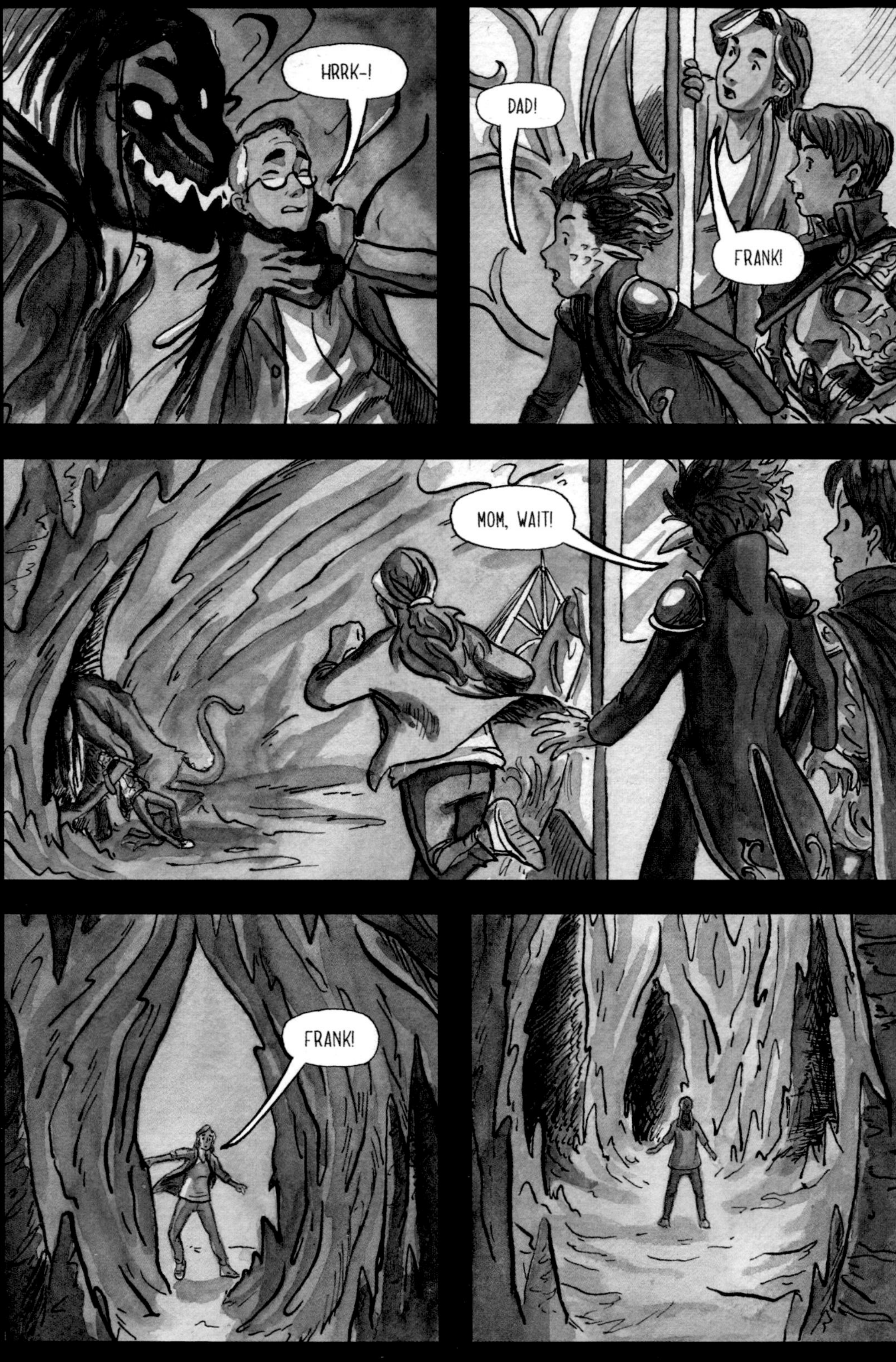
HRRK-!
DAD!
FRANK!
MOM, WAIT!
FRANK!

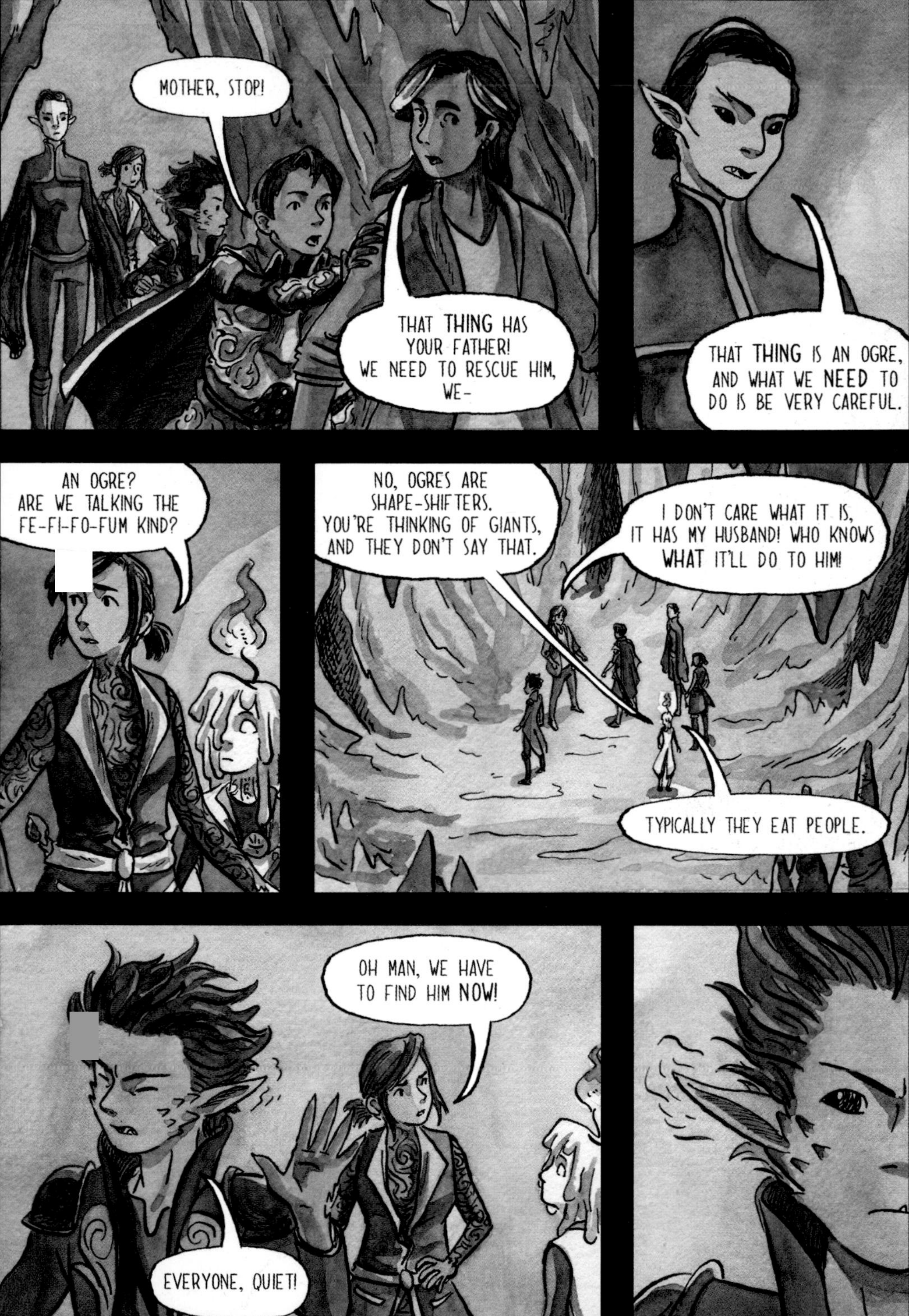
MOTHER, STOP!
THAT THING HAS YOUR FATHER! WE NEED TO RESCUE HIM, WE-
THAT THING IS AN OGRE, AND WHAT WE NEED TO DO IS BE VERY CAREFUL.
AN OGRE? ARE WE TALKING THE FE-FI-FO-FUM KIND?
NO, OGRES ARE SHAPE-SHIFTERS. YOU'RE THINKING OF GIANTS, AND THEY DON'T SAY THAT.
I DON'T CARE WHAT IT IS, IT HAS MY HUSBAND! WHO KNOWS WHAT IT'LL DO TO HIM!
TYPICALLY THEY EAT PEOPLE.
OH MAN, WE HAVE TO FIND HIM NOW!
EVERYONE, QUIET!

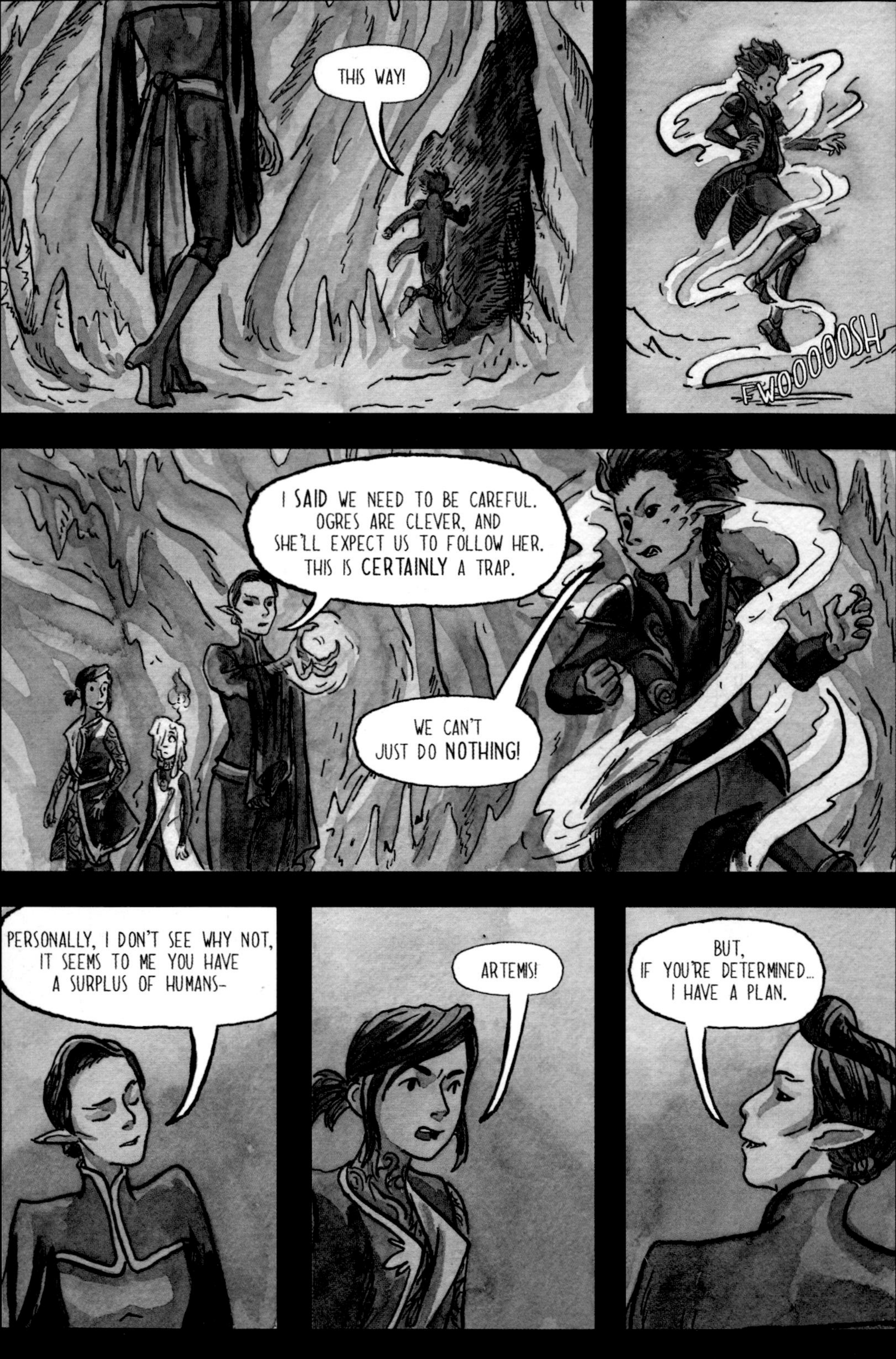

THIS WAY!
FWOOOOOSH
I SAID WE NEED TO BE CAREFUL. OGRES ARE CLEVER, AND SHE'LL EXPECT US TO FOLLOW HER. THIS IS CERTAINLY A TRAP.
WE CAN'T JUST DO NOTHING!
PERSONALLY, I DON'T SEE WHY NOT, IT SEEMS TO ME YOU HAVE A SURPLUS OF HUMANS-
ARTEMIS!
BUT, IF YOU'RE DETERMINED... I HAVE A PLAN.

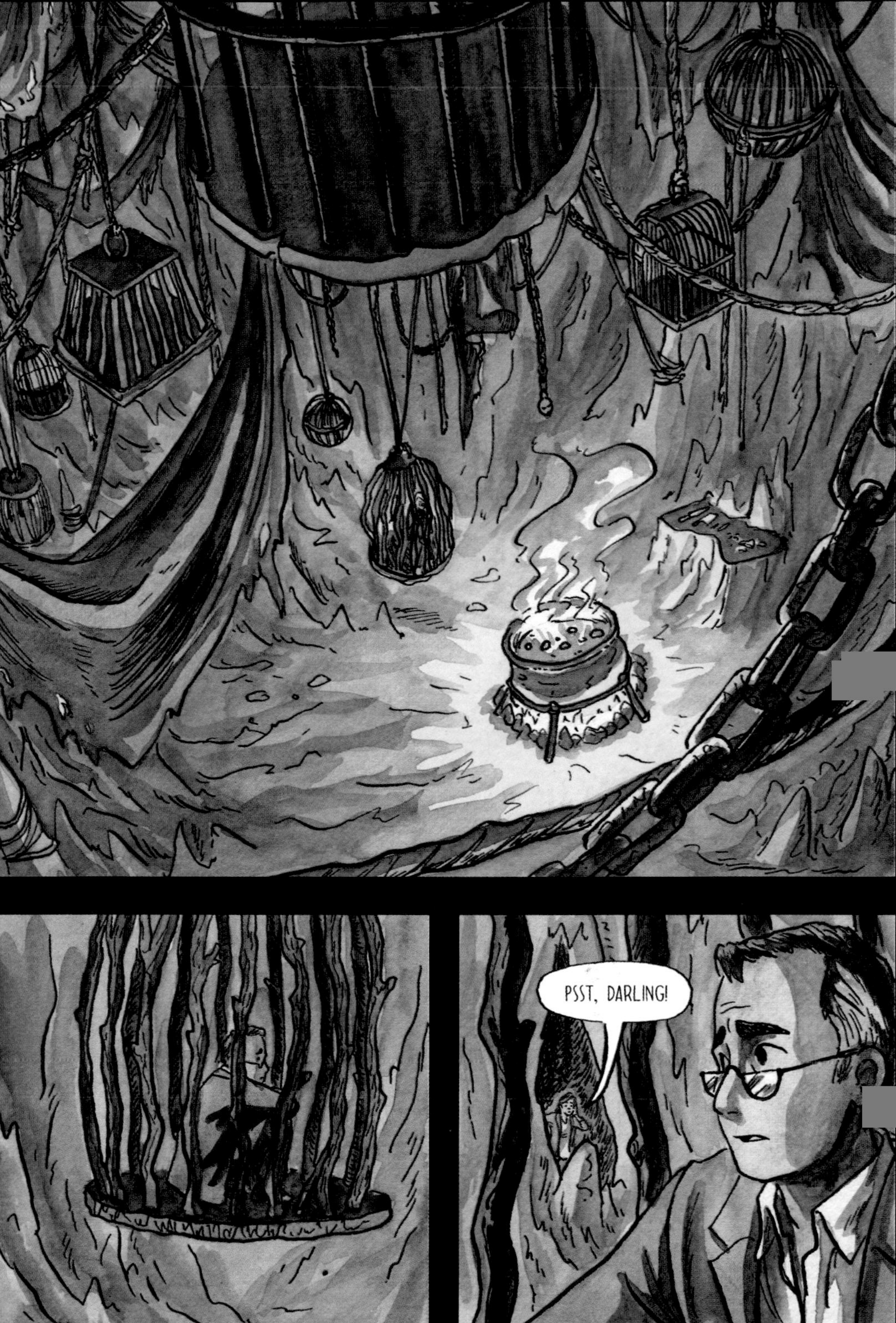
PSST, DARLING!

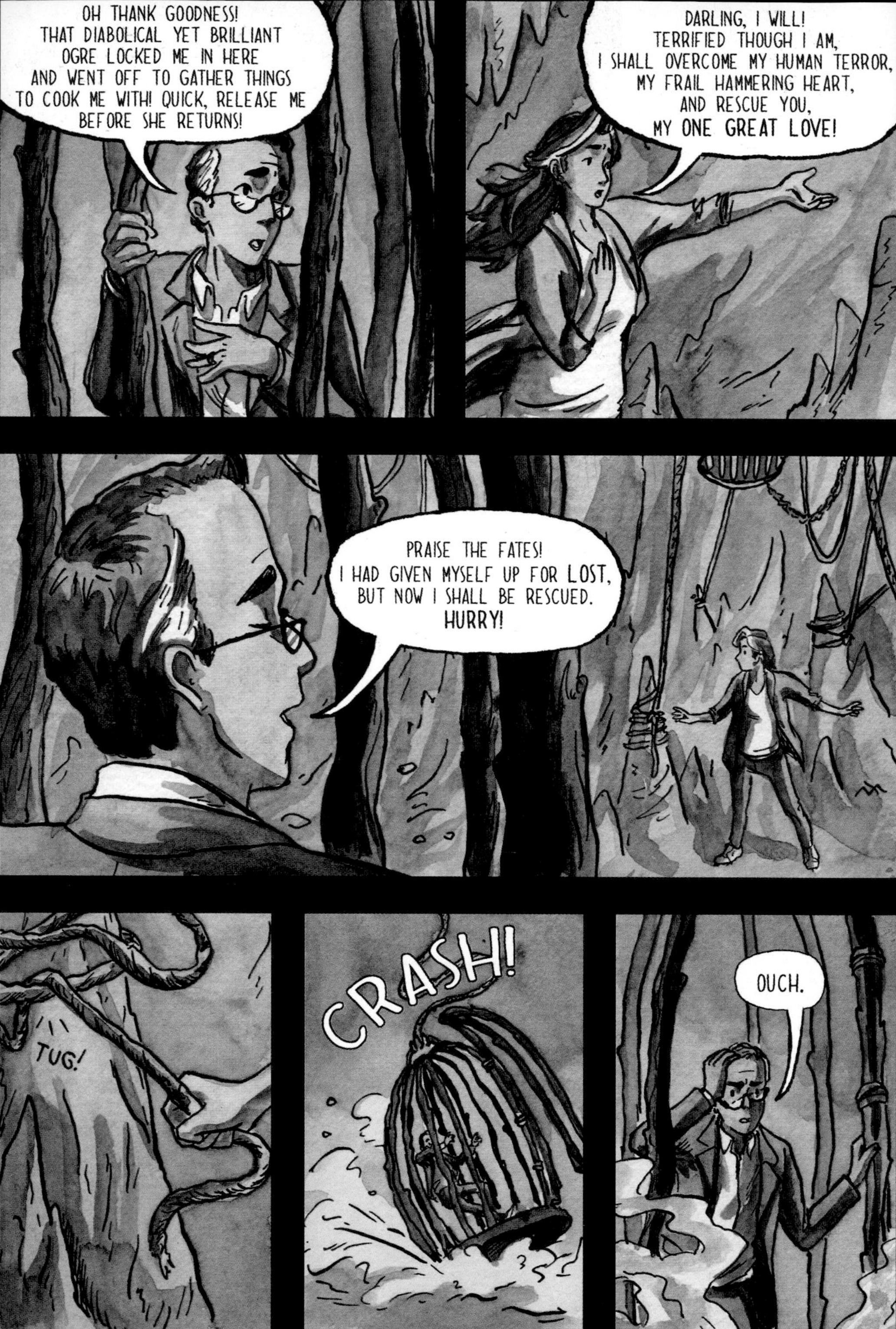
OH THANK GOODNESS! THAT DIABOLICAL YET BRILLIANT OGRE LOCKED ME IN HERE AND WENT OFF TO GATHER THINGS TO COOK ME WITH! QUICK, RELEASE ME BEFORE SHE RETURNS!
DARLING, I WILL! TERRIFIED THOUGH I AM, I SHALL OVERCOME MY HUMAN TERROR, MY FRAIL HAMMERING HEART, AND RESCUE YOU, MY ONE GREAT LOVE!
PRAISE THE FATES! I HAD GIVEN MYSELF UP FOR LOST, BUT NOW I SHALL BE RESCUED. HURRY!
TUG!
CRASH!
OUCH.

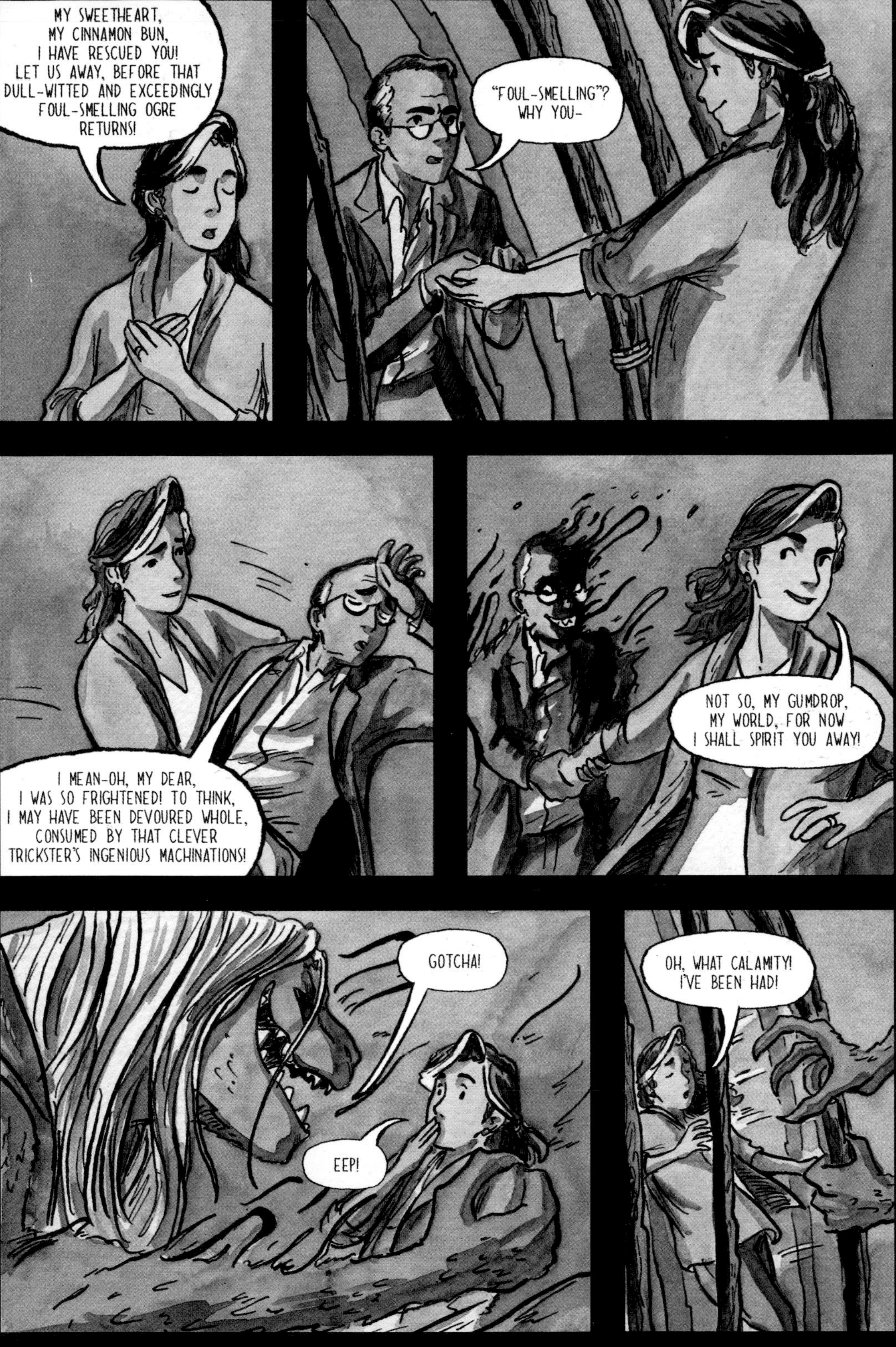
MY SWEETHEART, MY CINNAMON BUN, I HAVE RESCUED YOU! LET US AWAY, BEFORE THAT DULL-WITTED AND EXCEEDINGLY FOUL-SMELLING OGRE RETURNS!
"FOUL-SMELLING"? WHY YOU-
I MEAN-OH, MY DEAR, I WAS SO FRIGHTENED! TO THINK, I MAY HAVE BEEN DEVOURED WHOLE, CONSUMED BY THAT CLEVER TRICKSTER'S INGENIOUS MACHINATIONS!
NOT SO, MY GUMDROP, MY WORLD, FOR NOW I SHALL SPIRIT YOU AWAY!
GOTCHA!
EEP!
OH, WHAT CALAMITY! I'VE BEEN HAD!

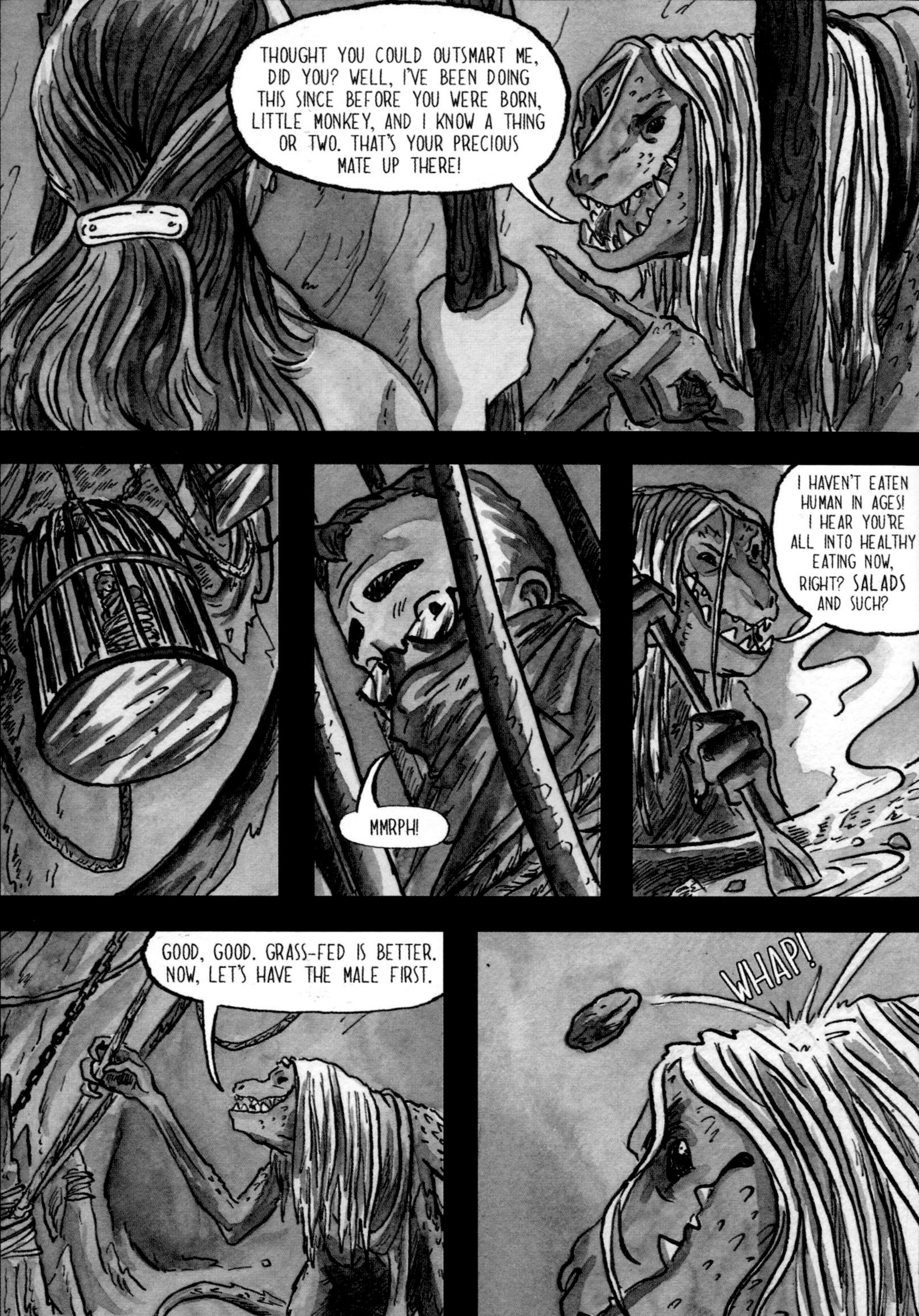
THOUGHT YOU COULD OUTSMART ME, DID YOU? WELL, I'VE BEEN DOING THIS SINCE BEFORE YOU WERE BORN, LITTLE MONKEY, AND I KNOW A THING OR TWO. THAT'S YOUR PRECIOUS MATE UP THERE!
MMRPH!
I HAVEN'T EATEN HUMAN IN AGES! I HEAR YOU'RE ALL INTO HEALTHY EATING NOW, RIGHT? SALADS AND SUCH?
GOOD, GOOD. GRASS-FED IS BETTER. NOW, LET'S HAVE THE MALE FIRST.
WHAP!

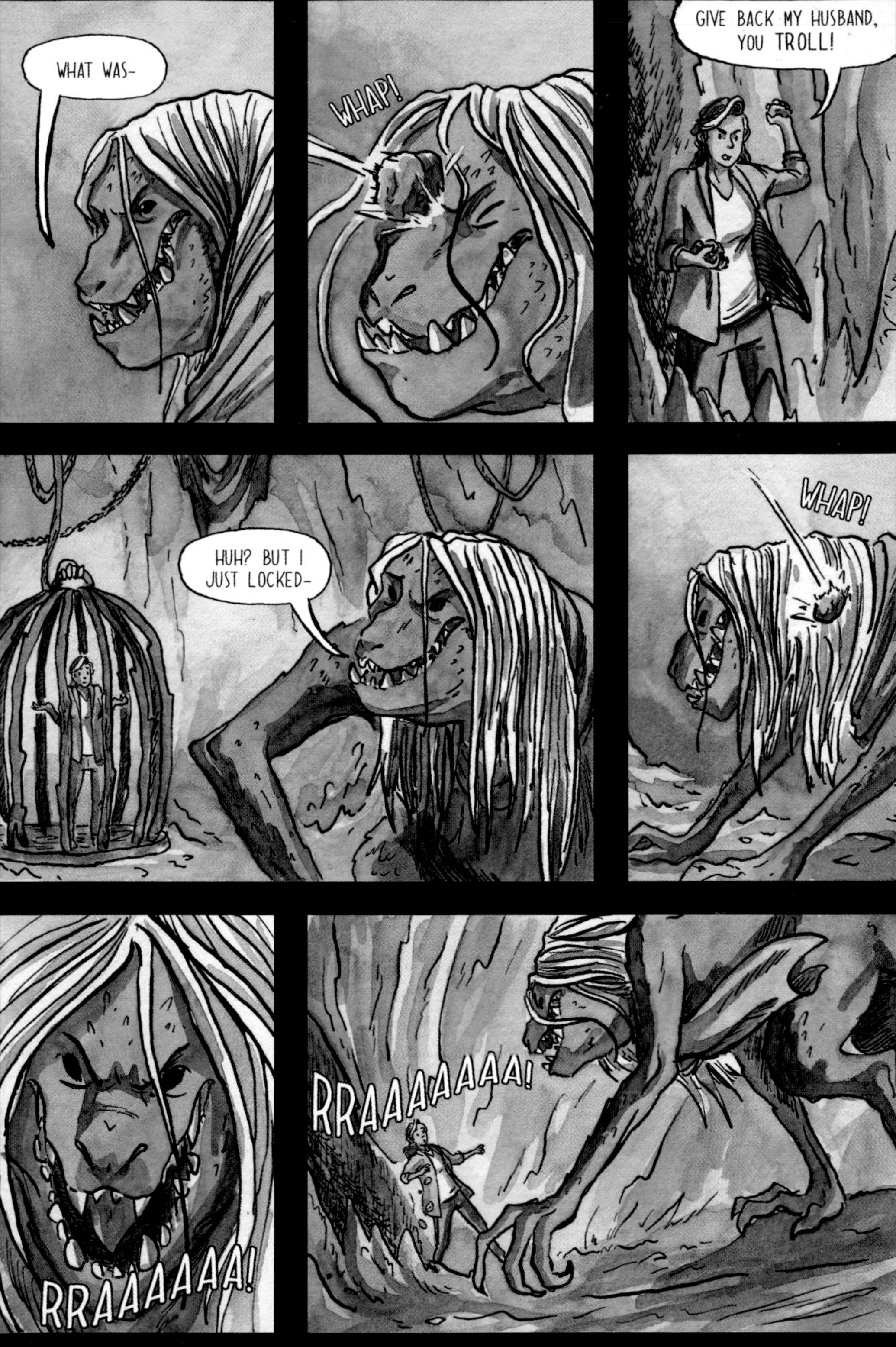
WHAT WAS-
WHAP!
GIVE BACK MY HUSBAND, YOU TROLL!
HUH? BUT I JUST LOCKED-
WHAP!
RRAAAAAAA!
RRAAAAAAAA!

BACK OFF!

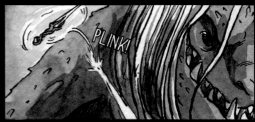

PLINK!

HA-HA, SKIN LIKE STONE, RUNT!

CRUNCH!

AAAAH!

STOP!

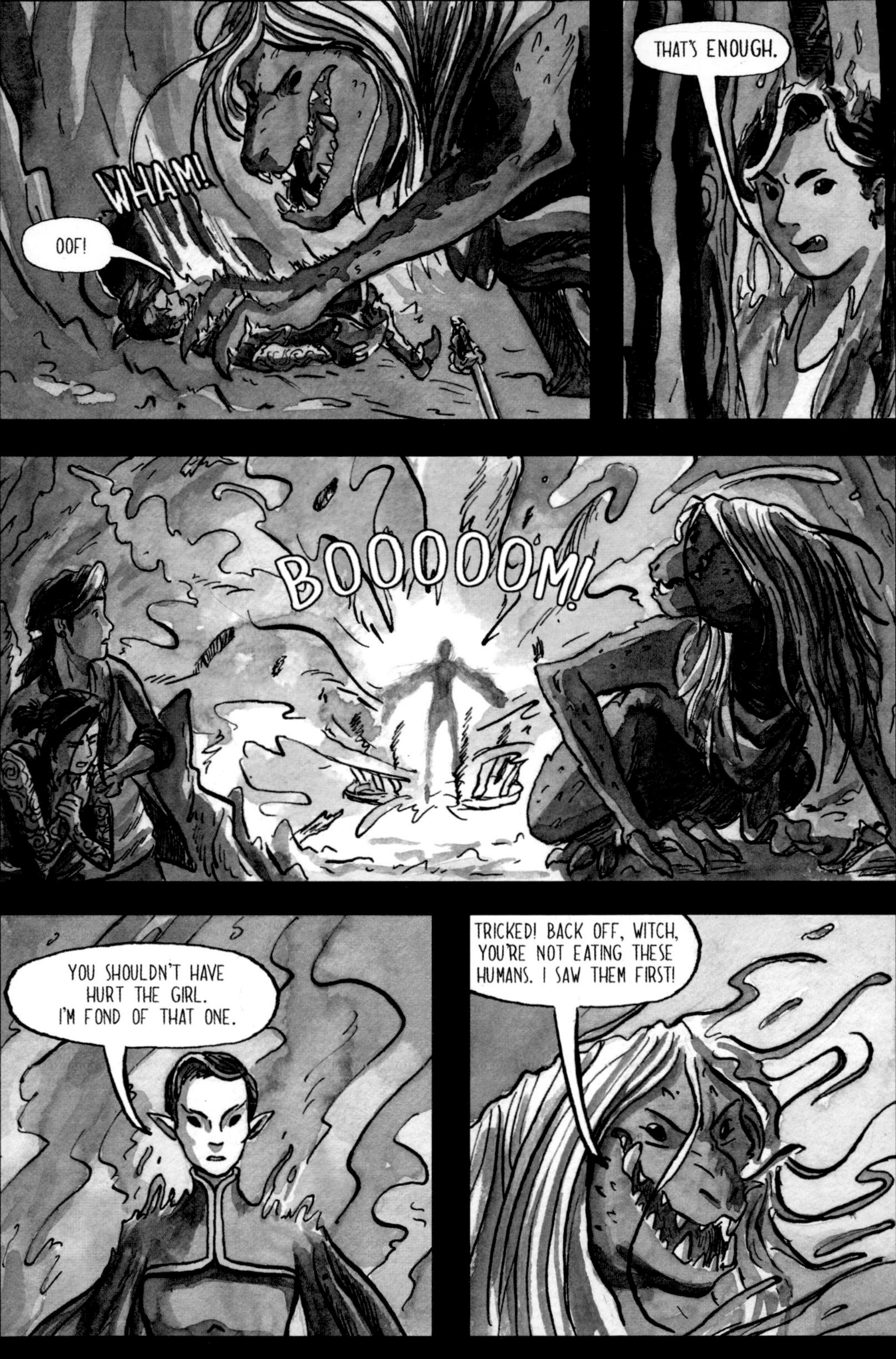
WHAM!
OOF!
THAT'S ENOUGH.
BOOOOOM!
YOU SHOULDN'T HAVE HURT THE GIRL. I'M FOND OF THAT ONE.
TRICKED! BACK OFF, WITCH, YOU'RE NOT EATING THESE HUMANS. I SAW THEM FIRST!

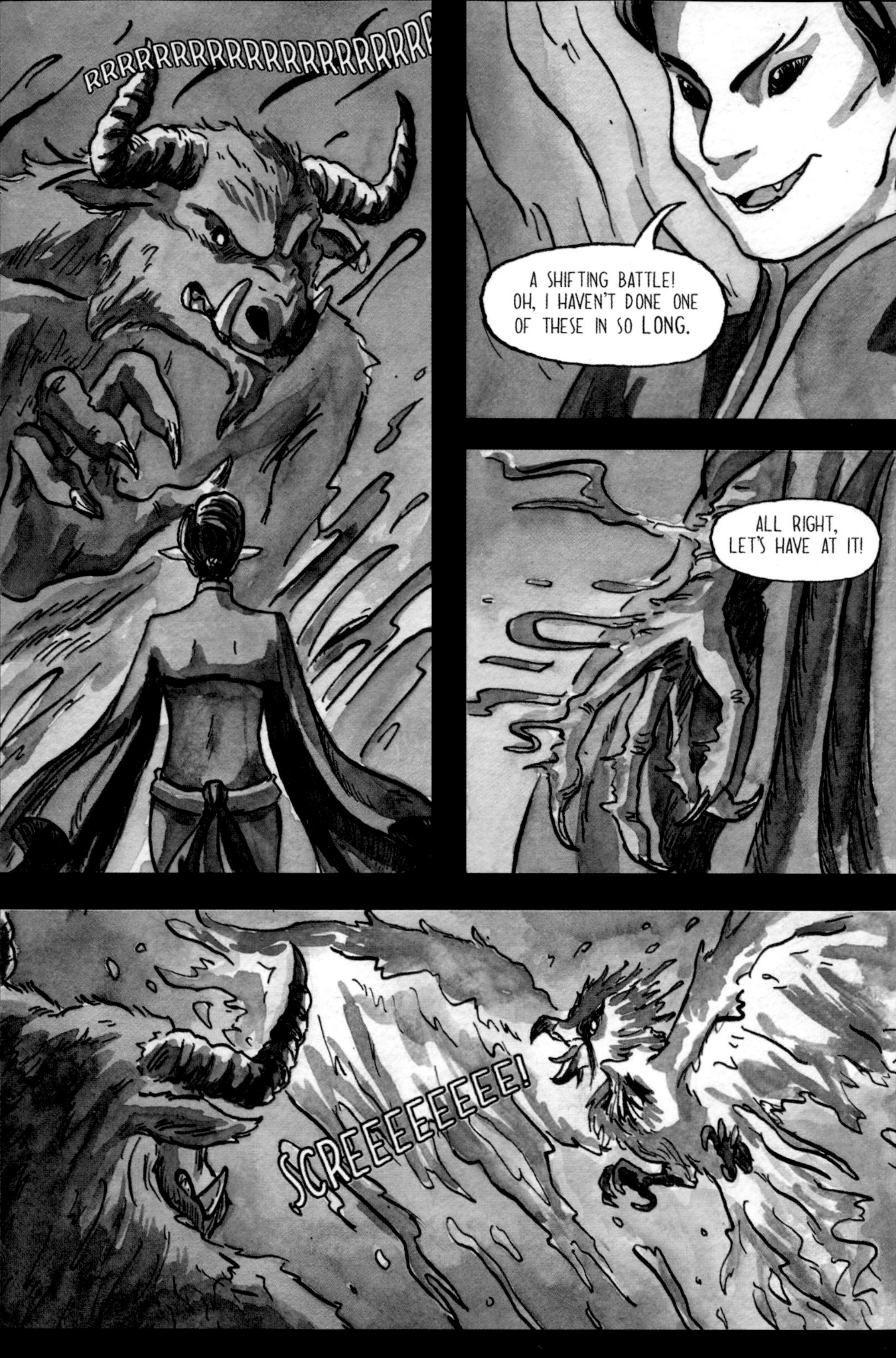
RRRRRRRRRRRRRRRRRRRRRRRR
A SHIFTING BATTLE! OH, I HAVEN'T DONE ONE OF THESE IN SO LONG.
ALL RIGHT, LET'S HAVE AT IT!
SCREEEEEEEEE!

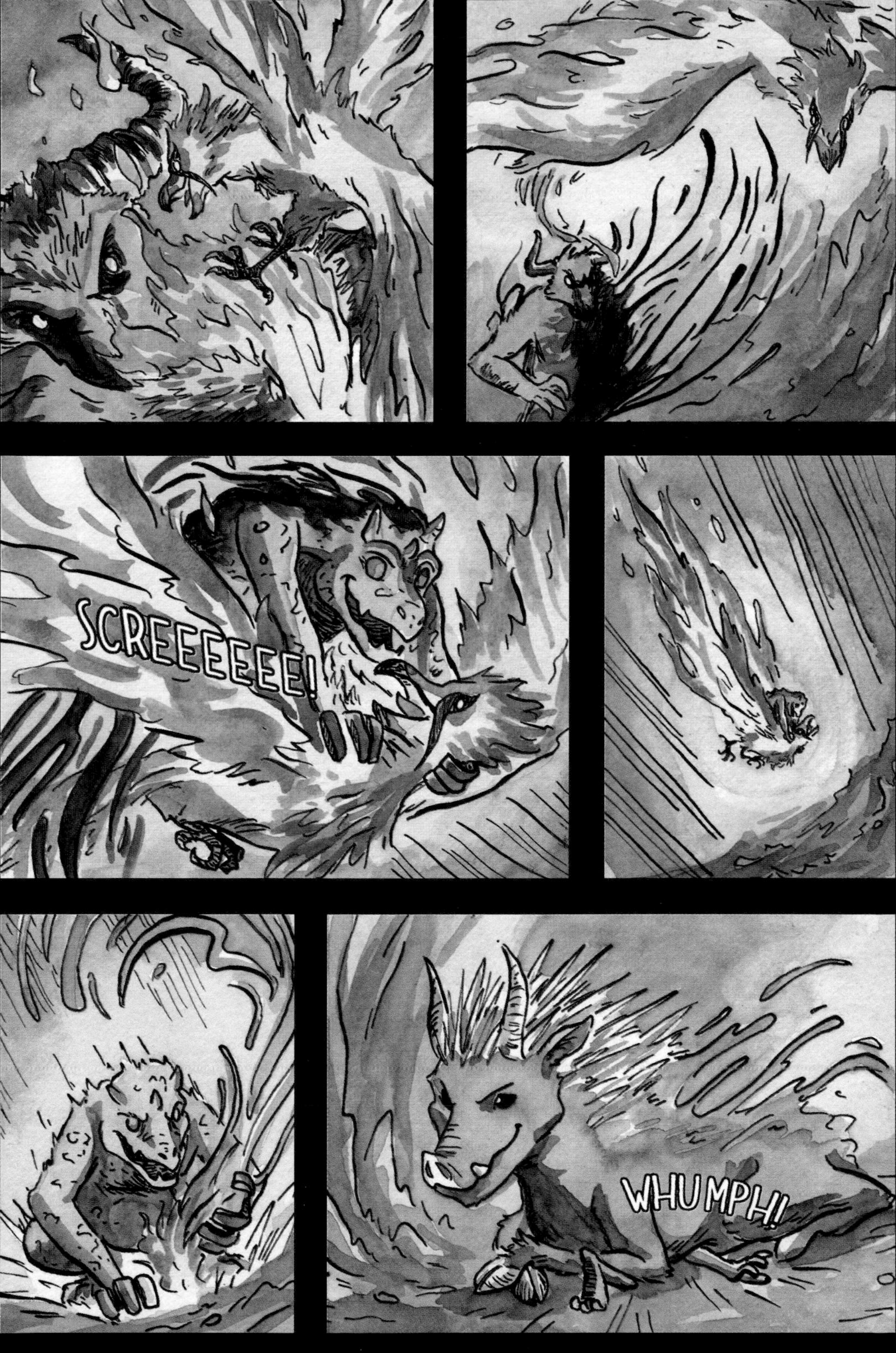
SCREEEEEEE!
WHUMPH!

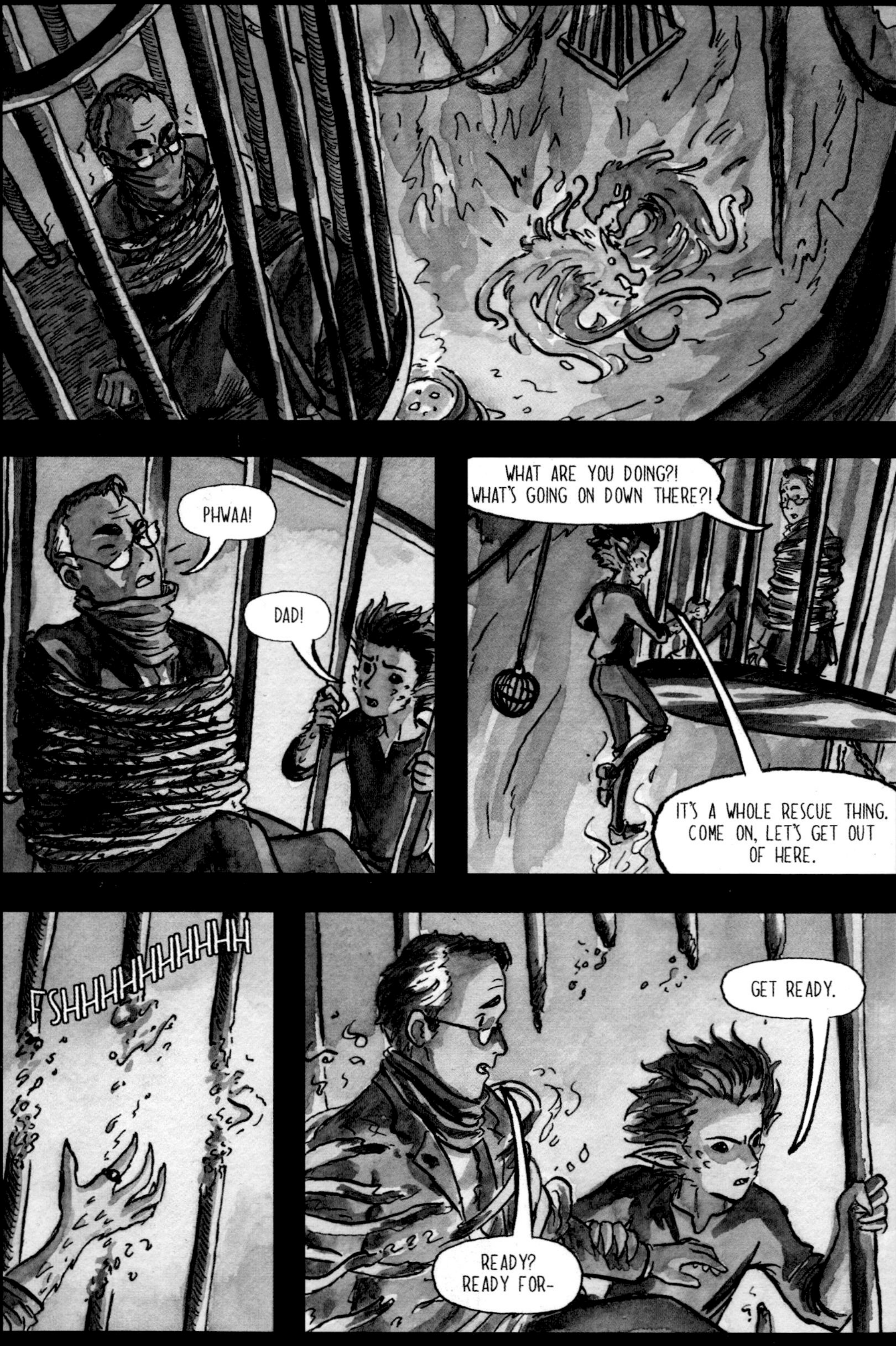
PHWAA!
DAD!
WHAT ARE YOU DOING?! WHAT'S GOING ON DOWN THERE?!
IT'S A WHOLE RESCUE THING. COME ON, LET'S GET OUT OF HERE.
FSHHHHHHHHHHHH
GET READY.
READY? READY FOR-

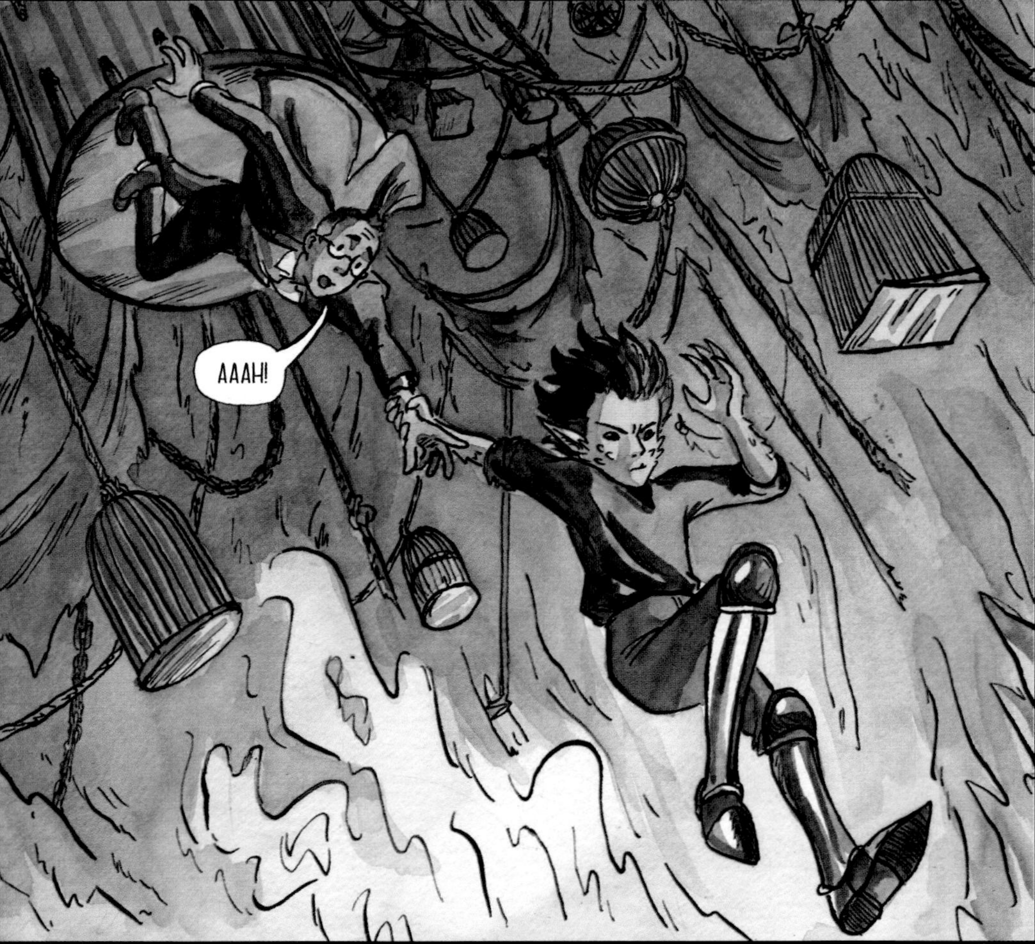
AAAH!

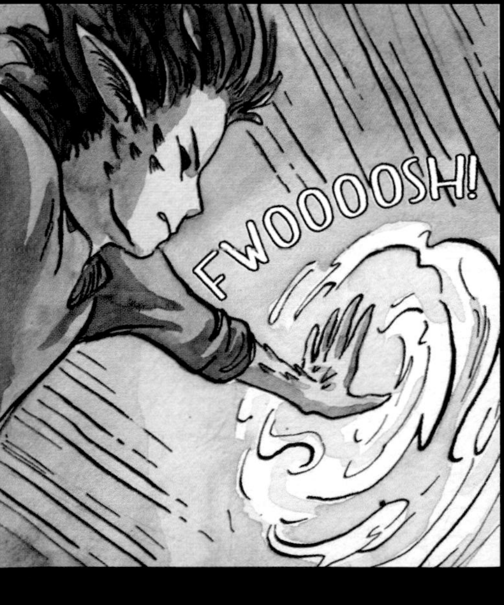
FWOOOOOSH!

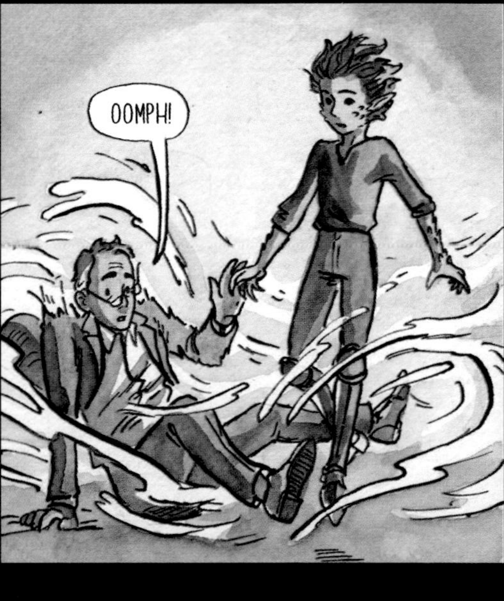
OOMPH!

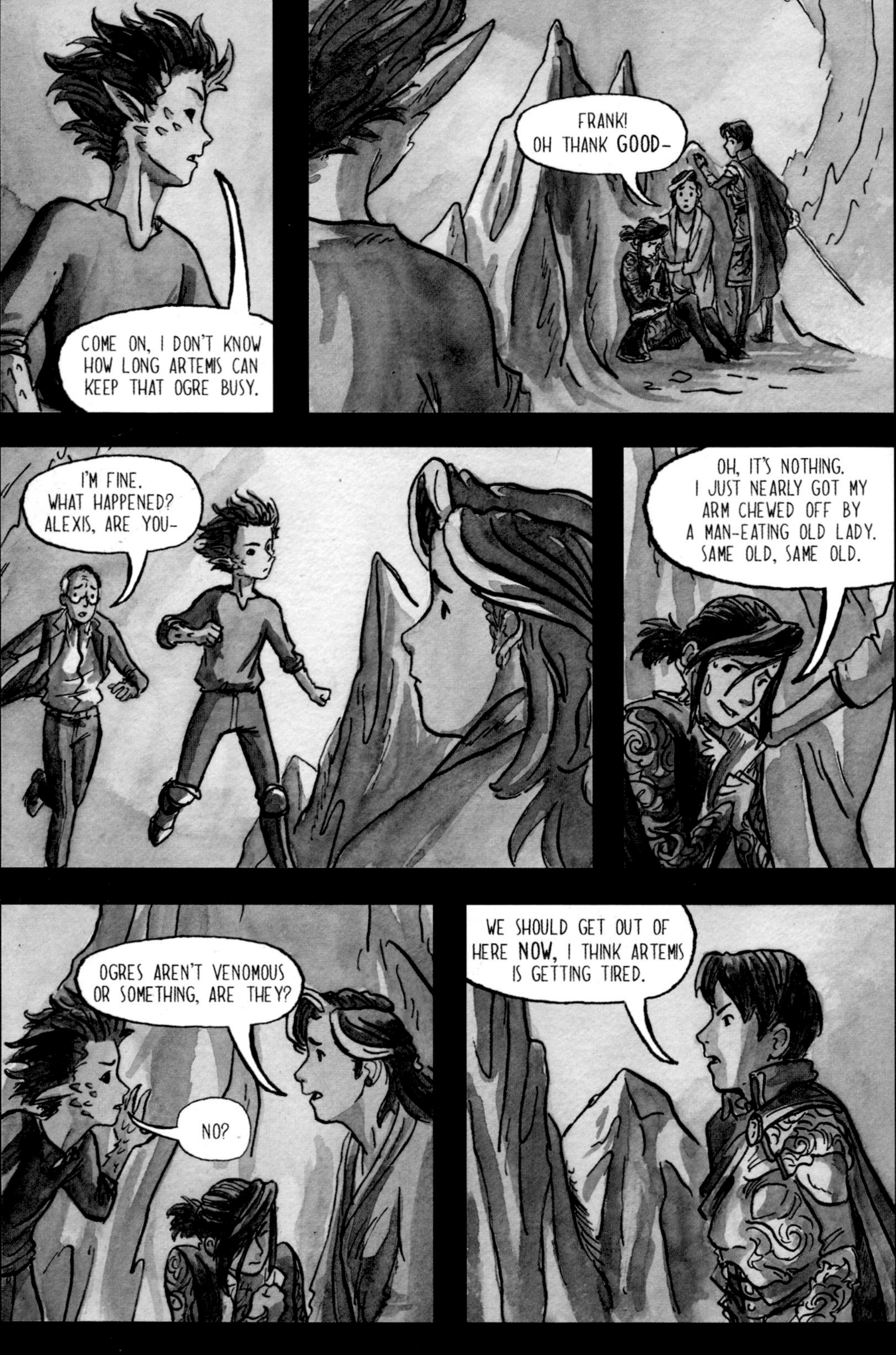
COME ON, I DON'T KNOW HOW LONG ARTEMIS CAN KEEP THAT OGRE BUSY.
FRANK! OH THANK GOOD-
I'M FINE. WHAT HAPPENED? ALEXIS, ARE YOU-
OH, IT'S NOTHING. I JUST NEARLY GOT MY ARM CHEWED OFF BY A MAN-EATING OLD LADY. SAME OLD, SAME OLD.
OGRES AREN'T VENOMOUS OR SOMETHING, ARE THEY?
NO?
WE SHOULD GET OUT OF HERE NOW, I THINK ARTEMIS IS GETTING TIRED.

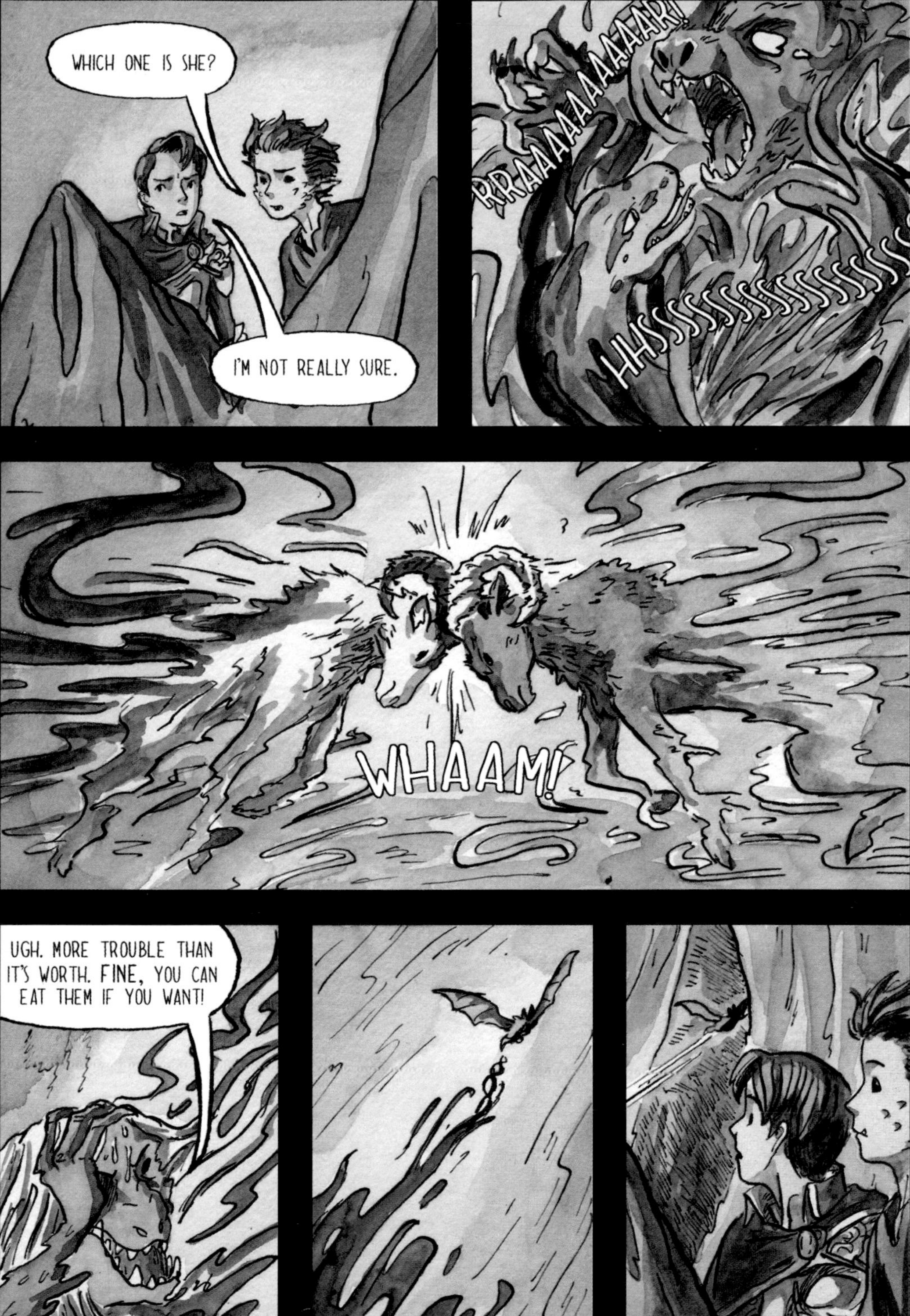

WHICH ONE IS SHE?
I'M NOT REALLY SURE.
RRAAAAAAAAAAAR!
HHSSSSSSSSSSSSSS
WHAAM!
UGH. MORE TROUBLE THAN IT'S WORTH. FINE, YOU CAN EAT THEM IF YOU WANT!

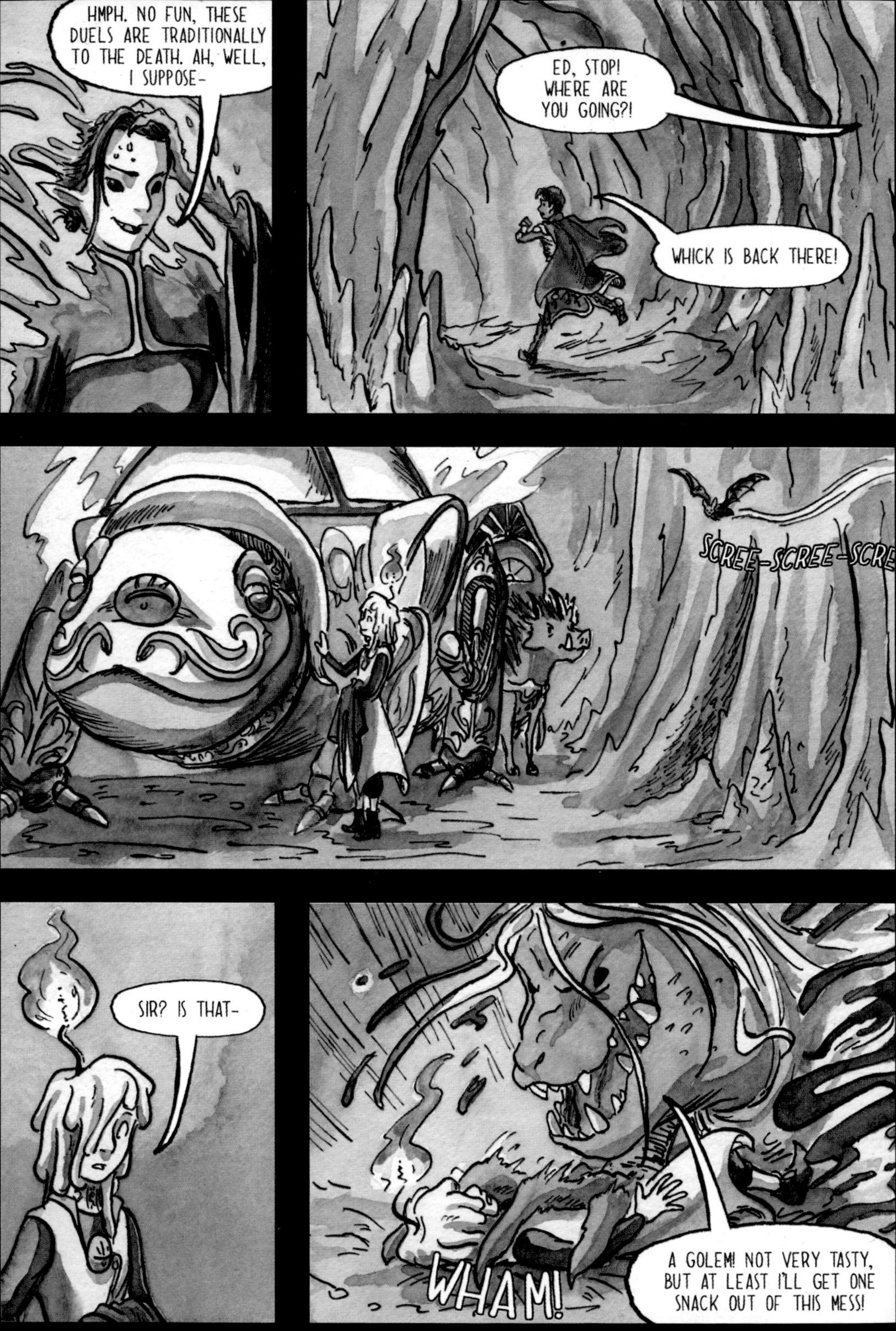
HMPH. NO FUN, THESE DUELS ARE TRADITIONALLY TO THE DEATH. AH, WELL, I SUPPOSE-
ED, STOP! WHERE ARE YOU GOING?!
WHICK IS BACK THERE!
SCREE-SCREE-SCRE
SIR? IS THAT-
A GOLEM! NOT VERY TASTY, BUT AT LEAST I'LL GET ONE SNACK OUT OF THIS MESS!
WHAM!

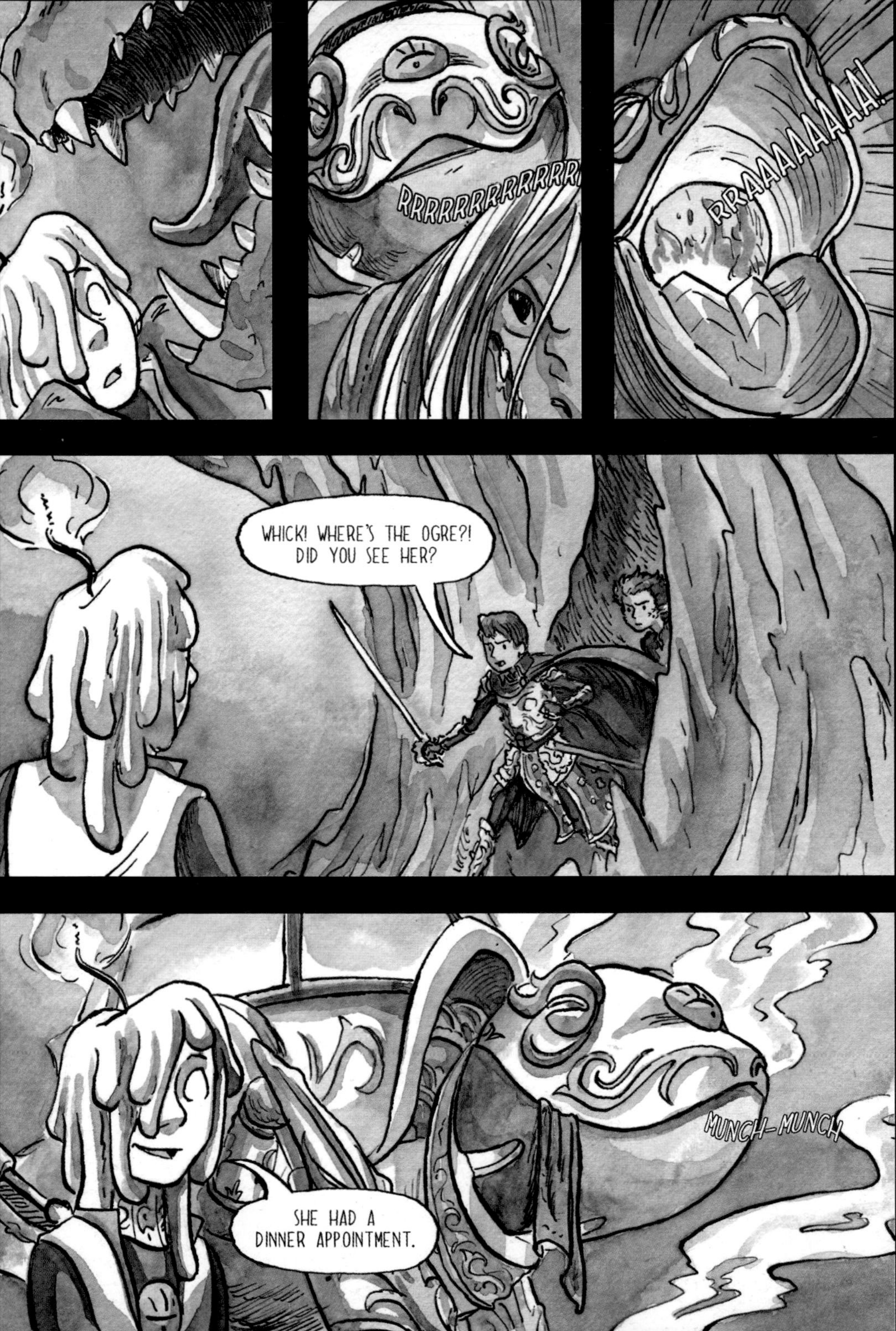
RRRRRRRRRRRRRR
RRAAAAAAAAAA!
WHICK! WHERE'S THE OGRE?! DID YOU SEE HER?
MUNCH-MUNCH
SHE HAD A DINNER APPOINTMENT.

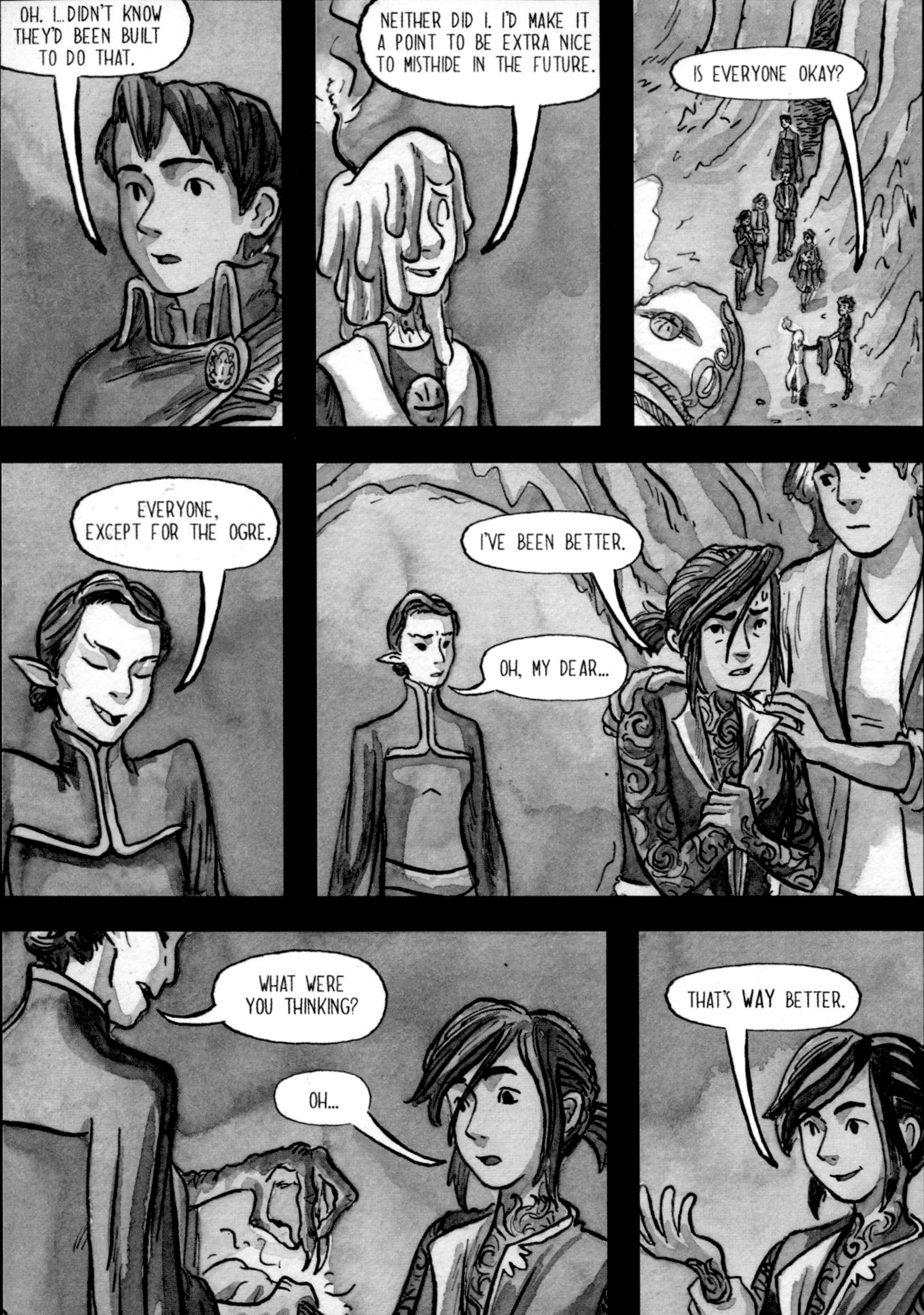
OH. I...DIDN'T KNOW THEY'D BEEN BUILT TO DO THAT.
NEITHER DID I. I'D MAKE IT A POINT TO BE EXTRA NICE TO MISTHIDE IN THE FUTURE.
IS EVERYONE OKAY?
EVERYONE, EXCEPT FOR THE OGRE.
I'VE BEEN BETTER.
OH, MY DEAR...
WHAT WERE YOU THINKING?
OH...
THAT'S WAY BETTER.

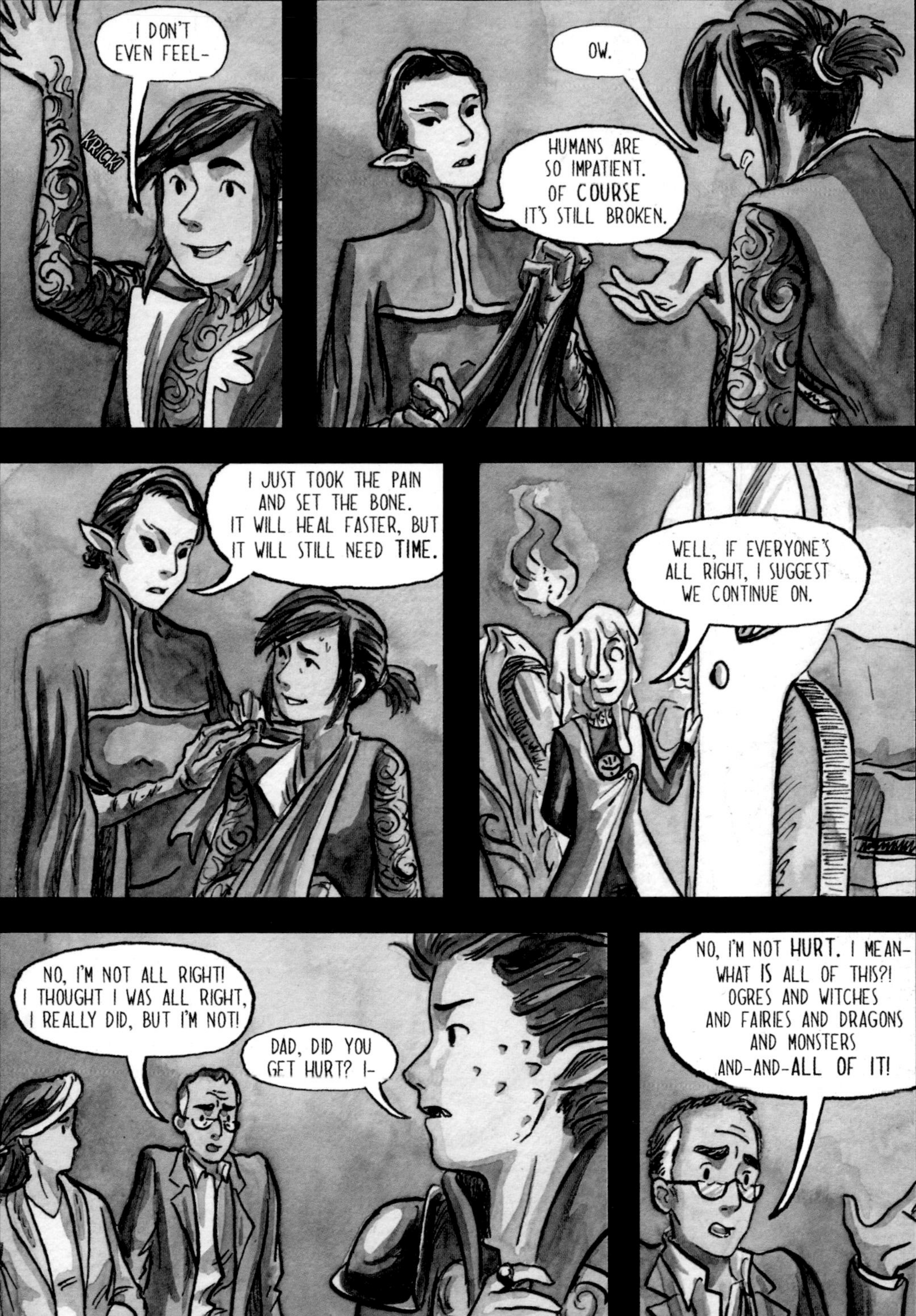
I DON'T EVEN FEEL-
KRICK!
OW.
HUMANS ARE SO IMPATIENT. OF COURSE IT'S STILL BROKEN.
I JUST TOOK THE PAIN AND SET THE BONE. IT WILL HEAL FASTER, BUT IT WILL STILL NEED TIME.
WELL, IF EVERYONE'S ALL RIGHT, I SUGGEST WE CONTINUE ON.
NO, I'M NOT ALL RIGHT! I THOUGHT I WAS ALL RIGHT, I REALLY DID, BUT I'M NOT!
DAD, DID YOU GET HURT? I-
NO, I'M NOT HURT. I MEAN- WHAT IS ALL OF THIS?! OGRES AND WITCHES AND FAIRIES AND DRAGONS AND MONSTERS AND-AND-ALL OF IT!

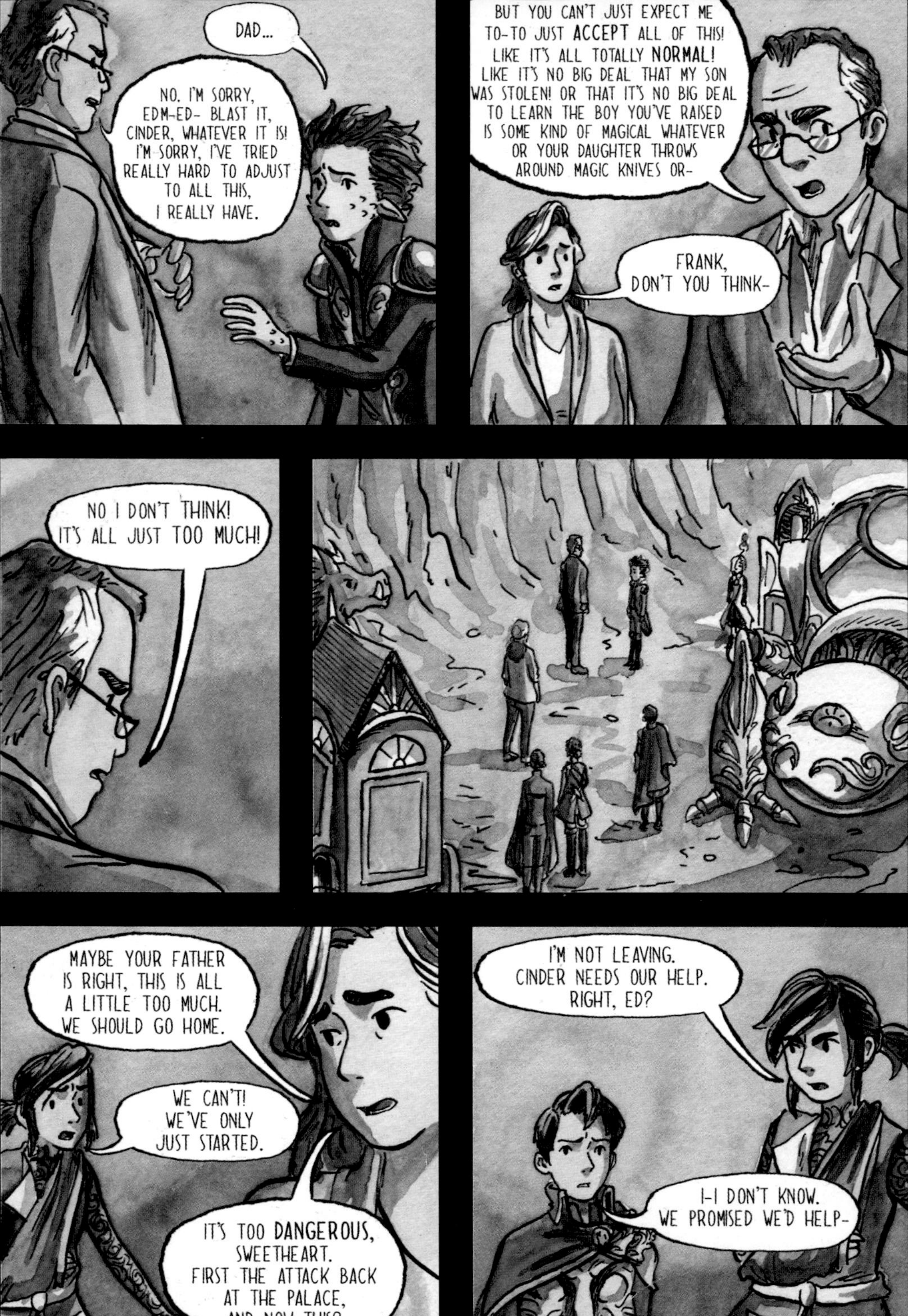
DAD...
NO. I'M SORRY, EDM-ED- BLAST IT, CINDER, WHATEVER IT IS! I'M SORRY, I'VE TRIED REALLY HARD TO ADJUST TO ALL THIS, I REALLY HAVE.
BUT YOU CAN'T JUST EXPECT ME TO-TO JUST ACCEPT ALL OF THIS! LIKE IT'S ALL TOTALLY NORMAL! LIKE IT'S NO BIG DEAL THAT MY SON WAS STOLEN! OR THAT IT'S NO BIG DEAL TO LEARN THE BOY YOU'VE RAISED IS SOME KIND OF MAGICAL WHATEVER OR YOUR DAUGHTER THROWS AROUND MAGIC KNIVES OR-
FRANK, DON'T YOU THINK-
NO I DON'T THINK! IT'S ALL JUST TOO MUCH!
MAYBE YOUR FATHER IS RIGHT, THIS IS ALL A LITTLE TOO MUCH. WE SHOULD GO HOME.
WE CAN'T! WE'VE ONLY JUST STARTED.
IT'S TOO DANGEROUS, SWEETHEART. FIRST THE ATTACK BACK AT THE PALACE, AND NOW THIS?
I'M NOT LEAVING. CINDER NEEDS OUR HELP. RIGHT, ED?
I-I DON'T KNOW. WE PROMISED WE'D HELP-

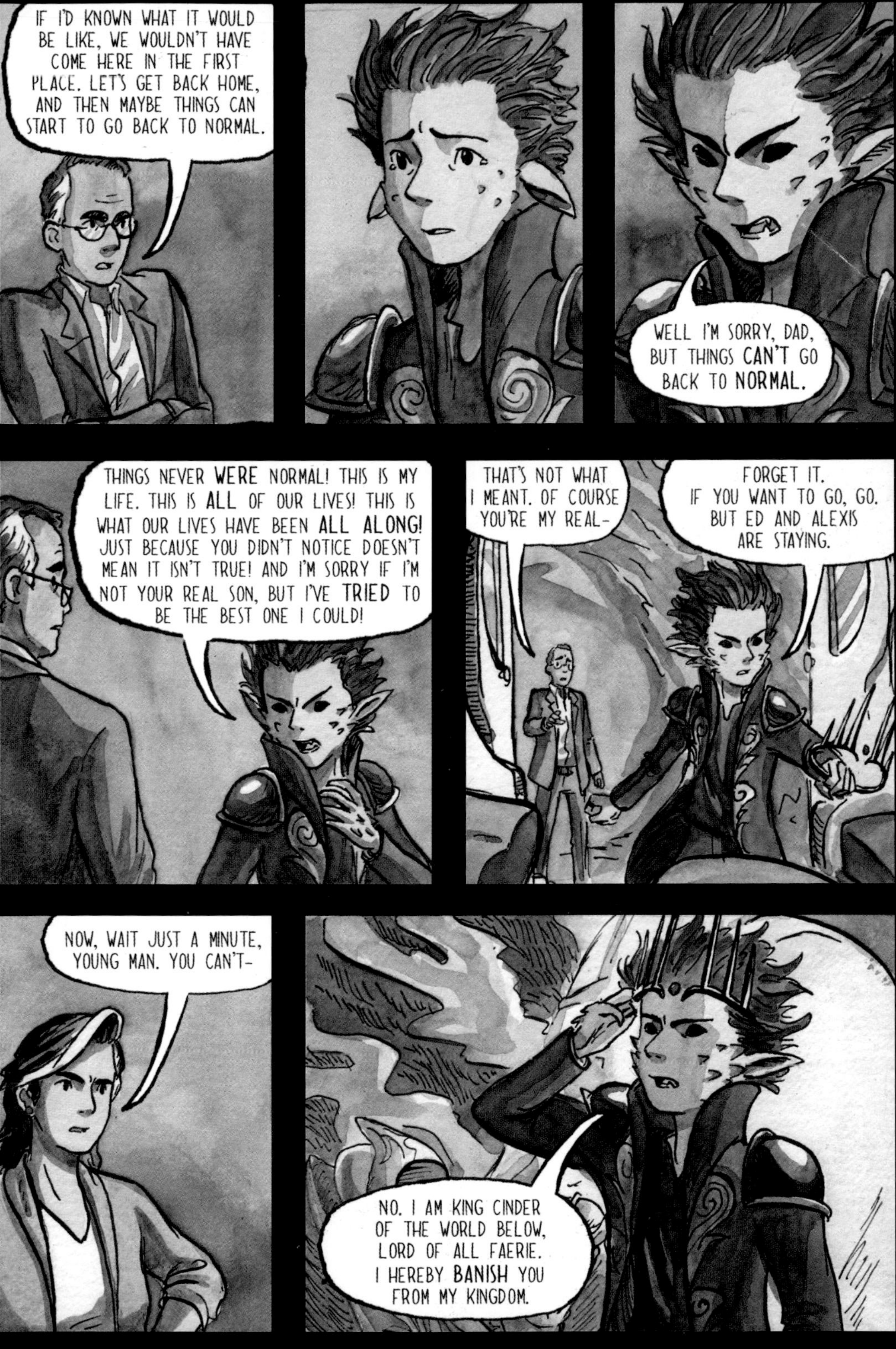
IF I'D KNOWN WHAT IT WOULD BE LIKE, WE WOULDN'T HAVE COME HERE IN THE FIRST PLACE. LET'S GET BACK HOME, AND THEN MAYBE THINGS CAN START TO GO BACK TO NORMAL.
WELL I'M SORRY, DAD, BUT THINGS CAN'T GO BACK TO NORMAL.
THINGS NEVER WERE NORMAL! THIS IS MY LIFE. THIS IS ALL OF OUR LIVES! THIS IS WHAT OUR LIVES HAVE BEEN ALL ALONG! JUST BECAUSE YOU DIDN'T NOTICE DOESN'T MEAN IT ISN'T TRUE! AND I'M SORRY IF I'M NOT YOUR REAL SON, BUT I'VE TRIED TO BE THE BEST ONE I COULD!
THAT'S NOT WHAT I MEANT. OF COURSE YOU'RE MY REAL-
FORGET IT. IF YOU WANT TO GO, GO. BUT ED AND ALEXIS ARE STAYING.
NOW, WAIT JUST A MINUTE, YOUNG MAN. YOU CAN'T-
NO. I AM KING CINDER OF THE WORLD BELOW, LORD OF ALL FAERIE. I HEREBY BANISH YOU FROM MY KINGDOM.

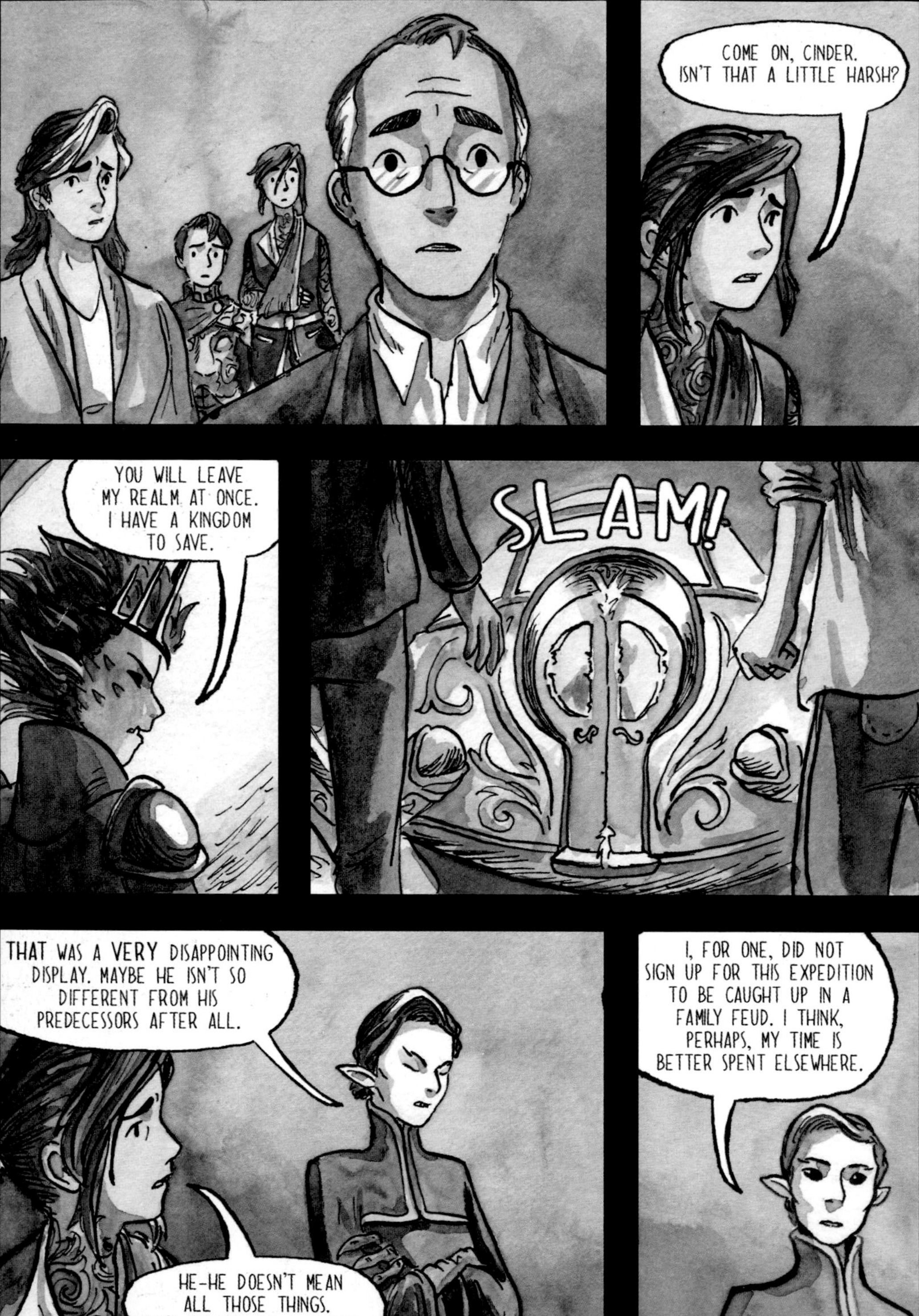
COME ON, CINDER. ISN'T THAT A LITTLE HARSH?
YOU WILL LEAVE MY REALM AT ONCE. I HAVE A KINGDOM TO SAVE.
SLAM!
THAT WAS A VERY DISAPPOINTING DISPLAY. MAYBE HE ISN'T SO DIFFERENT FROM HIS PREDECESSORS AFTER ALL.
HE-HE DOESN'T MEAN ALL THOSE THINGS. HE'S ALWAYS HAD A TEMPER.
I, FOR ONE, DID NOT SIGN UP FOR THIS EXPEDITION TO BE CAUGHT UP IN A FAMILY FEUD. I THINK, PERHAPS, MY TIME IS BETTER SPENT ELSEWHERE.

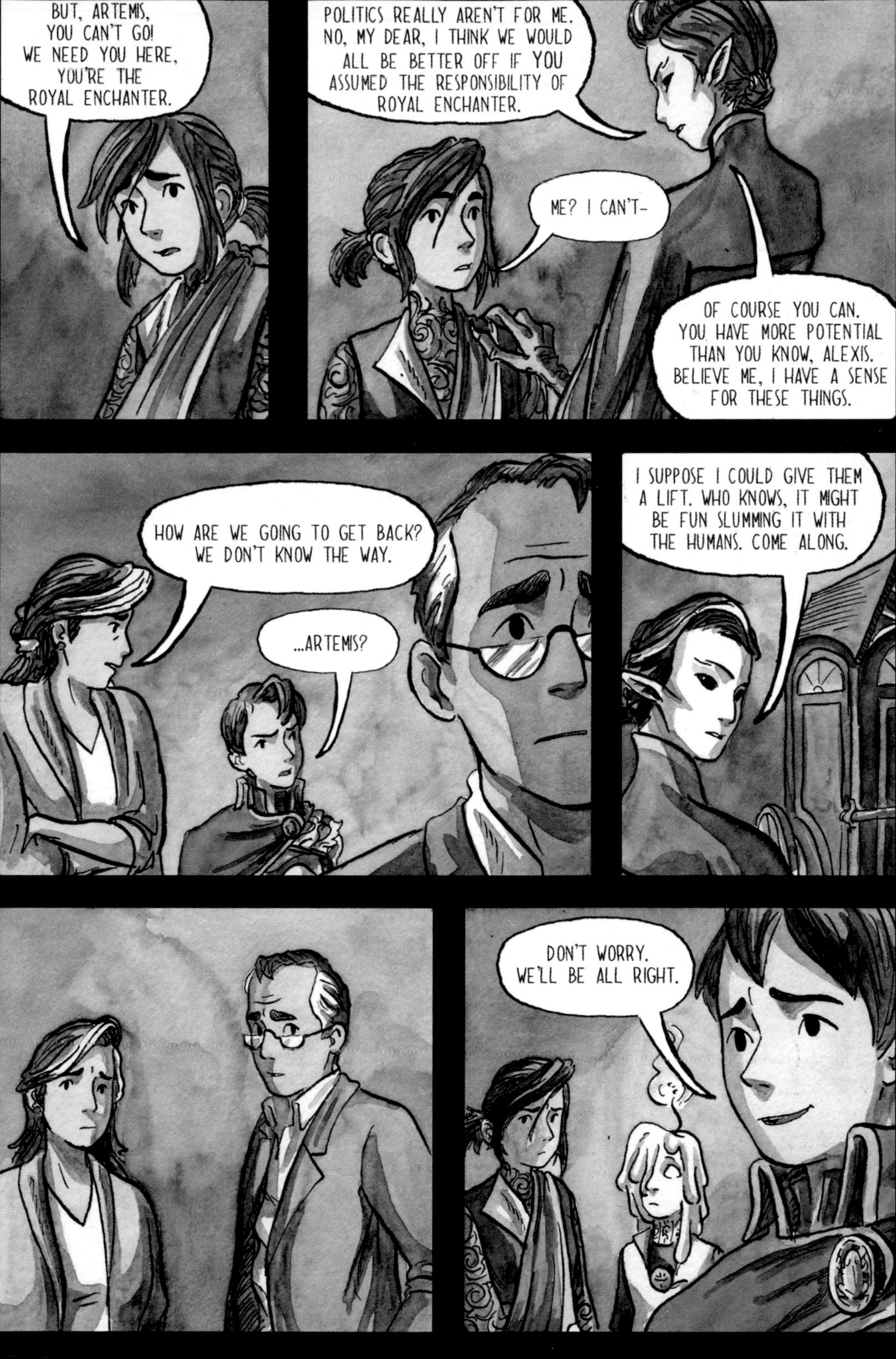
BUT, ARTEMIS, YOU CAN'T GO! WE NEED YOU HERE, YOU'RE THE ROYAL ENCHANTER.
POLITICS REALLY AREN'T FOR ME. NO, MY DEAR, I THINK WE WOULD ALL BE BETTER OFF IF YOU ASSUMED THE RESPONSIBILITY OF ROYAL ENCHANTER.
ME? I CAN'T-
OF COURSE YOU CAN. YOU HAVE MORE POTENTIAL THAN YOU KNOW, ALEXIS. BELIEVE ME, I HAVE A SENSE FOR THESE THINGS.
HOW ARE WE GOING TO GET BACK? WE DON'T KNOW THE WAY.
...ARTEMIS?
I SUPPOSE I COULD GIVE THEM A LIFT. WHO KNOWS, IT MIGHT BE FUN SLUMMING IT WITH THE HUMANS. COME ALONG.
DON'T WORRY. WE'LL BE ALL RIGHT.

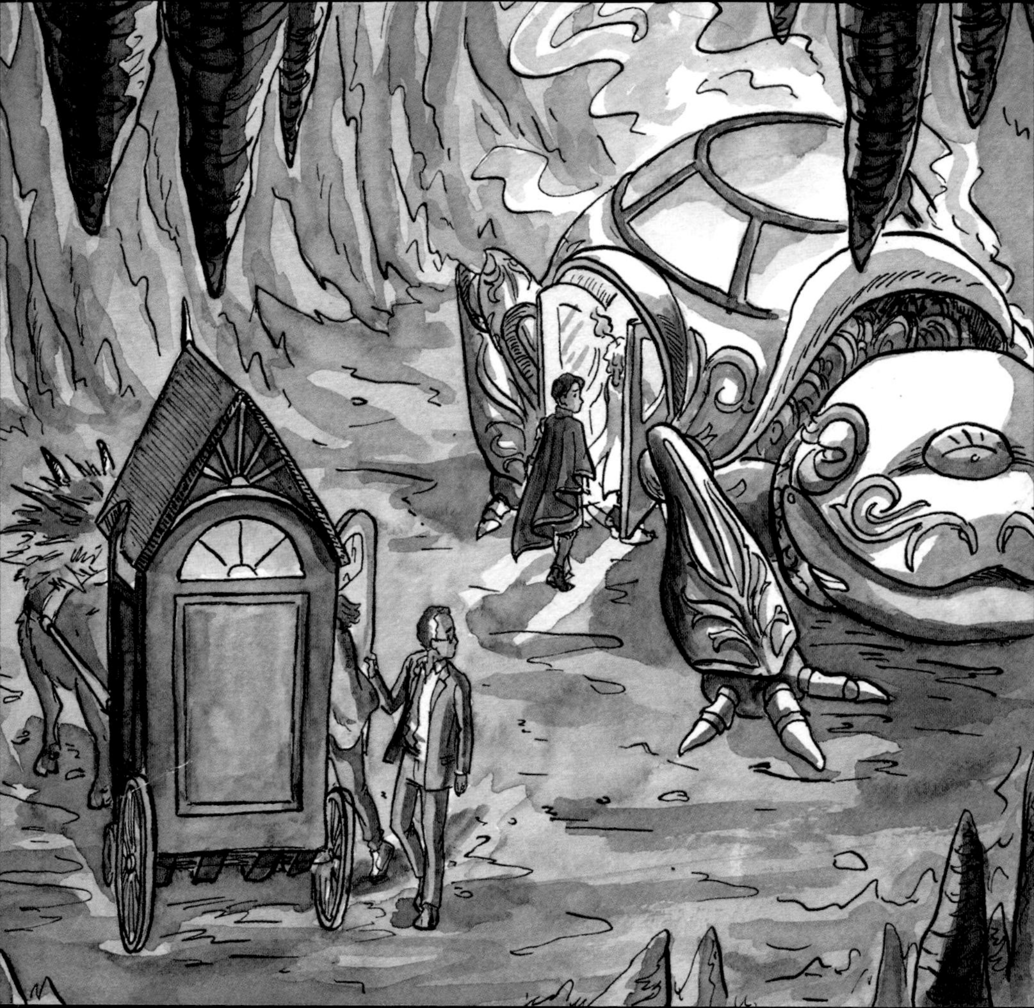

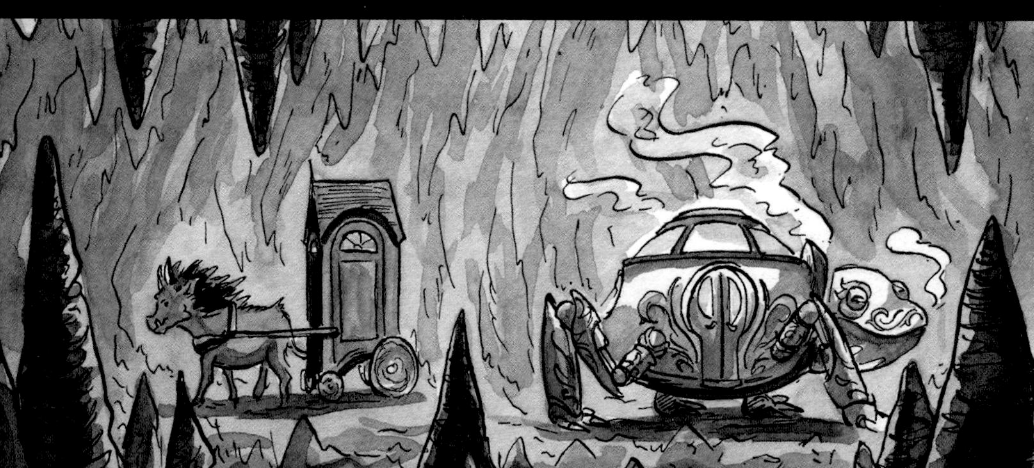

Chapter

Seven

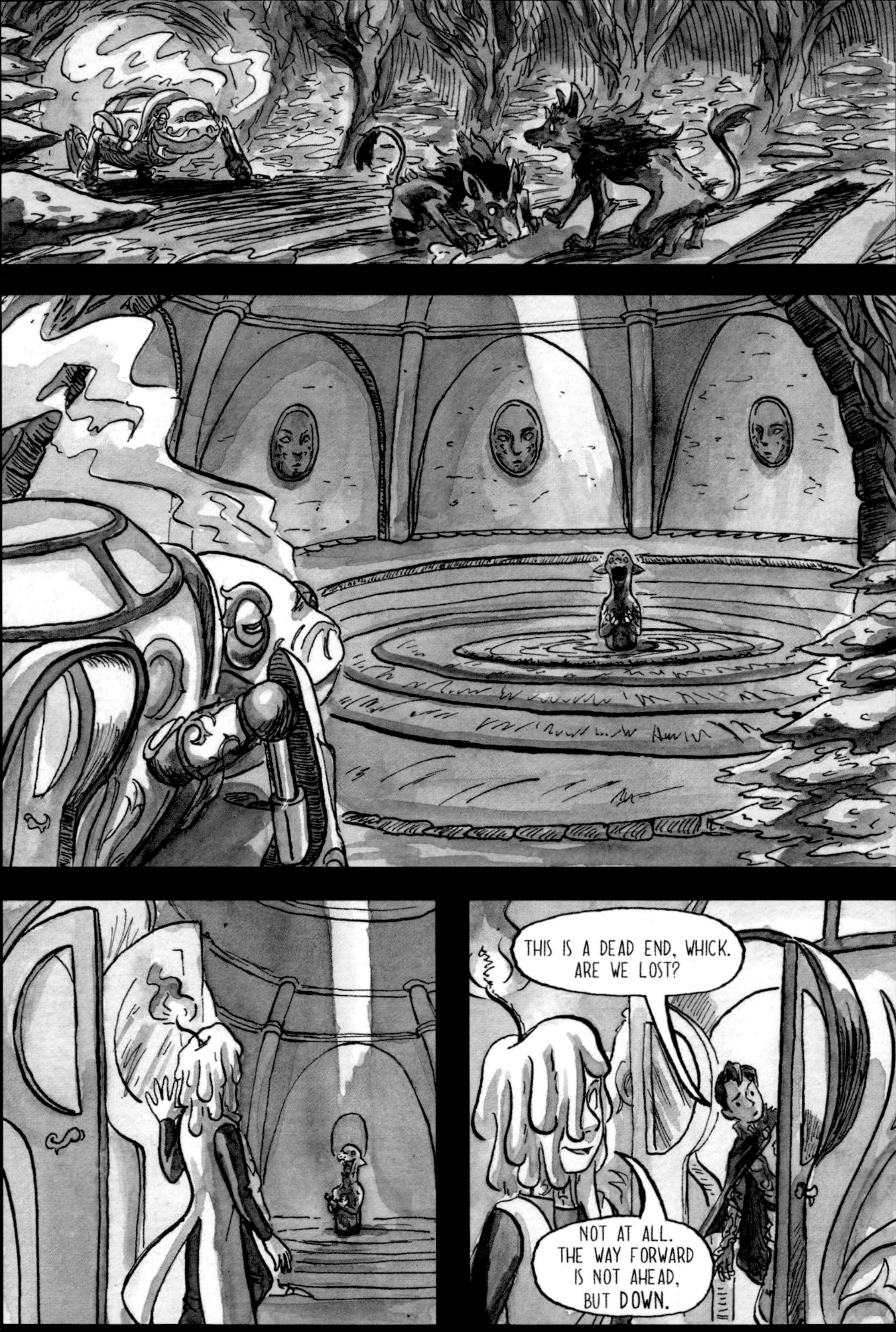
THIS IS A DEAD END, WHICK. ARE WE LOST?
NOT AT ALL. THE WAY FORWARD IS NOT AHEAD, BUT DOWN.

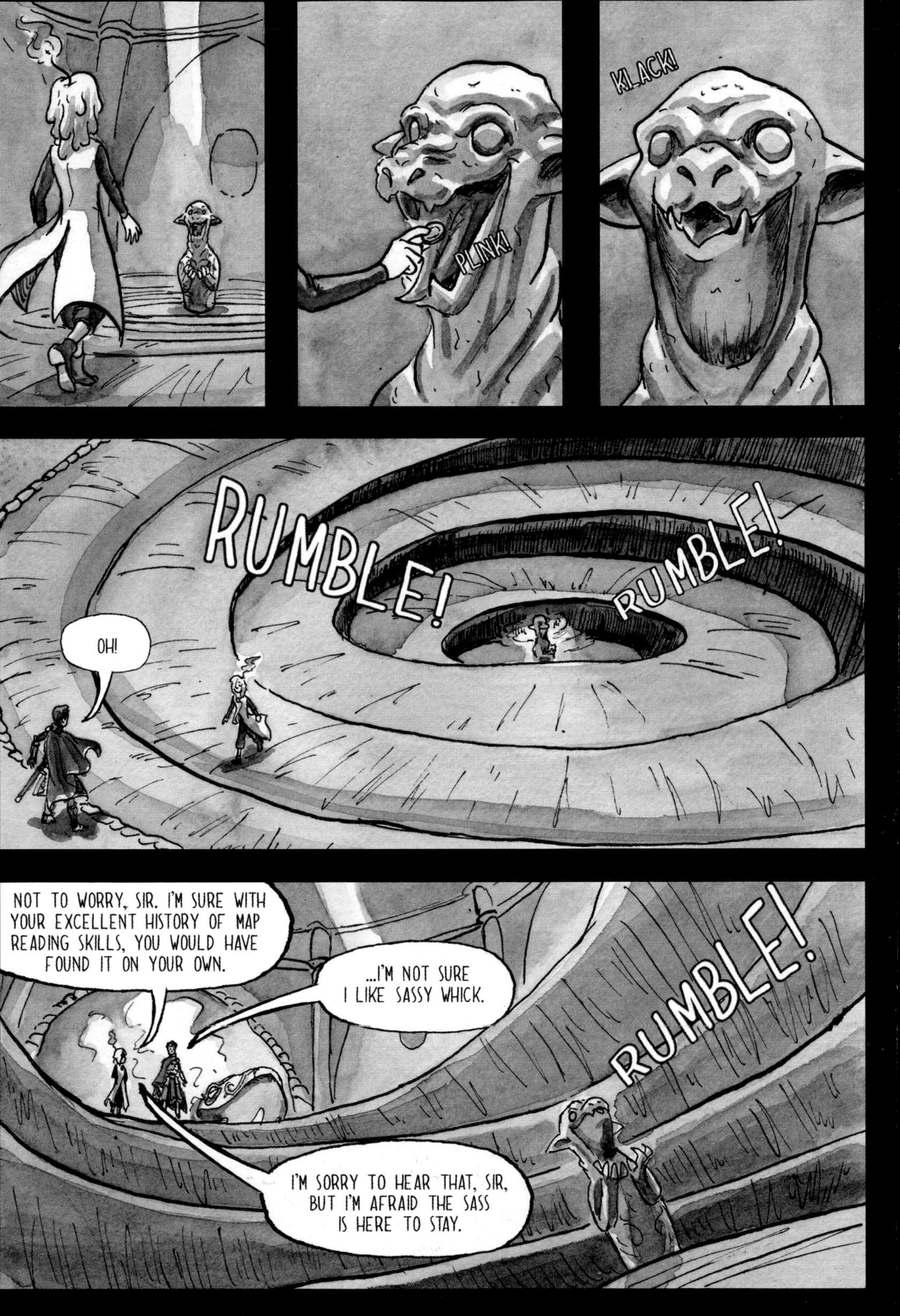
PLINK!
KLACK!
RUMBLE!
RUMBLE!
OH!
NOT TO WORRY, SIR. I'M SURE WITH YOUR EXCELLENT HISTORY OF MAP READING SKILLS, YOU WOULD HAVE FOUND IT ON YOUR OWN.
...I'M NOT SURE I LIKE SASSY WHICK.
RUMBLE!
I'M SORRY TO HEAR THAT, SIR, BUT I'M AFRAID THE SASS IS HERE TO STAY.

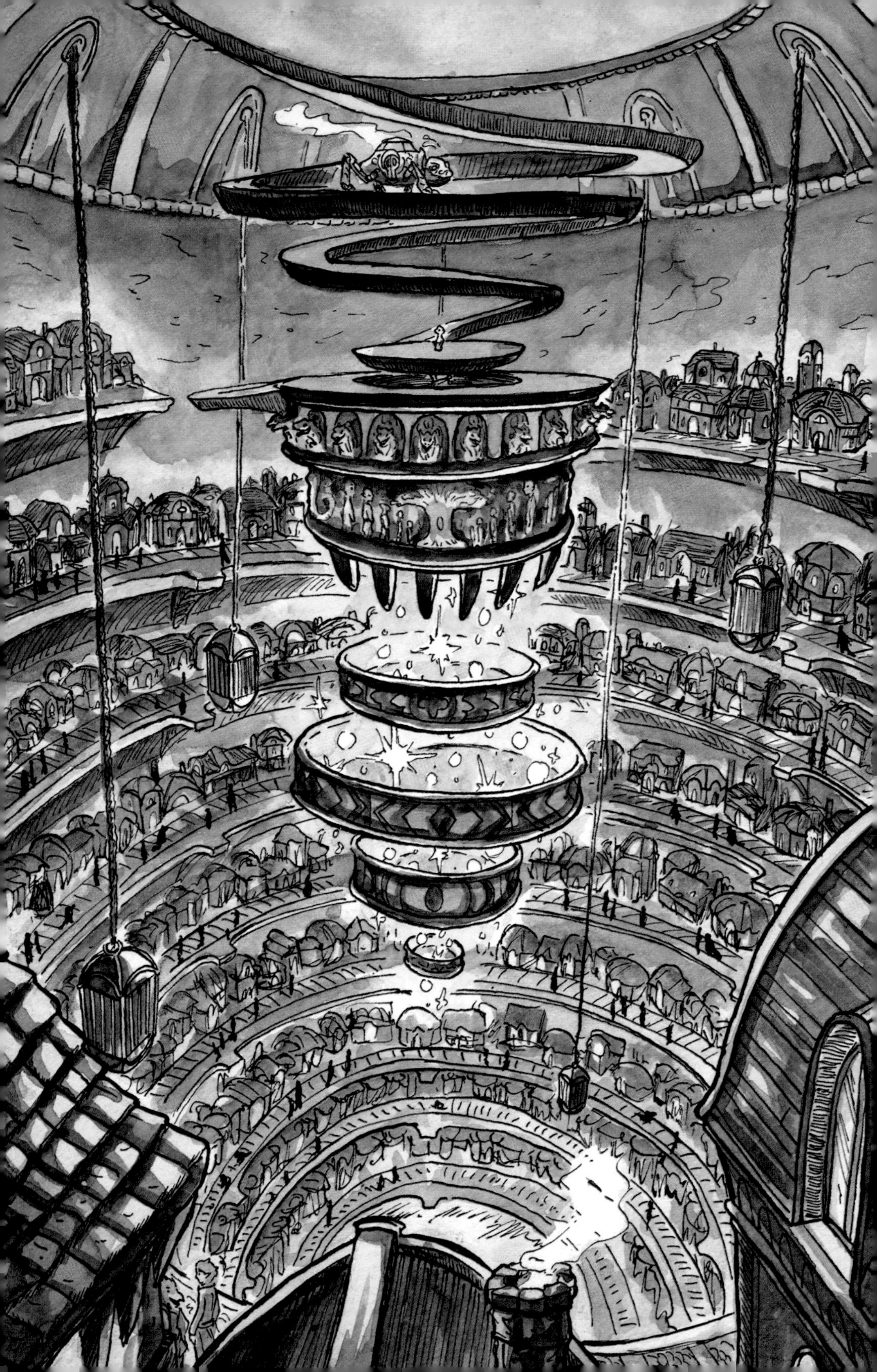

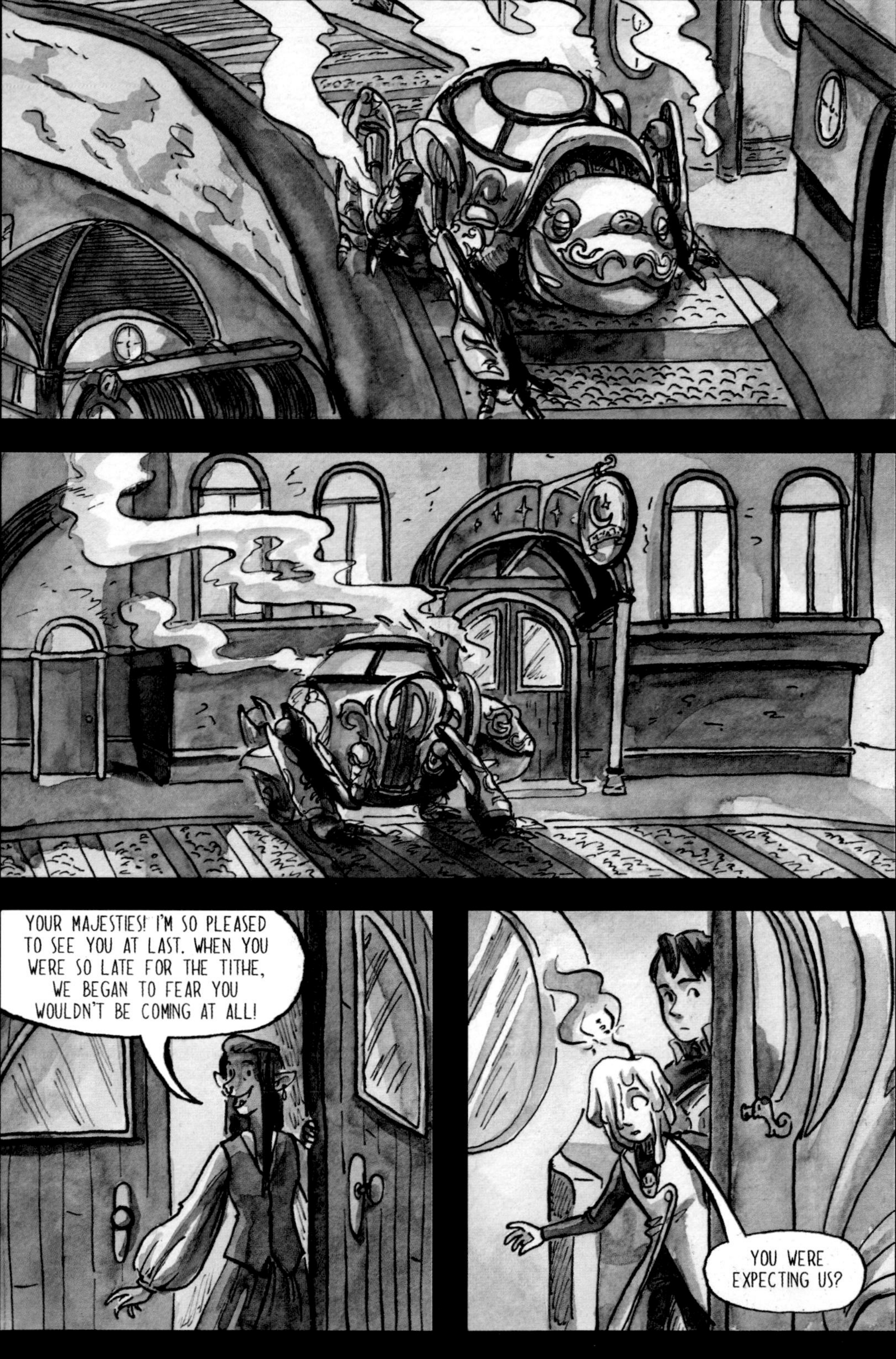
YOUR MAJESTIES! I'M SO PLEASED TO SEE YOU AT LAST. WHEN YOU WERE SO LATE FOR THE TITHE, WE BEGAN TO FEAR YOU WOULDN'T BE COMING AT ALL!
YOU WERE EXPECTING US?

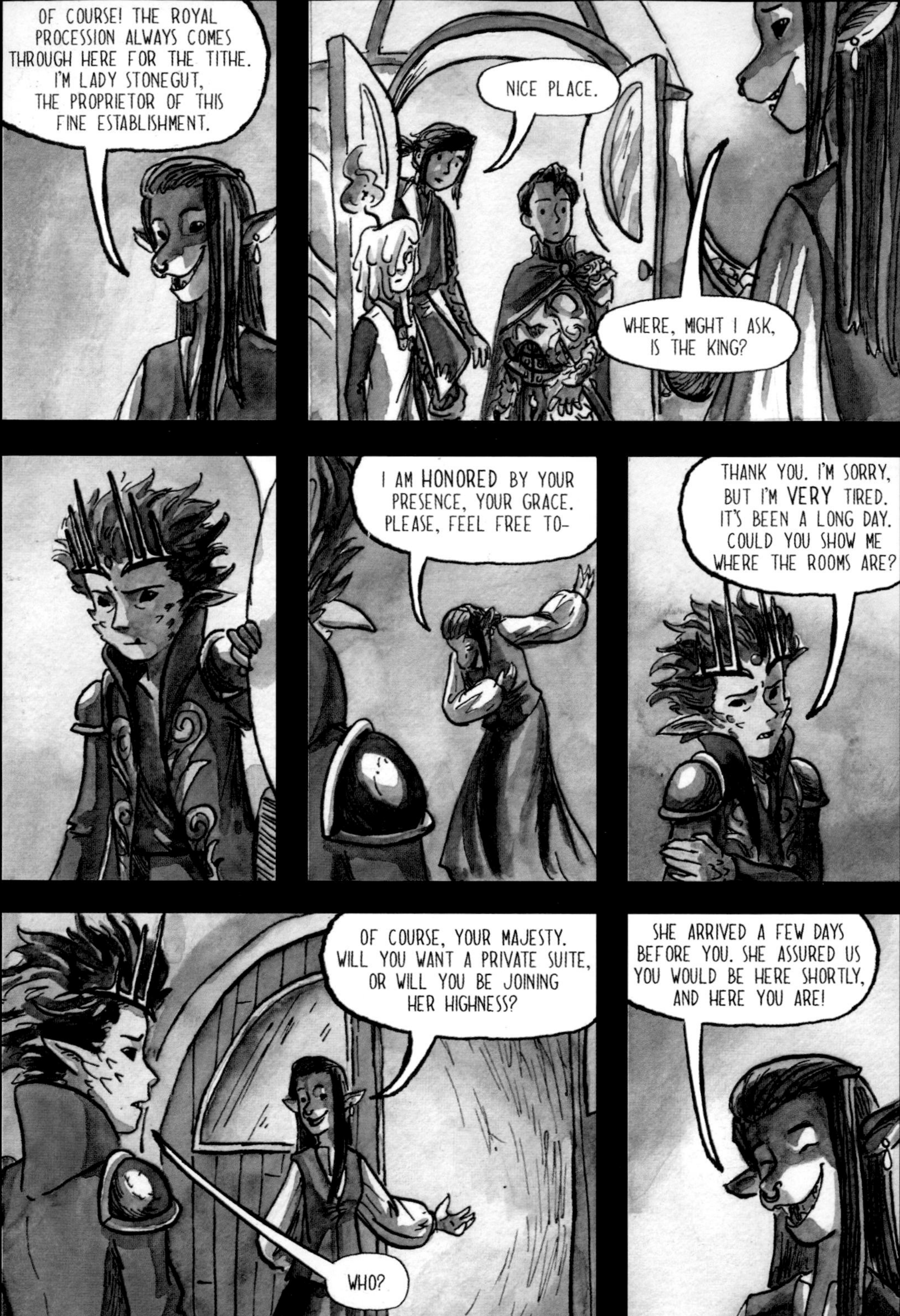
OF COURSE! THE ROYAL PROCESSION ALWAYS COMES THROUGH HERE FOR THE TITHE. I'M LADY STONEGUT, THE PROPRIETOR OF THIS FINE ESTABLISHMENT.
NICE PLACE.
WHERE, MIGHT I ASK, IS THE KING?
I AM HONORED BY YOUR PRESENCE, YOUR GRACE. PLEASE, FEEL FREE TO-
THANK YOU. I'M SORRY, BUT I'M VERY TIRED. IT'S BEEN A LONG DAY. COULD YOU SHOW ME WHERE THE ROOMS ARE?
OF COURSE, YOUR MAJESTY. WILL YOU WANT A PRIVATE SUITE, OR WILL YOU BE JOINING HER HIGHNESS?
WHO?
SHE ARRIVED A FEW DAYS BEFORE YOU. SHE ASSURED US YOU WOULD BE HERE SHORTLY, AND HERE YOU ARE!

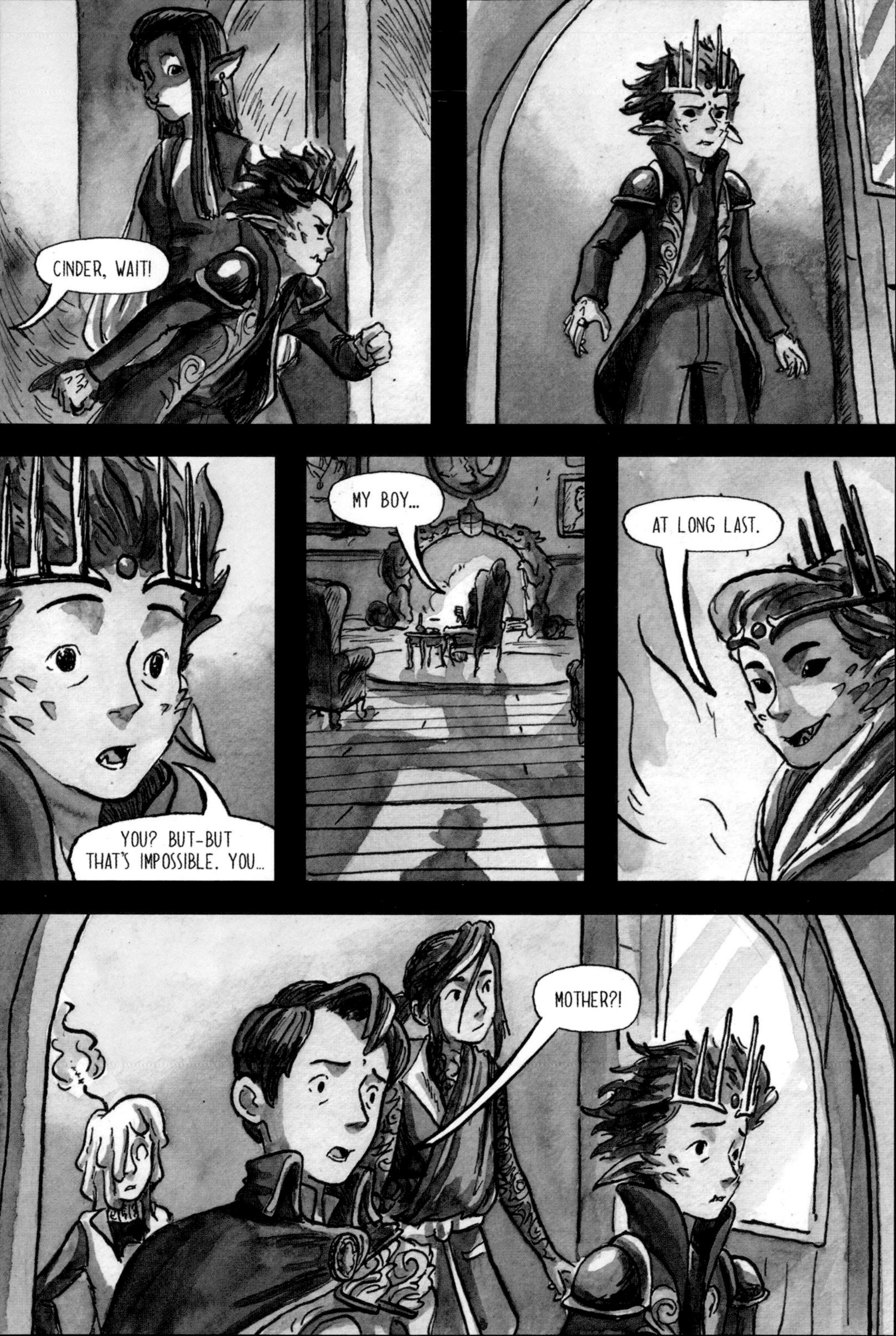
CINDER, WAIT!
YOU? BUT-BUT
THAT'S IMPOSSIBLE. YOU...
MY BOY...
AT LONG LAST.
MOTHER?!

CHAPTER
EIGHT

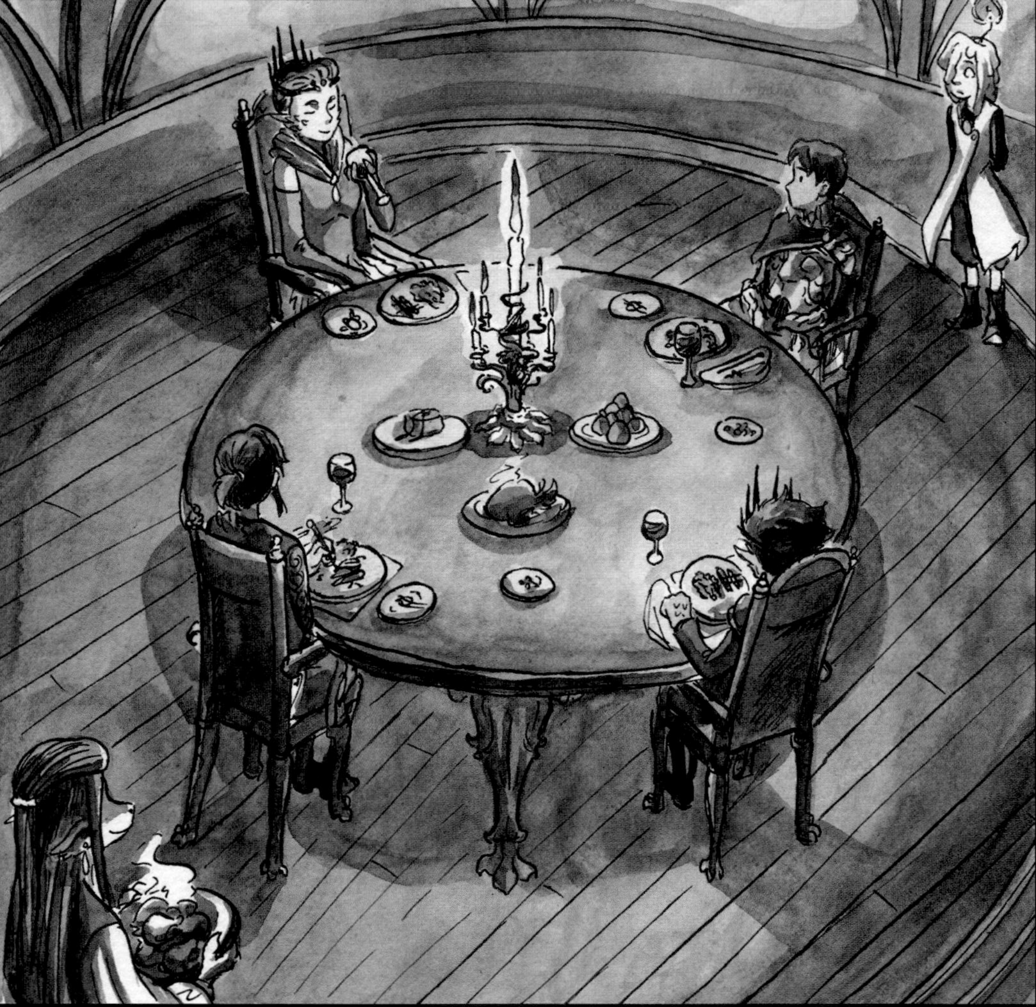

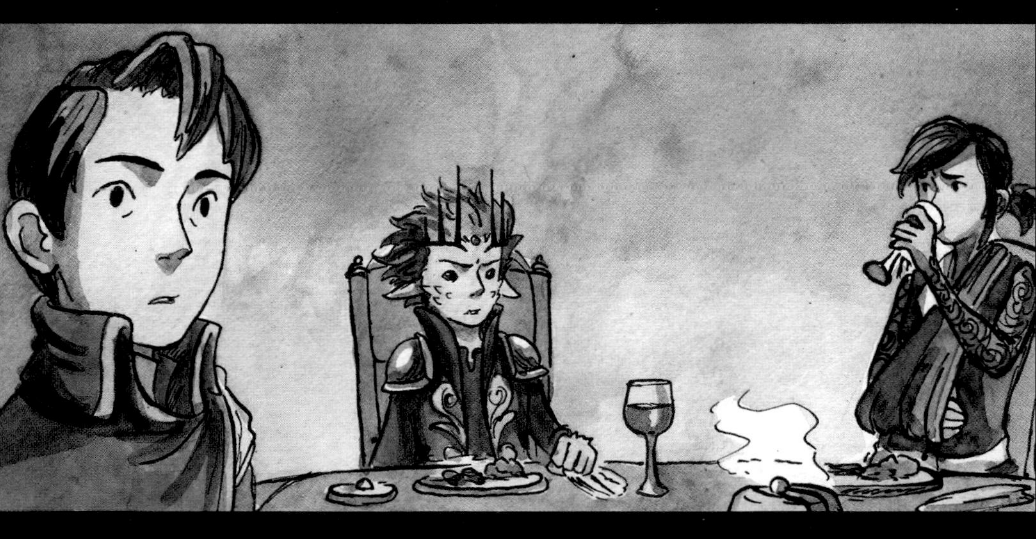

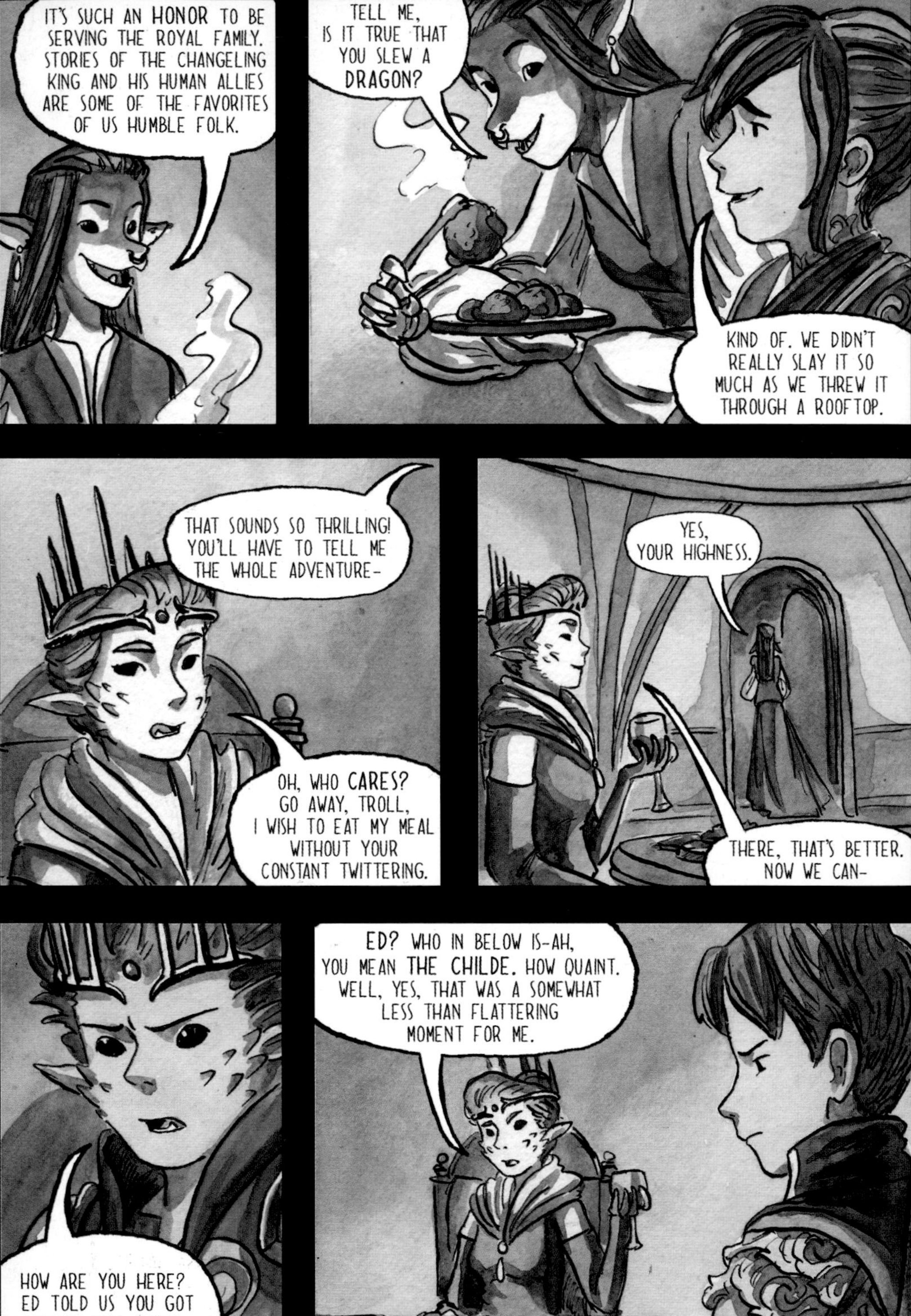
IT'S SUCH AN HONOR TO BE SERVING THE ROYAL FAMILY. STORIES OF THE CHANGELING KING AND HIS HUMAN ALLIES ARE SOME OF THE FAVORITES OF US HUMBLE FOLK.
TELL ME, IS IT TRUE THAT YOU SLEW A DRAGON?
KIND OF. WE DIDN'T REALLY SLAY IT SO MUCH AS WE THREW IT THROUGH A ROOFTOP.
THAT SOUNDS SO THRILLING! YOU'LL HAVE TO TELL ME THE WHOLE ADVENTURE-
OH, WHO CARES? GO AWAY, TROLL, I WISH TO EAT MY MEAL WITHOUT YOUR CONSTANT TWITTERING.
YES, YOUR HIGHNESS.
THERE, THAT'S BETTER. NOW WE CAN-
HOW ARE YOU HERE? ED TOLD US YOU GOT TURNED INTO A RAT.
ED? WHO IN BELOW IS-AH, YOU MEAN THE CHILDE. HOW QUAINT. WELL, YES, THAT WAS A SOMEWHAT LESS THAN FLATTERING MOMENT FOR ME.

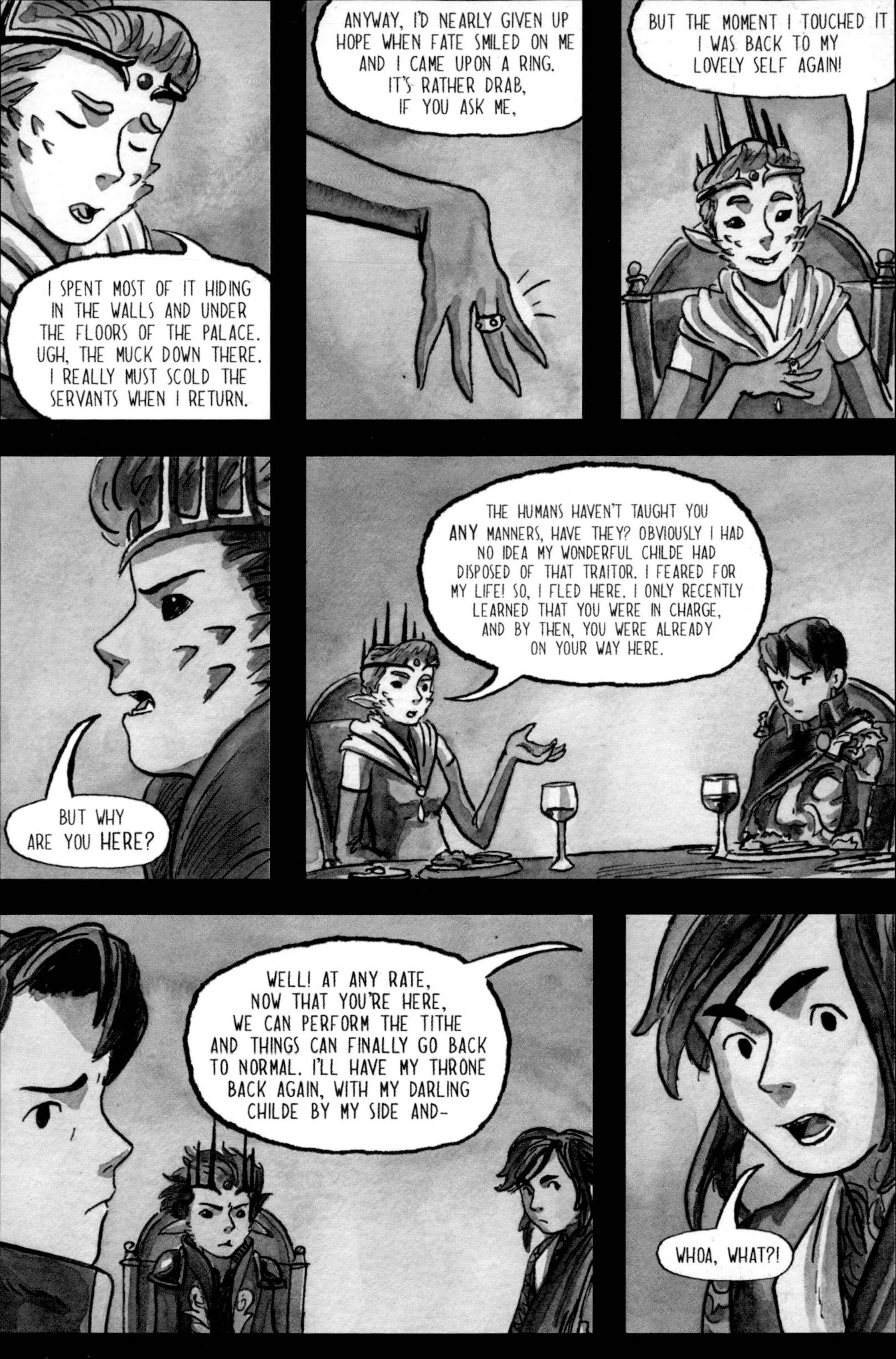

I SPENT MOST OF IT HIDING IN THE WALLS AND UNDER THE FLOORS OF THE PALACE. UGH, THE MUCK DOWN THERE. I REALLY MUST SCOLD THE SERVANTS WHEN I RETURN.
ANYWAY, I'D NEARLY GIVEN UP HOPE WHEN FATE SMILED ON ME AND I CAME UPON A RING. IT'S RATHER DRAB, IF YOU ASK ME,
BUT THE MOMENT I TOUCHED IT I WAS BACK TO MY LOVELY SELF AGAIN!
BUT WHY ARE YOU HERE?
THE HUMANS HAVEN'T TAUGHT YOU ANY MANNERS, HAVE THEY? OBVIOUSLY I HAD NO IDEA MY WONDERFUL CHILDE HAD DISPOSED OF THAT TRAITOR. I FEARED FOR MY LIFE! SO, I FLED HERE. I ONLY RECENTLY LEARNED THAT YOU WERE IN CHARGE, AND BY THEN, YOU WERE ALREADY ON YOUR WAY HERE.
WELL! AT ANY RATE, NOW THAT YOU'RE HERE, WE CAN PERFORM THE TITHE AND THINGS CAN FINALLY GO BACK TO NORMAL. I'LL HAVE MY THRONE BACK AGAIN, WITH MY DARLING CHILDE BY MY SIDE AND-
WHOA, WHAT?!

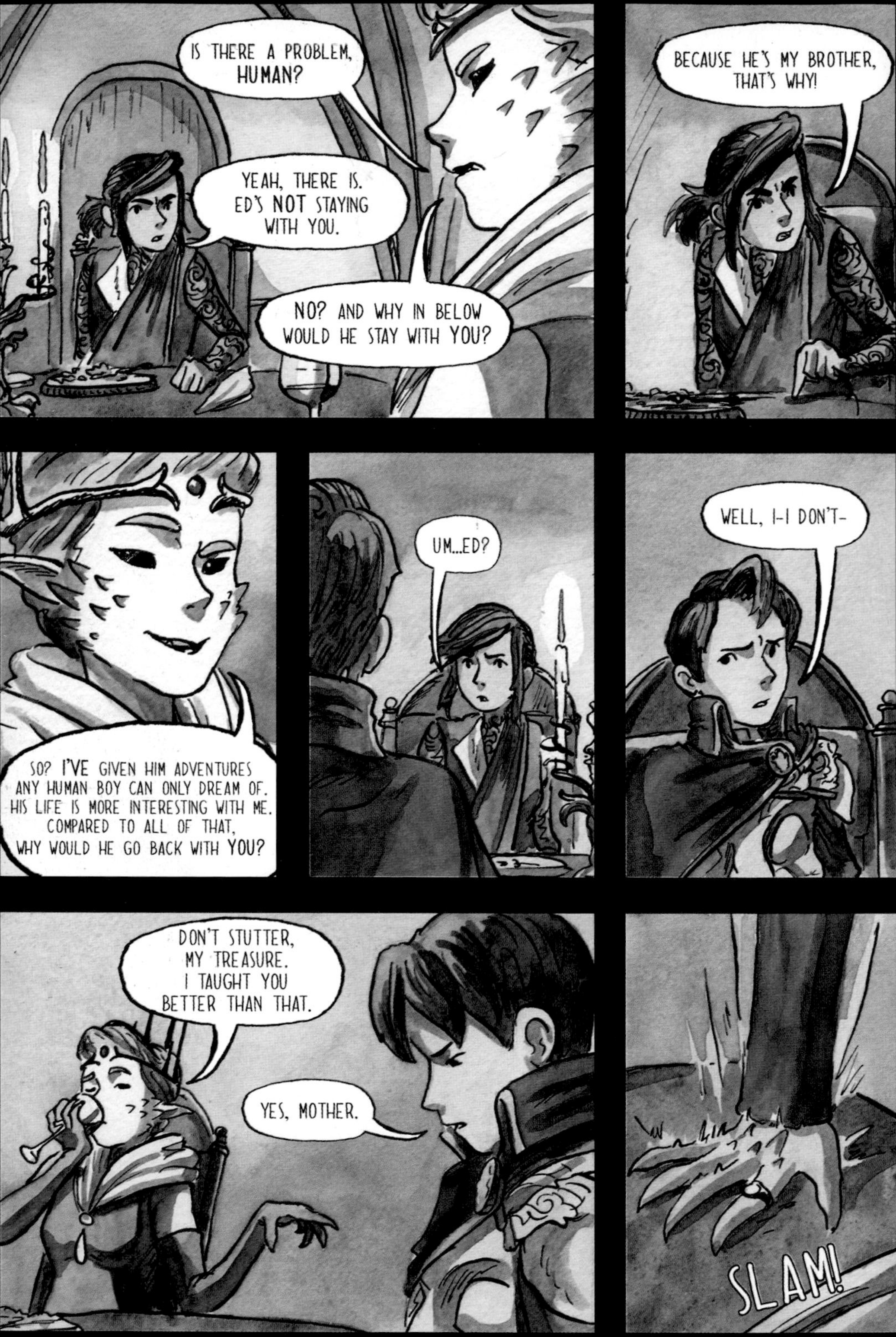

IS THERE A PROBLEM, HUMAN?
YEAH, THERE IS. ED'S NOT STAYING WITH YOU.
NO? AND WHY IN BELOW WOULD HE STAY WITH YOU?
BECAUSE HE'S MY BROTHER, THAT'S WHY!
SO? I'VE GIVEN HIM ADVENTURES ANY HUMAN BOY CAN ONLY DREAM OF. HIS LIFE IS MORE INTERESTING WITH ME. COMPARED TO ALL OF THAT, WHY WOULD HE GO BACK WITH YOU?
UM...ED?
WELL, I-I DON'T-
DON'T STUTTER, MY TREASURE. I TAUGHT YOU BETTER THAN THAT.
YES, MOTHER.
SLAM!

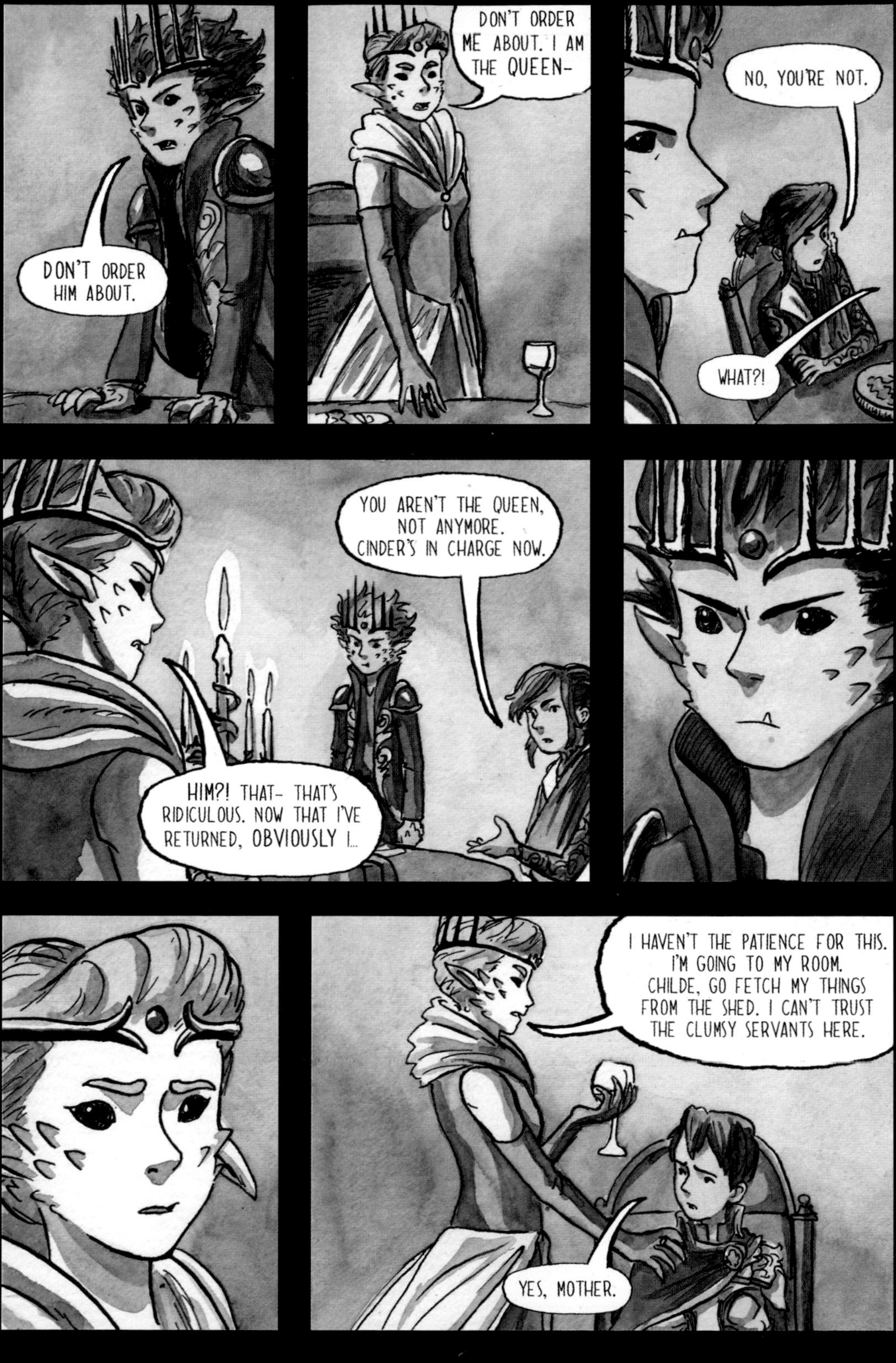
DON'T ORDER HIM ABOUT.
DON'T ORDER ME ABOUT. I AM THE QUEEN-
NO, YOU'RE NOT.
WHAT?!
YOU AREN'T THE QUEEN, NOT ANYMORE. CINDER'S IN CHARGE NOW.
HIM?! THAT- THAT'S RIDICULOUS. NOW THAT I'VE RETURNED, OBVIOUSLY I...
I HAVEN'T THE PATIENCE FOR THIS. I'M GOING TO MY ROOM. CHILDE, GO FETCH MY THINGS FROM THE SHED. I CAN'T TRUST THE CLUMSY SERVANTS HERE.
YES, MOTHER.

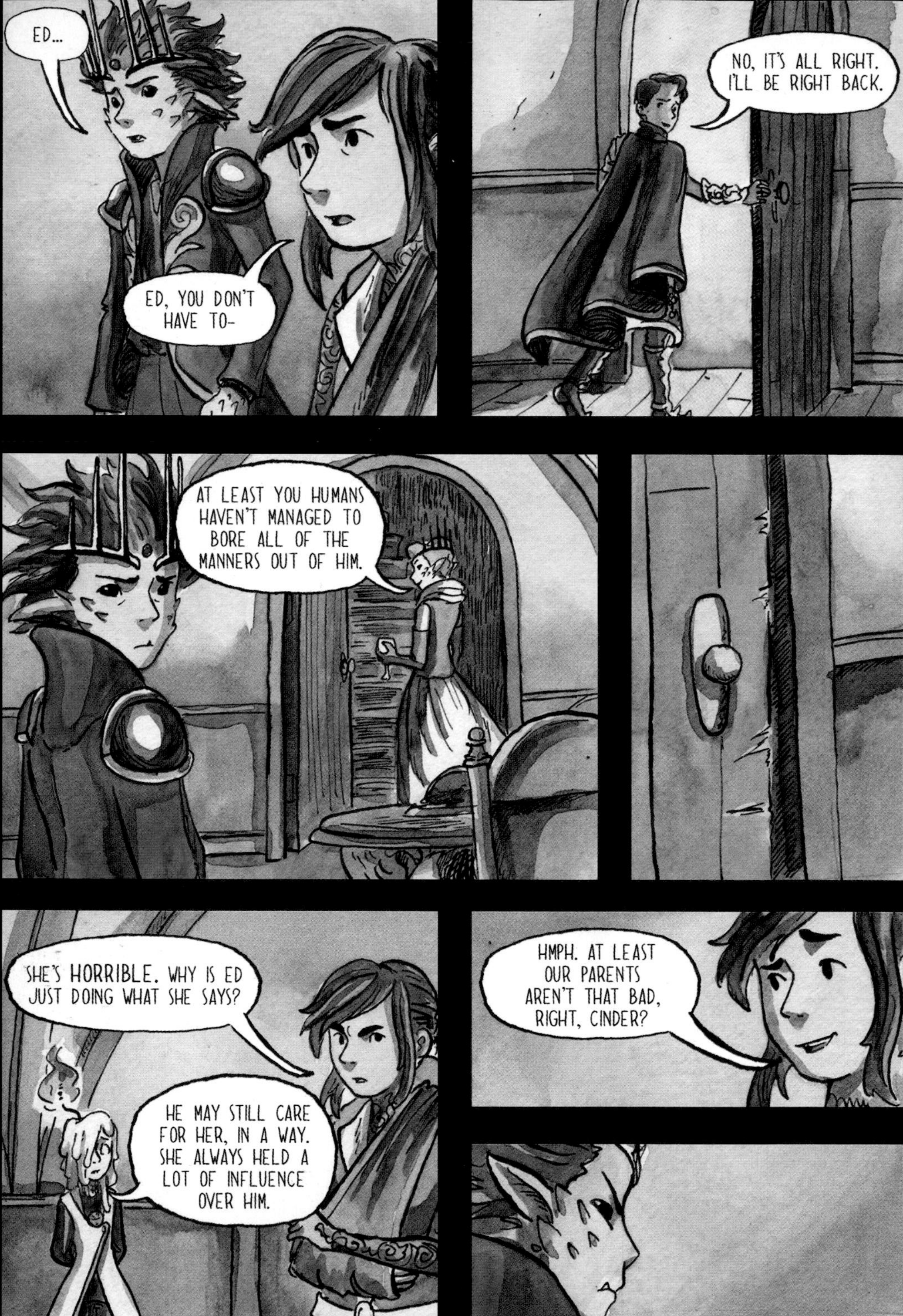
ED...
ED, YOU DON'T HAVE TO-
NO, IT'S ALL RIGHT. I'LL BE RIGHT BACK.
AT LEAST YOU HUMANS HAVEN'T MANAGED TO BORE ALL OF THE MANNERS OUT OF HIM.
SHE'S **HORRIBLE**. WHY IS ED JUST DOING WHAT SHE SAYS?
HE MAY STILL CARE FOR HER, IN A WAY. SHE ALWAYS HELD A LOT OF INFLUENCE OVER HIM.
HMPH. AT LEAST OUR PARENTS AREN'T THAT BAD, RIGHT, CINDER?

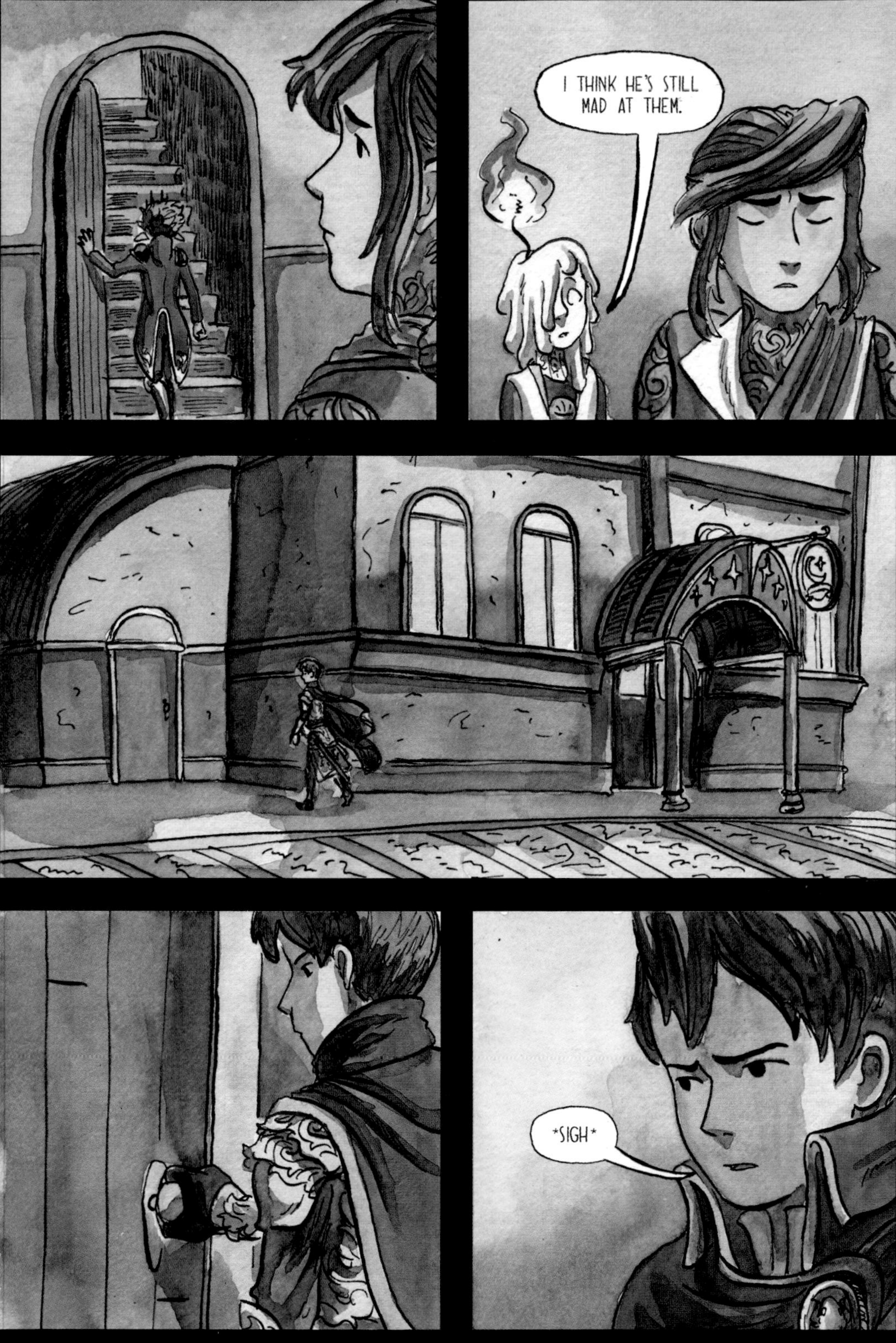
I THINK HE'S STILL MAD AT THEM.
SIGH

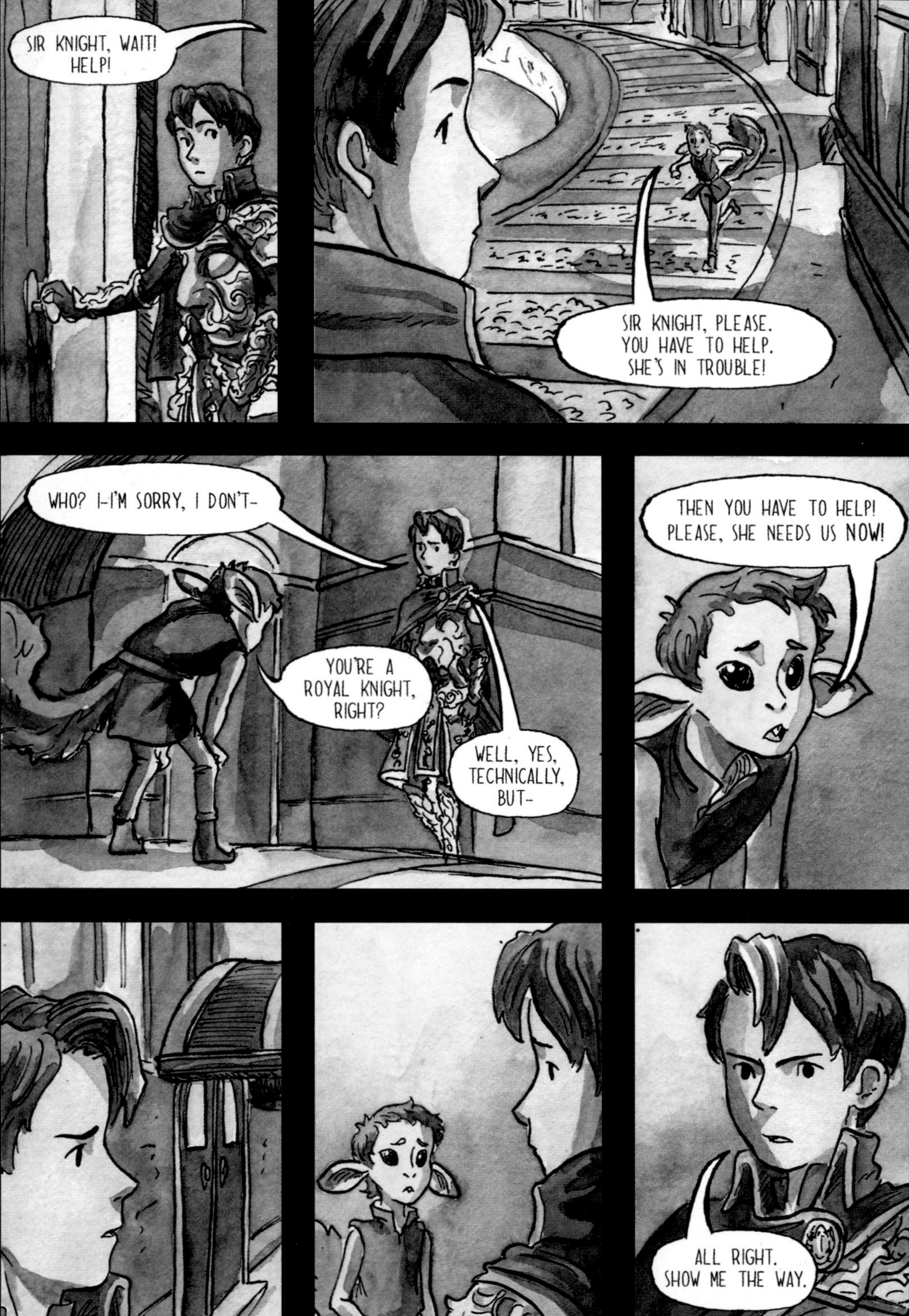
SIR KNIGHT, WAIT! HELP!
SIR KNIGHT, PLEASE. YOU HAVE TO HELP. SHE'S IN TROUBLE!
WHO? I-I'M SORRY, I DON'T-
YOU'RE A ROYAL KNIGHT, RIGHT?
WELL, YES, TECHNICALLY, BUT-
THEN YOU HAVE TO HELP! PLEASE, SHE NEEDS US NOW!
ALL RIGHT. SHOW ME THE WAY.

CHAPTER
NINE

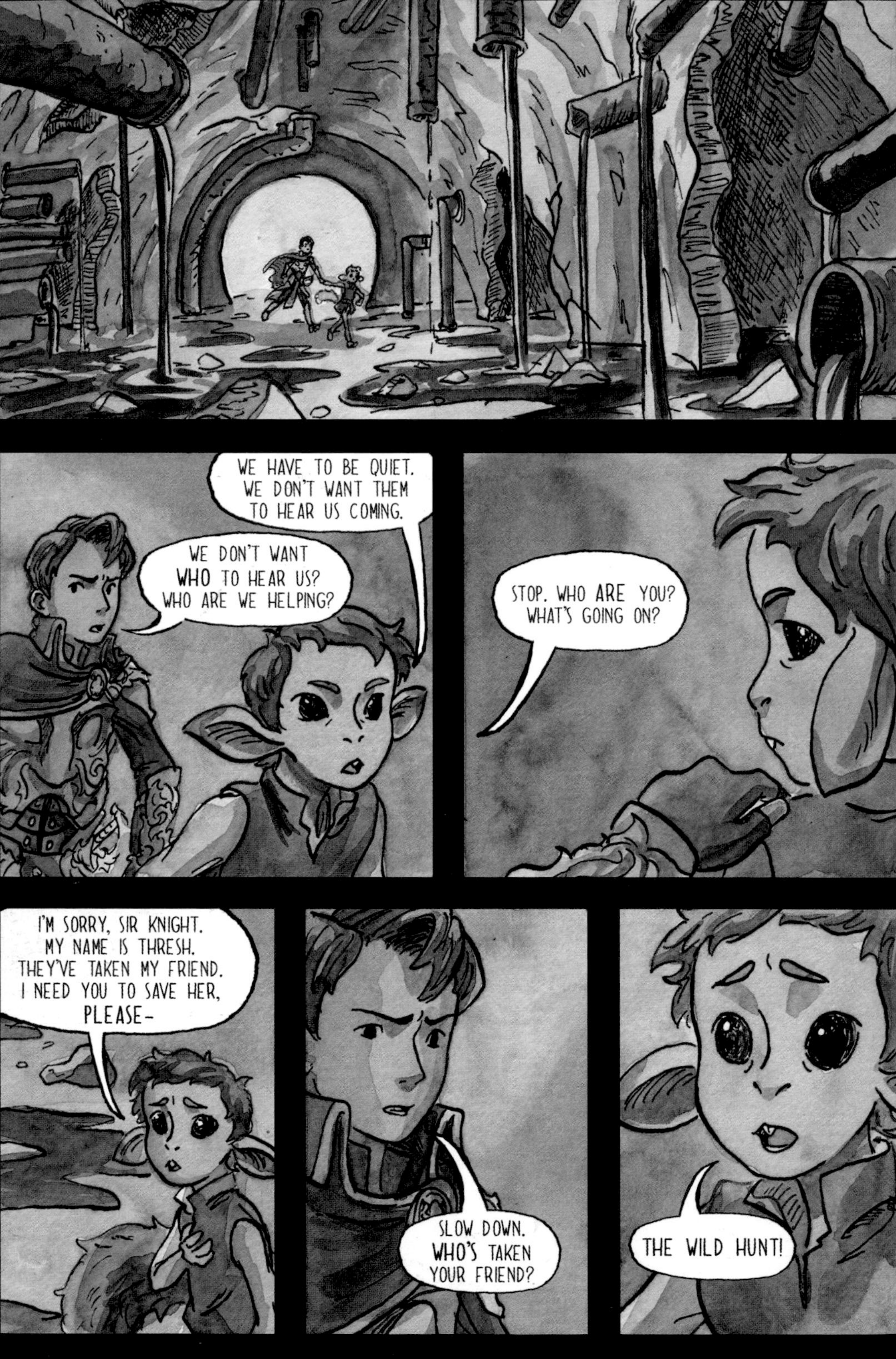
WE HAVE TO BE QUIET. WE DON'T WANT THEM TO HEAR US COMING.
WE DON'T WANT WHO TO HEAR US? WHO ARE WE HELPING?
STOP. WHO ARE YOU? WHAT'S GOING ON?
I'M SORRY, SIR KNIGHT. MY NAME IS THRESH. THEY'VE TAKEN MY FRIEND. I NEED YOU TO SAVE HER, PLEASE-
SLOW DOWN. WHO'S TAKEN YOUR FRIEND?
THE WILD HUNT!

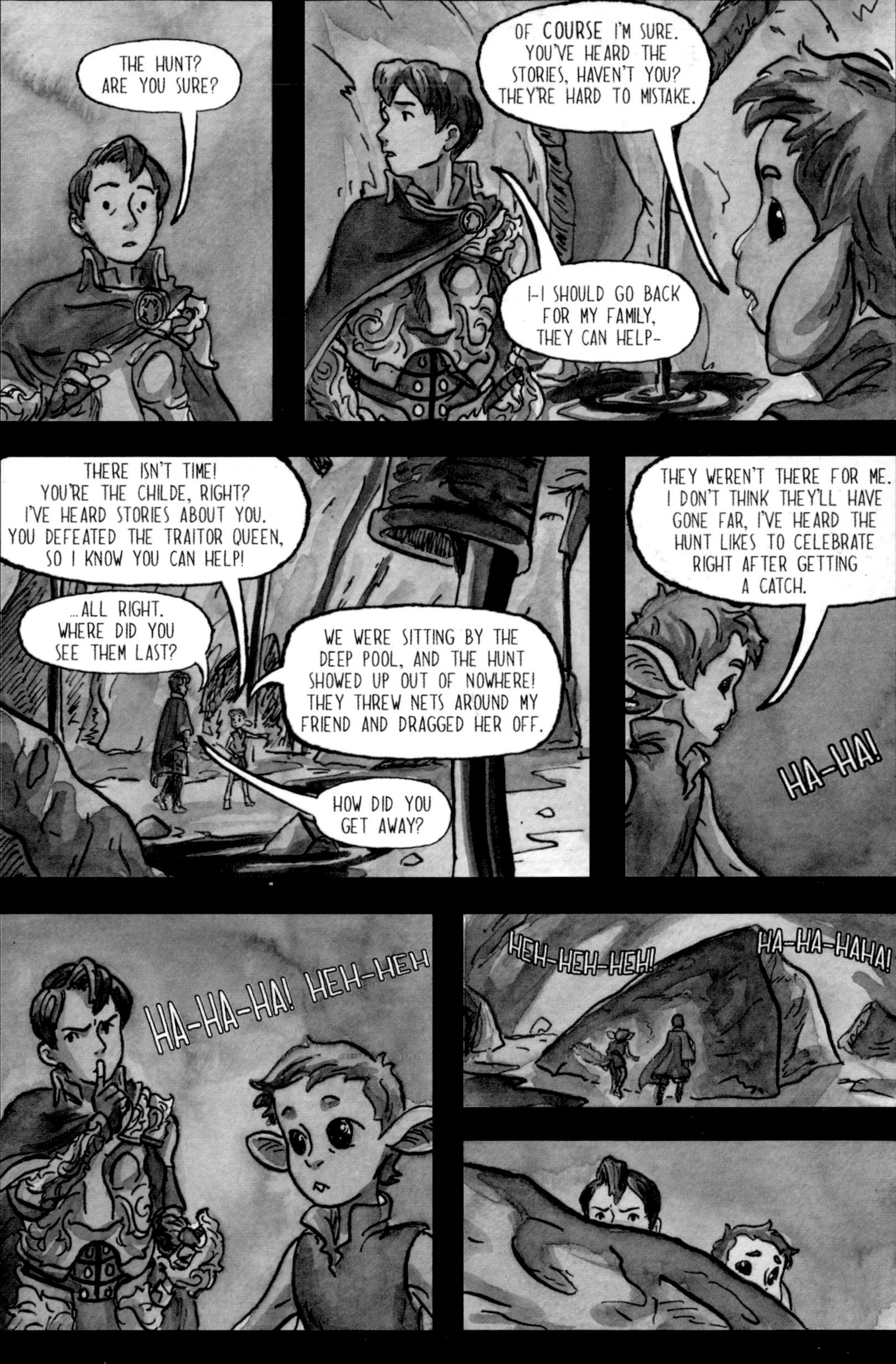
THE HUNT? ARE YOU SURE?
OF COURSE I'M SURE. YOU'VE HEARD THE STORIES, HAVEN'T YOU? THEY'RE HARD TO MISTAKE.
I-I SHOULD GO BACK FOR MY FAMILY, THEY CAN HELP-
THERE ISN'T TIME! YOU'RE THE CHILDE, RIGHT? I'VE HEARD STORIES ABOUT YOU. YOU DEFEATED THE TRAITOR QUEEN, SO I KNOW YOU CAN HELP!
...ALL RIGHT. WHERE DID YOU SEE THEM LAST?
WE WERE SITTING BY THE DEEP POOL, AND THE HUNT SHOWED UP OUT OF NOWHERE! THEY THREW NETS AROUND MY FRIEND AND DRAGGED HER OFF.
HOW DID YOU GET AWAY?
THEY WEREN'T THERE FOR ME. I DON'T THINK THEY'LL HAVE GONE FAR, I'VE HEARD THE HUNT LIKES TO CELEBRATE RIGHT AFTER GETTING A CATCH.
HA-HA!
HA-HA-HA! HEH-HEH
HEH-HEH-HEH!
HA-HA-HAHA!

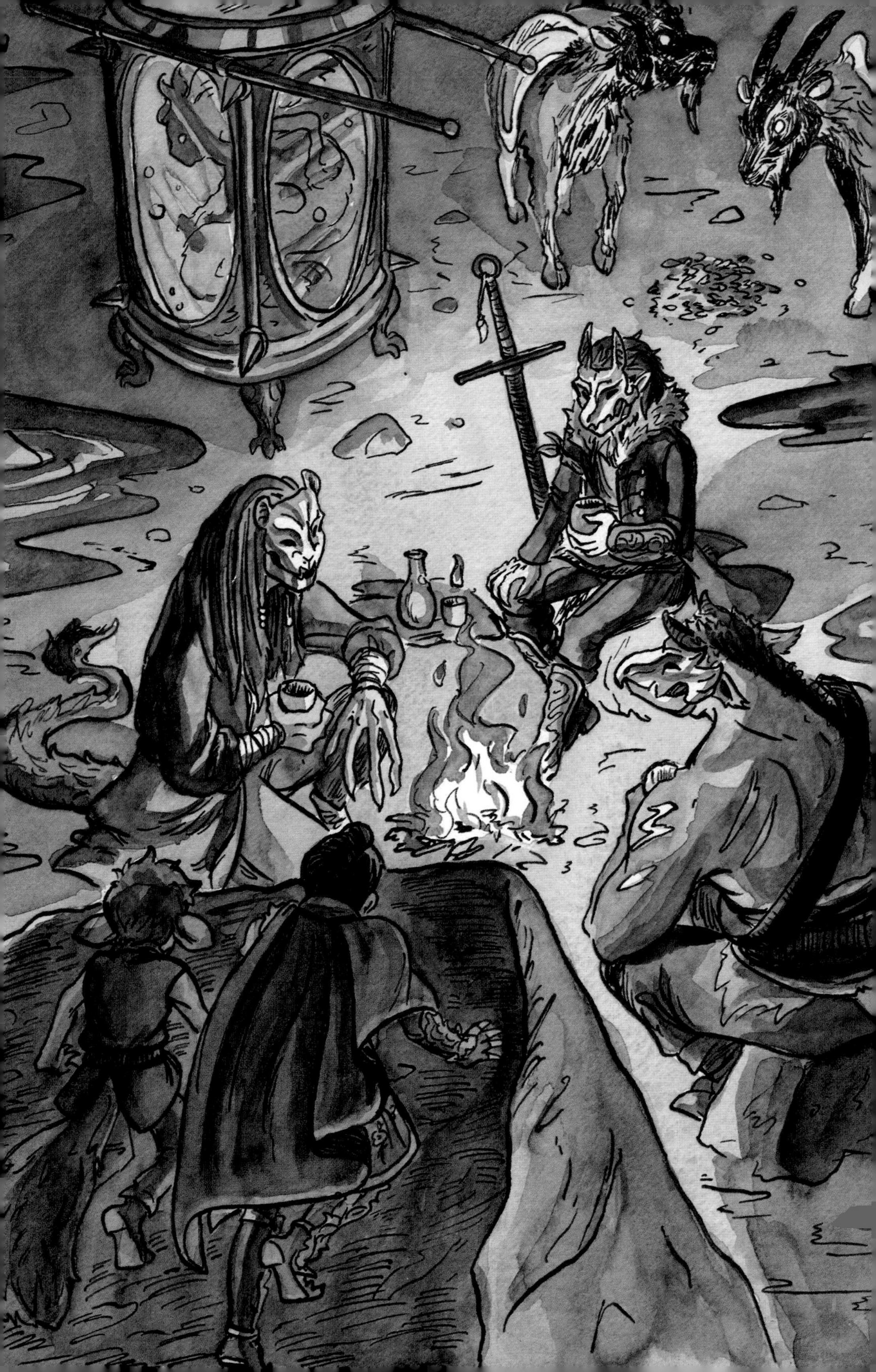

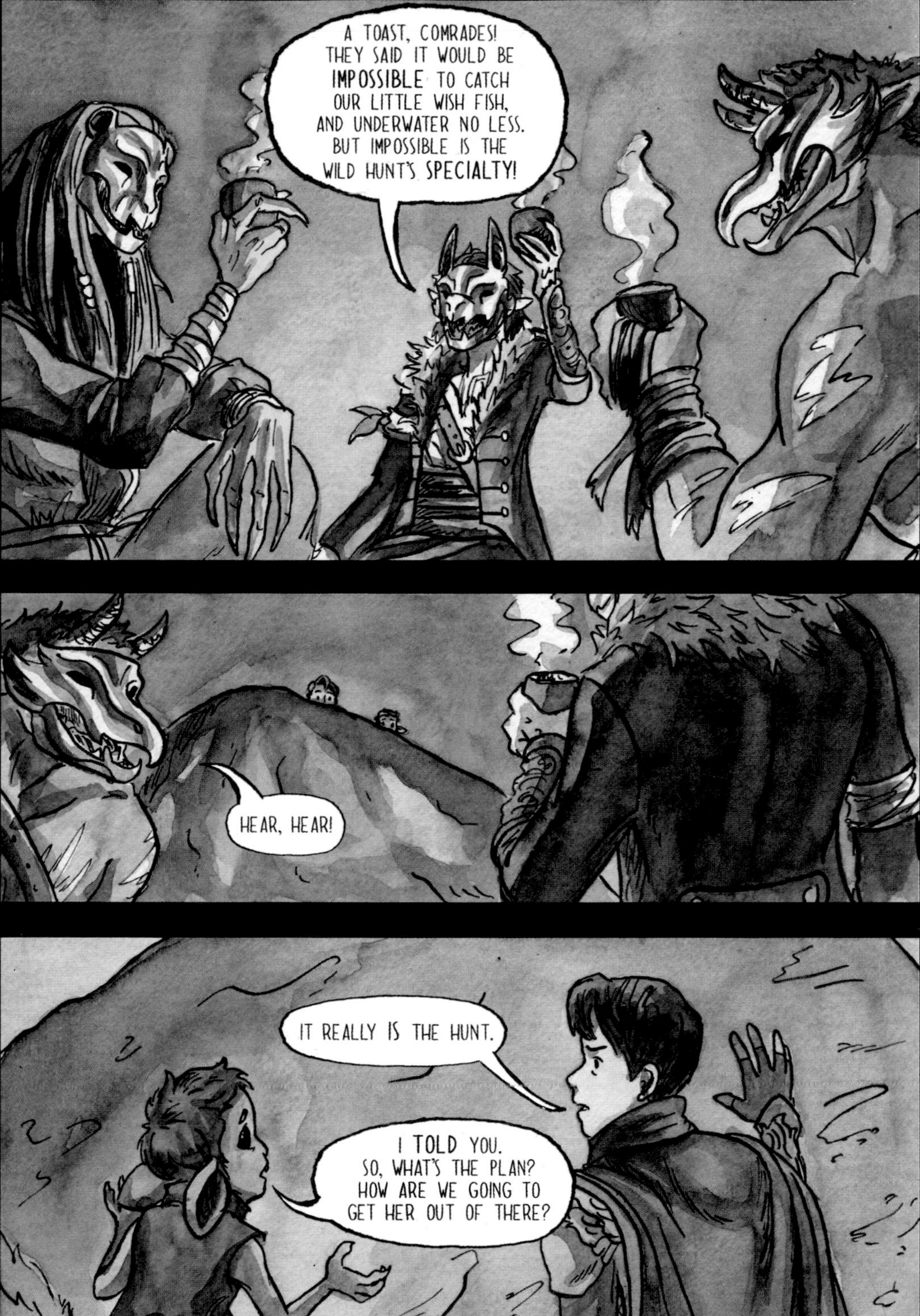
A TOAST, COMRADES! THEY SAID IT WOULD BE IMPOSSIBLE TO CATCH OUR LITTLE WISH FISH, AND UNDERWATER NO LESS. BUT IMPOSSIBLE IS THE WILD HUNT'S SPECIALTY!
HEAR, HEAR!
IT REALLY IS THE HUNT.
I TOLD YOU. SO, WHAT'S THE PLAN? HOW ARE WE GOING TO GET HER OUT OF THERE?

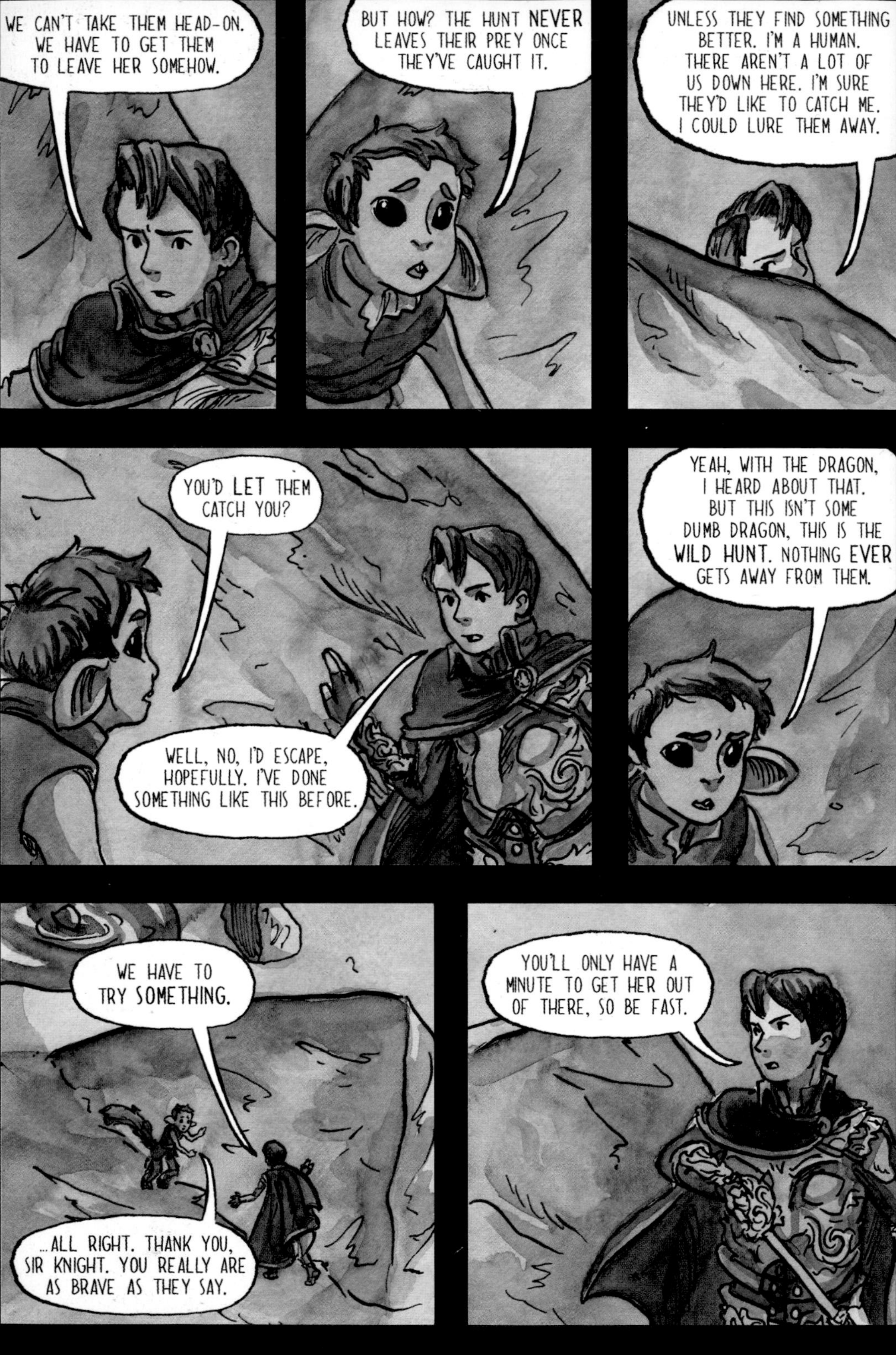

WE CAN'T TAKE THEM HEAD-ON. WE HAVE TO GET THEM TO LEAVE HER SOMEHOW.
BUT HOW? THE HUNT NEVER LEAVES THEIR PREY ONCE THEY'VE CAUGHT IT.
UNLESS THEY FIND SOMETHING BETTER. I'M A HUMAN. THERE AREN'T A LOT OF US DOWN HERE. I'M SURE THEY'D LIKE TO CATCH ME. I COULD LURE THEM AWAY.
YOU'D LET THEM CATCH YOU?
WELL, NO, I'D ESCAPE, HOPEFULLY. I'VE DONE SOMETHING LIKE THIS BEFORE.
YEAH, WITH THE DRAGON, I HEARD ABOUT THAT. BUT THIS ISN'T SOME DUMB DRAGON, THIS IS THE WILD HUNT. NOTHING EVER GETS AWAY FROM THEM.
WE HAVE TO TRY SOMETHING.
...ALL RIGHT. THANK YOU, SIR KNIGHT. YOU REALLY ARE AS BRAVE AS THEY SAY.
YOU'LL ONLY HAVE A MINUTE TO GET HER OUT OF THERE, SO BE FAST.

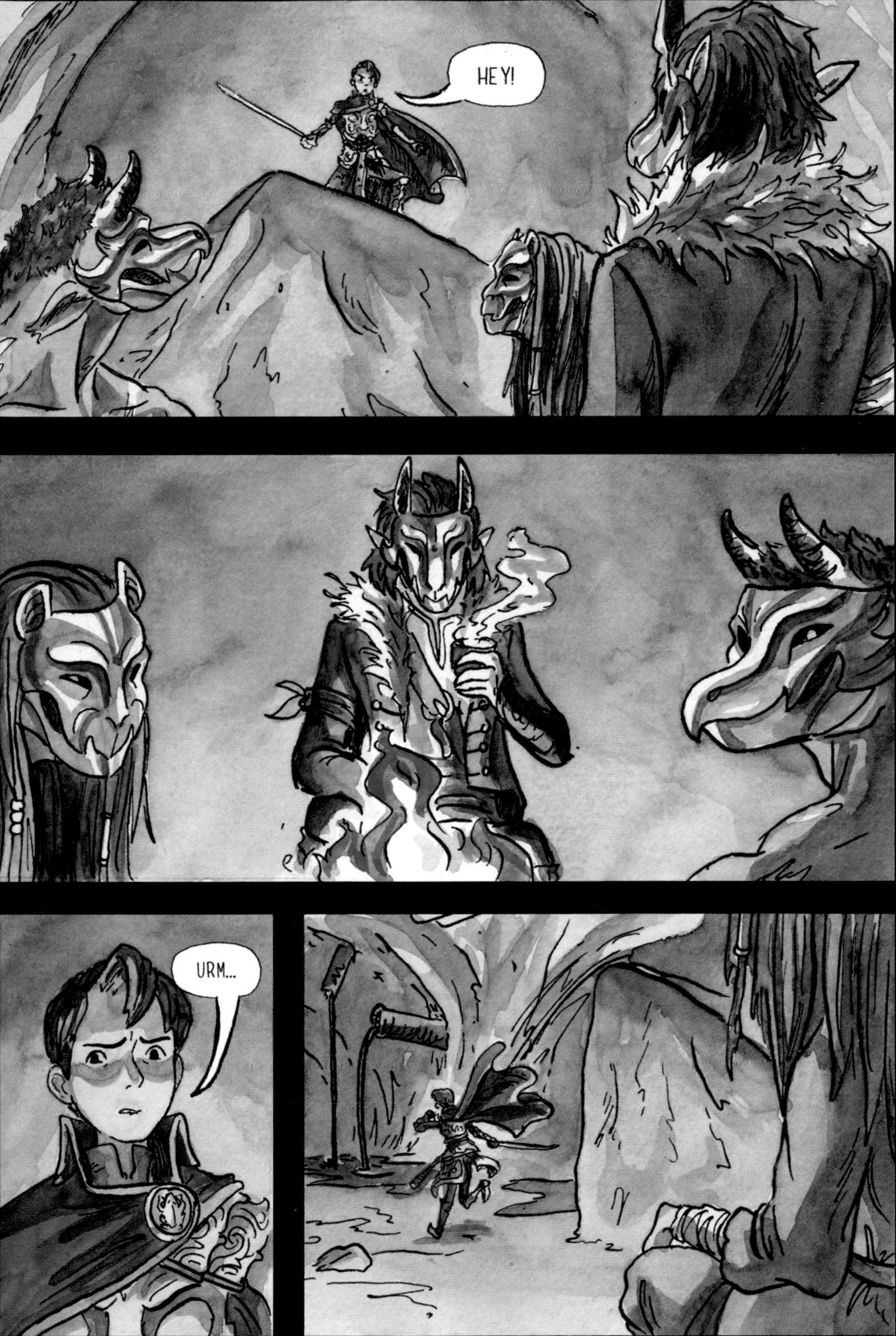
HEY!
URM...

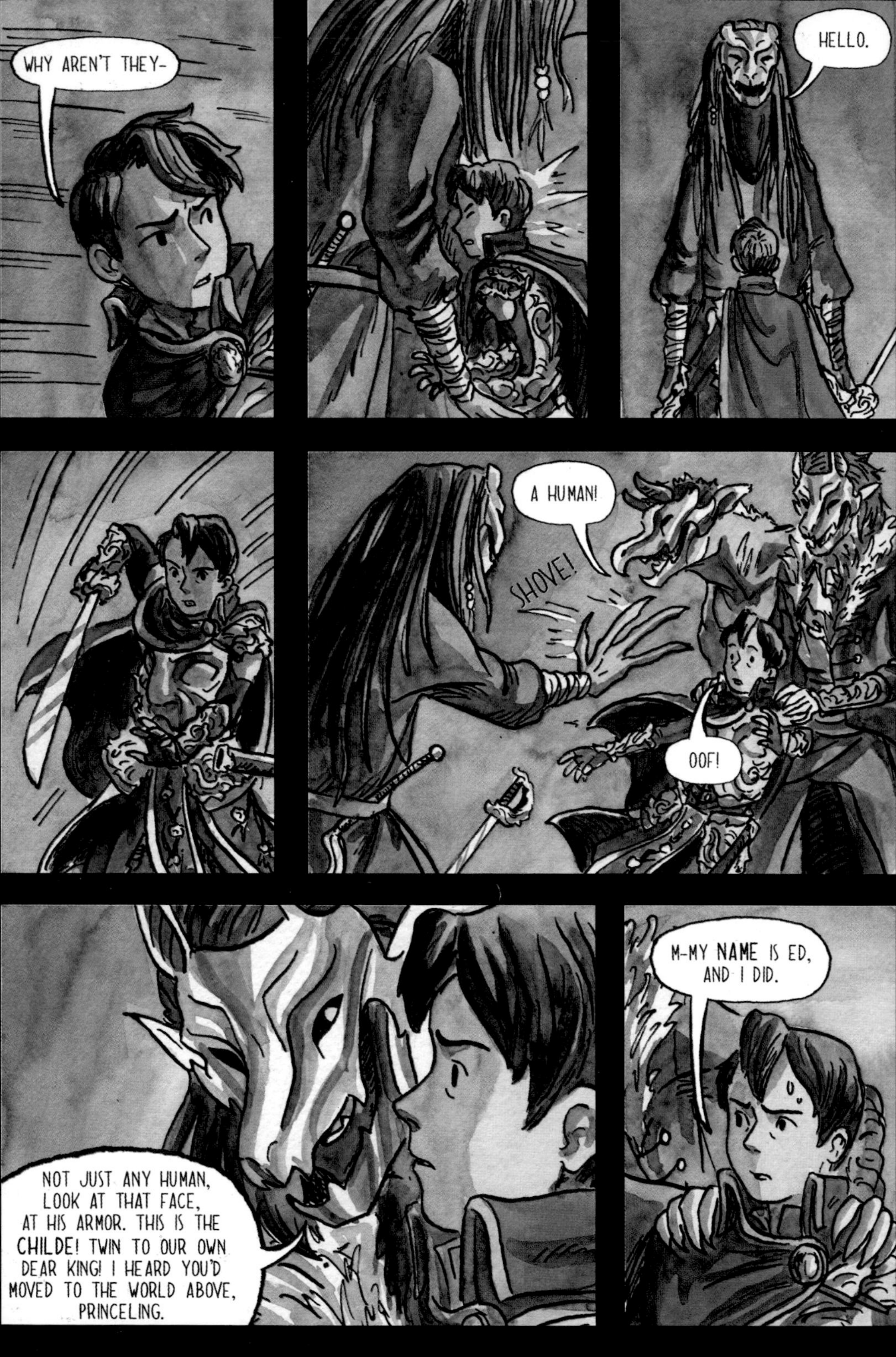
WHY AREN'T THEY-
HELLO.
A HUMAN!
SHOVE!
OOF!
NOT JUST ANY HUMAN, LOOK AT THAT FACE, AT HIS ARMOR. THIS IS THE CHILDE! TWIN TO OUR OWN DEAR KING! I HEARD YOU'D MOVED TO THE WORLD ABOVE, PRINCELING.
M-MY NAME IS ED, AND I DID.

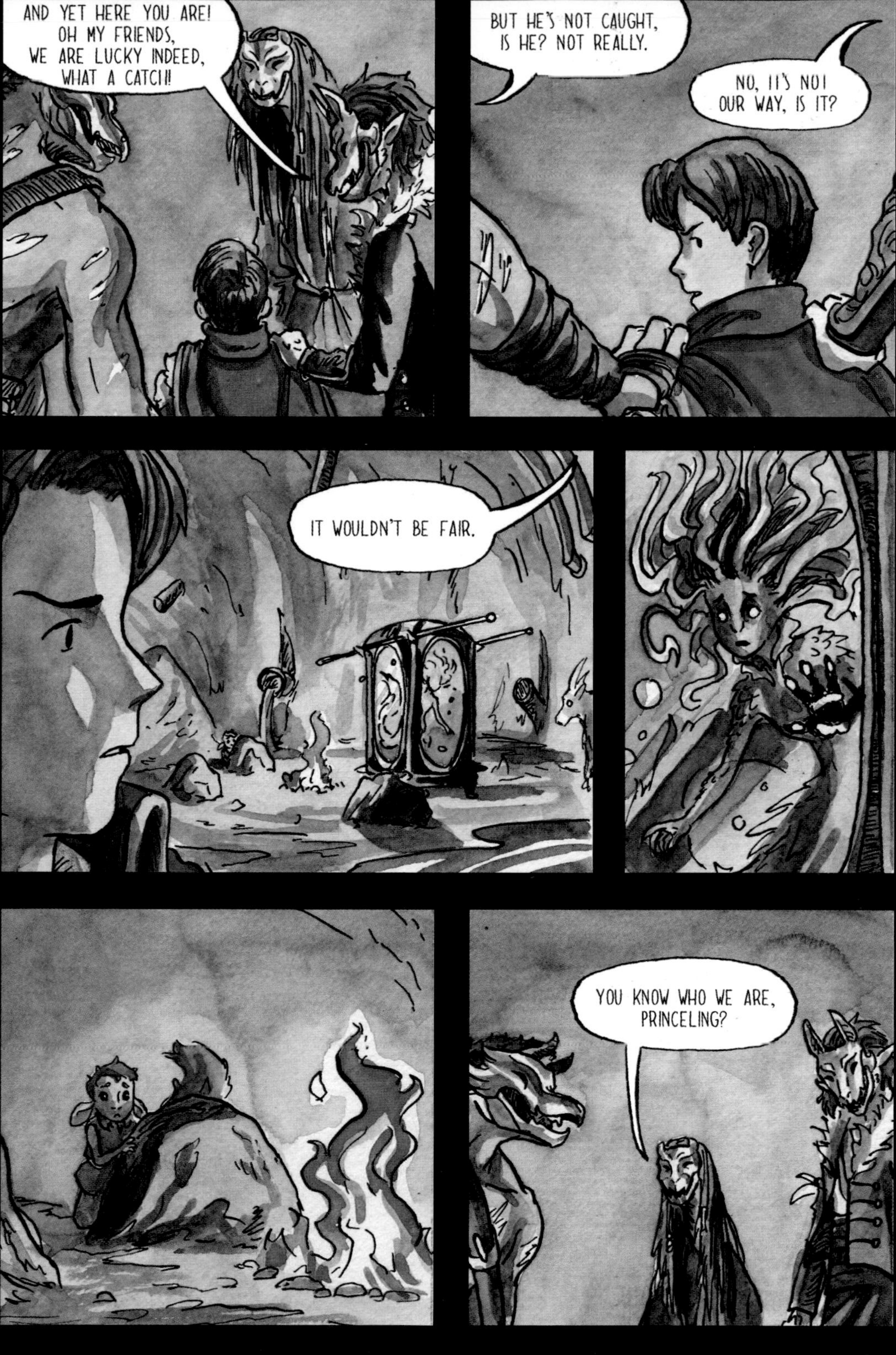
AND YET HERE YOU ARE! OH MY FRIENDS, WE ARE LUCKY INDEED, WHAT A CATCH!
BUT HE'S NOT CAUGHT, IS HE? NOT REALLY.
NO, IT'S NOT OUR WAY, IS IT?
IT WOULDN'T BE FAIR.
YOU KNOW WHO WE ARE, PRINCELING?

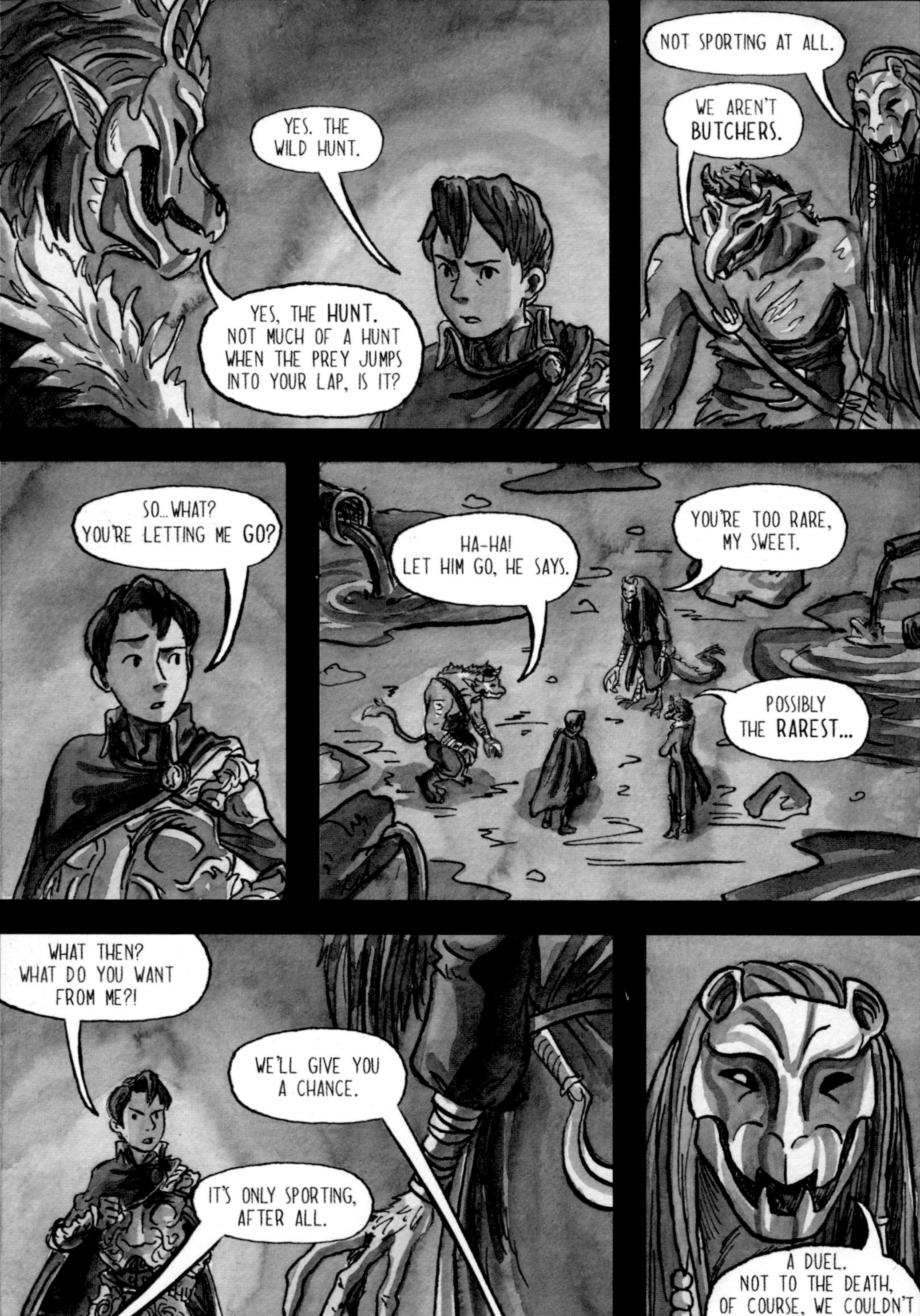
YES. THE WILD HUNT.
YES, THE HUNT. NOT MUCH OF A HUNT WHEN THE PREY JUMPS INTO YOUR LAP, IS IT?
NOT SPORTING AT ALL.
WE AREN'T BUTCHERS.
SO... WHAT? YOU'RE LETTING ME GO?
HA-HA! LET HIM GO, HE SAYS.
YOU'RE TOO RARE, MY SWEET.
POSSIBLY THE RAREST...
WHAT THEN? WHAT DO YOU WANT FROM ME?!
WE'LL GIVE YOU A CHANCE.
IT'S ONLY SPORTING, AFTER ALL.
A DUEL. NOT TO THE DEATH, OF COURSE, WE COULDN'T KILL SOMETHING AS PRECIOUS AS YOU.

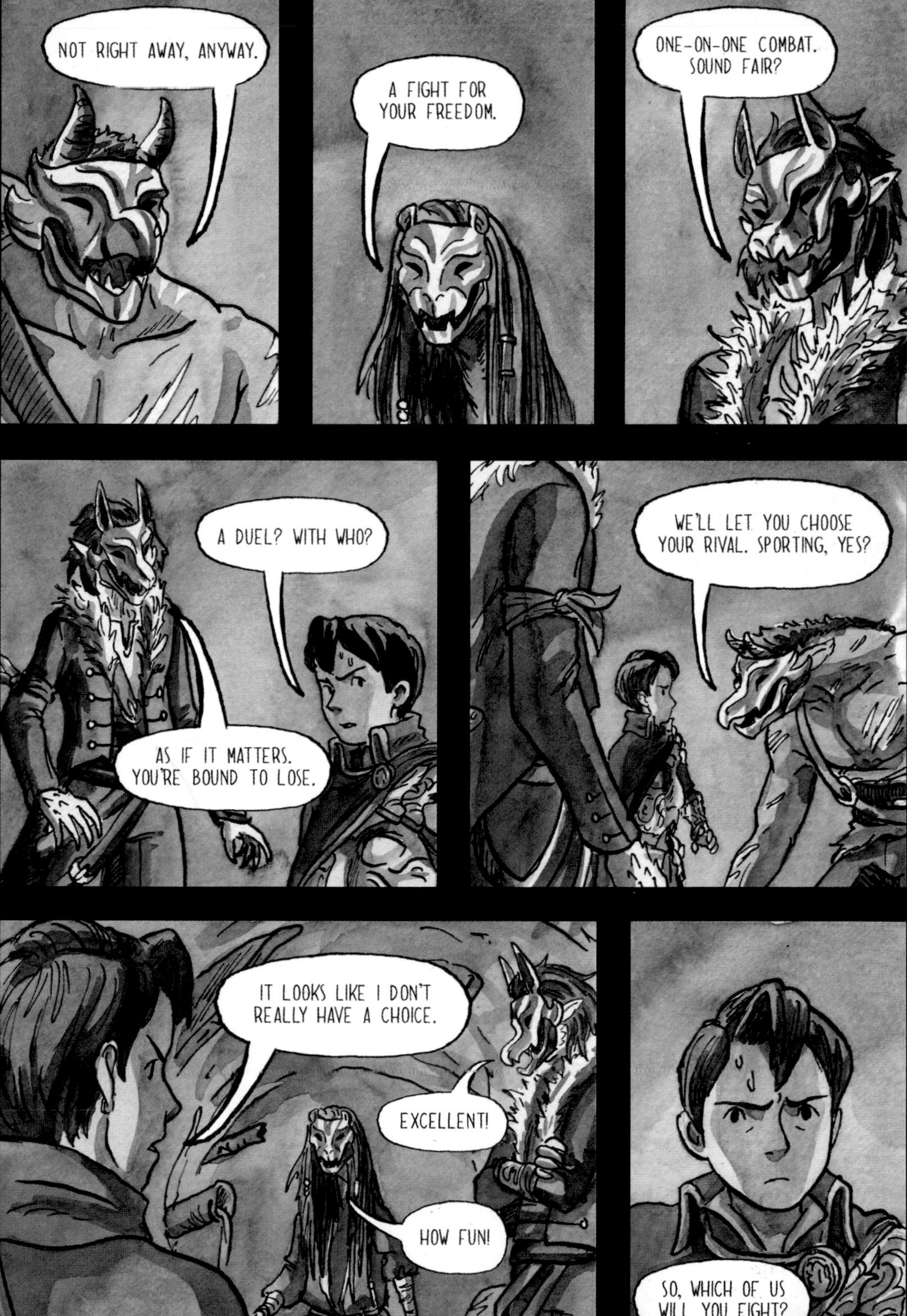
NOT RIGHT AWAY, ANYWAY.
A FIGHT FOR YOUR FREEDOM.
ONE-ON-ONE COMBAT. SOUND FAIR?
A DUEL? WITH WHO?
AS IF IT MATTERS. YOU'RE BOUND TO LOSE.
WE'LL LET YOU CHOOSE YOUR RIVAL. SPORTING, YES?
IT LOOKS LIKE I DON'T REALLY HAVE A CHOICE.
EXCELLENT!
HOW FUN!
SO, WHICH OF US WILL YOU FIGHT?

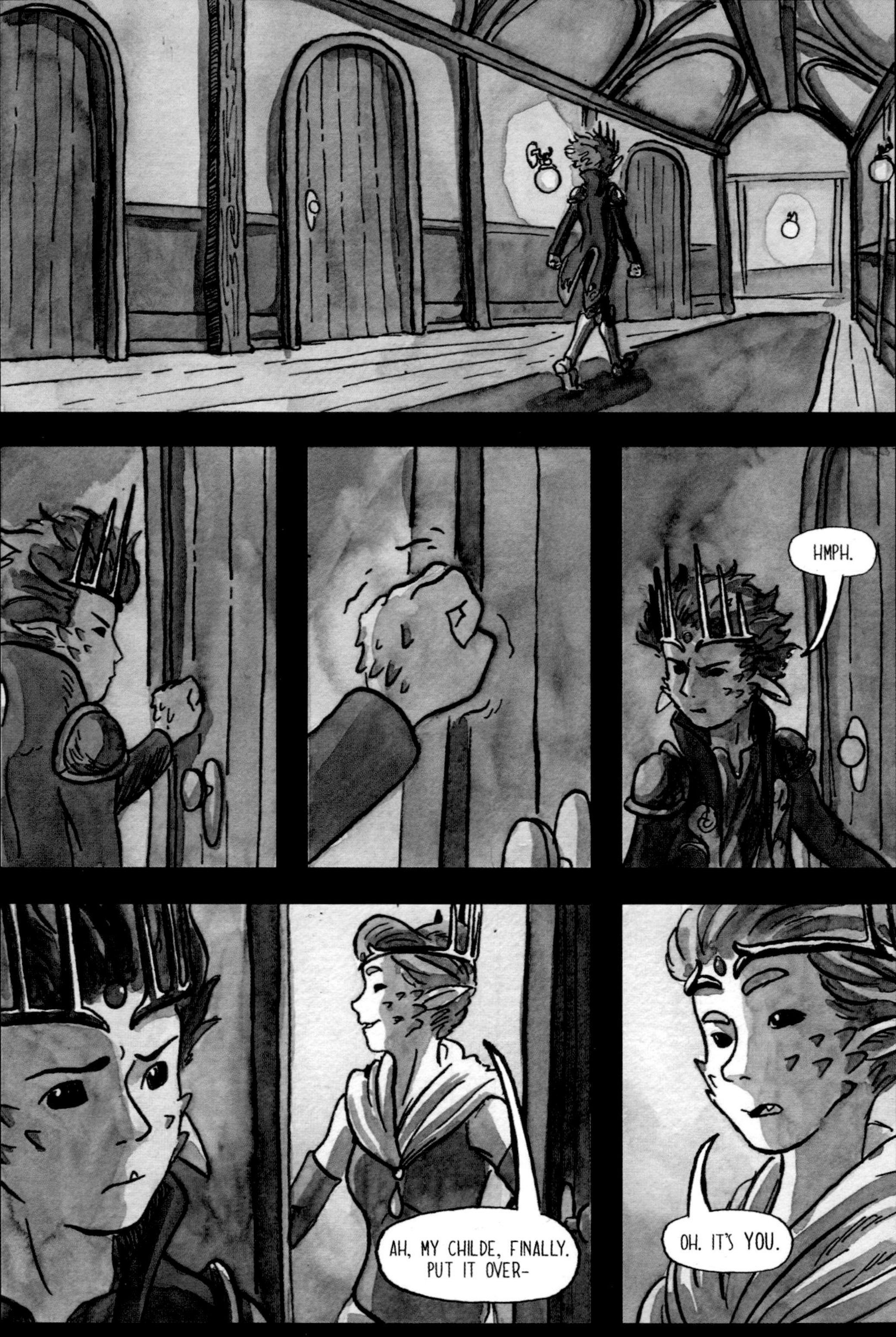
HMPH.
AH, MY CHILDE, FINALLY. PUT IT OVER-
OH. IT'S YOU.

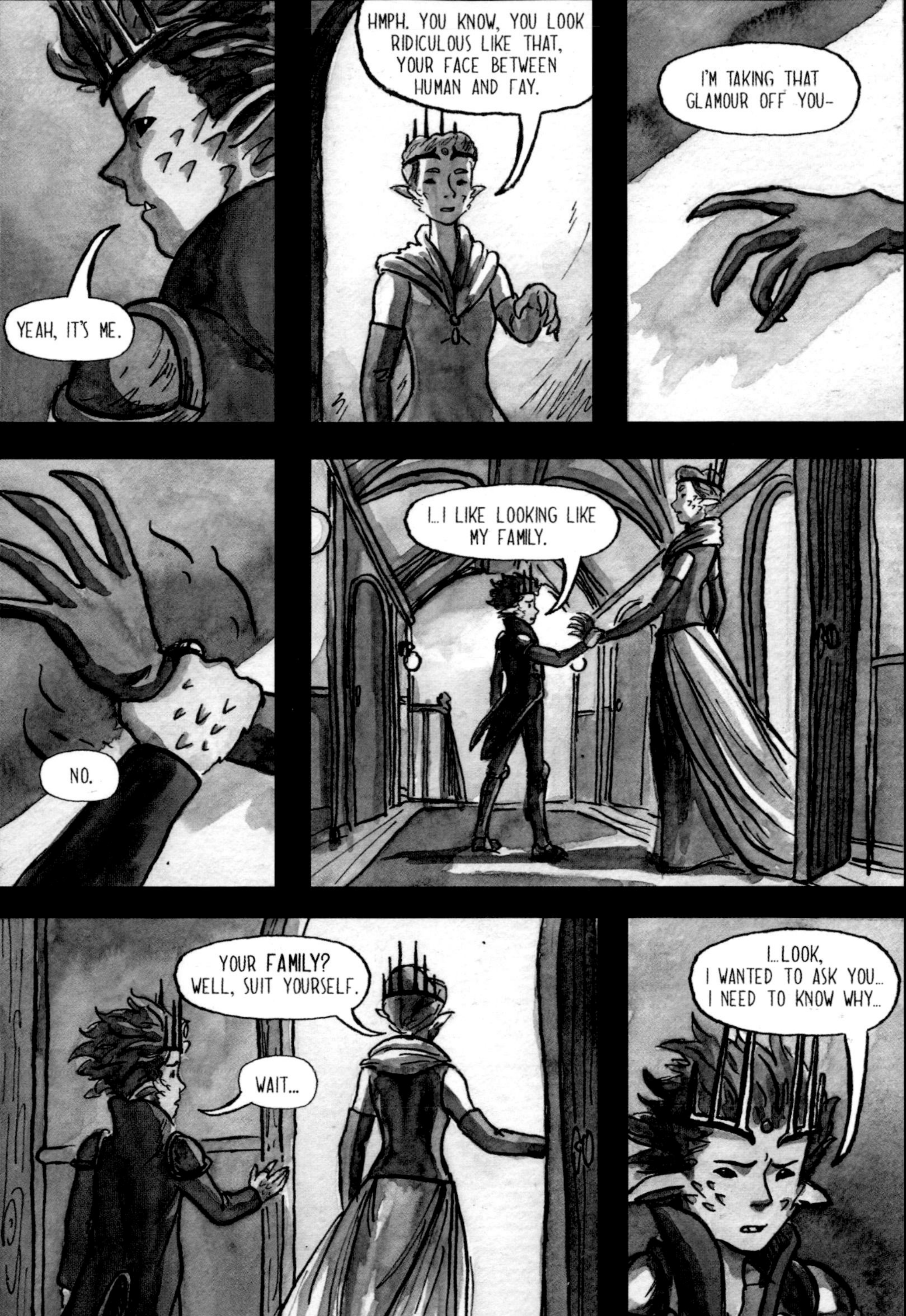
YEAH, IT'S ME.
HMPH. YOU KNOW, YOU LOOK RIDICULOUS LIKE THAT, YOUR FACE BETWEEN HUMAN AND FAY.
I'M TAKING THAT GLAMOUR OFF YOU-
NO.
I...I LIKE LOOKING LIKE MY FAMILY.
YOUR FAMILY? WELL, SUIT YOURSELF.
WAIT...
I...LOOK, I WANTED TO ASK YOU... I NEED TO KNOW WHY...

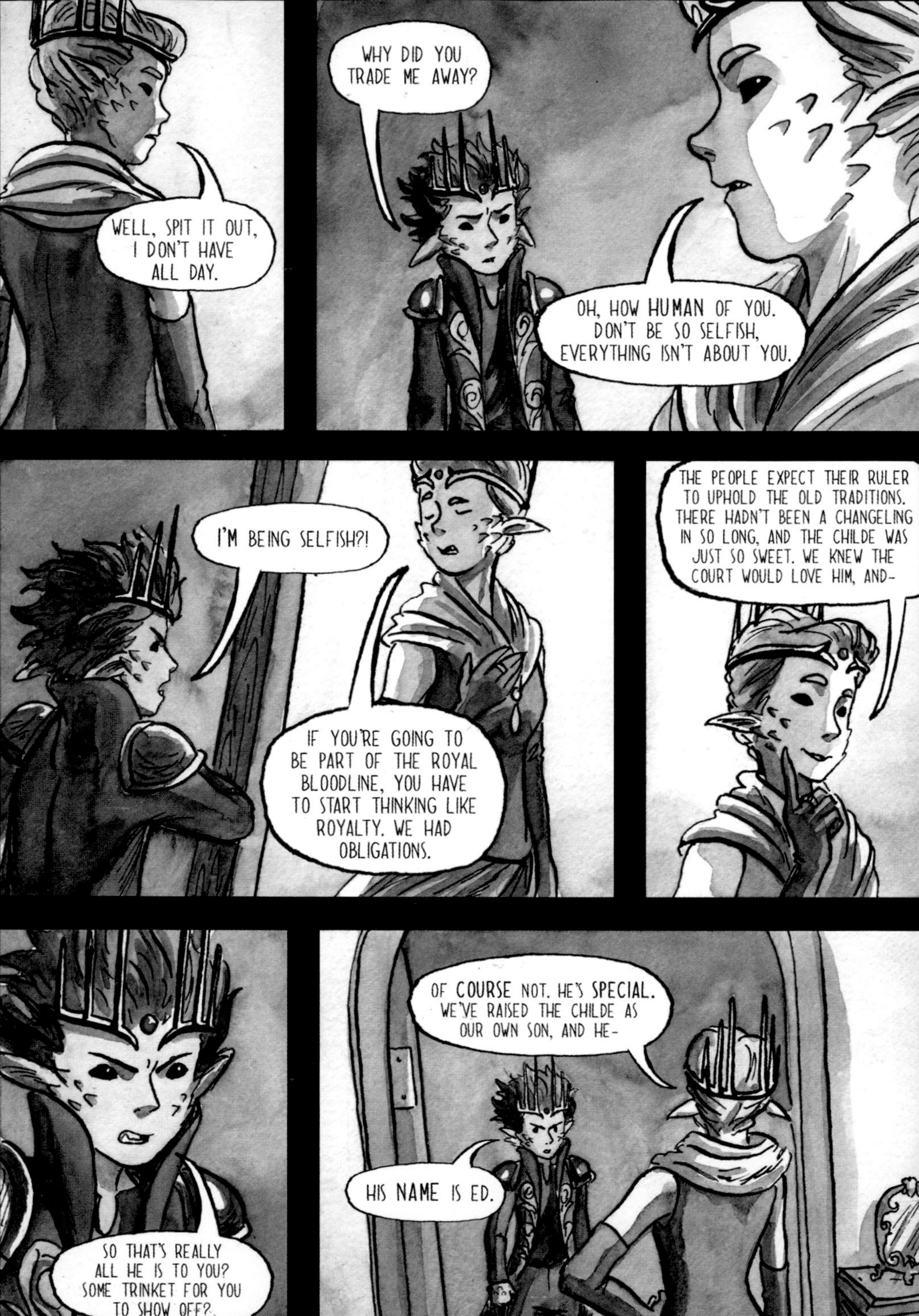

WELL, SPIT IT OUT, I DON'T HAVE ALL DAY.
WHY DID YOU TRADE ME AWAY?
OH, HOW HUMAN OF YOU. DON'T BE SO SELFISH, EVERYTHING ISN'T ABOUT YOU.
I'M BEING SELFISH?!
IF YOU'RE GOING TO BE PART OF THE ROYAL BLOODLINE, YOU HAVE TO START THINKING LIKE ROYALTY. WE HAD OBLIGATIONS.
THE PEOPLE EXPECT THEIR RULER TO UPHOLD THE OLD TRADITIONS. THERE HADN'T BEEN A CHANGELING IN SO LONG, AND THE CHILDE WAS JUST SO SWEET. WE KNEW THE COURT WOULD LOVE HIM, AND-
SO THAT'S REALLY ALL HE IS TO YOU? SOME TRINKET FOR YOU TO SHOW OFF?
OF COURSE NOT. HE'S SPECIAL. WE'VE RAISED THE CHILDE AS OUR OWN SON, AND HE-
HIS NAME IS ED.

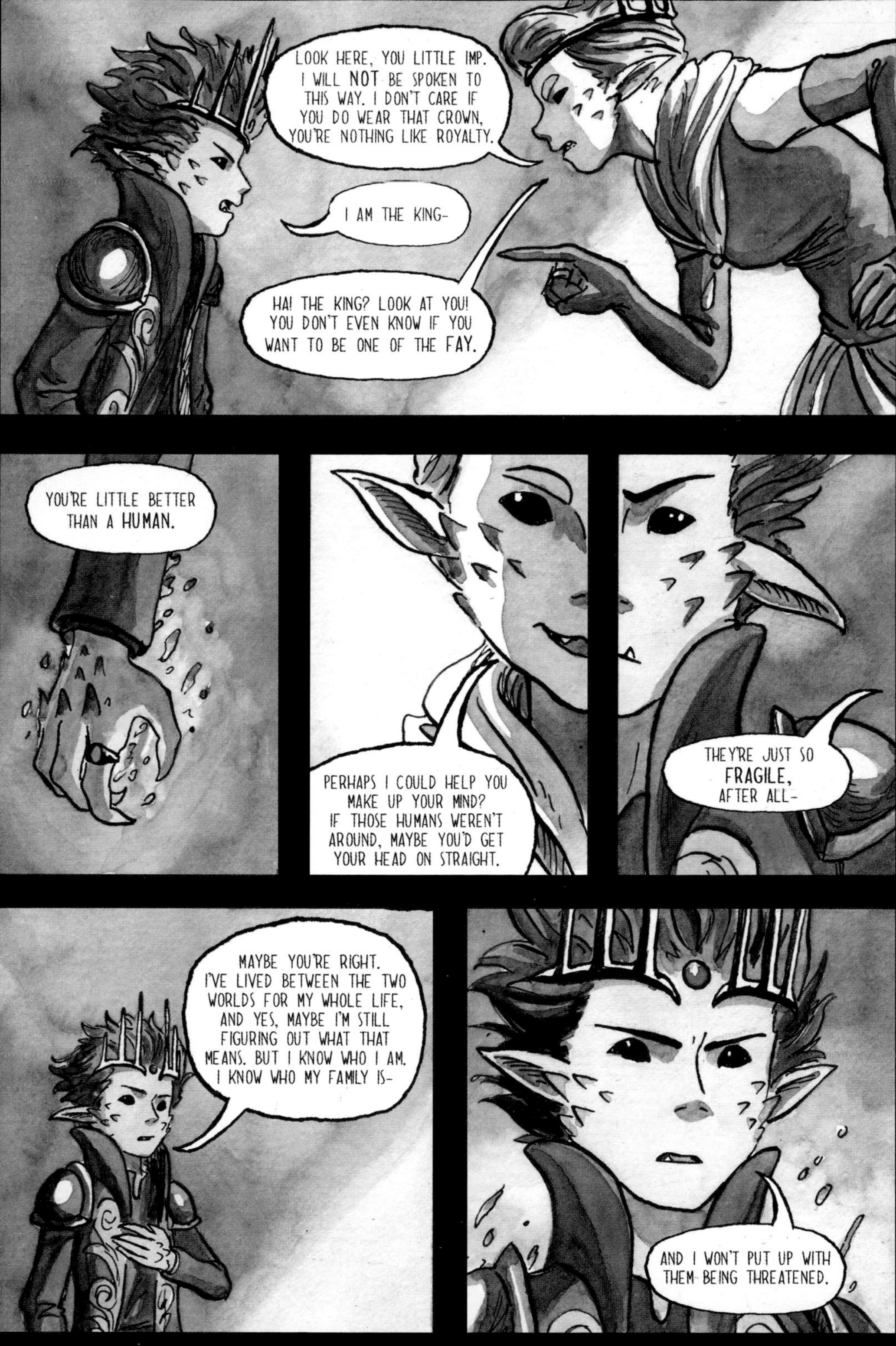

LOOK HERE, YOU LITTLE IMP. I WILL NOT BE SPOKEN TO THIS WAY. I DON'T CARE IF YOU DO WEAR THAT CROWN, YOU'RE NOTHING LIKE ROYALTY.
I AM THE KING-
HA! THE KING? LOOK AT YOU! YOU DON'T EVEN KNOW IF YOU WANT TO BE ONE OF THE FAY.
YOU'RE LITTLE BETTER THAN A HUMAN.
PERHAPS I COULD HELP YOU MAKE UP YOUR MIND? IF THOSE HUMANS WEREN'T AROUND, MAYBE YOU'D GET YOUR HEAD ON STRAIGHT.
THEY'RE JUST SO FRAGILE, AFTER ALL-
MAYBE YOU'RE RIGHT. I'VE LIVED BETWEEN THE TWO WORLDS FOR MY WHOLE LIFE, AND YES, MAYBE I'M STILL FIGURING OUT WHAT THAT MEANS. BUT I KNOW WHO I AM. I KNOW WHO MY FAMILY IS-
AND I WON'T PUT UP WITH THEM BEING THREATENED.

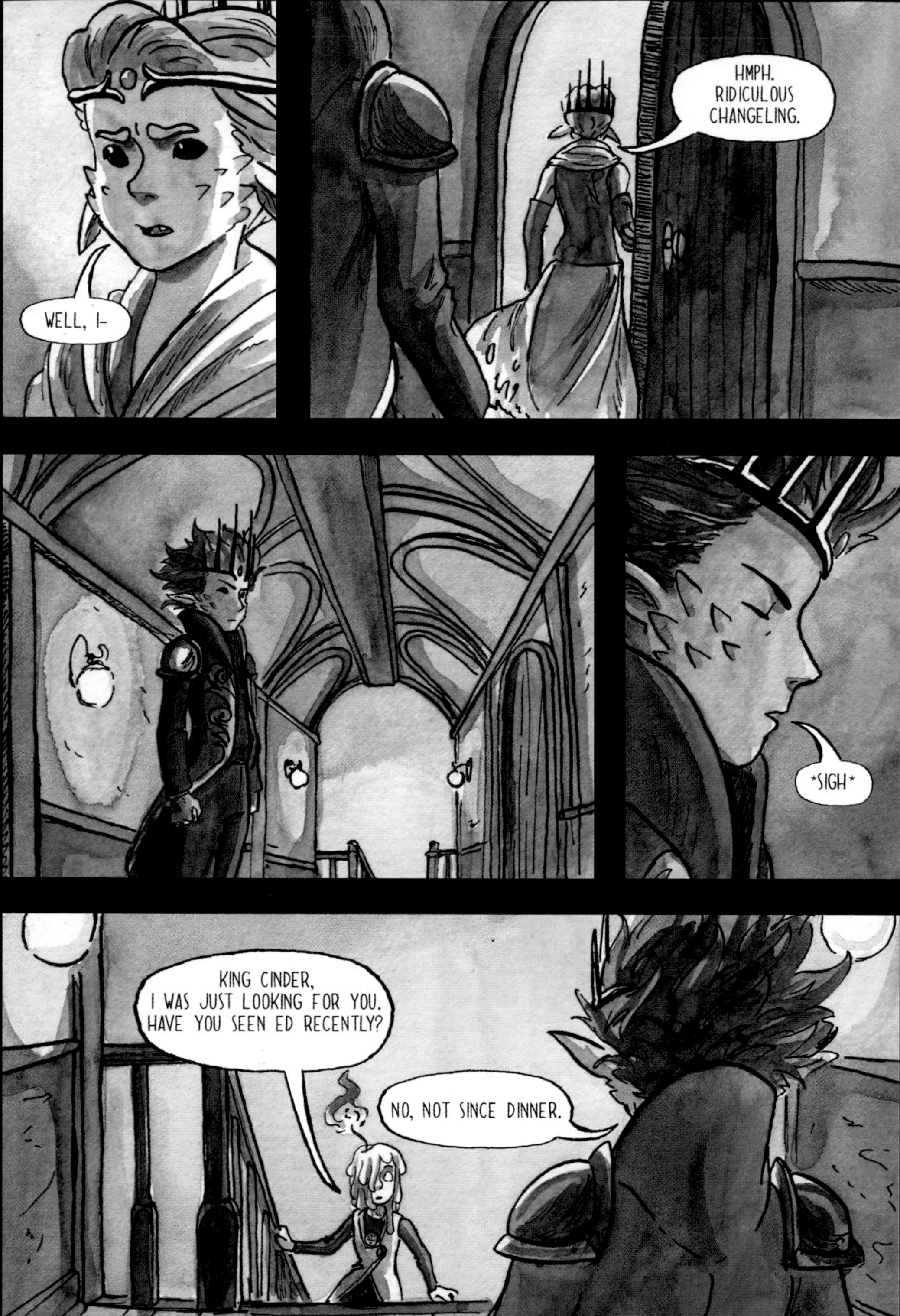
WELL, I-
HMPH. RIDICULOUS CHANGELING.
SIGH
KING CINDER, I WAS JUST LOOKING FOR YOU. HAVE YOU SEEN ED RECENTLY?
NO, NOT SINCE DINNER.

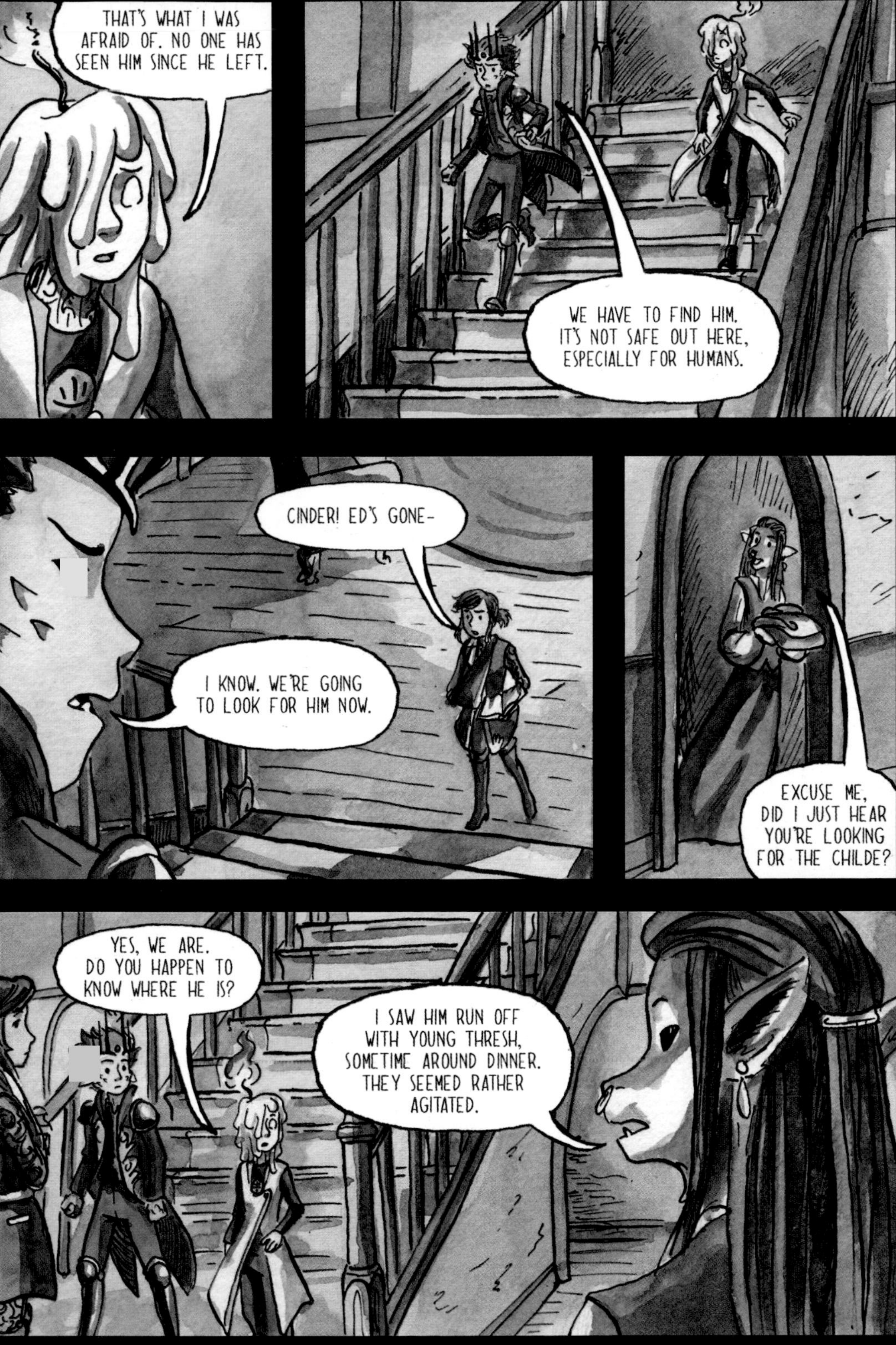
THAT'S WHAT I WAS AFRAID OF. NO ONE HAS SEEN HIM SINCE HE LEFT.
WE HAVE TO FIND HIM. IT'S NOT SAFE OUT HERE, ESPECIALLY FOR HUMANS.
CINDER! ED'S GONE-
I KNOW. WE'RE GOING TO LOOK FOR HIM NOW.
EXCUSE ME, DID I JUST HEAR YOU'RE LOOKING FOR THE CHILDE?
YES, WE ARE. DO YOU HAPPEN TO KNOW WHERE HE IS?
I SAW HIM RUN OFF WITH YOUNG THRESH, SOMETIME AROUND DINNER. THEY SEEMED RATHER AGITATED.

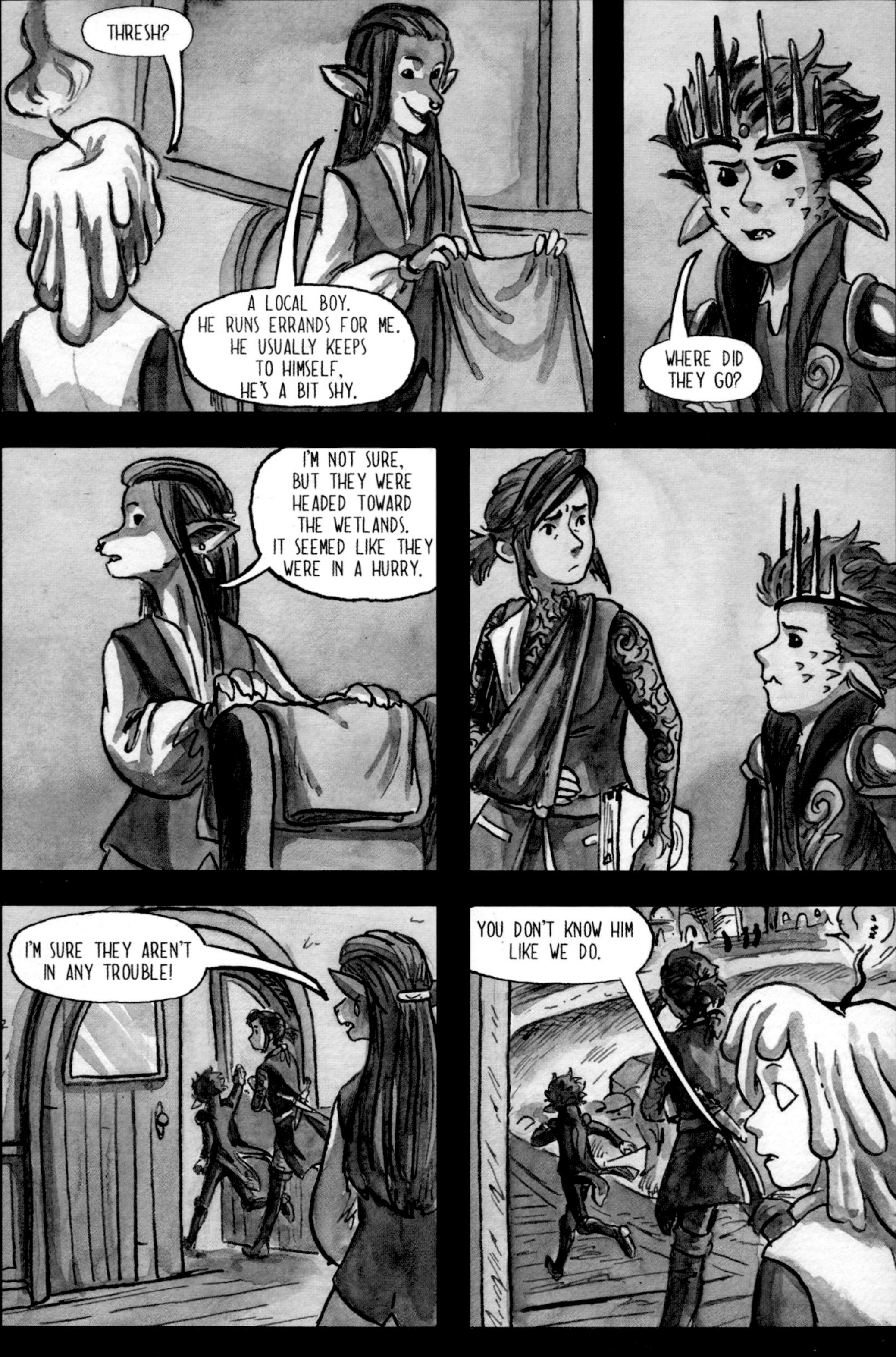
THRESH?
A LOCAL BOY. HE RUNS ERRANDS FOR ME. HE USUALLY KEEPS TO HIMSELF, HE'S A BIT SHY.
WHERE DID THEY GO?
I'M NOT SURE, BUT THEY WERE HEADED TOWARD THE WETLANDS. IT SEEMED LIKE THEY WERE IN A HURRY.
I'M SURE THEY AREN'T IN ANY TROUBLE!
YOU DON'T KNOW HIM LIKE WE DO.

Chapter Ten

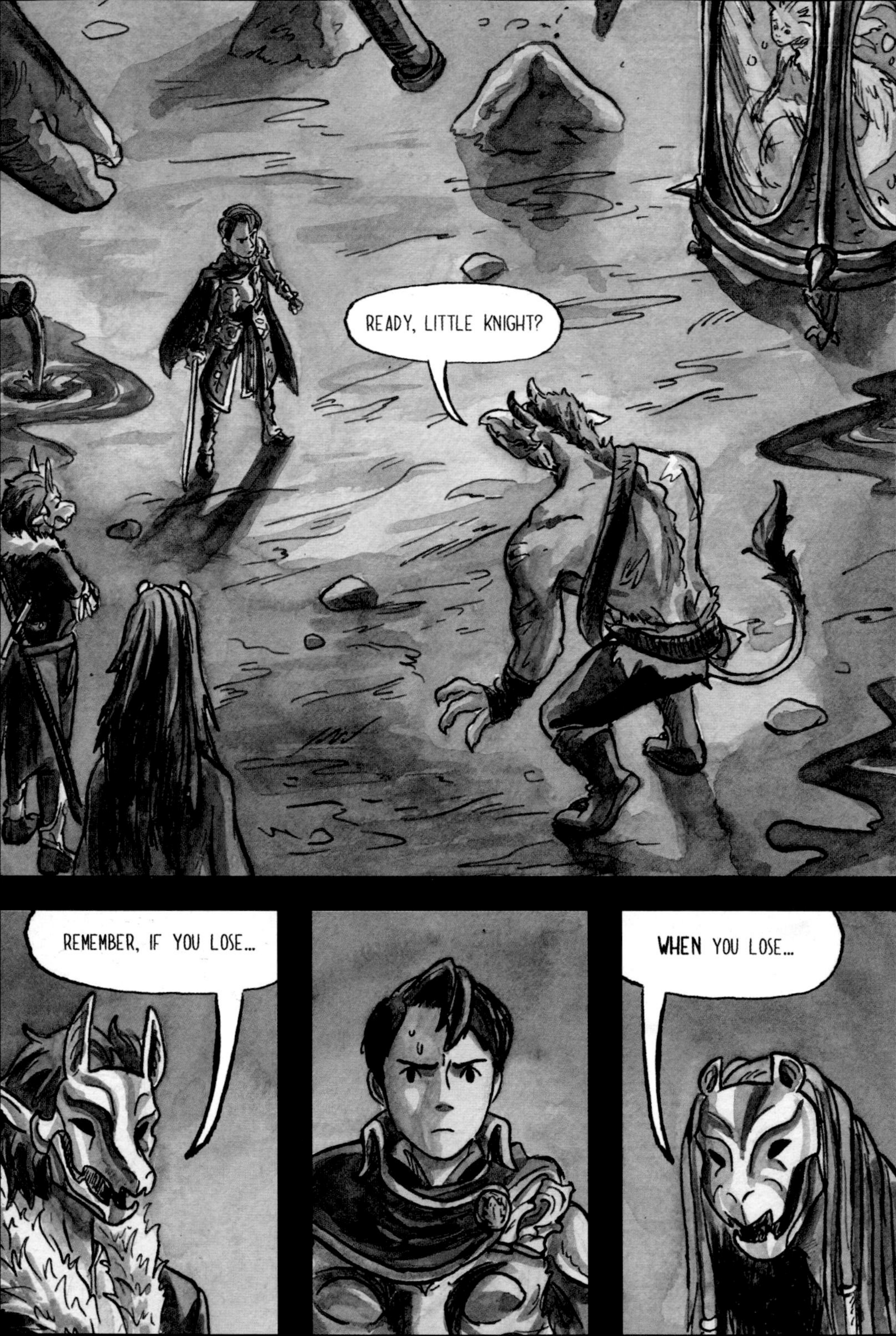
READY, LITTLE KNIGHT?
REMEMBER, IF YOU LOSE...
WHEN YOU LOSE...

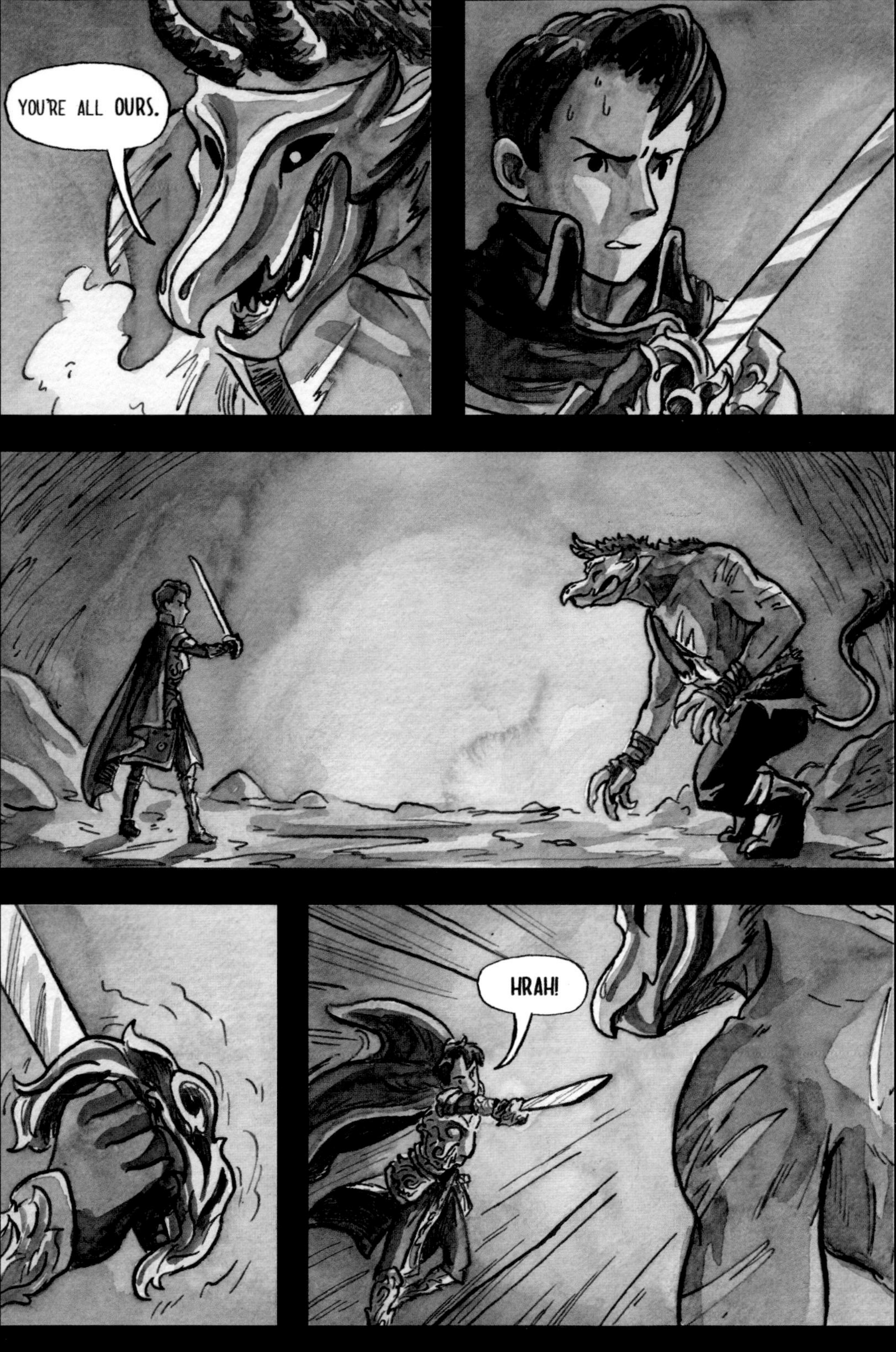
YOU'RE ALL OURS.
HRAH!

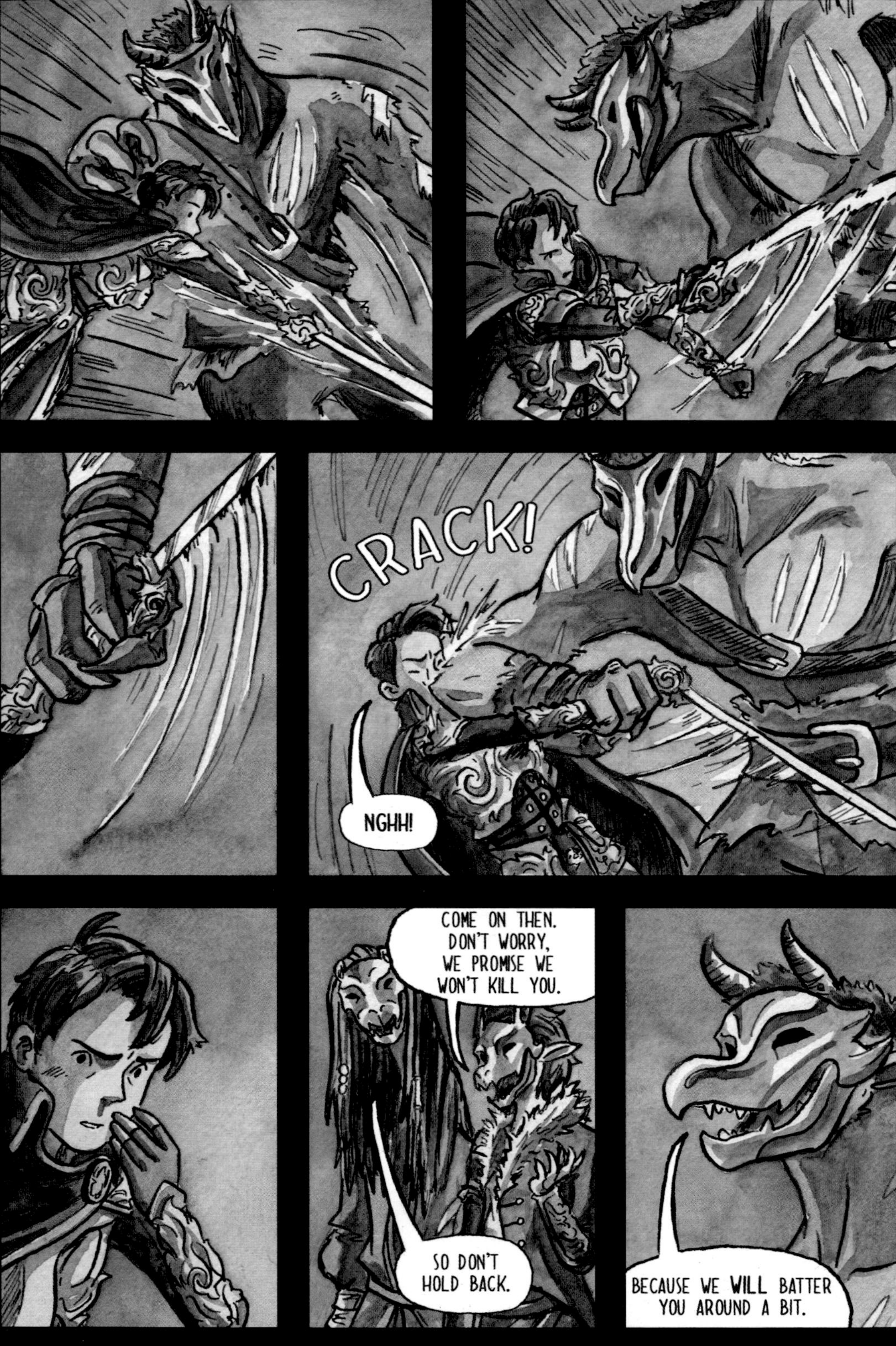
CRACK!
NGHH!
COME ON THEN. DON'T WORRY, WE PROMISE WE WON'T KILL YOU.
SO DON'T HOLD BACK.
BECAUSE WE WILL BATTER YOU AROUND A BIT.

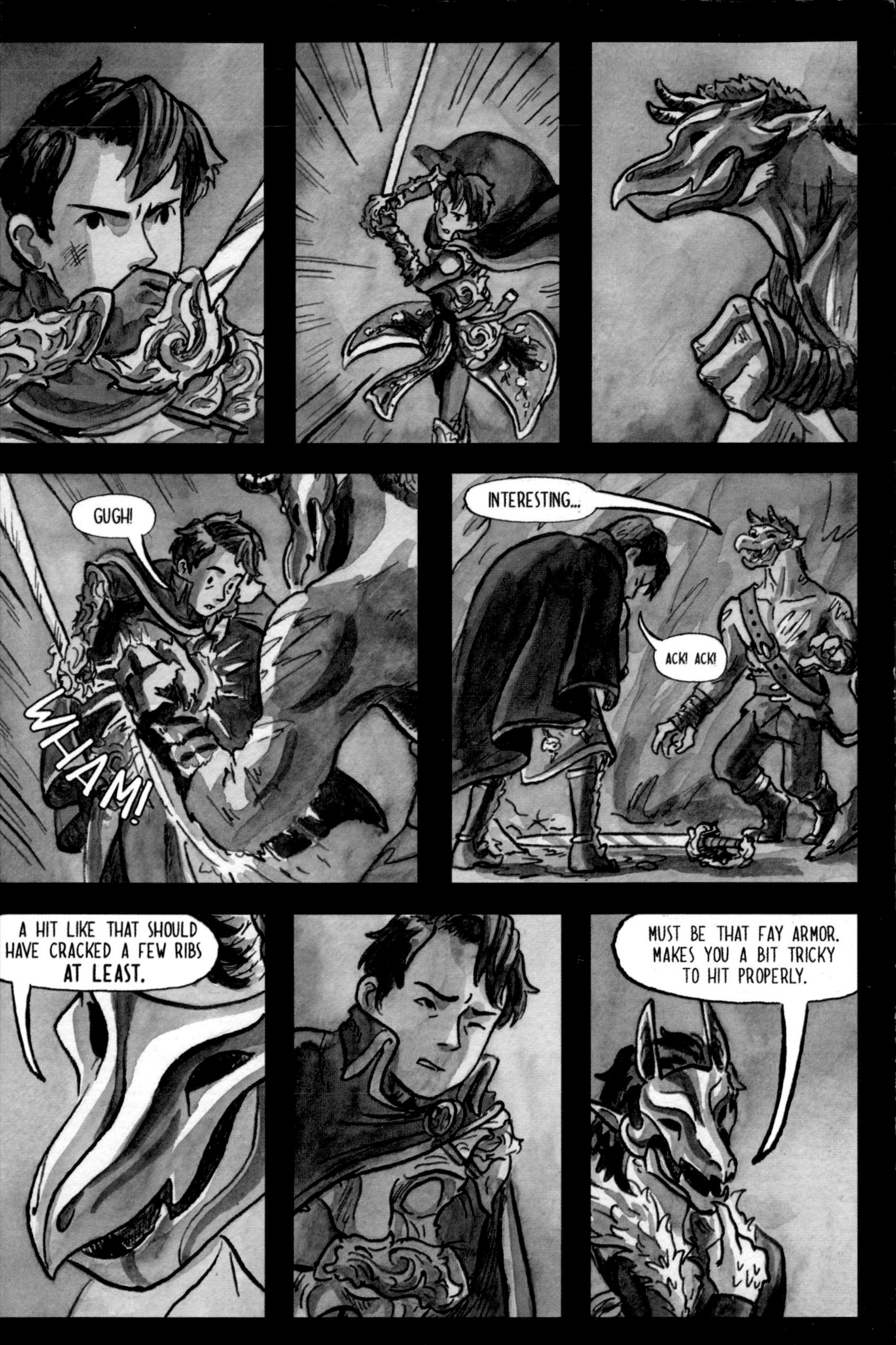
GUGH!
WHAM!
INTERESTING...
ACK! ACK!
A HIT LIKE THAT SHOULD HAVE CRACKED A FEW RIBS AT LEAST.
MUST BE THAT FAY ARMOR. MAKES YOU A BIT TRICKY TO HIT PROPERLY.

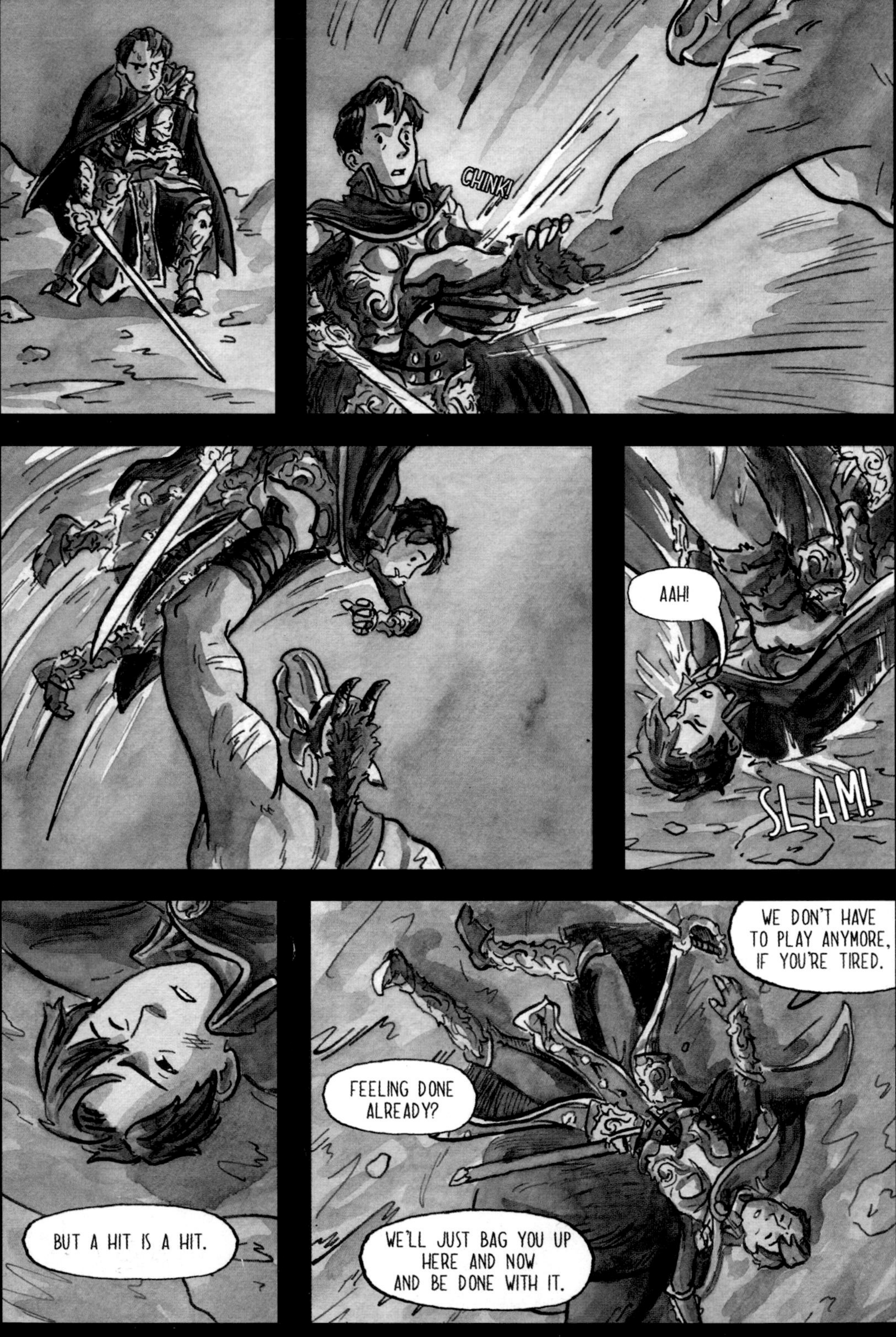
CHINK!
AAH!
SLAM!
BUT A HIT IS A HIT.
WE DON'T HAVE TO PLAY ANYMORE, IF YOU'RE TIRED.
FEELING DONE ALREADY?
WE'LL JUST BAG YOU UP HERE AND NOW AND BE DONE WITH IT.

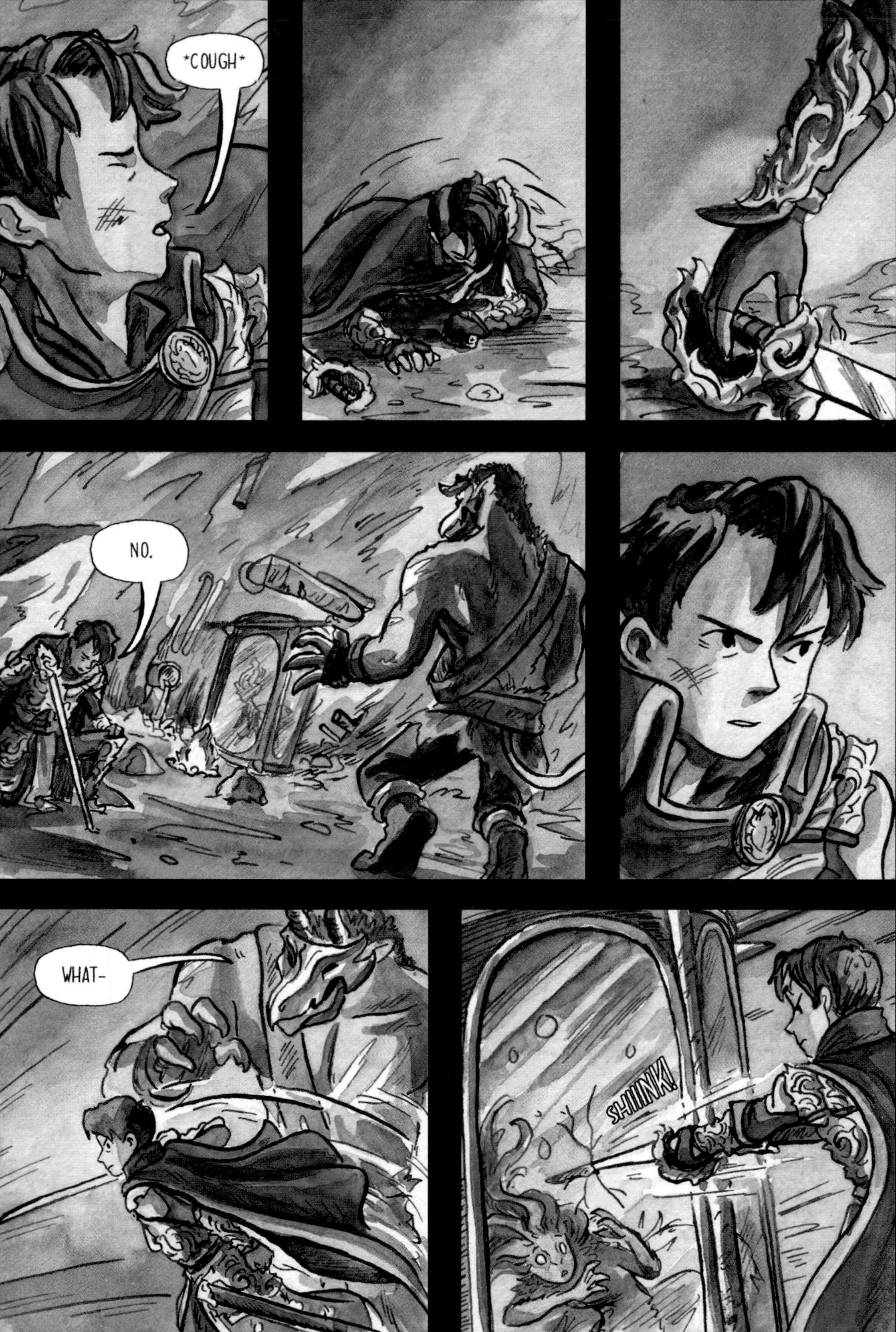
COUGH
NO.
WHAT-
SHIIINK!

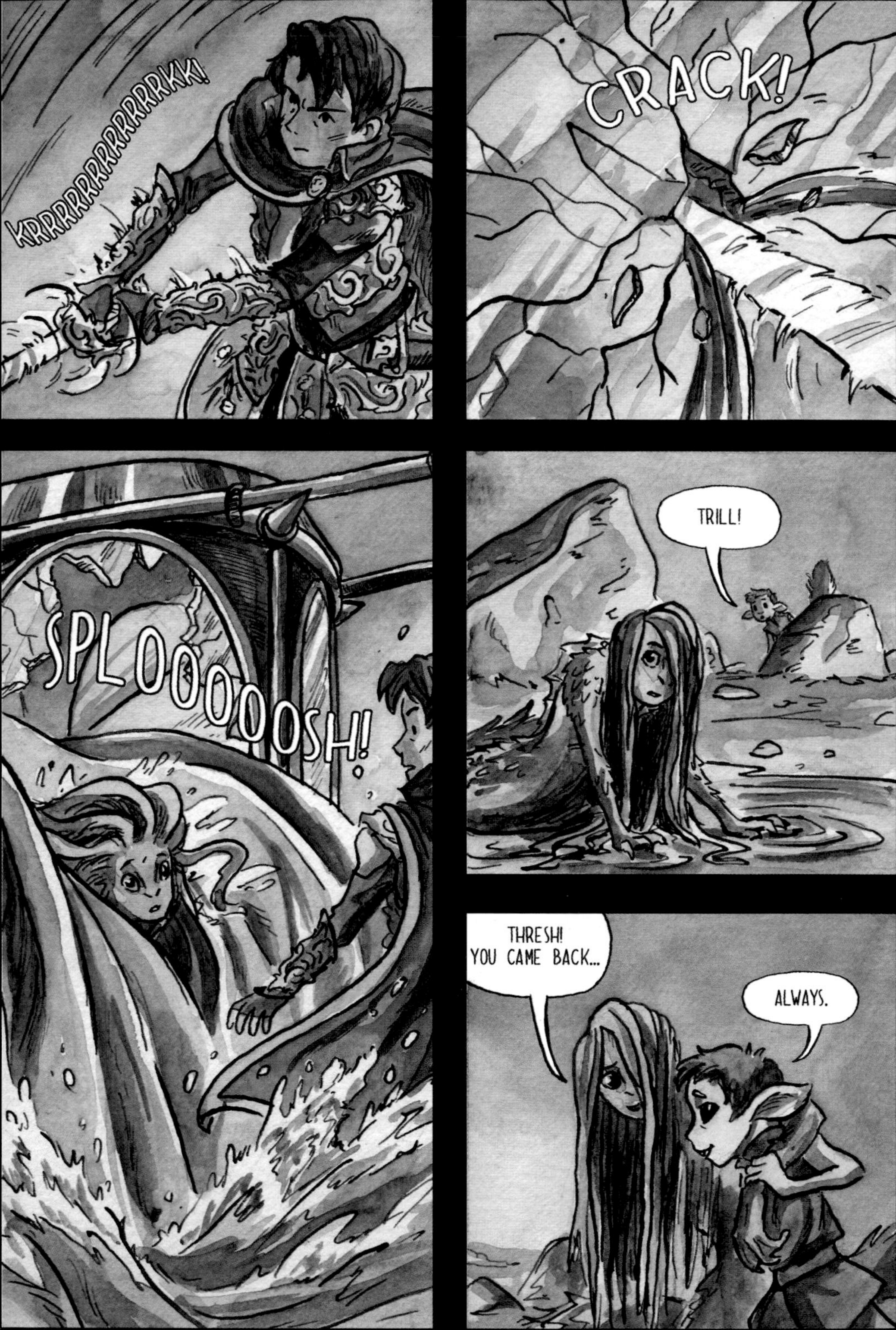

KRRRRRRRRRRRRRKK!
CRACK!
SPLOOOOOOSH!
TRILL!
THRESH! YOU CAME BACK...
ALWAYS.

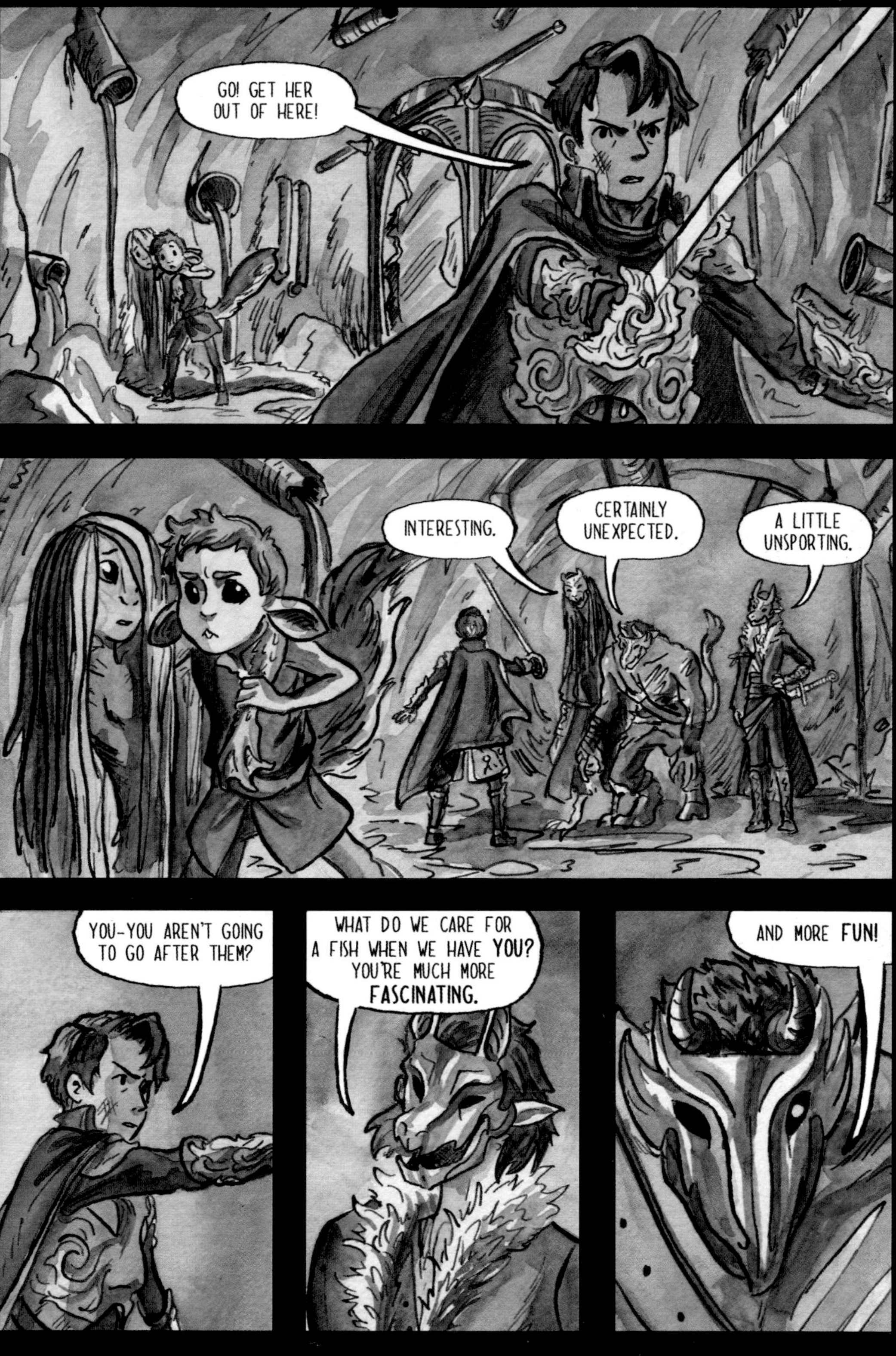
GO! GET HER OUT OF HERE!
INTERESTING.
CERTAINLY UNEXPECTED.
A LITTLE UNSPORTING.
YOU-YOU AREN'T GOING TO GO AFTER THEM?
WHAT DO WE CARE FOR A FISH WHEN WE HAVE YOU? YOU'RE MUCH MORE FASCINATING.
AND MORE FUN!

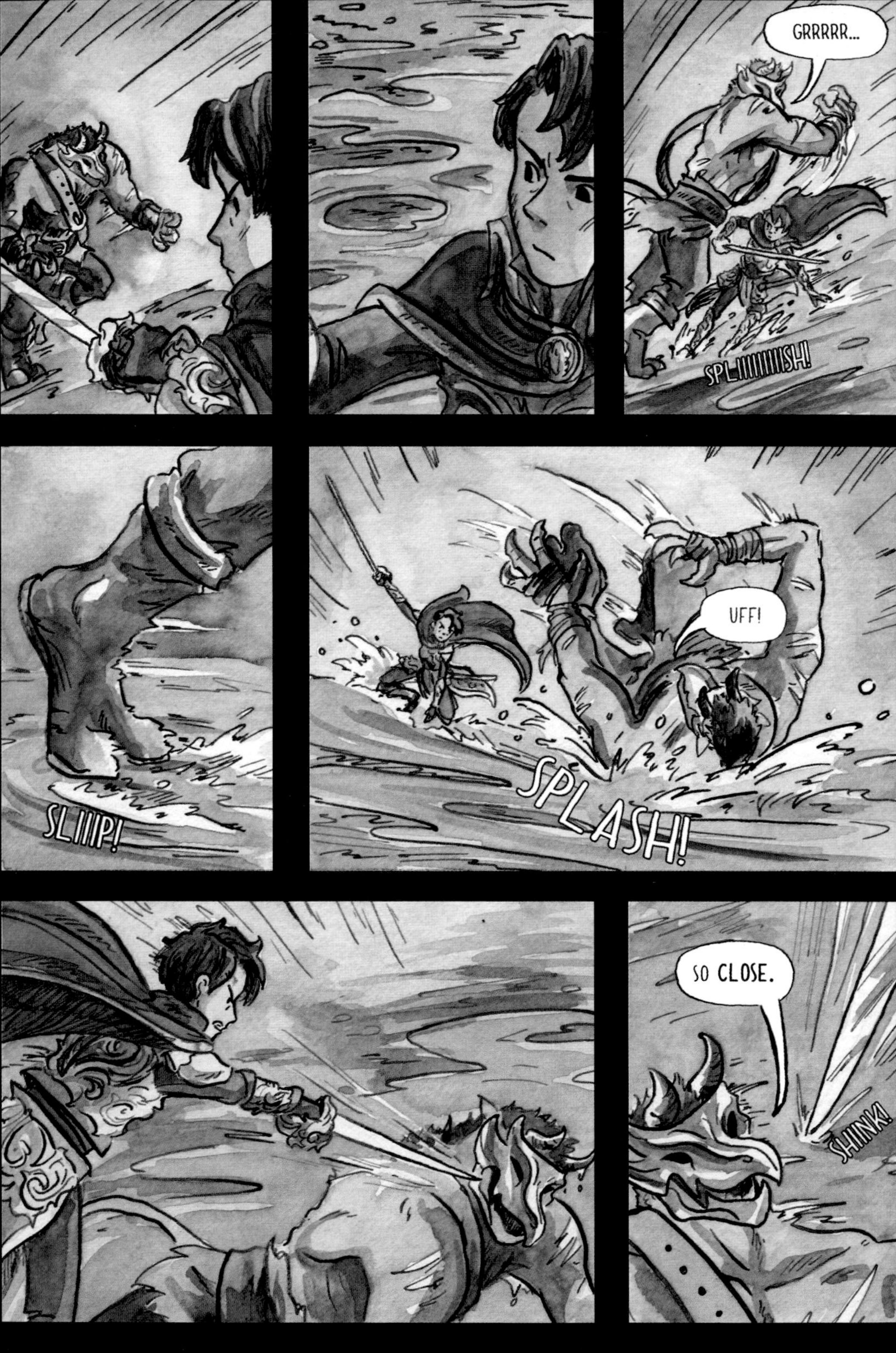
GRRRRR...
SPLIIIIIIIISH!
SLIIIP!
UFF!
SPLASH!
SO CLOSE.
SHINK!

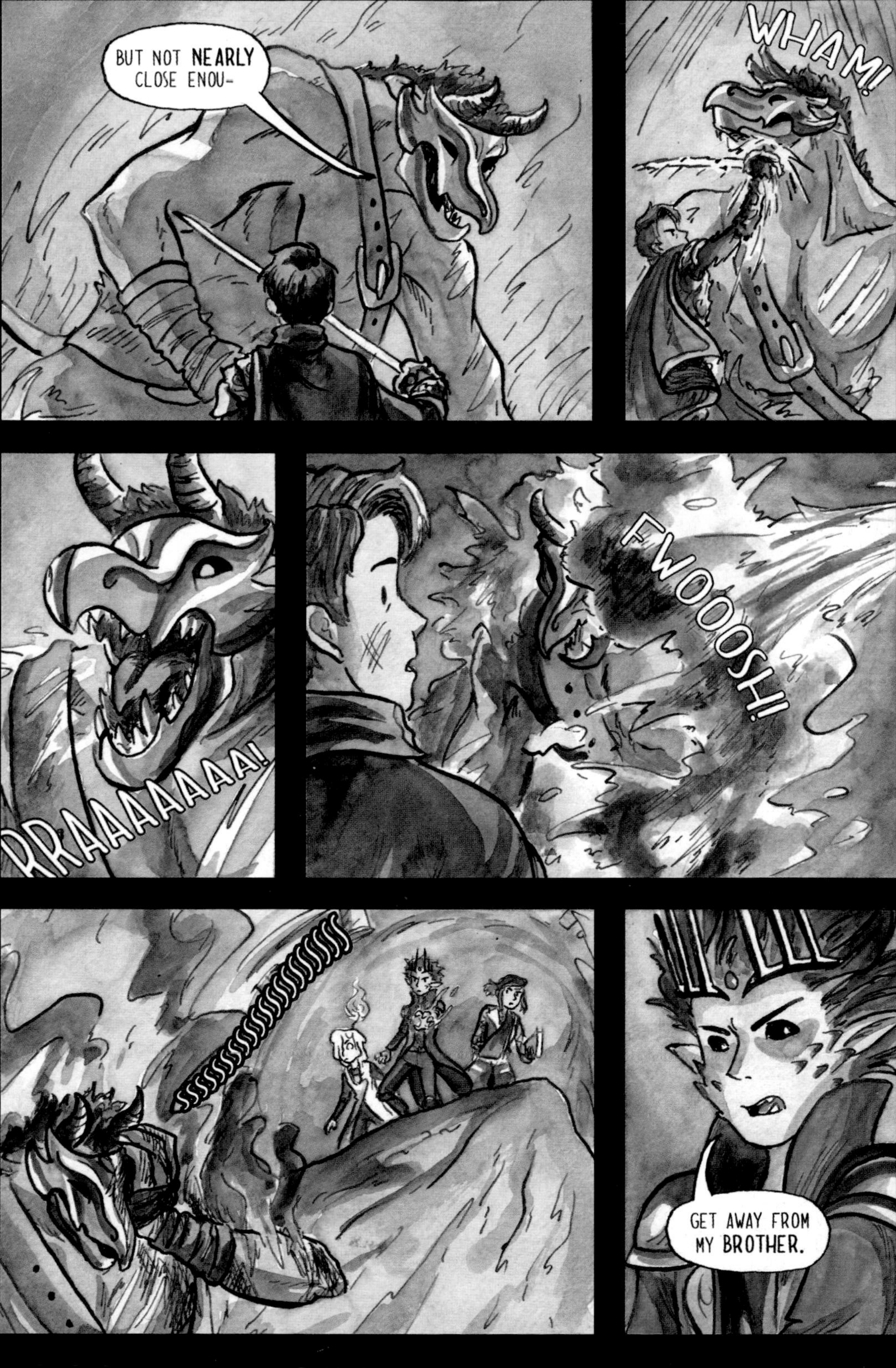

BUT NOT **NEARLY** CLOSE ENOU-
WHAM!
RRAAAAAAAA!
FWOOOOSH!
SSSSSSSSSSSSSSSSS
GET AWAY FROM MY **BROTHER.**

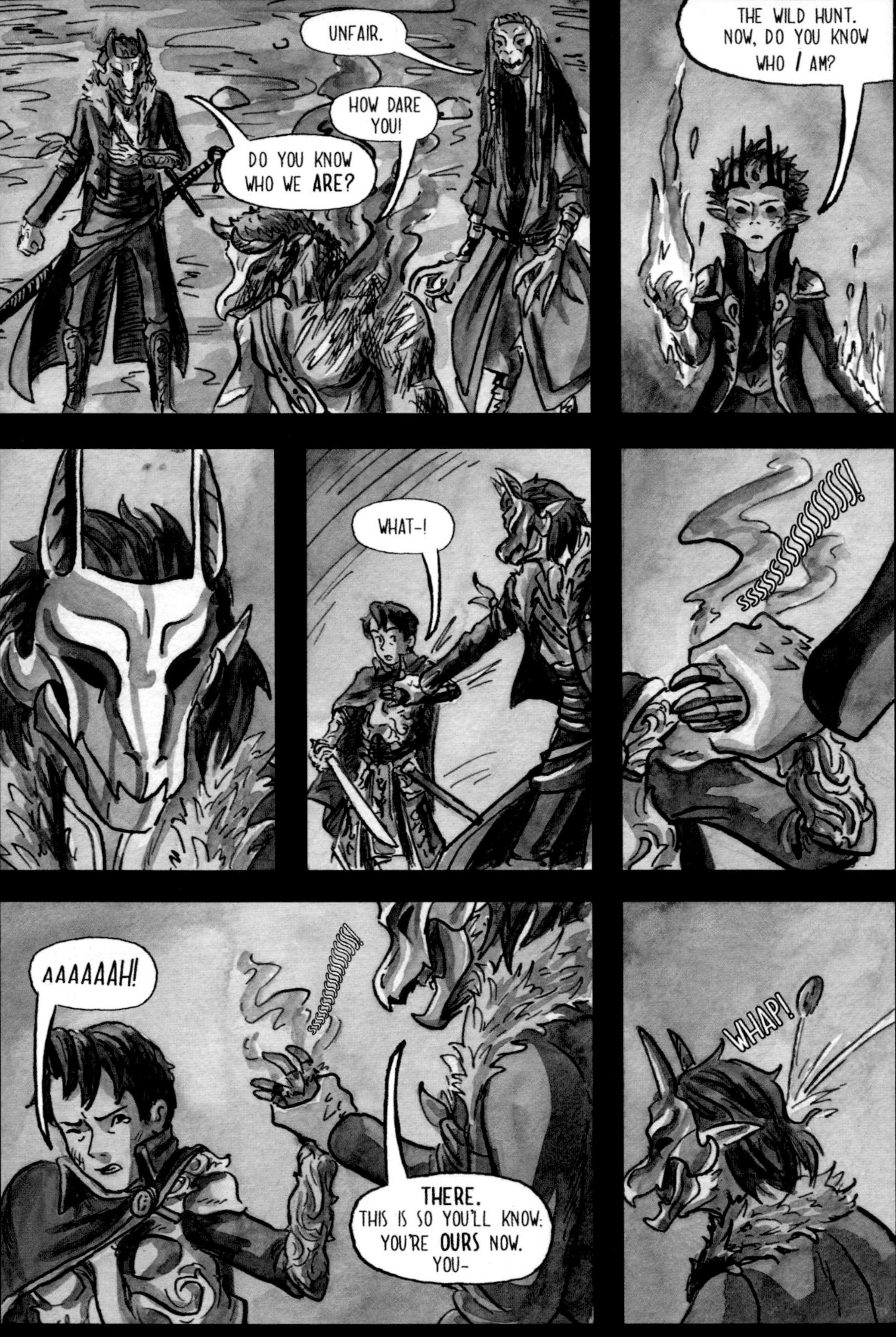
UNFAIR.
HOW DARE YOU!
DO YOU KNOW WHO WE ARE?
THE WILD HUNT. NOW, DO YOU KNOW WHO I AM?
WHAT-!
SSSSSSSSSSSSSS!
AAAAAAH!
SSSSSSSSSSSSSS!
THERE. THIS IS SO YOU'LL KNOW; YOU'RE OURS NOW. YOU-
WHAP!

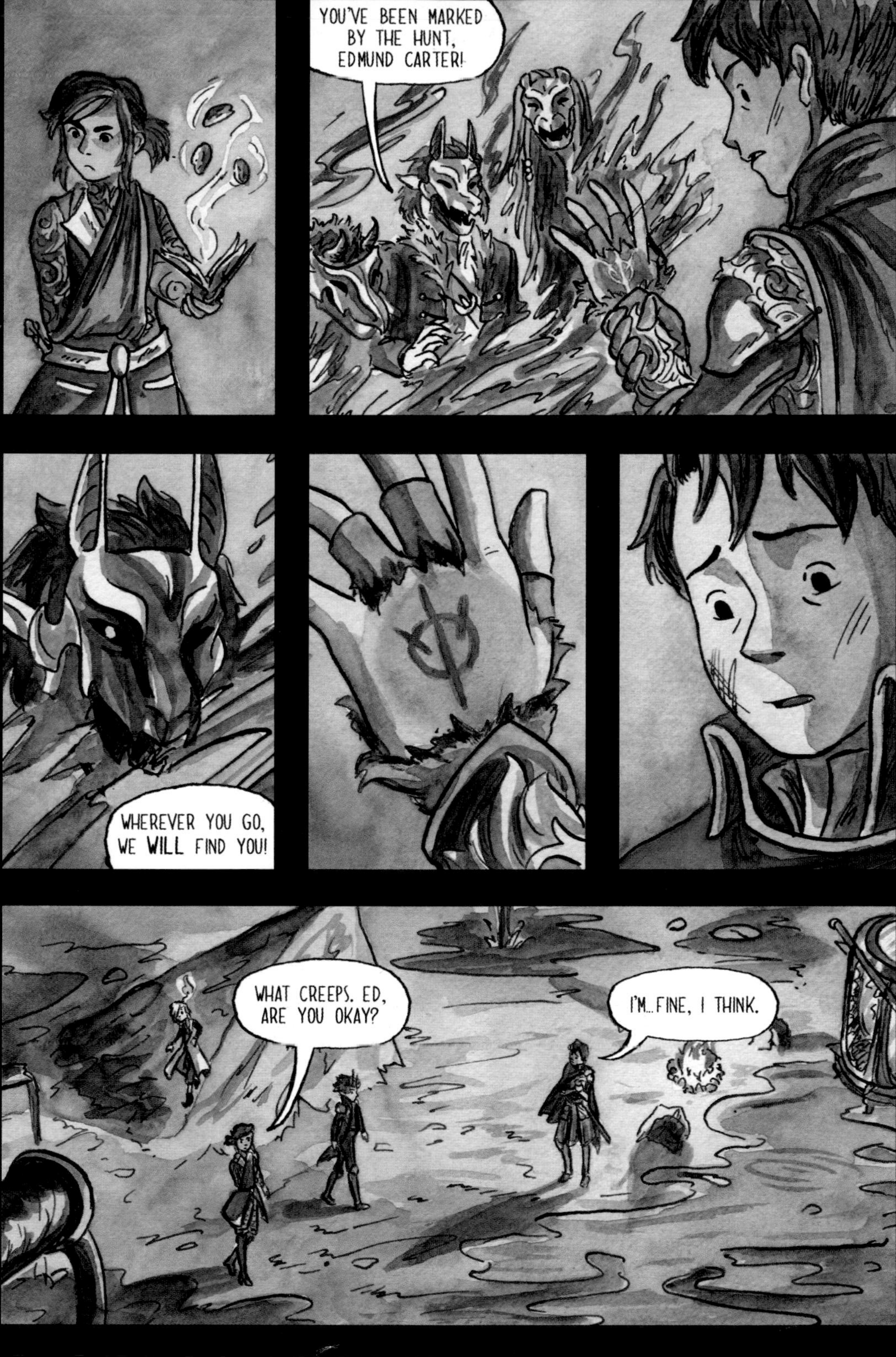
YOU'VE BEEN MARKED BY THE HUNT, EDMUND CARTER!
WHEREVER YOU GO, WE WILL FIND YOU!
WHAT CREEPS. ED, ARE YOU OKAY?
I'M...FINE, I THINK.

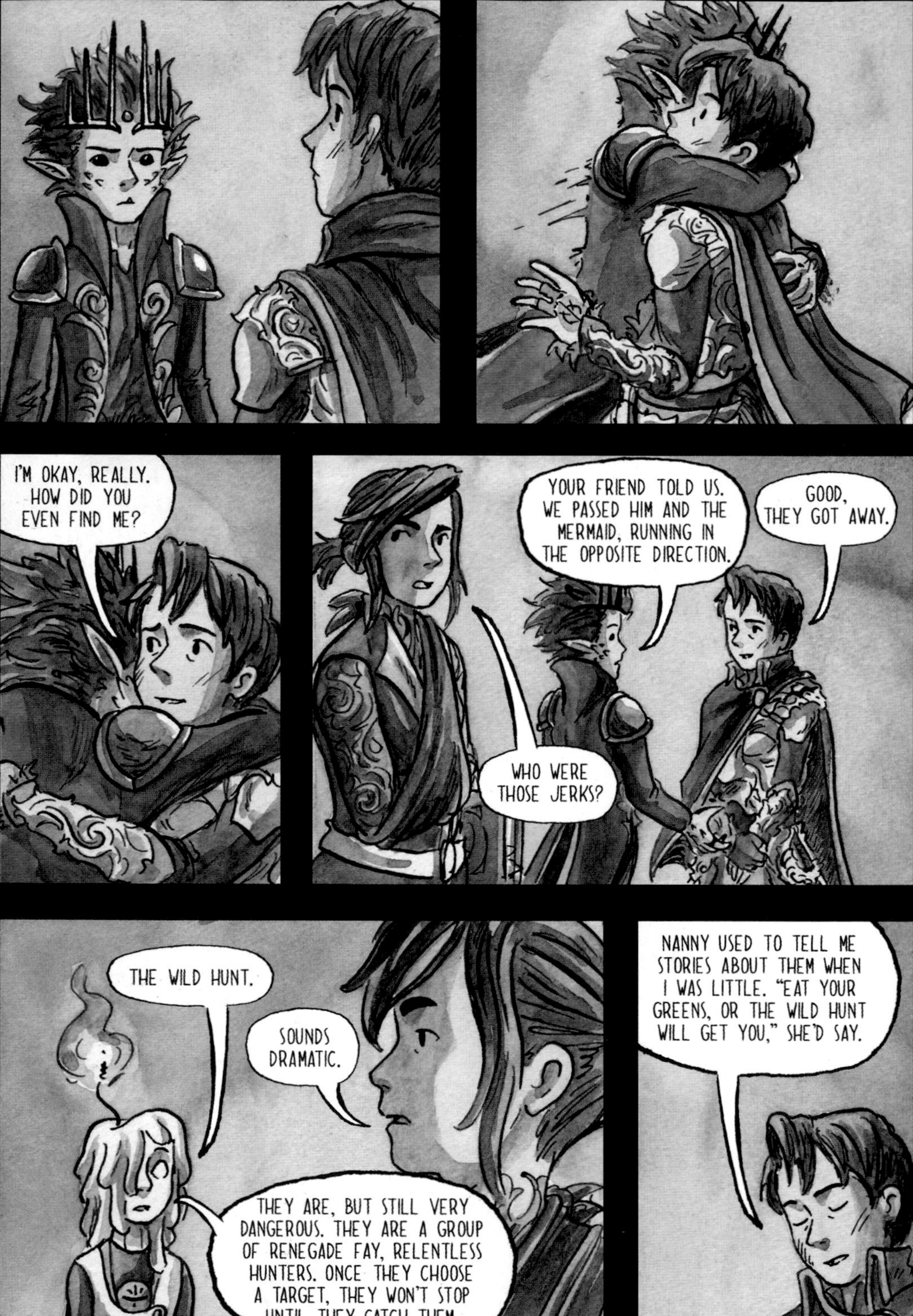
I'M OKAY, REALLY. HOW DID YOU EVEN FIND ME?
YOUR FRIEND TOLD US. WE PASSED HIM AND THE MERMAID, RUNNING IN THE OPPOSITE DIRECTION.
GOOD, THEY GOT AWAY.
WHO WERE THOSE JERKS?
THE WILD HUNT.
SOUNDS DRAMATIC.
THEY ARE, BUT STILL VERY DANGEROUS. THEY ARE A GROUP OF RENEGADE FAY, RELENTLESS HUNTERS. ONCE THEY CHOOSE A TARGET, THEY WON'T STOP UNTIL THEY CATCH THEM.
NANNY USED TO TELL ME STORIES ABOUT THEM WHEN I WAS LITTLE. "EAT YOUR GREENS, OR THE WILD HUNT WILL GET YOU," SHE'D SAY.

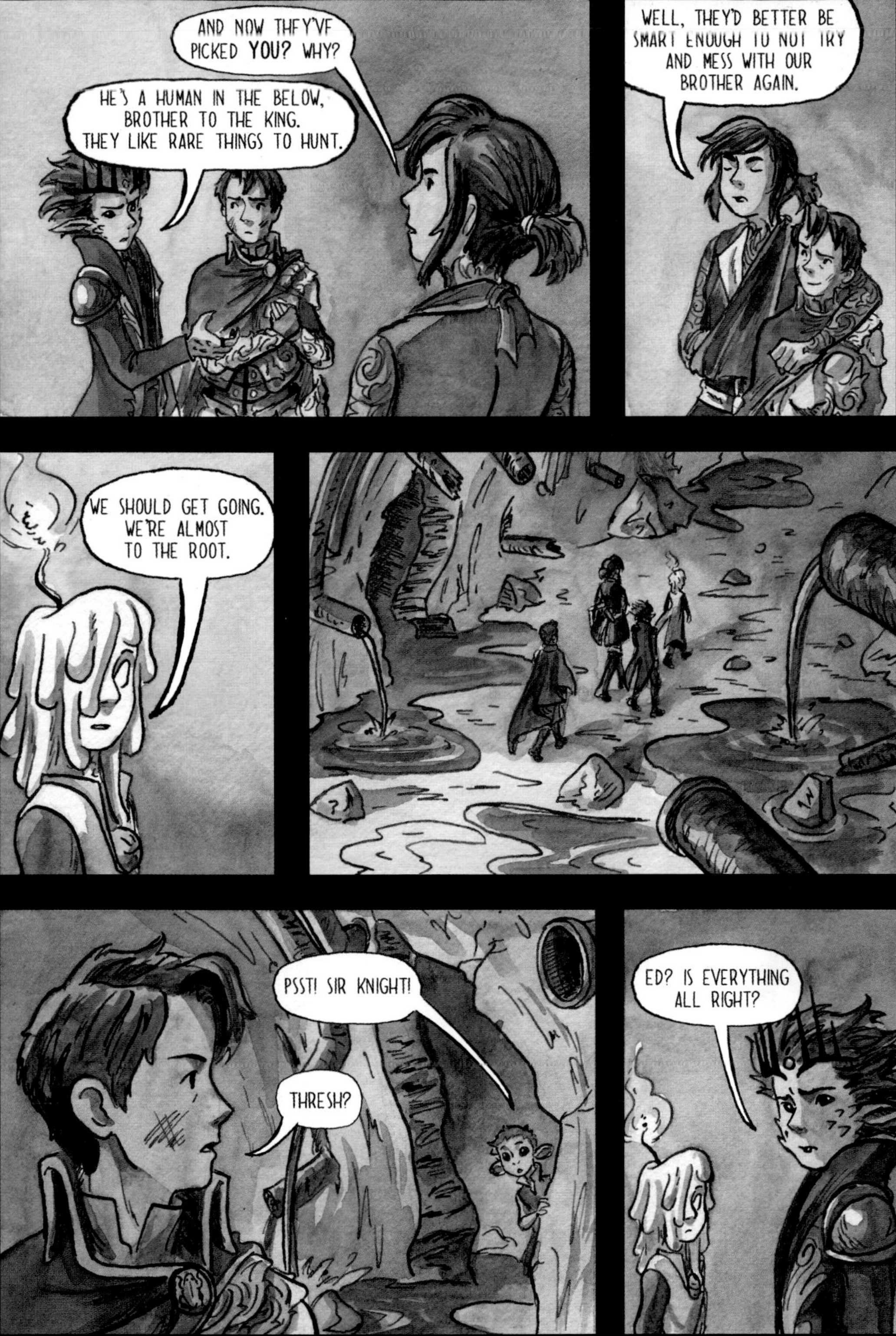
AND NOW THEY'VE PICKED YOU? WHY?
HE'S A HUMAN IN THE BELOW, BROTHER TO THE KING. THEY LIKE RARE THINGS TO HUNT.
WELL, THEY'D BETTER BE SMART ENOUGH TO NOT TRY AND MESS WITH OUR BROTHER AGAIN.
WE SHOULD GET GOING. WE'RE ALMOST TO THE ROOT.
PSST! SIR KNIGHT!
THRESH?
ED? IS EVERYTHING ALL RIGHT?

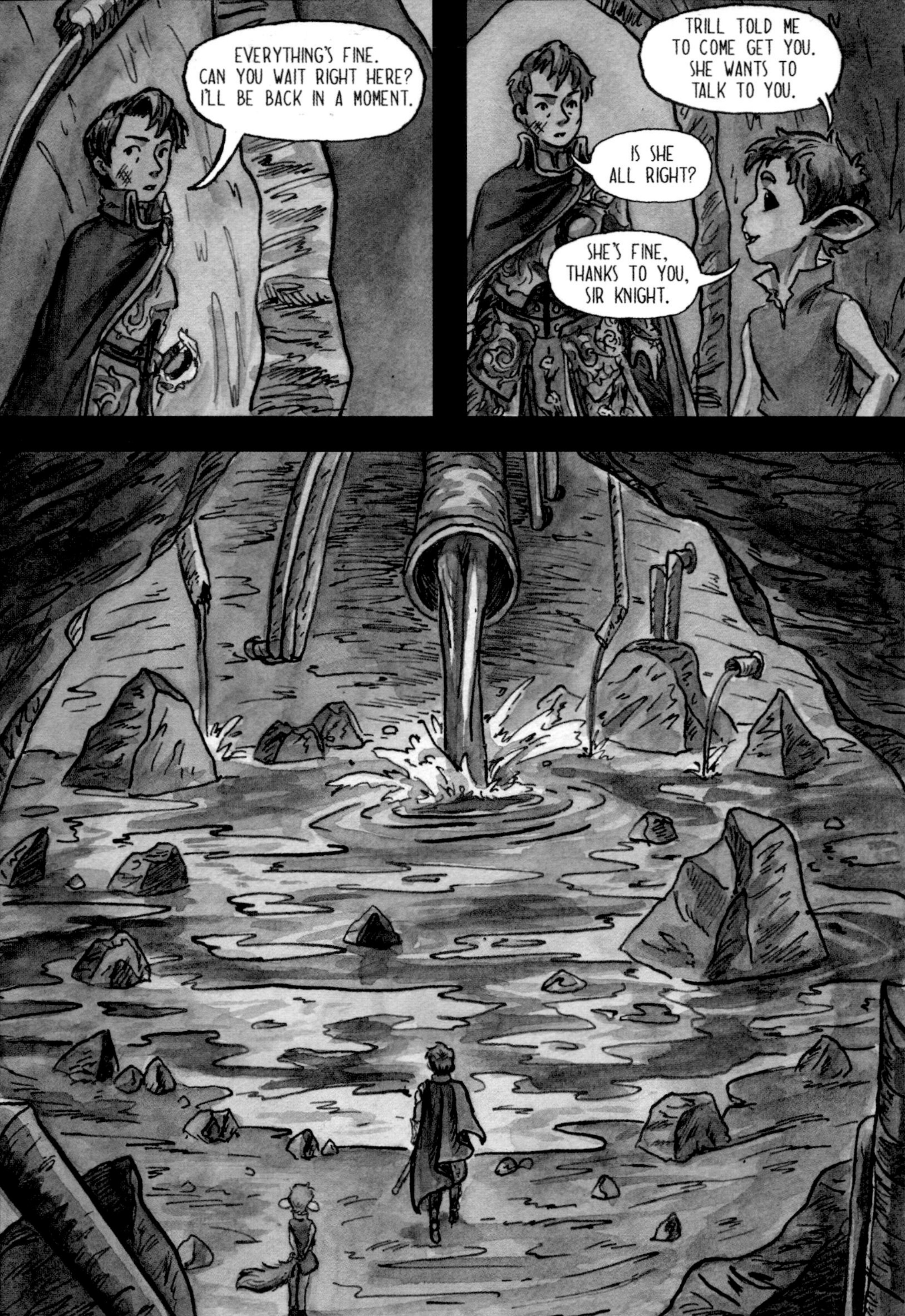
EVERYTHING'S FINE. CAN YOU WAIT RIGHT HERE? I'LL BE BACK IN A MOMENT.
TRILL TOLD ME TO COME GET YOU. SHE WANTS TO TALK TO YOU.
IS SHE ALL RIGHT?
SHE'S FINE, THANKS TO YOU, SIR KNIGHT.

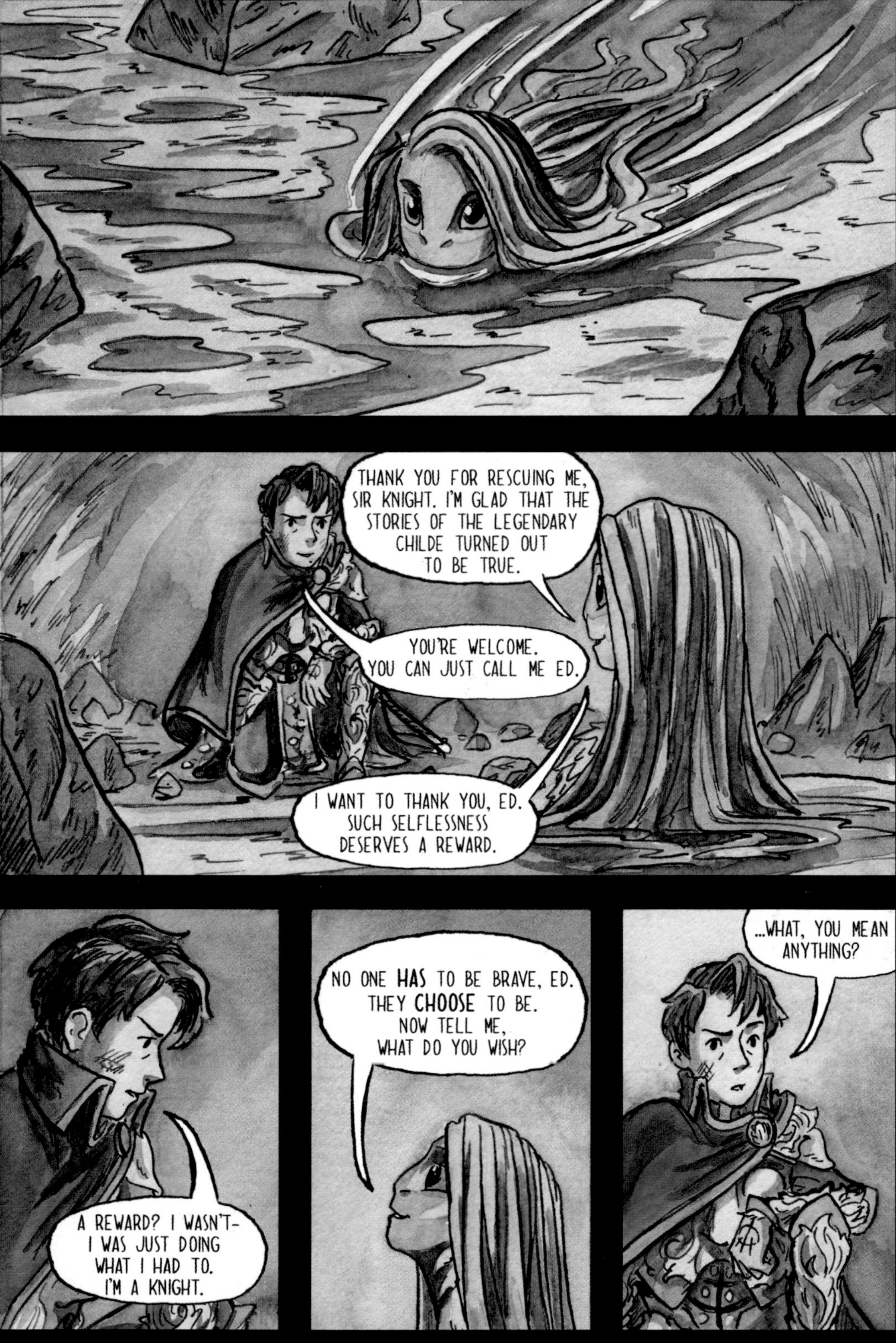
THANK YOU FOR RESCUING ME, SIR KNIGHT. I'M GLAD THAT THE STORIES OF THE LEGENDARY CHILDE TURNED OUT TO BE TRUE.
YOU'RE WELCOME. YOU CAN JUST CALL ME ED.
I WANT TO THANK YOU, ED. SUCH SELFLESSNESS DESERVES A REWARD.
A REWARD? I WASN'T- I WAS JUST DOING WHAT I HAD TO. I'M A KNIGHT.
NO ONE **HAS** TO BE BRAVE, ED. THEY **CHOOSE** TO BE. NOW TELL ME, WHAT DO YOU WISH?
...WHAT, YOU MEAN ANYTHING?

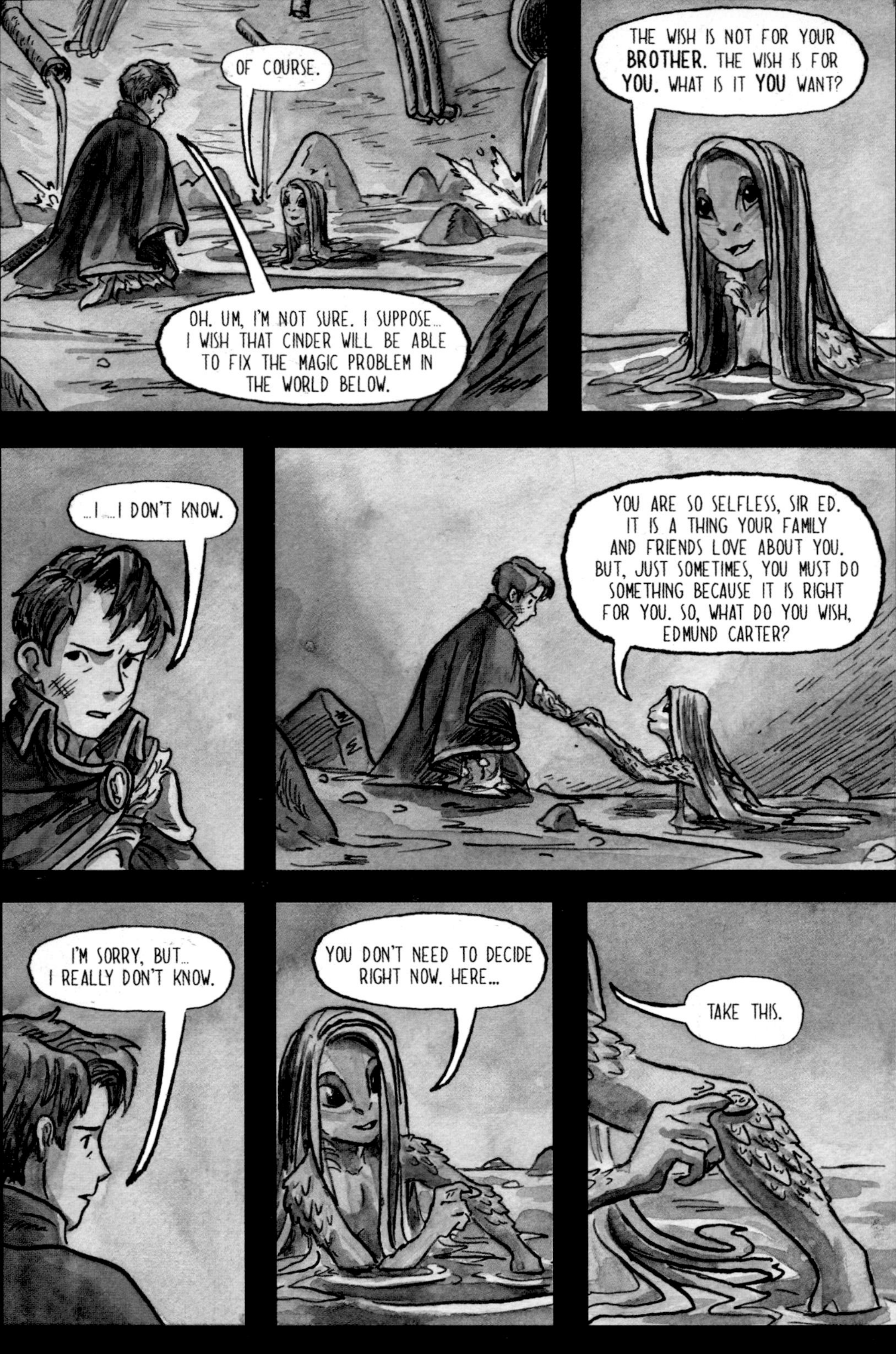
OF COURSE.
OH. UM, I'M NOT SURE. I SUPPOSE... I WISH THAT CINDER WILL BE ABLE TO FIX THE MAGIC PROBLEM IN THE WORLD BELOW.
THE WISH IS NOT FOR YOUR **BROTHER**. THE WISH IS FOR **YOU**. WHAT IS IT **YOU** WANT?
...I ...I DON'T KNOW.
YOU ARE SO SELFLESS, SIR ED. IT IS A THING YOUR FAMILY AND FRIENDS LOVE ABOUT YOU. BUT, JUST SOMETIMES, YOU MUST DO SOMETHING BECAUSE IT IS RIGHT FOR YOU. SO, WHAT DO YOU WISH, EDMUND CARTER?
I'M SORRY, BUT... I REALLY DON'T KNOW.
YOU DON'T NEED TO DECIDE RIGHT NOW. HERE...
TAKE THIS.

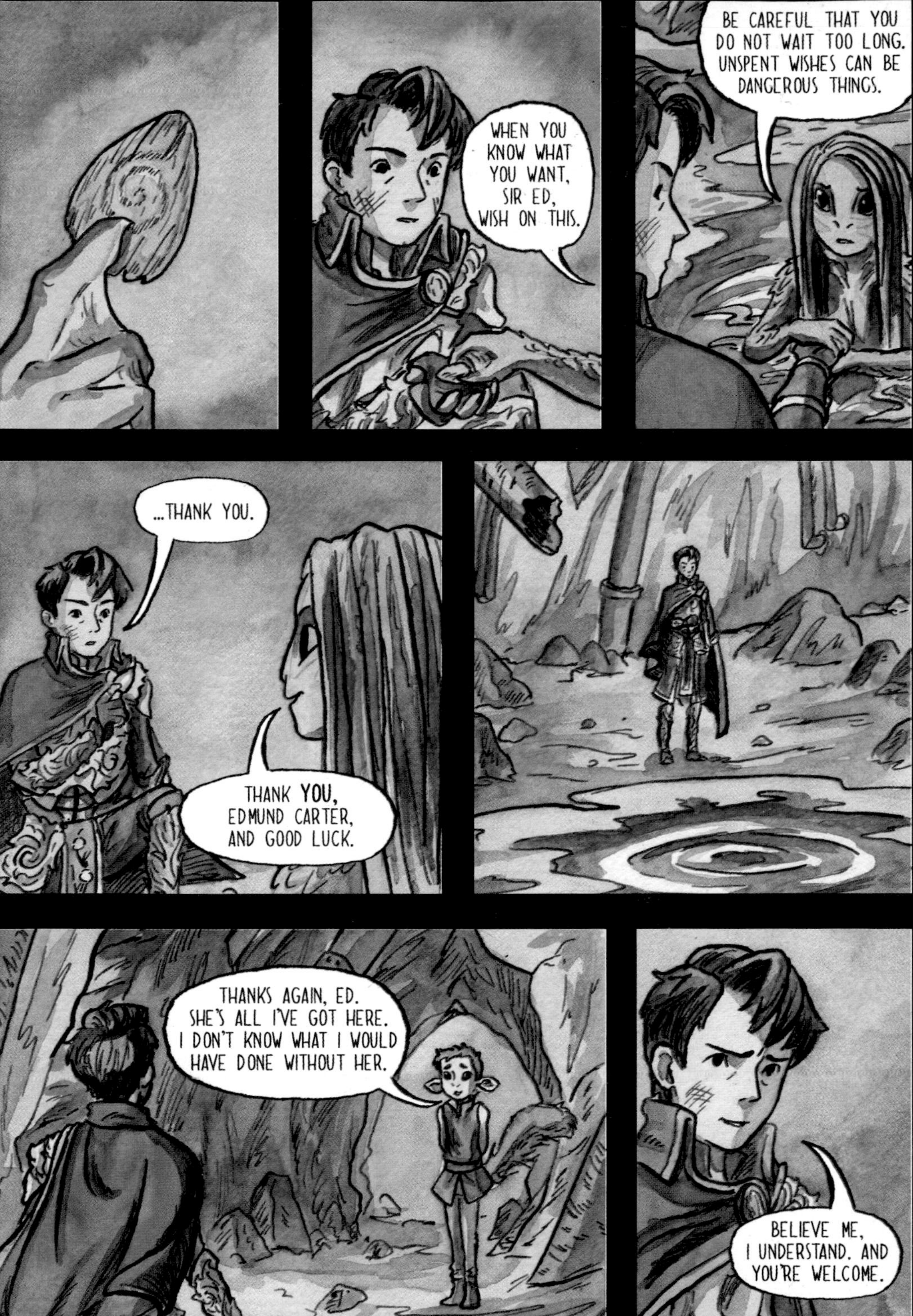
WHEN YOU KNOW WHAT YOU WANT, SIR ED, WISH ON THIS.
BE CAREFUL THAT YOU DO NOT WAIT TOO LONG. UNSPENT WISHES CAN BE DANGEROUS THINGS.
...THANK YOU.
THANK **YOU,** EDMUND CARTER, AND GOOD LUCK.
THANKS AGAIN, ED. SHE'S ALL I'VE GOT HERE. I DON'T KNOW WHAT I WOULD HAVE DONE WITHOUT HER.
BELIEVE ME, I UNDERSTAND. AND YOU'RE WELCOME.

CHAPTER
ELEVEN

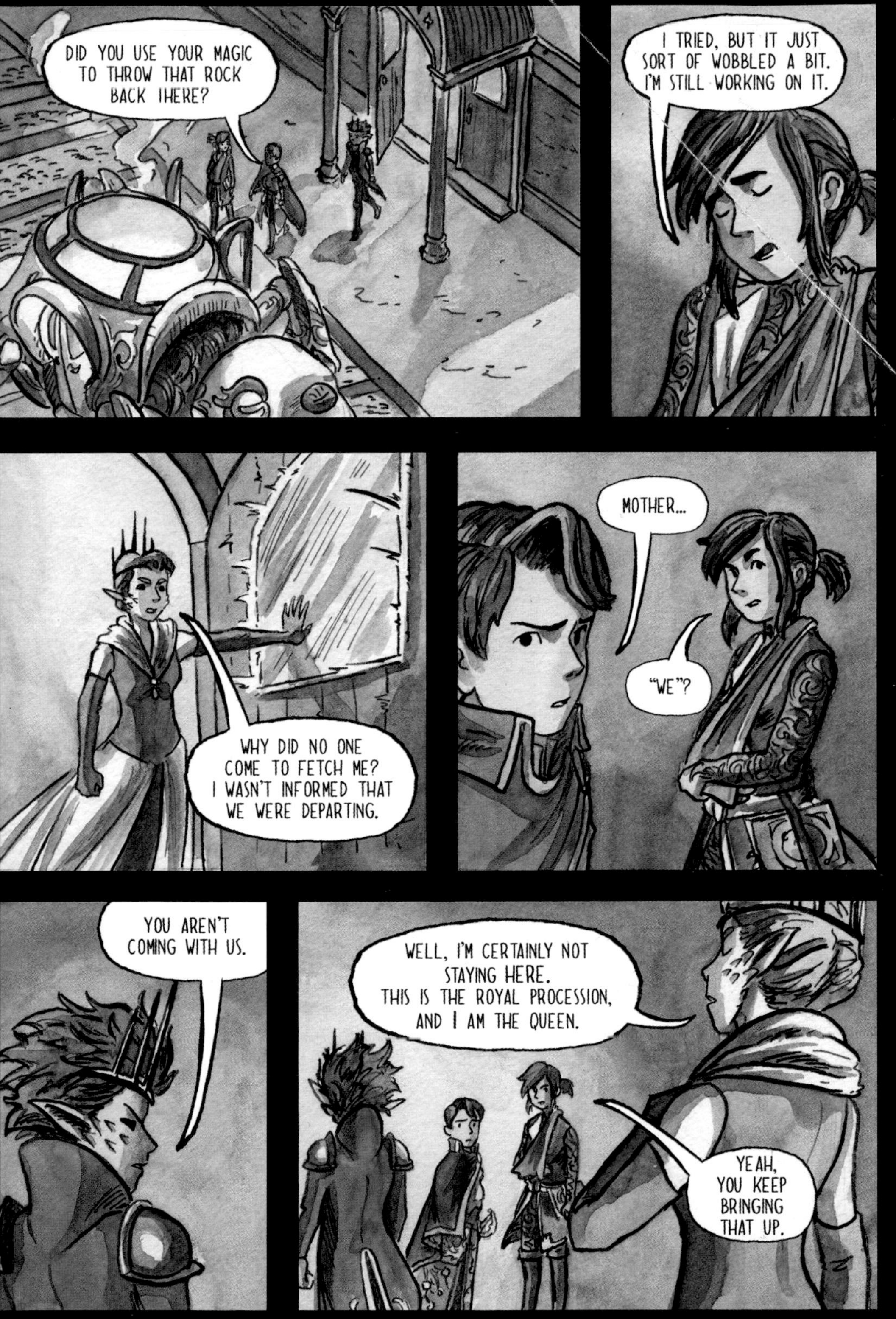
DID YOU USE YOUR MAGIC TO THROW THAT ROCK BACK THERE?
I TRIED, BUT IT JUST SORT OF WOBBLED A BIT. I'M STILL WORKING ON IT.
WHY DID NO ONE COME TO FETCH ME? I WASN'T INFORMED THAT WE WERE DEPARTING.
MOTHER...
"WE"?
YOU AREN'T COMING WITH US.
WELL, I'M CERTAINLY NOT STAYING HERE. THIS IS THE ROYAL PROCESSION, AND I AM THE QUEEN.
YEAH, YOU KEEP BRINGING THAT UP.

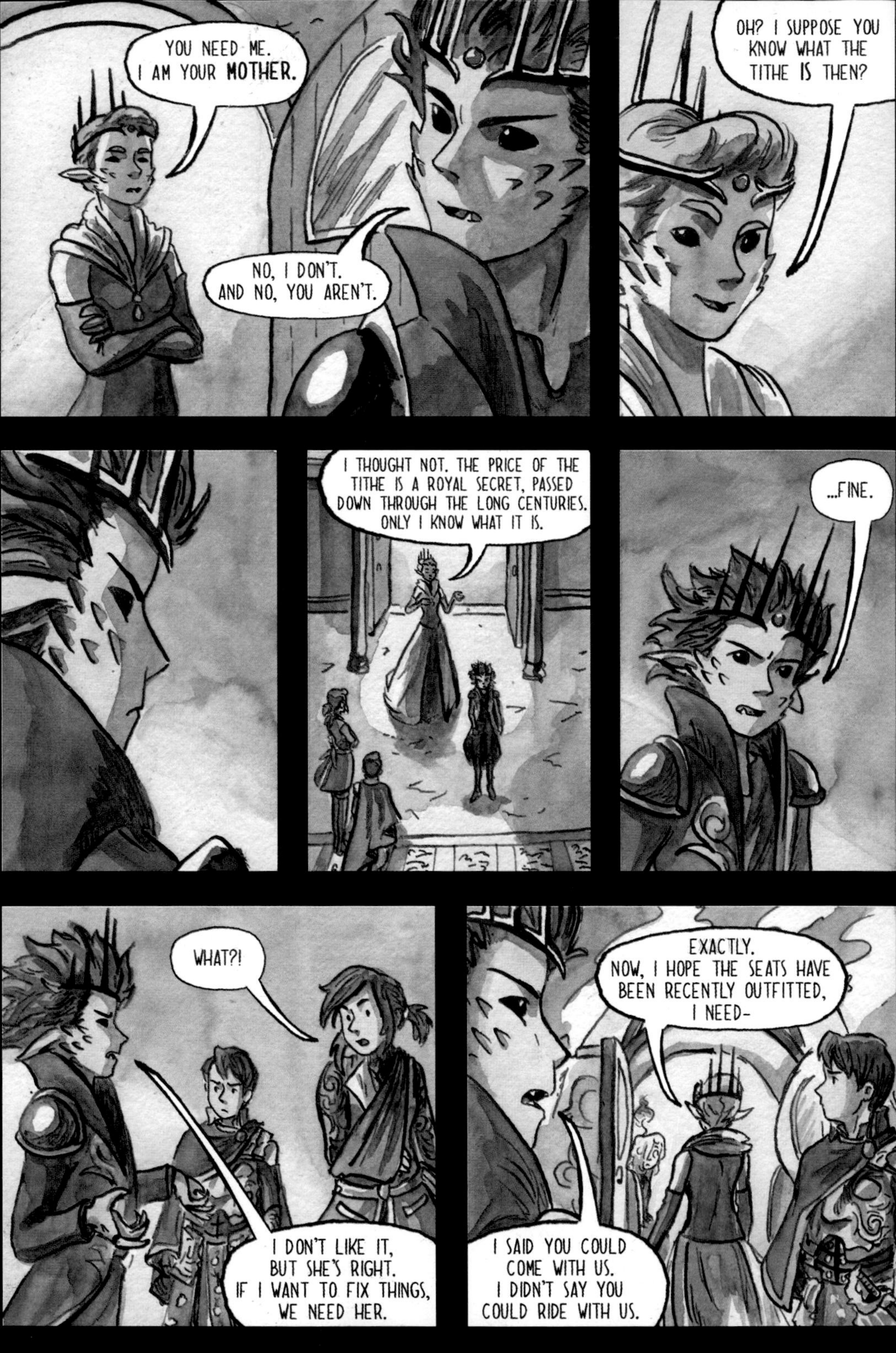
YOU NEED ME. I AM YOUR **MOTHER.**
NO, I DON'T. AND NO, YOU AREN'T.
OH? I SUPPOSE YOU KNOW WHAT THE TITHE **IS** THEN?
I THOUGHT NOT. THE PRICE OF THE TITHE IS A ROYAL SECRET, PASSED DOWN THROUGH THE LONG CENTURIES. ONLY I KNOW WHAT IT IS.
...FINE.
WHAT?!
I DON'T LIKE IT, BUT SHE'S RIGHT. IF I WANT TO FIX THINGS, WE NEED HER.
EXACTLY. NOW, I HOPE THE SEATS HAVE BEEN RECENTLY OUTFITTED, I NEED-
I SAID YOU COULD COME WITH US. I DIDN'T SAY YOU COULD RIDE WITH US.

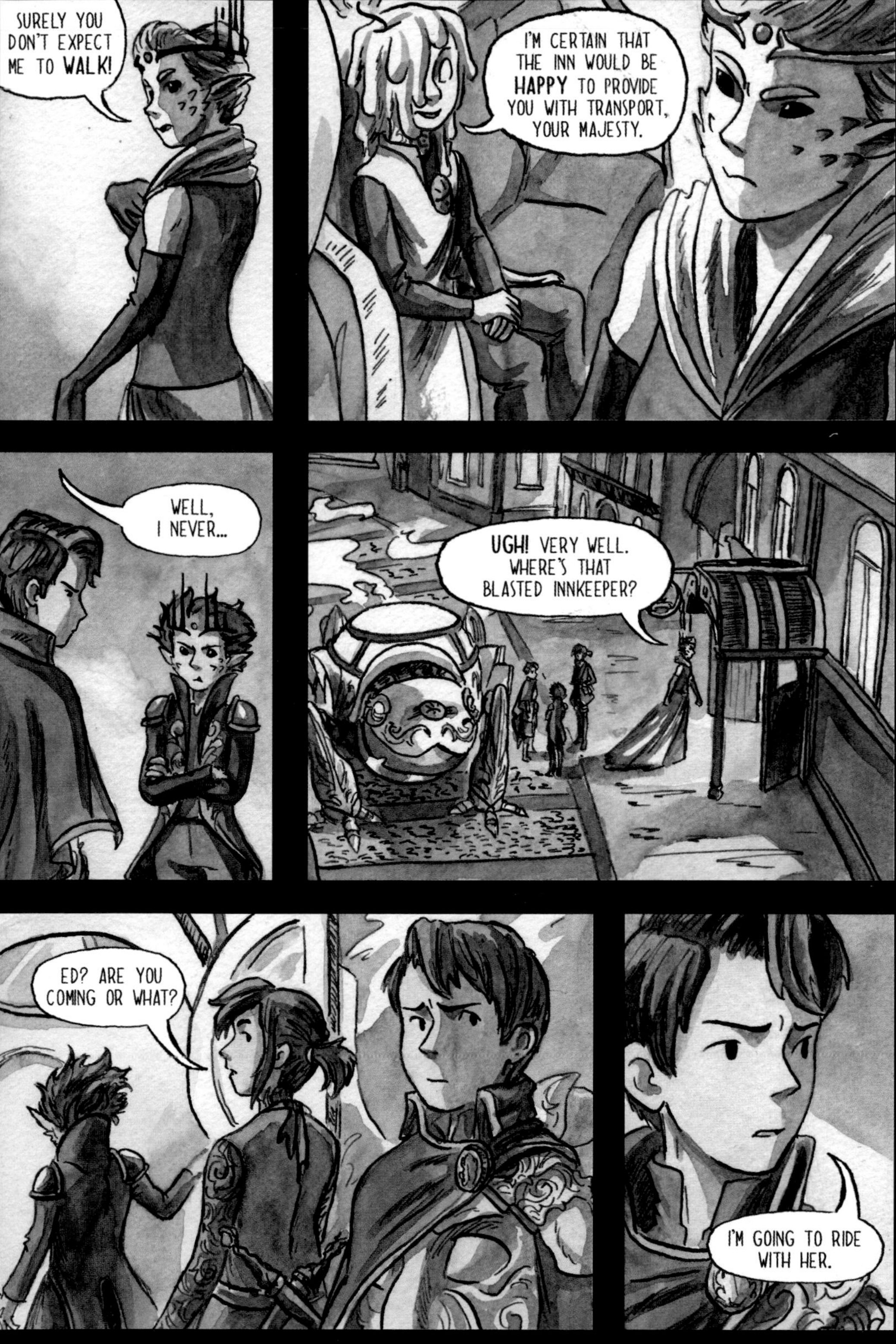
SURELY YOU DON'T EXPECT ME TO WALK!
I'M CERTAIN THAT THE INN WOULD BE HAPPY TO PROVIDE YOU WITH TRANSPORT, YOUR MAJESTY.
WELL, I NEVER...
UGH! VERY WELL. WHERE'S THAT BLASTED INNKEEPER?
ED? ARE YOU COMING OR WHAT?
I'M GOING TO RIDE WITH HER.

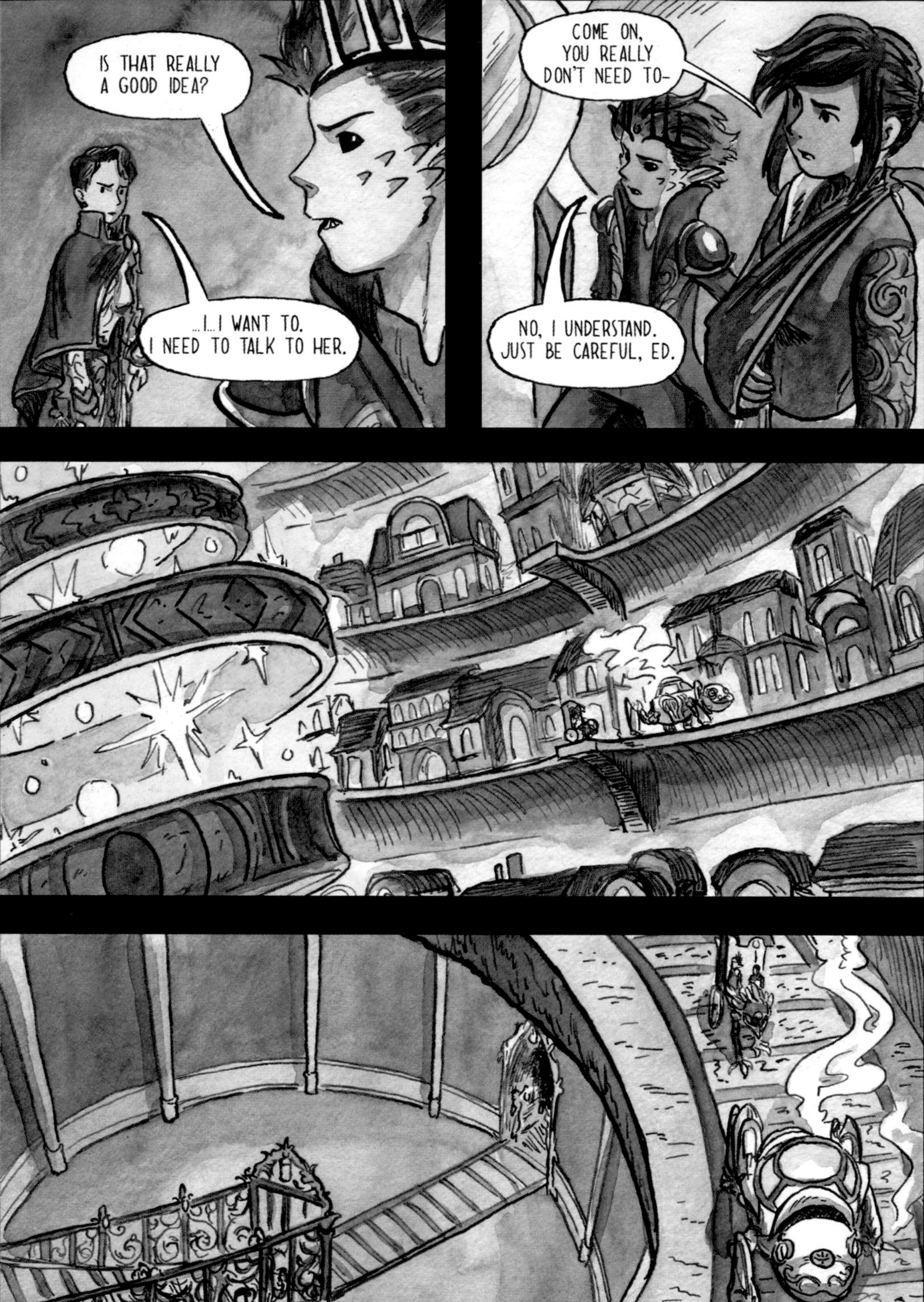
IS THAT REALLY A GOOD IDEA?
...I...I WANT TO. I NEED TO TALK TO HER.
COME ON, YOU REALLY DON'T NEED TO-
NO, I UNDERSTAND. JUST BE CAREFUL, ED.

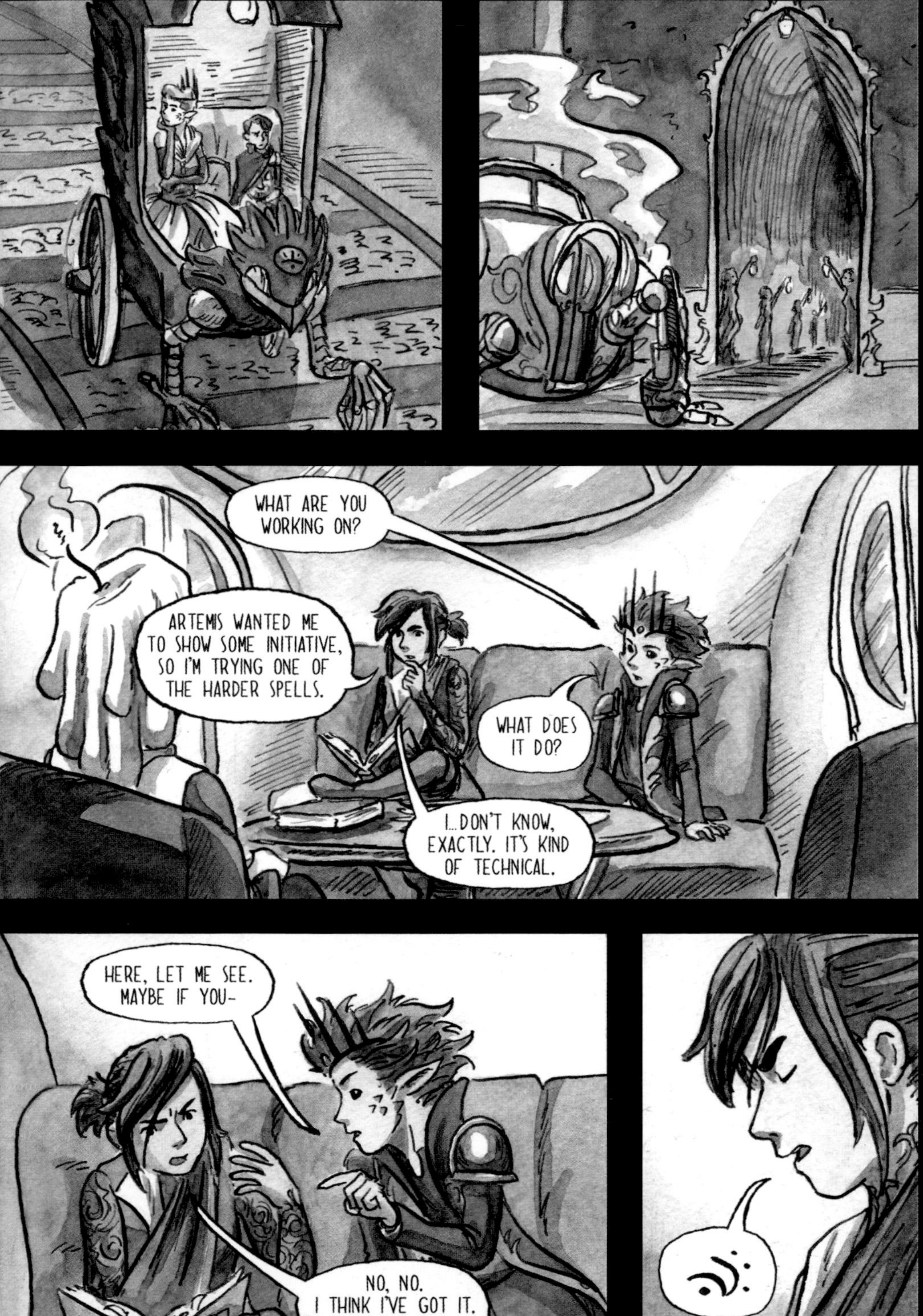

WHAT ARE YOU WORKING ON?
ARTEMIS WANTED ME TO SHOW SOME INITIATIVE, SO I'M TRYING ONE OF THE HARDER SPELLS.
WHAT DOES IT DO?
I...DON'T KNOW, EXACTLY. IT'S KIND OF TECHNICAL.
HERE, LET ME SEE. MAYBE IF YOU-
NO, NO. I THINK I'VE GOT IT. SOMETHING LIKE...

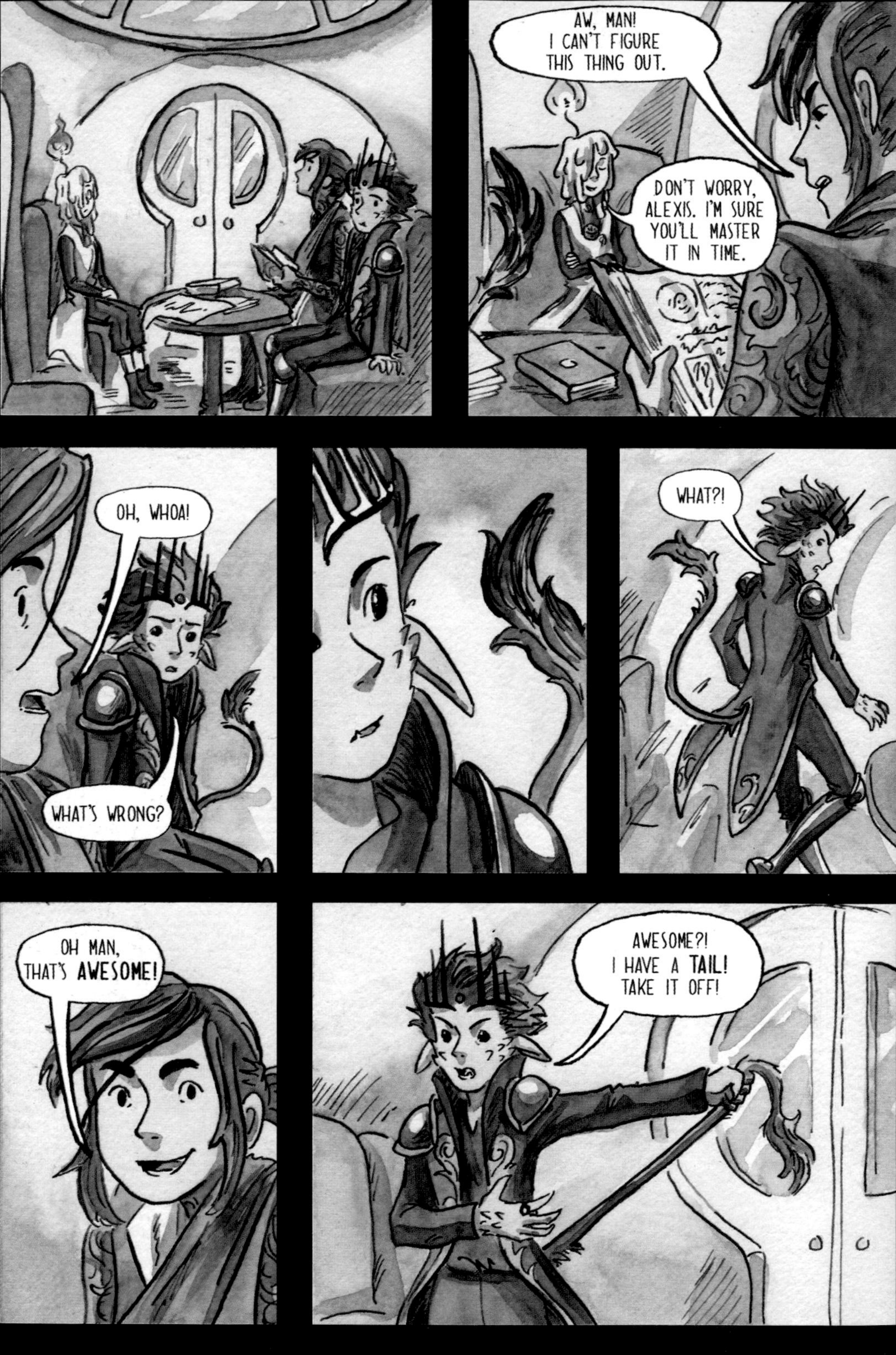
AW, MAN! I CAN'T FIGURE THIS THING OUT.
DON'T WORRY, ALEXIS. I'M SURE YOU'LL MASTER IT IN TIME.
OH, WHOA!
WHAT'S WRONG?
WHAT?!
OH MAN, THAT'S **AWESOME**!
AWESOME?! I HAVE A **TAIL**! TAKE IT OFF!

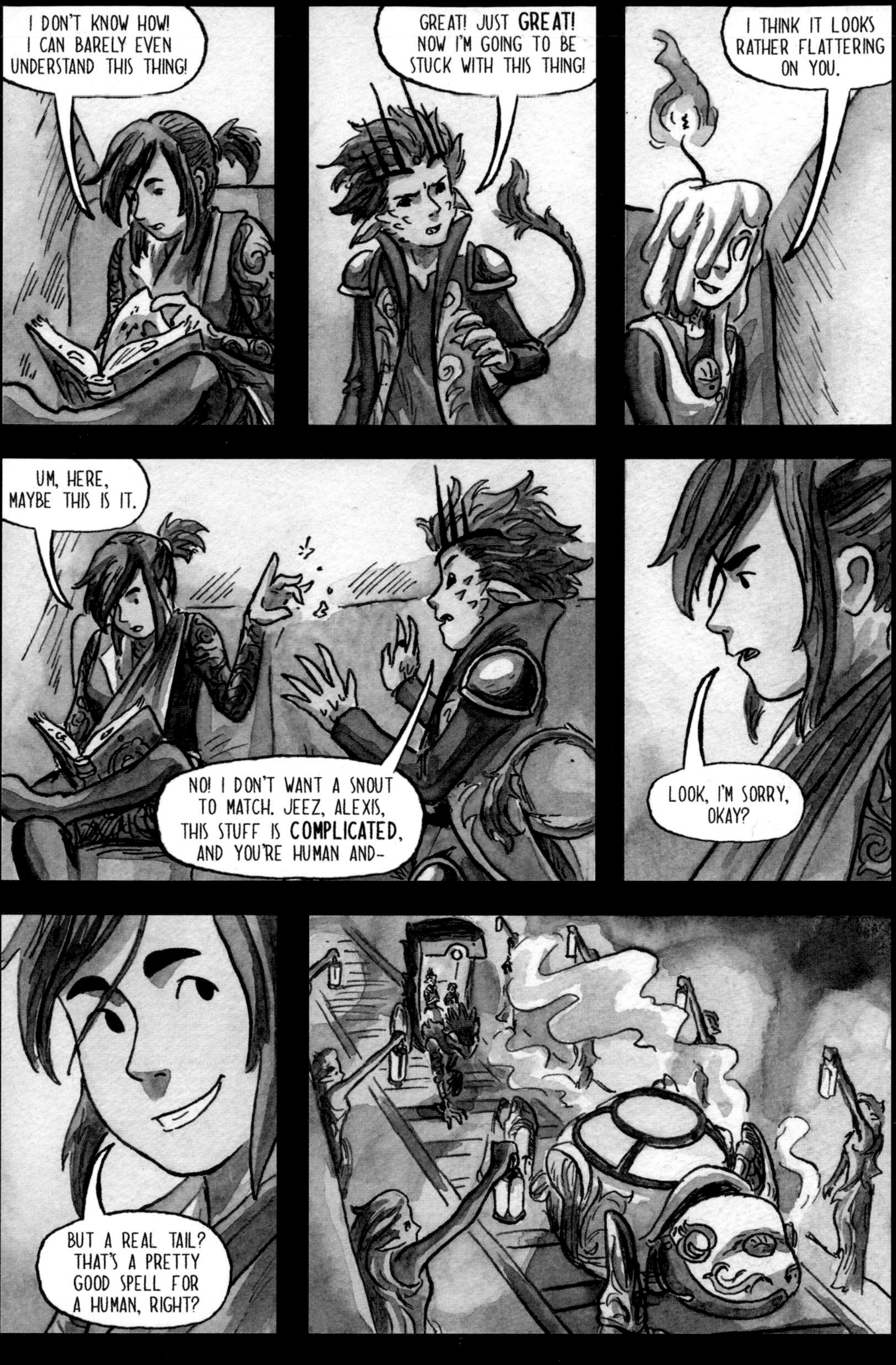
I DON'T KNOW HOW! I CAN BARELY EVEN UNDERSTAND THIS THING!
GREAT! JUST **GREAT!** NOW I'M GOING TO BE STUCK WITH THIS THING!
I THINK IT LOOKS RATHER FLATTERING ON YOU.
UM, HERE, MAYBE THIS IS IT.
NO! I DON'T WANT A SNOUT TO MATCH. JEEZ, ALEXIS, THIS STUFF IS **COMPLICATED**, AND YOU'RE HUMAN AND-
LOOK, I'M SORRY, OKAY?
BUT A REAL TAIL? THAT'S A PRETTY GOOD SPELL FOR A HUMAN, RIGHT?

REALLY, IT'S JUST APPALLING. THE STATE OF THINGS HERE. I HADN'T REALIZED THINGS HAD GOTTEN SO OUT OF HAND. AS SOON AS WE RETURN, THERE ARE GOING TO BE SOME MUCH-NEEDED CHANGES PUT INTO PLACE.

YES, MOTHER.

AND WHO DO THOSE HUMANS THINK THEY ARE?! BOSSING ME ABOUT, THE NERVE! NO GRATITUDE AT ALL.

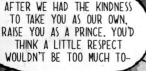

AFTER WE HAD THE KINDNESS TO TAKE YOU AS OUR OWN, RAISE YOU AS A PRINCE. YOU'D THINK A LITTLE RESPECT WOULDN'T BE TOO MUCH TO—

MOTHER?

HM? YES, SWEETHEART?

WHY DID YOU CHOOSE ME?

OH, NOT YOU TOO. EVERYONE WANTS TO HAVE THESE LITTLE HEART-TO-HEARTS TODAY. IT'S TEDIOUS, DEAR, IT REALLY IS. IT'S THAT HUMAN INSTINCT.

OH, ALL RIGHT MY DEAR, IF YOU MUST KNOW. I NEVER COULD SAY NO TO YOU.

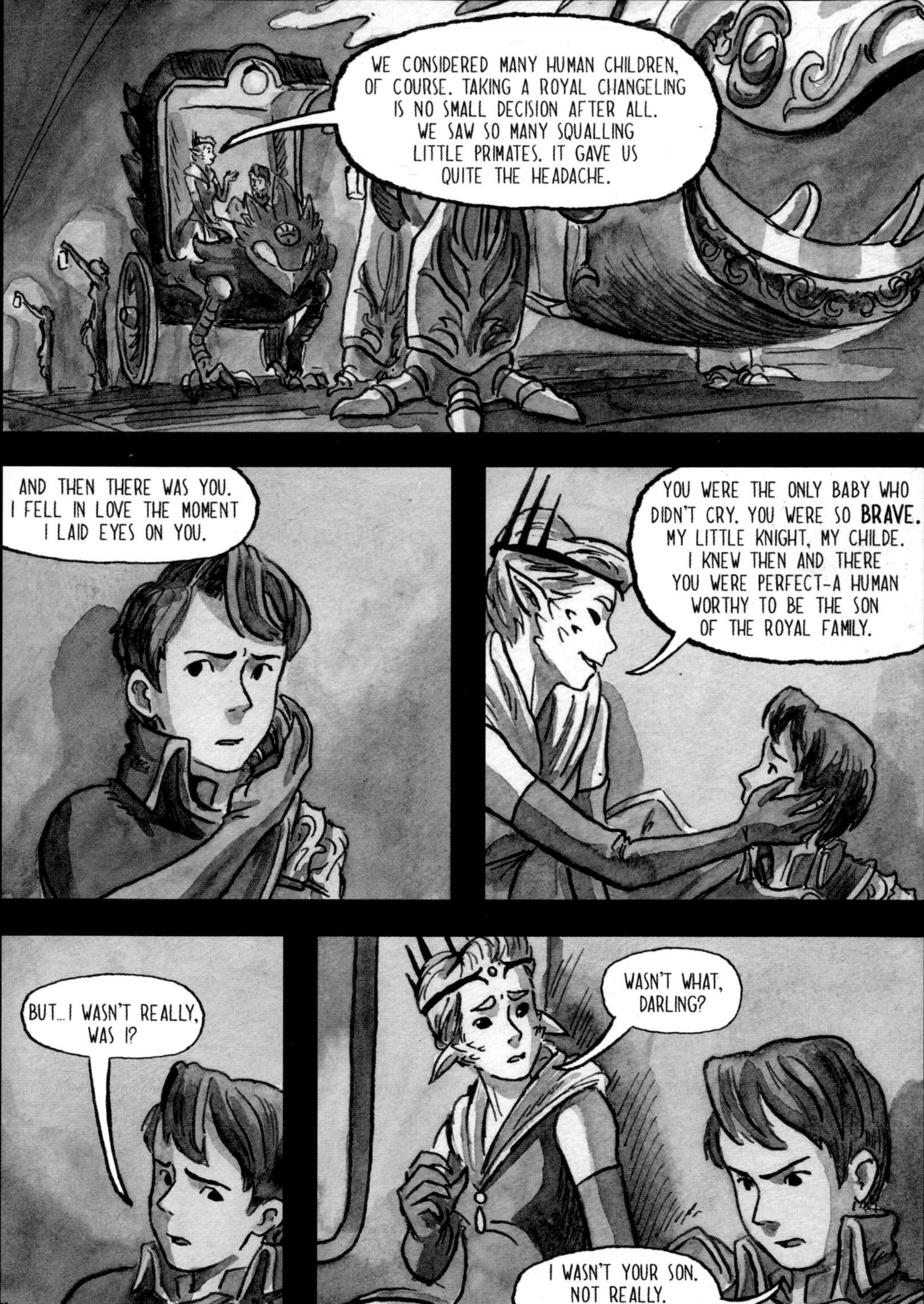
WE CONSIDERED MANY HUMAN CHILDREN, OF COURSE. TAKING A ROYAL CHANGELING IS NO SMALL DECISION AFTER ALL. WE SAW SO MANY SQUALLING LITTLE PRIMATES. IT GAVE US QUITE THE HEADACHE.
AND THEN THERE WAS YOU. I FELL IN LOVE THE MOMENT I LAID EYES ON YOU.
YOU WERE THE ONLY BABY WHO DIDN'T CRY. YOU WERE SO **BRAVE.** MY LITTLE KNIGHT, MY CHILDE. I KNEW THEN AND THERE YOU WERE PERFECT-A HUMAN WORTHY TO BE THE SON OF THE ROYAL FAMILY.
BUT...I WASN'T REALLY, WAS I?
WASN'T WHAT, DARLING?
I WASN'T YOUR SON. NOT REALLY. I WAS ONLY EVER "THE CHILDE."

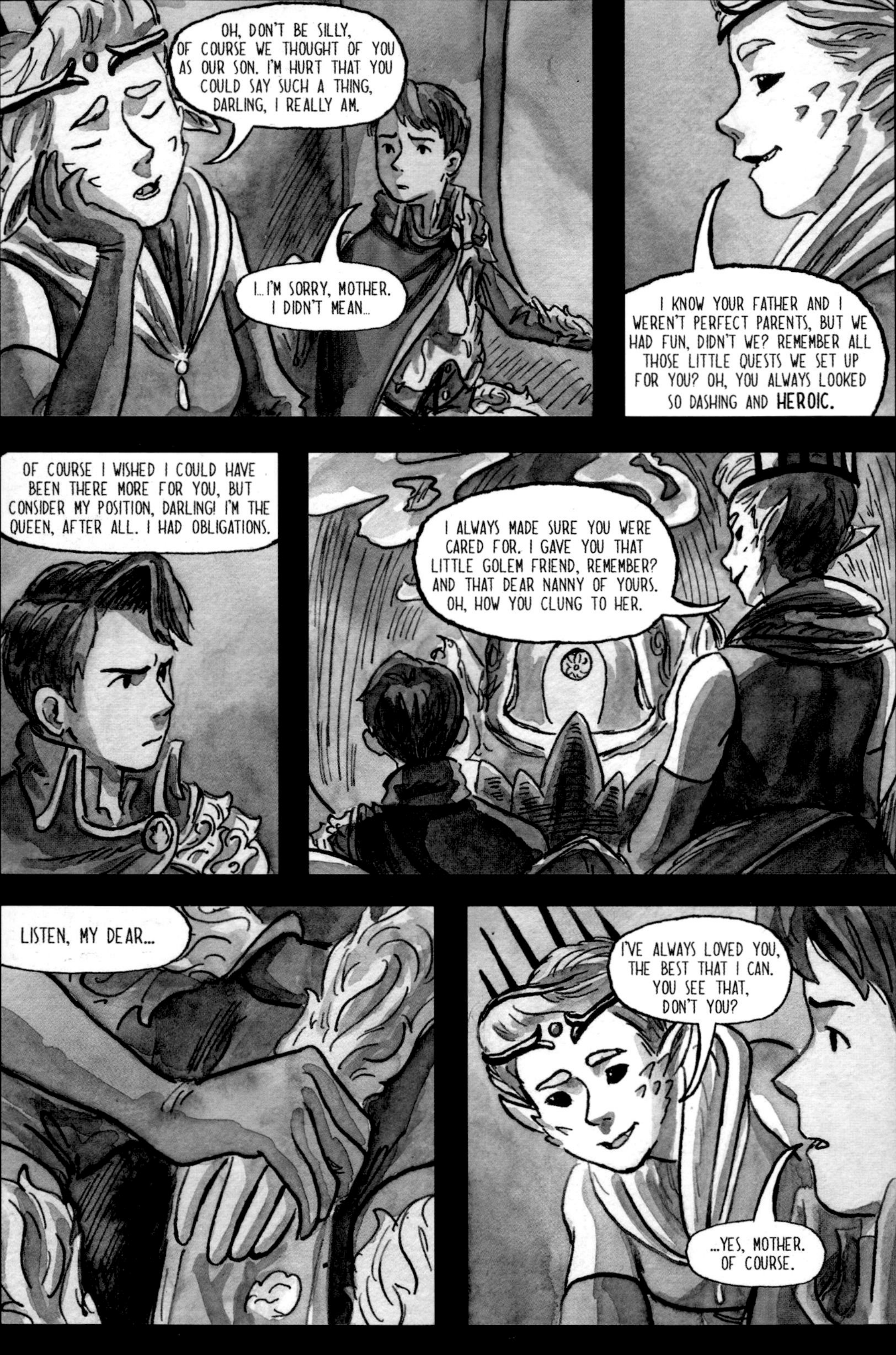
OH, DON'T BE SILLY, OF COURSE WE THOUGHT OF YOU AS OUR SON. I'M HURT THAT YOU COULD SAY SUCH A THING, DARLING, I REALLY AM.
I... I'M SORRY, MOTHER. I DIDN'T MEAN...
I KNOW YOUR FATHER AND I WEREN'T PERFECT PARENTS, BUT WE HAD FUN, DIDN'T WE? REMEMBER ALL THOSE LITTLE QUESTS WE SET UP FOR YOU? OH, YOU ALWAYS LOOKED SO DASHING AND **HEROIC.**
OF COURSE I WISHED I COULD HAVE BEEN THERE MORE FOR YOU, BUT CONSIDER MY POSITION, DARLING! I'M THE QUEEN, AFTER ALL. I HAD OBLIGATIONS.
I ALWAYS MADE SURE YOU WERE CARED FOR. I GAVE YOU THAT LITTLE GOLEM FRIEND, REMEMBER? AND THAT DEAR NANNY OF YOURS. OH, HOW YOU CLUNG TO HER.
LISTEN, MY DEAR...
I'VE ALWAYS LOVED YOU, THE BEST THAT I CAN. YOU SEE THAT, DON'T YOU?
...YES, MOTHER. OF COURSE.

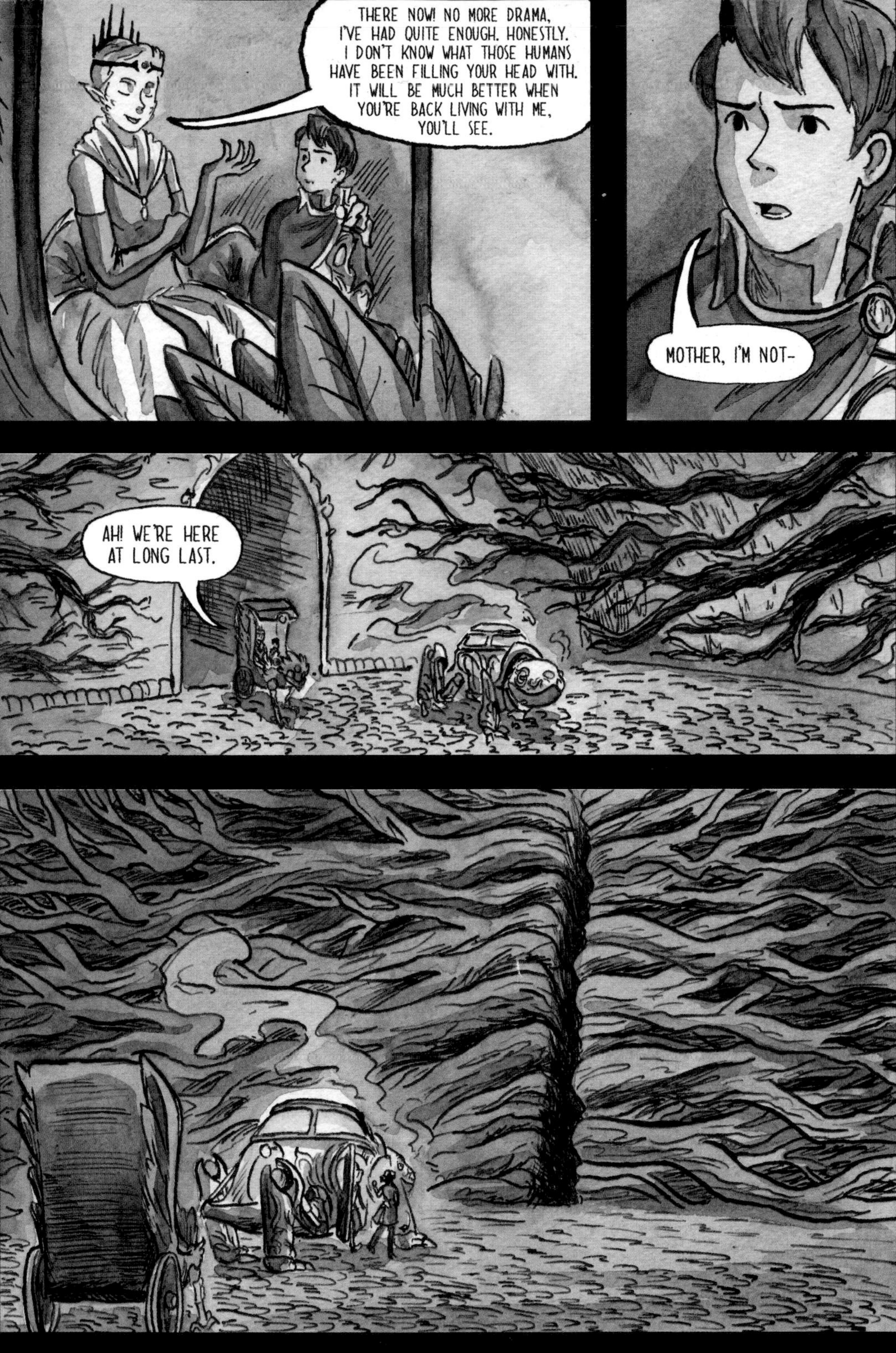
THERE NOW! NO MORE DRAMA, I'VE HAD QUITE ENOUGH. HONESTLY. I DON'T KNOW WHAT THOSE HUMANS HAVE BEEN FILLING YOUR HEAD WITH. IT WILL BE MUCH BETTER WHEN YOU'RE BACK LIVING WITH ME, YOU'LL SEE.
MOTHER, I'M NOT-
AH! WE'RE HERE AT LONG LAST.

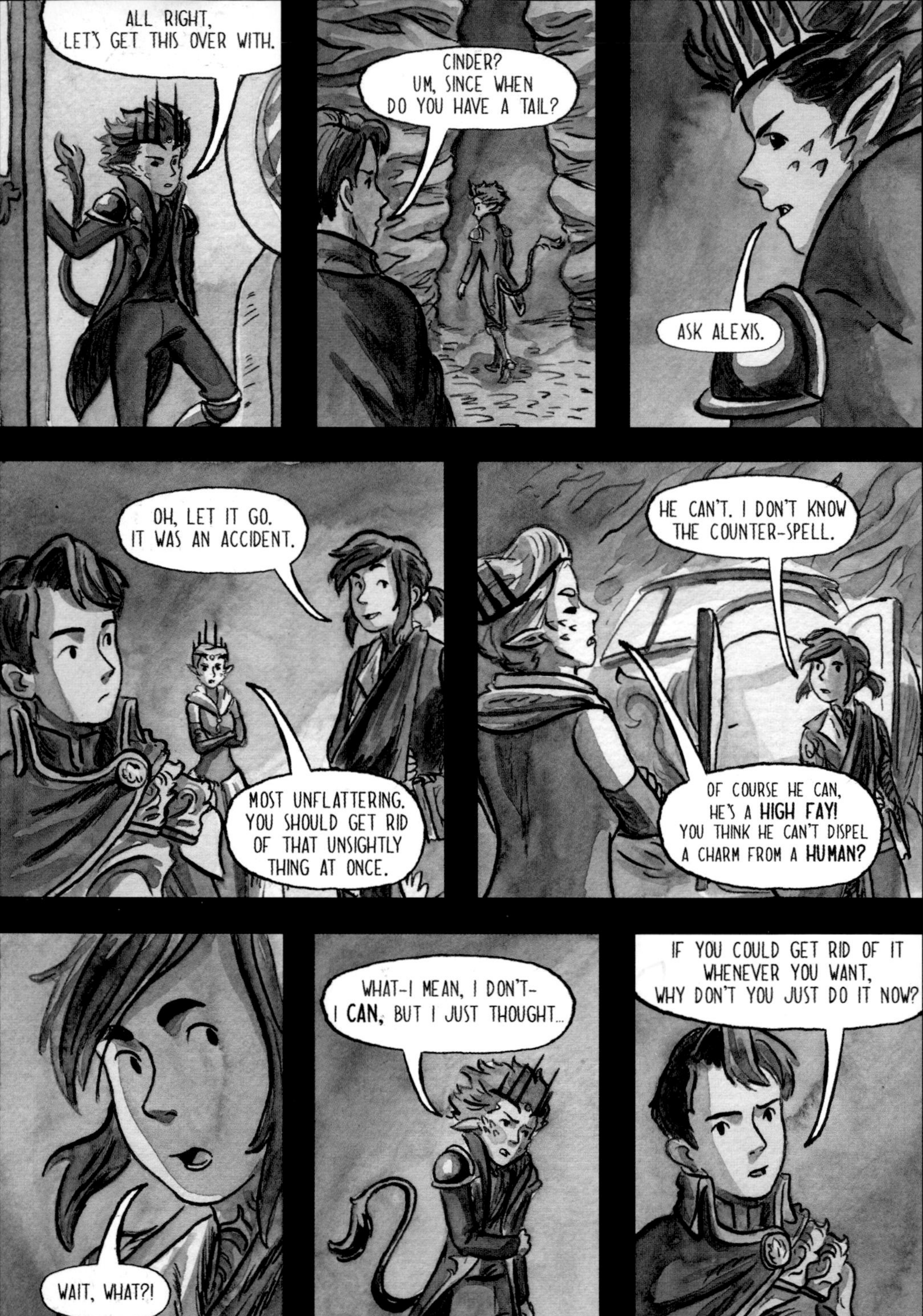
ALL RIGHT, LET'S GET THIS OVER WITH.
CINDER? UM, SINCE WHEN DO YOU HAVE A TAIL?
ASK ALEXIS.
OH, LET IT GO. IT WAS AN ACCIDENT.
MOST UNFLATTERING. YOU SHOULD GET RID OF THAT UNSIGHTLY THING AT ONCE.
HE CAN'T. I DON'T KNOW THE COUNTER-SPELL.
OF COURSE HE CAN, HE'S A HIGH FAY! YOU THINK HE CAN'T DISPEL A CHARM FROM A HUMAN?
WAIT, WHAT?!
WHAT-I MEAN, I DON'T- I CAN, BUT I JUST THOUGHT...
IF YOU COULD GET RID OF IT WHENEVER YOU WANT, WHY DON'T YOU JUST DO IT NOW?

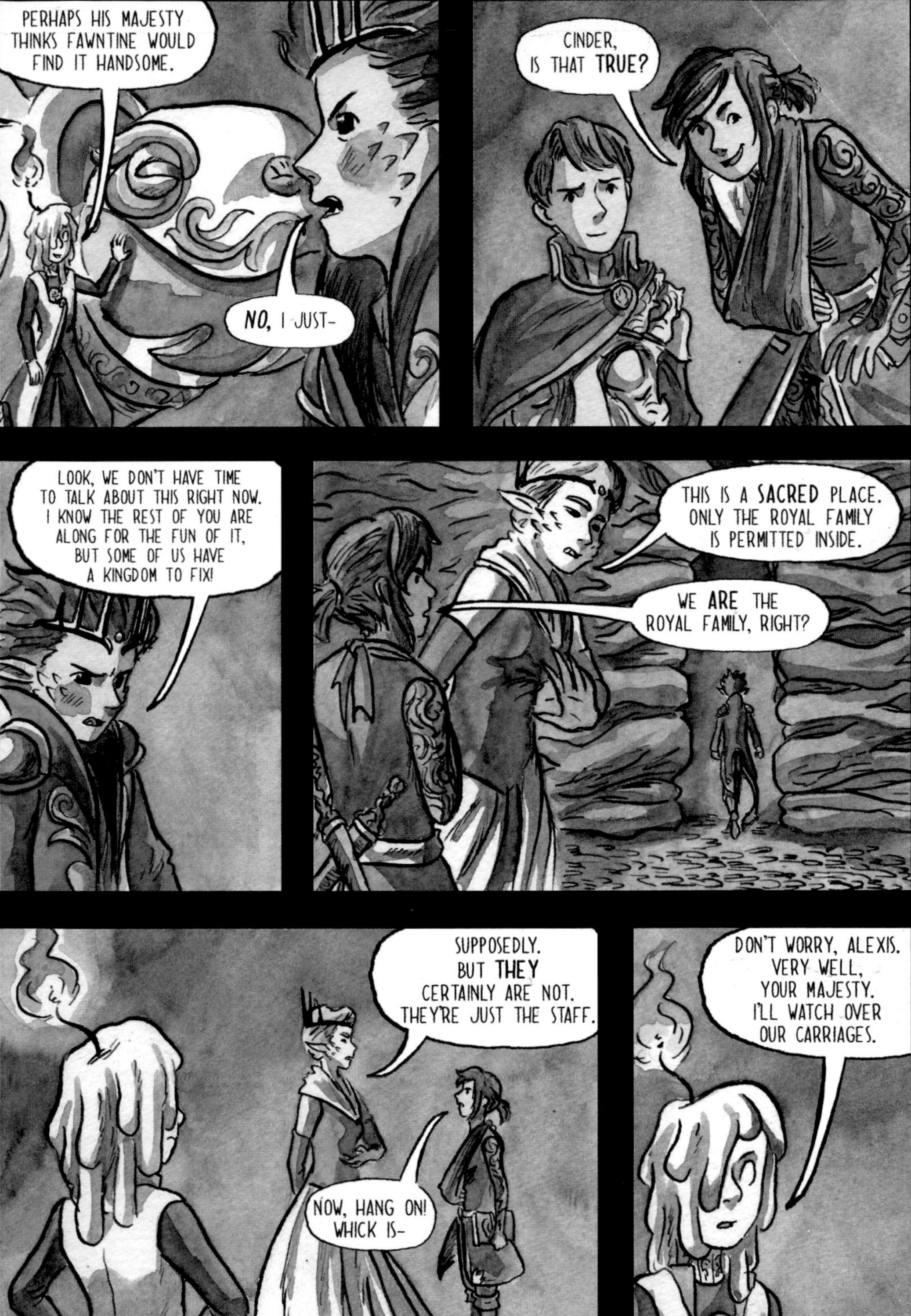
PERHAPS HIS MAJESTY THINKS FAWNTINE WOULD FIND IT HANDSOME.
NO, I JUST-
CINDER, IS THAT TRUE?
LOOK, WE DON'T HAVE TIME TO TALK ABOUT THIS RIGHT NOW. I KNOW THE REST OF YOU ARE ALONG FOR THE FUN OF IT, BUT SOME OF US HAVE A KINGDOM TO FIX!
THIS IS A SACRED PLACE. ONLY THE ROYAL FAMILY IS PERMITTED INSIDE.
WE ARE THE ROYAL FAMILY, RIGHT?
SUPPOSEDLY. BUT THEY CERTAINLY ARE NOT. THEY'RE JUST THE STAFF.
NOW, HANG ON! WHICK IS-
DON'T WORRY, ALEXIS. VERY WELL, YOUR MAJESTY. I'LL WATCH OVER OUR CARRIAGES.

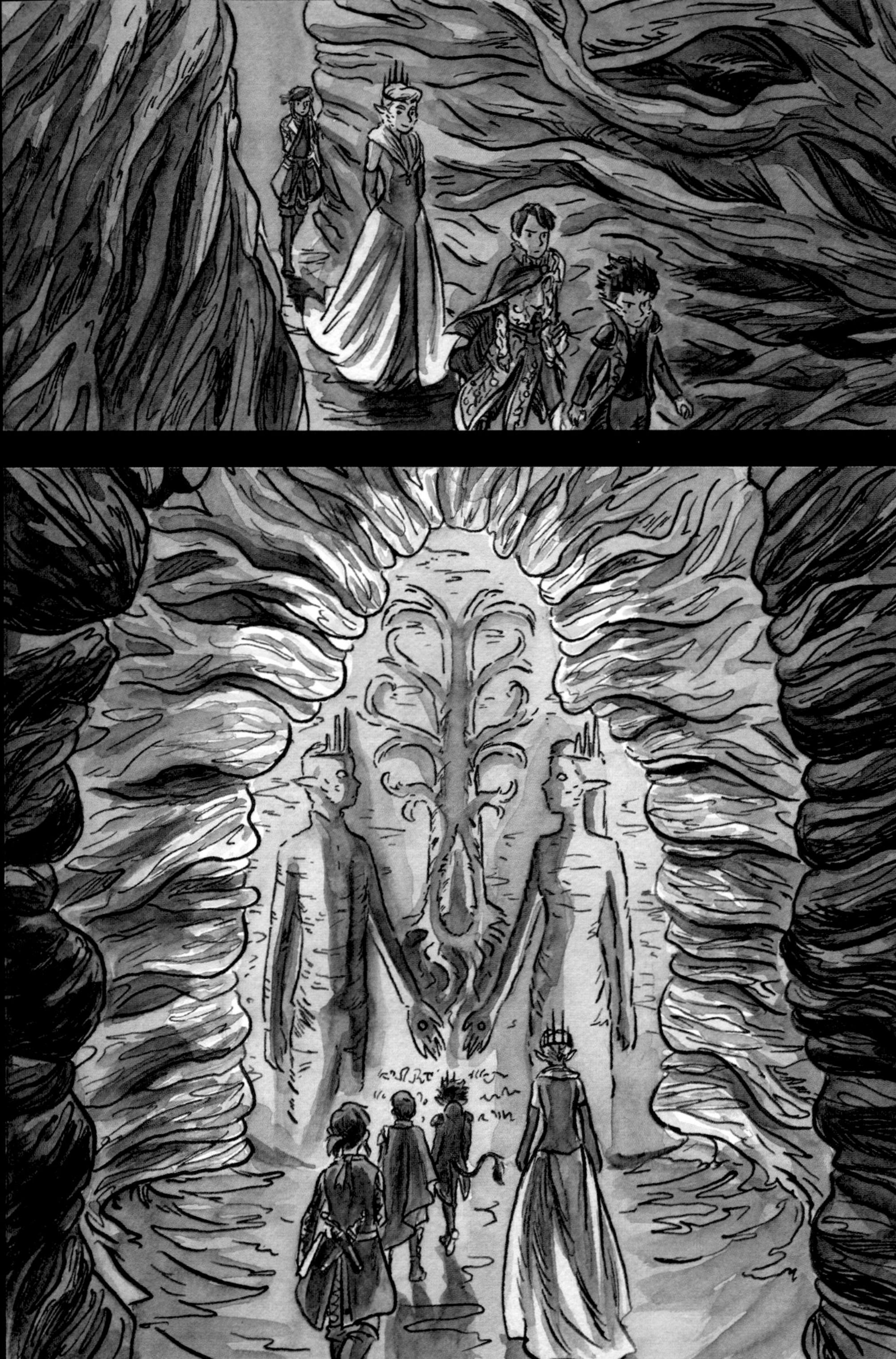

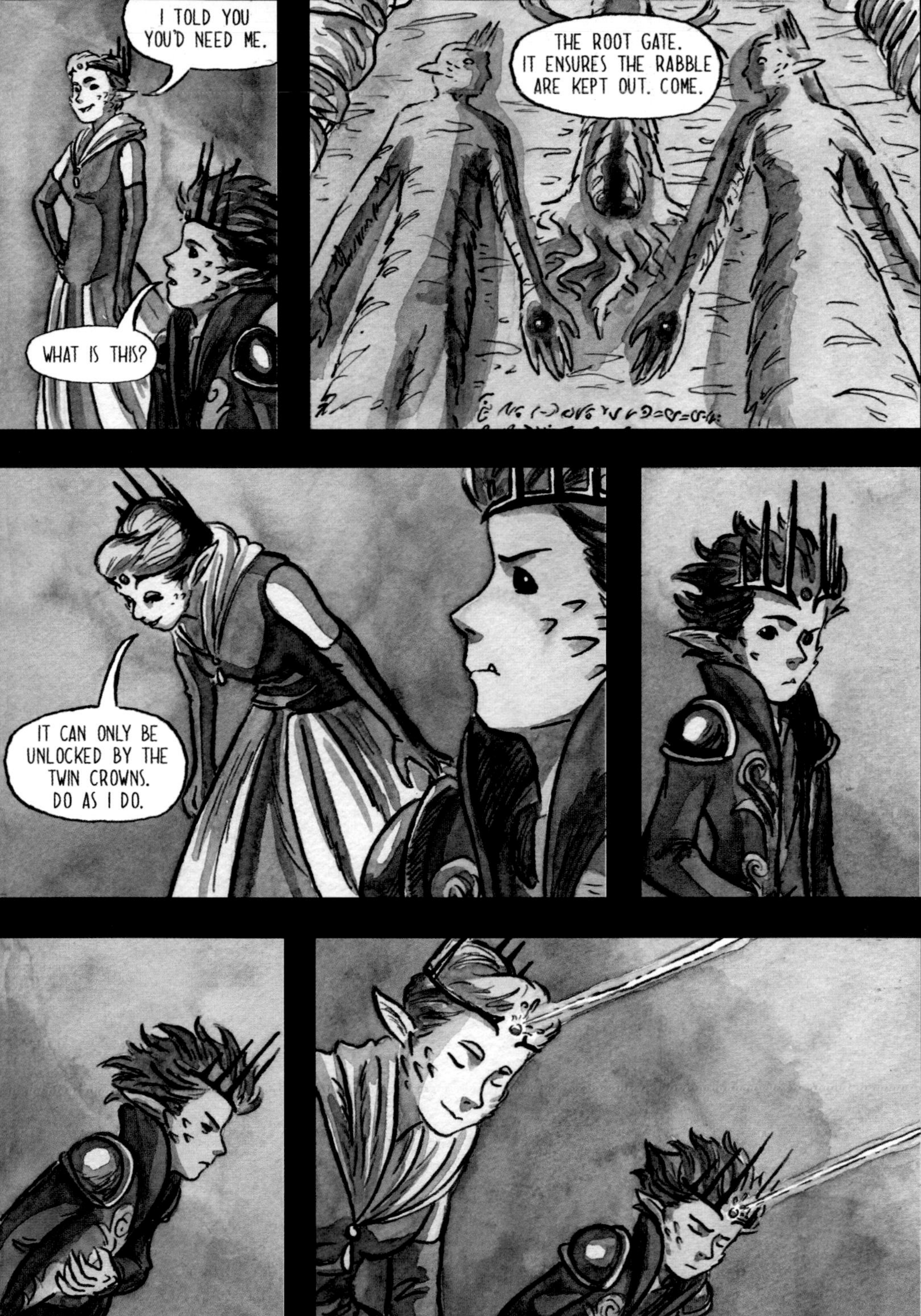
I TOLD YOU YOU'D NEED ME.
WHAT IS THIS?
THE ROOT GATE. IT ENSURES THE RABBLE ARE KEPT OUT. COME.
IT CAN ONLY BE UNLOCKED BY THE TWIN CROWNS. DO AS I DO.

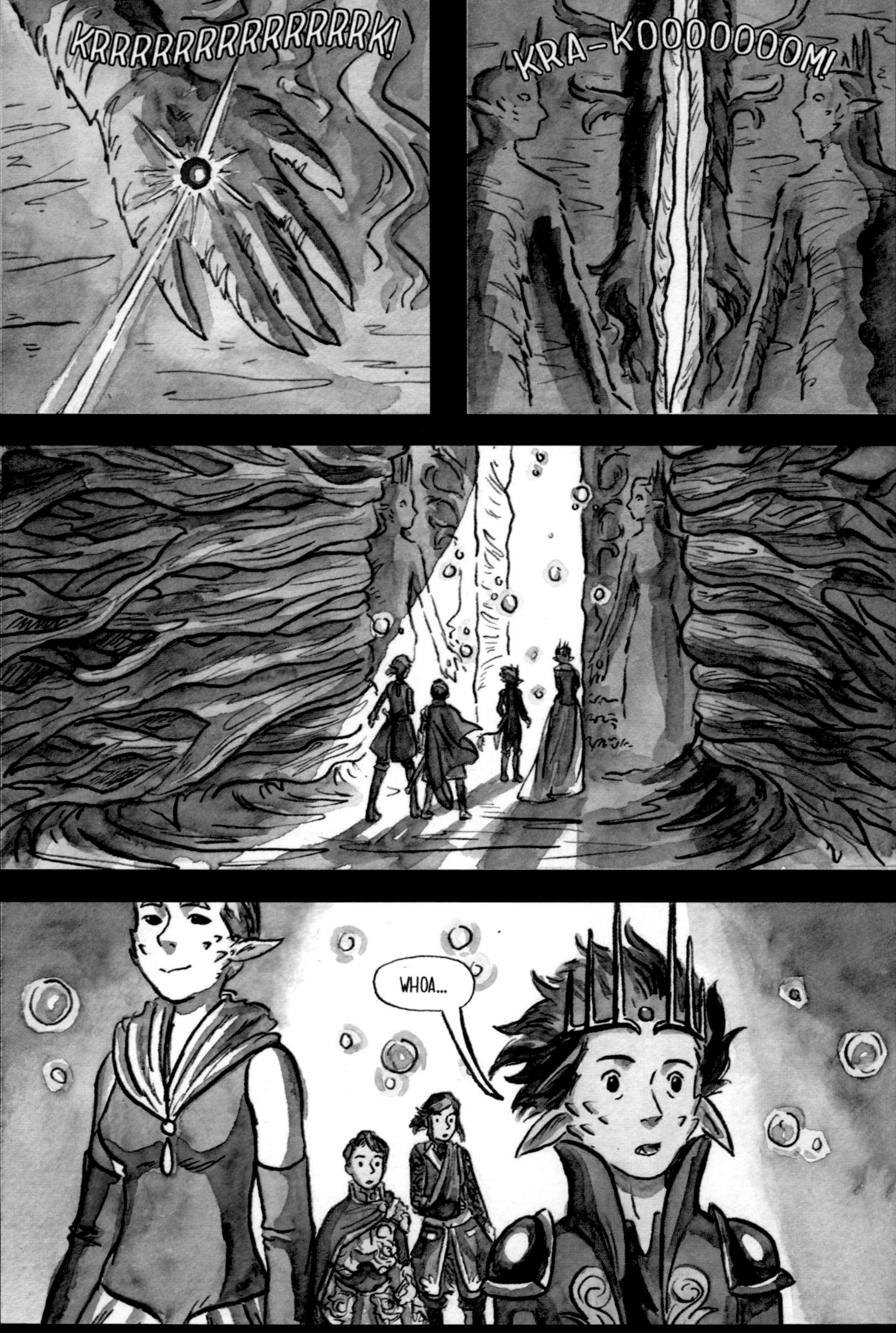

KRRRRRRRRRRRRRRK!
KRA-KOOOOOOOOM!
WHOA...

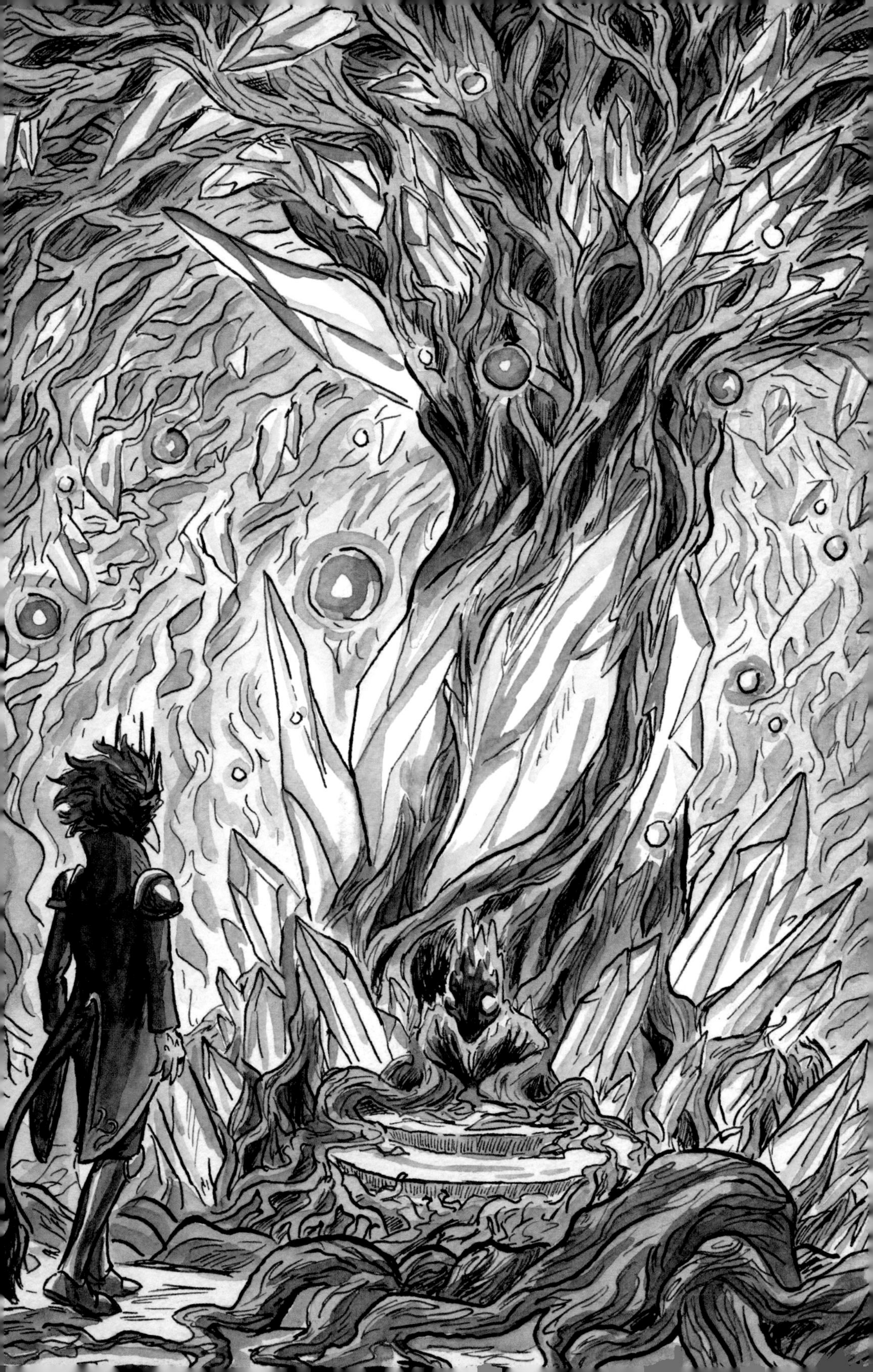

CHAPTER
TWELVE

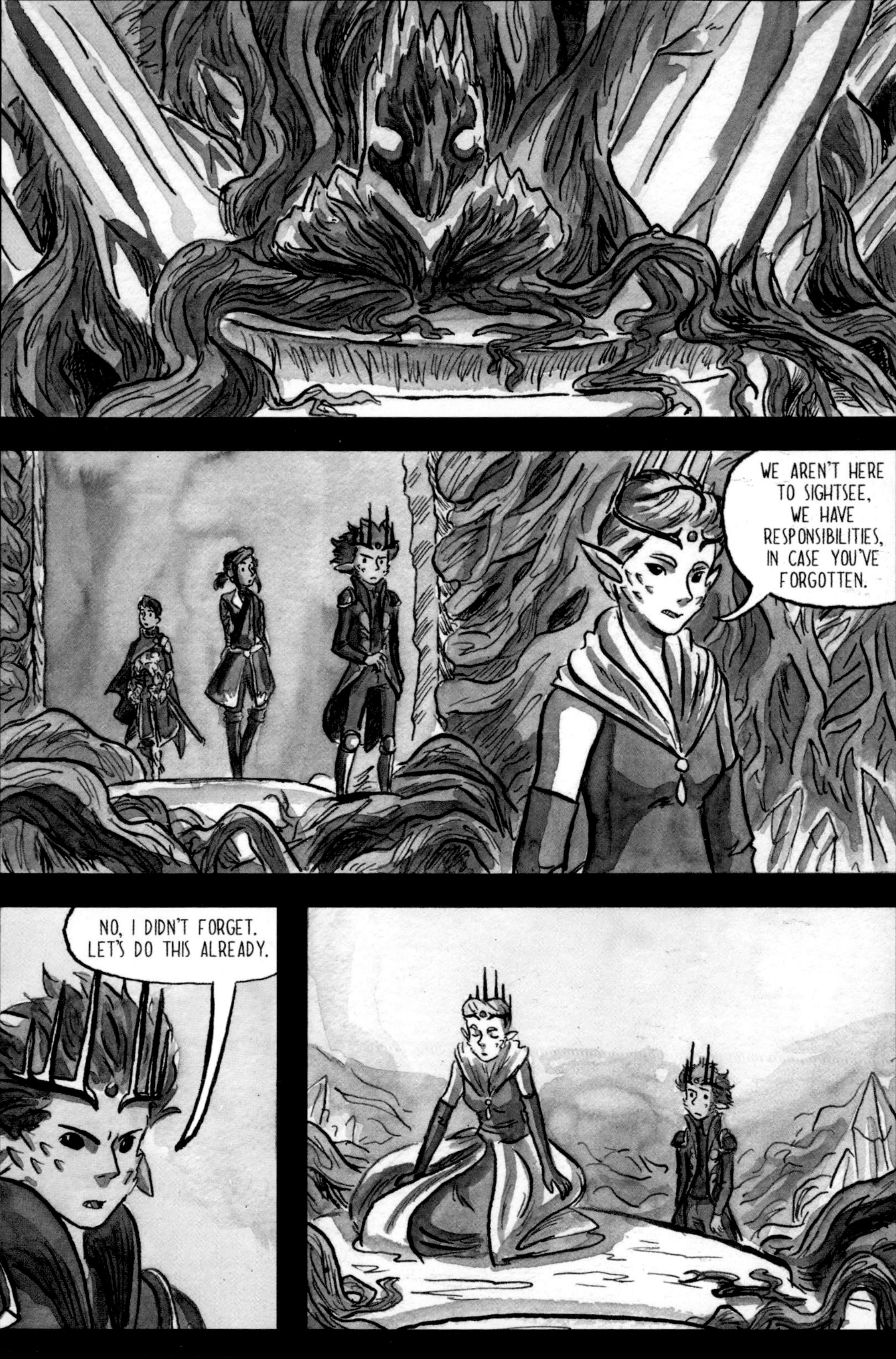
WE AREN'T HERE TO SIGHTSEE, WE HAVE RESPONSIBILITIES, IN CASE YOU'VE FORGOTTEN.
NO, I DIDN'T FORGET. LET'S DO THIS ALREADY.

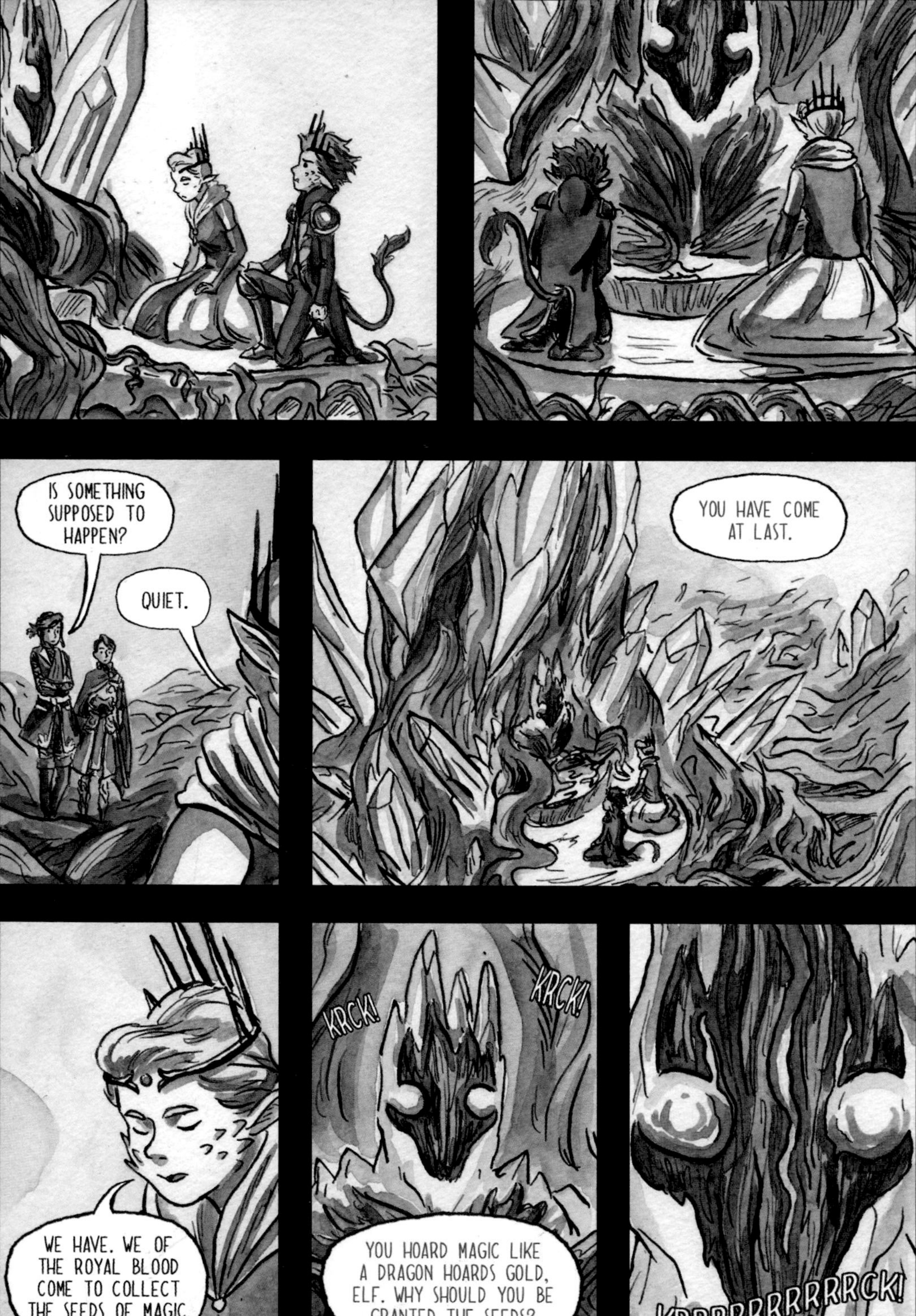

IS SOMETHING SUPPOSED TO HAPPEN?
QUIET.
YOU HAVE COME AT LAST.
WE HAVE. WE OF THE ROYAL BLOOD COME TO COLLECT THE SEEDS OF MAGIC.
KRCK!
KRCK!
YOU HOARD MAGIC LIKE A DRAGON HOARDS GOLD, ELF. WHY SHOULD YOU BE GRANTED THE SEEDS?
KRRRRRRRRRRCK!

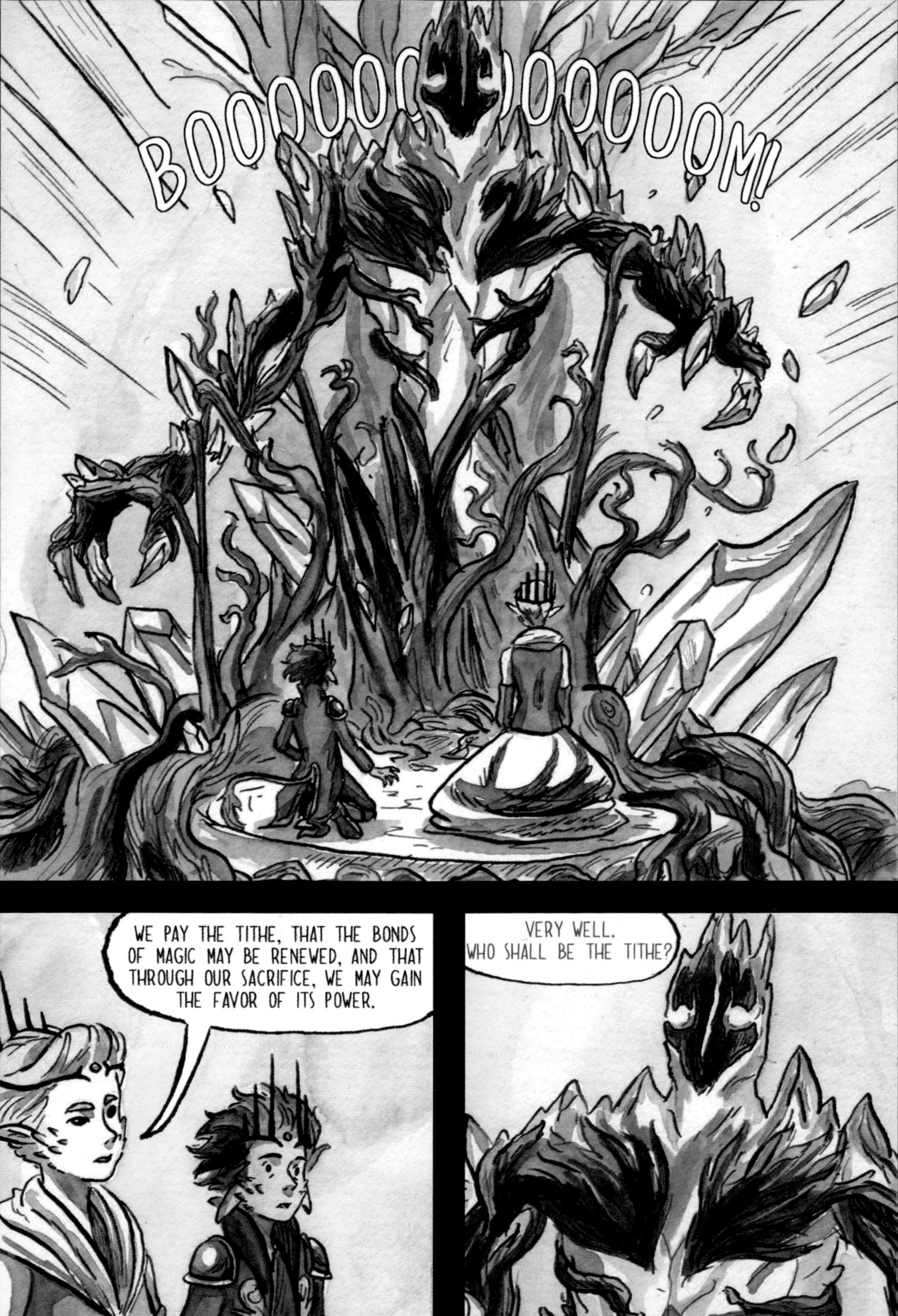
BOOOOOOOOOOOOOM!
WE PAY THE TITHE, THAT THE BONDS OF MAGIC MAY BE RENEWED, AND THAT THROUGH OUR SACRIFICE, WE MAY GAIN THE FAVOR OF ITS POWER.
VERY WELL. WHO SHALL BE THE TITHE?

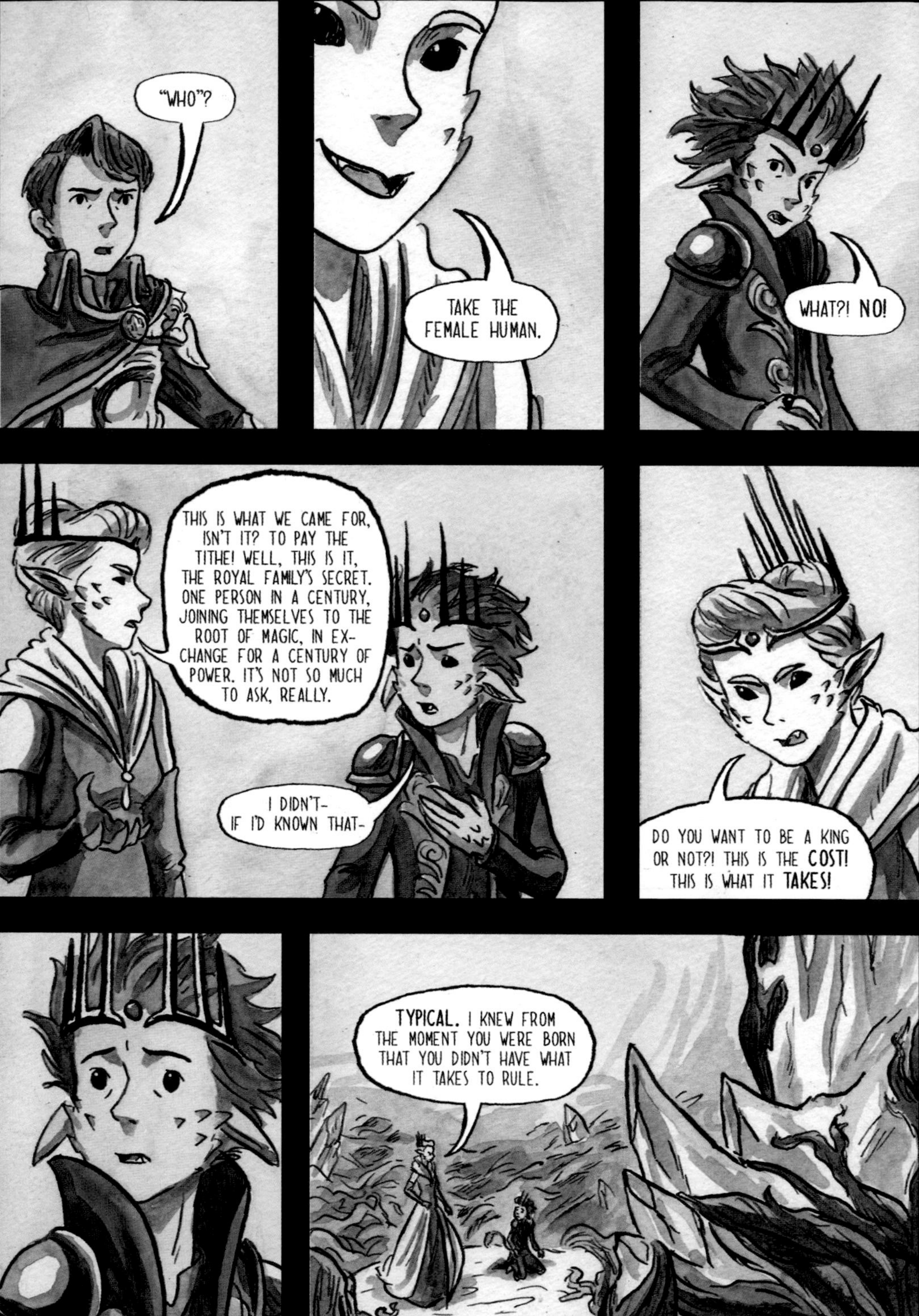
"WHO"?
TAKE THE FEMALE HUMAN.
WHAT?! NO!
THIS IS WHAT WE CAME FOR, ISN'T IT? TO PAY THE TITHE! WELL, THIS IS IT, THE ROYAL FAMILY'S SECRET. ONE PERSON IN A CENTURY, JOINING THEMSELVES TO THE ROOT OF MAGIC, IN EX-CHANGE FOR A CENTURY OF POWER. IT'S NOT SO MUCH TO ASK, REALLY.
I DIDN'T- IF I'D KNOWN THAT-
DO YOU WANT TO BE A KING OR NOT?! THIS IS THE **COST!** THIS IS WHAT IT **TAKES!**
TYPICAL. I KNEW FROM THE MOMENT YOU WERE BORN THAT YOU DIDN'T HAVE WHAT IT TAKES TO RULE.

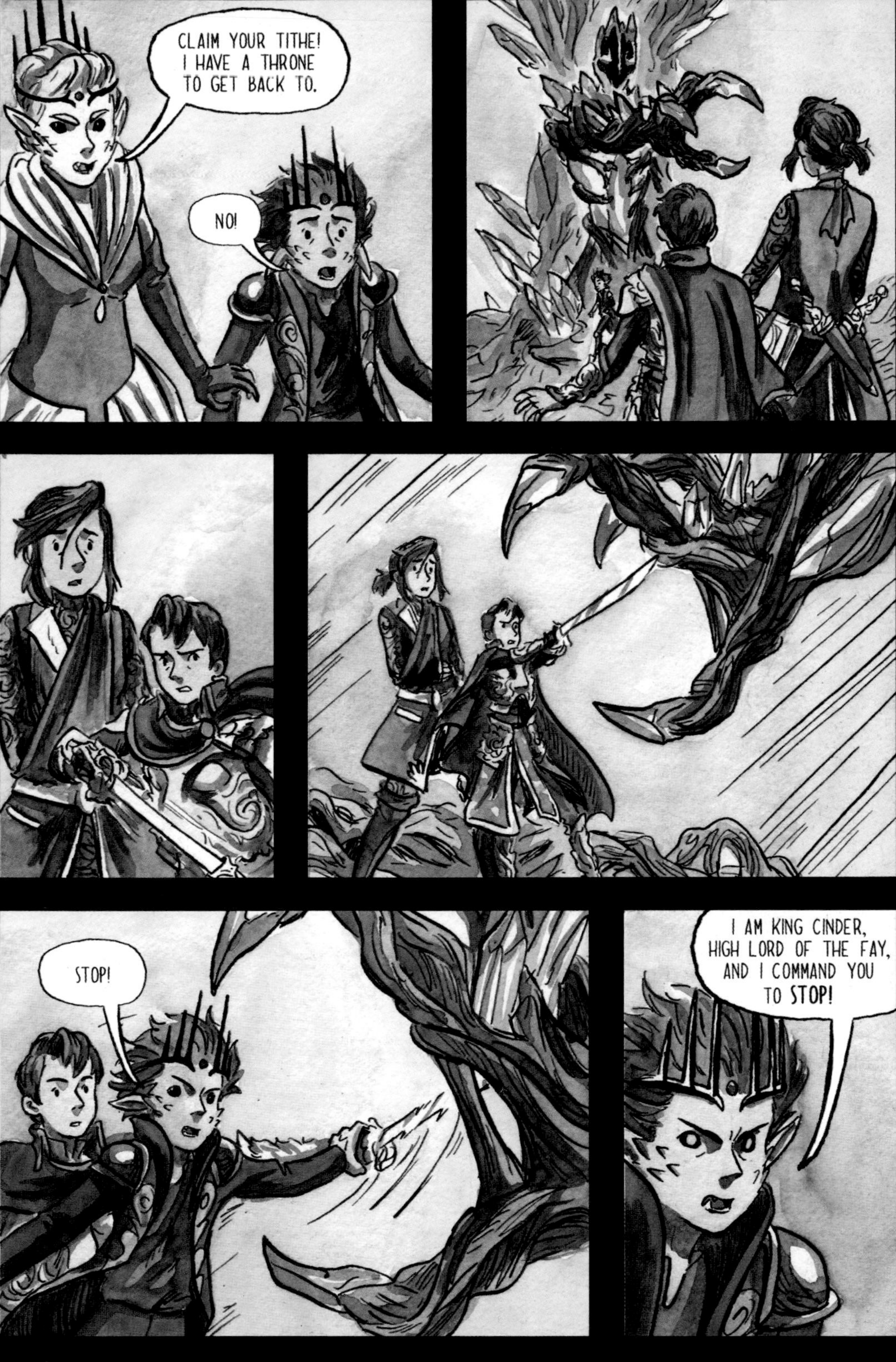
CLAIM YOUR TITHE! I HAVE A THRONE TO GET BACK TO.
NO!
STOP!
I AM KING CINDER, HIGH LORD OF THE FAY, AND I COMMAND YOU TO **STOP!**

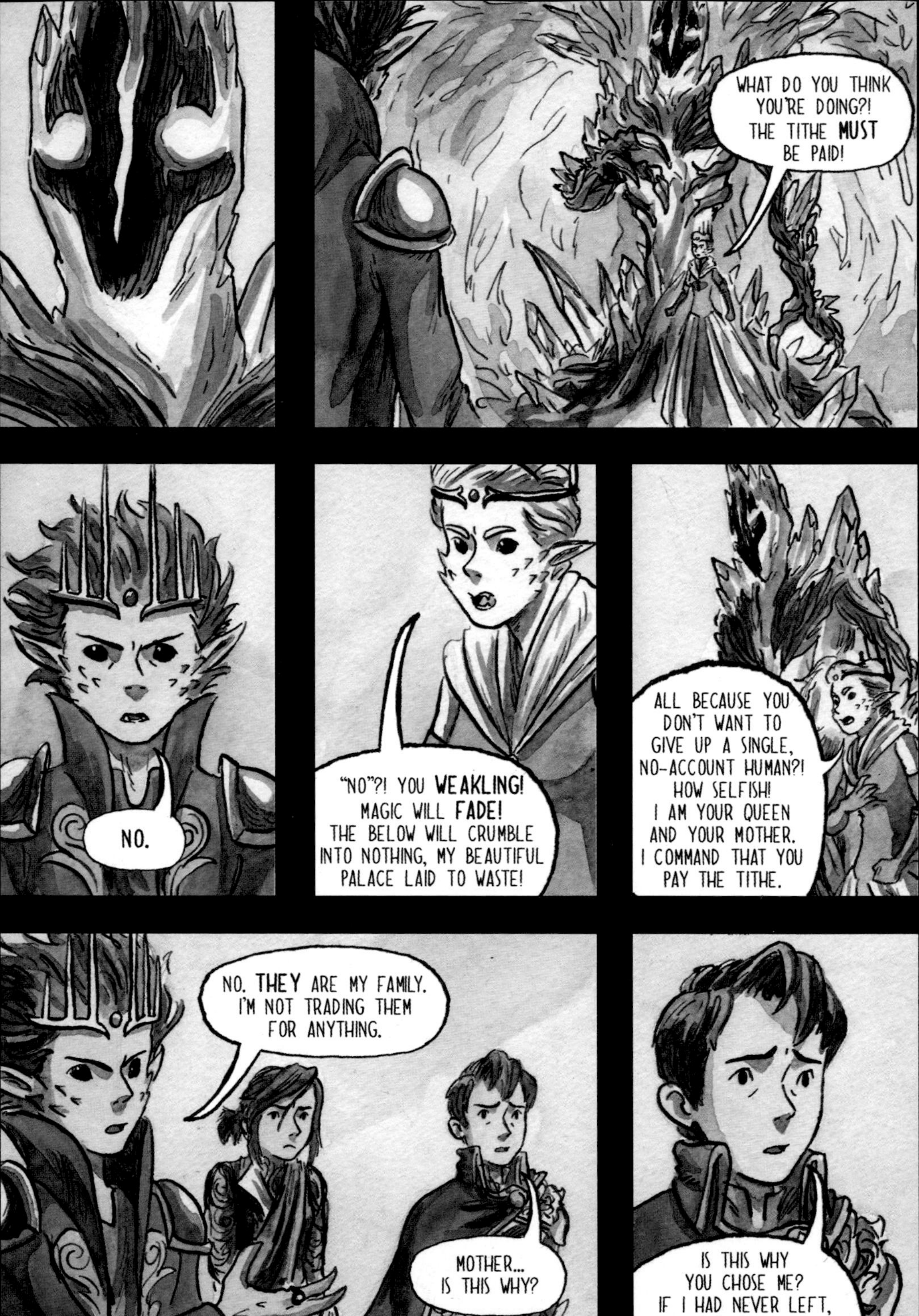
WHAT DO YOU THINK YOU'RE DOING?! THE TITHE **MUST** BE PAID!
NO.
"NO"?! YOU **WEAKLING!** MAGIC WILL **FADE!** THE BELOW WILL CRUMBLE INTO NOTHING, MY BEAUTIFUL PALACE LAID TO WASTE!
ALL BECAUSE YOU DON'T WANT TO GIVE UP A SINGLE, NO-ACCOUNT HUMAN?! HOW SELFISH! I AM YOUR QUEEN AND YOUR MOTHER. I COMMAND THAT YOU PAY THE TITHE.
NO. **THEY** ARE MY FAMILY. I'M NOT TRADING THEM FOR ANYTHING.
MOTHER... IS THIS WHY?
IS THIS WHY YOU CHOSE ME? IF I HAD NEVER LEFT, WOULD YOU HAVE GIVEN ME TO THIS?

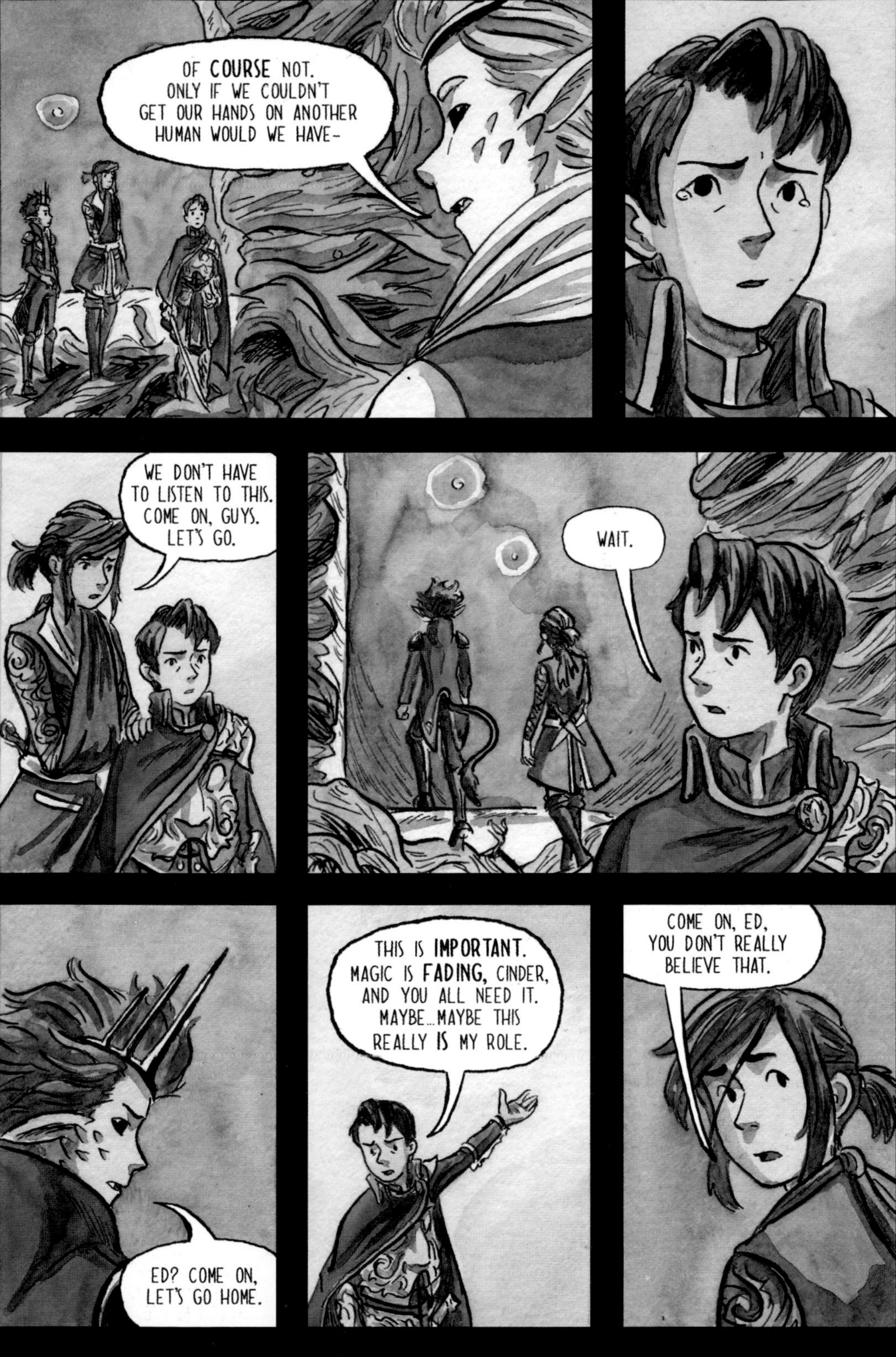

OF COURSE NOT. ONLY IF WE COULDN'T GET OUR HANDS ON ANOTHER HUMAN WOULD WE HAVE-
WE DON'T HAVE TO LISTEN TO THIS. COME ON, GUYS. LET'S GO.
WAIT.
ED? COME ON, LET'S GO HOME.
THIS IS IMPORTANT. MAGIC IS FADING, CINDER, AND YOU ALL NEED IT. MAYBE...MAYBE THIS REALLY IS MY ROLE.
COME ON, ED, YOU DON'T REALLY BELIEVE THAT.

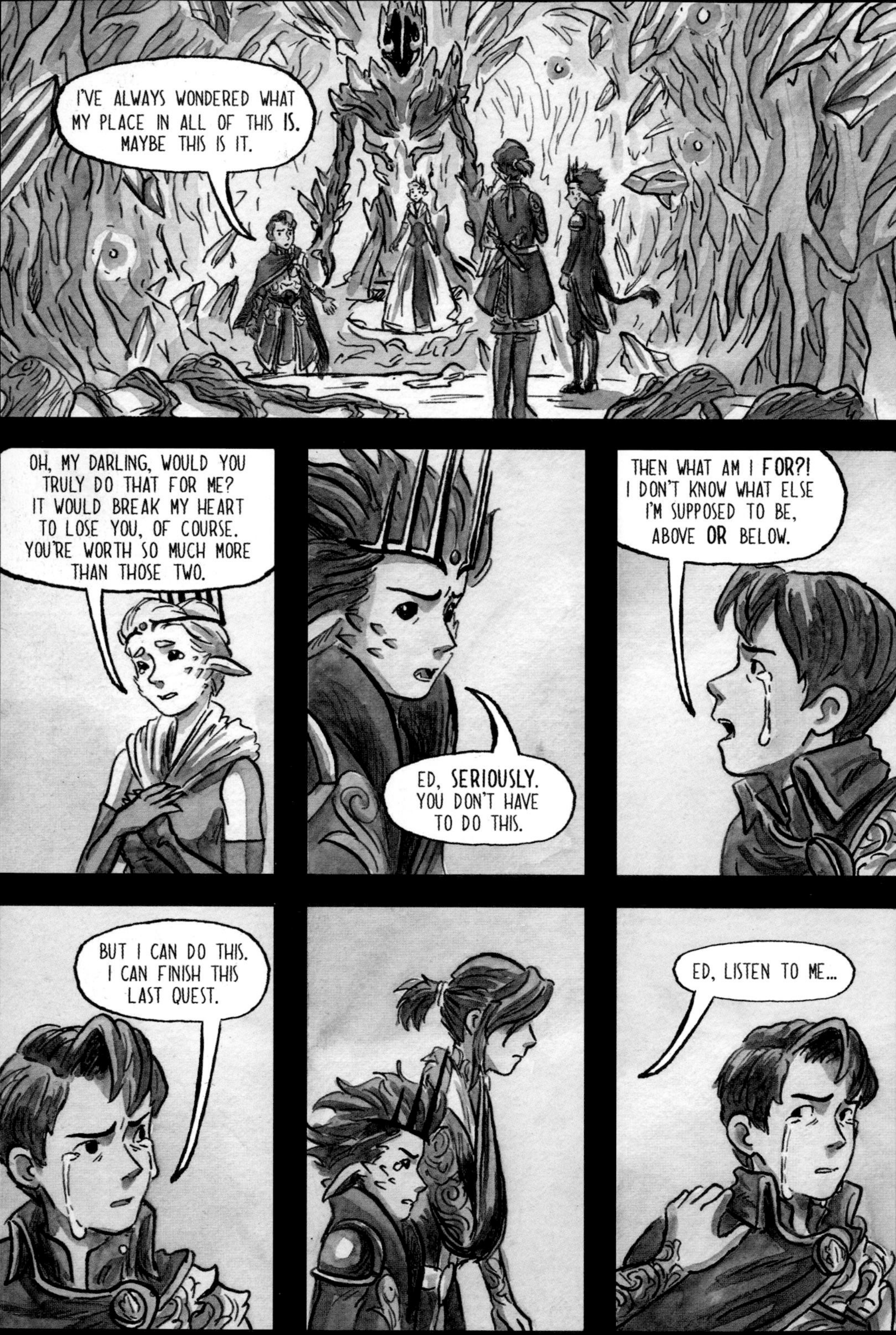
I'VE ALWAYS WONDERED WHAT MY PLACE IN ALL OF THIS IS. MAYBE THIS IS IT.
OH, MY DARLING, WOULD YOU TRULY DO THAT FOR ME? IT WOULD BREAK MY HEART TO LOSE YOU, OF COURSE. YOU'RE WORTH SO MUCH MORE THAN THOSE TWO.
ED, SERIOUSLY. YOU DON'T HAVE TO DO THIS.
THEN WHAT AM I FOR?! I DON'T KNOW WHAT ELSE I'M SUPPOSED TO BE, ABOVE OR BELOW.
BUT I CAN DO THIS. I CAN FINISH THIS LAST QUEST.
ED, LISTEN TO ME...

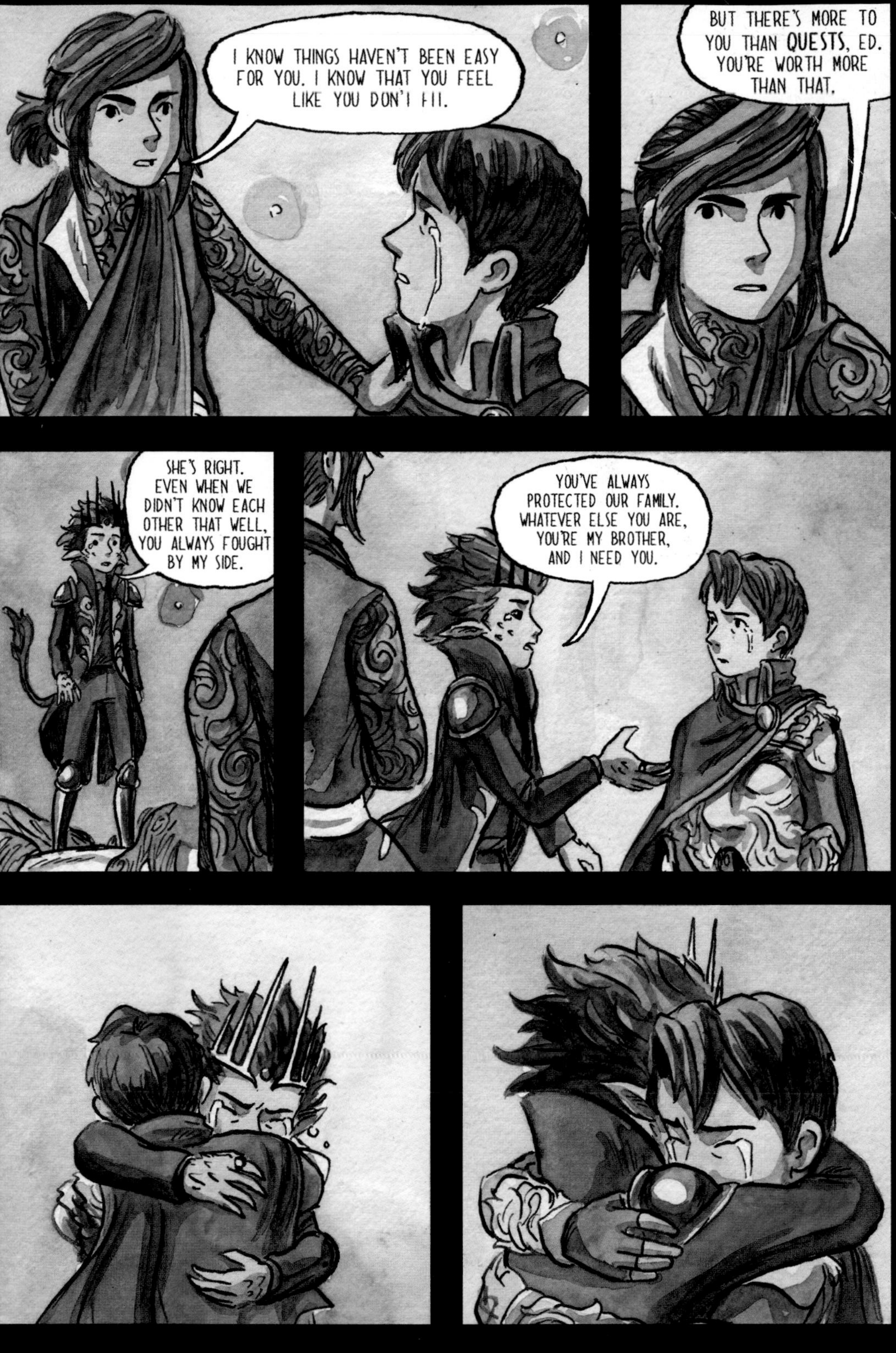
I KNOW THINGS HAVEN'T BEEN EASY FOR YOU. I KNOW THAT YOU FEEL LIKE YOU DON'T FIT.
BUT THERE'S MORE TO YOU THAN **QUESTS**, ED. YOU'RE WORTH MORE THAN THAT.
SHE'S RIGHT. EVEN WHEN WE DIDN'T KNOW EACH OTHER THAT WELL, YOU ALWAYS FOUGHT BY MY SIDE.
YOU'VE ALWAYS PROTECTED OUR FAMILY. WHATEVER ELSE YOU ARE, YOU'RE MY BROTHER, AND I NEED YOU.

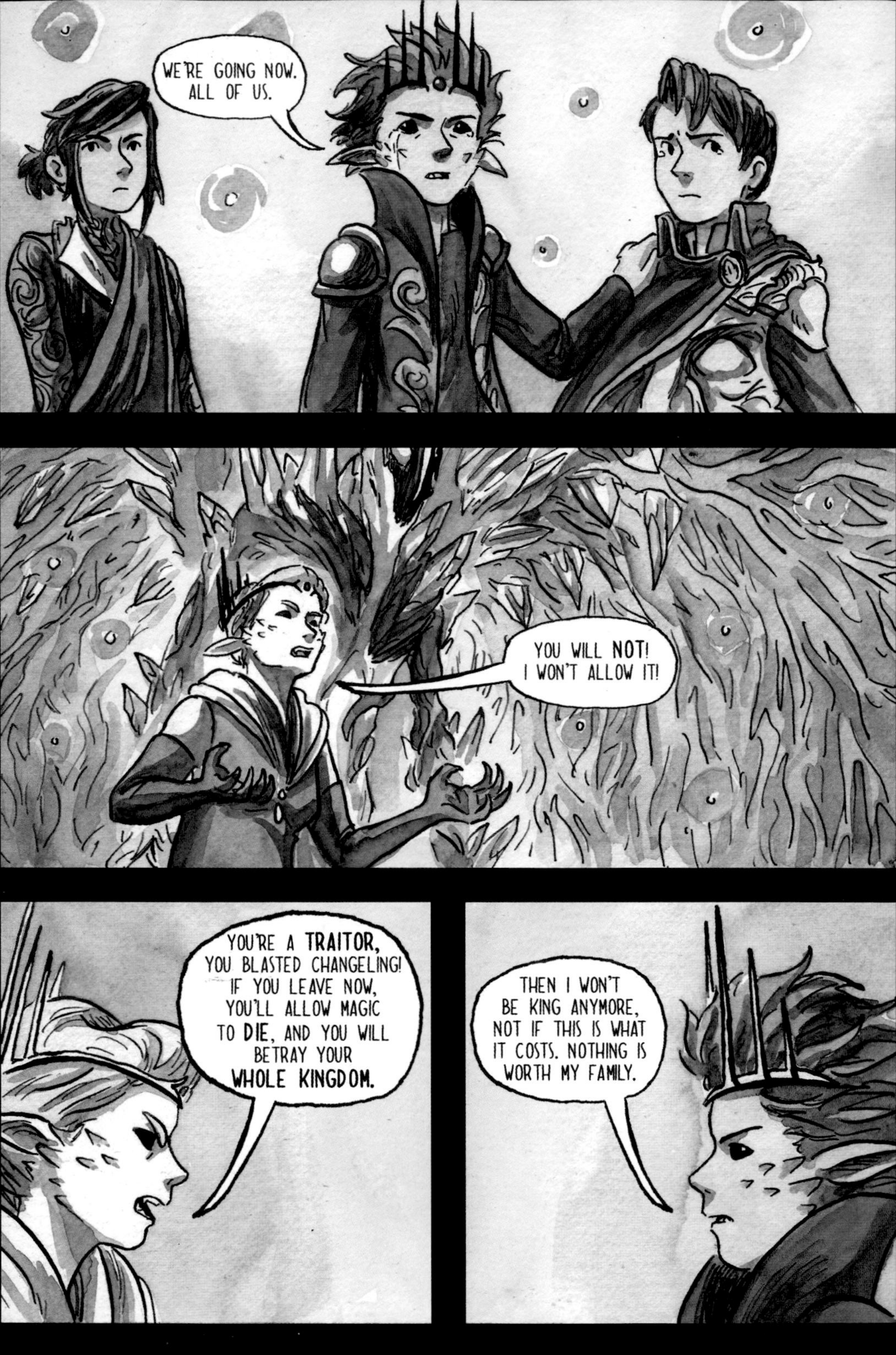
WE'RE GOING NOW. ALL OF US.
YOU WILL NOT! I WON'T ALLOW IT!
YOU'RE A TRAITOR, YOU BLASTED CHANGELING! IF YOU LEAVE NOW, YOU'LL ALLOW MAGIC TO DIE, AND YOU WILL BETRAY YOUR WHOLE KINGDOM.
THEN I WON'T BE KING ANYMORE, NOT IF THIS IS WHAT IT COSTS. NOTHING IS WORTH MY FAMILY.

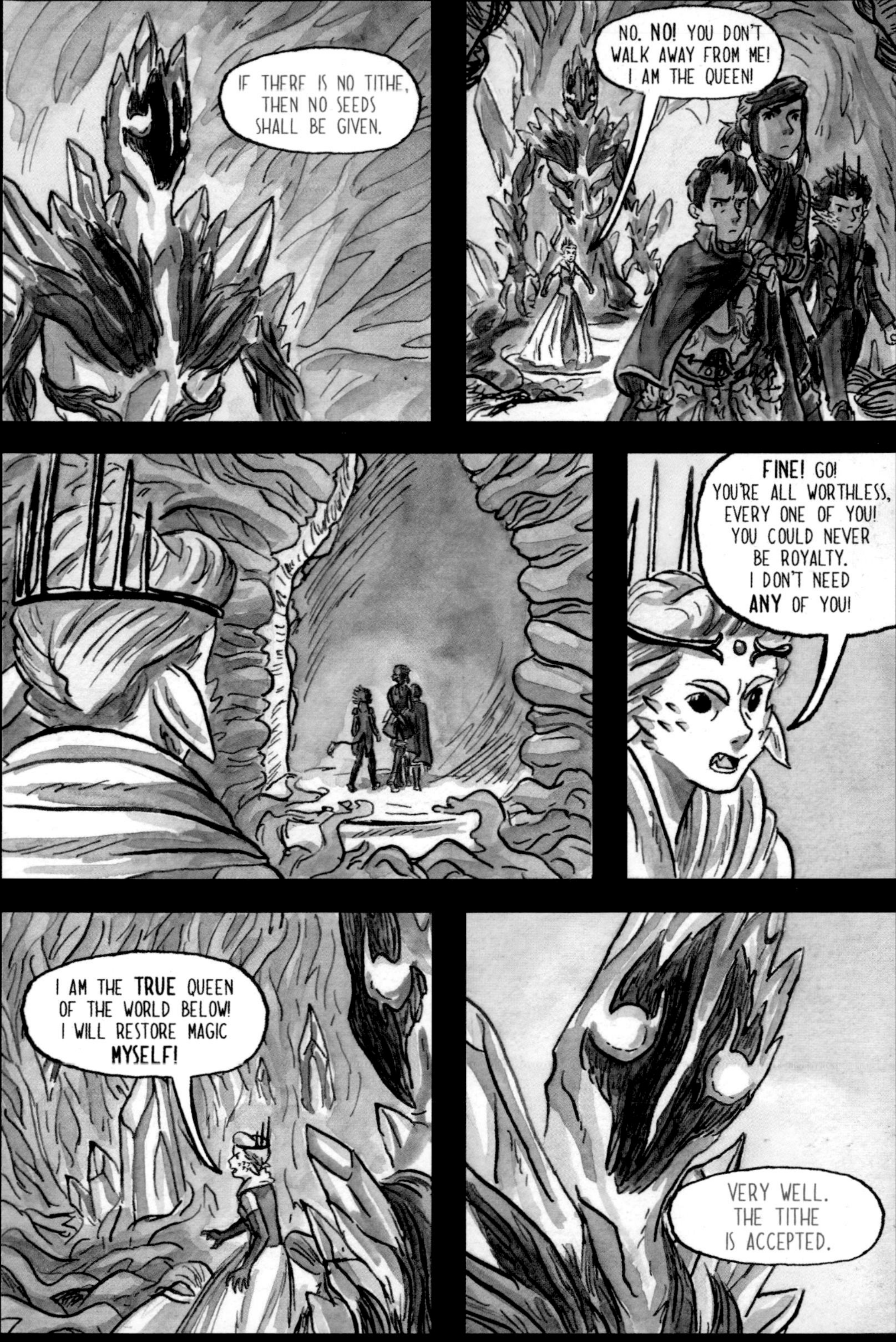
IF THERE IS NO TITHE, THEN NO SEEDS SHALL BE GIVEN.
NO. **NO!** YOU DON'T WALK AWAY FROM ME! I AM THE QUEEN!
FINE! GO! YOU'RE ALL WORTHLESS, EVERY ONE OF YOU! YOU COULD NEVER BE ROYALTY. I DON'T NEED **ANY** OF YOU!
I AM THE **TRUE** QUEEN OF THE WORLD BELOW! I WILL RESTORE MAGIC **MYSELF!**
VERY WELL. THE TITHE IS ACCEPTED.

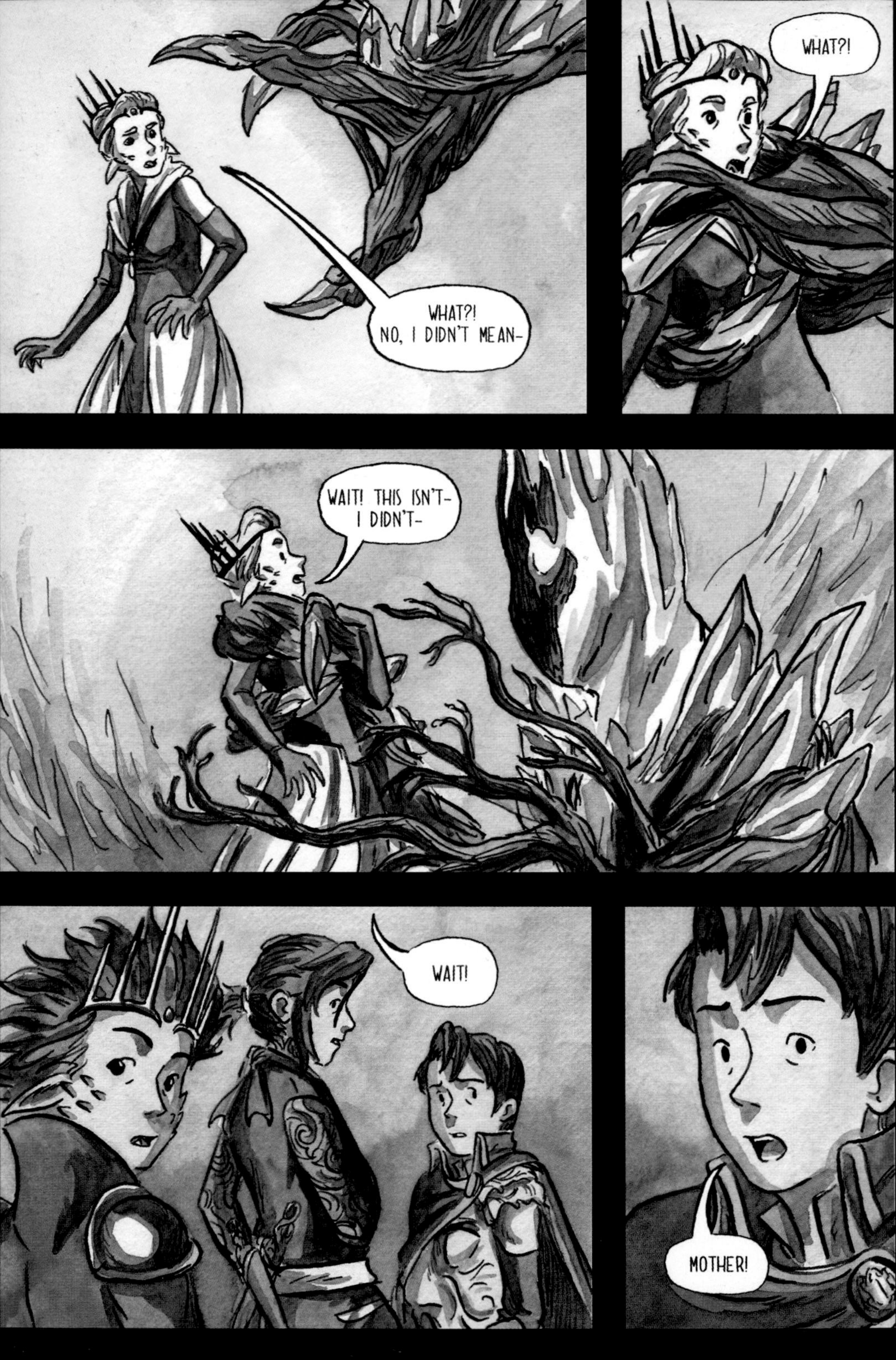
WHAT?!
NO, I DIDN'T MEAN-
WHAT?!
WAIT! THIS ISN'T-
I DIDN'T-
WAIT!
MOTHER!

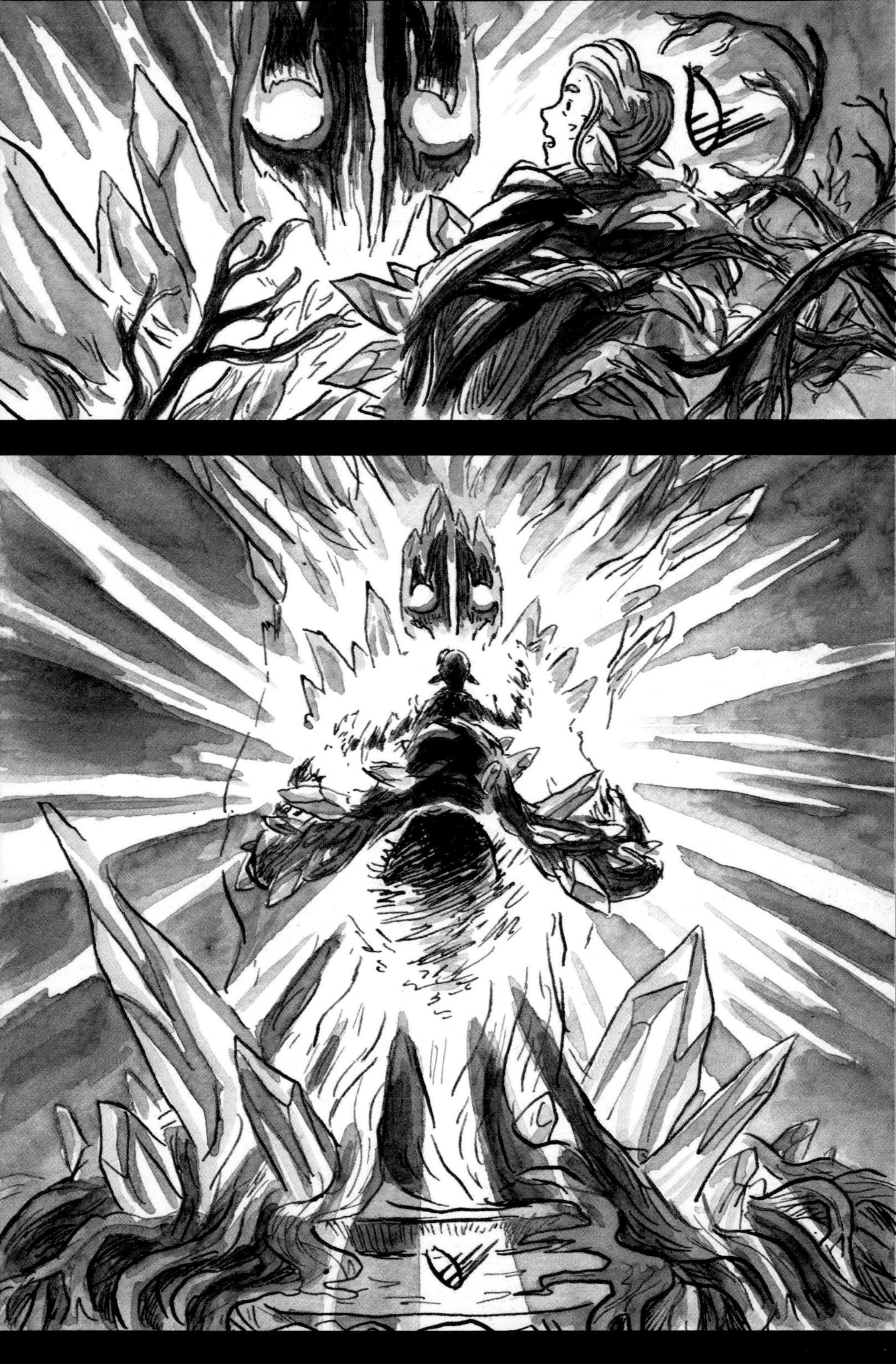

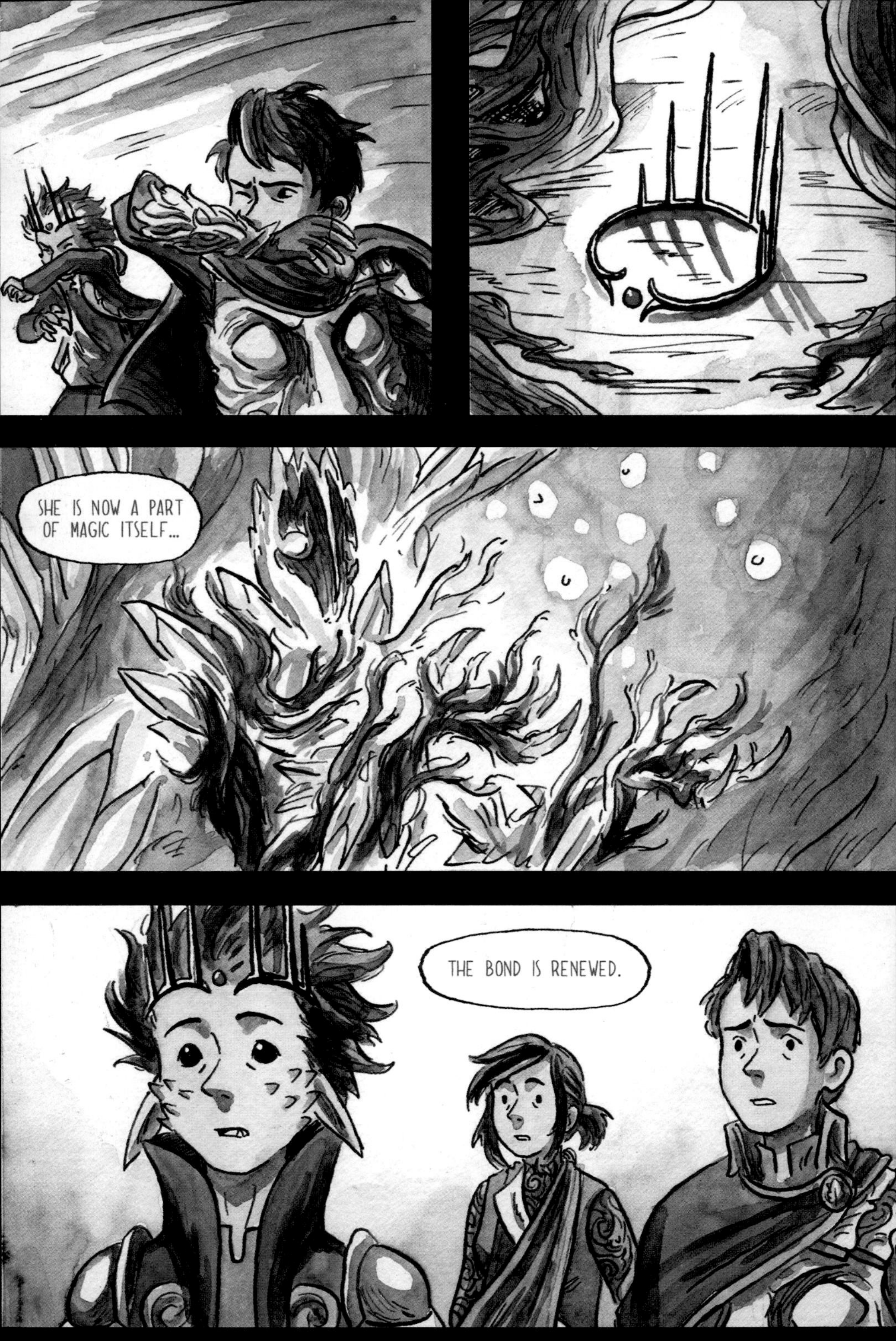
SHE IS NOW A PART OF MAGIC ITSELF...
THE BOND IS RENEWED.

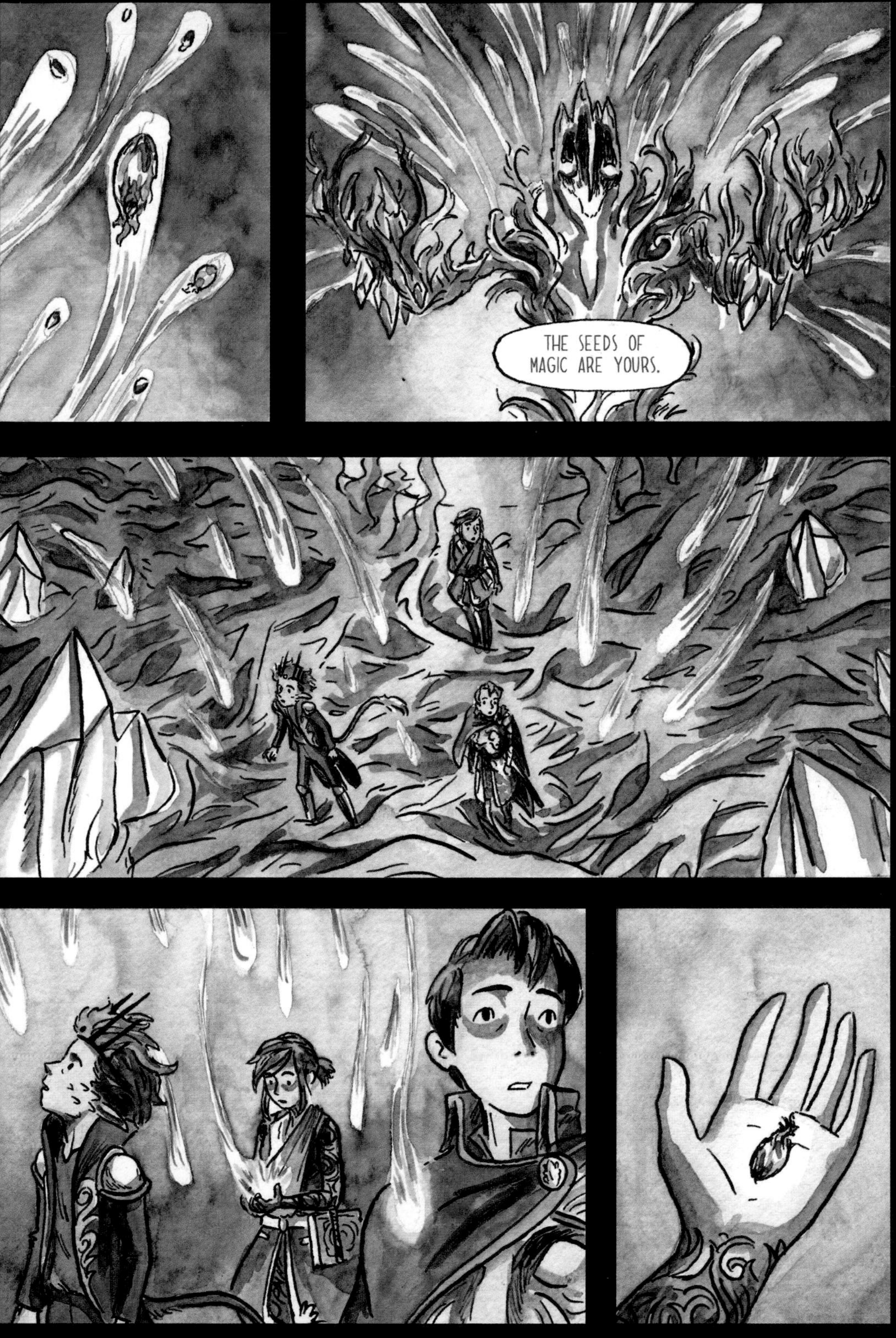
THE SEEDS OF
MAGIC ARE YOURS.

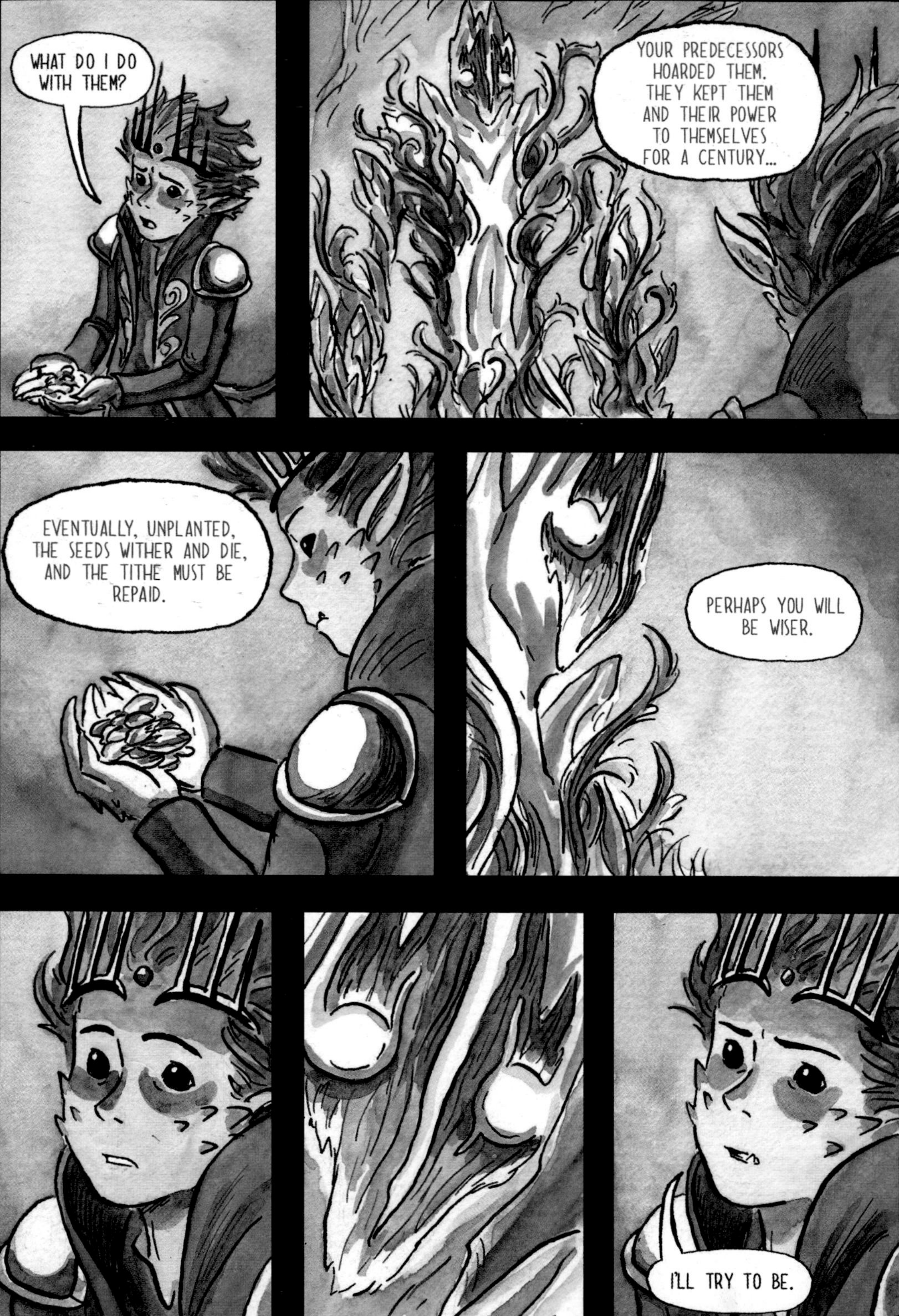
WHAT DO I DO WITH THEM?
YOUR PREDECESSORS HOARDED THEM. THEY KEPT THEM AND THEIR POWER TO THEMSELVES FOR A CENTURY...
EVENTUALLY, UNPLANTED, THE SEEDS WITHER AND DIE, AND THE TITHE MUST BE REPAID.
PERHAPS YOU WILL BE WISER.
I'LL TRY TO BE.

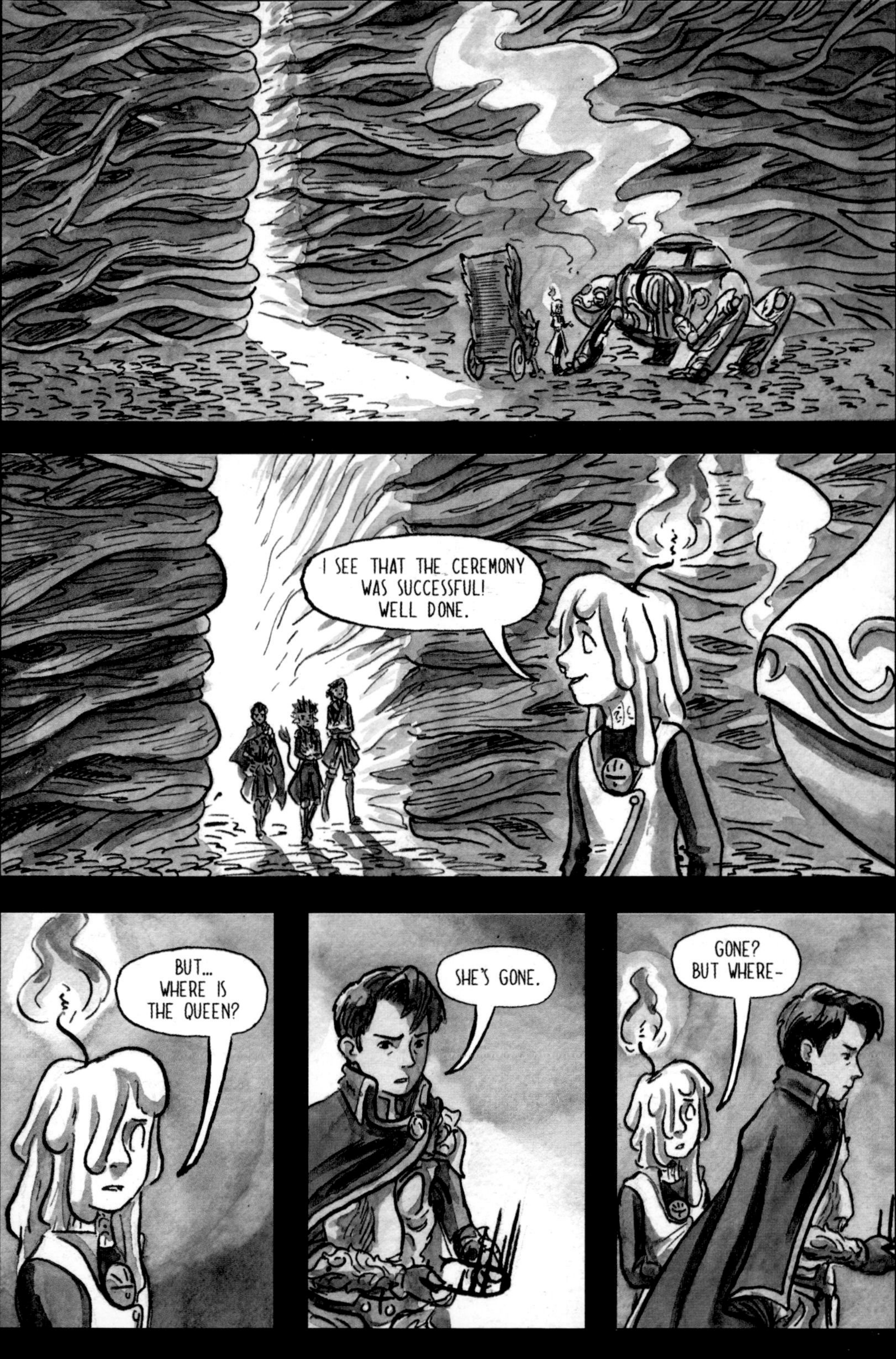
I SEE THAT THE CEREMONY WAS SUCCESSFUL! WELL DONE.
BUT... WHERE IS THE QUEEN?
SHE'S GONE.
GONE? BUT WHERE-

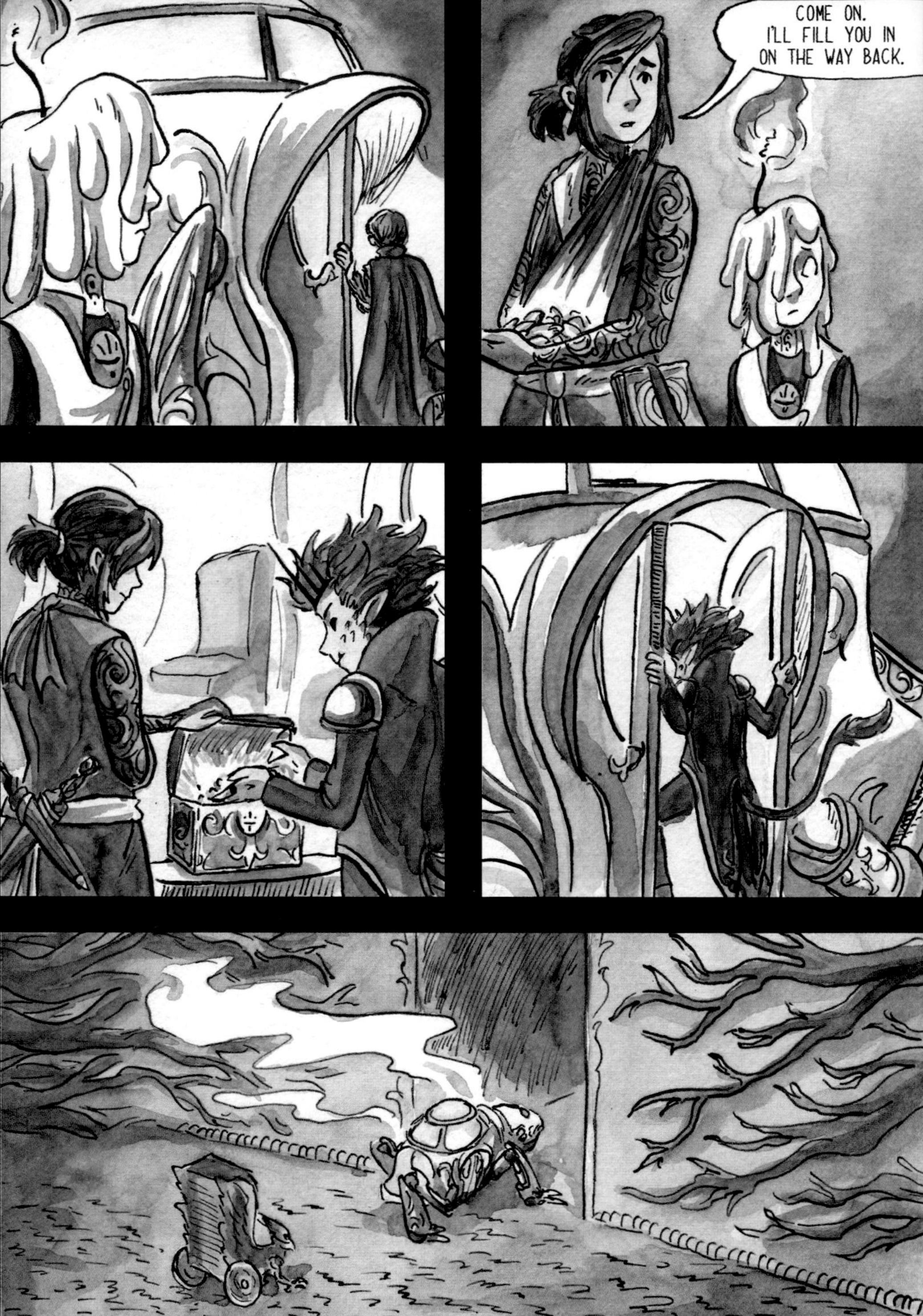
COME ON.
I'LL FILL YOU IN
ON THE WAY BACK.

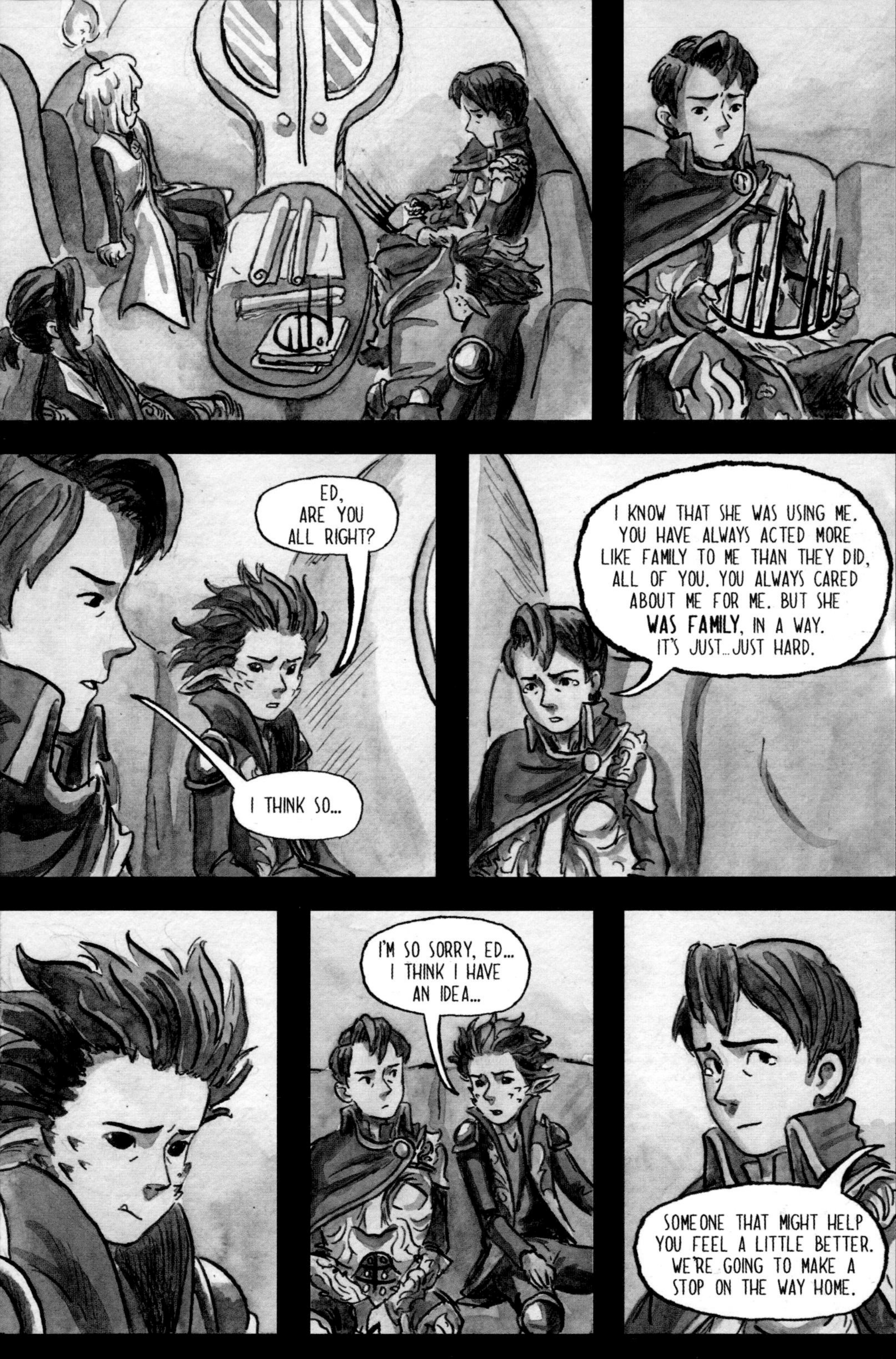
ED, ARE YOU ALL RIGHT?
I THINK SO...
I KNOW THAT SHE WAS USING ME. YOU HAVE ALWAYS ACTED MORE LIKE FAMILY TO ME THAN THEY DID, ALL OF YOU. YOU ALWAYS CARED ABOUT ME FOR ME. BUT SHE **WAS FAMILY**, IN A WAY. IT'S JUST...JUST HARD.
I'M SO SORRY, ED... I THINK I HAVE AN IDEA...
SOMEONE THAT MIGHT HELP YOU FEEL A LITTLE BETTER. WE'RE GOING TO MAKE A STOP ON THE WAY HOME.

CHAPTER
THIRTEEN

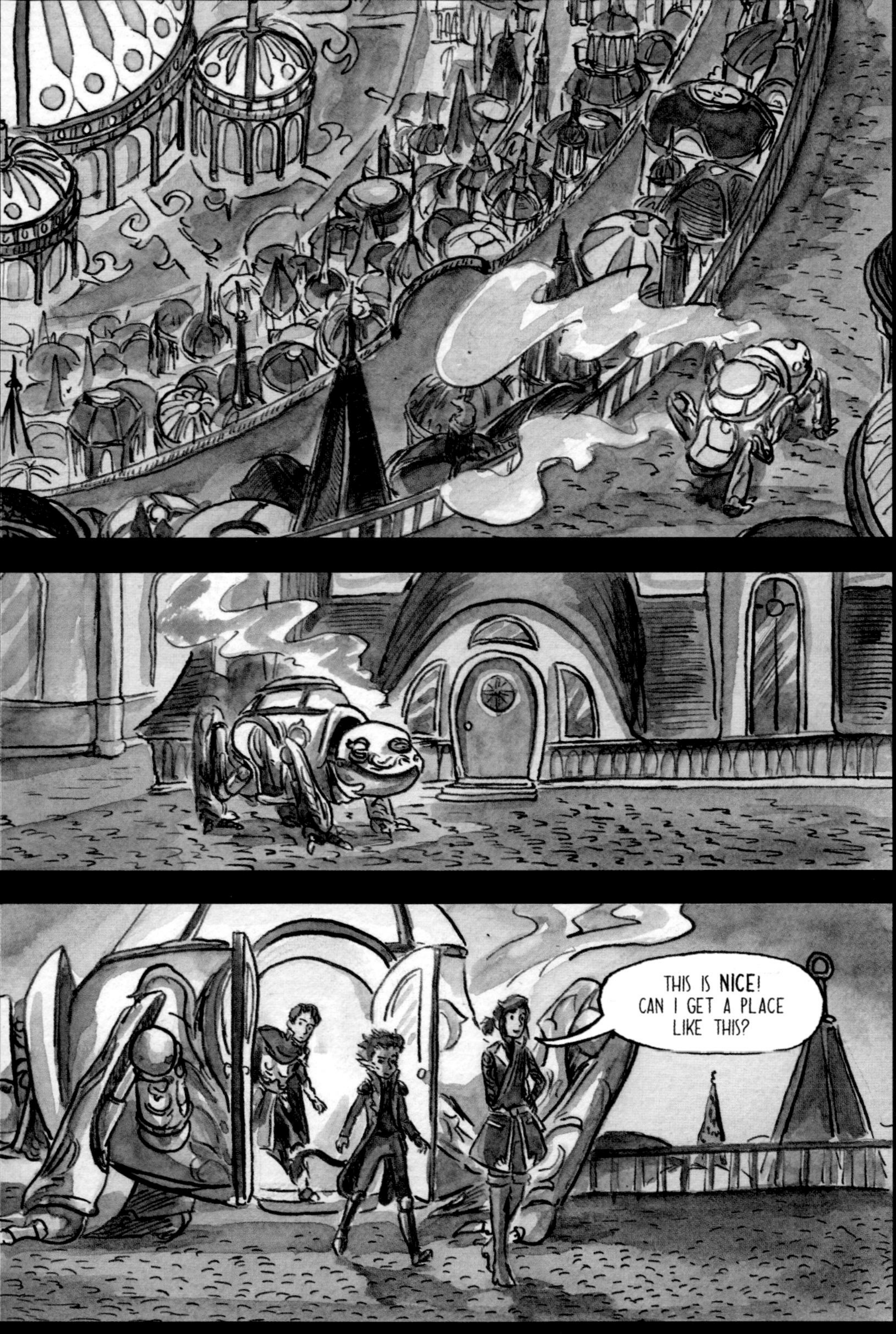
THIS IS NICE!
CAN I GET A PLACE LIKE THIS?

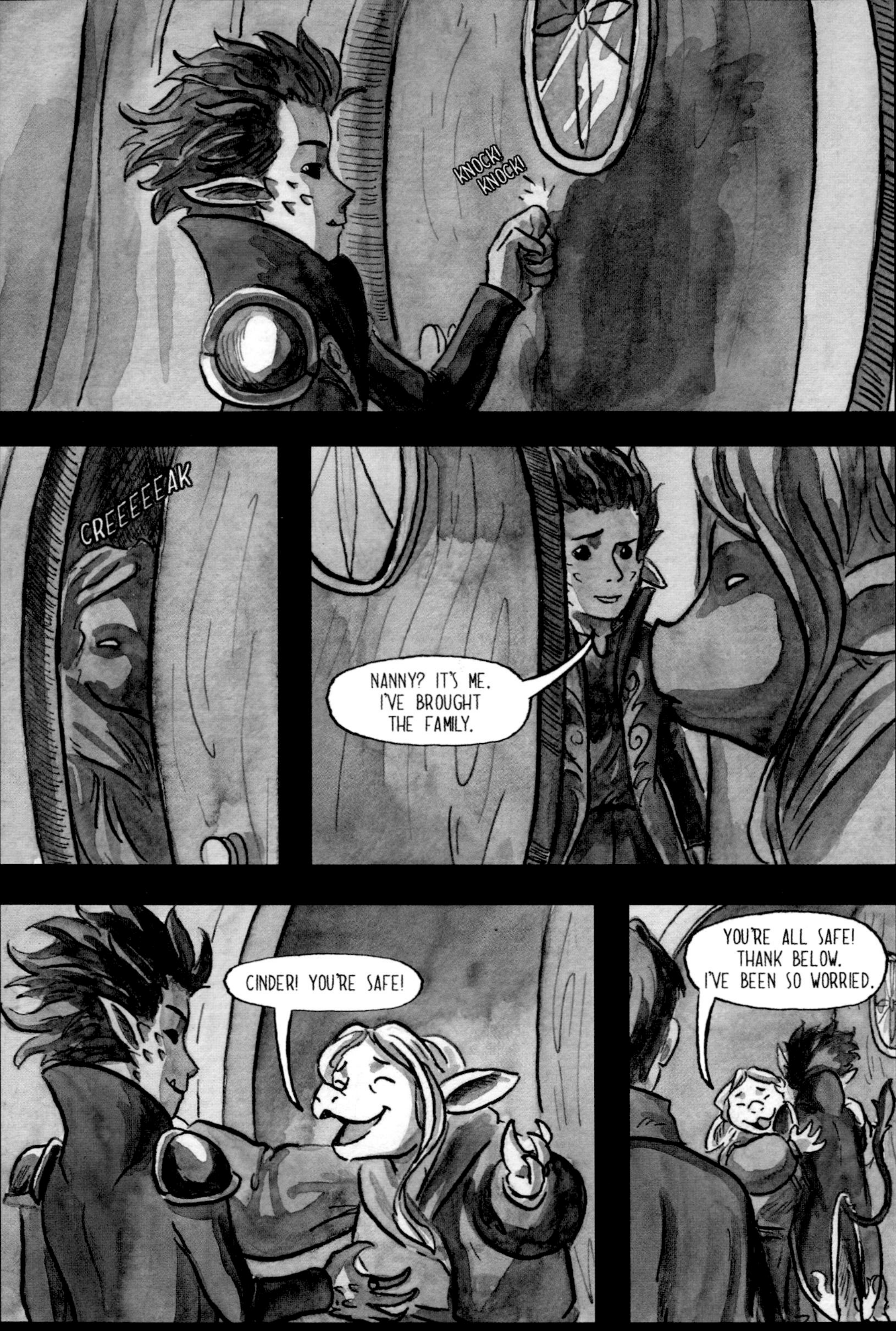
KNOCK! KNOCK!
CREEEEEEAK
NANNY? IT'S ME. I'VE BROUGHT THE FAMILY.
CINDER! YOU'RE SAFE!
YOU'RE ALL SAFE! THANK BELOW. I'VE BEEN SO WORRIED.

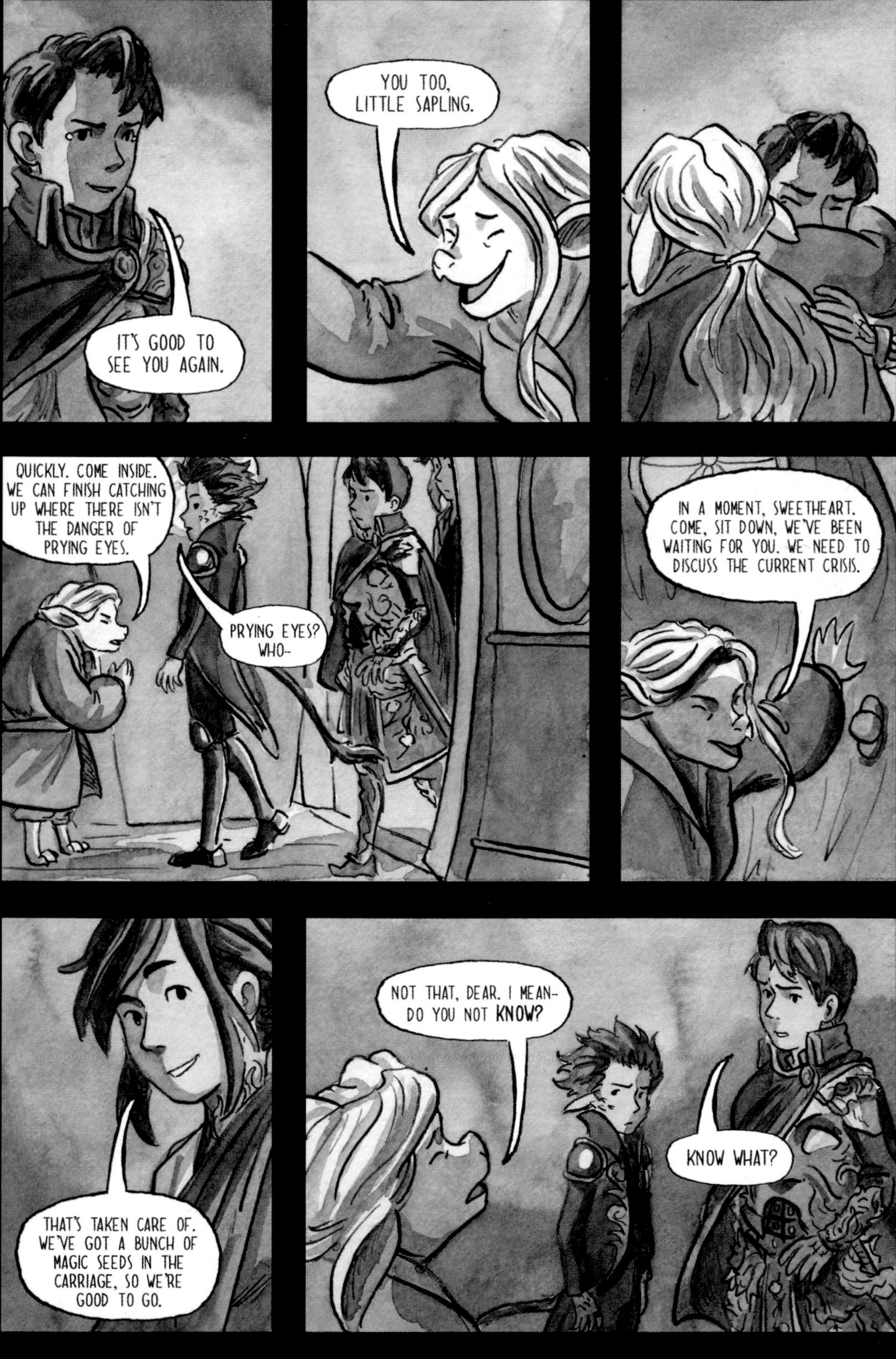
IT'S GOOD TO SEE YOU AGAIN.
YOU TOO, LITTLE SAPLING.
QUICKLY. COME INSIDE. WE CAN FINISH CATCHING UP WHERE THERE ISN'T THE DANGER OF PRYING EYES.
PRYING EYES? WHO-
IN A MOMENT, SWEETHEART. COME, SIT DOWN, WE'VE BEEN WAITING FOR YOU. WE NEED TO DISCUSS THE CURRENT CRISIS.
THAT'S TAKEN CARE OF. WE'VE GOT A BUNCH OF MAGIC SEEDS IN THE CARRIAGE, SO WE'RE GOOD TO GO.
NOT THAT, DEAR. I MEAN- DO YOU NOT **KNOW**?
KNOW WHAT?

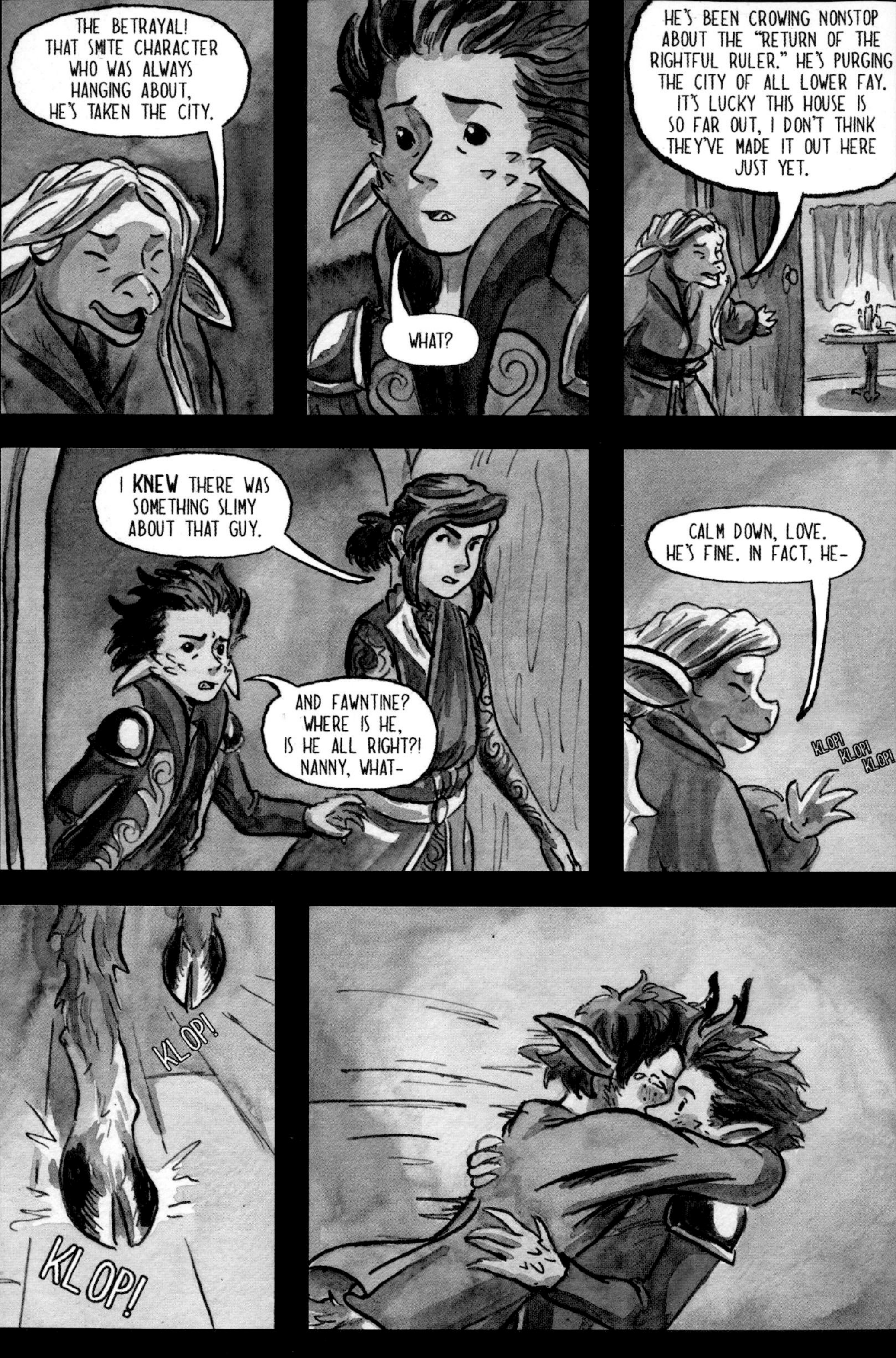
THE BETRAYAL! THAT SMITE CHARACTER WHO WAS ALWAYS HANGING ABOUT, HE'S TAKEN THE CITY.
WHAT?
HE'S BEEN CROWING NONSTOP ABOUT THE "RETURN OF THE RIGHTFUL RULER." HE'S PURGING THE CITY OF ALL LOWER FAY. IT'S LUCKY THIS HOUSE IS SO FAR OUT, I DON'T THINK THEY'VE MADE IT OUT HERE JUST YET.
I **KNEW** THERE WAS SOMETHING SLIMY ABOUT THAT GUY.
AND FAWNTINE? WHERE IS HE, IS HE ALL RIGHT?! NANNY, WHAT-
CALM DOWN, LOVE. HE'S FINE. IN FACT, HE-
KLOP! KLOP! KLOP!
KLOP!
KLOP!

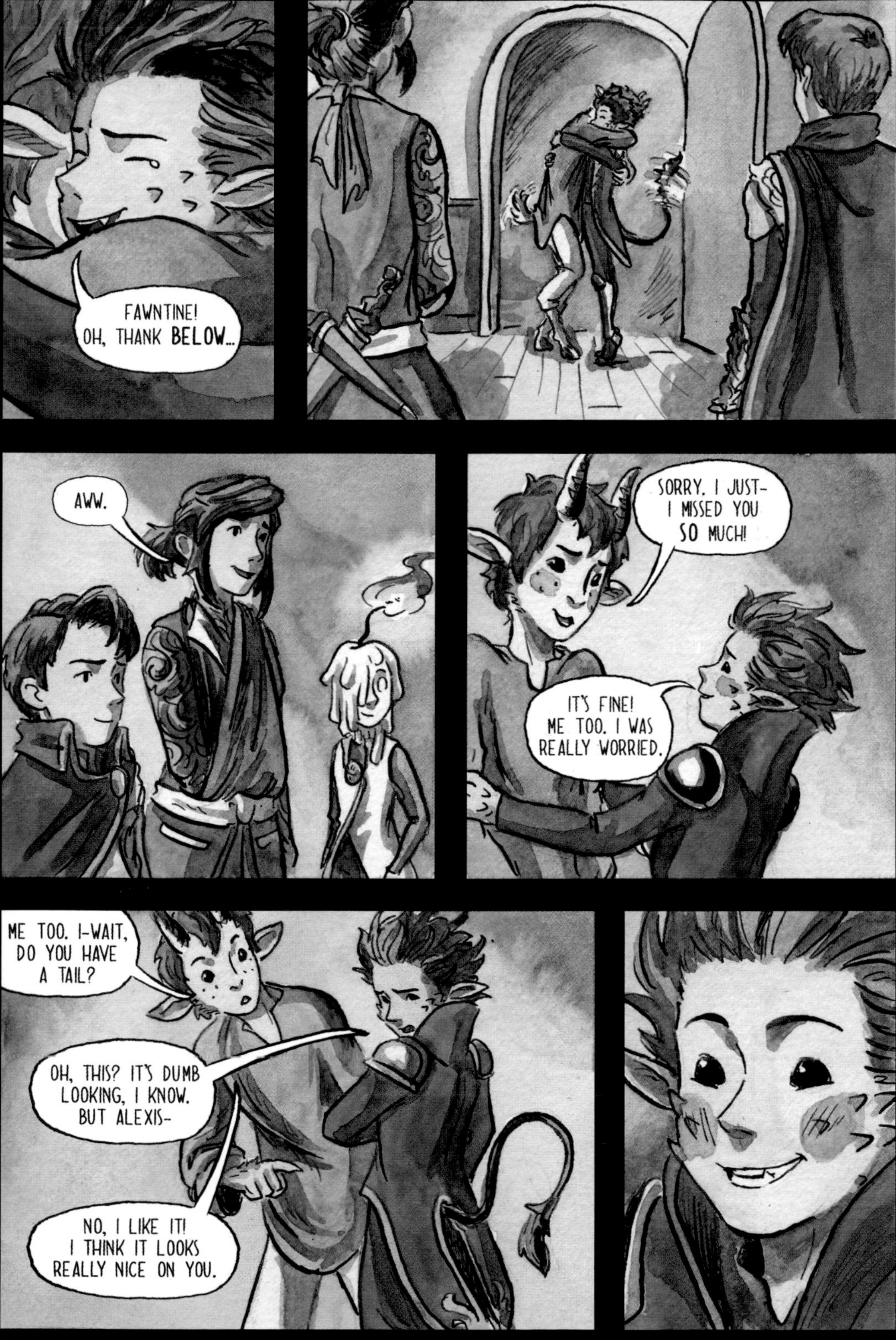
FAWNTINE! OH, THANK BELOW...
AWW.
SORRY. I JUST- I MISSED YOU SO MUCH!
IT'S FINE! ME TOO. I WAS REALLY WORRIED.
ME TOO. I-WAIT, DO YOU HAVE A TAIL?
OH, THIS? IT'S DUMB LOOKING, I KNOW. BUT ALEXIS-
NO, I LIKE IT! I THINK IT LOOKS REALLY NICE ON YOU.

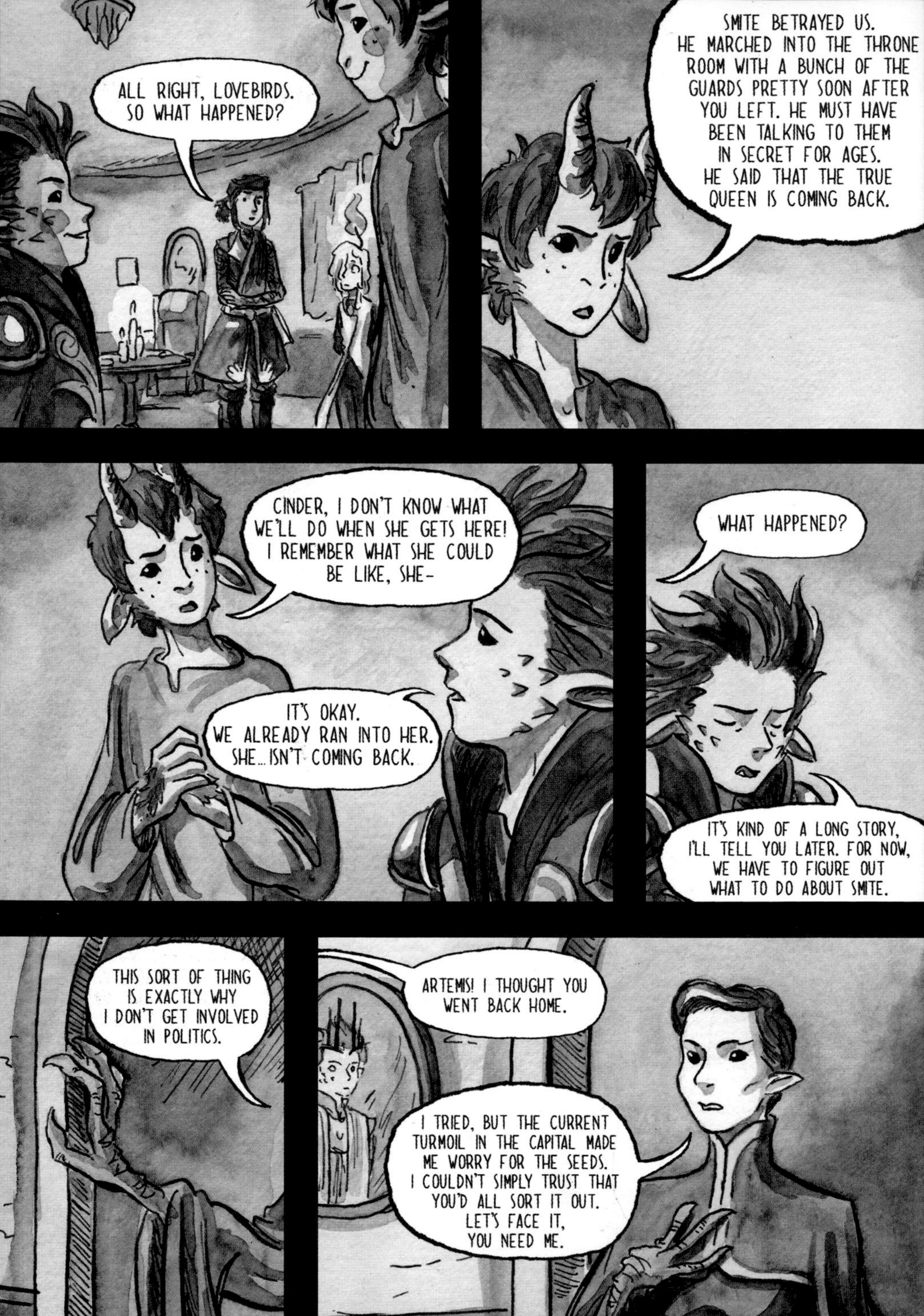
ALL RIGHT, LOVEBIRDS. SO WHAT HAPPENED?
SMITE BETRAYED US. HE MARCHED INTO THE THRONE ROOM WITH A BUNCH OF THE GUARDS PRETTY SOON AFTER YOU LEFT. HE MUST HAVE BEEN TALKING TO THEM IN SECRET FOR AGES. HE SAID THAT THE TRUE QUEEN IS COMING BACK.
CINDER, I DON'T KNOW WHAT WE'LL DO WHEN SHE GETS HERE! I REMEMBER WHAT SHE COULD BE LIKE, SHE-
IT'S OKAY. WE ALREADY RAN INTO HER. SHE... ISN'T COMING BACK.
WHAT HAPPENED?
IT'S KIND OF A LONG STORY, I'LL TELL YOU LATER. FOR NOW, WE HAVE TO FIGURE OUT WHAT TO DO ABOUT SMITE.
THIS SORT OF THING IS EXACTLY WHY I DON'T GET INVOLVED IN POLITICS.
ARTEMIS! I THOUGHT YOU WENT BACK HOME.
I TRIED, BUT THE CURRENT TURMOIL IN THE CAPITAL MADE ME WORRY FOR THE SEEDS. I COULDN'T SIMPLY TRUST THAT YOU'D ALL SORT IT OUT. LET'S FACE IT, YOU NEED ME.

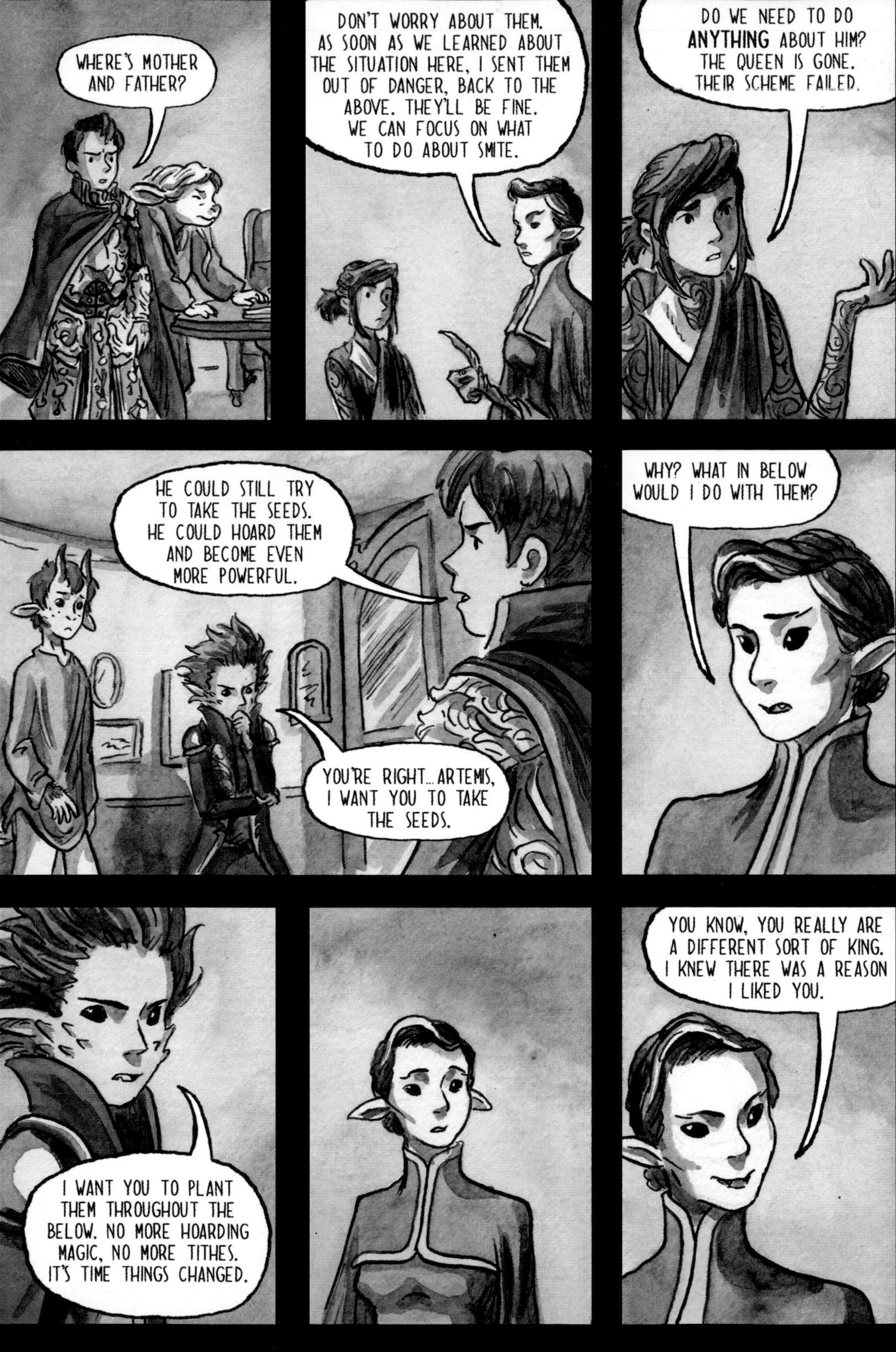
WHERE'S MOTHER AND FATHER?
DON'T WORRY ABOUT THEM. AS SOON AS WE LEARNED ABOUT THE SITUATION HERE, I SENT THEM OUT OF DANGER, BACK TO THE ABOVE. THEY'LL BE FINE. WE CAN FOCUS ON WHAT TO DO ABOUT SMITE.
DO WE NEED TO DO **ANYTHING** ABOUT HIM? THE QUEEN IS GONE. THEIR SCHEME FAILED.
HE COULD STILL TRY TO TAKE THE SEEDS. HE COULD HOARD THEM AND BECOME EVEN MORE POWERFUL.
YOU'RE RIGHT... ARTEMIS, I WANT YOU TO TAKE THE SEEDS.
WHY? WHAT IN BELOW WOULD I DO WITH THEM?
I WANT YOU TO PLANT THEM THROUGHOUT THE BELOW. NO MORE HOARDING MAGIC, NO MORE TITHES. IT'S TIME THINGS CHANGED.
YOU KNOW, YOU REALLY ARE A DIFFERENT SORT OF KING. I KNEW THERE WAS A REASON I LIKED YOU.

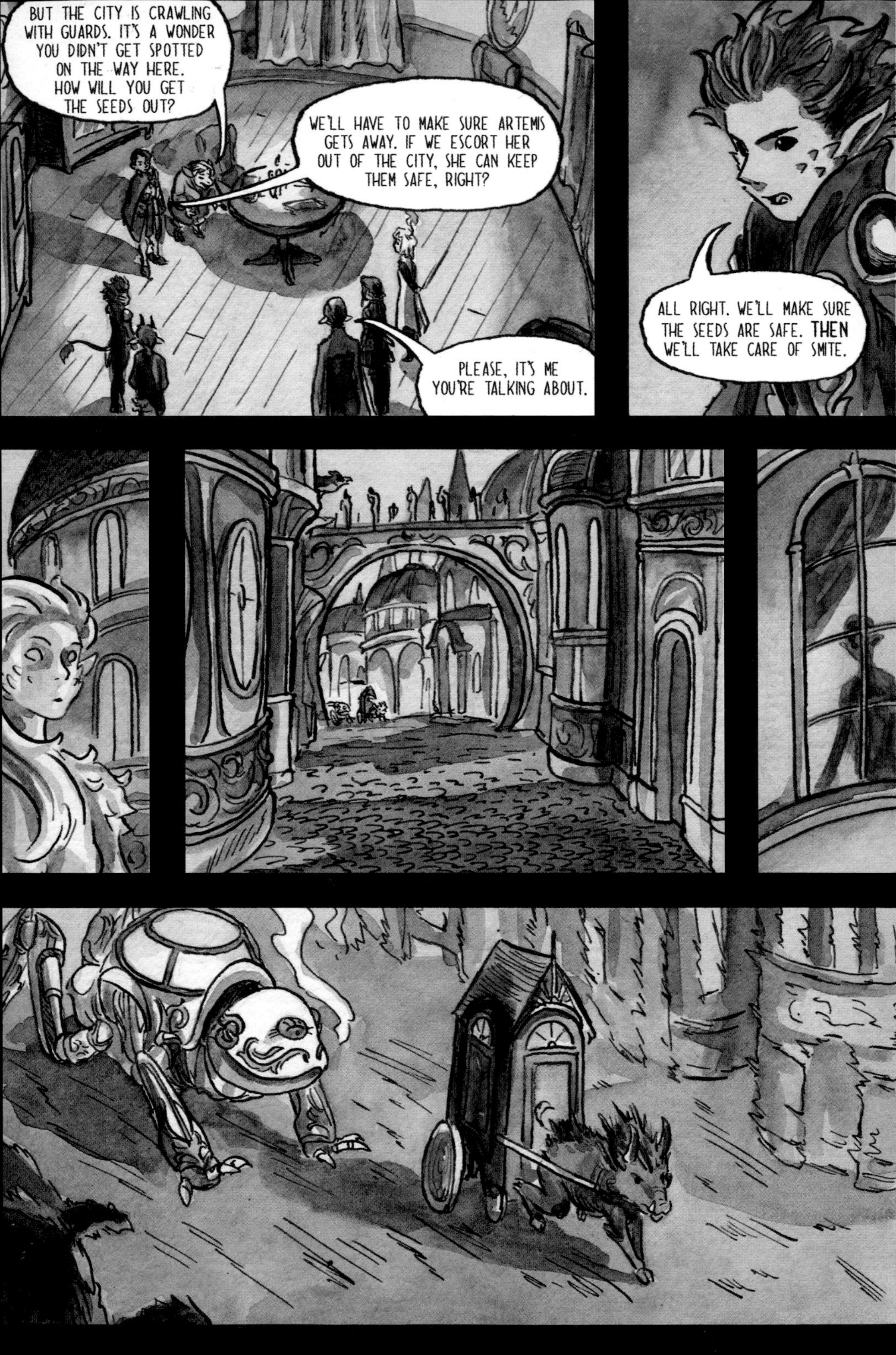
BUT THE CITY IS CRAWLING WITH GUARDS. IT'S A WONDER YOU DIDN'T GET SPOTTED ON THE WAY HERE. HOW WILL YOU GET THE SEEDS OUT?
WE'LL HAVE TO MAKE SURE ARTEMIS GETS AWAY. IF WE ESCORT HER OUT OF THE CITY, SHE CAN KEEP THEM SAFE, RIGHT?
PLEASE, IT'S ME YOU'RE TALKING ABOUT.
ALL RIGHT. WE'LL MAKE SURE THE SEEDS ARE SAFE. **THEN** WE'LL TAKE CARE OF SMITE.

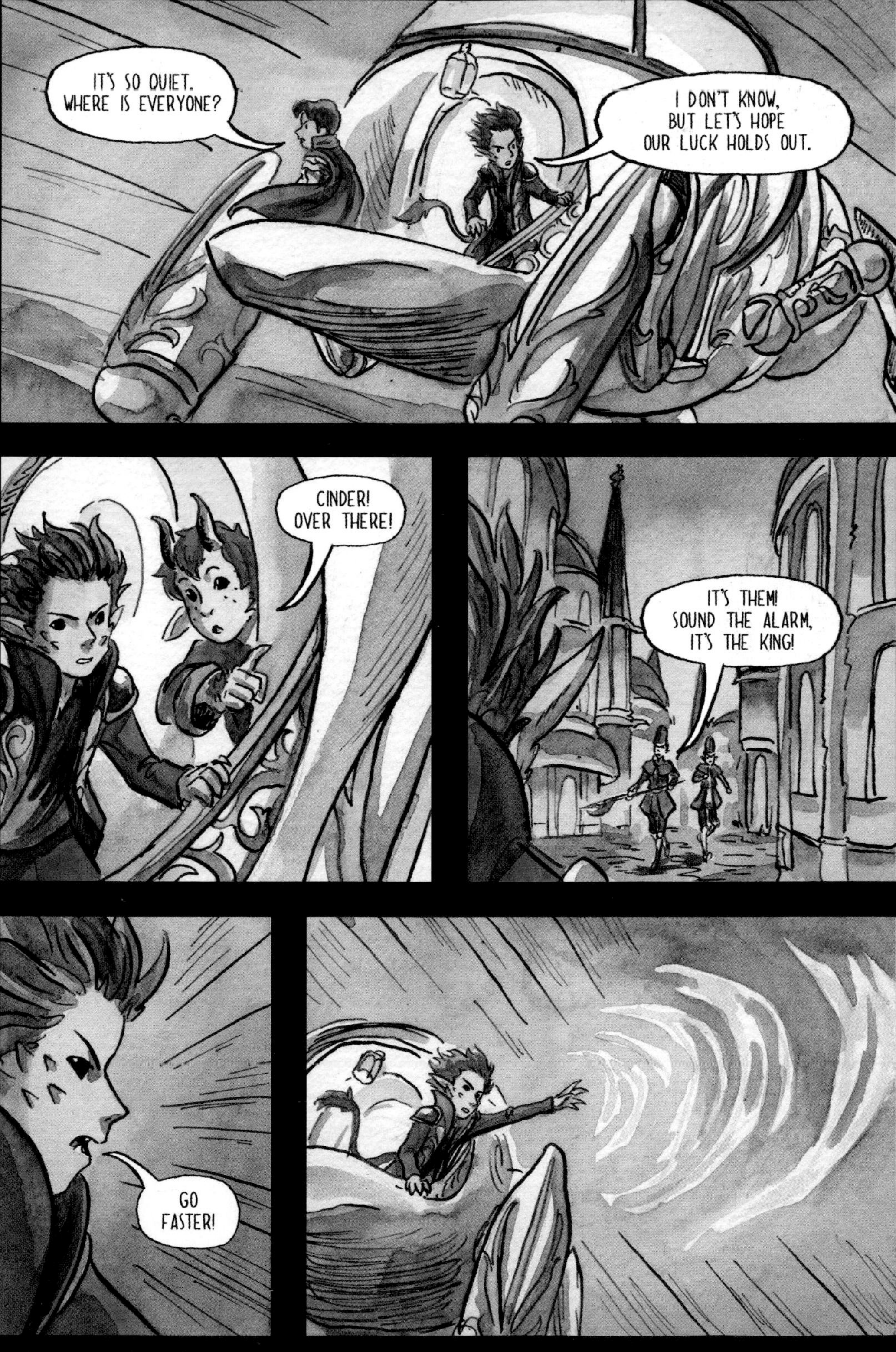
IT'S SO QUIET. WHERE IS EVERYONE?
I DON'T KNOW, BUT LET'S HOPE OUR LUCK HOLDS OUT.
CINDER! OVER THERE!
IT'S THEM! SOUND THE ALARM, IT'S THE KING!
GO FASTER!

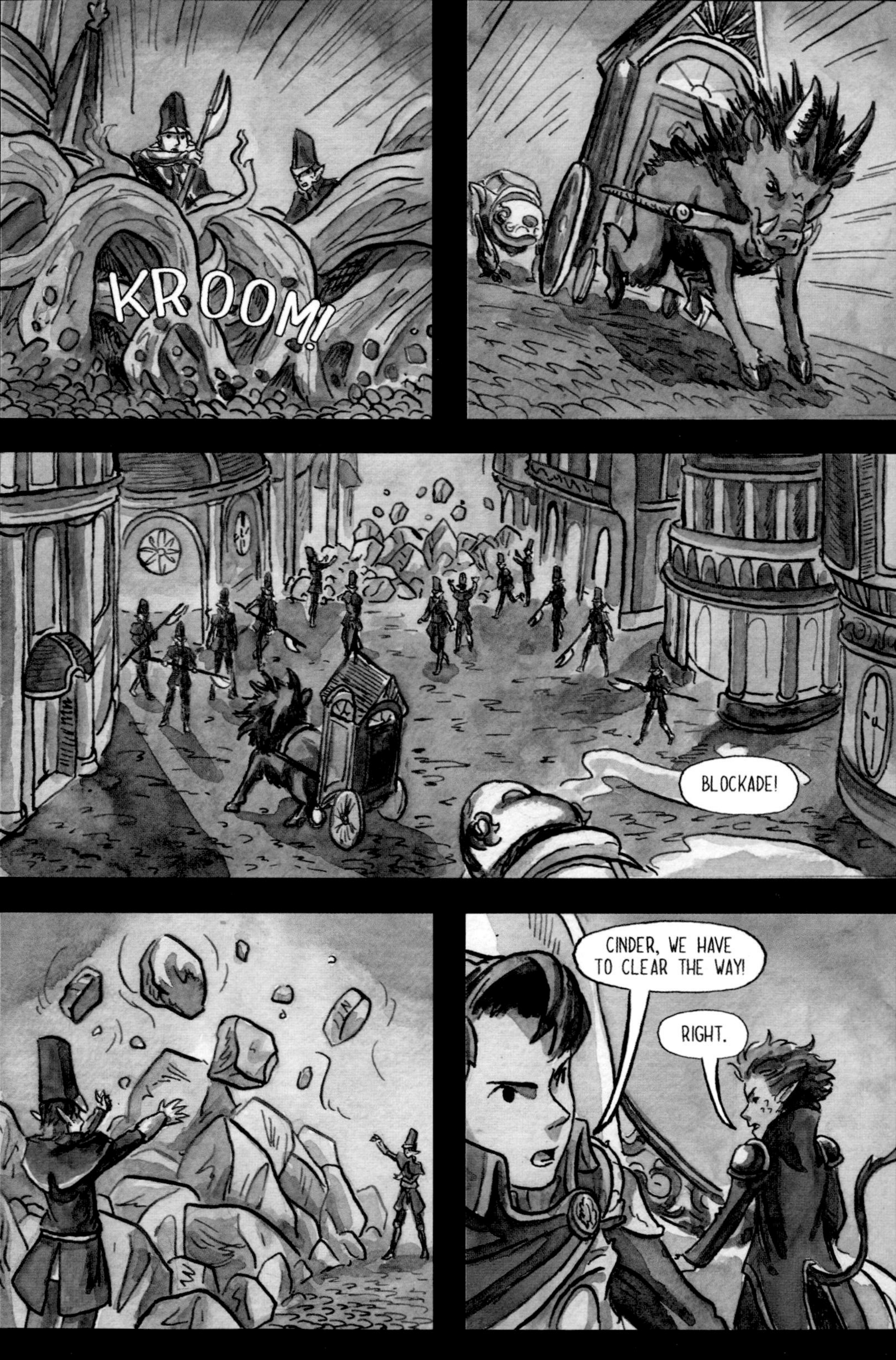
KROOM!
BLOCKADE!
CINDER, WE HAVE TO CLEAR THE WAY!
RIGHT.

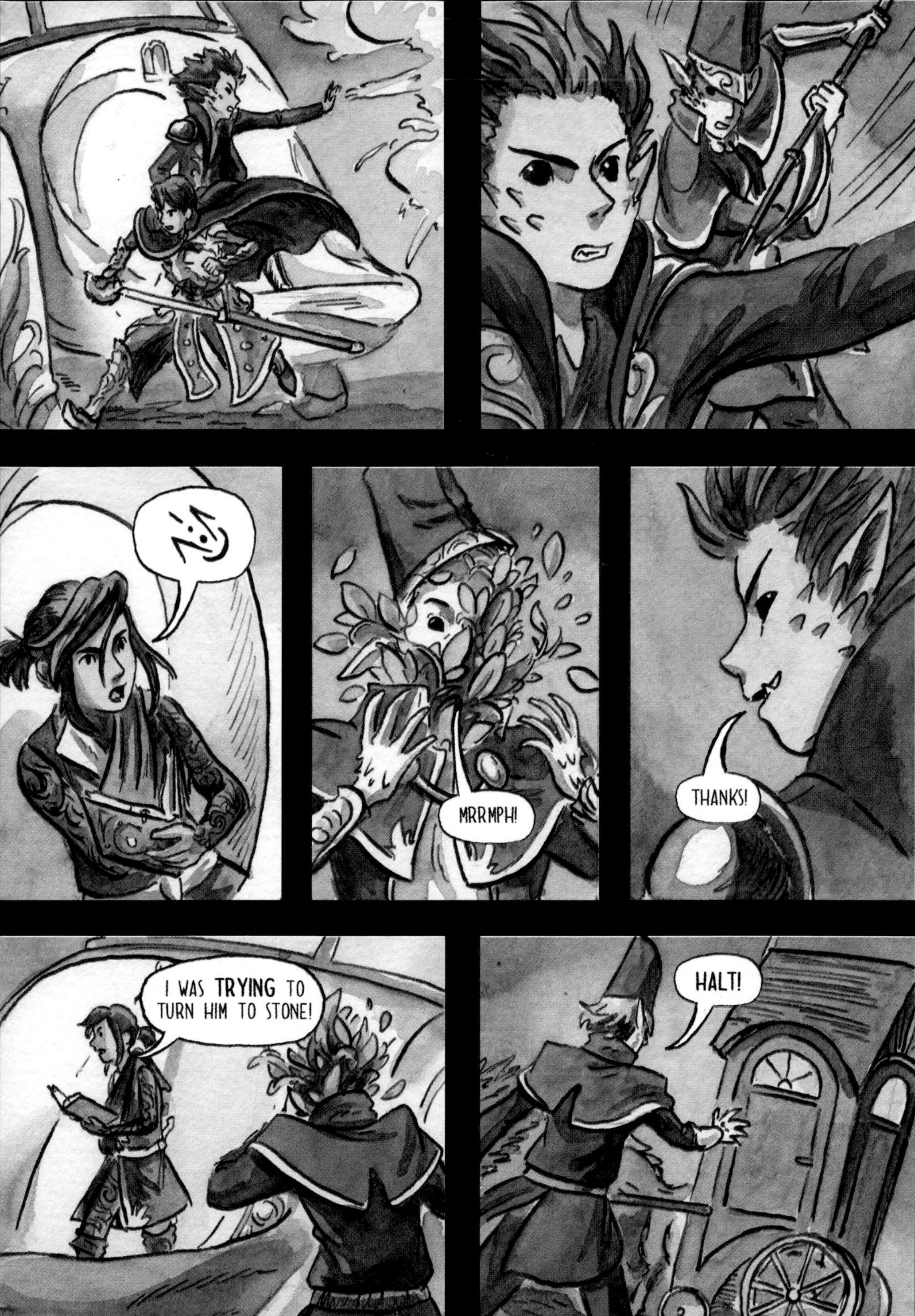
MRRMPH!
THANKS!
I WAS TRYING TO TURN HIM TO STONE!
HALT!

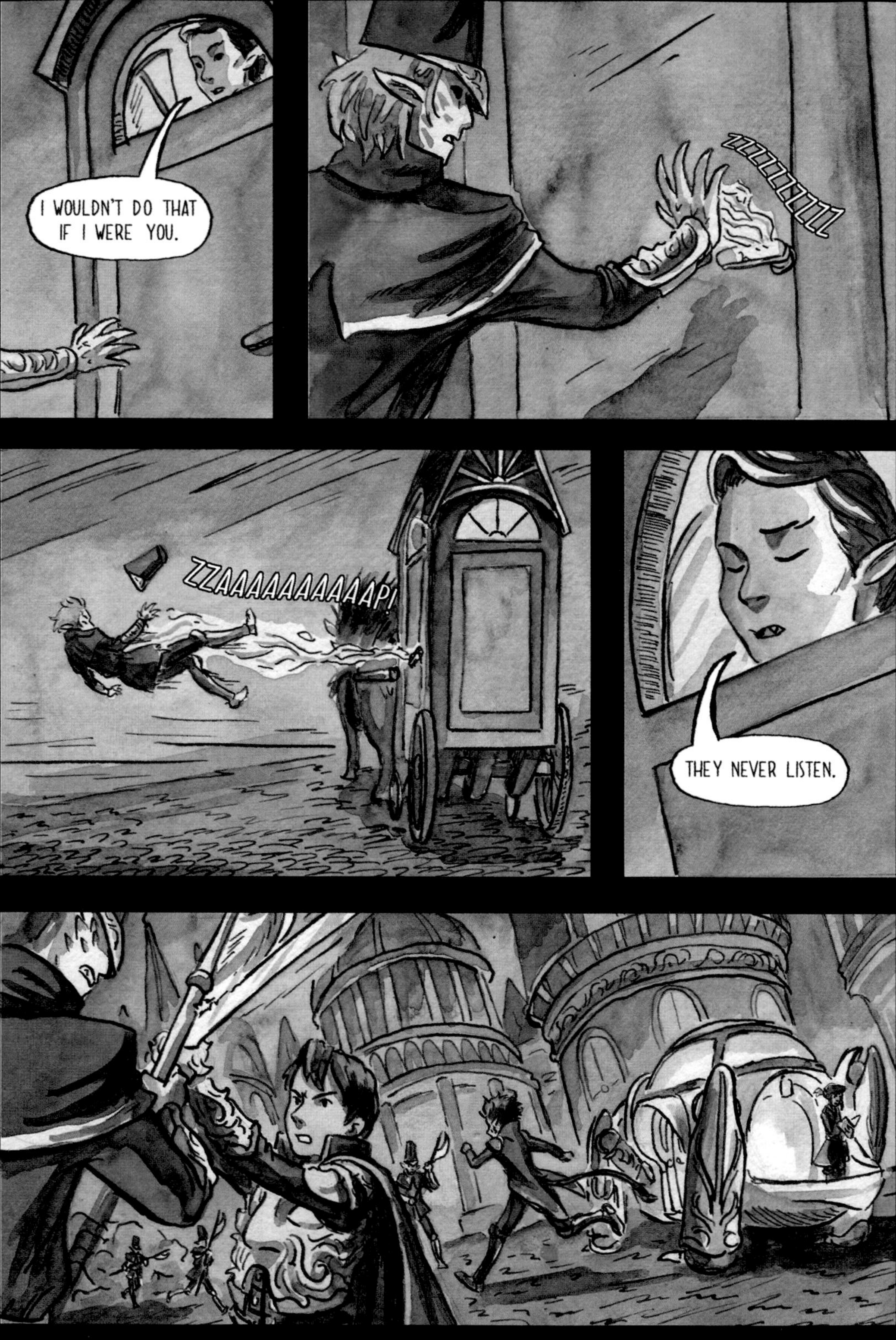
I WOULDN'T DO THAT IF I WERE YOU.
ZZZZZZZZZZZ
ZZAAAAAAAAAAAP!
THEY NEVER LISTEN.

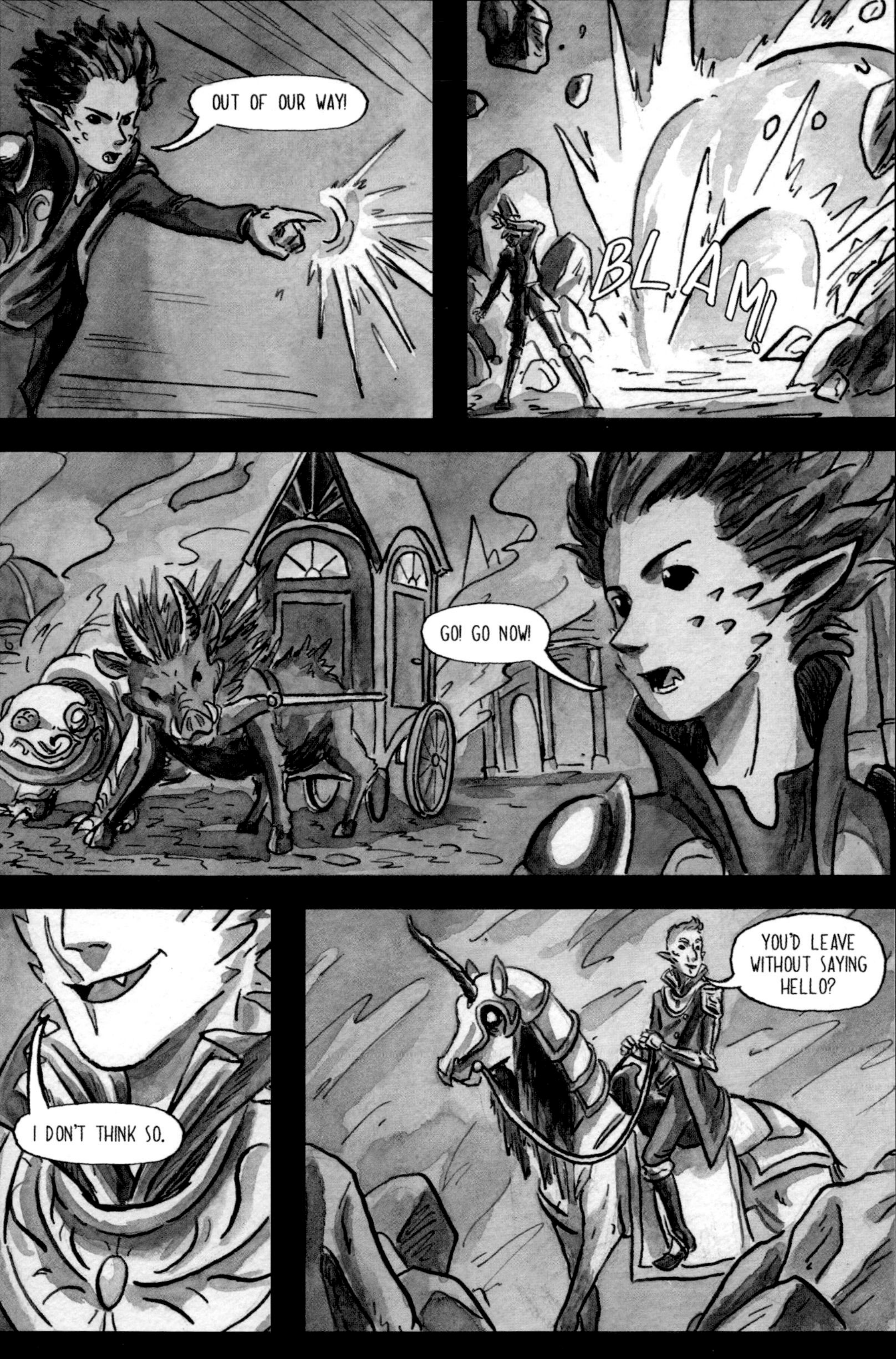
OUT OF OUR WAY!
BLAM!
GO! GO NOW!
I DON'T THINK SO.
YOU'D LEAVE WITHOUT SAYING HELLO?

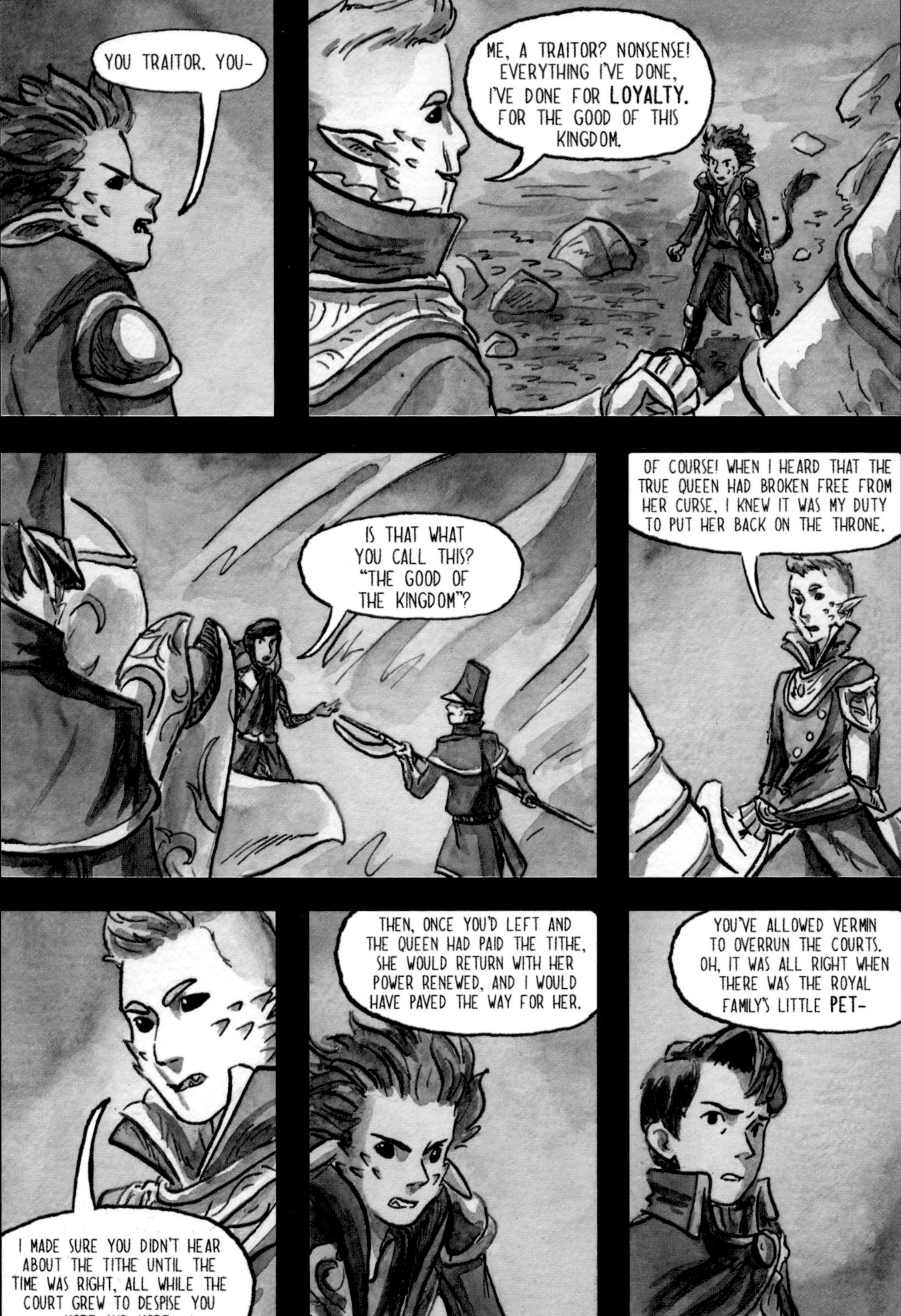
YOU TRAITOR. YOU-
ME, A TRAITOR? NONSENSE! EVERYTHING I'VE DONE, I'VE DONE FOR LOYALTY. FOR THE GOOD OF THIS KINGDOM.
IS THAT WHAT YOU CALL THIS? "THE GOOD OF THE KINGDOM"?
OF COURSE! WHEN I HEARD THAT THE TRUE QUEEN HAD BROKEN FREE FROM HER CURSE, I KNEW IT WAS MY DUTY TO PUT HER BACK ON THE THRONE.
I MADE SURE YOU DIDN'T HEAR ABOUT THE TITHE UNTIL THE TIME WAS RIGHT, ALL WHILE THE COURT GREW TO DESPISE YOU MORE AND MORE.
THEN, ONCE YOU'D LEFT AND THE QUEEN HAD PAID THE TITHE, SHE WOULD RETURN WITH HER POWER RENEWED, AND I WOULD HAVE PAVED THE WAY FOR HER.
YOU'VE ALLOWED VERMIN TO OVERRUN THE COURTS. OH, IT WAS ALL RIGHT WHEN THERE WAS THE ROYAL FAMILY'S LITTLE PET-

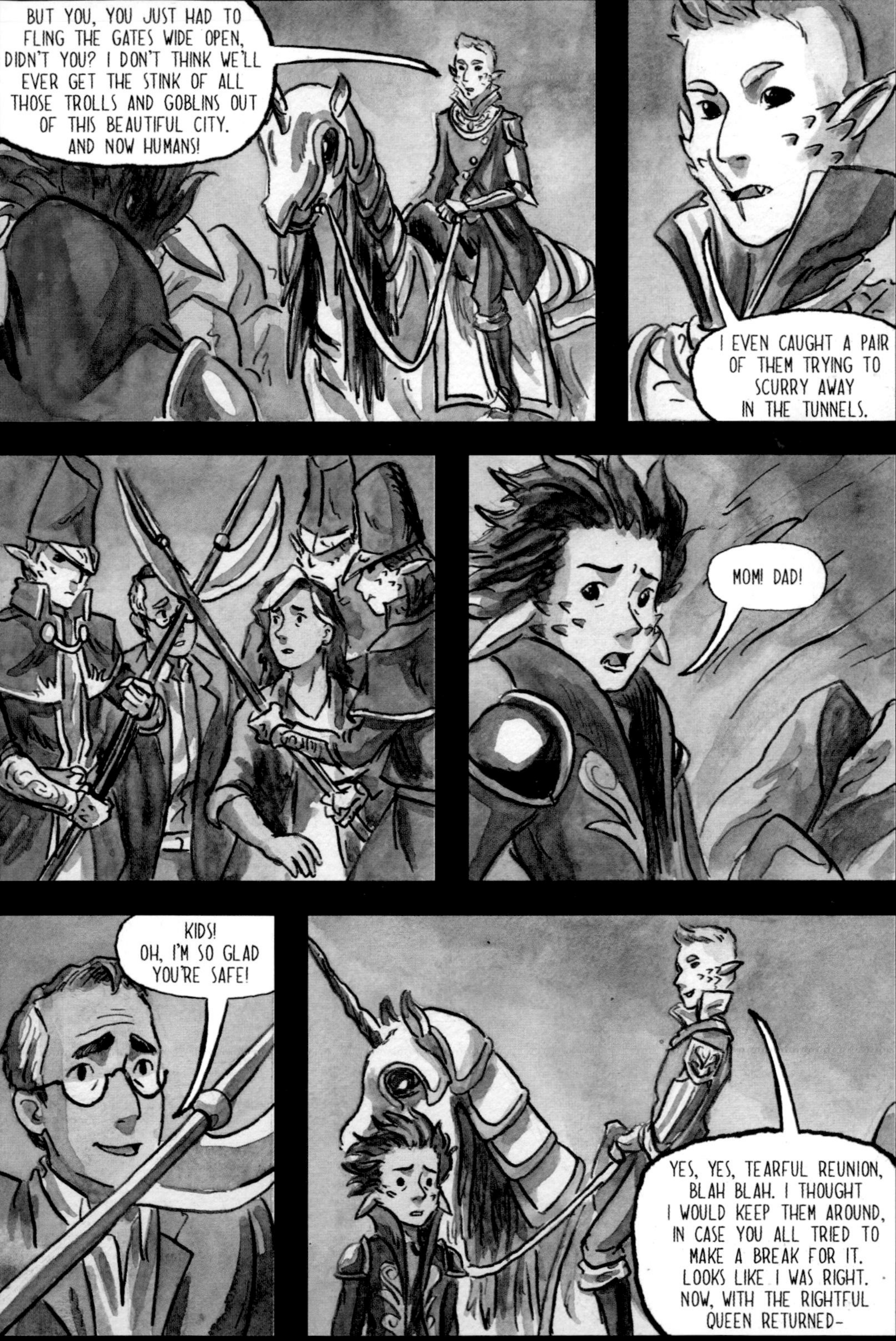
BUT YOU, YOU JUST HAD TO FLING THE GATES WIDE OPEN, DIDN'T YOU? I DON'T THINK WE'LL EVER GET THE STINK OF ALL THOSE TROLLS AND GOBLINS OUT OF THIS BEAUTIFUL CITY. AND NOW HUMANS!
I EVEN CAUGHT A PAIR OF THEM TRYING TO SCURRY AWAY IN THE TUNNELS.
MOM! DAD!
KIDS! OH, I'M SO GLAD YOU'RE SAFE!
YES, YES, TEARFUL REUNION, BLAH BLAH. I THOUGHT I WOULD KEEP THEM AROUND, IN CASE YOU ALL TRIED TO MAKE A BREAK FOR IT. LOOKS LIKE I WAS RIGHT. NOW, WITH THE RIGHTFUL QUEEN RETURNED-

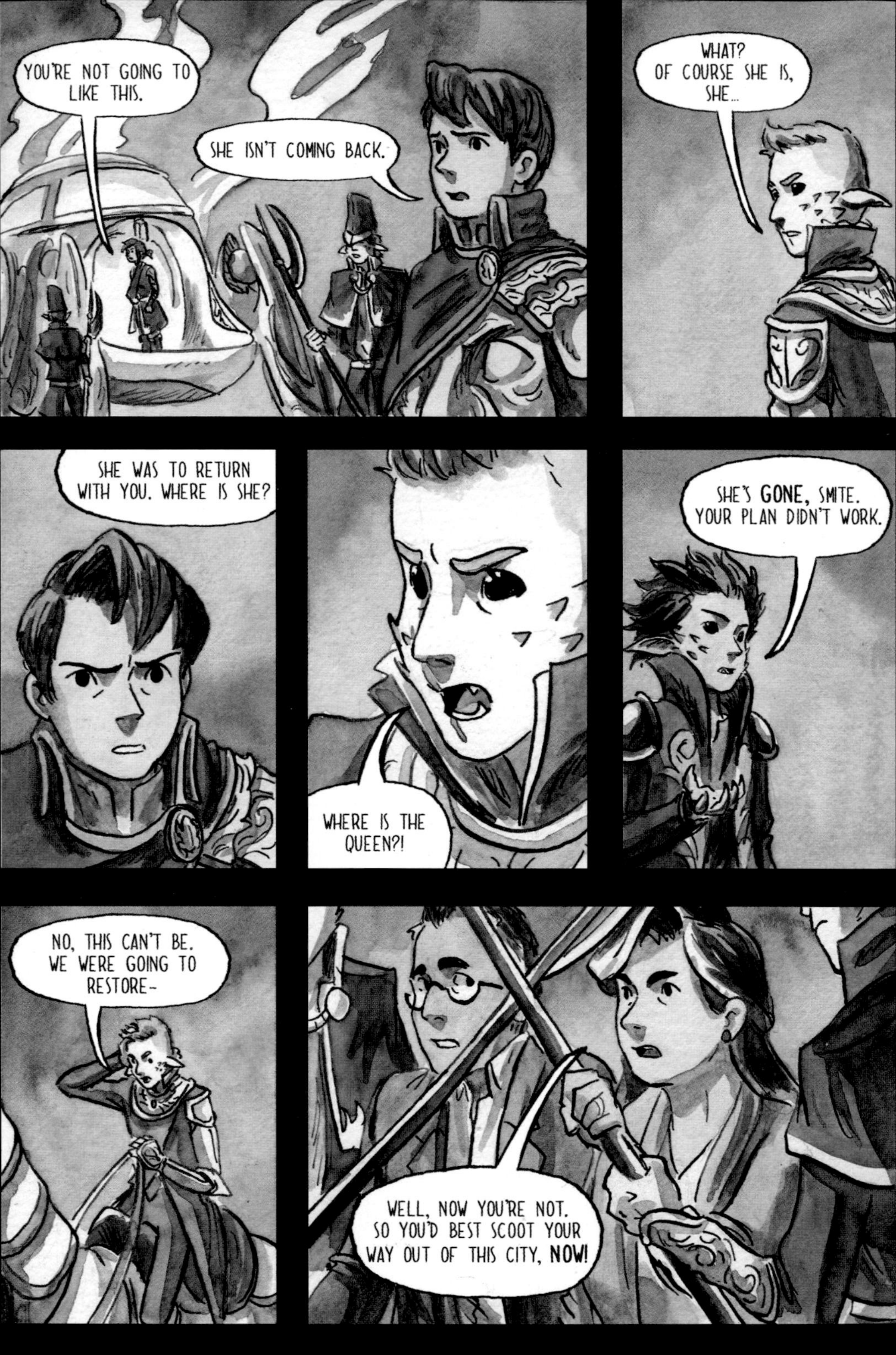

YOU'RE NOT GOING TO LIKE THIS.
SHE ISN'T COMING BACK.
WHAT? OF COURSE SHE IS, SHE...
SHE WAS TO RETURN WITH YOU. WHERE IS SHE?
WHERE IS THE QUEEN?!
SHE'S **GONE,** SMITE. YOUR PLAN DIDN'T WORK.
NO, THIS CAN'T BE. WE WERE GOING TO RESTORE-
WELL, NOW YOU'RE NOT. SO YOU'D BEST SCOOT YOUR WAY OUT OF THIS CITY, **NOW!**

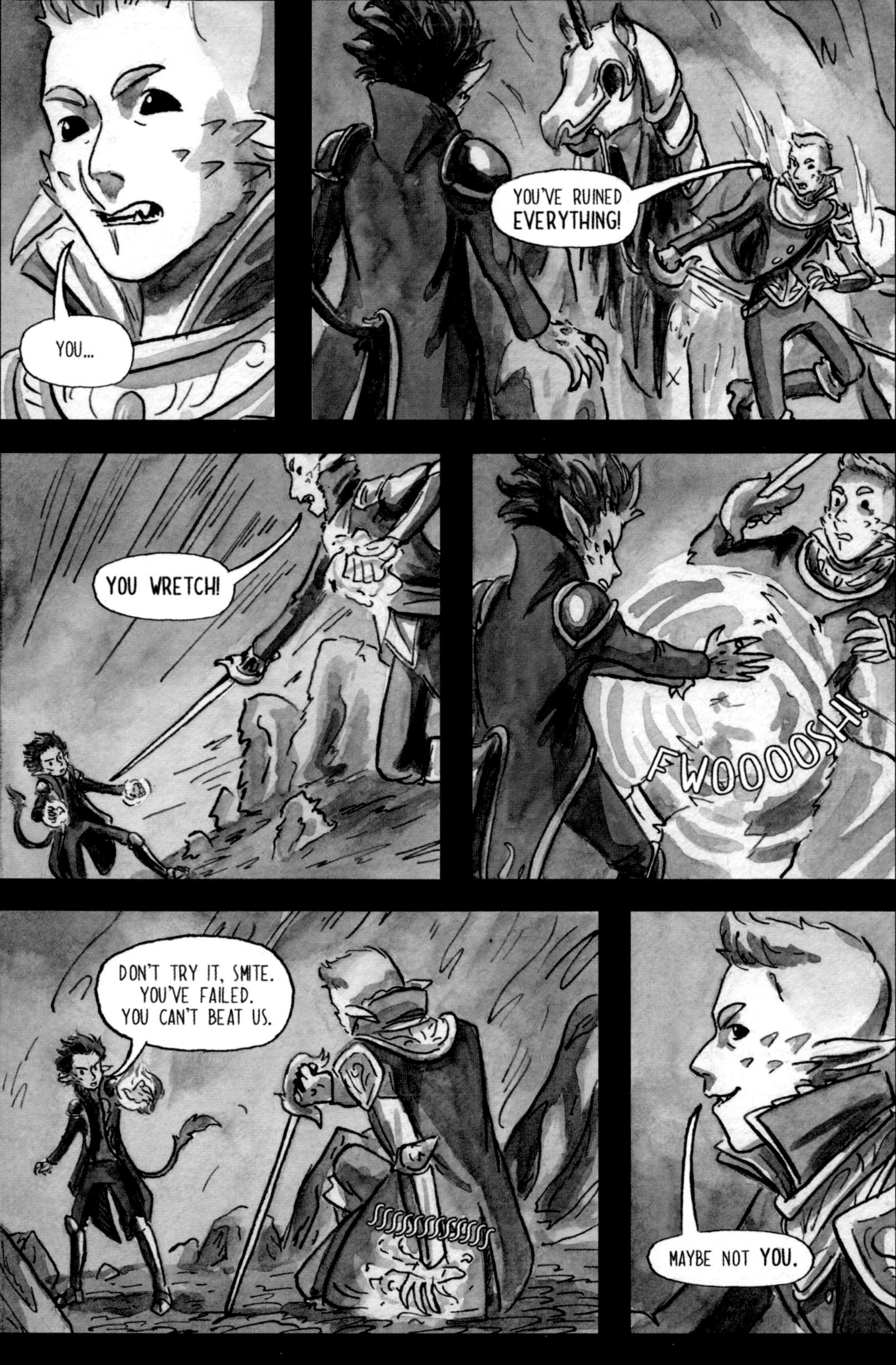

YOU...
YOU'VE RUINED EVERYTHING!
YOU WRETCH!
FWOOOOSH!
DON'T TRY IT, SMITE. YOU'VE FAILED. YOU CAN'T BEAT US.
SSSSSSSSSSS
MAYBE NOT YOU.

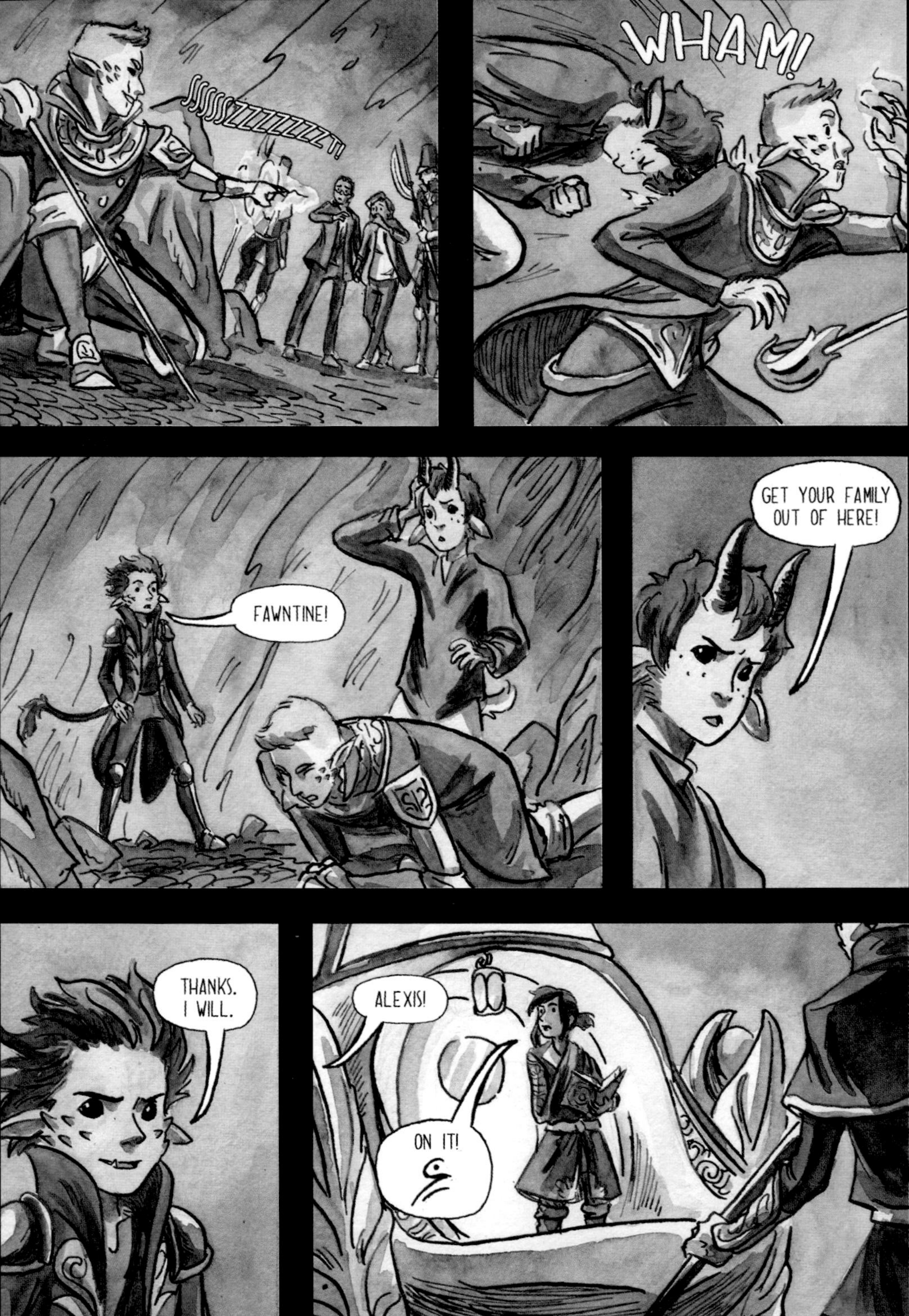
SSSSSZZZZZZZZT!
WHAM!
FAWNTINE!
GET YOUR FAMILY OUT OF HERE!
THANKS. I WILL.
ALEXIS!
ON IT!

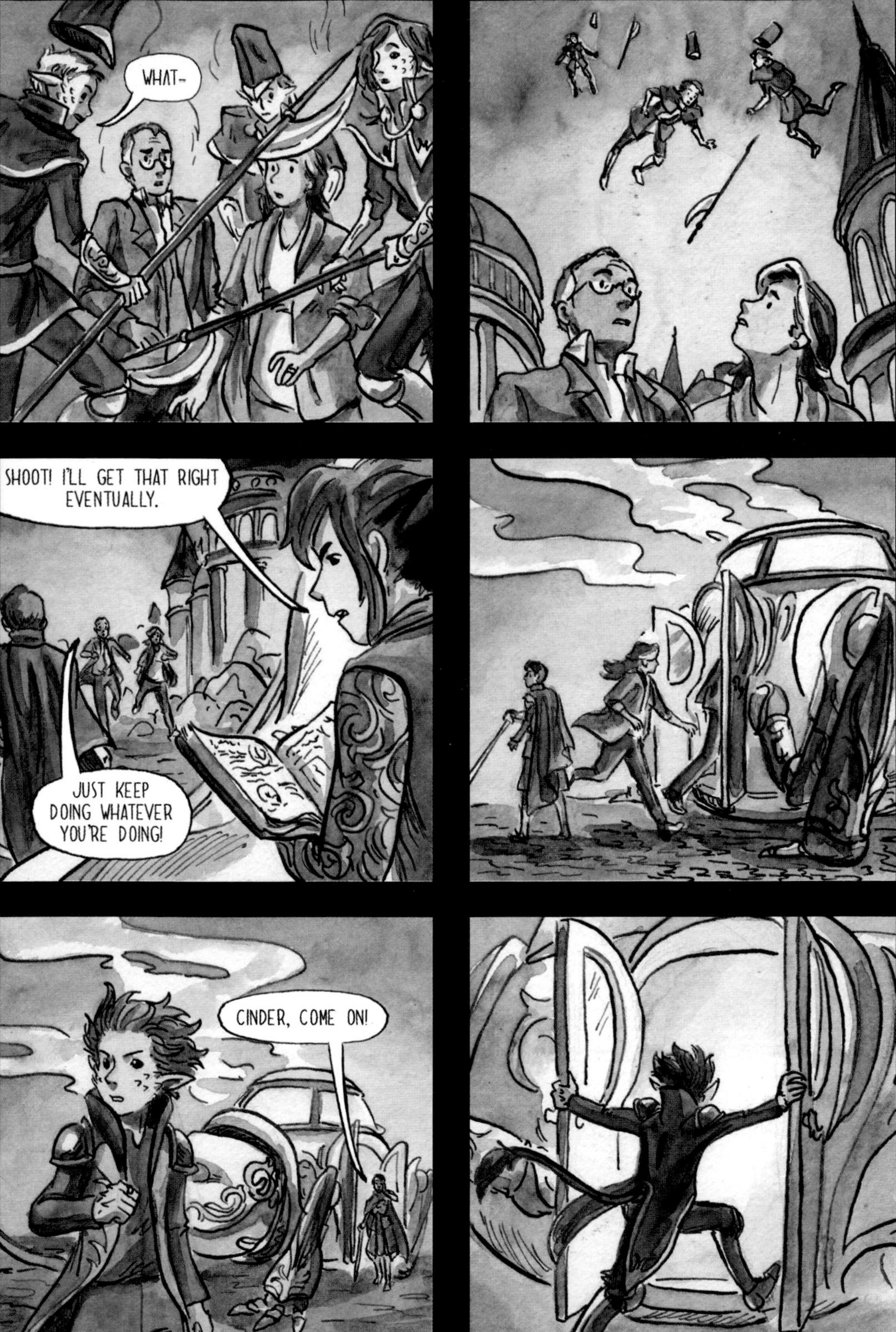
WHAT–
SHOOT! I'LL GET THAT RIGHT EVENTUALLY.
JUST KEEP DOING WHATEVER YOU'RE DOING!
CINDER, COME ON!

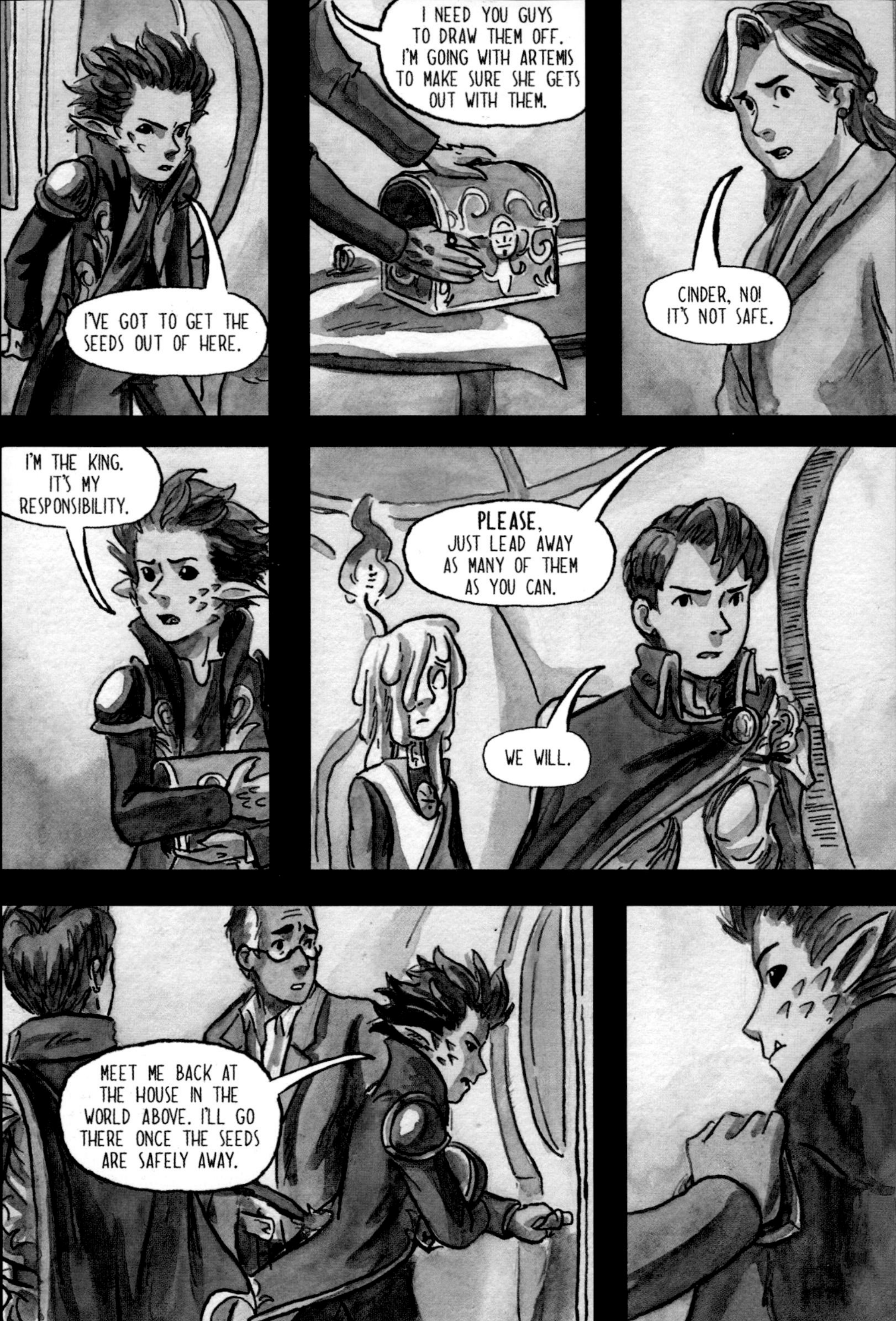
I'VE GOT TO GET THE SEEDS OUT OF HERE.
I NEED YOU GUYS TO DRAW THEM OFF. I'M GOING WITH ARTEMIS TO MAKE SURE SHE GETS OUT WITH THEM.
CINDER, NO! IT'S NOT SAFE.
I'M THE KING. IT'S MY RESPONSIBILITY.
PLEASE, JUST LEAD AWAY AS MANY OF THEM AS YOU CAN.
WE WILL.
MEET ME BACK AT THE HOUSE IN THE WORLD ABOVE. I'LL GO THERE ONCE THE SEEDS ARE SAFELY AWAY.

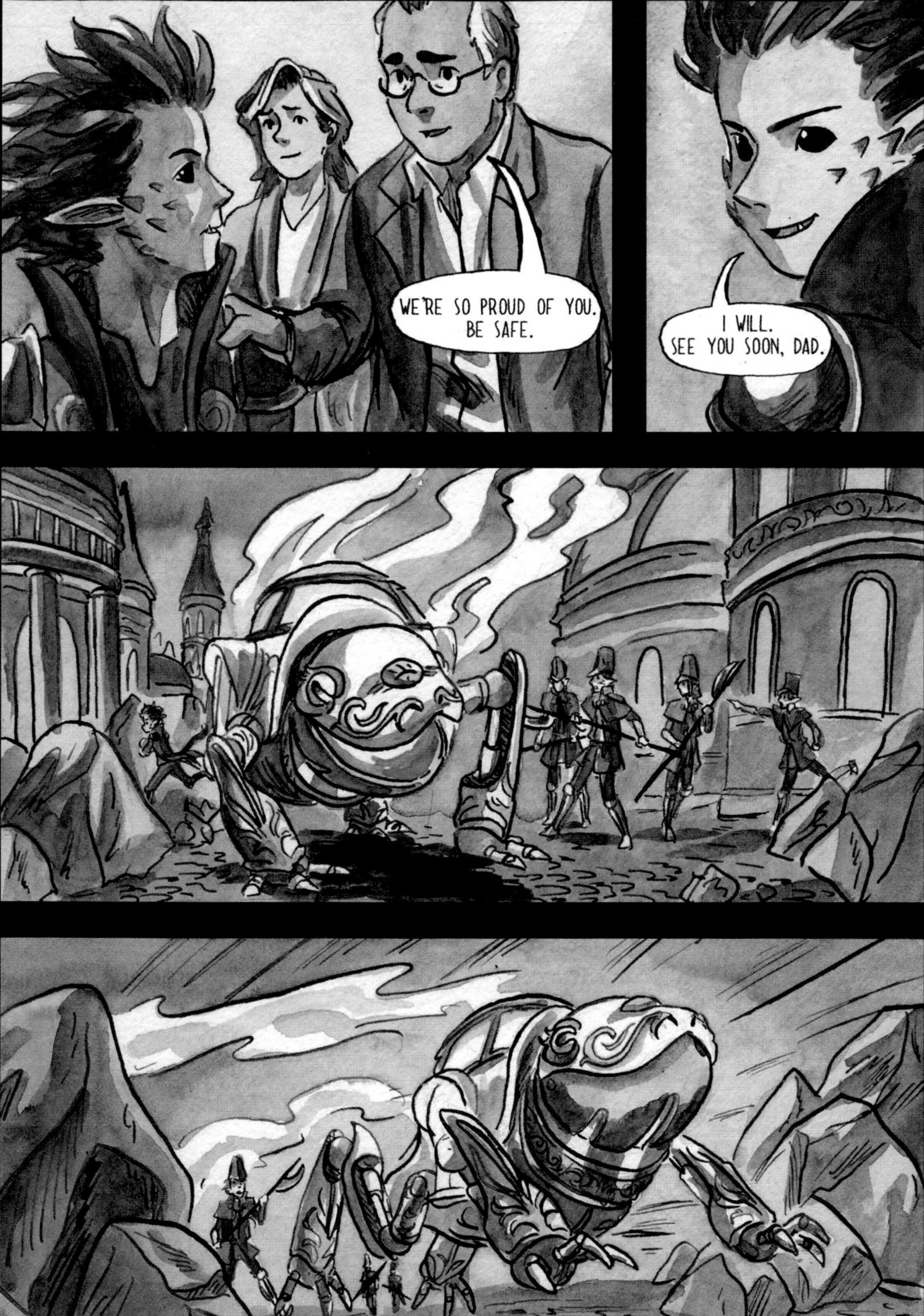
WE'RE SO PROUD OF YOU. BE SAFE.
I WILL. SEE YOU SOON, DAD.

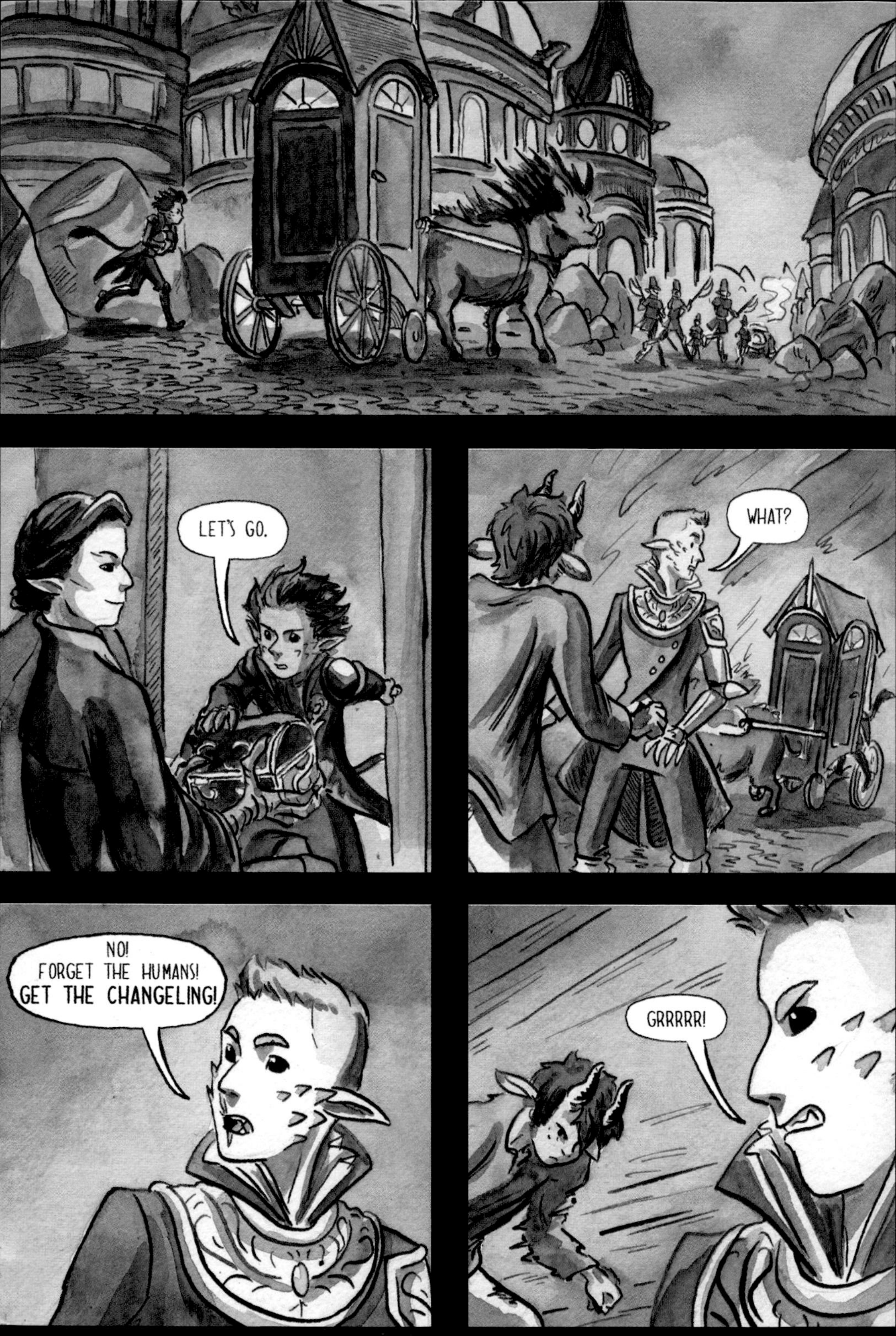
LET'S GO.
WHAT?
NO!
FORGET THE HUMANS!
GET THE CHANGELING!
GRRRRR!

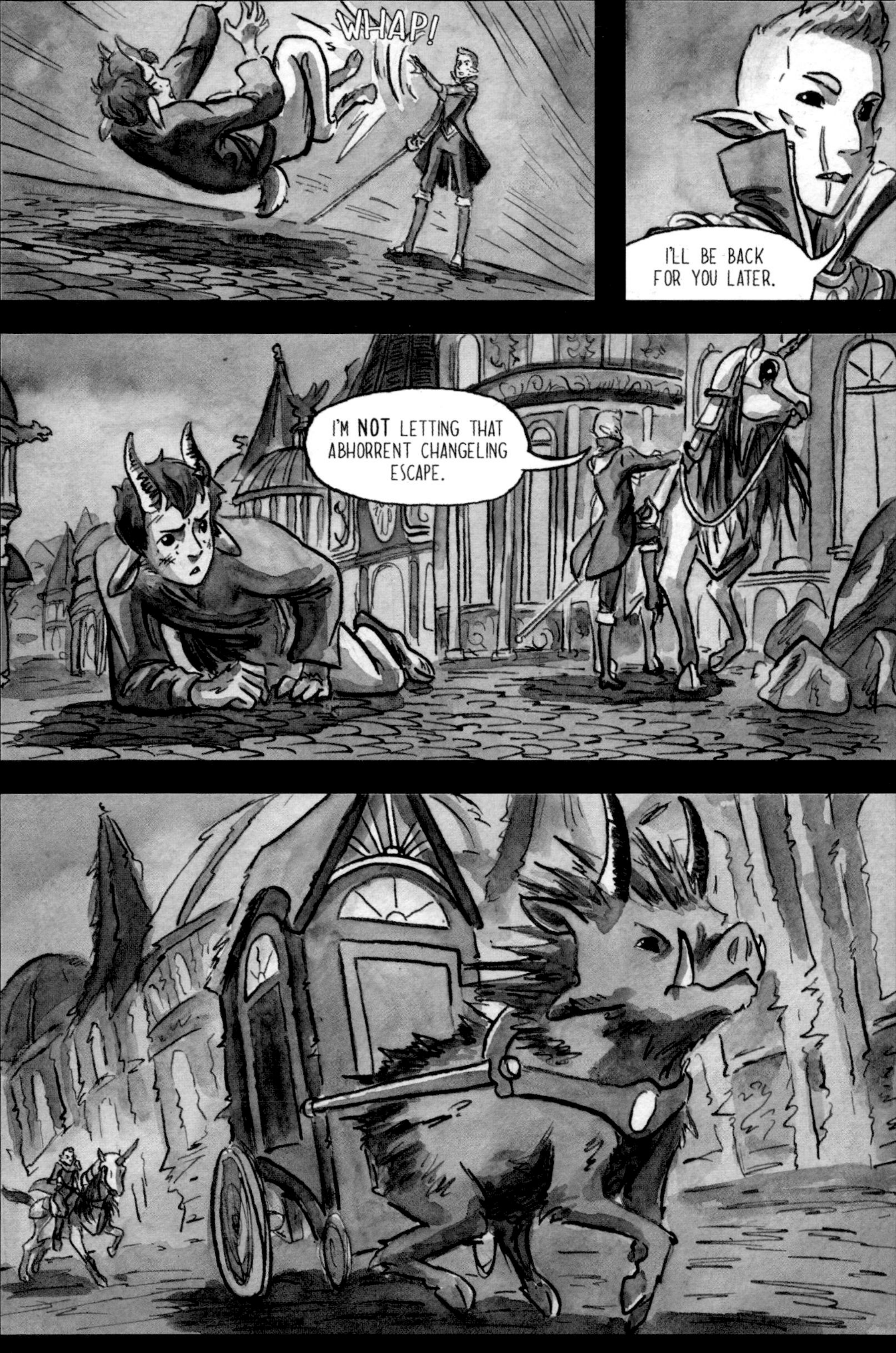
WHAP!
I'LL BE BACK FOR YOU LATER.
I'M NOT LETTING THAT ABHORRENT CHANGELING ESCAPE.

CHAPTER
FOURTEEN

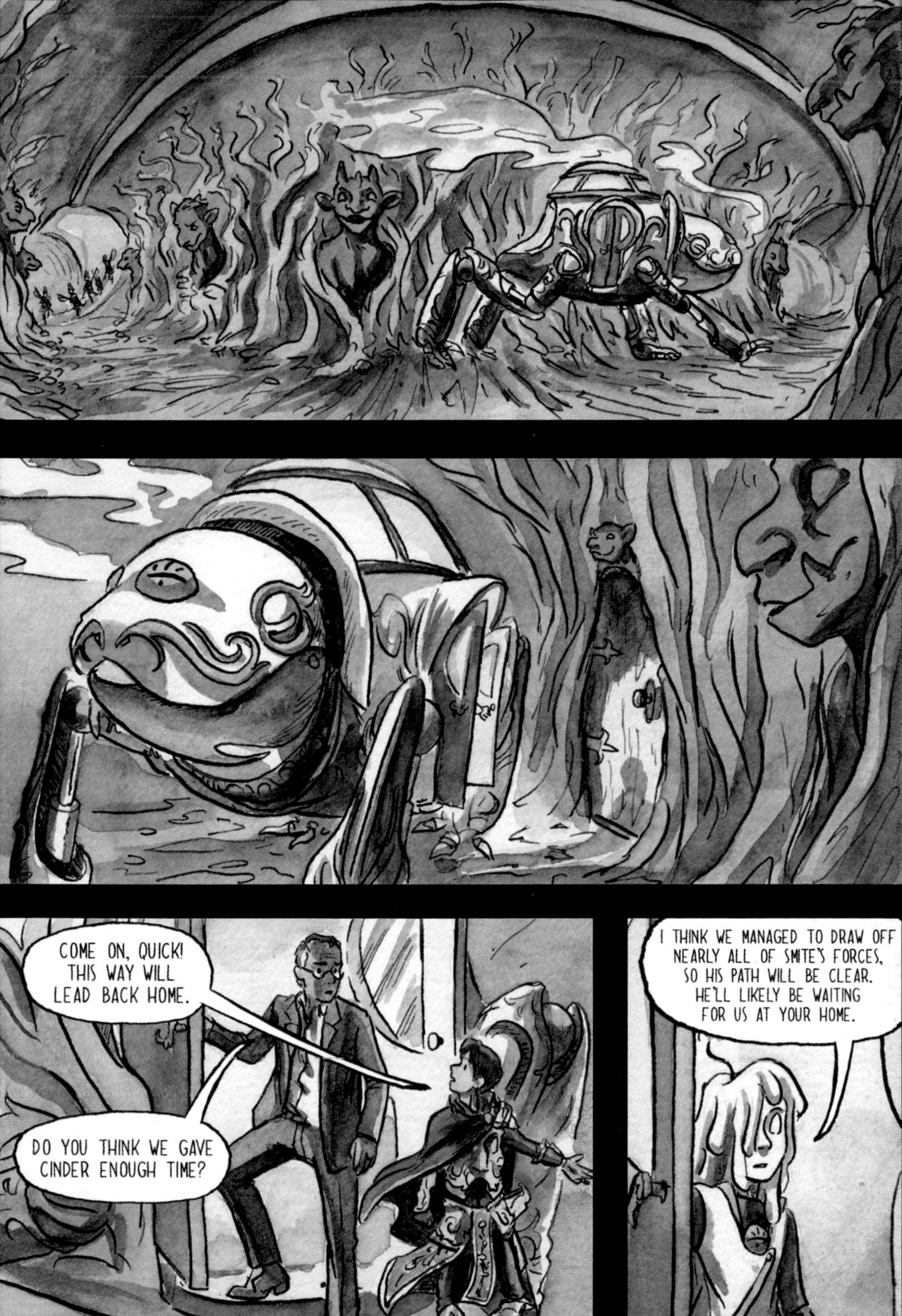
COME ON, QUICK! THIS WAY WILL LEAD BACK HOME.
DO YOU THINK WE GAVE CINDER ENOUGH TIME?
I THINK WE MANAGED TO DRAW OFF NEARLY ALL OF SMITE'S FORCES, SO HIS PATH WILL BE CLEAR. HE'LL LIKELY BE WAITING FOR US AT YOUR HOME.

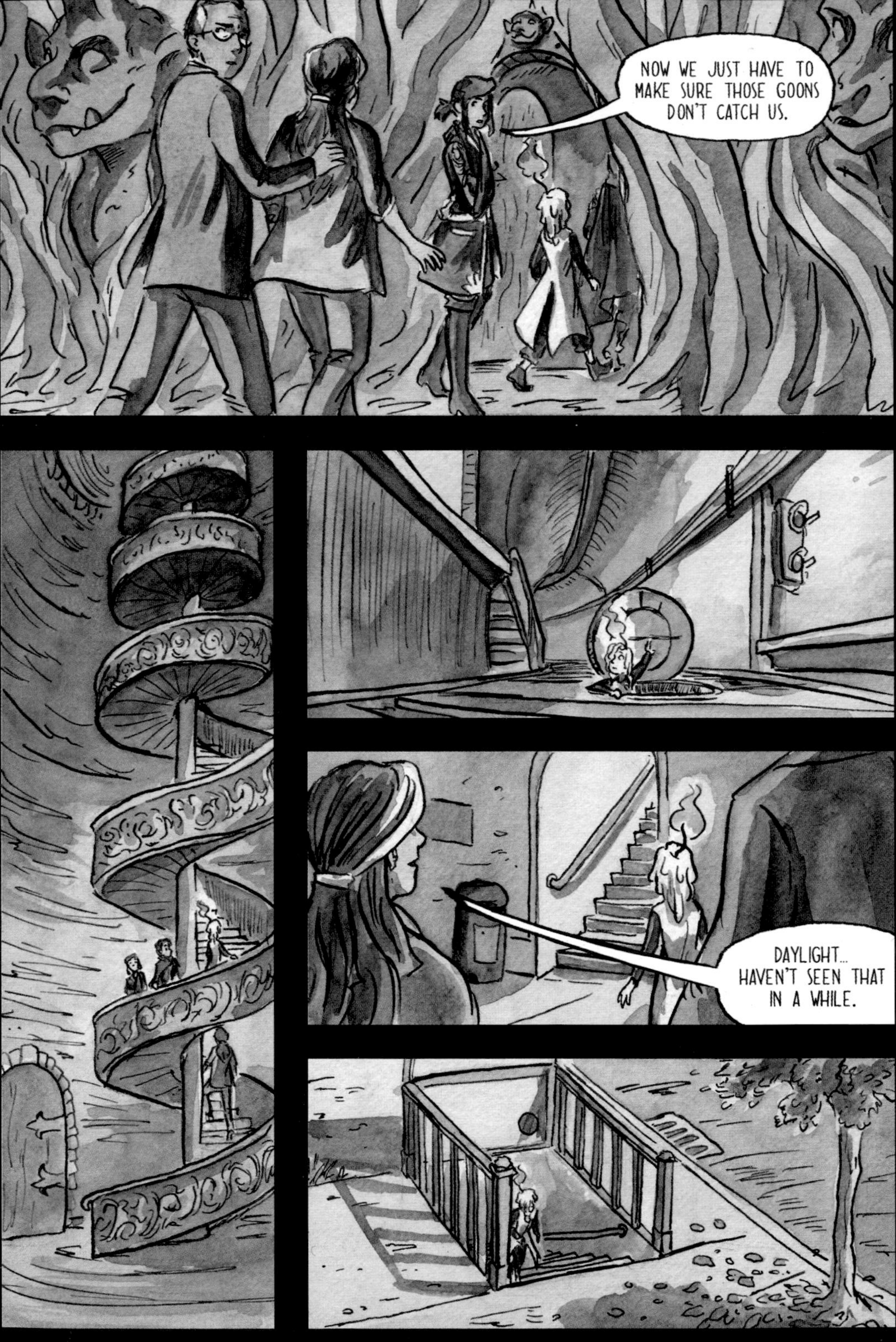
NOW WE JUST HAVE TO MAKE SURE THOSE GOONS DON'T CATCH US.
DAYLIGHT... HAVEN'T SEEN THAT IN A WHILE.

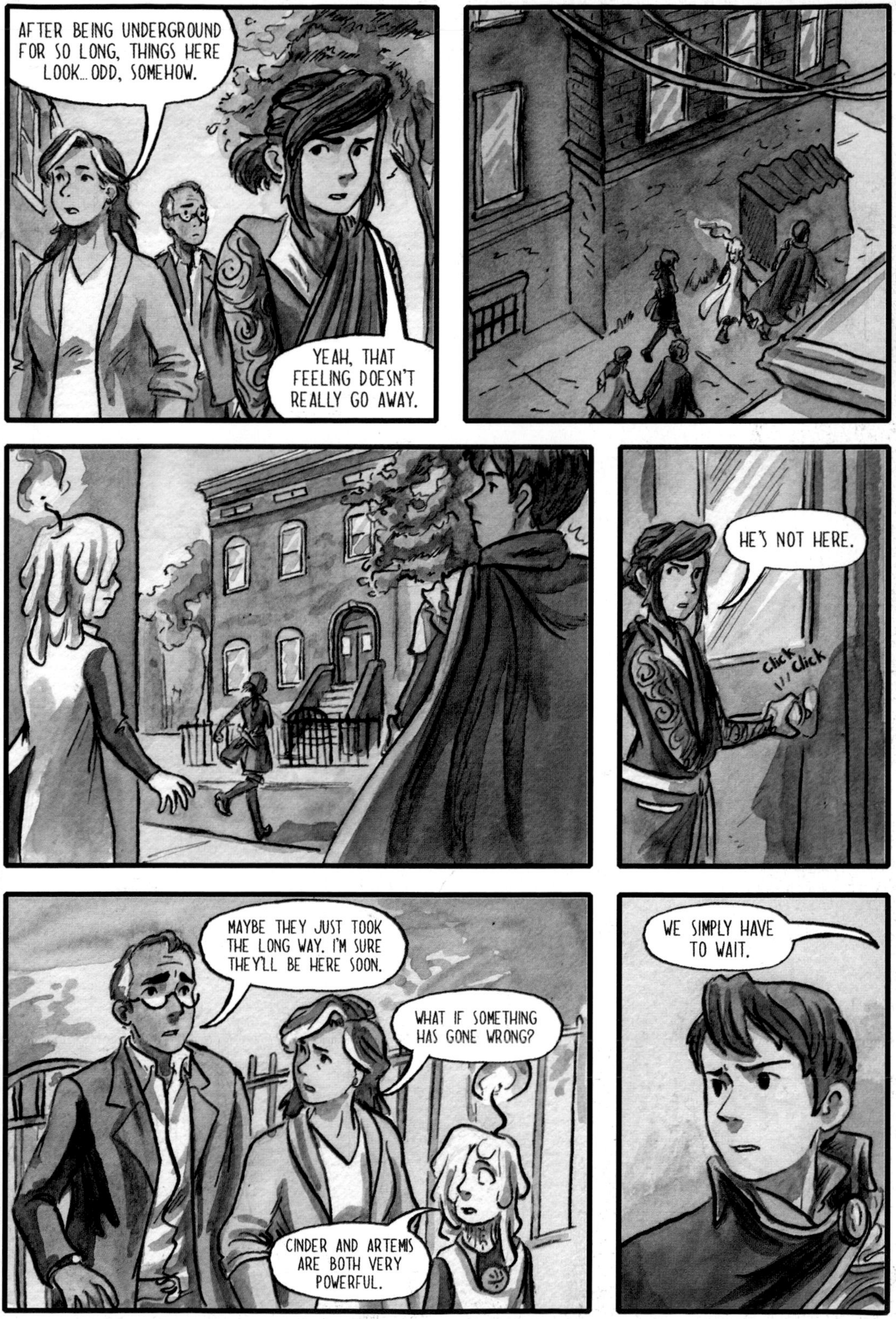
AFTER BEING UNDERGROUND FOR SO LONG, THINGS HERE LOOK... ODD, SOMEHOW.
YEAH, THAT FEELING DOESN'T REALLY GO AWAY.
HE'S NOT HERE.
CLICK CLICK
MAYBE THEY JUST TOOK THE LONG WAY. I'M SURE THEY'LL BE HERE SOON.
WHAT IF SOMETHING HAS GONE WRONG?
CINDER AND ARTEMIS ARE BOTH VERY POWERFUL.
WE SIMPLY HAVE TO WAIT.

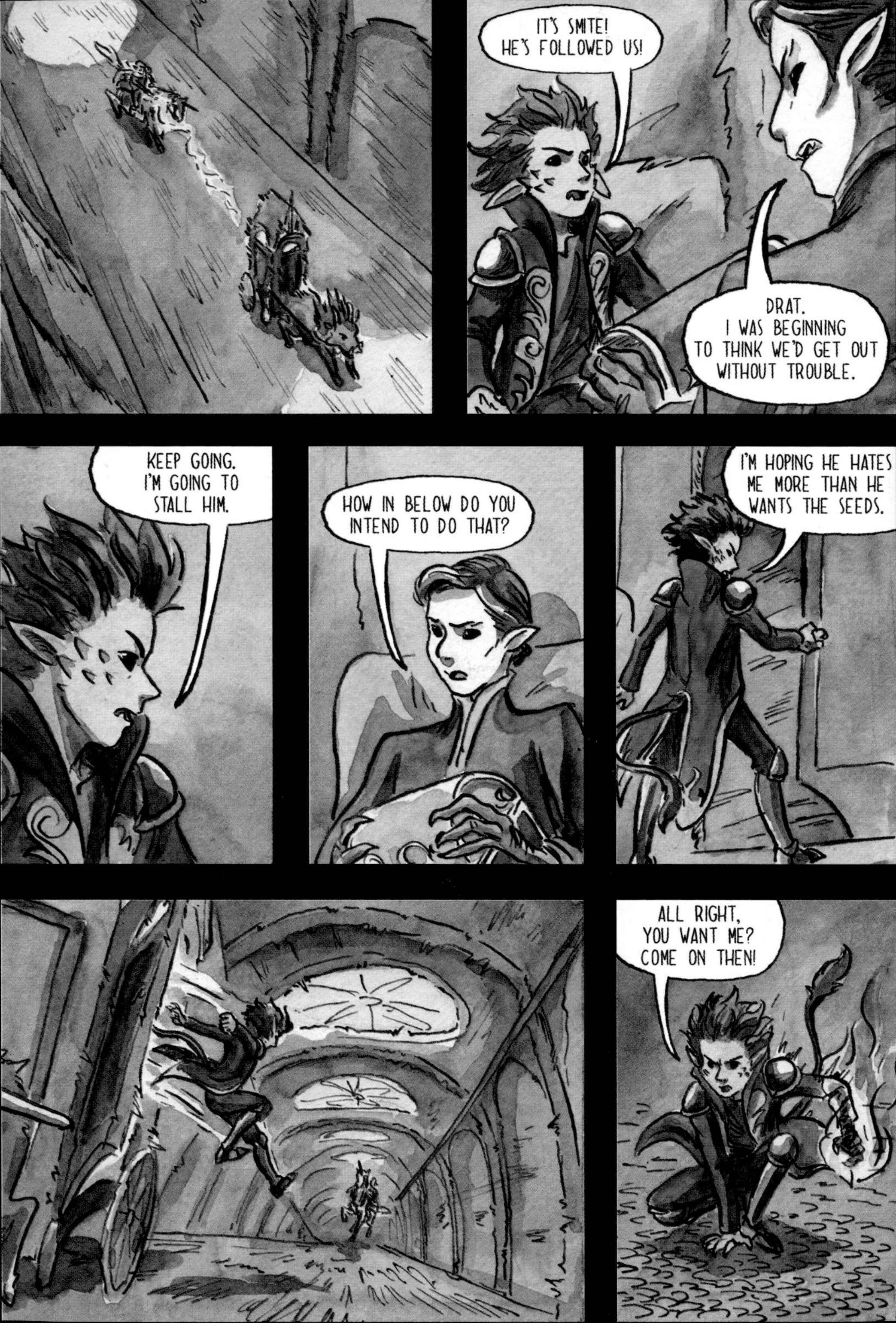
IT'S SMITE! HE'S FOLLOWED US!
DRAT. I WAS BEGINNING TO THINK WE'D GET OUT WITHOUT TROUBLE.
KEEP GOING. I'M GOING TO STALL HIM.
HOW IN BELOW DO YOU INTEND TO DO THAT?
I'M HOPING HE HATES ME MORE THAN HE WANTS THE SEEDS.
ALL RIGHT, YOU WANT ME? COME ON THEN!

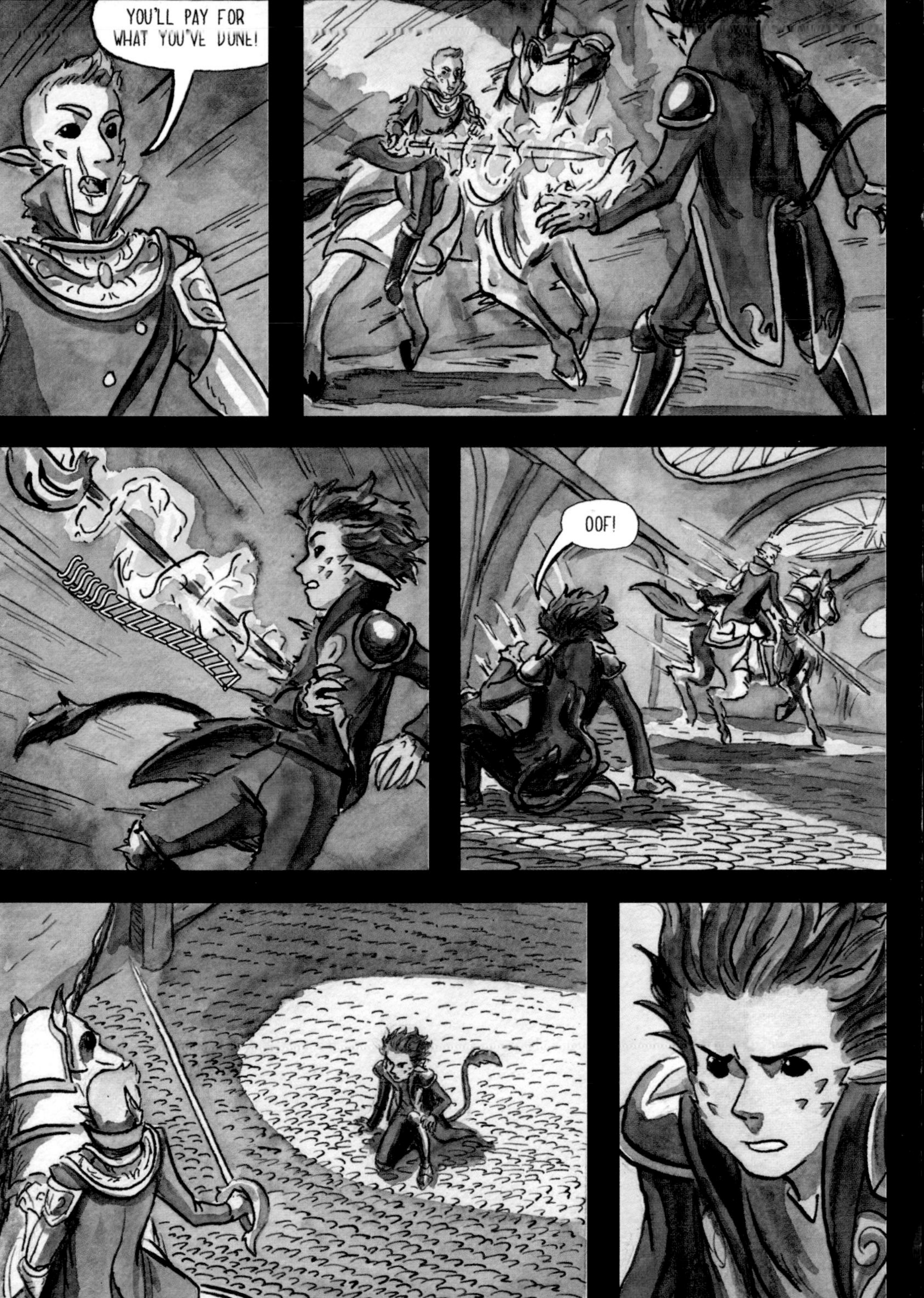
YOU'LL PAY FOR WHAT YOU'VE DONE!
SSSSSZZZZZZZZZZZT
OOF!

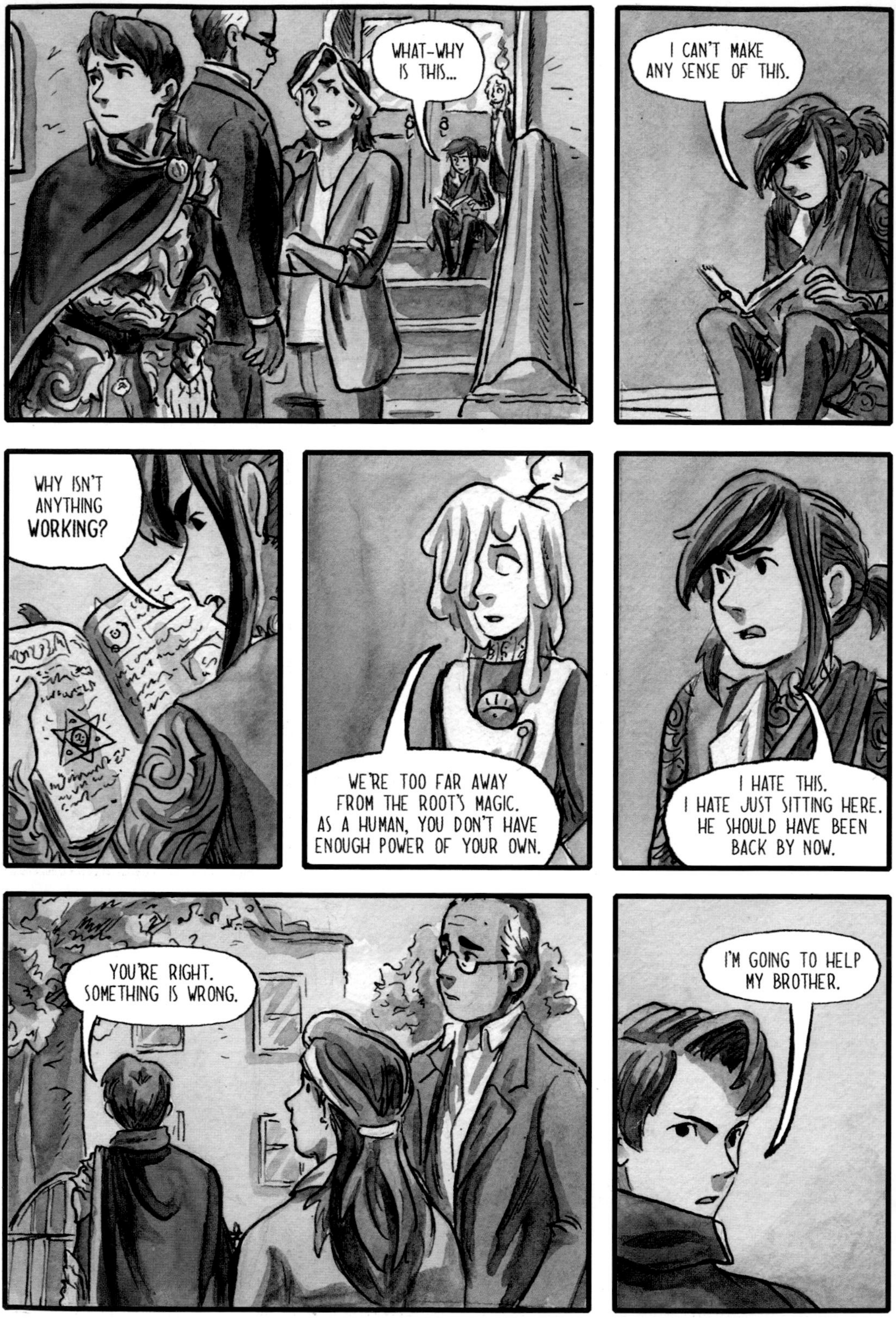
WHAT-WHY IS THIS...
I CAN'T MAKE ANY SENSE OF THIS.
WHY ISN'T ANYTHING WORKING?
WE'RE TOO FAR AWAY FROM THE ROOT'S MAGIC. AS A HUMAN, YOU DON'T HAVE ENOUGH POWER OF YOUR OWN.
I HATE THIS. I HATE JUST SITTING HERE. HE SHOULD HAVE BEEN BACK BY NOW.
YOU'RE RIGHT. SOMETHING IS WRONG.
I'M GOING TO HELP MY BROTHER.

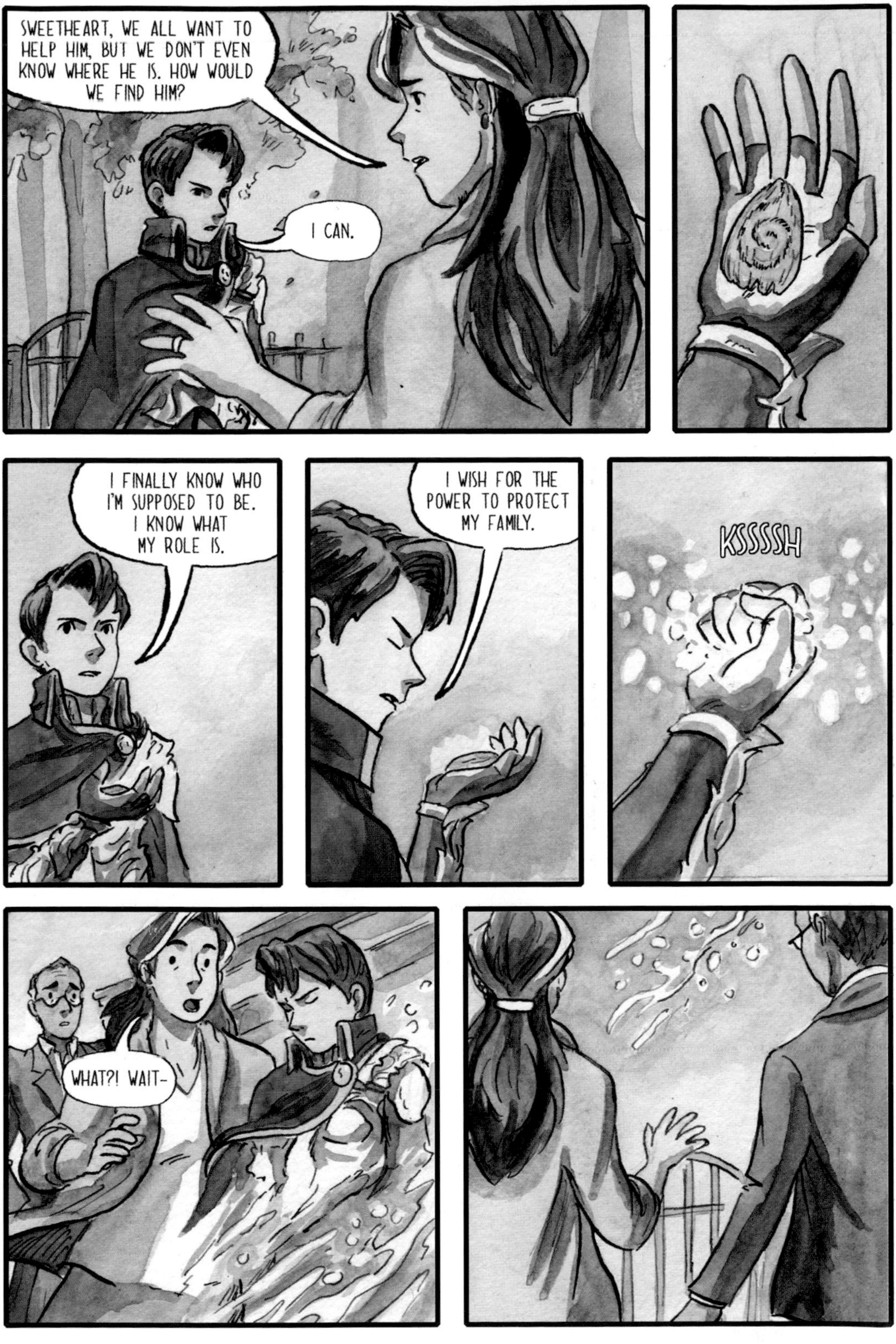
SWEETHEART, WE ALL WANT TO HELP HIM, BUT WE DON'T EVEN KNOW WHERE HE IS. HOW WOULD WE FIND HIM?
I CAN.
I FINALLY KNOW WHO I'M SUPPOSED TO BE. I KNOW WHAT MY ROLE IS.
I WISH FOR THE POWER TO PROTECT MY FAMILY.
KSSSSH
WHAT?! WAIT-

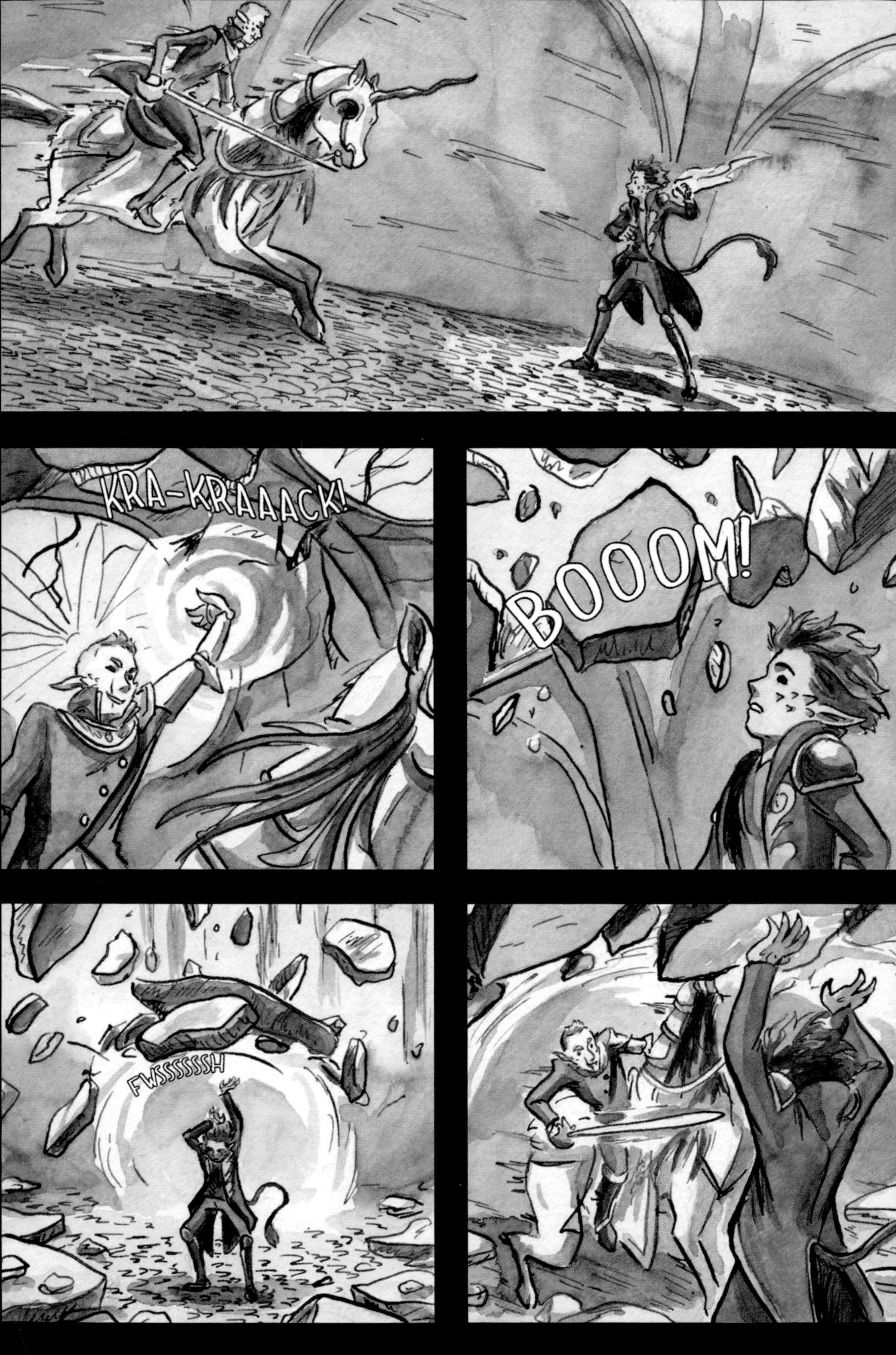
KRA-KRAAACK!
BOOOM!
FWSSSSSSH

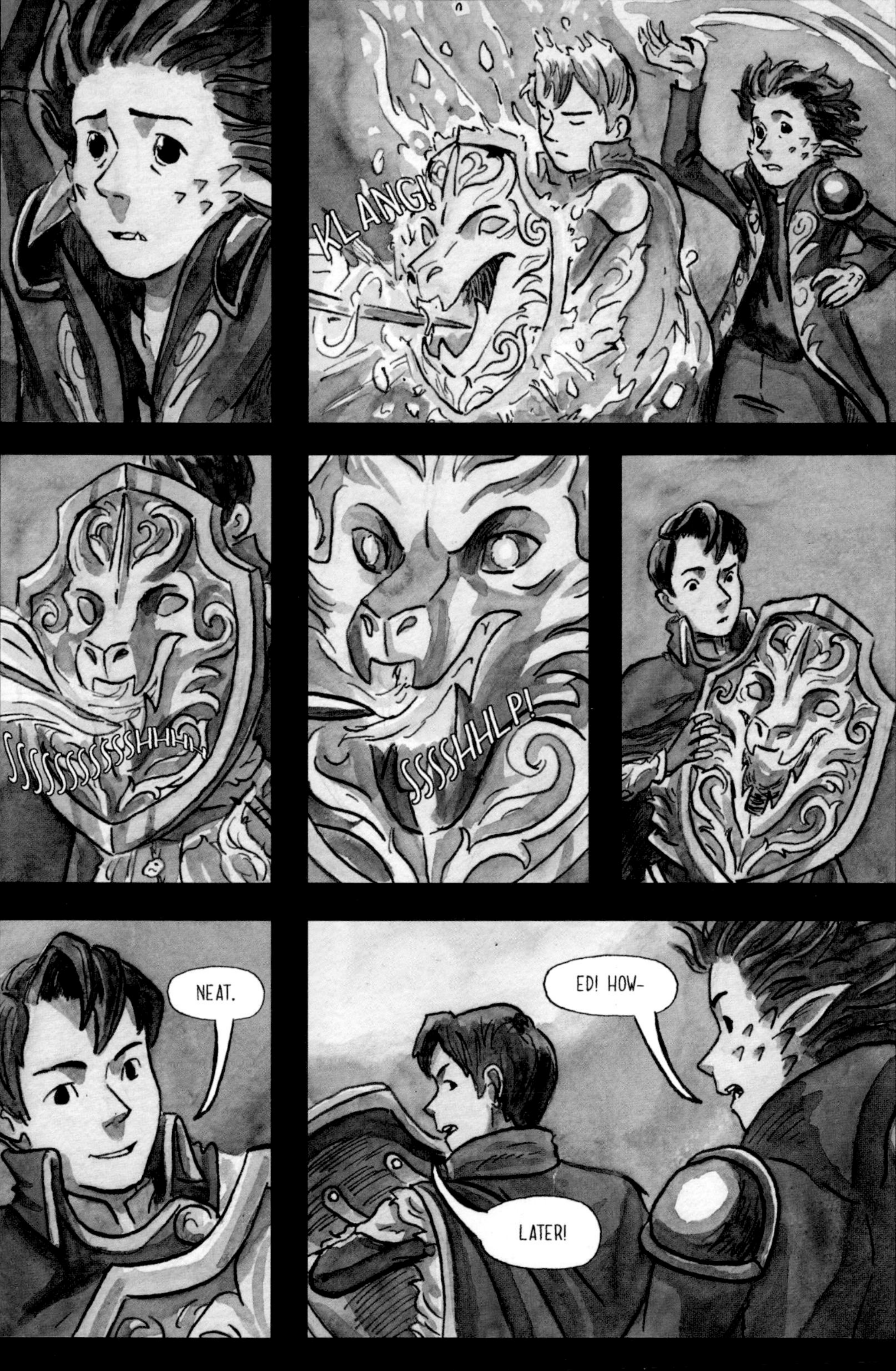
KLANG!
SSSSSSSSSSSSHHHH
SSSSHHLP!
NEAT.
ED! HOW-
LATER!

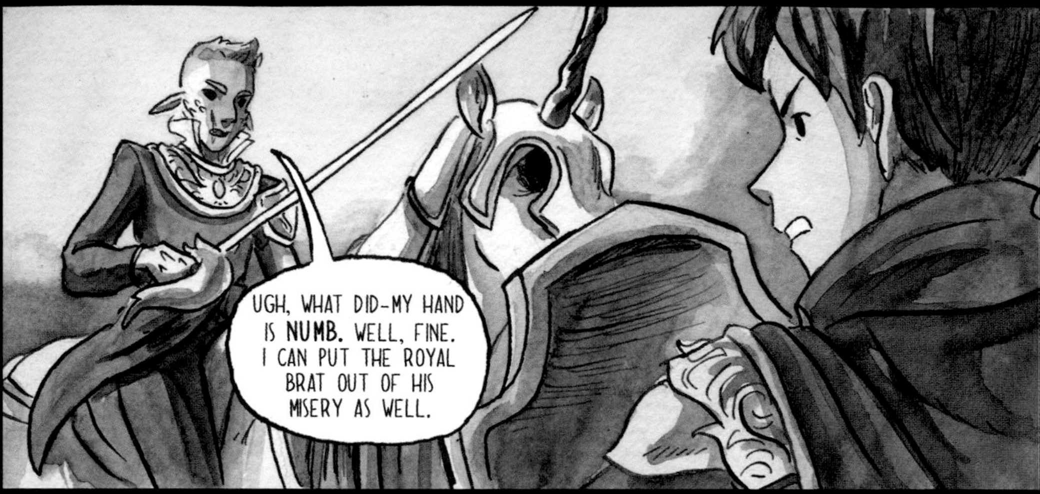
UGH, WHAT DID-MY HAND IS **NUMB.** WELL, FINE. I CAN PUT THE ROYAL BRAT OUT OF HIS MISERY AS WELL.

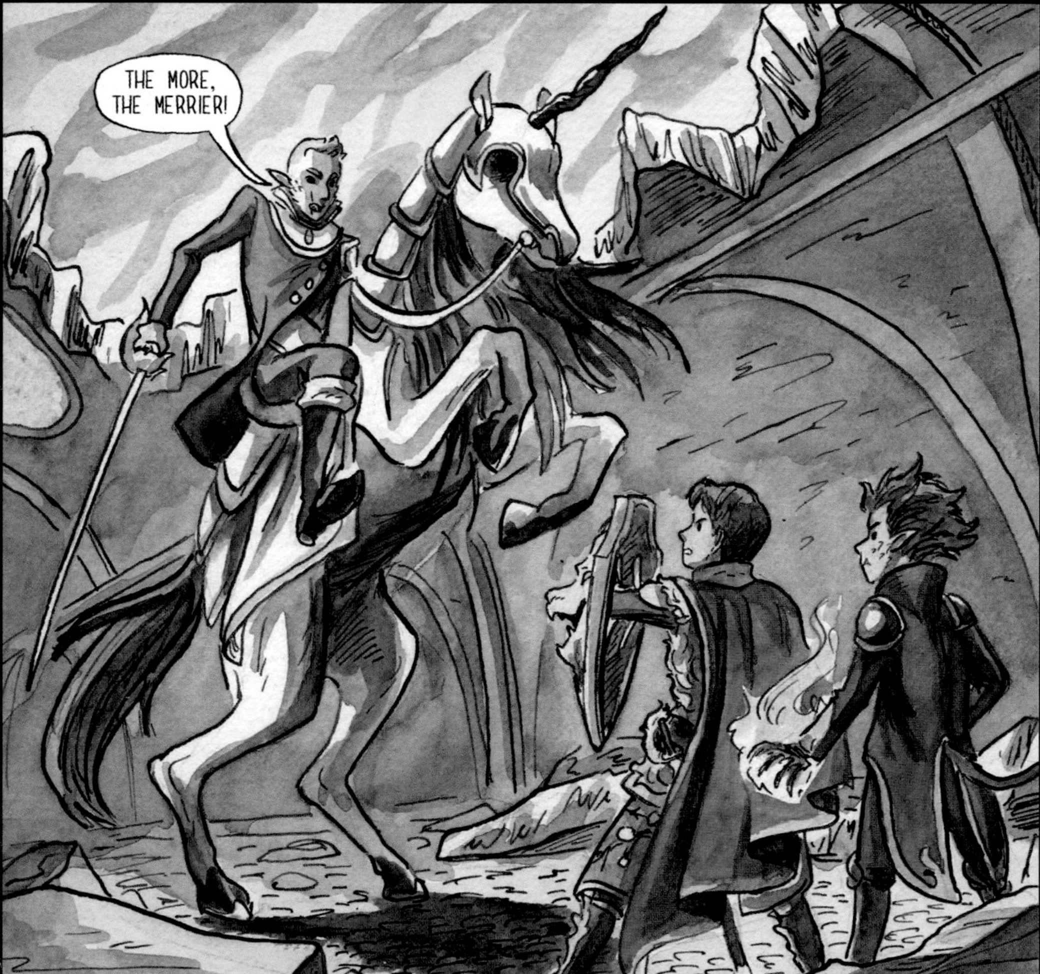
THE MORE, THE MERRIER!

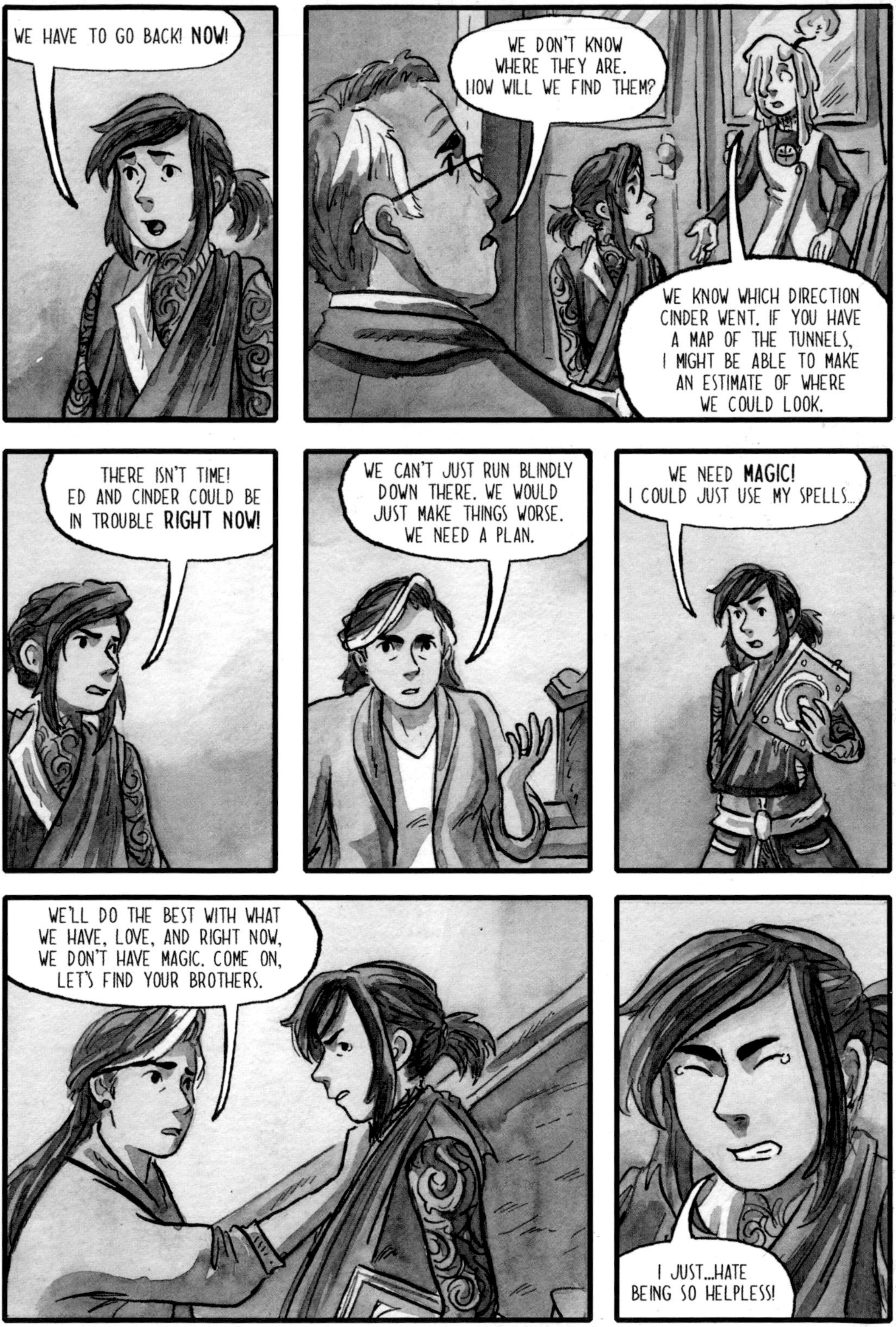
WE HAVE TO GO BACK! **NOW!**
WE DON'T KNOW WHERE THEY ARE. HOW WILL WE FIND THEM?
WE KNOW WHICH DIRECTION CINDER WENT. IF YOU HAVE A MAP OF THE TUNNELS, I MIGHT BE ABLE TO MAKE AN ESTIMATE OF WHERE WE COULD LOOK.
THERE ISN'T TIME! ED AND CINDER COULD BE IN TROUBLE **RIGHT NOW!**
WE CAN'T JUST RUN BLINDLY DOWN THERE. WE WOULD JUST MAKE THINGS WORSE. WE NEED A PLAN.
WE NEED **MAGIC!** I COULD JUST USE MY SPELLS...
WE'LL DO THE BEST WITH WHAT WE HAVE, LOVE, AND RIGHT NOW, WE DON'T HAVE MAGIC. COME ON, LET'S FIND YOUR BROTHERS.
I JUST...HATE BEING SO HELPLESS!

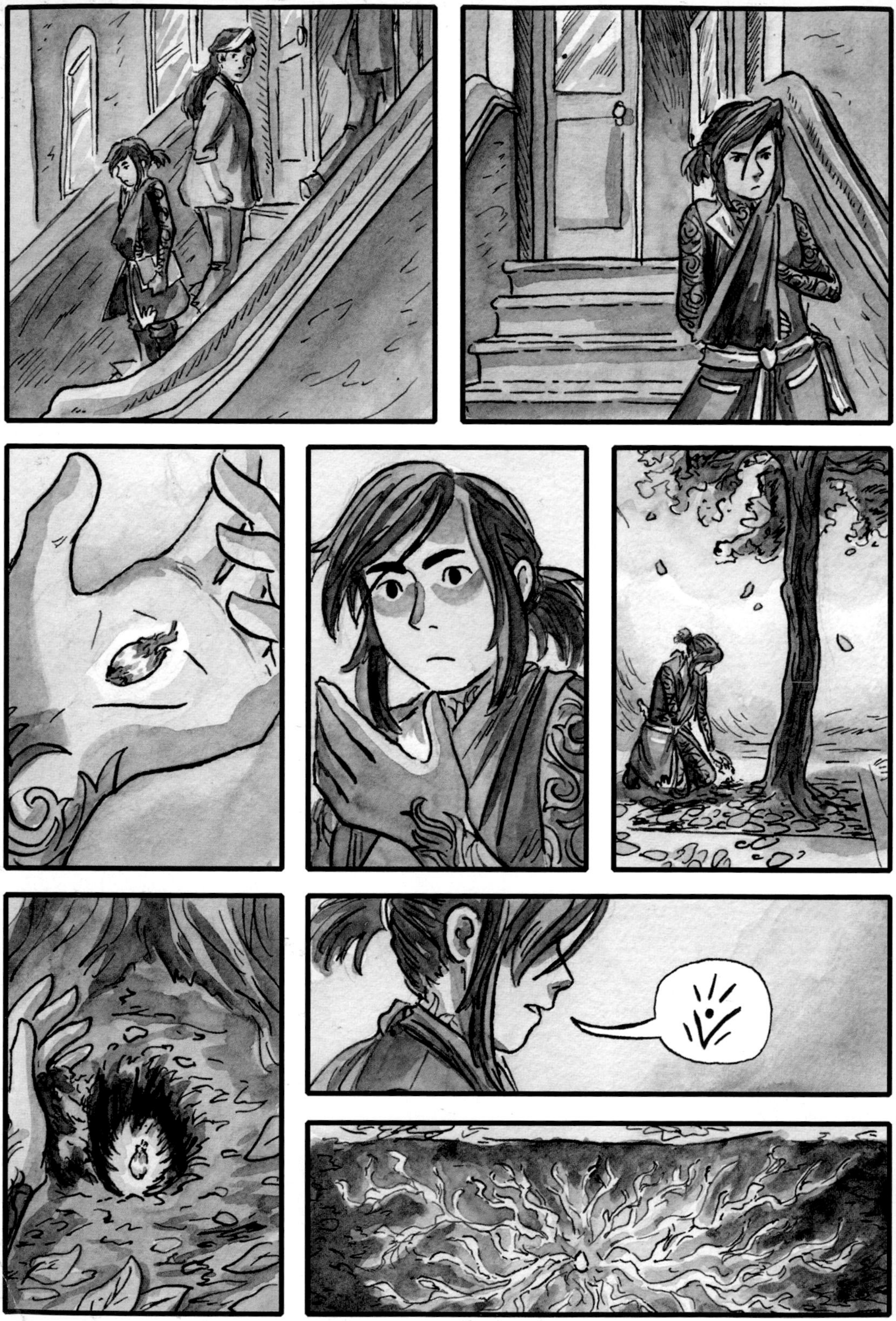

CHAPTER
FIFTEEN

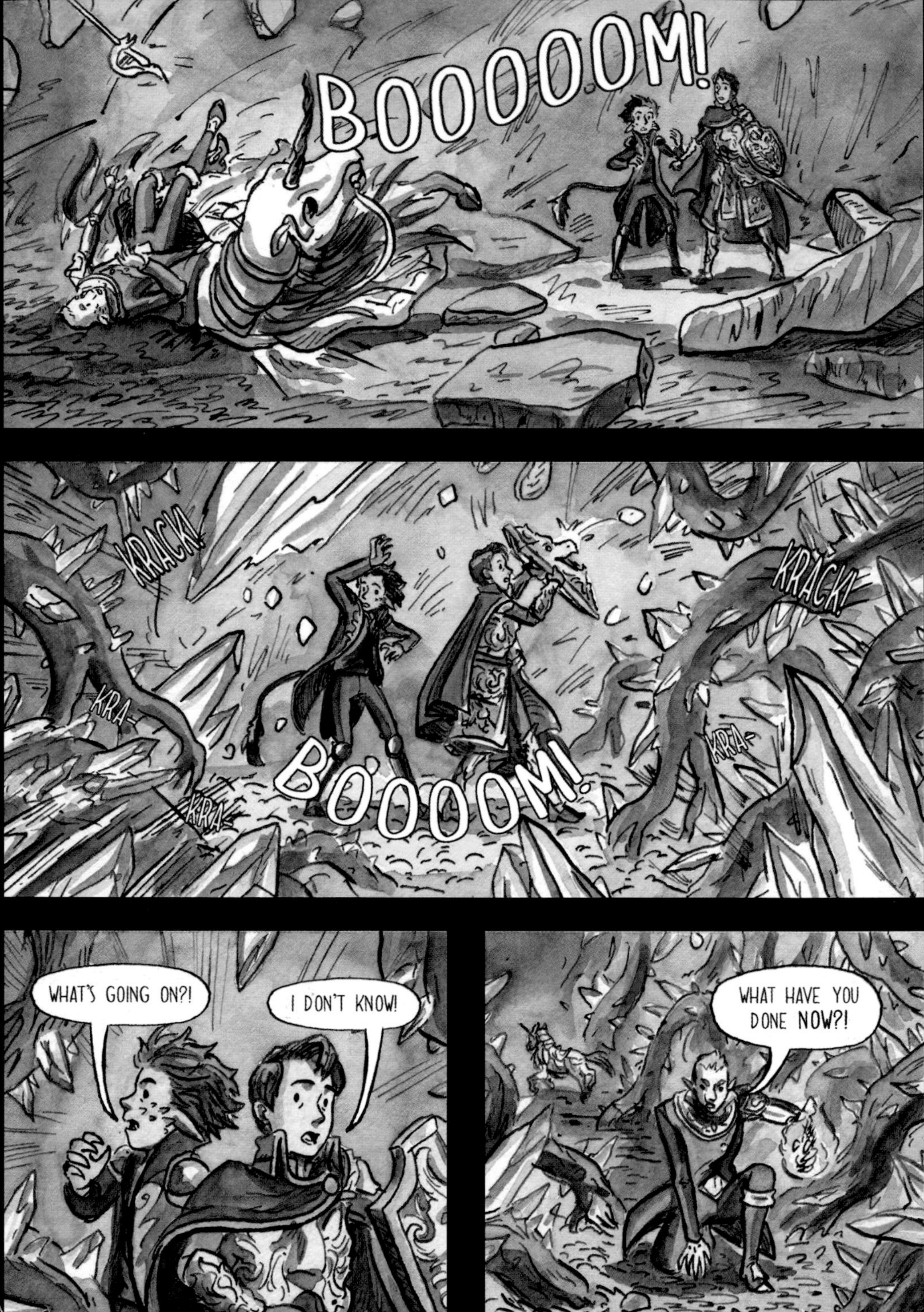
BOOOOOM!
KRACK!
KRACK!
KRA-
KRA-
KRA-
BOOOOM!
WHAT'S GOING ON?!
I DON'T KNOW!
WHAT HAVE YOU DONE NOW?!

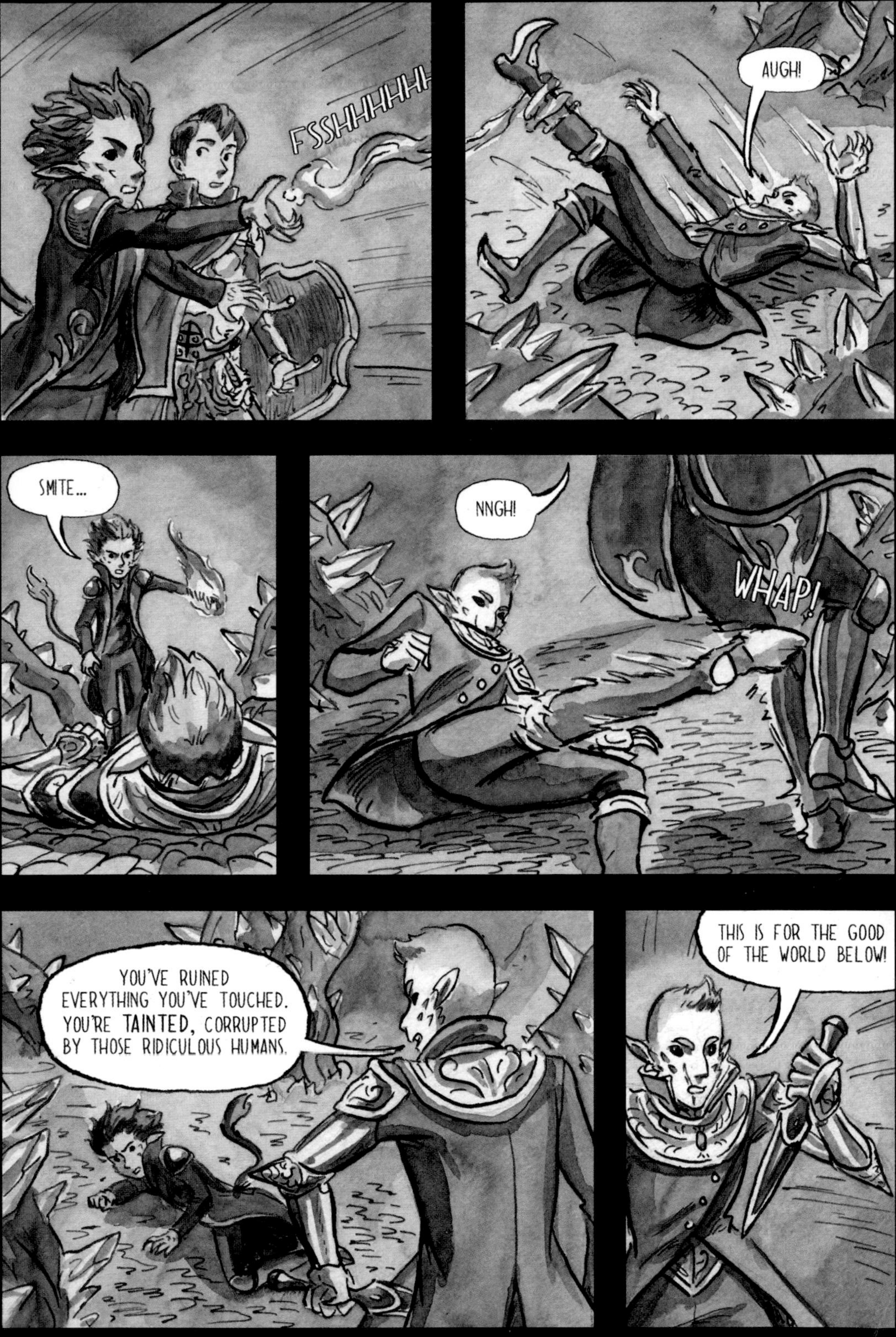
FSSHHHHHH
AUGH!
SMITE...
NNGH!
WHAP!
YOU'VE RUINED EVERYTHING YOU'VE TOUCHED. YOU'RE **TAINTED,** CORRUPTED BY THOSE RIDICULOUS HUMANS.
THIS IS FOR THE GOOD OF THE WORLD BELOW!

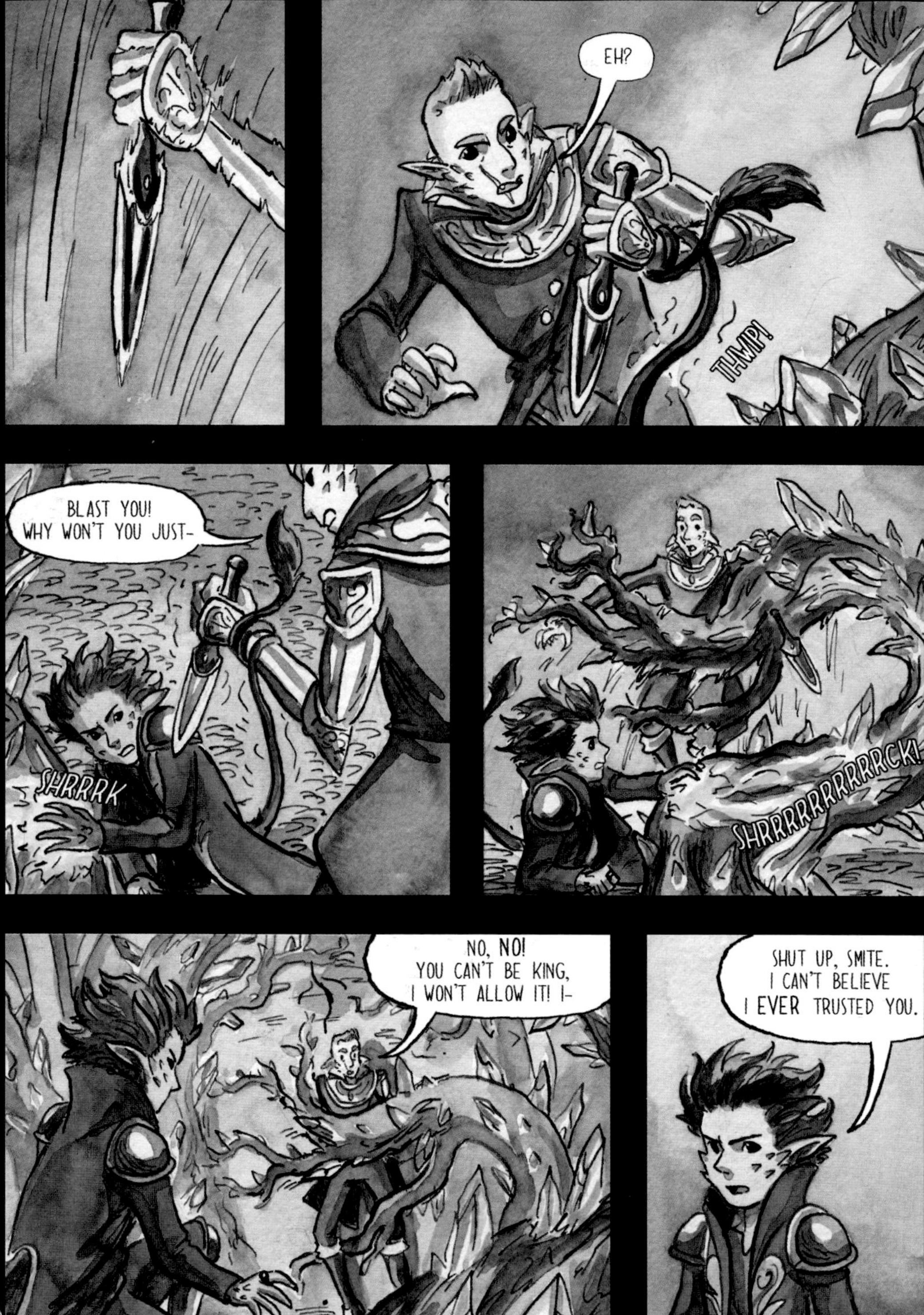
EH?
THMP!
BLAST YOU!
WHY WON'T YOU JUST-
SHRRRK
SHRRRRRRRRRRRRCK!
NO, NO!
YOU CAN'T BE KING,
I WON'T ALLOW IT! I-
SHUT UP, SMITE.
I CAN'T BELIEVE
I EVER TRUSTED YOU.

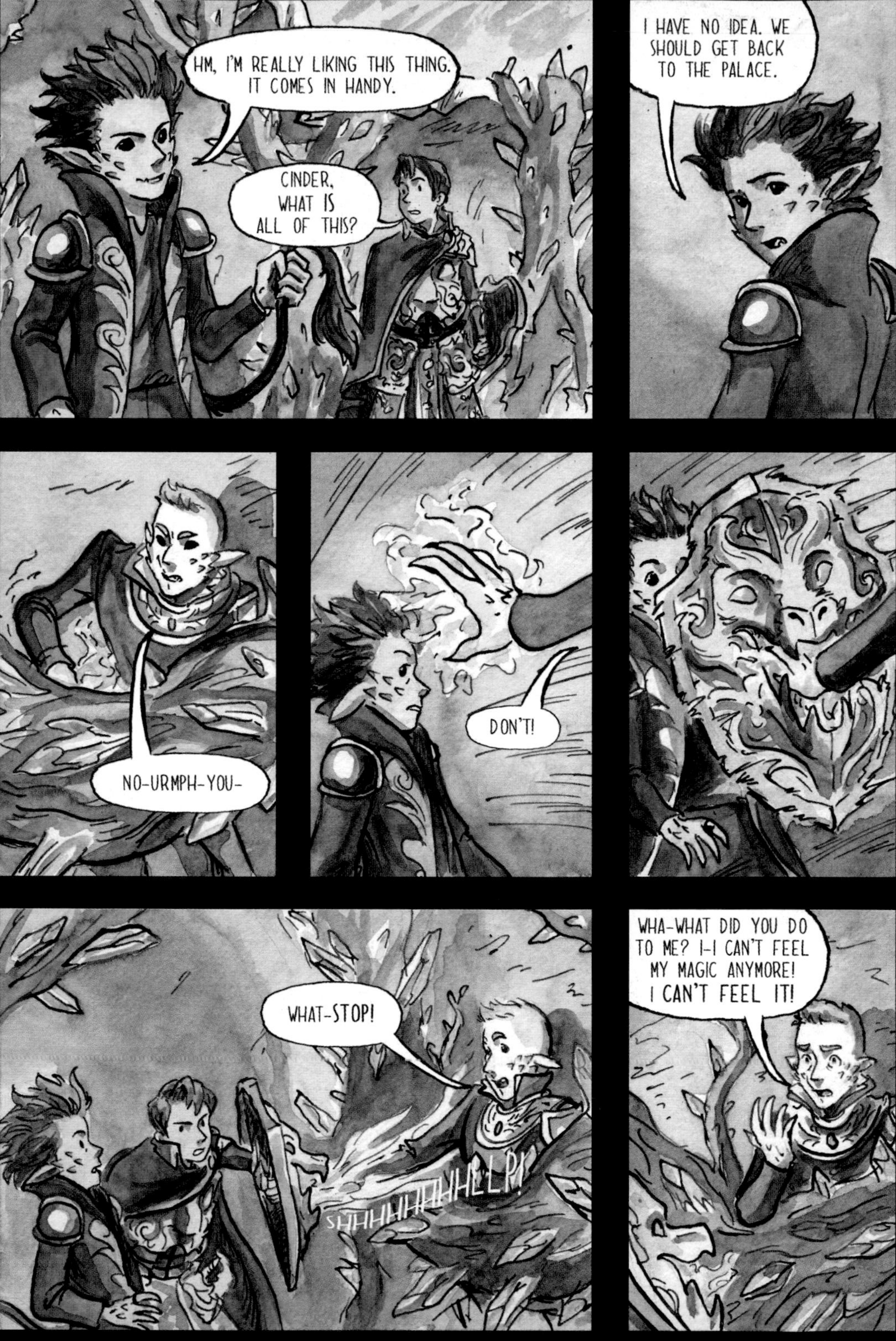
HM, I'M REALLY LIKING THIS THING. IT COMES IN HANDY.
CINDER, WHAT IS ALL OF THIS?
I HAVE NO IDEA. WE SHOULD GET BACK TO THE PALACE.
NO-URMPH-YOU-
DON'T!
WHAT-STOP!
SHHHHHHHHHHHHELP!
WHA-WHAT DID YOU DO TO ME? I-I CAN'T FEEL MY MAGIC ANYMORE! I CAN'T FEEL IT!

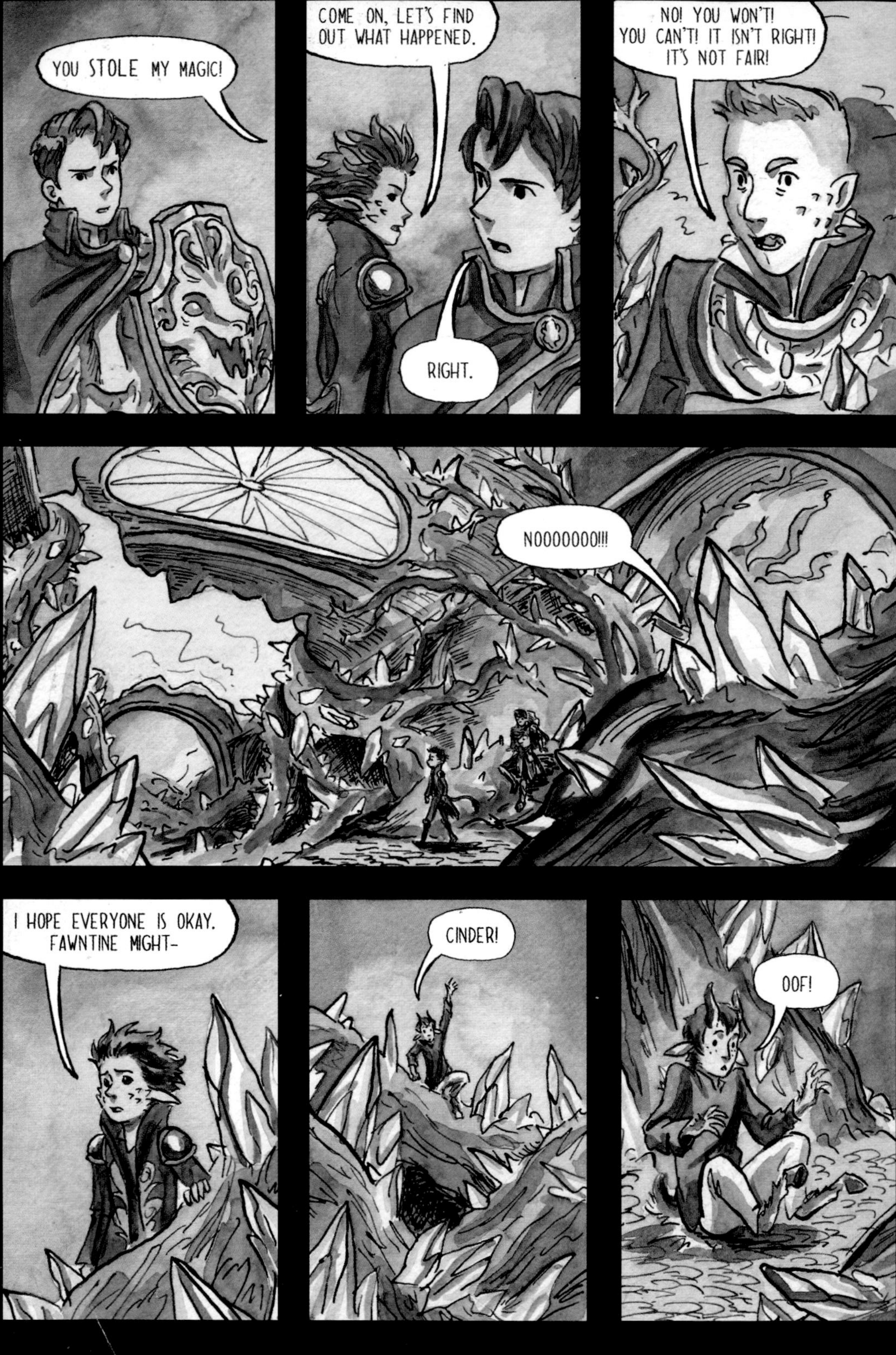
YOU STOLE MY MAGIC!
COME ON, LET'S FIND OUT WHAT HAPPENED.
RIGHT.
NO! YOU WON'T! YOU CAN'T! IT ISN'T RIGHT! IT'S NOT FAIR!
NOOOOOOO!!!
I HOPE EVERYONE IS OKAY. FAWNTINE MIGHT-
CINDER!
OOF!

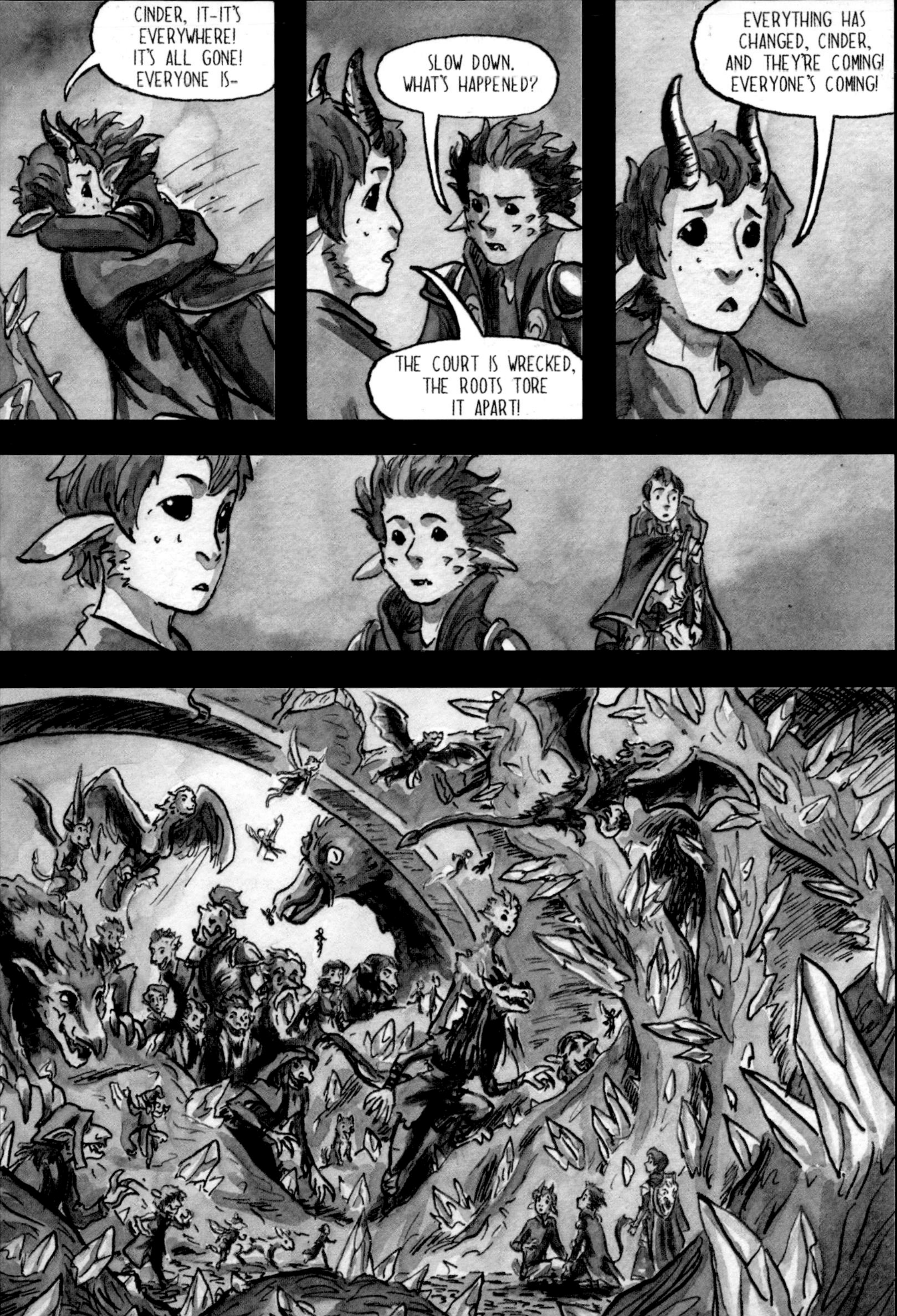
CINDER, IT-IT'S EVERYWHERE! IT'S ALL GONE! EVERYONE IS-
SLOW DOWN. WHAT'S HAPPENED?
THE COURT IS WRECKED, THE ROOTS TORE IT APART!
EVERYTHING HAS CHANGED, CINDER, AND THEY'RE COMING! EVERYONE'S COMING!

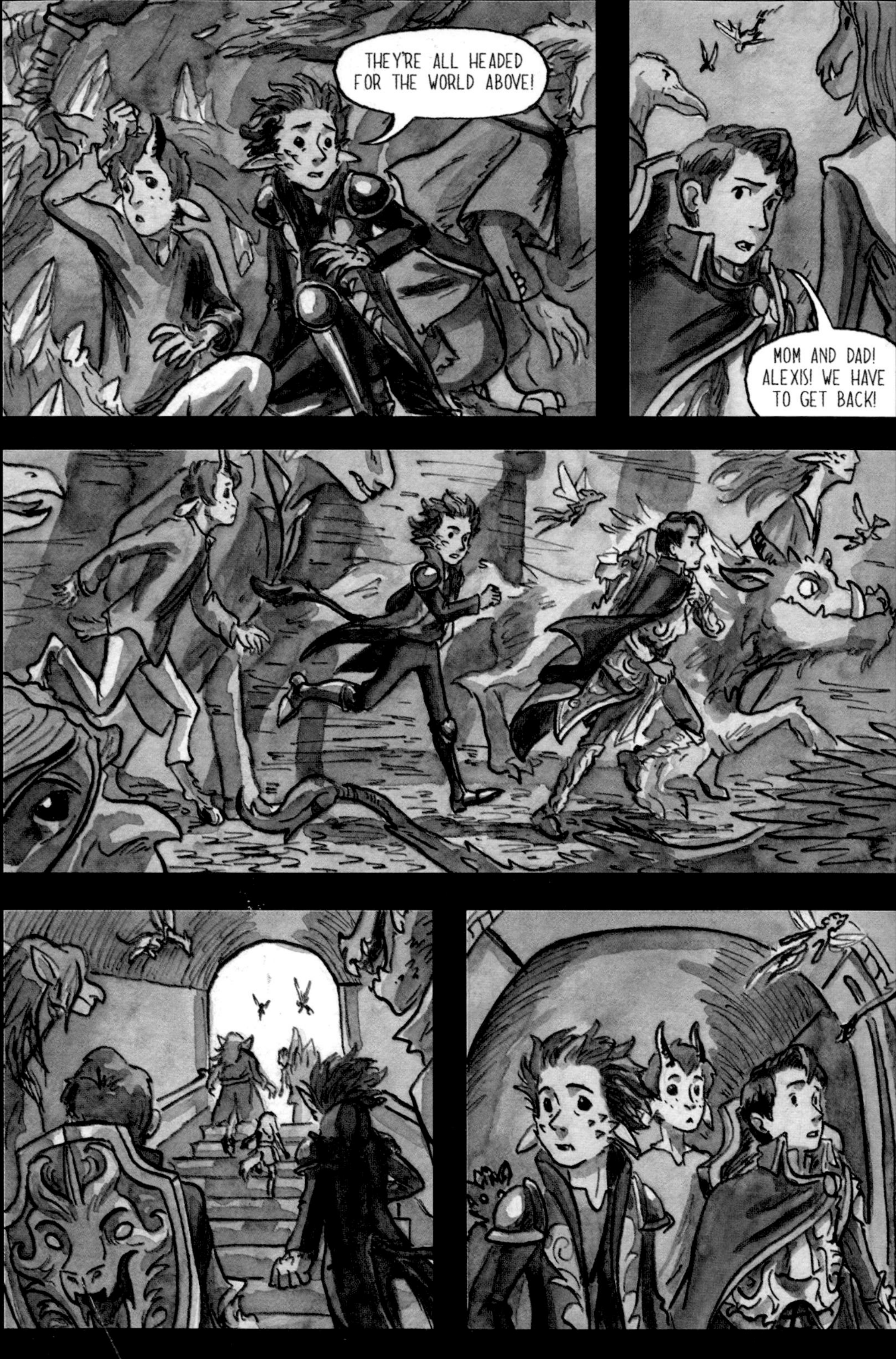
THEY'RE ALL HEADED FOR THE WORLD ABOVE!
MOM AND DAD! ALEXIS! WE HAVE TO GET BACK!

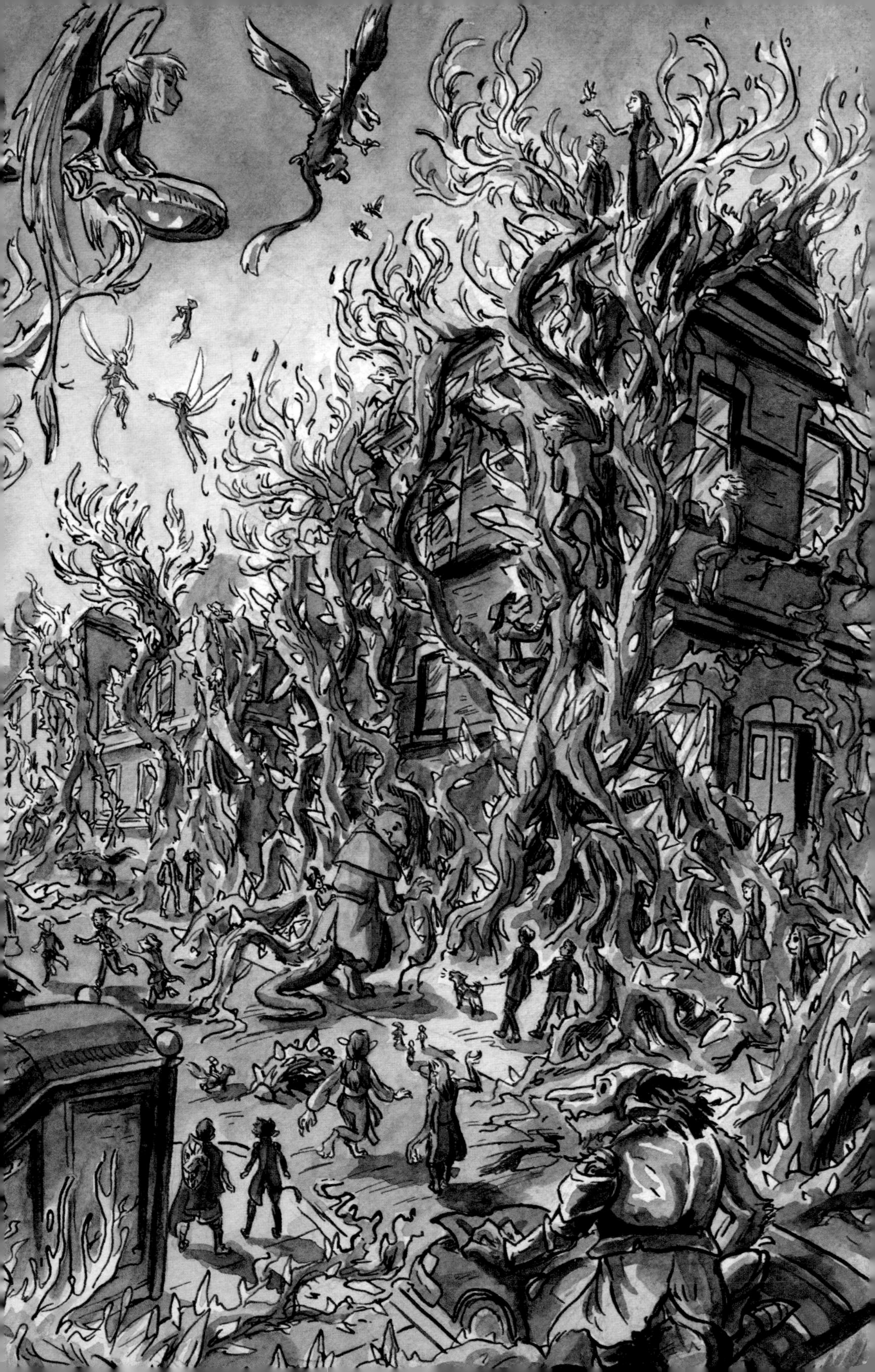

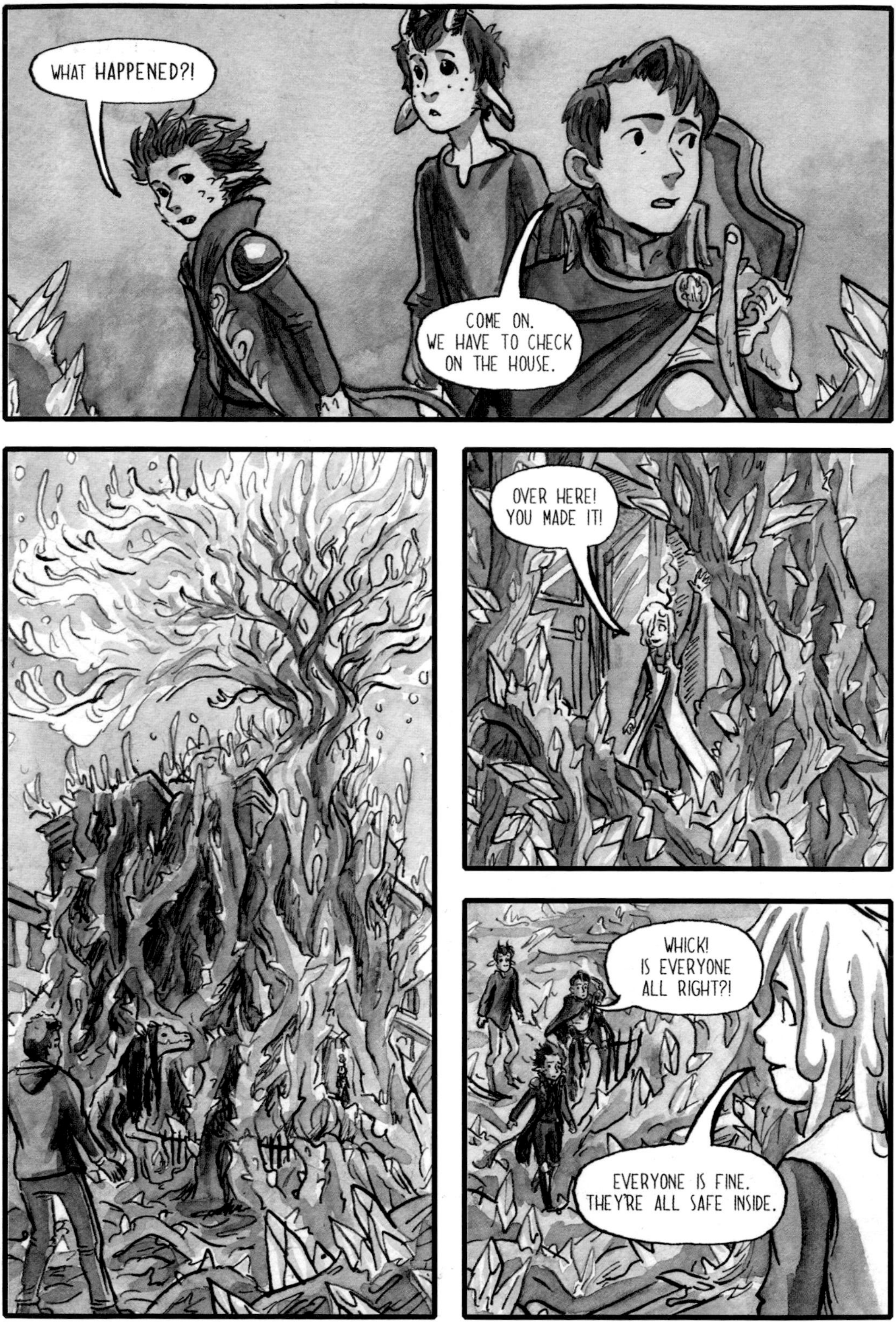
WHAT HAPPENED?!
COME ON. WE HAVE TO CHECK ON THE HOUSE.
OVER HERE! YOU MADE IT!
WHICK! IS EVERYONE ALL RIGHT?!
EVERYONE IS FINE. THEY'RE ALL SAFE INSIDE.

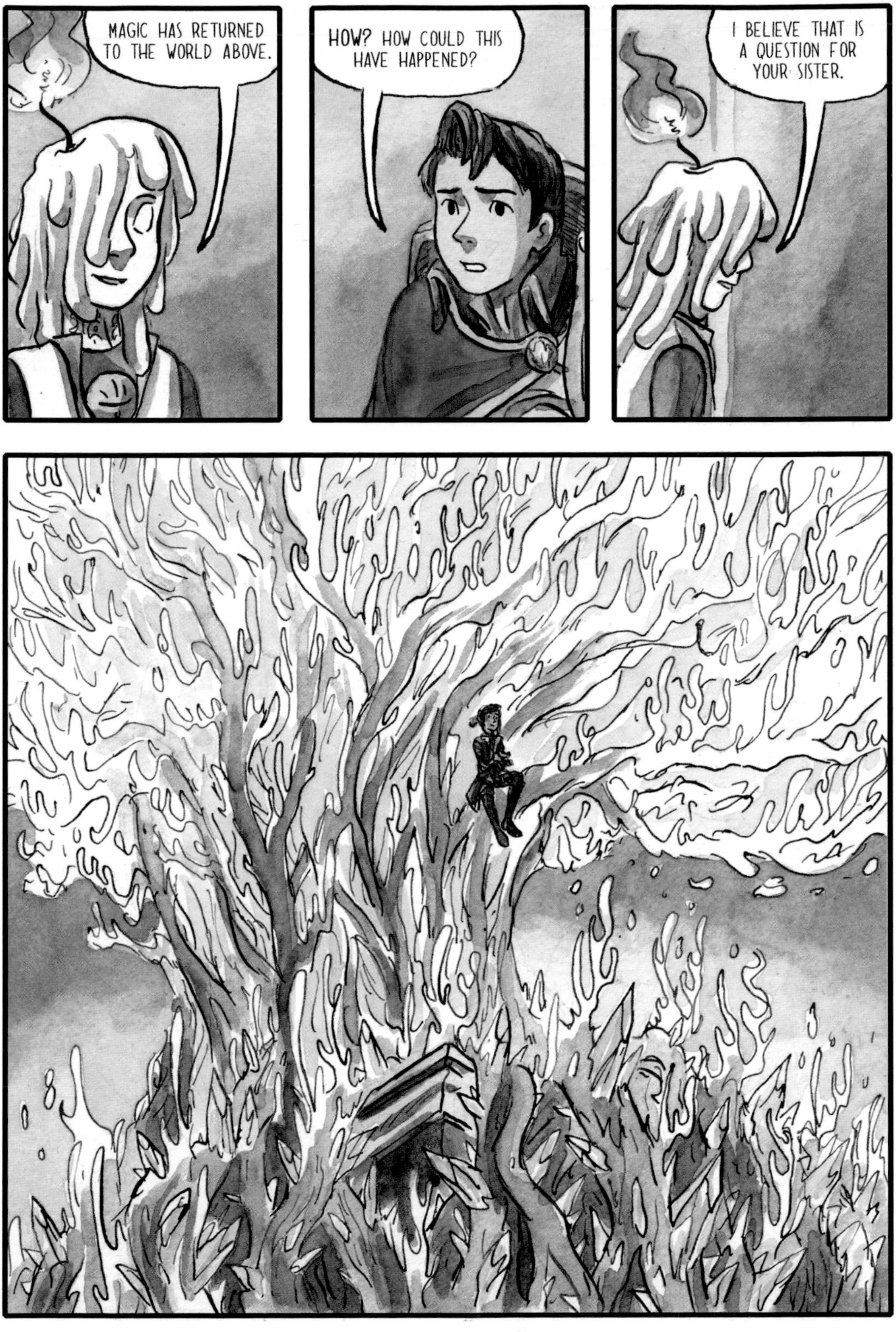
MAGIC HAS RETURNED TO THE WORLD ABOVE.
HOW? HOW COULD THIS HAVE HAPPENED?
I BELIEVE THAT IS A QUESTION FOR YOUR SISTER.

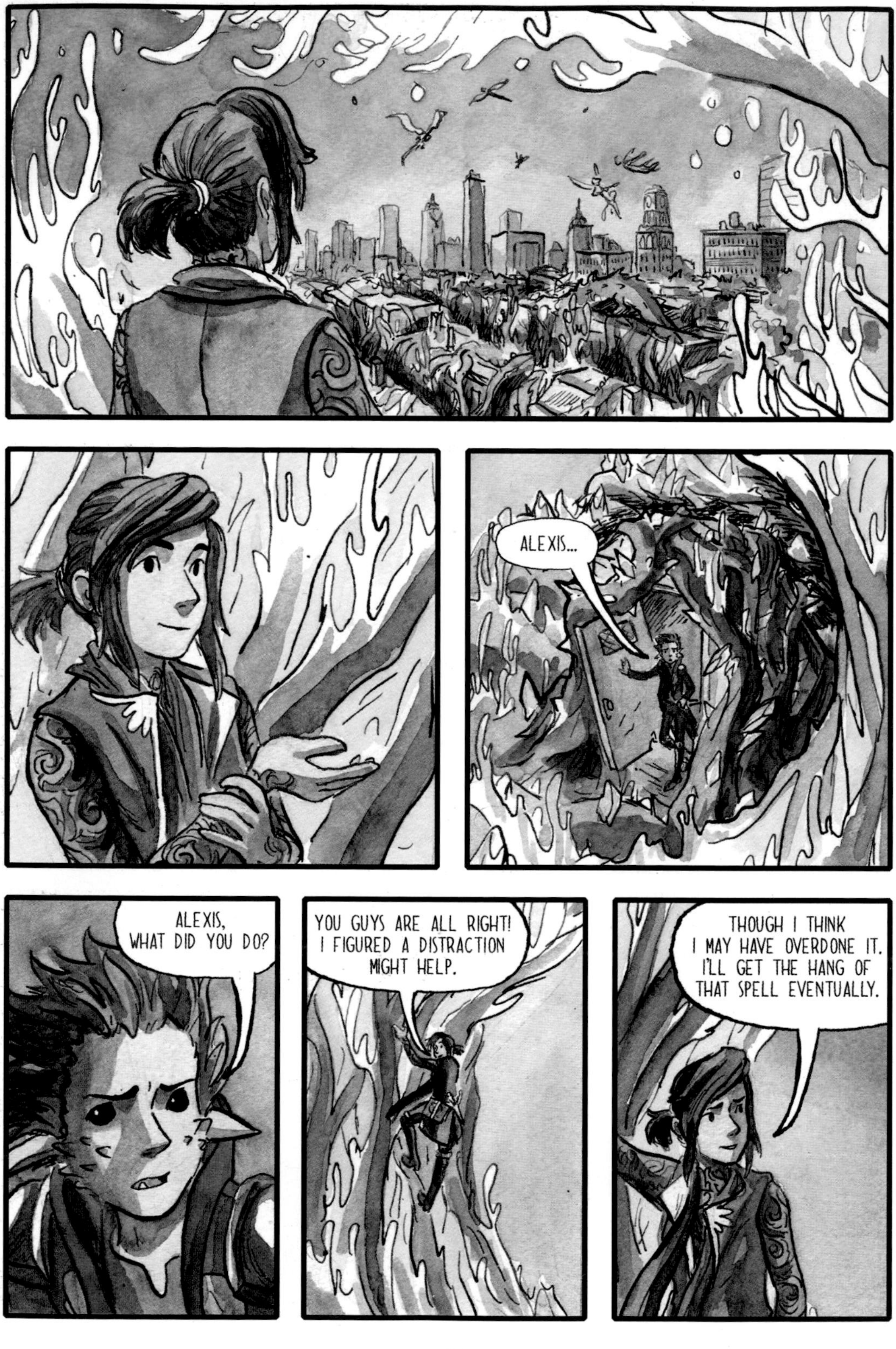
ALEXIS...
ALEXIS, WHAT DID YOU DO?
YOU GUYS ARE ALL RIGHT! I FIGURED A DISTRACTION MIGHT HELP.
THOUGH I THINK I MAY HAVE OVERDONE IT. I'LL GET THE HANG OF THAT SPELL EVENTUALLY.

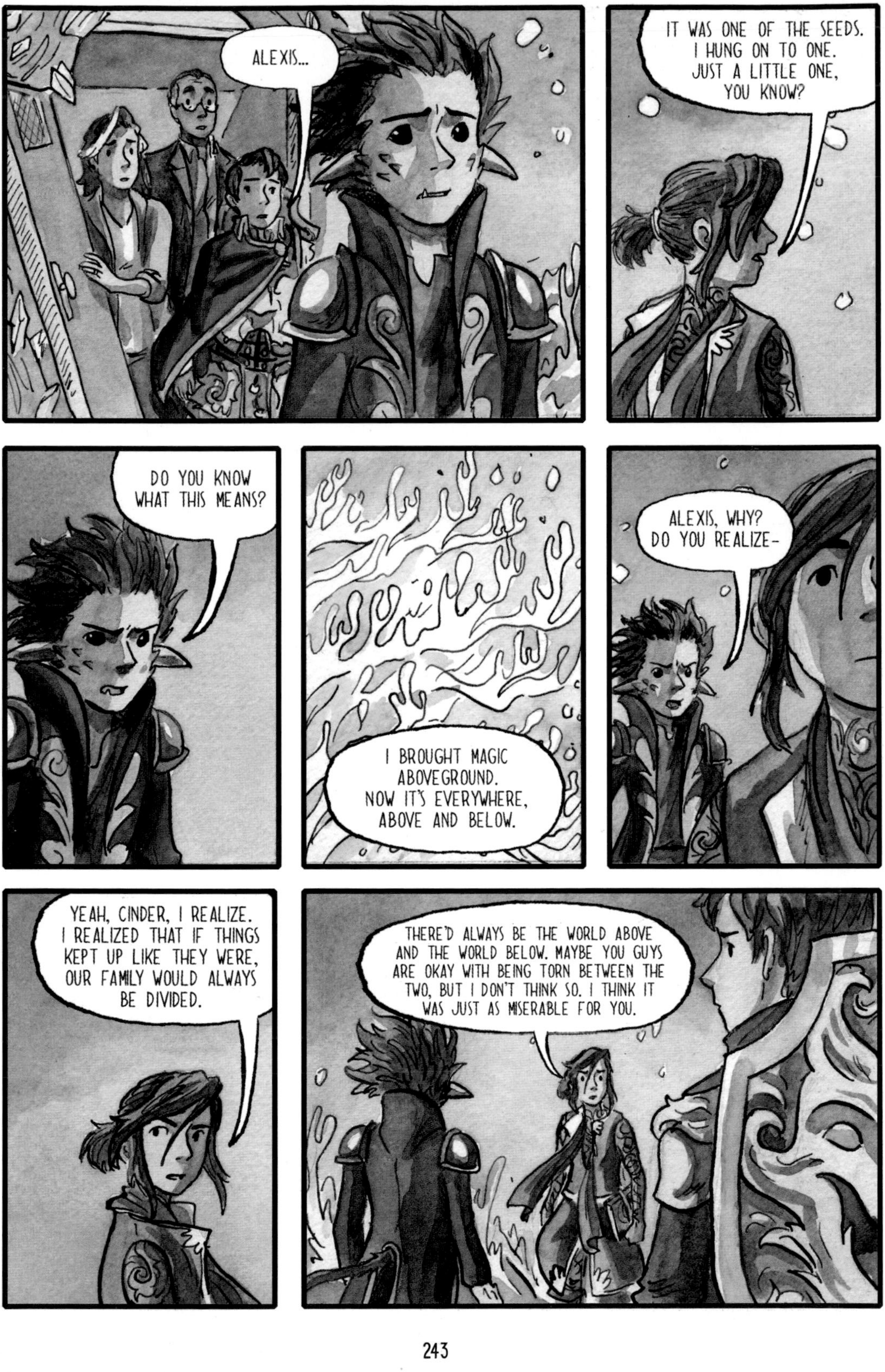
ALEXIS...
IT WAS ONE OF THE SEEDS. I HUNG ON TO ONE. JUST A LITTLE ONE, YOU KNOW?
DO YOU KNOW WHAT THIS MEANS?
I BROUGHT MAGIC ABOVEGROUND. NOW IT'S EVERYWHERE, ABOVE AND BELOW.
ALEXIS, WHY? DO YOU REALIZE-
YEAH, CINDER, I REALIZE. I REALIZED THAT IF THINGS KEPT UP LIKE THEY WERE, OUR FAMILY WOULD ALWAYS BE DIVIDED.
THERE'D ALWAYS BE THE WORLD ABOVE AND THE WORLD BELOW. MAYBE YOU GUYS ARE OKAY WITH BEING TORN BETWEEN THE TWO, BUT I DON'T THINK SO. I THINK IT WAS JUST AS MISERABLE FOR YOU.

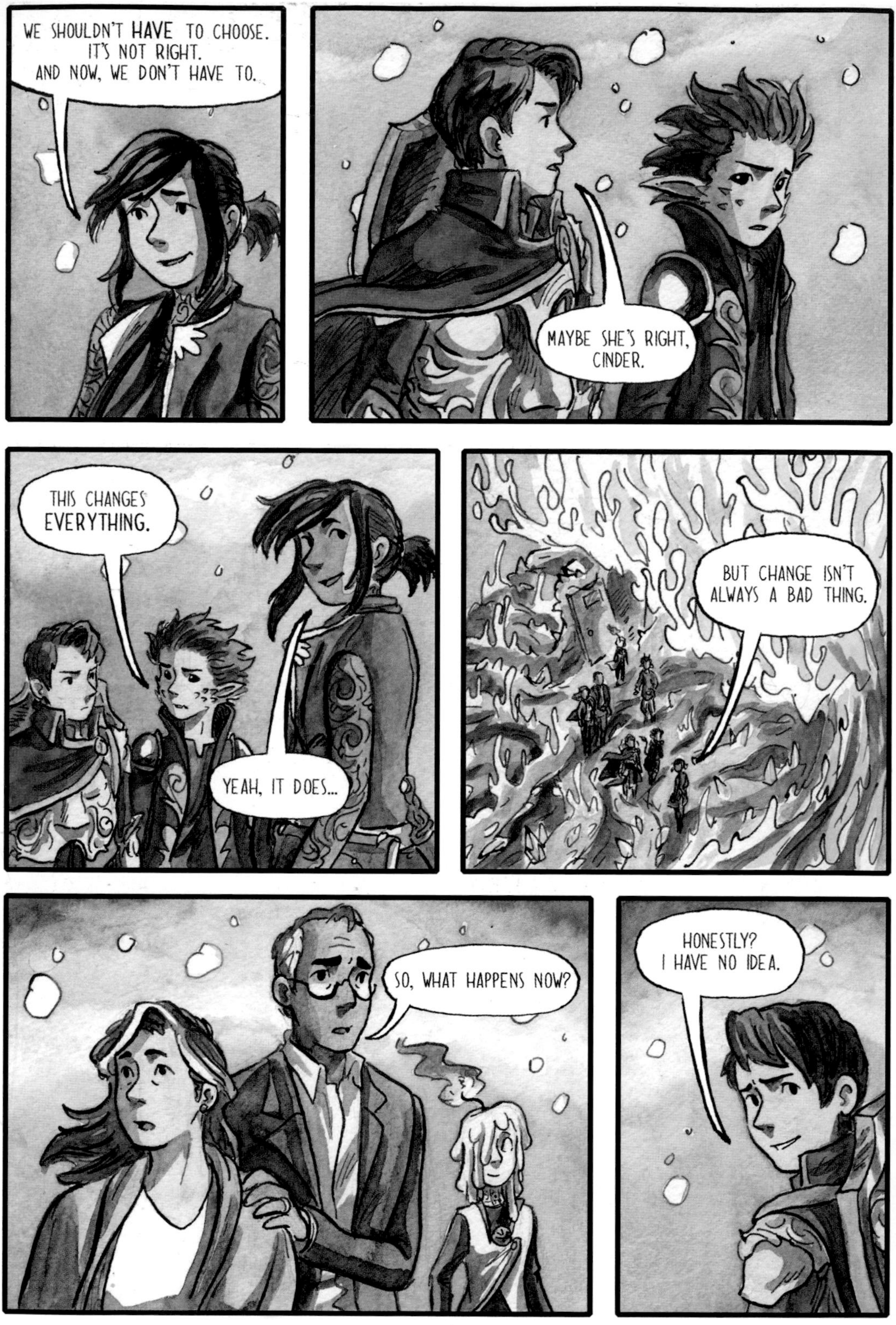
WE SHOULDN'T HAVE TO CHOOSE. IT'S NOT RIGHT. AND NOW, WE DON'T HAVE TO.
MAYBE SHE'S RIGHT, CINDER.
THIS CHANGES EVERYTHING.
YEAH, IT DOES...
BUT CHANGE ISN'T ALWAYS A BAD THING.
SO, WHAT HAPPENS NOW?
HONESTLY? I HAVE NO IDEA.

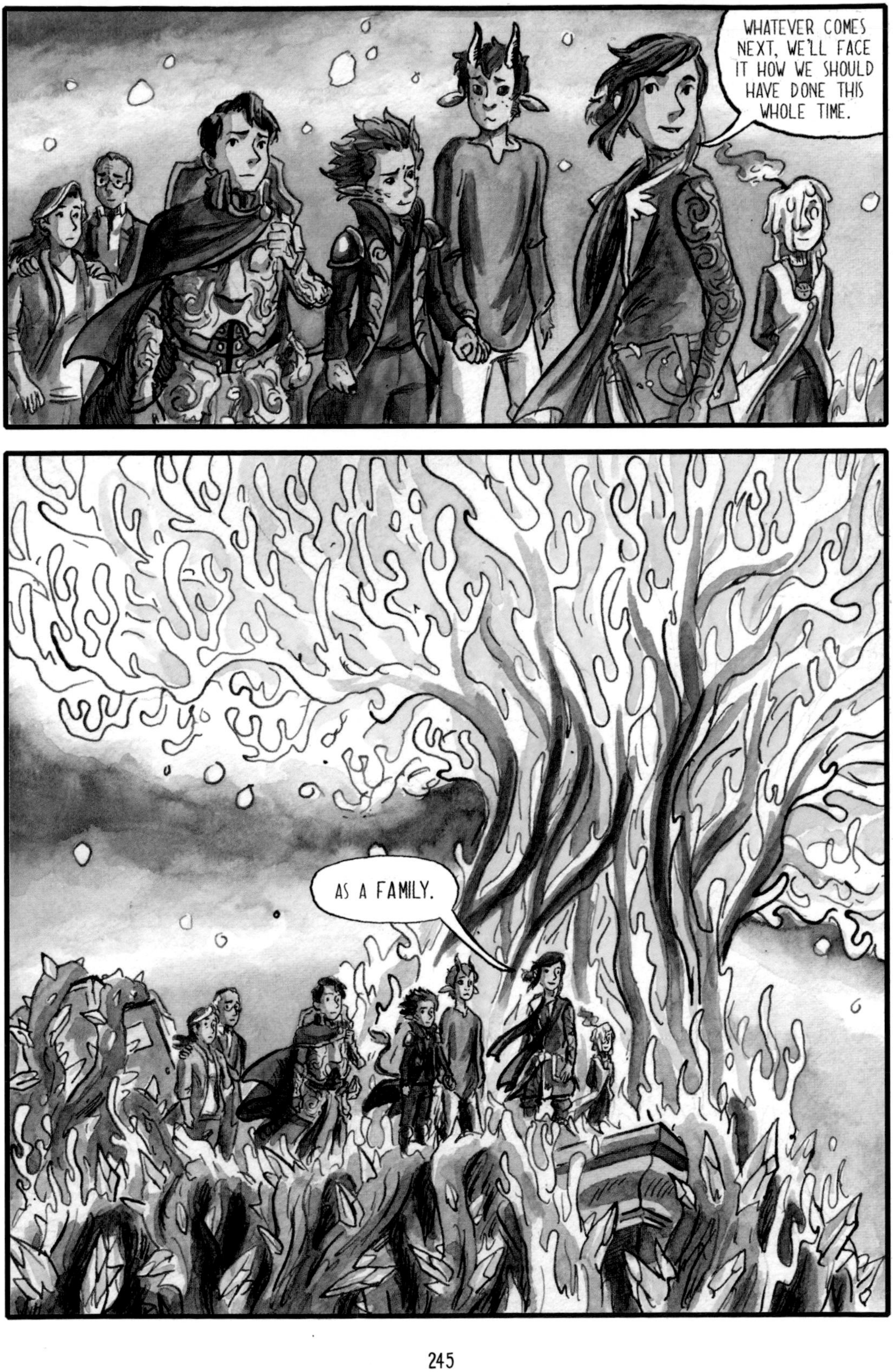
WHATEVER COMES NEXT, WE'LL FACE IT HOW WE SHOULD HAVE DONE THIS WHOLE TIME.
AS A FAMILY.

THE END

ACKNOWLEDGMENTS

This book was a large one, and a lot of people helped me make it a reality. First, I'd like to thank MY PARENTS, as well as MY SIBLINGS and THEIR SPOUSES, for their unending support, their willingness to listen to me complain while working on the more difficult bits of the book, and for acting appropriately impressed when I told them I would be writing a book series.

Thank you to fellow artist WENDY XU, for providing helpful feedback and joining me on long working afternoons. Thanks to BRANDON THORPE for all his insight and for the brilliant conversations on what fantasy is capable of.

I owe a big thank-you to all my patrons, and in particular XANDER, BRAXTON, ERIKA, STEPHEN, and DUSTIN. Many of you believed in this story from the very beginning, and I can't thank you enough.

Thank you as always to my wonderful agent, STEPHEN BARBARA, whose instinct, wit, and drive gave me the confidence to finish this book.

Thanks to my editor, ANDREW ELIOPULOS; art director, ERIN FITZSIMMONS; designer, CATHERINE SAN JUAN; and the whole team at Harper. This wouldn't be half the book it is without all the love and hours of hard work you poured into it.

Finally, the biggest of thanks and love to my incredible husband, MATTHEW, for the late nights ironing out the story, the endless support and encouragement, and the title of this book. There's no one else I'd rather be on this adventure with.

Development of
Estranged
The Changeling King

KING CINDER

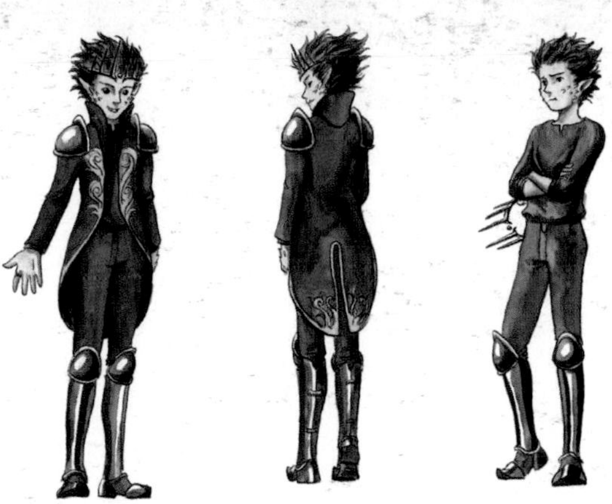

ED CARTER

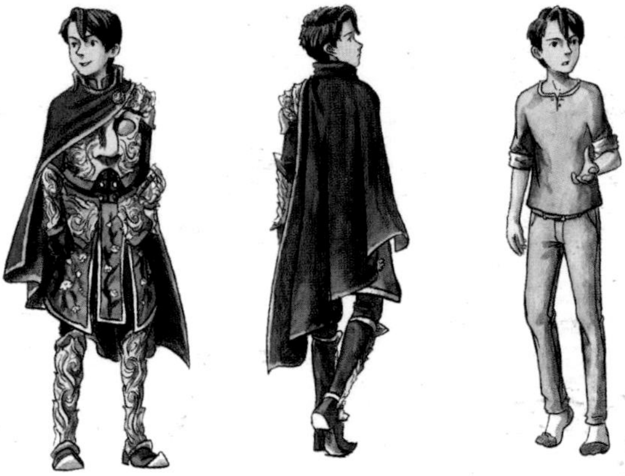

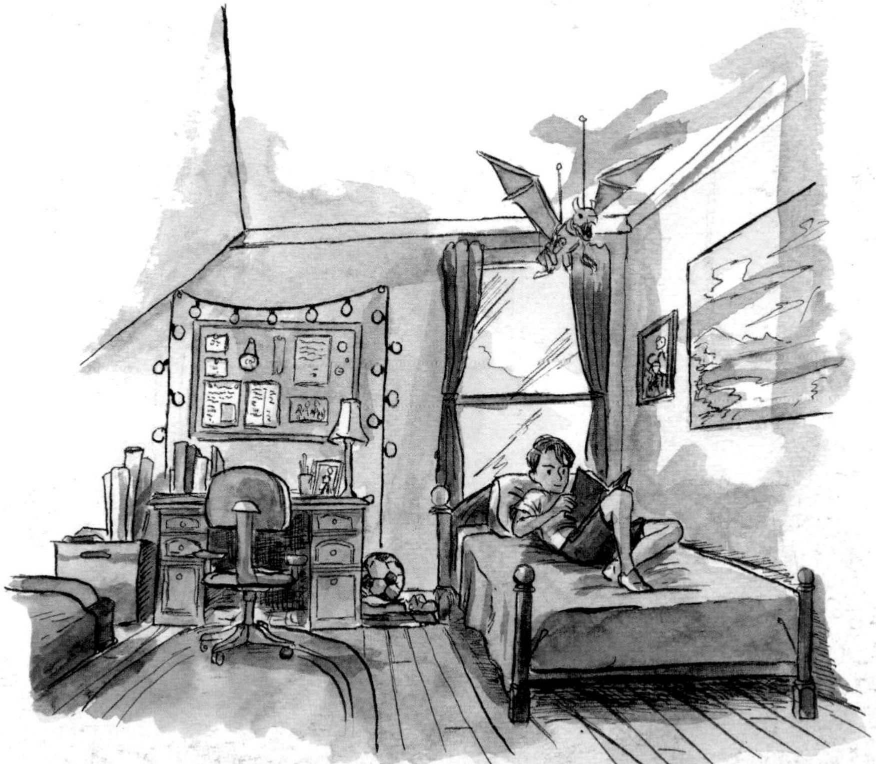

ALEXIS CARTER

OCT 2019

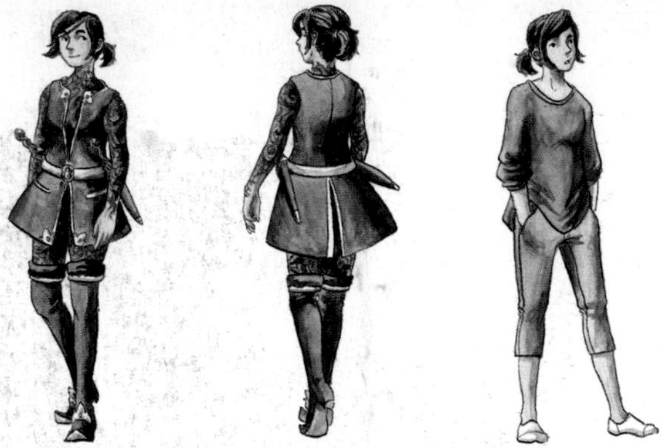

WHICK

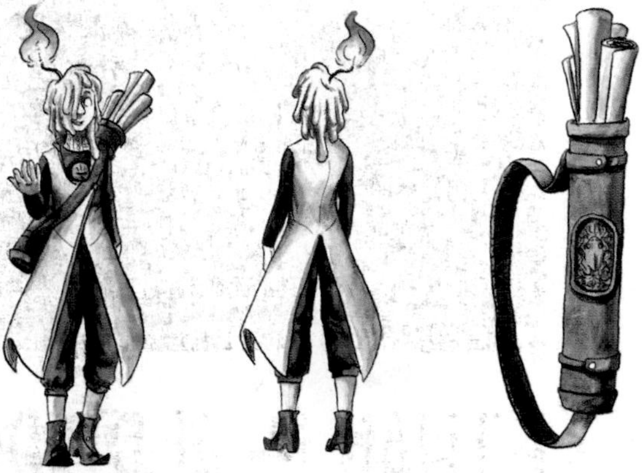

THE WILD HUNT

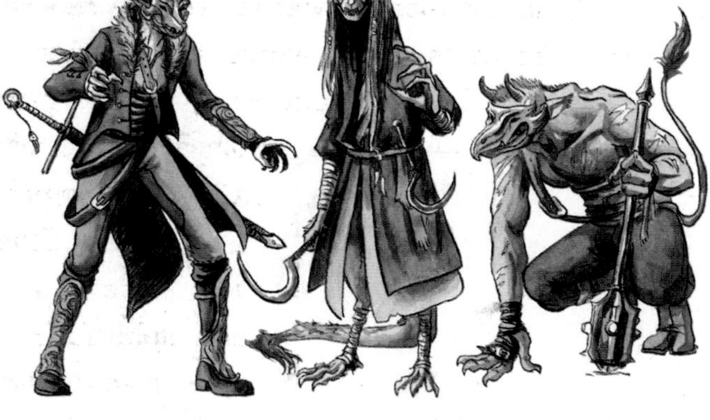

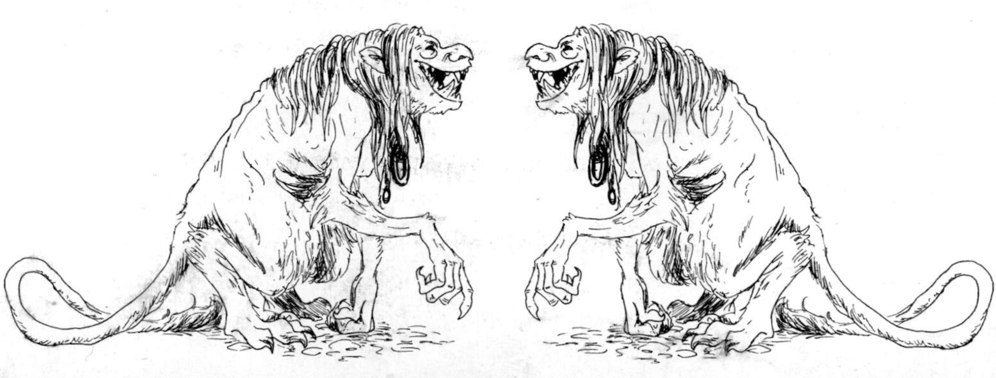